High Bottom Drunk

High Bottom Drunk

A Novel...and the Truth
about
Addiction & Recovery

Charles N. Roper, PhD

Small Change Publishing Co.
Buda, Texas

High Bottom Drunk: A Novel...and the Truth about Addiction & Recovery
Copyright 1999 © by Charles N. Roper

Small Change Publishing Co.
320 N. Main St., #300
Buda, Texas 78610

Publisher's Cataloging-in-Publication

Roper, Charles N.
High Bottom Drunk: A Novel...and the Truth about Addiction & Recovery / Charles N. Roper. First Edition.
ISBN 0-9677529-0-6

Library of Congress Cataloging-in-Publication

Roper, Charles N.
High Bottom Drunk: A Novel...and the Truth about Addiction & Recovery / Charles N. Roper.
CIP 00-190301

First Printing: December 1999; Printed in the United States of America at Morgan Printing; Austin, Texas.

Second Printing: February 2001; Printed in Canada at Hignell Book Printing; Winnipeg, Manitoba.

For:

Louise Yelvington Denham

&

Mary Lois Alderman

ACKNOWLEDGMENTS

I have been blessed with wonderfully supportive family and friends. I wish to thank them all, especially the following:

Louise Yelvington Denham, my beloved high school English teacher, who taught me to write and to appreciate simple words.

Mary Alderman, my mom, who stretched her tolerance enough to love my work, and who listened to me read and read and read and...

Chet Alderman, my stepdad, and the kindest, sweetest man I've ever been fortunate enough to know.

Joan Roper, my wife, who shared my dream, my tears, and my joy from start to finish, and who finally said, "No more revisions!"

Andrew Roper and Kathryn Roper, my two kids still in the nest, who never thought it weird that I would rather write for free than work for money. And Kim Roper Gibbons and Grady Roper, my two kids out of the nest, who seem to like me, warts and all, at least most of the time.

Tim Wright, Joe Kahler, Joe Grady Tuck, and Tisa Bean, my buds, who consistently encouraged me to follow my heart, and with whom I made a pact that I would really publish this book.

Jay Edwards, who profoundly challenged my thinking. Travis Sebera, who insisted that I be "present." And Leigh Sebera, my hero, who is a constant source of inspiration.

Earl Pomerleau, who gently nudged me toward a recovery path.

Ulysses "Mac" McLester, who inspired me to seek recovery at a deeper, more meaningful level.

Alcoholics and addicts everywhere—both those in recovery and those not yet there.

CONTENTS

INTRODUCTION

As a therapist and counselor, I have learned about people from people. I respect academia and have spent more than my fair share of time in the classroom. Over the years, I've earned three academic degrees, attended hundreds of workshops and seminars, and read literally thousands of books, journal articles, and other scholarly works. Still, most of what I know about the human spirit, human nature, human behavior, and change has come directly from people, especially my patients.

People in emotional pain are exceptional teachers. Without trying, they show us how to nurture suffering and/or how to release it. To feed pain, they fight it. They develop coping skills and defenses that soften or deaden the feelings but guarantee their continuation. To starve pain, they surrender. They listen to voices wiser than the ones in their heads, and they give up the fight. Either way—fight or surrender—they lay it right out there for us to learn or ignore.

People in emotional pain are also exceptional storytellers. No fictional tale in God's universe can rival the profundity of a suffering man's story, as long as that story is unyieldingly true and told from the heart. Likewise, no academic text in existence can inspire understanding like the true-life story of an anguished human being.

I have listened intently to people's emotional pain—to their stories—for over thirty years. For many of those years, I listened with the ear of a conscientious, well-trained therapist. I applied the tools of my trade with great care. I developed detailed treatment plans and kept copious case notes. I worked hard and felt good about my therapeutic skills.

Then, some years ago, I had an experience that altered my perspective. I was working with Doug M., a very bright but troubled young man who as a child had been emotionally and physically abused by his father. The case was interesting and challenging so I obtained his permission to write up his story and present it as a case study to a class of university psychology students. When I finished the project, I asked him to read it and give me feedback on its accuracy. His reaction surprised me.

"It's accurate, I guess, but where's the story?" he asked.

"What do you mean, Doug?" I replied.

"Well," he said, "The details are here, but it's colorless and flavorless. I mean, it isn't me. This isn't my story. This is a chronology of life events." He handed the paper back to me. "Maybe it's just because I've never read a case study before, but I gotta tell you, Charles, I'm kind of disappointed."

"Really?" I asked. "This is the way I've always written case studies. It's objective, and it gives a lot of information without compromising your privacy or confidentiality."

Doug smiled and shook his head. "Man, what do I care about privacy and confidentiality? I mean, what are the chances of one of your students knowing or even caring who the hell I am? And speaking of your students, if I were in your class, I think I'd yawn all over this assignment. Listen, Charles, if you want to use my life experience to teach someone something about insanity, at least make me interesting. You know, make me warm-blooded. Let them in on the good stuff. Tell them how I feel."

I thought a lot about what Doug had said. I decided to take the case study back to the drawing board, where I turned it into short story "fiction." I built a detailed story line around the people and events that had shaped Doug's life. I invented dialogue between characters; I exposed their secrets, at least as I imagined them. I gave Doug what he wanted—a real life, very warm blood, and lots of feelings.

The outcome exceeded anything I could have imagined. Everything changed.

I changed. By the time I finished writing Doug's story, I knew him. Conceptualizing his life in my mind and writing it with my own hand placed me squarely into his experience. I felt his feelings. I cried his tears. I knew his pain.

Doug changed. Seeing his life story through another's eyes broadened his vision and objectivity. He tightened his focus. He started seeing solutions as clearly as he did problems. He zeroed in on the real issues and tackled them with greater courage. His healing process accelerated.

Our patient-therapist relationship changed. Barriers came down. Mutual trust and respect strengthened. He knew that I knew who he was and that I loved and accepted him unconditionally.

My students jumped headfirst into Doug's story. They studied him. They discussed him. They analyzed dialogue for subtle messages and meaning. They compared his thoughts with his feelings and behavior. Within the context of his story, Doug became more than a case study; he became a live human being. To my delight, they learned, understood, and remembered the elements of post-traumatic stress disorder.

Doug completed his work. He left therapy, and we eventually lost touch. Our shared experience, though, permanently altered my understanding of and approach to therapeutic practice and teaching. I learned to listen to people's emotional pain—their stories—with the ear of a storyteller. And I became a writer.

High Bottom Drunk breaks new ground for me as a writer. It is neither a short story nor a case study. The protagonist, Steve Campbell, was never my patient. Under different circumstances, he could have been. He carried more emotional baggage than most of the people who pay me for psychological help, and he rummaged through that baggage like a man possessed. Had we met in my office instead of in the back alley that separated our homes, I would have welcomed him as a patient.

I cannot honestly say that Steve and I were friends. We liked each other. We spent a great amount of time together. But our relationship lacked the reciprocity required for true friendship. For the better part of three years, Steve talked and I listened. This arrangement worked out well, for Steve had one hell of a story to tell, and I'm a writer of people's stories.

I met Steve in September 1973, a few days following his move to Austin, Texas. He had just taken a small rent house on the outer edge of what is known locally as the "university district." Our backyard gates opened to the same alley, where we happened to run into each other on a Saturday afternoon. I was setting out my trash. Steve was walking home from the nearby convenience store with a six-pack of Shiner beer in each hand. We spent the better part of the rest of the day in my living room. That was the first few of what turned into hundreds of hours together in that room, with Steve talking and me listening.

Many of those hours were given to what might be called fairly meaningless chatter. Every so often, though, Steve opened his heart. Most of *those* conversations occurred late night/early morning, when Steve was struggling, hurting, unable or unwilling to sleep, and somehow able to coax me out of my bed and into my living room chair. The intrusions were usually worth the effort. There were a few times when Steve rambled and bored me to tears. But when he was *on,* he held me spellbound.

I knew from our first meeting that Steve was good story material, and I wrote the first few pages of *High Bottom Drunk* not long after our first visit. When I told him what I had in mind regarding his story he laughed out loud. "Yeah, right," he said. "Like there's anything interesting enough about me to put in a fucking book." I assured him that there was. "Yeah, whatever," he said with a dismissing wave of his hand.

I began sharing the *High Bottom Drunk* manuscript with Steve when I was two years into the project, about six months following a very significant turn in his life. When he realized the extent of my work he was dumbfounded.

"This is unbelievable, man. I mean, I knew you were kind of working on my story, but this is a goddamn epic. Look at this. I don't even remember telling you some of this stuff."

"It's fiction, Steve. It's a novel," I said, smiling.

He laughed. "A novel, huh? That's a good one. Man, what are all of these people going to think when they see this? Holy shit, what's my mom gonna say?"

I said, "Just tell them the truth. It's a novel. It's fiction. It says so right there on the opening pages of the book."

Steve caught his breath, got his feet under him, and shook his head slowly. "Well...I guess you know what you're doing," he said.

"Does it scare you?" I asked.

He looked at the manuscript in his hands and spoke softly. "Yeah, I guess it does. I mean, there's just so much of it, you know? And it's so damn graphic."

Fortunately, Steve's doubts concerning *High Bottom Drunk* faded quickly. Within a couple of weeks he had gathered enthusiasm for the project and had climbed on board to support it. He helped edit some of the more difficult parts of the story. He convinced me to leave myself and our relationship out of the story line altogether, suggesting instead that I simply tell the story from the viewpoint of an invisible, omniscient observer.

"Ah, sort of a God-like J. D. Salinger hiding in the shadows, huh?" I asked.

He laughed and replied, "Well, isn't that pretty much the way you see yourself?"

I didn't ask him how much, if at all, he was kidding.

As *High Bottom Drunk* approached completion, Steve pushed me hard to finish it. "Man, I can hardly wait," he said. "There will finally be a truly honest text on addiction and recovery that people will actually read." He paused for a moment and then added, "You *do* think people will read it, don't you?"

I nodded cautiously. "Yeah, I think it will find its niche, at least among people who have had any kind of personal experience with addiction and recovery. I think those folks will find it compelling. And who knows, the greater reading public may just jump all over it. Stranger things have happened."

When Steve smiled, I continued. "It sounds as though your fear of people reading it is gone," I said.

"Yeah, it's long gone. Hell, I don't care who sees it. In fact, the truth be known, this book should be required reading for anyone who's ever known me, or even anyone like me, for that matter."

High Bottom Drunk is Steve Campbell's story. It's his real story—absolutely unyieldingly true. Calling it fiction is technicality correct, but it's a stretch. Names and dates have been altered, but that's about it. Characters in this story will, in fact, recognize themselves. Please note: That is not an apology.

I salute Steve Campbell's courage. And yours.

Section One:

What It Was Like

CHAPTER 1

High Bottom Drunk, if nothing else, is a nice, catchy little phrase. I dropped it on a university psychology class a couple of years ago, and one student said it made him think of a lush with an oddly placed body part. I caught the image, and despite myself, I had to smile. I informed him that while the term does refer to a particular type of alcoholic, it has nothing to do with human anatomy. Genetics, perhaps, but not anatomy.

High bottom drunks are addicts. They are addicted to the drug alcohol. Indeed, the terms *high bottom drunk* and *high bottom addict* are interchangeable. They refer to exactly the same people.

High bottom drunks' addictions are very real. They spawn very real life problems. Those problems are seldom catastrophic, but they always cause harm.

High bottom drunks hurt themselves and others, and they pay a price for that. Generally speaking, though, the price they pay is minimal. They land on people's resentment lists but almost never make the morning papers.

Some high bottom drunks escape condemnation by offsetting the negative with the positive. They minimize the significance of their alcohol and drug abuse by flaunting their accomplishments. They can do that because high bottom drunks are notoriously functional. Some are quite successful. A few stand at the top of the heap.

Low bottom drunks and *low bottom addicts,* on the other hand, are the really bad ones. They're the ones whose problems are exceptional, tragic, and frequently public.

Some low bottom drunks simply get lost. They live in alleyways and under bridges; they pursue anonymity and die before their time. People call them disgusting. Other low bottom drunks go the opposite direction and achieve immortality. Janis Joplin and Jimmy Hendrix are remembered as much for their alcohol and drug-related deaths as they are for their music. People call their lives tragic.

Fortunately, perhaps, *most* alcoholics and addicts have high bottoms rather than low ones.

Steve Campbell could have been a high bottom drunk poster boy. His alcohol and other drug addictions caused problems. And those problems caused suffering. But they appeared pretty minor within the context of his successful life.

Steve graduated college. He worked hard. He made good money, paid his bills, and provided for his family. He never got arrested. Never shot dope. Never even fell into the proverbial

16

punchbowl. People liked and respected him. Some called him a golden boy. No one called him an addict.

Steve knew he drank too much. And he knew it caused him problems. He even got down on himself from time to time. But like all good high bottom drunks, he rationalized, justified, and minimized his alcohol and drug use to the extent that he continued to use in relatively good conscience.

During the course of his seemingly inauspicious drinking and drugging career, Steve only one time—one day—really experienced the worst nature and fullest extent of his problem. That was not the night that a cop gave him a stern warning instead of a DWI. It was not the evening he acted like an idiot in front of his best friend's parents and was asked to leave his friend's home. It was not the night that Bev caught him in the downstairs closet with one of her best friends. It wasn't the morning he awoke at 4:00 o'clock in a field behind a country western dance hall with puke covering the front of his shirt. It was not the day his three best friends confronted him about his escalating alcohol and drug use. It was just one summer day when he drank too much alcohol and mixed it with too many drugs.

On that day, Steve humiliated and degraded himself and put his life directly in harm's way. Luck, or perhaps it was grace, forgave him and let him off the hook. The experience left him feeling lost, alone, confused, and afraid. It convinced him once and for all that he had to change the nature of his relationship with alcohol and drugs. It did not convince him to quit drinking and using, but it brought him to that threshold.

In terms of alcohol and drug addiction, Steve Campbell's story is neither shocking nor tragic. Like most high bottom drunks, Steve was a fundamentally good person who crossed the invisible line that separates individuals who drink and use drugs for fun and pleasure from those who drink and use out of necessity. The line is a thin one. The side of the line on which a person resides is not always obvious.

Steve Campbell resided on the alcoholic/addict side of the line. Despite his own and others' perception of him, he was a man addicted to alcohol and drugs. A high bottom addict. A high bottom drunk.

CHAPTER 2

Lois had exactly three sources for information regarding Steve: His sister, Sheri; his estranged wife, Bev; and Steve. Of the three, Sheri was the most reliable.

17

"Honey, have you seen Steve lately? I think he's avoiding me."

Sheri smiled. "Your radar must be up today, Mother. He dropped by the house last night."

"Was he alright?" Lois asked.

"Well, I've seen him better. He was in one of his 'I need to talk' moods."

"What did he need to talk about?"

"Oh, I don't know, Mother. I'm not all that anxious to go into it again. You know how he gets when he's like that."

"No, Sheri, I don't know how he gets. Not really. He doesn't come to me when he needs to talk. I wish he would, but he doesn't. I wish you'd tell me what's going on."

"Mother, I don't know what's going on with Steve. I'm not sure anyone does. He was drinking. He was upset. He didn't say so, but I think he must have had another run-in with Dad. I guess he still wants Dad's approval, and he can't seem to accept the fact that Dad just doesn't *give* his approval."

"That's for damn sure," Lois said. "I know I never got it from him. None of us did. Your dad doesn't love people that way. I don't think he can."

Sheri nodded. "I know, but Steve takes it personally. And sometimes when he drinks too much, old issues and feelings come up, and he can't control them. When that happens, I just sit and listen. I don't know what else to do; there's no way to console him."

"Well, you might as well tell me. What was it that came up last night?"

Sheri stared at her mom. "You're a glutton for punishment, aren't you, Mother. Why do you insist on hearing all of this stuff? It's all from the past—the long past. And it's not really even about you."

Lois nodded. "It is about me. It's easy to blame your dad for all of those old issues, but they're not just his fault. He didn't operate in a vacuum. I was there every step of the way. Your dad and I were both sick. Neither of us had any respect for ourselves or for each other. There were times when we hated each other's guts. I believe there were even times when we wanted to kill each other.

"And do you know what? We drug Steve right through the middle of it—time after time after time. We used him; he was our pawn. So don't tell me that it's not about me. And maybe I am a glutton for punishment, but for whatever reason, it helps me to know what's happening with Steve. It helps me to understand him. And maybe, just maybe, it will give me something that I can use to help him."

Sheri held her hands up as if being robbed at gunpoint. "Okay, I give up, but I'm going to keep it short," she said. "If

Steve had a theme, I'd say it was abandonment and rejection. He talked about how Dad always ran off and left us when the going got tough between you and him, especially after I went away to school.

"He brought up that time when he went off with Dad and tried to live with him in that motel. He's still very bitter about that. He feels as though Dad's rejection of him, or his unwillingness to accept him or approve of him, or whatever it is that Dad has done to him is responsible for his problems and for the way he feels about himself. He said that sometimes he thinks he's a bad seed, a third or fourth generation piece of you-know-what, who is destined to live and die that way.

"He also feels as though none of us understand him, and I suppose when you get right down to it, he's probably right about that. He knows we love him, but he feels like he's alone, and he's starting to think that he'll always be alone. He thinks he doesn't have the wherewithal to be in a loving relationship, and even if he did, he doesn't deserve to have one. He's terrified that Lynn and Eddie will grow up feeling about him the way he feels about Dad."

Sheri paused for a moment. "Mother, none of this is new. You know that. I've had these conversations with Steve plenty of times. And it's always been when he's had too much to drink. I've never heard him say these things when he's sober. And I don't think he feels like that when he's sober. I'd be willing to bet you anything he's not feeling like that today."

Lois closed her eyes and took a breath. "I know how Steve feels. I understand it a lot better than either of you think I do. I've been there. I've felt that way about myself. I've felt worthless and alone. I've gone to sleep at night hoping and praying that I would never wake up. The only difference is that I didn't have bad parents to blame it on like he does. I only had myself."

"Mother, please. Give yourself some credit. You're not like that anymore."

"Maybe not, but I'll tell you, Honey, it was pretty damn awful for Steve. I'll never forgive myself for what we did to him those last couple of years that he was at home. It was a nightmare. It was a nightmare for all of us, but he got the brunt of it."

"Well, I promise you, Mother, he doesn't blame you. In fact, I think he feels like all three of us were Dad's victims."

Lois shook her head. "That's ironic when you think about it. In some ways, I was worse than Henry. At least when he blew up and took off, he was gone. I stayed around, but I abandoned Steve in every other way. I was there physically, but mentally and emotionally I was totally absent. I had nothing to give him. I was empty inside, and he had to see me like that every day. A young man should not have to go through that with his mother."

19

Sheri sighed. "Well, Mother, I'll say it again, and I wish you'd hear me. That's not what he was saying last night, and I'm quite sure that's not the way he feels. I think he would have told me if it was."

"Well...." said Lois, quietly now, "There's one thing I do know for sure. He's drinking too much, and I know he's taking drugs. He won't admit it, but I know he is. It just breaks my heart to see what's happening to him.

"Do you remember what a sweet little boy Steve was? There wasn't a mean bone in his body. Everyone adored him. When y'all were little, when we still lived with Mama and Papa, Steve would wander around the neighborhood, going from door to door, just to say 'Hello' to people—mostly old people. Sometimes he was gone for hours at a time. Now when I see him or talk to him, what I feel is his distance. He has his guard up with me, and I can't penetrate it. We don't connect. It's not that I blame him. It's just that I don't know what to do about it."

Sheri touched her mother's arm. "He's still a good person, Mother. At least his intentions are good. His heart is good. You know, he's great with the kids—his and mine both. Bobbie and Brandi are crazy about him. He's just going through a rough time right now. He's confused, and to tell you the truth, I think he's scared. He's got a lot on his plate, especially the divorce and everything that goes along with it. He knows he's going to get murdered on the property settlement. He's worried about Lynn and Eddie. And then there's that whole thing about being alone. I think it would be hard on anyone.

"You know, Mother, Steve goes through these things, but he snaps out of them. He's resilient. He always has been. One day he's down, and the next day he's up. But regardless, it's his stuff, not yours. You did not hurt Steve on purpose, and as far as I can see, you've made your amends many times over. Honestly, Mother, more than anything, I think Steve is just drinking too much."

"Sheri, people drink like that for a reason. In the best case scenario, he's medicating something, like I was when I started drinking. I was so unhappy that I drank just to feel half-normal. Then the drinking got to be such a part of my life that I couldn't stop, even when I wanted to. That's the worst case scenario, and I'm afraid Steve's already there. I'm afraid that he's an alcoholic just like I was and just like your dad is still."

"Well, I don't know. You might be right. I hope not, but you might be," Sheri said.

Lois leaned forward in her chair. "Sheri, tell me the truth. You don't think Steve would do anything to hurt himself, do you?"

20

Sheri returned her mother's gaze. "Mother, you're taking this thing too far. Steve's not the kind of person who would do that. He's never even hinted at it."

Lois nodded. "Okay. I just needed to ask."

When Lois got home, she fixed lunch and sat alone at her kitchen table. As she reflected on her conversation with Sheri, her imagination ran wild. She pictured Steve all alone, Steve drunk and depressed, Steve drunk and driving, Steve drunk and blowing his brains out. She picked up the phone to call him but at the last second dialed Bev's number instead.

Lois liked Bev. She hadn't always. When Bev got pregnant at 19, Lois privately accused her of trapping Steve into marriage. She encouraged Bev to terminate the pregnancy rather than saddle Steve with a wife and child when he was so obviously not ready. Bev had felt offended, but instead of resenting Lois, she set out to prove herself to her. She succeeded.

Bev had kept her distance from Lois and the rest of Steve's family since she and Steve separated. The first time they split up, two years previous, she stayed in constant contact with Lois and Sheri in order to track Steve's whereabouts, his moods, and his intentions. This time, however, she understood that he was not coming back, and she had little interest in his whereabouts, moods, or intentions.

"Hi, Bev. It's Lois. How are you?"

"Hello, Lois. I'm fine. Yourself?"

"Pretty good. I was just thinking about you, wondering how you and the kids are doing. And to be honest, I was wondering if you've seen Steve."

"Well, the first part is easy. The kids and I are fine. As for the second, yes, Steve dropped by unannounced yesterday afternoon. He said he wanted to see the kids, but he hardly paid any attention to them. He only stayed for about half an hour. Actually, I think he came by to show off his new car. I guess you've seen it—a new Corvette convertible. He had Lenny Miller with him, and he knows full well how I feel about that S.O.B. I've asked Steve not to bring Lenny around here. I can hardly stand the sight of him."

"I know. I feel the same way. He's nothing but trouble. Anyway, Bev, I'm just a little worried about Steve. I hope you don't mind my asking, but did he seem okay to you?"

"I don't know, Lois. We ended up angry, as usual. We're not really even supposed to be talking to each other. Both of our lawyers have said we should leave each other alone until the divorce is final. It's hard to do, though, especially with the kids. I want them to see Steve, and I want Steve to feel free to come by and see them. Lately, though, we've found something to argue about every time we've seen each other."

"I'm sorry to hear that. It must be hard on all of you, especially Lynn."

"It is. We try to stay out of earshot, but you know Lynn. She has very big ears. Plus, she's incredibly perceptive. And smart. I can't hide much of anything from her."

Lois took a breath. "Bev, I hate to ask this, but was Steve drinking when you saw him? The reason I ask is that he showed up at Sheri's last night, and he was drinking and feeling down. He said some things to her that have me worried. He gets pretty depressed, you know, and I guess I'm afraid that he might try to hurt himself."

Bev hesitated for a moment and then said, "Lois, Steve's not my responsibility. And, really, he's not your responsibility, either. The only thing I need to worry about is what he does when he has Lynn and Eddie, and so far, as far as I know, he hasn't done anything to hurt them or put them in danger. Maybe I should be more concerned about him, but you know, Lois, I worried about him enough when he was still here. I have other things that I need to deal with now. I hope that doesn't sound too cold. It's just the reality of my situation."

"I'm sorry, Bev. I probably shouldn't even be talking to you about this. I know it's not your problem. I also know how hard it must be for you right now. I know what it's like to be left alone with two little kids. He is helping you out, isn't he?"

Bev's voice softened. "Yes. He is. Actually, he's been very helpful. It's hard, though. I mean, I'm okay, but Lynn really misses him. She cries for him all the time, and when she tries to call him, he's hardly ever there. He doesn't even seem to be at his store anymore. But to answer your question, yes, he is helping us. I've got to give him credit for that."

"Well, Bev, do you need anything? I mean, is there anything I can do to help?"

"No, Lois. Really, we're fine." There was a brief silence, and then Bev continued. "Lois, listen. I don't know what Steve's problem is. He and I can't talk. We try, but we just can't do it. There's too much animosity between us right now. I don't want to see Steve hurting. I really don't. But I have accepted the fact that he is gone. I didn't ask for it to be this way, and I didn't want it to be this way. But I've accepted it. He doesn't love me, and we aren't going to get back together this time. So I need to be thinking about me and the kids. I'm sure that Steve is drinking a lot. My guess is that he's also doing drugs, too, but that's not my problem unless it affects the kids.

"I'm doing my best to let go of Steve. I'm trying to move on. Steve is a smart, enterprising man. I've never seen him stay down for too long. I think he'll figure it out and be okay. And I know it's none of my business, Lois, but why don't you give yourself a break and let go of him, yourself?"

Lois replied slowly. "I know, Bev. I know. I really should. Worrying about him doesn't do anyone any good. I guess I still feel responsible for him, though. Sometimes I catch myself thinking of him as my little boy, even though he hasn't been that for a very long time. I can't help it; that's just the way I am." She paused. "Anyway, Bev, I should let you go. Give me a call, okay? Especially if you need anything. I'd be glad to keep the kids if you want to get out."

Bev hung up the phone. She caught an image of Steve in her mind. She imagined him alone and depressed. Then she recalled his brief visit the day before, in his new car—a Corvette no less, and with Lenny Miller in tow. She shook her head slowly back and forth. "Fuck him," she whispered to herself.

Lois hung up her phone. She pictured Steve as a little boy, smiling, happy, totally carefree. She wiped tears from her eyes.

She thought about her own alcoholism. She recalled the worst of it, toward the end of her marriage to Henry. The public intoxication arrest, which she demanded even though the cop begged her to shut up, go back into the house, and sleep it off. Passing out on the living room floor during her own dinner party, leaving Henry, drunk, angry, and embarrassed, to send their guests home. Starting fights with Henry that she knew would escalate into violence, oftentimes in front of Steve. Forcing Steve to kneel with her beside her bed while she sobbed and slurred prayers for forgiveness and salvation. Cursing Steve and slapping his face when he confronted her behavior.

For one three-month stretch during Steve's last year at home, when she and Steve lived there alone, she isolated herself behind a locked bedroom door. She left the house only during the day, when Steve wasn't around, to buy vodka, wine, and TV dinners. She unlocked her door at night to fight with Henry when he happened to drop by. Steve was fifteen. He fended for himself.

Lois recalled the bitterness of her divorce from Henry and its aftermath, which she later recognized as the bottoming out stage of her alcoholism. She seldom ate. She talked to no one. She cried herself to sleep. She had little of value—materially or spiritually. She had very little hope. She wanted to die but could not kill herself.

Instead of dying, Lois stumbled into Alcoholics Anonymous and got sober. With abundant support from other sober alcoholics, she took back her life. She slowly regained her health and rediscovered her sanity. She married Chester, another sober member of AA, on her one-year sober birthday. She found some semblance of peace. That had been almost nine years ago. In every respect, her life had improved. But she agonized over Steve. Her guilt haunted her.

23

CHAPTER 3

Lois and Henry did not make Steve an addict. Alcoholics and drug addicts are born and then they make themselves. They are born with bodies receptive to addiction. It's part of their genetic structure. Then, in response to the circumstances of their lives, they perceive the need to change the way they feel. When they discover that alcohol and/or other drugs do the trick, they act predictably. They use. Without understanding the implications of their actions, they feed addictive substances to their addiction-prone bodies. Unfortunately, it's a perfect fit. Body, mind, and environment collaborate to produce addictive disease.

Steve Campbell was born fully wired for addiction. Alcoholism ran in his family the way that dark hair and brown eyes run in others. Henry and Henry's father were full-blown alcoholics. Henry's mother secretly sipped vodka and abused prescription drugs. His maternal grandparents, who helped raise him, drank beer from morning till night. Lois was a late-blooming alcoholic. She took up regular social drinking at age 30 and crossed the line into alcohol addiction within a year. Lois' parents did not drink alcohol, but her paternal grandparents were both alcoholics and pill junkies.

Despite this legacy of addiction, Steve had little direct contact with drinking and virtually none with alcoholic behavior for the first six years of his life. During that time, Lois' parents, Mama and Papa Rogers, provided Lois, Steve, and Sheri a sane, safe, secure home. And while living with her parents, Lois rarely took a drink and never drank in front of her family. Henry lived 200 miles away and did not visit. The other grandparents and great grandparents seldom drank in front of the little kids. When they did, Mama and Papa quietly took Steve and Sheri home.

Within that environment, Steve felt secure, confident, and happy. He trusted everyone.

Then things changed. Shortly before his sixth birthday, Steve's secure world came apart at the seams. Henry and Lois remarried, and Steve met his dad for the first time in his memory. Henry re-enlisted in the Army and signed up for an overseas tour of duty. Before Steve and Sheri understood what was happening, they were on a ship bound for Sasebo, Japan with their father and mother. And the chaos had begun.

During the two-week voyage, Henry drank heavily. While intoxicated, he complained loudly about everything from the sleeping quarters and the food to the watered-down drinks in the bar. He used profanities that Steve and Sheri had never heard. He criticized them in front of other people; he disparaged them in

24

private. He yelled at Lois for no apparent reason. One night when she yelled back, he shoved her up against a wall and held her there while he screamed in her face. He vomited in his bunk and blamed the ship's cook for making him sick.

Halfway through the trip, Lois received word from home that Papa Rogers had died from a ruptured brain aneurysm.

The altered circumstances of Steve's life took their toll. During two years in Japan, he lost his gentle, friendly nature. He lost his confidence in himself and other people. He built walls around himself. He became vigilant and cautious when Henry drank alcohol. He ran scared when Henry and Lois drank together. He taught himself how to sleep in the midst of his parents' screaming matches.

Steve, Sheri, Lois, and Henry returned to the states when Steve was eight. Steve came back angry and afraid. He began lying in earnest at age nine, stealing at 10, smoking cigarettes at 11, and fighting at 12. By his 13th birthday, he hated his life. He trusted no one.

During the summer of his 13th year, Steve stumbled upon a solution. He discovered alcohol. A neighborhood friend sold him a quart of beer. As he drank it, he gained confidence and courage. By the time he finished it, he felt happy and carefree. He forgot about everything except being high and at peace.

From that day forward through his adolescent and early adulthood years, Steve seldom passed up a chance to drink. That he might follow in his ancestors' footsteps and become an alcoholic never crossed his mind. And furthermore, had someone laid it all out for him (addiction-prone body plus addictive substances typically equals addictive disease) he would have chosen to take his chances.

"Well, I guess we'll see, won't we," he would have said.

CHAPTER 4

The day following her conversations with Sheri and Bev, Lois decided not to wait any longer for Steve to get in touch. She called his apartment, expecting to get his answering machine. To her surprise, he answered the phone.

"Steve's Bar & Grill. What's your pleasure?"

"For crying out loud, Steve, why do you answer the phone like that? This is your mother."

"Hey, mom. I don't know. In a playful mood, I guess. Gotta take advantage of them when they come along, you know? What's up?"

"What's up is that I want you to come over here for dinner tonight. I feel like I never see you anymore, so I'm going to bribe you with your favorite meal—roast beef, mashed potatoes and gravy, fresh green beans, and cornbread. What do you think?"

"Well, I think that if you're going to offer a bribe, that's a pretty compelling one. The only problem is that I've got a hot date tonight. Can we eat early? Or would you like me to bring her with me?"

"No, let's just plan to eat early. Would 6:00 o'clock work?"

"Yeah, I think it would. It doesn't give me a whole lot of time, but I bet I can handle it. Want me to bring anything?"

"No, Honey. Just bring yourself."

"Okay then, it sounds like you've got company coming. I'll be there. Anything else, Mother?"

"No. Why, are you in a hurry?"

"Well, kind of. A friend dropped by a little while ago, and we're in the middle of a very serious conversation."

"Okay, I won't keep you. Don't be late, now. We'll eat right about 6:00. Okay?"

"You got it. See you then." Steve hung up the phone and winked at Debbie, who was sitting next to him on the sofa in a pair of white cotton bikini panties. She was nineteen, very pretty, very sweet, very naïve, and very infatuated with Steve.

"Your mom, huh? Checking up on her little boy? Good thing she didn't just drop by, right?" She took a hit on the joint they had been sharing and handed it to Steve.

He laughed. "Yeah, I guess so. She's a great mom, but she worries too much. She insists on seeing me every so often to make sure I'm still breathing. Anyway, enough about that. Being stoned and naked in the middle of the day with you is a hell of a lot more interesting than my mother's paranoia." Steve took a hit and passed the joint back to Debbie.

"You know what, Debbie?" he said. "You are a very, very beautiful woman. You have the face of an angel, and as perfect a body as I have ever seen. What do you do to make yourself look so good?"

Debbie smiled and blushed slightly. "It's no big deal, really. I probably just inherited it. My mom's almost forty, and she still looks great. You know, you look pretty good yourself, Stevey." Debbie inhaled deeply, passed the joint, and slipped her hand up through the leg of Steve's boxers.

Steve closed his eyes. He rested his head on the back of the couch, and while he smoked, Debbie rubbed his penis gently until it was erect. Then she took it out. She leaned over and put him into her mouth for a minute and then brought her face up to his. She kissed him softly and slipped her tongue into his mouth. "How do you taste to yourself?" she whispered.

"Not bad," he whispered back. "But to tell you the truth, I'm more curious about how you might taste."

"Oh, yeah? Well, you can go there whenever you're ready."

Steve repositioned her onto her back and slowly removed her panties. He perused her body from head to toe. Then he went down on her—gently, deliberately, savoring her completely. She came once while he gave her head and again during intercourse.

Afterwards, they dozed off in each other's arms. Just before dropping off to sleep, Steve caught the sweet smell of pot and sweat and semen in the air and the soft voice of Rita Coolidge on the stereo. He awoke an hour later to the sound of Debbie's breathing. He nudged her awake.

"I need to get up and shower, Debbie. Want to join me?"

"Yeah, I'll join you. But first, can I ask you something?"

"Sure. Shoot."

"Was I good for you?"

Steve smiled and kissed her. "You were incredible. The best. I've never had better."

Debbie pulled him closer and stroked his back. "By any chance am I the hot date you told your mom about?"

Steve laughed. "Yeah, sure you are. What did you think?"

"I didn't know. I was hoping, but I wasn't sure."

Steve winked at her. "You're crazy if you think I'd let you slip away that easily. You can hang out around here if you want to—you know, make yourself at home while I go over to my mother's. I'll come back and pick you up around 8:00. We'll go do something fun and then come back here. You can spend the night if you'd like."

"That sounds great, Steve. Where are you going to take me?"

"Hey, you name it, Babe. Mexico? New Orleans? Singapore? Wherever your sweet little heart desires."

Debbie laughed. "I don't need Singapore, Steve. A movie would work for me. Really, I just want to be with you. I want to give you whatever *your* sweet little heart desires. I'm yours till 9:00 o'clock tomorrow morning. Church, you know? Is that okay?"

"That's perfect. In the meantime, how about walking your perfect little ass over to the fridge and grabbing us a cold beer while I warm up the shower?"

Steve watched Debbie walk to the kitchen. "Sweet, sweet, sweet young thing," he thought to himself. "I've finally died and gone to heaven, and lo and behold, it was worth the wait."

Steve arrived at Lois and Chester's fifteen minutes late. On the way there, he stopped at the convenience store and bought breath mints to mask the smell of alcohol and eye drops to remove the redness from the pot.

"It's good, Mom," he said as he ate his favorite meal. "It's really good. I'm glad to have some home cooking for a change. I miss it."

"I bet you do. You're as thin as a rail. I wish you'd come over and eat with us more often. So who's the big date with?"

"Oh, just a girl I know from the bank. Very nice. Very safe. Nothing even remotely serious, so don't ask, and don't worry. I think we're just going to a movie."

Lois shook her head. "I wasn't going to ask, and I'm not worried. I was just curious. I know you're smart enough not to jump into another relationship anytime soon. I did want to talk to you about something else, though, Steve. Can we be serious for a few minutes?"

Steve looked up from his plate. "Ah, the price of the meal is about to be revealed," he said. He looked at Chester and said, "What do you think, Ches? Is it safe to talk seriously with her tonight?"

Chester smiled. "I'm afraid I can't promise you anything, my friend. You know Mama. She's liable to come up with almost anything."

"Yeah, you've got that right. Oh well, what the hell. I guess I can stand it. As long as it doesn't relate to my sex life, my morals, my drinking, or money."

Chester laughed. "A man your age, what else would you have to be serious about?"

They all laughed, but when Steve looked at Lois again, her smile was gone. "Okay, Mother, go ahead. Let me have it." Steve said.

Lois hesitated for a moment and then started. "Actually, Steve, it *is* about your drinking. I haven't said a whole lot about it for some time now, but I need to tell you that I'm worried about it, and I'm worried about you. It seems as though every time I see you or talk to you these days, you have been drinking. I also keep up with you through my grapevine, and I hear the same report from other people. Long story short, I'm afraid you're drinking too much. Frankly, I'm scared that you'll wind up just like your dad and me. Sometimes, I even think you're hell bent on it.

"Steve, I don't want to pry, and God knows I don't want to run you off, but I felt as though I had to say something. I wouldn't even bring it up if I didn't love you, and if it wasn't for the fact that unfortunately, I know so much about problem drinking, as you well know. Anyway, that's what I want to talk about."

Steve watched his mother's face while she spoke. Now he looked away from her and down at his plate. He ran his fork through his potatoes. "Well," he said, "You're not going to run me off, not as long as you can cook this good, anyway." He flashed her a smile. She remained expressionless.

"Okay," he relented. "I hear you. But listen, stop worrying about me. Everything's cool. Nothing's wrong. Nothing's out of hand. I'm just having a good time being a bachelor for the first time in my adult life. That's all. I promise. I'm all right. Really I am. Okay?"

"No, Steve, it's not that simple. I know you think I'm meddlesome, but I can't help it. You're my son. I love you. And I'm afraid you're in trouble and you don't even know it. Chewing gum and breath mints don't cover up the smell of alcohol. Your happy-go-lucky disposition feels phony; it feels like an act. You think I'm blind because I'm old and square, but I know you better than you think I do."

Steve looked at Lois and smiled. "Boy, you're on a tear tonight. I'm starting to feel less like a guest and more like a suspected criminal under bright lights. Listen, Mother, I promise you I'm okay. I had a bad night over at Sheri's that I'm sure you know all about, but those are very rare. Most of the time, I'm as happy as a lark. There's nothing to worry about. If there was, I'd tell you. Okay? Come on, can we just finish eating now?"

Lois shook her head slowly. "What am I going to do with you, Steve? I want so much for you to have a good life. You have so much going for you. Please don't throw it away.

"The least you can do is promise me something. If you do start seeing that your drinking is a problem, I want you to talk to me about it. I've been there. I understand alcoholism, and I can help. Chester's been there, too. He helped save my life nine years ago. Isn't that right, Chester?"

"Yes, dear. I suppose that's right." He looked at Steve and nodded his head. "I'm here for you if you need me, Steve. As long as I'm living and breathing, you can count on that. You know I love you."

"I know that, Ches. I would never question that," Steve said sincerely.

"Steve," Lois continued, "we know how insidious alcoholism can be. With almost no effort at all, it can trick you into believing that you're all right when you're really not. It happens all the time, every day, and it happens to people who are much worse off than you are. For Christ's sake, look at your dad. He says he's a social drinker. And he believes it. Do you? Do you think for one minute that he's not an alcoholic?"

Steve raised his hand for Lois to stop. "Okay, Mother. I get it. I promise. I even swear. If there's a problem, I'll call you. But I want you to stop worrying. I'm not like Dad. I'm not an alcoholic. I've been there, too, don't forget. I lived with you and Dad until I was sixteen. Remember? I know exactly what alcoholism looks like. I've seen plenty of it."

Lois took a deep breath. "That's true, Steve, but believe me, it always looks different on someone else than it does on yourself. It's easier to see on someone else than it is to see on yourself. And besides that, you don't have to sink as low as your dad and I did in order for it to be a problem. If you take it as far as we did, you may not survive the trip. We were damn lucky. At least I was. I can't speak for him."

Steve nodded. "I know, Mother."

Lois waited for Steve to look her in the eye. When he did, she said, "Remember your promise. You'll call me. I have your word on it. Am I right?"

"Yes, you have my word. Can we talk about something else now? I'd like to finish my dinner."

Steve left Lois and Chester's with a full stomach, a doggie bag, weakly suppressed anger, and wounded pride. As he pulled away from the house, he caught a glimpse of them in his rearview mirror. They were smiling and waving goodbye.

"Just because you're a goddamn alcoholic doesn't mean I'm one," he said to the mirror. "And another thing; I'll never, fucking ever, be like Dad. That's the goddamn promise you can take to the goddamn bank."

Steve picked up Debbie at his apartment at 8:30. They went to a movie and afterwards stopped off at one of Steve's watering holes for beer and snacks. They talked and laughed and at 2:00 AM went back to Steve's for drugs and very good sex. Debbie missed church the next morning. When Steve dropped her at her parents' house, she got his word that he would call her again soon. He never did. It wasn't because he didn't like her. He just didn't feel like calling. Instead, he gave her phone number to Lenny Miller.

CHAPTER 5

Most high bottom drunks get married, have kids, make friends, hold jobs, and pay bills. They live in houses, mow their lawns, take out the trash, change the oil in their cars, and call their mothers on Mother's Day. Many go to church. Some hold high office. For the most part, they are functional, regular people who drink too much. They always damage but seldom destroy their lives. Steve was a high bottom drunk. Not so Lenny Miller.

Lenny Miller and Steve Campbell were best friends through high school and a little beyond. Actually, they were more than best friends. They were a team. They partied hard. They drank hard. No one kept up with them when they got on a roll. They played off of each other like a seasoned comedy act, and although they were offensive to some people, they were the life of the party to most.

Steve and Lenny were incorrigible. They knew very few limits. Unenlightened women of the early-to-mid 1960's adored them. They especially liked Lenny, the rascal, who slept with more beautiful women than anyone could count but seldom slept with the same one more than twice.

Lenny was a gifted athlete. He went to college on a full basketball scholarship but only played one season because of poor work habits and pitiful grades. He eventually flunked out of three different colleges and never accumulated enough college credits to be classified a sophomore.

Through carelessness and impaired judgment, Steve and Lenny both impregnated and married their girlfriends during the summer of 1966, when they were both twenty years old. Each threw the other a memorable bachelor party. Each served as the other's best man.

Lenny's wife filed for divorce on the date of their first wedding anniversary. His only comment was, "Fuck the bitch if she can't take a joke." Steve named his daughter, Lynn, after Lenny. Bev went along with the idea despite her contempt for Lenny and everything he stood for.

Shortly after his divorce, Lenny landed the job of his dreams. He interviewed, hired, and helped train stewardesses for a major airline company. He loved his job dearly, but his drinking and drug use sabotaged his best efforts to hang on to it. The company had a liberal impaired employee policy, but Lenny was fired when he went AWOL from his third turn at alcoholism treatment. He slipped out one night to have a couple of beers and got caught. It was not the first time he sneaked out. It was just the first time he got caught.

Lenny avoided accepting responsibility for his loss by blaming the treatment center. "Man, can you believe that shit? Those motherfuckers sneak into my goddamn private room and look under my goddamn bed covers. Is that invasion of privacy, or what? I'm telling you, man, I ought to sue the goddamn sons of bitches! They made me lose the best fucking job I've ever had!"

Bev never liked or trusted Lenny, even during the early years of her and Steve's relationship, when Lenny was still Steve's best friend. Lenny sucked up to Bev, but she saw through his act. She could not see through Steve's, but she saw straight through Lenny's.

Bev tolerated Steve and Lenny's behavior, even though they found trouble almost every time they got together. She blamed Lenny for his bad influence on Steve. Lenny considered that a compliment. Steve gladly let him take the heat.

Lenny Miller was no high bottom drunk. Wild and funny at 17, he was reckless, annoying, and offensive at 23. At 27, he crossed the line that separates high bottom from low bottom alcoholics. He held one menial job after another. He wrote hot checks and ignored his bills. He hid his car at night to avoid repossession. He ripped people off. Friends avoided him like the plague.

Even Steve gave up on him. In July 1973, following a party at Steve's apartment, Lenny informed Steve that he was going to crash on the sofa. Instead of sleeping, though, he sat up all night and drank the rest of the beer, played the stereo on high volume, and made long distance calls on Steve's phone. At 5:00 AM, he got naked, threw open Steve's bedroom door, and loudly propositioned Steve's girlfriend, Rachel, while Steve and Rachel were sleeping together in Steve's bed. Rachel told him to screw himself, which he did.

Lenny did not remember the incident the next day. He accused Steve and Rachel of making the whole thing up as a way to get rid of him. He became enraged and punched Steve in the face when Steve told him to leave. Their friendship, which had been deteriorating anyway, did not survive the episode.

Over the next three years, Lenny's luck ran out. By the time he turned 30, he had nothing left—no friends, no family, and no possessions that anyone would bother to steal. His parents refused to accept his collect telephone calls. Old drinking buddies disclaimed him and held him up to their wives and girlfriends as an example of a *real* alcoholic.

Lenny called Steve one night from the Salvation Army and said he would like to see him, just for old times' sake. Steve declined, and Lenny lashed out.

"Man, you and me, we've got too much fucking history for you to blow me off like that. Who made you so goddamn high and mighty that you can't take 15 minutes to see an old friend?"

"It's not that," Steve said.

"Well, what is it, then, asshole?"

Steve closed his eyes and took a breath. "Lenny, I've got enough going on right now. I don't want to take you on, too."

Lenny's voice got louder. "Fuck you, man. You think you're hot shit, but you're nothing. You think you're better than me. Ha! That's a fucking joke. I know you, motherfucker. You and me, we're just alike. We always have been, and we always will be."

"I have to go, Lenny. Don't call me again. I mean it." Steve hung up the phone and sat down on the edge of his bed. "Please, God," he whispered, "if you can hear me, and if you care about me even a little bit, please don't ever let me be like that. I don't ask for much, but I'm asking you for this."

CHAPTER 6

Rachel Anders, the woman that Lenny frightened with his early morning indiscretion, came into Steve's life just about the time that Lenny was leaving. Rachel filled the vacancy in Steve's life following his separation from Bev. He filled the vacancy in hers following her divorce from her first husband.

Steve met Rachel on a blind date. He agreed to take her out because his friend described her as not only pretty but also newly divorced and lots of fun. That combination made her a promising, worthwhile target. When he saw her for the first time, though, he flipped.

Rachel was gorgeous. She was tall and blond; her body, muscular and lithe; her movements, graceful. She was shy in the most attractive way—coy, alluring, and completely unpretentious.

Instantly enamored, Steve turned on the charm and pulled out all the stops. They ate steak and lobster and drank fine wine at his favorite restaurant on the San Antonio Riverwalk. Following dinner, they proceeded to a downtown nightclub, where they danced and matched each other drink for drink until the club closed its doors. They talked and laughed like long lost friends. They held hands as they walked to the car.

Before Steve opened the car door, he turned and faced Rachel. "I don't suppose you believe in love at first sight, do you?" he asked her.

Rachel smiled and glanced away. "I don't know, Steve. Why? Do you?"

"If I didn't before, I do now." He gently pulled her body against his and kissed her on the lips.

Rachel went home with Steve that night, and they became glued at the hip for the rest of the summer. They included Lynn and Eddie and Rachel's son, Sammy, occasionally, but for the most part, it was Steve and Rachel—alone, crazy for each other, touching, talking, getting high, and making love. Steve ignored his business. Rachel ignored her family. During one four-day stretch they never left Steve's apartment, never answered the phone, never got fully dressed, and never sobered up. They dubbed themselves *The Hideaways* and secretly challenged anyone to find them.

Toward the end of August, *The Hideaways* jumped in Steve's Corvette and took an unplanned road trip through New Mexico and Colorado. With an ice chest full of beer strapped to the back of the car and two ounces of pot in the bottom of Rachel's purse, Steve and Rachel headed for the mountains. They dropped in on her friends in Durango and his in Telluride. They soaked in the hot springs at Ouray. They hit every little juke joint bar they passed. And they slept under the stars almost every night.

On the drive home, they got serious.

Steve reached over and nudged Rachel's leg. "Hey, you're awfully quiet this morning," he said.

Rachel patted his hand lightly. "Yeah, I guess I am," she said.

"Are you okay?" he asked.

"Yeah, I'm fine. I was just thinking about the summer—what a blast it's been. Kind of like old times, you know? School's out and anything goes."

Steve smiled. "Yeah, it's been fun. You look pretty serious, though. What else is going on?"

Rachel leaned over and rested her head against Steve's shoulder. "I was thinking about our timing, about how impossible it is. I've been divorced for all of four months, and you're still married. Sammy and I are living with my parents, and none of them even know where I am right now. I promised Mom and Dad that I would get a job and move out by the end of summer, and here it is already—the end of summer. It's not fair to them.

"It's not fair to Sam, either. I've been thinking a lot about him today. I miss him. I feel guilty about leaving him alone with Mom and Dad for the last two months, and even though I know in my heart I'm a good mother, today I'm feeling like a very bad one."

Steve nodded. "Yeah, I understand. I've had some of those thoughts myself. I'm feeling very disconnected from Lynn and Eddie. Lord knows what Bev has been telling them about me while I've been absent. Maybe worse yet, Lord knows what she's been telling her lawyers. And I need to get back to work. John and Sheri have been covering for me at the store for four months now. I told them I needed a couple of weeks to get my shit together after I left Bev and the kids. But like you said, here it is—end of summer."

Rachel put her hand on Steve's thigh and rubbed it gently. "Maybe we need to take a break, Steve. You know, revisit our lives, make our apologies, clean up our messes."

"Yeah, maybe so," Steve said softly.

After a few minutes of silence, Rachel left Steve's shoulder and sat up in her seat. "Steve, there's something else that's been on my mind. I haven't been dwelling on it or anything, but it's been poking around in there off and on for the last couple of weeks. It's about my drinking and pot smoking. I'm kind of concerned about it."

Steve turned his head and looked at her. "You're kidding, right?"

"No, I'm not kidding. And this isn't the first time it's come up for me, either. I've had some problems with it in the past. I've even gone on the wagon a few times. In fact, when you and I went out the first time I hadn't had a drink for almost two months, not since I came home late one night and puked on the kitchen floor of my parents' house. Anyway, like I said, it's not a big deal or anything; it's just something that's been on my mind."

"Well, now you've got my curiosity up. What kind of problems are you talking about? I mean, I've seen people with drinking problems up close and personal, and I'm having a hard time picturing you in there with them."

Rachel laughed. "Oh, you might be surprised, my friend. I've never robbed a bank or killed anyone, but surely you know by now that I'm no saint. Actually, it's nothing that obvious; it's more like exceeding limits I set for myself, or saying and doing stupid things that I wouldn't normally say or do. Stuff like that."

"Can you give me an example?"

"Well, how about this trip? You know, running off with you to Colorado without telling anyone where I was going. I mean, we're sitting around in our underwear at 10:00 o'clock in the morning, loaded to the gills. The idea pops up, and 30 minutes later, we're on the road. I'm not saying there's anything inherently wrong with that kind of spontaneity; I'm just saying it's not something I would do when I'm sober, especially when my kid is probably wondering where the hell his mother is."

Steve shook his head. "I don't think that's an alcohol and drug problem, Rachel. I mean, if it's a problem at all, which I'm not convinced it is, it's more like a temporary lapse in judgment issue. Or maybe you're having some kind of guilt attack or something. But I don't think we made this trip just because we were loaded. Hell, I would have been up for it regardless. If that's your best drinking problem story, you've failed to convince me that you have much of problem."

"Well, I don't know why I should have to convince you of anything, Steve, but in the spirit of fair play, I'll give you a better one. I met Sammy's dad at a bar. He was drunk, and I was blasted. I took him home with me, and we drank some more. Before I knew it, we were naked, I was on my back on the floor, and he was slipping into a condom. I said, 'No way, baby. No raincoats for this little girl tonight.'

"He tossed the rubber on the floor, and I turned up pregnant a few weeks later. Then, for some strange, stupid reason, I married the asshole, and he proceeded to abuse me all kinds of ways for the next two and a half years. But that's beside the point. The point is that if I had not been drunk, I would not have taken him home with me, and I would not have had sex with him, especially unprotected sex, for Christ's sake. I really didn't even like the son of a bitch.

"If you need more examples, I can give you a hundred of them. I screwed a guy one night when I was drunk because he had hash oil, and I wanted some of it. I spent $175 buying rounds of beer at a club one night and couldn't pay my electric bill that month. I lost my goddamn purse at an outdoor concert because I was too stoned to pay attention to what was going on around me. One time, I..."

Steve reached over and touched Rachel's arm. "Whoa, girl. Slow down a bit. I wasn't calling you liar. At least I didn't mean to. And I sure as hell didn't mean to piss you off."

Rachel relaxed her shoulders and lowered her voice. "I know you didn't, Steve. I'm sorry. You didn't do anything to deserve that tirade. Let's just drop it, okay? It's not important. I don't even know why I brought it up. In fact, where's the stupid dope box? I think I'll roll us one. I don't know about you, but I could stand to lighten my mood a little."

The Hideaways got high and spent the rest of the morning leisurely twisting and turning their way along the mountain roads of southern Colorado and northern New Mexico, the car top down and the stereo blaring southern rock.

After lunch in downtown Santa Fe, they relaxed in the grass on the square. Steve looked through the newspaper, and Rachel watched people stream by.

"Steve, do you ever wish your life was different than what it is?" Rachel said softly.

"Yeah, sure I do. Doesn't everyone?"

Rachel shook her head. "I don't think so. I think there are people who love their lives just the way they are and feel as though they have made good choices right down the line."

Steve chuckled. "Maybe so, but I don't think I know any of those folks. It could be that I've always chosen to hang out with all the wrong people, but I doubt it. I mean, who in the world doesn't have regrets?"

"I don't know. Maybe people who have a real strong belief in fate? They might say that everything happens for a reason, and they don't need to know what that reason is. Or maybe people with really strong spiritual beliefs. You know, people with the kind of faith in God that lets them believe that He's in charge and has everything under control. I mean, I have to believe that there's such a thing as God's will, and if God is really God, then surely His will shall prevail. Otherwise, He wouldn't be God, right? And so if it's God's will that prevails, then everything is always just exactly the way it's supposed to be."

Steve scratched his head in exaggerated mock confusion. "Rachel, are you trying to go somewhere with this line of thought? Because if you are, I think you've wandered off to some other planet."

Rachel smiled weakly. "I'll try to get to the point. It might take a few minutes so be patient. I just hope it comes out right.

"While we were driving through the mountains this morning, I thought a lot about our earlier conversation, you know, the one where we agreed that we have messes to clean up when we get home. I started making a mental list of those messes and other things I need to take care of when we get back. It quickly grew into a pretty long list—making peace with Sam and with Mom and Dad, finding a job, finding daycare, finding a place to live, moving, getting the new place set up, caring for Sammy and me and our home, etc., etc.

"At first it was a little overwhelming, but then I got into it and got kind of excited, you know, like 'Yeah, this is a chance to start over fresh and clean, a chance to do it over again without making the same mistakes I've made before.'

"I pictured myself going here and there, doing this and that, being organized, getting things done, and in general acting like a reasonable, responsible, sane woman. I'm almost embarrassed to say it, but I saw myself acting like an adult.

"Then, Steve, I realized that you weren't anywhere in the picture, and a wave of panic shot through me. At first I thought the panic was about your absence, about not having you with me. But then the more I thought about it, I realized that it was really the opposite of that. It was about my not being able to do those things and become this strong, competent woman if you *are* there with me.

"I thought to myself, on the one hand there's us—you and me. On the other hand, there's everything else—me being an adult. And the two hands don't seem to compliment each other."

Steve held up his hand for Rachel to stop talking. "Rachel, it's not that black and white. You don't have to exclude me from your life in order to be who you want to be."

"I'm not so sure about that, Steve. I mean, it might feel different if we had started out dating and had gradually integrated each other into our real lives. But we skipped that whole ritual. You know what we did? We jumped out of the frying pan into the fire. We went from our marriages—turmoil that we did not like—to this fairy tale we're in now, that sometimes seems like turmoil we like too intensely.

"Steve, you and I have been more deeply involved in the last two months than Sammy's father and I were in the last two years. You and I have talked more and made love more times than he and I did during the entire two and a half years of our marriage.

"You and I have consumed each other. I'm not saying that's good or bad. I'm just saying that's who we are as a couple, as a relationship. I don't think it's possible for us to back up and start over more slowly and responsibly. At least not now. Maybe later, after we've taken a break from each other and done what we need to do to put our lives on some kind of right track, or at least better track.

"That's what I feel like I need—to get my life on track. That's what I want. And it's just about me. It's not about you. I love you; you know that. I've loved you from the moment that you looked at me and asked me if I believed in love at first sight. But I feel like I'm losing myself, and I need to get myself back."

Steve frowned. "So you're saying, 'I love you, goodbye?'"

"Not in those words, no. But could we say, 'Let's take a break and see what happens?'"

Steve nodded. "Yeah, we can do that if that's what you want. I mean, I'm not blind to what you're saying. I'm not all that happy or proud of who I am, either. Six months ago, I blamed Bev for my unhappiness and figured that if I could just get the hell away from her I'd be fine. But I'm not really that naïve. In my heart I know she didn't make me unhappy. She didn't make me crazy. I was crazy before I ever met her. I know I have work to do on myself. And I never did plan to live in this kind of fantasy world for the rest of my life.

"At the same time, though, I hate the thought of losing you. I feel like there's something very special and solid between us, and I really don't believe that our feelings for each other are dependent on alcohol, drugs, and/or sex, even though those things have been a big part of what we do.

"And, too, my experience has been that taking a break from a relationship usually means the end of that relationship. You know what I mean, don't you, Rachel?"

Rachel nodded. "I do. I need to take that chance, though, Steve. And honestly, I think you do, too."

CHAPTER 7

Steve pulled into an Amarillo Ramada Inn at about 6:00 PM. They unpacked a few things, smoked a joint, shed their clothes, and lay on the bed in each other's arms until they both fell asleep.

Steve awoke a little after 9:00 PM. He silently reviewed the Santa Fe conversation in his mind. He considered what Rachel had said about starting over with a clean slate. He pictured himself letting her go and imagined himself alone again. To his surprise, he felt curiously at peace with the idea.

Steve woke Rachel by gently rubbing her back and neck. Without opening her eyes, she found his face with her hands and kissed him. They made love slowly and tenderly.

At midnight, Steve called Domino's for pizza delivery, and *The Hideaways* watched *Butch Cassidy & the Sundance Kid* on TV over a large supreme deluxe and cans of Pepsi Cola. It was early morning when they turned off the light.

After laying quietly for a few minutes, Rachel whispered, "Steve, do you realize that was the first time we've made love when we weren't loaded."

Steve nodded and smiled. "Yeah, I do," he said. "I thought about it as soon as I realized where we were headed, and to tell you the truth, I almost stopped us so that we could get high first."

"Why is that, Steve?"

"Well, having sex without being drunk or stoned is something I'm pretty unfamiliar with. I haven't done it since I was a teenager. I guess I was a little nervous about how things would turn out."

Rachel looked up at Steve. "I don't understand. What did you think was going to happen?"

"Hell, I don't know, Rachel. Impotence, maybe. Premature ejaculation. Whatever. The thing is, I've always had reservations about myself as a lover. I've always been afraid that I wouldn't be good, you know, like I'd come up short somehow. No pun intended.

"I don't know why I'm like that. I love sex; I've always loved it. No one has ever complained about my performance, and over the years I've only had one erection failure. Still, I have this anxiety about it, at least until I get high. When I'm high, I might think about it, but it's just a fleeting thought. Hence, the lack of sex without being high. And hence, my relief about how well things turned out for us when we did it straight tonight."

"That's so weird, Steve, because it was great. It was sweet and gentle. I loved it."

Steve nodded. "Yeah, it was very nice."

"Why do you think you have that fear, Steve?"

"I don't know. I got a pretty shaky start sexually. Maybe I just never quite recovered. I was a compulsive masturbater as a kid, and I had a couple of homosexual experiences when I was about ten or eleven. And then my first real girlfriend and I didn't know much about what we were doing. I came in my pants almost every time we made out lying down, which was usually in the back seat of my dad's car. I felt terribly embarrassed about that. Not that she ever said anything. In fact, I'm not sure she even knew about it. She was more ignorant about sex than I was.

"I remember the first time she actually saw me with an erection. She was flabbergasted. She thought I was going to look like the little boys she had babysat over the years. Actually, I think it scared her. She couldn't imagine that something like that could fit up inside of her without it hurting like hell. She and I tried really hard to figure things out. We tried to be good sex partners, you know, like we tried to be good for each other. We weren't miserable failures, but we never really got it right, either. I ended up feeling pretty inadequate.

"Anyway, it's been different with you. I've felt more confident with you, and that's been very good for me and for how I feel about myself as a lover and as a man. I'm very glad we made love tonight when we did."

Rachel whispered in Steve's ear, "You're the best lover I've ever had, Steve. Drunk or sober. I promise." She kissed him softly on the mouth, and they made love again. It was the second time they had made love sober.

CHAPTER 8

Rachel woke up first. She studied Steve's face while he slept. She watched the darting movements of his eyes beneath their lids and wondered what he was dreaming.

"One more day together on the road," she thought. "One more day. And then what? No more *Hideaways*. No more daily dose of fantasy world. No more daily dose of love making. No more getting drunk and stoned every day. Maybe no more getting drunk and stoned at all."

She shook him gently. "Hey, sleepyhead, we better get moving if we're going to make it home tonight."

Steve opened one eye. "Do we have to? I hear Amarillo is beautiful and exciting this time of year."

"Funny boy. Yes, we have to. I need to go home."

Steve opened both eyes and leaned up. "You're sure about all of this? You're really ready to move on? Ready for adulthood?"

Rachel nodded. "At this moment, I'm ready."

Even after a late start, Steve and Rachel made good time. They picked up sandwiches and beer and ate lunch on the road. After her second beer, Rachel fell asleep. Steve picked a half-smoked joint out of the ashtray and finished it off. Then he adjusted the rear view mirror so that he could see Rachel's face. She was lovely. He would miss her.

Steve was deep into his own thoughts when he felt Rachel's hand on the back of his neck. "Well, good morning again, lazy bum," he said.

Rachel yawned. "Why didn't you wake me up?"

"I don't know. I was enjoying watching you sleep and appreciating how incredibly beautiful you are."

Rachel looked away and smiled. "Steve, I want to tell you something. Yesterday you said that you aren't happy with yourself and that you need to work on yourself. Remember?"

"Yeah, I remember. Why? Did you dream up some answers for me?"

"I don't know, maybe. I spent a lot of time yesterday fantasizing about and plotting the course for my so-called new life. And I feel stronger about it today than I did yesterday. Today I'm not afraid, and I don't feel apologetic about wanting to grow up and take responsibility for myself. Instead, I feel excited and optimistic."

Steve laughed. "Let me guess. You want me to grow up and be an adult, too?"

"No, not at all. I just want you to know that I believe in you. I believe that you deserve to be happy, and I believe that you are fully capable of finding happiness. You said yesterday that you are crazy. Well, I don't think you're crazy. I just think you're like me—kind of lost, you know, like you haven't figured out where you fit into this stupid world. You don't seem very interested in your business. I know you like the money it brings you, but you never talk about it being fun or challenging or fulfilling."

"Well, I don't know about the craziness, but you're sure right about the business. It's a great big damn bore. I mean, think about it. I sell expensive preppy clothes to rich assholes and their arrogant, spoiled kids.

"The ironic thing is that I thought I was buying my freedom and independence when I went into business for myself. Let me tell you something; it didn't work that way. The store and my partnership with John and Sheri have me trapped. If I was working for someone else, I'd just quit, but hell, I can't even do that.

"And you're right about the money; it's been good. The problem is that it hasn't done what it was supposed to. It hasn't made me happy. In fact, sometimes I think it may be the biggest trap of all."

Rachel sat up straight and faced Steve. "That's the point, Steve. That's what I wanted to tell you. I believe that I can change my life. By God, if I want to be independent, I can be independent. If I want to be a good mother, I can be a good mother. I know deep inside that I have what it takes to pull that off. And so do you.

"Steve, you're not trapped in anything. You walked away from an unfulfilling marriage. Why can't you walk away from unfulfilling work? If you're bored, why not create some excitement?

"Man, you're just 27. That's still really young, right? You're smart, too. You've got two college degrees and good, solid business experience. You don't have to worry about money. You're not responsible for anyone but yourself. If you're trapped, it's certainly not obvious. When I look at you, I see someone with no barriers, and I mean *none*. I see someone who is free to do anything he wants and has everything he needs right at his fingertips."

Steve smiled and glanced at Rachel. "Boy, it sounds pretty damn simple when you put it like that. All I have to do is go home, quit the store, abandon my partners, one of whom is my only sister, and...and then what? What am I supposed to do next? I don't know what would make me happy. I know I'm not ready to follow you into adulthood. I don't want to settle down and be responsible and predictable. Not yet anyway."

"Come on, Steve. I think you're bluffing. You don't lack imagination, and I know damn good and well you've thought about this before today. You tell *me* what's next. Imagine for a minute that what I said is absolutely true. Imagine that starting at 6:00 o'clock tomorrow morning, you don't have one single barrier to doing whatever you want to do and being whoever you want to be. Come on. Humor me. Describe for me the life and times of the new, happier Steve Campbell. No holds barred. Anything goes."

Steve took a deep breath and shook his head. "I'd rather talk about the new, happier Rachel Anders, but okay. I'll humor you. First thing, of course, I get out from under the store. I sell out my half to John and Sheri, and I stash the money away to take care of the divorce settlement. Next, I slow things down— not to a crawl, but to a nice, easy jog. I get rid of this ridiculous car and pick up something more comfortable, more practical, and less pretentious. I give my suits and ties and button-down collars to the Salvation Army. I keep the jeans and the pullovers. Goodwill gets the TV. I keep the stereo.

"Then...then I move. I get the hell out of San Antonio. I put some distance between Bev and me and between my family and me. I stay just close enough to see Lynn and Eddie on weekends. And you, too, hopefully, at least every once in a while."

"Where do you move to?" Rachel asked.

"Austin, I suppose. When I get there I rent a small, old, very inexpensive house with hardwood floors and an attic fan. I furnish it very simply—pretty much just the basics. I turn part of the backyard into a garden and grow my own vegetables. If it's safe, I put in a couple of pot plants. I cook for myself every day— healthy stuff only. I give up greasy burgers and fries completely. I let my hair grow long. Maybe I grow a beard.

"I have a little cash, so I skate by without a job for a while. That gives me time to read. I do *Walden's Pond* first. Then *The Dhammapada*. Then, I don't know, maybe *War and Peace*. I don't just read them; I study them. I hang out at coffee shops instead of bars, and while I'm there I write letters to family and friends and discuss politics and literature with graduate students and old hippies.

"Then I suppose since I'm already in Austin, and I don't have a job, I enroll in UT and study something interesting and possibly even useful. Psychology, perhaps. I eventually become a college teacher, or better yet, a therapist. Actually, therapist would be good; then I could look at myself with intelligence and insight and figure out what the hell's wrong with me."

As Steve spoke, he caught the images in his mind. Steve Campbell, the scruffy, long-haired, intellectual retro-hippie, bent over an old desk in the small, dimly lit bedroom of his wood frame and hardwood floor house—coffee cup in hand, simmering joint in the ashtray, quietly and earnestly searching for and discovering the secrets to mental health and spiritual well-being. He chuckled to himself.

"What's funny, Steve?"

"Oh, I don't know, Rachel. I just got a glimpse of myself in my supposed new life. It was quite a sight. Not much like the present clean cut Steve Campbell in his new Corvette, tooling down a long Texas highway with the top down and a beautiful, mature, adult woman-to-be by his side. I guess the image just tickled me."

"Does that life really appeal to you?" Rachel asked.

Steve thought for a moment. He let the image return, and then he nodded his head. "Yeah, it does. Or at least I think it does. I didn't get to do that trip when I was in college. I had Bev and Lynn to take care of, and I was determined to get an education that would launch me into the big bucks as soon as I finished school. I don't know, maybe somewhere deep down inside I feel like I missed out on something. But anyway, yeah, I like the thought.

"Of course, I'd be the only one who liked it. The rest of my family would freak. They would have me committed. Man, my dad would shit. Ha! I'd love to see the look on his goddamn face if I pulled up in front of his house in some old clunker car, looking like a 'goddamn long-haired hippie bum.' Those would be his exact words. God, that would be so damn funny."

Rachel smiled at the thought. "Well, I haven't met your infamous father, but from what you've told me about him, I can see why you might enjoy that."

Rachel paused and looked out the window. Then she looked at Steve and said, "Do it, Steve."

He glanced over and caught her eye. "Do what? Fuck with my dad's head?"

"No, silly. The whole thing. Do the whole thing. The store, the car, the clothes, the hair, the move, school, all of it. We can be like partners in change. I'll be growing up, and you'll be growing down. We can stay in touch and encourage each other. We can get together every so often and compare notes. You think I'm kidding, but I'm as serious as death. Do it, Steve. I dare you."

Steve laughed. "I thought I was crazy, but you're the crazy one. You're a goddamn nut case is what you are."

"Not true, Steve. I mean, think about it. Honestly, what could possibly stand in your way? Do you really feel trapped? Step out of the trap. What's to lose? The prestige? The money? You already know those things don't work. You said so yourself."

"Well, maybe so, but that doesn't mean I'm ready to give them up. Am I crazy? Yeah. Am I stupid? No, I don't think so. Listen, I can't tell for sure if you're being serious or not, but if you are, you're talking about a very complicated major life change. You're telling me, 'Take everything you've worked for and throw it out the window.' Actually, you're saying more than that; you're saying, 'Take everything you are and turn yourself into the opposite.' Am I right, or am I right?"

"Yes, you're right. But don't you see? That's the point. Your life's not working for you. You're not happy with what you're doing. You're not happy with who you are. Why *not* turn it over and try the opposite? Again, where's the big risk? If it fails, you can always go back to the way things were.

"Here, I'll even make it simple and easy for you. I'll give you the whole plan, step-by-step, right now, right off the top of my head. What do you say? Will you listen?"

"Yeah, sure. Why not? As long as you're flipping people's lives over like pancakes, go ahead. Lay it on me. Go easy, though. I'm not as receptive to change as you are."

Rachel started talking. She talked nonstop for over an hour. She laid it out for him just like she said she would—step by step. At first, he laughed and played along. But the more she talked, the more he listened. Before long, he softened a little. Then he wavered. And by the time Rachel stopped talking, Steve had fallen silent.

She waited for a few moments, and then she nudged him. "Well? What do you think?" she asked.

Steve shook his head slowly. "I don't know, Rachel. I still think it's crazy, but maybe it's not totally insane. I don't know. Maybe I'll kick it around. Maybe I'll think about it."

"You should do it, Steve. You won't be hurting anyone. You will see your kids the same amount, and you'll enjoy them more. Maybe they'll enjoy you more. Sheri and John have already been running your business by themselves for four months. Who knows, they may be relieved to see you go. Just think about what an incredible adventure it would be."

"Yeah, I'll do that. I'll think about it. I really will."

CHAPTER 9

The Hideaways reached Steve's apartment a little after midnight and went straight to bed. Steve gave up trying to sleep at 4:00 AM. He sat down at the table with a cup of coffee in one hand and pencil, paper, and calculator in the other. He sketched out a balance sheet of assets and liabilities. Then he worked up a budget that included estimates on child support payments and bottom-dwelling living expenses. Finally, he crunched the numbers until they produced the answer he wanted.

"It's possible," he said to himself. "Not exactly a piece of cake, but possible."

He leaned back in his chair and recreated the previous day's conversations and mental images. Neither seemed as absurd as they had the day before. He played with the images until they took him back to Henry's living room. "Hi, there, Dad. Guess who. It's me, Steve, your goddamn long-haired, dope-smoking, happy-feeling, hippie bum son." He chuckled.

He picked up his coffee cup and walked outside. The air was warm and heavy. Daylight was near. He walked slowly along the path to the community swimming pool area, where he sat down on the edge of the pool and dangled his legs in the water.

Again, he let his imagination take him to Austin and to the possibilities that a new life might offer. He pictured himself handing over his store keys to John and Sheri and ripping off his tie and coat. He pictured his Corvette transforming into a Volkswagen bug with a bicycle rack attached to the back. He pictured ragged old men gleefully pulling his $600 suits off of the racks at the Salvation Army Retail Store. He pictured himself in jeans and T-shirt, with a ponytail and beard, a cold beer in one hand and a joint in the other. The image made him smile.

Gradually, his thoughts shifted from appearances and activities to attitudes and feelings. Just for fun, he placed himself on the flip side of his beliefs. He imagined himself a bleeding-heart liberal, a card-carrying socialist, a people-centered idealist. Again, he smiled. "That might be a bit of a stretch," he muttered.

Then he imagined himself fully at peace. He pictured himself sitting in a chair on the back porch of his new home, relaxed and at peace with himself and the world, looking out over his vegetable garden, smoking a joint rolled from his own home-grown plants, and casually reading a Kerouac novel. That image did it for him. It knocked him out.

"Hey, Rachel. Wake up. I need to tell you something."

Rachel opened her eyes. "What time is it, Steve? I feel like I just got to sleep."

"No, man, you've been asleep all night. It's morning. Are you awake enough to talk?"

"Yeah, I guess so. What's going on?"

"I'm gonna do it, Rachel. I'm gonna do major life change with you. You growing up, and me growing down, just like you said. I may be an idiot, and it may be the dumbest thing I've ever done in my life, but I'm gonna fucking do it."

CHAPTER 10

The Hideaways came out of hiding at about 11:00 AM on August 28, 1973.

Leaning against the side of Steve's car in the driveway of Rachel's parents' house, they kissed and held each other close.

"I love you, Rachel," Steve whispered. "If our situation was different, I'd be asking you to marry me instead of telling you goodbye."

"I love you, too, Steve. And if that was the case, I'd be saying, 'Yes.'"

"Good friends, right?" Steve asked.

"The best, for life," Rachel said. Then she kissed him one more time and walked into her parents' house.

Steve pulled out of Rachel's driveway and jumped into his new life with both feet. The sadness that he felt as he watched Rachel walk away quickly dispersed. In its place, he found unrestrained optimism. His day-to-day moods soared as he pushed through details of the move to Austin and rehearsed in his mind the images of his upcoming adventure.

"Finally, everything is going to be okay" became his mantra.

CHAPTER 11

The moment the phone rang at 7:00 AM, Steve knew it was Lois. "Good morning, Mother," he answered.

"Hello, Steve. I'm sorry to wake you, but I didn't want to take a chance on missing you. Sheri just called and told me that you're pulling out of the business and moving to Austin. What's the story? Is this some kind of joke?"

Steve sat up in bed. "Mother, you have the story. I'm pulling out of the business and moving to Austin. It's a decision I made on my trip, and I'm committed to it. I think it's the right thing for me to do."

"But, Honey, why? What happened? Did you and John have a falling out?"

"No. Nothing happened, Mother. It's just everything. It's me. I need a change. I'm tired of treading water. I'm bored with my life. I'm bored with the business."

"Steve, how could you be bored with the business? You've hardly set foot inside the store since the end of March."

"Mother, it's not just the store. I'm not happy. I don't really have any friends here anymore. Bev has taken over our couple friends. I have Rachel, but she and I are heading off in different directions. John and Sheri are sick and tired of my crap. You and Chester are cool, but you're not what I need right now.

"And it's not just that, either. I need to get away from Bev. I need some miles between us. She and I are constantly at each other's throats, and I think it's hurting Lynn and Eddie.

"I don't know, Mother, I just need something different. I need something to wake up to in the morning, and I don't think I can find it here."

"Steve, you need to think about this. Moving away from San Antonio isn't going to make you happy. You know what the term 'geographical cure' means; you've heard me talk about it before. You think that moving to Austin is going to change your life, but I'm telling you, Honey, it won't. There's a lot more to it than that. Geographical cures don't work. None of the easy solutions to major problems work."

Steve sighed loudly. "Whatever, Mother. You can say whatever you want, but I'm going. Geographical cure or no geographical cure, it's a done deal in my mind."

"This is a mistake, Steve. It's a big mistake. Don't you see what you're doing? You're running away. You say you're bored, and you need a change, but underneath all that, you're just running away. But Honey, you can't run away from yourself, no matter where you go."

"Now, wait a damn minute, Mother. Who says I'm running away from anything? Hell, I think I'm running toward something, not away from something. I'm burned out on San Antonio, and I'm damn tired of my life the way it is. I want something different. I want something better.

"When Sheri gave you her early morning news flash, did she tell you that I'm also planning to go back to school? To find a new direction for my life? To develop something meaningful? I mean, how long can a person stay fulfilled selling clothes, especially overpriced preppy clothes? I want something more. What's wrong with that? Why does that have to mean I'm running away?"

"Steve, I hear what you're saying, and I know you believe it. I've been where you are now. I've said the same things you're saying. When I was so terribly unhappy with my life, I did the geographical cures. I changed where I lived; I changed where I worked; I changed my friends. I even changed the way I wore my hair. Believe me, Steve. It doesn't work that way. It just isn't that easy.

"The *only* way to find happiness for yourself and feel good about yourself is to make your changes on the inside, not the outside. If you don't do that, then you end up feeling exactly the same way about yourself and your life, regardless of where you're living or what you're doing.

"Listen to me for a minute, Honey. There's a story in AA that an old timer named Dr. Paul O. tells. He's an AA legend, and his story is in the Big Book. When he talks about his life before he

47

got into recovery from alcohol and drug addiction, he says, 'Wherever I went, there I was. I'd go over here, and there I was. I'd go over there, and there I was. No matter where I went, there I'd be.'

"Steve, that's the way geographical cures are. That's why they don't work. A different city is just a different city if you're the same person on the inside. Please believe me, Steve. I know what I'm talking about."

"Mother, I don't doubt that you know what's best for you. I know you've overcome a lot, and I respect what you've done for yourself. But I don't think you know what's best for me. How could you? You don't know what's going on inside of me. I do. And I'm telling you that I know for absolute certain that moving away from here and starting over is the best thing for me right now. It's really not something for you and me to argue about. Okay?"

"Damn it, Steve. Doesn't my experience count for anything?"

"Sure it does, Mother. But that's the point. It's your experience. It's not mine. I need my own experience. I need to live my life the way I think is best. You can't do it for me. You need to stop worrying about me. You need to let me live my life, even if it means making mistakes. I mean, what's the worst that could happen? If it doesn't work out, I'll come back. It's that simple. But I think it is going to work out. I think it's the answer for me. And I'm going to do it, with or without your blessing. And I'm going to do it real soon—as soon as I can get up there and find a place to live."

Lois sighed deeply into the phone. "Why are you so damn hard-headed? And why Austin, anyway? If you need to move, there are parts of San Antonio that you have never even seen. Move to one of them. And if it's really about going back to college, there are very good colleges right here."

"You're missing the point, Mother. I don't want to be in San Antonio. I want to get out of San Antonio. San Antonio is wrong for me right now. Austin just makes sense. It's close enough so that I can come back often. The university is there. It's a beautiful, progressive city with lots of stuff to do. And on top of everything else, Tucker and James are there. I'll be with some good friends again."

"Oh, great, Steve. Surely you don't think that helps. If anything, that just makes it worse. I know for a fact that Tucker drinks like a fish and gets himself into all kinds of trouble over it. And the last I heard, James was in prison for dealing drugs."

"Yeah, well, James was in prison for a short while, but he's out now, and he's doing just fine. And Tucker is a very good friend, even if he does drink a little too much."

48

"Honey, neither one of those guys are any good for you, especially that James. The two of you got into trouble every damn time you got together."

"Mother, for Christ's sake, get real. You're talking about junior high school. You're starting to sound desperate."

Lois gave another deep sigh. "What are you planning to do for work? What can you do in Austin to make the kind of living you make here?"

"Well, to start with, I don't plan to make that kind of money there. I plan to live a lot more simply than what I've been used to. Actually, I've been thinking about maybe opening a little furniture refinishing shop. I'm good at that, and I like doing it. Plus, I'll have some money set aside from selling the store, even after the divorce. Anyway, it doesn't matter. You know me. I'll come up with something. I've made enough money to pay my own way since I was twelve years old."

"Well...I don't know what else to say, Steve. I'm very upset about this. I know you're going to do exactly what you want, but I want it on the record that I don't approve. I think it's a big mistake, and I think you will live to regret it."

"Okay, Mother. Your warning has been recorded, but I think you'll be surprised. Now that we have that settled, I'd like to get a few more minutes of shuteye before I have to get up and get my day going. Okay?"

"Alright. I just wish you would think about what I said."

Steve laughed. "You got it. I will. Are we okay now?"

"Yeah, we're okay. We never were not okay. Call me later, will you?"

"Yes, I will."

Steve's geographical cure was sudden and sensational. Twenty-one days following Rachel's dare, Steve rolled into Austin, Texas.

He took little with him: A few pieces of furniture, his stereo and record collection, some clothes, a few kitchen items, a half-pound of fresh, sticky red-haired smoke, and his fantasy of a brand new, happy, trouble-free life.

He left behind a lot: Rachel, his kids, his family, his career, his car, his lifestyle, and, he hoped, his unhappy past.

Steve took heart in the fact that he was traveling light. Looking over all of his belongings in the back of a small U-Haul truck, he asked himself, "How complicated could a life be when it requires only this much space?" Then he smiled and answered. "Not very damn complicated. No sir, not very complicated at all."

CHAPTER 12

High bottom drunks gravitate to geographical cures for the sure-fire large-scale life changes that they promise. Psychologically, though, geographical cures serve a deeper, less obvious purpose. By directing attention away from the real problem—addiction and addictive behavior—and placing it squarely on a false solution—the move—they foster, maintain, and protect *denial.*

Denial is endemic to alcoholics and addicts. It represents the heart of their defense systems. It is their lifeblood. It allows them to rationalize, justify, and excuse irrational, unjustifiable, and inexcusable behavior. It allows them to continue doing what they do and still live with themselves.

Addicts in denial can explain away inexplicable behavior so masterfully that they appear absolutely believable. They are convincing because they believe themselves. If they did not believe themselves, they would not be in denial. They would just be lying.

Denial and lying are siblings, but they are not twins. When Steve looked Bev in the eye and swore that he had not been smoking pot, as he did quite often, he was lying. When he looked her in the eye, however, and swore that he was not an alcoholic, as he also did quite often, he was not lying. Both remarks were untrue. He *had* been smoking pot, and he *was* addicted to alcohol and marijuana. The first remark was an intentional untruth. Steve lied. The second was unintentional. Steve thought he was telling the truth.

Steve Campbell's denial was strong. It was not, however, invisible. When he told Lois that he had his life under control, he believed that he had his life under control. Lois knew that he didn't. When he told her that all he needed was a fresh start in a new place, he believed that his geographical cure would bring him happiness. Lois knew better.

When he told Sheri that his problems all stemmed from his relationship with his father, he believed that Henry was, in fact, the root cause of his unhappy, dysfunctional life. Sheri was sympathetic, but she knew there was more to it than that.

When Steve looked in the mirror and told himself that he was no goddamn alcoholic and that he bore no resemblance whatsoever to Henry, he truly believed his own ruse.

Denial is the defense that opens death's door to alcoholics and addicts. Because of their denial, addicts sometimes remain blind to the truth until it is too late. Steve's childhood idol, Mickey Mantle, drank himself to death. An uncle on his mother's side quit breathing when he took too many sedatives before retiring for the night.

There's a saying about denial—that it's not a river in Egypt. What it is instead is an insidious psychological defense against the truth. Until the addict's denial cracks, there is little chance that he or she will recover from his or her disease.

Steve was not stupid. On the contrary, he was quite intelligent. Unfortunately, intelligence does not encourage movement through denial. In fact, it often precludes it. This happens, for example, when highly intelligent alcoholics use their intellectual power to create and articulate eloquent rationalizations to justify behavior which simpler minds could not defend.

Such was the case with Tucker Taylor, one of Steve's Austin-based friends. While Steve's denial was substantial and powerful, Tucker's was absolute. It was a work of art. Tucker Taylor brought denial fully to life.

Tucker was exceptionally bright. High school teachers and college professors called him brilliant. His professional peers turned to him for advice. To compliment his intelligence, he possessed a delightful personality and engaging presence. He was witty and funny, an extraordinary teller of jokes and stories, and the life of many a party.

The connection between Tucker and Steve ran deep. They met in military high school, where they shared a dorm room for a year and a half. During that time they gave up just about all of their secrets to each other and in the process molded a rich, enduring friendship.

Tucker influenced Steve in many ways. He taught him to appreciate reading, especially the classics, just for the fun of reading. He introduced Steve to conservative politics and the critical value of money and wealth. He taught Steve how to sing harmony on country western songs and how to tell a dirty joke in any crowd without appearing crude.

When Steve went to college, Tucker convinced him to abandon his interest in science in favor of business administration as a course of study.

Steve introduced Tucker to marijuana. He taught him how to roll a joint, take hits on a bong, make marijuana brownies, and brew marijuana tea.

Tucker consumed alcohol and drugs like a man with the proverbial hollow leg. He kept his wits about him regardless of how much he drank, smoked, or snorted. He once gave a near perfect after dinner talk to a group of CPAs on the heels of a full afternoon of drinking beer and smoking pot in the backyard at Steve's house.

But while Tucker looked cool and in control, the consequences of his addictions, though relatively few in number, were dreadful. He broke his back and lost his son in a car crash that would not have happened had he not been drunk. Several years later, a counselor asked him about the connection between his drinking and the accident. He responded in a deadpan voice. "Listen, that was a freak accident. If you don't believe me, check the reports. They show clearly that it wasn't my fault. Anyway, I don't want to talk about it. I've already dealt with that, and I won't discuss it again."

Three different women divorced Tucker because of his alcohol and drug-affected judgment and behavior. When the same counselor asked about the divorces, Tucker laughed and said, "Those three bitches could have been sisters. They were great to look at, but they were ball-busters from the ball-buster hall of fame. Bitches from hell. To borrow a phrase from country music radio, 'Thank God and Greyhound they're gone.' If my drinking ran them off, then here's a salute to the drink that did the trick."

Tucker was a highly competent accountant who worked hard and produced a sizable income. But he struggled constantly to keep his head above water financially. He complained endlessly about being strapped for money. But he could always scrape together enough cash for a quarter ounce of coke and a night on the town.

Tucker declared bankruptcy in 1972. He explained it thusly: "Here I am, working my poor, bleeding fingers to the bone, and I still can't get ahead. My damn employees make more than I do. And what I don't give them, I hand over to those asinine Democrats in Congress who turn around and hand it to welfare trash who don't pay back a dime. It's the epitome of liberal politics; Tucker works his ass off, and everyone gets fat and happy except him."

When a counselor told Tucker that he fit the profile of a classic high bottom alcoholic, Tucker shook his head in an exaggerated show of disbelief. "Man, you have got to be putting me on. If I'm an alcoholic, then the goddamn Pope is a Hasidic Jew. I don't even drink that much. I don't drink every day. I don't hang out in bars. I've never missed a day's work in my life. Hell, I never even take a drink until 5:30 in the afternoon unless something special is going on.

"I got the one DWI that brought me here, but that wasn't because I was drunk. It was because I invited the cop to insert his breath test into a lower orifice.

"Listen, I know some guys who drink hard, and I'm not like them. I just like to relax and have a good time. I'm not saying I'm perfect. I've made some bad decisions. And God knows I've had some rotten luck. But that doesn't make me an alcoholic. Trust me on this one, Doc. I know what I'm talking about."

Tucker admitted himself into alcohol and drug abuse treatment two different times following that one session with a drug counselor. Steve drove him there the first time. During the ride Tucker puked all over the floorboard of Steve's truck. Three weeks into treatment, Tucker's counselor pushed Tucker really hard to get honest about his apparent dependency on alcohol and drugs. To placate the counselor, Tucker referred to himself as "probably an alcoholic of sorts." He knew deep down inside, however, that he had lied. The next day he called Steve and told him what had happened.

"Why did you say that you were an alcoholic when you believe you aren't?" Steve asked him.

"Well, I figured it would get him off of my back and make him feel indebted to me, you know, like I was one of his success stories. Anyway, it's not like I'm denying that I've screwed up a few times around booze. God knows, I have.

"The thing is, Steve, I'm not like the rest of this riffraff. With the exception of one mildly attractive topless dancer, they're all big time losers. They drink, they fuck up; they drink, they fuck up; they drink some more, they fuck up some more. They remind me of that friend of yours from San Antonio—that Lenny Miller character. Now, if I were Lenny Miller, I'd be begging on my hands and knees for alcoholism treatment. I'd be taking to heart every goddamn thing these counselors said. But Steve, I ain't him.

"Listen, when I need to, I can control my drinking. It's never been a 'have to' thing with me. Now, does that sound like a real alcoholic to you? You better say 'no' unless you want to look stupid."

When he started drinking and using again, shortly after completing the treatment program, Tucker rationalized his failure to remain sober by attacking the chemical dependency treatment industry. "Treatment is bull shit, man. You know that. All they really want to do is take your money, convince you that you have some fatal disease, and shove God down your throat, or up your tush, depending on your perspective. I'm not buying it. I'll let those gullible losers go down that road alone. I don't need it. I've learned what I need to know about drinking alcohol and doing drugs. You won't see this old boy having any more problems in that department. *That* I can guarantee."

Tucker was Steve's all-time favorite drinking partner. Tucker never went home early. He never ran out of interesting conversation or funny stories. He kept the party going at almost any cost. And if he happened to have a stash, he never failed to share. He was a prince of a guy whose denial was a thing of beauty.

James Shannon, Steve's other Austin-based old friend, owned a different denial style. Tucker was steadfast; he simply shut and locked the door on critical self-examination. James, on the other hand, was slippery. He actively pursued self-examination. He possessed strong personal insight and appeared

53

to accept himself fully, warts and all. In therapeutic settings, he was unflappable. He self-disclosed openly and offered razor sharp feedback to others. Group therapy peers looked to him as often as they did to the counselors. Indeed, James left seasoned counselors thoroughly confused regarding how to work with him therapeutically.

James Shannon's brand of brilliance was also different. While Tucker was quick, witty, and articulate, James was abstract and arcane. His high school teachers and college professors called him provocative and gifted. Some found him intimidating. A couple questioned his sanity. None thought of him as endearing.

James read everything except the newspaper and recalled in great detail everything he read. He got lost in art and music, both of which he created effortlessly. He drew pictures with his eyes closed and played the guitar, mandolin, banjo, and piano by ear. He gave away his art and his music to those who appreciated its deceptive beauty.

James shot out the picture tube of his younger brother's television set with a 9mm pistol. Then he looked at his brother and said, "Don't worry, brother. You can thank me later."

Steve and James met in Mrs. Andrew's sixth grade class at Olmos Elementary. James had attended school there since first grade. Steve was a new student. By the luck of the draw, they wound up sitting next to each other on the back row.

After a minute or two of small talk, James said, "So why are you talking to me? Don't you know that everybody thinks I'm a weirdo?"

Steve shook his head. "No, I'm new here. I haven't heard anything about anybody."

James laughed out loud and replied, "Well, we'll see how it goes. Who knows, maybe you're smart enough to think for yourself."

Steve did not understand what James meant, but he liked his laugh. Within a week, they were buddies and hanging out together during and after school.

As an adult, James smuggled and sold marijuana. Texas drug dealers knew him for his fairness and his madness. He once stole his own airplane from storage at a government-owned facility. Federal DEA officers had impounded the plane following a drug bust and were holding it for evidence. James and his business partner boarded the plane in the middle of the night and took off while two guards chased them down the runway.

The United States government charged James three times with drug related offenses—once for smuggling and twice for dealing. Juries convicted him on two of those charges. He spent several years in federal prison.

James' philosophy about his line of work was, "This is what I do, man. It's what I know and what I believe in. I know it sounds strange, but I look at it as a service I perform, and no one that I know does it better than I do. Besides, it's exciting, the money's decent, and the hours suit my lifestyle."

No court ever tagged James an addict, either high bottom or low. To the court system, he was just another criminal. He did go through a yearlong substance abuse treatment program, however, as an automatic condition of his parole from federal prison.

While in treatment, he became fascinated with addiction and recovery as concepts. He read and studied everything on the subject he could get his hands on. He talked extensively with counselors and with visiting speakers from outside the treatment agency. Over the course of the year, he acquired a knowledge base which exceeded that of his counselors.

Steve asked James why he smoked so much. James smiled and said, "From where I sit, man, the better question is, 'Why do you smoke so little?' I mean, think about it. You have a choice. You can be straight, or you can be high. It's an easy choice for me, man. I feel better high than I do straight. I'm easier to get along with high than I am straight. Hell, I'm a better person high than I am straight. So why would I want to be straight?"

Steve asked him if he was addicted to pot. "That's a meaningless question, man," he said. "Addiction is just a word. It's a concept. In reality, it doesn't exist. If I take the 20-question test and answer the questions honestly, then sure, I'll meet the diagnostic criteria for addiction. But what the hell does that mean? It's some egotistical academic's opinion of what an addict looks like. What's that worth?

"Listen, man, I smoke exactly as much weed as I want to, which happens to be a lot. It's my lifestyle. It's my choice. If it causes me problems, so be it. I don't mind. To me, it's worth it."

James totally rejected speed, coke, and narcotic drugs. He believed they were dangerous, and he hated them. He had reservations about alcohol, but he drank it anyway, at least occasionally. When he did drink, he usually drank too much. Nothing horrible happened, but unexpected things did. One night he and Steve were at a bar. He insulted a woman by drawing attention to a pimple on her back. She poured half a pitcher of beer over his head. He laughed it off like a good sport, but Steve could tell that he was embarrassed. Steve asked him about it the next day. James replied, "Yeah, man, I get stupid when I drink that much alcohol. That's why I don't do it very often."

Steve liked James a lot. He enjoyed his quirky, sometimes bizarre take on things. He respected his brand of intelligence. He appreciated James' ability to throw seemingly disparate physical, metaphysical, intellectual, and spiritual ideas together in such a way that he could comprehend them. James challenged Steve. Steve appreciated the challenge.

Steve's other friends tolerated James because he was Steve's friend. None, however, felt totally comfortable around him. Tucker summed it up for most of them. "He's a lunatic, Steve. He's demented. He's got a brilliant mind, and sometimes his ideas are quite compelling. But as often as not, his logic reads like riddles. Hell, sometimes he makes William S. Burroughs seem normal. I trust James' intelligence, but I wouldn't bet a nickel on his sanity. He's about as weird as they come, my friend."

Bev was afraid of James and didn't mind saying so behind his back. She and Steve had more than one argument about how welcome James was in their home. Lois didn't trust him. She believed that his criminal activity reflected his worth as a human being. Lenny Miller despised him because James saw right through Lenny and summarily dismissed him as a punk.

Rachel met James once and said to Steve afterwards, "I guess he's an acquired taste." Rachel was correct.

Steve did not choose Austin as the destination of his geographical cure in order to reconnect with James and Tucker. Their presence there, however, was the icing on the cake. Although they were as different from each other as night and day, they were two of Steve's oldest and best friends. They were his kindred spirits.

Coincidence, fate, or perhaps grace threw the three of them together during the summer of 1973 in Austin, Texas, where they played significant roles in each other's addictive disease and in each other's denial around that disease.

CHAPTER 13

Tucker came through for Steve. As soon as Steve called him and told him that he was moving to Austin, Tucker went to work finding him a place to live. Within an hour, he had located someone who knew someone who knew about a house for rent that was cheap and close to campus.

It was an exceptional find, a nice old house owned by a nice old lady, renting for half its value, with no security deposit and no written contract or rules of conduct. By mid-afternoon of his first day in town, Steve had secured the perfect spot to hang his hat.

Steve's good fortune with the house convinced him more than ever that his decision to move to Austin was the right one. "Providence," he said to himself, as he opened a beer, lit a joint, and walked around his new digs. It was basic—five small rooms, hardwood floors, faded wallpaper, unpolished brass light fixtures and doorknobs, wooden Venetian blinds, and an attic fan in the hall.

"Well, here it is, Stevey boy," he said to himself. "This is what you asked for, and this is what you got—a simple house in which to live your simple life. You're a free man. No more pressures. No more hassles. No more deadlines. No more customers. No more employees. No more bitching and moaning from bitches and moaners. No more goddamn neckties. Holy shit, can you even believe it?"

He grabbed another beer from the ice chest and ambled from the kitchen into the living room. He lay on the living room floor, cushioned his head with his hands, and closed his eyes.

Soon, images of Rachel emerged in his mind. "Dear, lovely Rachel," he whispered. He saw her shy smile, her expectant blue eyes, and her strong, athletic body. He pictured her in shorts and tank top, jogging gracefully along a trail, her leg muscles standing out, her arms churning, and wisps of blond hair sticking to her neck and the side of her face. "Beautiful," he said softly.

His thoughts shifted to their lovemaking. He visualized them in each other's arms on the bed, on the floor, in the shower, in the car, in the grass. He recalled the warmth and security of their bodies pressed against each other. He lingered in the dream, then let the image fade.

"How different from Peggy," he whispered. He recalled the first time he noticed Peggy Sue Martin, his first true love. It was January 14, 1960, on the covered walkway between Building A and the gym at Robert E. Lee Junior High. Peggy told him later that she had noticed him, too. Same time, same place.

Peggy not only caught Steve's eye. She stopped him dead in his tracks and turned him around. He followed her, literally, until she stopped and spoke briefly to someone. He asked that person who she was. Then he went to work. Within a week, Steve and Peggy were arm in arm. They stayed that way almost without a hitch for three and a half years.

He sang softly, "Peggy Sue, Peggy Sue, oh, how my heart yearns for you. I love you, girl, and I need you, Peggy Sue."

A melancholy smile came to Steve's face as he recalled their struggles. Two kids, urgently in love, intensely desiring each other, but inexperienced and clumsy in their expression of that desire.

Steve remembered his part. A year of making out, yearning for more, and masturbating. Another year and a half of petting, heavy petting, dry humping, coming in his pants, wet dreams, and masturbating. And finally, a year of working through the particulars of going all the way, and still masturbating.

Steve recalled the disappointment of their first try at making love. Young, firm, and beautiful in their nakedness. Hot, sweaty, and trembling against each other in the back seat of Steve's Plymouth. Fervent desire, tempered with anticipation and apprehension. Breathing deeply into each other's faces and hair, fogging the windows all around the car. Peggy deliciously full and wet and open, receptive to Steve's hands and fingers. But when the rubber went on, and she felt his penis against her, she stopped breathing, and her body said, "No."

She tightened up, and in his confusion and frustration, Steve tried to force his way into her, only to come into the rubber before he realized that it just wasn't going to work.

They both felt embarrassed. Steve felt ashamed. They tried to talk about it, but the best they could do was apologize to each other. Neither of them had anyone else to discuss it with.

As Steve recalled the experience, he regretted his ignorance. He reminded himself that their lovemaking did get better, though they never did get it quite right. He continued to ejaculate prematurely, and Peggy never conquered her guilt.

"It would be different today," Steve said softly to himself. Then in a whisper, "I still love you, Peggy. I hope it got better for you."

Steve let go of Peggy's image as his thoughts drifted back to *Roxy*, his Plymouth, the car in which virginity was offered and taken. Roxy was a two-tone green, four-door 1953 sedan, purchased originally by Mama Rogers, brand new off of the showroom floor from Mixon Motor Company in Kenedy, Texas.

Steve bought her from Mama Rogers on his sixteenth birthday. She was nine years old and as straight and clean as a brand new car. The odometer showed 17,222 miles. And when Steve picked her up, she sported four new tires and a new battery.

Mama Rogers' price was $200.00, payable at $25.00 down and $25.00 per month for seven months. She sold the car to Steve for that price and those terms because she loved him, and she wanted him to have it. She treated the transaction like a straightforward business deal. Steve did not realize until after her death, seven years later, what a thoughtful and generous gift to him the car had been.

Steve owned Roxy for exactly seven months. Two weeks after making the last $25.00 payment, he sold her and went away to The Academy, a military boarding school.

Steve recalled driving up to his house and seeing four familiar cars in the driveway. It was late afternoon, August 20, 1962. He knew that something was up because as a rule, the owners of those four cars—Henry, Lois, Mama Rogers, and Grandmother Campbell—did not come together under the same roof unless there was a problem.

He walked into a living room filled with silence and with all eight eyes fixed on him. "This is pretty interesting. What's the deal?" he said. Then he sat quietly as four anxious adults tried to sell him on the benefits of going away to school. They pitched it from the positive: "It's an excellent school; it has a rich tradition; there's a nine-hole golf course; it's a great opportunity." And they pitched it from the negative: "You're getting into trouble at home and school; your grades were bad last year; you're running around with the wrong crowd; we can't trust you to do what's right."

Steve felt bewildered. "I don't get it," he said. "What did I do that was so terrible? What did I do to deserve being sent away?"

The coalition of adults fell into an uneasy silence. Lois stared at the floor. Henry opened his mouth to speak but then said nothing. Finally, Mama Rogers, the one person in the group that Steve trusted, spoke up.

"Steve, I wouldn't be here if this was a hatchet job. The truth is, at least the way I see it, this is not really about you. It may look and sound that way, and others in this room may want you to see it that way. But let me tell you what I think.

"I know you've had some problems this year. I know your mom and dad have worried about you, as we all have. My guess is that you've had more problems than any of us even know about. I also know it hasn't been easy for you around here. From what your mother has told me about what goes on between her and your dad, I can only imagine how much you have been through.

"Please understand, I'm not trying to place blame. At this point, I don't think it matters who does what to whom or why. What matters to me is what's best for you.

"So here's the bottom line, Steve. To my way of thinking, if you leave home now to attend high school in a different town, you won't have to live in this house for the next two years. You will be free of whatever it is that goes on here. With you away at school, your mom and dad can say and do whatever it is they need to say and do, and you won't have to be involved in it. From where I sit, that's your great opportunity."

Steve nodded. "Could I come and live with you instead?"

"Of course you could. You are always welcome in my home. I wouldn't recommend it, though. Rural South Texas schools aren't much to brag about, and I think ours are some of the worst. I think you deserve better. Nevertheless, as far as I'm concerned, it's up to you. I just want you to get away from here."

Steve held his grandmother's gaze for a moment and then said, "Okay. Thank you, Mama Rogers. I'll do the boarding school thing."

Steve's memory of that event triggered images of the chaos of the last few months before he left home. He remembered feeling lost and alone. Most of all, he remembered the paralyzing fear. He visualized his mother and father standing at the foot of his bed, their red, puffy faces just inches apart, raging at each other, yelling hateful statements, accusations, and threats that saner people would reserve for their bitterest enemies.

Henry backhanding Lois hard on one side of her face, then slapping her on the other, screaming at her, "You fucking whore! You goddamn slut!" Then pointing at Steve in his bed and yelling, "Look at him and tell him what you are! Look at him, and tell him, goddamn it! He has a right to know what his mother is!" Grabbing her by her shoulders and jerking her body around to face Steve squarely. Shaking her viciously and pushing her face close to Steve's. "Tell him, goddamn it, or I'll break your fucking neck!"

Lois' face red and swollen, her eyes bloodshot and wide with rage and fear, her hair disheveled and damp with sweat, her pajama top torn open, exposing her breasts, her breath stinking of alcohol and cigarettes, but her voice strong and controlled. "He's a pitiful, lying son of a bitch, Steve. A pitiful, desperate, lying son of a bitch!"

Those words pushed Henry over the edge. He slammed Lois' body face first into the bedroom wall. "THUD!" Lois bounced off the wall and landed on her back on the floor. With her eyes closed, waiting for the next blow, she stated flatly through her pain and tears, "You're a pitiful goddamn son of a bitch, Henry."

Henry stood over her for a long moment, glaring at her on the floor, breathing very hard, his hands clenched tightly into fists. Steve fully expected him to strike her in the face, and the thought crossed his mind that he would kill her, right then and there. Instead, he bent down over her so that his face almost touched hers, and he screamed, "FUCK YOU!" at the top of his lungs. He hesitated for one split second and then stood up and stomped out of Steve's bedroom and out of the house, slamming the front door with such force that it shook Steve's bedroom walls.

Steve lay motionless, paralyzed, the bed covers pulled up tightly to just under his eyes. He heard Henry's car laying rubber out of the driveway and for half a block down the street. Then silence, until he heard his mother moving. She slowly rolled onto her stomach, put one hand on the foot of Steve's bed, and cautiously pulled herself up to her knees and then to standing. She covered her chest with her arms. Her face was bloody, her features contorted. Her eyelids drooped. "He's lying, Steve," she said. "I'm not a slut. I've never cheated on him, regardless of how bad he's treated me. He's just a damn liar, and he's running out of ways to hurt me, except for trying to turn you against me."

She turned slowly and walked out of Steve's bedroom and down the hall. She closed and locked her bedroom door. The incident had taken about four or five minutes, perhaps, but it had felt like an eternity to Steve. Throughout it, he had not moved a muscle except for his eyes. He remained fixed in that position until he fell asleep several hours later.

Steve recalled the day following the fight. He came home from school late, having spent the afternoon with Peggy, to a quiet, dark house. He walked into the kitchen, assuming that Lois was in her bedroom. As he stood in front of the freezer, considering his options for dinner, he heard Lois' voice in the den. "Come here, Steve," she said.

He hesitated and then walked to the doorway. Lois sat in the dark in a chair against the opposite wall, facing him. "What do you want?" he asked.

When she spoke, the words rolled out of her mouth in a slur. "I want to apologize to you for what happened last night. I'll never forgive your father for what he did to me in front of you. He robbed me of my pride. He treated me like a worthless animal. He broke my arm and my nose and bruised my ribs. I'm sorry you had to see it. I hope I never see his face again as long as I live."

As Lois spoke, Steve's eyes adjusted to the dark. He saw that her right arm was in a cast, and her nose and face were bandaged. "Where is he now?" he asked.

"I don't know, and furthermore, I couldn't care less."

"Okay," Steve replied. It was all he had to say. He felt nothing. He walked into his bedroom, closed the door, and did not open it again until the next morning when he left for school.

Henry moved back into the house two weeks later.

Steve realized that tears were trickling down both sides of his head, and suddenly he felt the full brunt of his sadness and grief and shame. He covered his face with his hands, and he cried hard. "Mother, I'm so sorry I didn't help you," he whispered through his sobs. "I'm so sorry I let him do that to you. I just didn't....." He searched, but the words were not there.

He sat up and wiped his tears on his shirtsleeve. "What the hell are you doing, Steve?" he said softly. "That shit is over and done. It's nothing any more. It's not even real. This here, this is real. This house, my fresh start, my new life. The slate is wiped clean. Leave it alone, man; just leave it alone."

Steve slowly stood and walked back into the kitchen. He opened the last beer and took a long swig. He walked through the house once more and visualized the placement of his furniture. It was an easy task. He did not have much.

"This will work," he said. "No room for lots of crap that I don't need—not in my house, and not in my life."

CHAPTER 14

The physical move from San Antonio to Austin was a snap. Rachel showed up early to help Steve pack, but her heart wasn't in it, and she quickly became more distraction than help. Steve thanked her and sent her home at 9:00 AM.

Then he finished packing, loaded the U-Haul, drove to Austin, unloaded, drove back to San Antonio, dropped off the truck, and arrived at Lois and Chester's by taxi just after dark. His helpers for the day included one appliance dolly, two amphetamine diet pills, three joints, and two six packs of Shiner. By the time he arrived at his mom's, he felt beat and looked strung out.

Lois struggled to keep her thoughts to herself. She wanted to say, "Where is this new man you promised, the one who has his life and his drinking under control?" Instead, she said, "I'll make a deal with you, Honey. If you'll hang around here with us tonight, I'll cook you dinner and give you a ride back to Austin in the morning." Steve gratefully agreed.

The next morning, Lois tried to bring up the issue of his condition the night before, but Steve declined. "Can we just keep it light today, Mother?" he said. "Yesterday was a tough one, and I'm still pretty worn out from it." She let it drop.

When they arrived at 2905 Columbus Street, they got out of the car and stood in front of Steve's new home. Steve noted the need for exterior paint and the rundown condition of the front yard. "Luckily, I'll have time to work on it," he said, smiling and winking at Lois.

She slowly turned a full circle, taking in the immediate surroundings. The house faced West. Next door, facing south, a 24-hour convenience store bustled with morning customers. Across the street, just catty corner from and facing Steve's front yard, stood The Roam In—a rustic looking bar and live music venue. Next door to the north sat a large old house with four bicycles chained to the front porch and two large dogs lying against the front door.

"So this is it?" Lois asked. "This is what you left San Antonio for?"

Steve laughed. "Come on, Mother. This is just the house. It isn't what I left San Antonio for. Anyway, it's not that bad. You'll see. It's actually pretty nice inside."

"But, Honey, couldn't you at least have found something in a better neighborhood? Something a little quieter, maybe? How are you ever going to sleep, much less study? And for crying out loud, you're right across the street from a bar."

"Hey, don't worry about it, Mother. It's part of the charm of the place. It'll be fine. Come on in for a minute. I'll give you the two-bit tour."

After the tour and a brief visit, Steve convinced Lois that he would be okay. He assured her that he could manage the cleaning, unpacking, and arranging without her help, and that he would call her the minute his phone was installed.

"I would feel a lot better if it was just cleaner, Steve, and if it wasn't across the street from a damn beer joint," she said.

"Mother, I've never felt better about anything in my life. I know it probably sounds silly and stupid to you, but I feel as though there's destiny at work here. I feel like I'm supposed to be in this city, in this neighborhood, and in this house. I feel like I've just stepped off of a train going nowhere and stepped into a wonderful new phase of my life. Please, just trust me and let it go at that."

Lois smiled. "Well, I wouldn't want to be someone who tried to interfere with destiny. I just want you to be healthy and happy." She reluctantly got into her car and drove away.

Steve sat on his front porch and watched her leave. When she was out of sight, he strolled next door to the convenience store and introduced himself to Mario, the store manager. Mario told Steve about the old lady who had lived and died in the house before Steve moved in.

"She was a cranky old bitch, man, but I got along with her pretty good. Whatever she said, I just said, 'Yes, ma'am, you're sure right about that, ma'am.' She stole little shit sometimes, but I just played like I didn't see it. Carla told me that the old bag lived in that house for sixteen years. Anyway, I watched them carry her out of there. Been a couple of months now. Hell, I can't believe it's been empty that long. They never even put up a 'For Rent' sign or anything. You're a lucky son bitch. You know that?"

"Yeah, I guess I am. So who's Carla?"

"Carla? She's your next door neighbor on the other side, man. She's a freaking Amazon, man, and she lives with a bunch of fruitcakes and weirdo's. Brings me cookies sometimes, and I turn her on to a smoke every now and then. You'll like her, man; she's real cool. Hey, listen, what kind of beer you drink?"

"Well, Shiner's my favorite, but I'll drink anything with alcohol in it."

"Yeah? Well, you're still a lucky son bitch. I carry Shiner, man, and I want to give you your first six for free. Grab you a six-pack out of the cooler there, and enjoy yourself. I gotta get back to work here, but don't be a stranger."

Steve took the beer and walked back to his house. "I've been in town for half an hour and already made a drug connection," he thought to himself. "I think I'm gonna love this place."

Steve spent the rest of the day cleaning the house, arranging his furniture, and unpacking his things. By evening, he was fairly organized and pretty loaded. He walked next door to the pay phone and called Tucker. No answer. He called James.

No answer. He called Rachel collect. No answer. He walked home, opened a beer, put a Doobie Brothers album on the stereo, sat down on the couch, and lit a joint. He looked around the room and smiled. "Not bad," he said. "Not bad at all. Low dollar house and high dollar antiques. Not a bad combination."

Halfway through the album, Steve wandered out onto his front porch. Then, almost as an afterthought, he strolled across the street to The Roam In. The inside of the place mirrored the outside—rustic, simple, and laid back. Rock and roll blared from the jukebox. A dozen or so people sat around at tables drinking beer. Steve walked up to the bar and ordered a Shiner.

"How nice. A new face on a weeknight," the bartender said as she drew the beer into a plastic cup.

Steve smiled. "I just moved into the house across the street. My name's Steve Campbell."

"Hello, Steve Campbell. I'm Dixie. Welcome to the neighborhood." She extended her hand and gave Steve a strong handshake. "You moved into the old bitch's place, huh? I hate to sound cruel, but I'm glad she's not around to harass us anymore. God rest her soul, she hated this place, and she didn't mind saying so.

"Anyway, I tend the bar Sunday through Thursday. How about you? What do you do to make a buck?"

"Well, nothing yet. I hope to be in school at UT in the fall, but in the meantime, I'm just hanging around and checking things out, trying to get the lay of the land. What do you do when you're not selling beer?"

"Oh, I sleep, go swimming, read, hang out. Nothing much. That guy over there goes to UT. Studying philosophy or something like that." She pointed to a man sitting alone at a table close to the door.

"Oh, yeah? He looks pretty serious. Is he a talker?" Steve asked.

Dixie laughed. "Is he a talker? Humph. Does Tim Leary get high? I'll say he's a talker. Go over there and say 'Hello' to him and see if he has anything to say. His name's Tommy."

Steve sat down at the table adjacent to Tommy's and looked him over. He was tall and wiry, probably mid- to late-thirties. He had long hair, a clean-shaven face, dark, very ruddy complexion, narrow eyes, and thin lips. "A face with character," Steve thought to himself.

Tommy had a pitcher of beer in front of him. He was reading what looked to Steve like some kind of tabloid newspaper written in a foreign language. After a few moments, Tommy looked up, smiled, and said, "Hello there, stranger. How the hell are you?"

"I'm good, I think," Steve answered. "I noticed your newspaper there. What is that? Spanish?"

64

"Yeah, it's pretty wild stuff, man. Central American political propaganda. Serious leftist bullshit. Fascinating stuff. Most people would be bored to tears, I guess, but I like to go to original sources for information if I can. Indicative of my cynical nature, I suppose. I don't trust North American reporters. Except for a few oddballs, they're all pretty much full of crap. Anyway, I don't remember ever seeing you around here. Are you a local?"

"No, not really. Well, I guess that's not true. I am now, I suppose. I just moved into that little white house across the street. How about you? Do you live close by?"

"Yeah, five doors down, on this side of the street. So you moved into Miss Sadie's old place. That's cool. That's a good old house. It's real solid. It needed someone in there. I hated seeing it sitting empty. She was a character, old Sadie. People around here complained about her because she thought her seniority gave her the right to run the neighborhood. She hated this place here with a passion. She hated the noise and the frat slob party boys that come around on Friday and Saturday nights when there's live music.

"I liked the old gal, myself. I lent her a hand around the house every so often, and we talked quite a bit. People don't know this about her, but she was smart. She knew more about the history of this area than anyone I've met, and I've been here a number of years myself. She died a couple of months ago. I hated to see her go. She didn't even have a goddamn funeral. But, that's life, right? Opened up a nice little house for you to move into. By the way, my name's Tommy Jefferson."

Steve took Tommy's outstretched hand. "I'm Steve Campbell. I'm glad to meet you, Tommy. Dixie tells me you're in school at UT."

"Yeah, that I am. Graduate school. I've got about two years left on my doctorate. Then I plan to travel the world and see how many people I can find to shoot the shit with. How about yourself? What's your racket?"

"Well, I don't have one at the moment. Until recently, I was in the retail clothing business in San Antonio, but I got out of that and came here to try my hand at graduate school, too. Dixie said you're studying philosophy."

Tommy grunted. "Yeah, well, she just thinks that because I'm the resident bull shit artist for The Roam In. Truth is, I'm studying psychology—counseling psychology to be exact. I'm in a professional training program to become a psychologist. Lord only knows why. I sure as hell don't think, act, or look much like one. In fact, some people think I need to see a psychologist more than I need to be one, if you get my drift."

"Well, I don't know about that, Tommy, but you know what? Psychology is exactly what I was thinking about getting into. Maybe we could get together sometime soon, and you could give me the lowdown. I'm pretty much in the dark about it. I don't know how to apply for admission or even whom to call. To tell you the truth, I just kind of picked Austin and UT out of a hat, and I'm flying by the seat of my pants. What do you think? I'll buy the beer. I'll even roll us up a few, if you're so inclined."

"Well, hell, now you're talking my language. You name the time and place. I'll be there."

Tommy Jefferson hailed from Deep South Texas. He claimed to be the only true intellectual atheist to come out of that part of the state in all recorded history. He was Steve's lucky find of the year. He was a generous, caring man and the consummate jack of all trades.

On the day following their first meeting, Tommy willingly helped Steve tie together loose ends. First, they hit the Telephone Company and the city utility departments. Then they bought, transported, and installed used kitchen appliances. Next, they mowed and trimmed the lawn. Then while Steve repaired Venetian blinds, Tommy fixed the toilet and the dining room light fixture and replaced the screen in both screen doors.

Tommy Jefferson was 42 years old. "An older-than-average student is what they call me," he told Steve. His passions, in addition to good conversation, were beer, marijuana, and bargains, not necessarily in that order.

Tommy smuggled pot by the ton out of Mexico during the 1960s. He quit the business after he got rich and before he got caught. He buried enough cash to carry him through the rest of his life. Even so, he was notoriously tight with a buck. He bought all of his belongings at thrift shops and garage sales. He drank cheap, off-brand beer or whatever was on sale by the case. His pickup truck's odometer registered 225,000+ miles and ran like a top.

He also kept accounts even. If Steve provided the beer and pot one night, Tommy showed up with it the next. "I'm frugal, and I'm fair," he told Steve. "That's how I hang onto my friends. You're welcome to the shirt off of my back, but keep your sticky fingers out of my wallet."

Tommy embodied one of the great paradoxes of high bottom drunks and their addictions. The ones who look the best are often the ones who have it the worst.

Tommy drank a lot but seldom got drunk. He smoked a lot of weed but seldom got ripped. He never looked wasted and never acted silly or stupid. "Well, if practice makes perfect, it's no wonder I've learned how to handle myself," he explained.

His ability to drink others under the table was not a measure of his manliness. Rather, it was a symptom of his alcoholism. It meant that his tolerance was high. Had he quit drinking abruptly, he would have experienced withdrawal symptoms, including, perhaps, seizures. At age 42, Tommy's addictions had already damaged his liver and his lungs.

Tommy compromised his dearest value—frugality—by spending more money on beer and pot than on any other part of his budget, including food and rent. He easily rationalized that fact. "Well, hell, man, that makes perfect sense. Beer and pot are more important than food and rent," he said.

As a graduate student in counseling psychology, Tommy stood out from the crowd. He had a good mind and a lot of gall. He cared little about theory and a lot about application. He asked tough questions and demanded understanding. At times, he challenged his professors to put up or shut up. They appreciated the challenge. They relished the debate.

Other students, especially younger ones, admired and respected Tommy. They looked to him to champion their causes.

On the other hand, he presented himself openly, to the extent that professors knew a lot about his past and present lifestyle. They privately expressed concern about turning out a psychologist who smuggled dope in the past and smoked it daily in the present. They consoled themselves by doubting that he would ever practice within the profession. They hoped and prayed that he would not.

Tommy gladly helped Steve explore his options at the university. He introduced Steve to the head of his department and gave him a good buildup. Steve learned that he could apply in November for admission to the graduate program the following September, a full year away. In the meantime, he could enter the university as a "special student" and take classes in any department, including graduate school, if the course instructor approved it.

Steve completed the admissions process and registered for two upper level undergraduate classes—social psychology and child development. He felt relieved to put graduate school on hold for a while, figuring that it would give him a chance to settle in and reacquaint himself with the academic world.

By mid-September, Steve felt like he was over the hump. The house was right. The clothes and shoes were right. The laid back attitude was getting there. The hair would continue to grow. Being without a car was a hassle, but he could handle it for the time being. Under Tommy's tutelage, the liberal political leanings were coming along. And he was stir frying vegetables and steaming rice as easily as he used to grill T-bone steaks.

Steve knew that his drinking and pot smoking had escalated somewhat. He ascribed that to new surroundings and new companions. It did not feel like a problem. He did not owe Lois a call.

CHAPTER 15

The first hint of hairline cracks in Steve's perfect world appeared during the last half of September and the first half of October.

"It's not quite as simple or romantic as I thought it would be," he told Rachel during one of their late night phone calls. "I hate to admit it, but I miss the money. I'm not used to denying myself anything, and I feel frustrated when there's something I want but can't just go out and buy it. I know it's stupid, but that's the way I feel. I've dipped into the divorce settlement money a couple of times even though my lawyer told me not to do that under any circumstances."

"What did you buy?" she asked.

"The first time it was stuff for the house, stuff I actually needed. The second time it was drugs—pot and coke. Last week I bought floor seat tickets to see Bruce Springstein. Then yesterday I went to the record store and blew $200.00 on records. I felt guilty every time, especially when I bought the coke. I don't know, Rachel, maybe I'm just permanently spoiled. I thought I left all of my bad habits in San Antonio, but I guess I brought some of them with me to Austin."

Steve enjoyed reading and studying but not as much as he had expected. He missed TV, especially when football season started. He tired of his own cooking and began eating out several times a week. He spent hours and hours across the street at The Roam In, drinking beer, talking to Dixie, listening to the jukebox, and playing pool and pinball.

The house was hot, even at night with the windows open and the attic fan on.

Steve reconnected easily with Tucker and James, but neither of them fulfilled his need for a reliable pal. Tucker worked a lot of hours and resisted Steve's invitations to play during the day. He also had weekend visitation with his two kids, which took him to Houston twice a month.

James' time was free, but he lived on the outskirts of town and seldom answered his phone unless he expected a call. His lack of respect for time, schedules, and routines left him unreliable. Plus, he disappeared without warning for days or weeks at a time, attending to his own mysterious business activities.

Tommy kept the welcome mat out, but when classes started up in September, he spent a fair amount of time with his studies, both at home and in the campus library. He never turned Steve away, but Steve did not want to become an unwelcome guest.

Steve's psychology classes held his interest, but they did not challenge him. He seldom studied beyond the basic reading assignments. He aced the first round of tests, setting the curve on one without much effort.

He attended graduate classes as Tommy's guest a few times but felt out of place and lost with the material. Then he felt self-conscious during the intellectually intense get-togethers with Tommy and his classmates after class at the coffeehouse.

He fit in better when Tommy invited him to join the group at the beer garden. Even then, though, they tended to drift into esoteric psychobabble and other unintelligible mumbo jumbo. Steve drank hard and fast to compensate for his fear of not measuring up.

Seeing Lynn and Eddie every week became a major chore without a car. By the end of September Steve cut his visitation back to every other weekend. Bev was unsympathetic and refused to drive them up, leaving Steve to scrounge rides and borrow vehicles.

"She's a mean, vindictive, selfish bitch," he grumbled to Tucker.

"Of course she is, you stupid shit," he answered. "What the hell do you expect? You left her, abandoned her, dumped her, and told her you didn't love her. So what do you think she's going to do? Race around to accommodate your needs just because you've chosen to live like a cheeseparer? I don't think so. Listen, man, her primary goal in life today is to make your life miserable. Take my word on that. I'm a guy with lots of experience in this department. I know what I'm talking about."

Steve missed Rachel a lot. He missed her support. He missed her shy smile. He missed her luscious body. At first, he called her often. As the weeks passed, though, they connected less often and less intimately, until neither was the other's first priority.

As Steve and Rachel drifted apart, Carla and the oddball crew next door took up the slack. The first time Carla saw Steve in his front yard, she walked over and introduced herself. Steve invited her in for a cold beer. They spent the next three hours drinking, smoking, eating ice cream, and listening to each other's stories.

Mario had not exaggerated about Carla's size. She was, indeed, an Amazon. She stood a full six feet and weighed at least 180. "Don't call me fat," she instructed Steve. "I'm just a big, rock-solid girl."

When Carla left, she kissed Steve on the cheek and said, "Hey, I'll do you a 'welcome wagon' thing tomorrow. After lunch sometime, I'll bring over some cookies and milk, and after you've had your fill, I'll give you a world-famous Carla Lott full body massage. How does that sound, Buddy-boy?"

True to her word, Carla showed up the next afternoon with two dozen of the best oatmeal raisin cookies that Steve had ever tasted. Later that evening she took him to her house and gave him the best full body massage that he had ever had.

When she finished, Steve offered to reciprocate. "I'm no expert, and I don't have your hand strength, but I am sincere," he said.

She smiled broadly, thanked him, and slipped out of her clothes and onto the table.

Carla's body flipped Steve's switch. She could tell. She heard his breathing quicken and felt his hands tremble slightly when he massaged her breasts, buttocks, and inner thighs.

When Steve was finished working on her, she rolled over and asked him in a soft voice if he liked her body.

Steve nodded. "I like your body a lot. When you said you were rock-solid, I didn't realize you were being so literal. I didn't expect you to be so firm and, I don't know, well proportioned. To tell you the truth, Carla, I've had a hard on for most of the last hour."

After saying that, he blushed. "Sorry, Carla, I didn't have to tell you that," he said.

Carla laughed. "You're funny, Steve. What's the matter? Are you afraid I might feel offended?"

"I don't know. It might have sounded like a come-on. I mean, it wasn't, but it might have sounded that way."

She was silent for a moment and then said, "Would you like to go to bed with me, Steve?"

"Are you serious?" he asked.

Carla nodded.

"Well, yeah, sure I would. Do you mean now?"

"Yeah, now," she said softly. She stepped down from the table and led Steve by the hand into her bedroom.

Relaxed and uninhibited, Carla led Steve through foreplay and intercourse by telling him what she liked and what she wanted and asking for the same guidance from him.

"You're a sweet lover, Steve," she said afterwards. "You're patient and responsive. I enjoyed it."

"So did I," Steve replied. "You're different from anyone I've ever been with. You seem so comfortable with yourself. I'm usually kind of up tight when I'm with someone for the first time, but you put me at ease. I liked talking about what we wanted. Maybe we can do it again sometime."

Carla smiled. "Yeah, I'd like that. Let's keep it simple, though, okay? I'm great with friends, but I don't do well when things get complicated. You're okay with that, aren't you?"

Steve turned his head to see Carla's face. Her expression was calm but serious. "Yeah, okay, Carla. I'm cool with that."

Another bright spot for Steve was Dixie, The Roam In's weekday bartender. Dixie had exactly ten years on Steve. She also had experience, having been married and divorced twice, both times to musicians who left her for younger, prettier women. She had no children and lived alone with her cat.

Steve and Dixie felt mildly attracted to each other sexually, but the attraction took a backseat to an easy friendship that sprang out of long afternoon talks at the bar. They expanded the talks into evening swims at Barton Springs, an occasional movie, and happy hour pool at the UT Student Union. Once or twice a week, Dixie walked across the street to Steve's house when she got off of work and ended up spending the night. Dixie liked Steve's youthful body and appreciated his attentiveness. Steve liked her mature, soft curves and appreciated her gentleness and patience. He felt no pressure to perform with Dixie. As a result, he had his first ever experience of climaxing after his partner instead of before.

Dixie and Carla both knew that the other one slept with Steve. Neither one seemed to mind, and they never compared notes. Carla did one time, however, mention to Steve that a threesome might be fun. Steve was interested, but Dixie said, "I don't think so, Steve. I'm not against people doing that, but it's just not my bag. A few years ago maybe, but not now. I guess I'll pass."

Steve did not say so, but he felt relieved more than disappointed. When he gave Carla the bad news, she just said, "Oh, well, that's cool; it was just a thought."

Steve nearly lost Dixie one night when he got very drunk at the bar and boasted to a couple of the regulars that he had been banging her. She felt hurt and betrayed. The incident reminded her of other men who had mistreated her and abused her trust.

The next day, Steve felt ashamed and genuinely remorseful. He apologized sincerely. Dixie forgave him, but she also questioned his drinking.

"I'm not being critical or judgmental, Steve. I'm just asking you, as a friend who cares, to take a look at it. At least be aware of it. That's all. It's not a big deal, but it is a suggestion."

"Yeah, okay," he said. "I'll look at it. It's funny, you know. When I moved here from San Antonio, I promised myself that I was going to slow down on my drinking and drugging. But I think I'm using more now than I was before. At first, I just passed it off as part of the move, you know, part of the process of getting my feet on the ground around here. I don't know, though. Maybe I need to revisit that promise. Maybe it's time for me to take it more seriously. So, yeah, I'll take a look at it. I really will."

That night, he asked Tommy what he thought. Tommy rubbed his chin for a moment and then said, "Well I like old Dixie too much to ever accuse her of being full of it. I'm sure she's coming from a good place with her concern. But I suspect there may be a little touch of covert incest going on, like maybe Dixie is trying to be both your lover and your mother. I'm probably wrong about that, but it does come to mind.

"Myself, I just don't see much of a problem. I've seen you drink and do drugs quite a bit over the last couple of months, and you seem to have pretty damn good control to me."

Steve respected Tommy's opinion, but Dixie's concern bothered him. It nudged him in the right direction at just the right time. It put a bug in his ear that did not readily disappear. He felt guilty about having hurt her. And he knew that he never would have done that if he had not been so drunk.

CHAPTER 16

Through the summer and fall of 1973, Steve and Bev's divorce attorneys tried to hammer out a property settlement that satisfied both parties. They came close twice, but fear, greed, and animosity got in the way both times.

In the end, Bev wanted everything. She felt entitled to it. She believed that Steve and John had conspired to cheat her out of a substantial amount of money by deliberately understating the price that John paid Steve for his half of the store.

She convinced her attorney to investigate this claim endlessly. She demanded that he subpoena the company's typewriter to compare its operation with samples of font type and ink density on various documents that appeared in company records. When he and his team failed to substantiate her claims, she fired them and hired a new firm. The new team did no better than the old one, leaving Beverly frustrated, bitter, and owing enormous attorney's fees.

By the end of October, everyone connected with the proceedings agreed that the only way to resolve it was to list the remaining assets and ask the court to divide them fairly. They set a November 11th court date.

When that day arrived, Steve awoke with a chip on his shoulder and something to prove. To his lawyer's utter dismay, Steve walked into the courthouse in his new persona—hair long, face unshaven, and dressed in jeans and polo-style shirt. Bev walked in behind him looking prim, proper, and perfect from head to toe. She arrived armed to the teeth for an all out war.

Bev took the stand eagerly. She informed the court that Steve and John had kept two sets of books since their first day in business. The private set reflected the true income and value of the business. The public set understated sales and profits, allowing them to "steal money from themselves," hide unreported income, pay reduced sales and income taxes, and understate the value of the business.

She claimed that Steve had received substantially more for his half of the business than the records reported and that he had hidden the difference between the real and the stated selling price in a place known only to him and John.

Bev argued convincingly that her unselfish willingness to work and put Steve through graduate school accounted for his business success in the first place. She was therefore entitled to most of the proceeds of the sale of the business, understated though they were.

Bev described tearfully and in great detail a number of Steve's more notorious alcohol and drug related indiscretions. She stated that his compulsive use of alcohol and drugs represented a form of covert spousal and child abuse.

She testified regarding Steve's marital infidelities, including one that never occurred. She painted a touching picture of her heroic efforts to provide for her children as a single parent on the paltry amount of money that Steve had been paying as temporary support. She related the story of Steve showing up at the house unannounced in a new Corvette convertible when she and the kids had barely enough money for food and clothing.

She claimed that when Steve had moved out of their home, he had taken with him the finest and most valuable pieces of antique furniture. She testified that he did this while she and the children were on a weekend visit to the Gulf Coast.

Bev pointed out Steve's failure to comply with his initial weekly visitation agreement. She described for the court Lynn's heartbreak when Steve stood up the kids on one of his designated visitations even after she had reluctantly agreed to him seeing them only twice a month.

She acknowledged that the children loved their father and that she did not want to deny him visitation rights. At the same time, she wanted the court's assurance that he would comply strictly with those rights. She also wanted the court's assurance that Steve would not hurt the kids in any way, including using drugs in front of them or while they were in his care.

Bev's testimony blew Steve away. It shocked him. It shattered his confidence. His arrogance turned into humiliation. He had grossly underestimated her, and for that he felt stupid and ashamed. His attorney's cross-examination ridiculed and effectively neutralized much of Bev's testimony. Even so, he knew that a smart, vindictive woman and her uptown lawyer had annihilated him.

When Steve took the stand, he felt and looked deflated and embarrassed. He deeply regretted his decision to wear his new persona into court, even "as a matter of principle." He regretted his choice of clothes. He lamented his decision to leave his hair long and his face unshaven. He wished that he could hide.

He denied most of Bev's allegations. He denied some because they misrepresented the truth. He denied others because their accuracy legally incriminated him and John. Overall, Steve was a poor witness on his own behalf.

The judge's decision reflected Bev's and Steve's performance and credibility on the stand. He awarded Steve $10,000 cash and the furniture and other incidental items in his possession. He awarded Beverly the house, its contents, her car, her personal belongings, including her jewelry, their stocks and bonds, and the balance of the business sale proceeds. Her award amounted to over $100,000. He set Steve's child support at $300.00 a month.

Steve took a tiny spot of solace from the fact that John did, in fact, owe him $15,000 under the table from the sale, to be paid out secretly, in cash at the rate of $300.00 per month. Ironically, John reneged on the debt after five payments. Since they had been careful to put nothing in writing, Steve had no recourse. He eventually let the matter drop.

After court, Steve ran into Bev on the courthouse steps. "You must feel pretty damn proud of yourself. I can't believe you said some of the things you did in there. What the hell's wrong with you? You didn't have to go that far, especially in front of all those people."

She looked him dead in the eye and said, "You got exactly what you deserved. You're a conniving, selfish son of a bitch, and you think you can treat people without regard for their needs or their feelings. Well, I want you to know that you can't always get away with it. As far as I'm concerned, you're lucky to have gotten anything. I told the truth. You lied. As far as I'm concerned, you can stick it up your ass." With that, she turned her back and walked away.

Steve stood motionless, startled by Bev's indignation and malice. "Jesus Christ, what's her goddamn problem?" he muttered to himself. "She got what she wanted. What the hell does she have to be pissed off about?"

Steve called Lois and asked her to pick him up at the courthouse. While he waited on the steps, he reviewed Bev's testimony in his mind. She had, indeed, told the truth, at least within the context of her bitterness toward him.

He and John had, indeed, kept two sets of books, one of which she had never seen but had heard about. And just as she suspected but could not prove, he and John had agreed on a higher under-the-table price for the business and had very carefully covered their tracks.

Steve considered Bev's assertion that she was responsible for his business success. He had never thought of her working while he obtained his master's degree as a sacrifice on her part, but perhaps it was.

He recalled the weekend when Bev took the kids to the beach so that he could move out. He had taken only a few things. Was it possible that he took more than his share? He had two of their nicest pieces, but he left so much more than he took.

Steve thought about the Corvette. "How stupid can one person be?" he said to himself. Buying the car was stupid enough. Showing it off to her the way he did was lunacy. As he thought about it now, he understood her anger. He had shown her up in front of Lynn and Eddie.

Then there was his disregard for her feelings when it came to drinking, drugging, and carousing. She accepted social drinking but refused to tolerate drunkenness and drug use. She condemned Steve when he crossed those lines. In response, he flaunted it. He wanted her to understand that he did not care what she thought and that she could not control him in any way.

Worse than the substance abuse, he had, in fact, been indiscreet in his relationships with other women. There had not been that many affairs, but two were blatant and must have hurt her deeply. One of those involved Bev's best friend and took place right under her nose. The other involved an eighteen-year-old girl and produced a pregnancy, an abortion, and a small scandal.

Steve had never considered the possibility that his behavior had been covertly abusive to Bev or the kids. He had, however, said disrespectful and hateful things to her over the years. He told her more than once that he had never really loved her and that he never would have married her if she had not trapped him into it by getting herself pregnant with Lynn.

Steve pictured Lynn and Eddie in his mind. He did love them, but he did not miss being with them day-to-day. He had felt hassled and overwhelmed by having to see them every week. Even every other week took quite an effort. Visitation sometimes felt like a chore rather than a gift.

Lois pulled up to the curb. Steve got into her car and gazed straight ahead. Lois looked at him for a moment and then pulled out into traffic. She felt his dark mood.

"Well? How bad was it?" she asked.

"Pretty bad," Steve answered.

"Are you going to tell me about it, or should I just guess what happened?"

"Not much to tell. She got most of it—the house, the investments, and most of the money. I got ten grand and pretty reasonable child support."

"Well, Honey, I hate to say it, but you asked for it."

Steve looked at her for the first time since getting into the car. "What the hell is that supposed to mean, Mother?"

"Well just look at you. You don't go into a courtroom looking like that and expect to be taken seriously. I warned you about that last week."

"Let's drop it," Steve said. "I'm in no mood to discuss it right now."

Lois remained quiet for a few minutes and then said, "I think you were feeling guilty, Steve, and this was your way of making sure that you'd be punished for what you did to Bev and the kids."

Steve sighed loudly and looked out the side window. "Whatever, Mother. Send me a bill for the diagnosis. Whose side are you on, anyway? I'm not Dad, you know. I'm Steve. Remember?"

"I'm not on anyone's side, Steve, and I know exactly who you are. If you were your father, I wouldn't be here. I'd be with Bev." Lois paused for a moment and then continued. "Beverly loved you. She was committed to making your marriage work. She tried to make it work. She overlooked and forgave you things that not many women would put up with. But I think you cast her aside in your own mind a long time ago, and you were just waiting for the right time to bail out. Steve, on some level you must realize that you did not do right by her. What I'm saying is, she made the effort, and you didn't."

Lois' rebuke hit home. Steve opened his mouth to defend himself but then stopped. He remained silent for a moment and then said softly, "I don't know, Mother. Maybe you're right. Maybe that's why she was still so angry even after she ripped me to shreds in court and got everything she could have possibly wanted.

"You know, there was a time, in the beginning, when I wanted to love Bev. I just didn't, though, and I didn't know how to tell her. I didn't want to be the bad guy. So I stuck around and kept thinking it might change, that something might happen to trigger a spark of something between us. I think that's why we had Eddie. I was the one who wanted us to have him; I was the one who suggested it. That just made things worse, though. I got what I wanted and then resented it. I felt more trapped than ever.

"Finally, I guess I came to accept the fact that I wasn't doing either one of us a favor, so I left. I don't think she ever would have, regardless of what I did. I don't regret leaving her. I have regrets about the way I treated her, but not about leaving. The truth is, I had to go."

Lois nodded. "I understand that," she said.

"I'll tell you something else, Mother," Steve added. "I'm glad I made the move to Austin. It's not perfect by any stretch of the imagination. In fact, it's been kind of hard, but I'm glad to be away from San Antonio. I've made some new friends, and I think

76

things are going to be better now that this thing isn't hanging over my head anymore."

"Well, I hope so, Steve. I really do hope so." She looked at him and said, "I hate to ask, but how much are you drinking?"

Steve looked back at her and smiled. "Not that much, Mother. Not enough for you to worry about."

She looked back at the road. "You remember your promise to me, don't you?"

"What promise is that?" he asked.

"Your promise that you will call me if your drinking starts causing you problems. You gave me your word, and I'm holding you to it."

Steve smiled. "If I were you, I wouldn't sit by the phone waiting for that call. Unless I'm sadly mistaken, it won't come."

Steve asked Lois to drop him off on the highway and let him hitchhike home, but she would not consider it. She did, however, promise not to bring up the divorce or his lifestyle on the drive to Austin. Instead, she challenged him to come up with at least one concrete, workable plan for earning a living.

He threw out a few ideas to antagonize her. He mentioned opening a retail condom and edible panties store, working as a disc jockey at a topless bar, and becoming a street mime on the UT drag. Then he brought up furniture refinishing and antique restoration. Lois liked the idea and insisted that they use the drive time to discuss it.

They talked about simplicity and practicality. Steve needed no partners or employees, no major financial investment, no inventory, no major overhead, no creditors, no credit sales, no set work hours, and no uniforms of any kind. Steve talked his way through a plan to turn his garage into a workshop and another one to market the business, all within the limits of his new financial situation.

Together, they chose a name: The WoodWorks, and a business plan: Do it now and keep it simple. By the time they parked in front of 2905 Columbus, Steve felt genuinely interested in turning the plan into reality.

Before leaving Austin, Lois pushed for and got one more concession from Steve. He promised to complete and submit his application for graduate school before the end of November.

CHAPTER 17

Steve waved goodbye to Lois as she drove away. "Thanks, Mom," he whispered.

He went inside, opened a beer, lit a joint, put Joni Mitchell's *Ladies of the Canyon* on the stereo, and stretched out on the sofa. He felt exhausted and relieved.

"Finally," he said. "Finally, it's a done damn deal. I am out."

Steve thought about Lois' assertion that he had sabotaged his chances for a fair court settlement in order to assuage his guilt. He wondered if it could be true.

He recalled the day the divorce had really begun. It was January 28th, three days after his twenty-seventh birthday. He had spent the previous evening with Lenny Miller, hanging out and drinking at a notorious eastside strip joint. He left Lenny in the hands of one of the strippers at 2:00 AM. On the way home, he stopped at a massage parlor and bought a $30.00 blowjob.

When he awakened on the morning of the 28th, he was hung over and alone in his and Bev's bed. He caught a glimpse of Bev walking down the hall, past the open bedroom door. She wore only panties and bra; her hair was wet and wrapped in a bath towel. Neither the scene nor the situation was anything out of the ordinary, but inside of that glimpse and without warning, Steve decided that the time had come. Without further thought or hesitation, he called her name.

"Bev?" She did not answer so he said it louder. "Beverly?"

She looked into the bedroom. "What do you want?" she asked.

"Come here for a minute," he said.

She walked across the room to the closet, took her robe from a hanger, and put it around her. She removed the towel from her head, shook her hair loose with her hand, and faced Steve. "Okay, here I am. What is it?"

"Come over here and sit on the bed. I need to talk to you about something."

She sat down on the edge of the bed. "You sound pretty serious for a man with blood-red eyes."

He took a deep breath. "Bev, it's time we talked seriously about ending this marriage—for real this time. I know, and you must know, too, that it's never going to get any better."

Bev's face tightened; her eyes narrowed. "So you want out, right?"

"Yes, I do," he said. "Don't you?"

"No, Steve, I don't. I don't want us to go on like this, but I don't want to quit. But then, I don't suppose what I want matters, does it?"

He looked down. "No, I guess not. Not really." He looked back up at her. "I'm sorry; I wish.... Well, never mind what I wish. I'll just leave it at that."

Bev stood up and started to move away from the bed, but she stopped and faced Steve again. Her face held no expression.

"Okay, Steve, so what's your plan? Do you already have a place to move into?"

"No. I haven't been planning this. But I'll start looking today. I'll stay here until I find something if that's alright with you."

She did not answer immediately. She stared at Steve impassively. "What are you going to tell Lynn and Eddie? This is going to crush Lynn. I hope you know that. She's been through this before with you, and it was hard enough the last time. This time will be worse. She's older, and she understands more. And this time I won't do it for you. I won't protect you the way I did before."

Steve took another deep breath. "Bev, maybe we should talk to Lynn together. Maybe we could present it to her in a positive way. I think that's possible because I believe that this will be a positive thing. And I mean for all of us."

"Oh, yeah? You think it's positive? That's great. You tell her. Then I think you'll find out how positive it is. I dealt with it by myself two years ago. It's your turn."

Again, Bev started to walk away, but again she turned around. This time, her anger showed. "I want to tell you something else, Steve Campbell, and I want you to listen. If you leave, it's over. No coming back again, no starting over again. If I'm going to live without you, then I want to live without you completely and forever. I want to have my own life without having to deal with your ambivalence. You can't come home when you 'get things worked out' or when you 'get your shit together.' I'm telling you right now. You better be damn sure that this is what you want, because I'm not kidding. If you leave, you don't come back. Do you understand what I'm telling you?"

Steve nodded. "Yes, Bev, I do. I understand completely, and I don't blame you."

She looked at him for a moment and then, impassive again, she said, "Find something fast, Steve. I don't want you here." She turned around, and this time she kept walking, out of the room and down the hall. She did not reappear while Steve was still in the house.

Steve opened his eyes and stared at the ceiling. He looked at his watch; it was 6:45. He heard the last few lines of *The Circle Game* on the stereo.

And the seasons they go round and round,
And the painted ponies go up and down.
We're captive on the carousel of time.
We can't return;
We can only look
Behind from where we came.
And go round and round and round

In the circle game.

Steve thought about how steadfast he and Bev had stood regarding the divorce once their decision was made. He rented an apartment the next day—a Thursday, and moved out on Saturday. Bev hired an attorney on Monday morning and filed within the week. They never discussed reconciliation.

"It really was the right thing," Steve muttered to himself.

His thoughts shifted to his talk with Lynn. He took her to the park on Friday afternoon. He tried to keep it simple and positive, but Bev had predicted Lynn's reaction correctly. She would not settle for simple. She wanted details. She wanted to understand. Unfortunately, her not quite six-year-old mind, bright though it was, did not work that way yet. She loved her father. She loved her mother. Why didn't her father love her mother?

Lynn sobbed. Steve held her close. "Listen to me, Sweetheart," he said. "I love you. I'll always love you. I'm not leaving you, and I'm not leaving because of you. What I'm leaving is my marriage to your mom. You and Eddie and I will still spend time together. I'll be living right up the road from you, and I'll come down and see you every weekend. It will be okay. I promise." As he spoke the words, he fully intended to keep his promise.

He had not done that. He knew that he could rationalize away his failure to keep up with weekly visitation. But the plain truth was that other things had taken precedent. First, there was Rachel—partying with Rachel, sleeping with Rachel, traveling with Rachel, being with Rachel.

Then there was distance and inconvenience. The eighty miles from Austin to San Antonio sometimes seemed like a long way and a lot of trouble. And there was apathy—days when he just did not have it in him to make the effort.

Finally, there was alcohol and drugs. As much as he hated to admit it to himself, being with the kids on weekends interfered with getting high and partying with his friends.

Steve looked at the ceiling again. He realized that the house was silent. He got up and opened another beer and put on another album—Bonnie Raitt's *Give It Up*. He listened to all of *Give It Up Or Let Me Go* and *Nothing Seems To Matter*, the song that he and Rachel had called their song.

Seems like such a long time
Since I've held you in my arms,
Felt you close and warm beside me.
Another night is getting late,
And I'm alone with just the ache
And the memory of you beside me.

Steve picked up the phone and dialed Rachel's number. A babysitter answered. He did not leave his name. He looked at his

80

watch; it was 8:05. He lay back down on the couch and closed his eyes.

"The WoodWorks," he thought. "How about The WoodWorks?" He visualized the shop set up in the garage. He saw it with workbenches and tools and projects in progress. Everything new. Everything clean. Everything organized and carefully arranged. The image brought a smile.

As a tradesman, a craftsman, yet, he did not compromise any values. Woodworking was honest work, real work, in a time-honored tradition. It required skill, but no dress code. It required time and patience, but no set hours. The WoodWorks was a good fit for the new man. He felt positive and optimistic.

Then he struck pay dirt, as his next thought nudged him across the line. "A pickup truck," he said out loud. "I'd have to have a pickup truck in order to be in business." A pickup would give him back his mobility—his freedom of movement, not only around Austin but also to and from San Antonio. Bingo. Suddenly the puzzle pieces fit together perfectly.

Steve sat up. "Okay," he said. "This is where we're headed, and it's the right place to go. I know it!" His and Lois' WoodWorks business plan popped into his head. *"Do it now and keep it simple,"* he shouted. "I'll start first thing in the morning. Tonight, though, I celebrate."

He opened another beer, walked briskly to Tommy's house, and drug him away from his books by announcing, "Come on, motherfucker; the beer is on me." He banged on Carla's door and made the same offer to all occupants. When he and his crew walked into The Roam In, he was all smiles and swagger.

Dixie grinned at him and said, "Well, it must have gone better than you expected."

"No, my friend, it didn't," he said. "As a matter of fact, it went worse. Much worse. But it went, by God. I am a free man, and I'm here to celebrate. I want to run a tab, and I want to start with six pitchers of Shiner. Spread them around, and if anyone doesn't like Shiner, then fuck 'em. Let them buy their own goddamn beer."

Steve drank one pitcher by himself in less than thirty minutes. He bought a second round and drank a second pitcher in less than twenty. He called for a third round and started on his third pitcher. The rest of the evening disappeared.

He awakened the next morning with a crushing headache and with Dixie, still asleep, snuggled up next to him in his own bed. He looked around the room, moving his head as little as possible. He looked at Dixie again and realized that he had no recollection of having been with her the night before. Indeed, he had no memory of leaving the bar or being in his house. No memory whatsoever.

He closed his eyes and tried to trace his steps. He remembered ordering the third round and drinking straight from a pitcher. He vaguely remembered putting quarters into the jukebox and dancing with Carla. He recalled placing his hands on her hips as she moved with the music. He faintly remembered standing on a chair, holding a pitcher of beer into the air, and proposing a toast to someone or something. Himself, perhaps. Then nothing; the rest was a complete blank.

Steve looked at his watch. It was 11:15. He put his hands over his face and rubbed his eyes and forehead. Then he carefully leaned up on one elbow and looked around the room again. Nothing appeared out of place. Their clothes lay on the floor by the bed. Two warm half-full beers and the tail end of a joint sat on the nightstand.

He slowly maneuvered his body into sitting on the edge of the bed. His head pounded; his body ached. He shuffled into the bathroom and then into the kitchen, where he downed four aspirin and a glass of milk. When he slipped back into bed, Dixie opened her eyes.

"How do you feel this morning, party boy?" she asked.

"Like hammered shit," he answered. "Worse than that if there's such a thing. What the hell happened?"

"What do you mean? What happened when?"

"What happened last night? I can't remember much past the second round of beer."

"Well, you missed a pretty wild time, then," she said, yawning into her hand. "Too bad you missed it, too, because you were without doubt the life of the party."

"Uh oh," he said. "What did I do?"

"Well, you danced on tables and chairs. You told some of the filthiest jokes I've ever heard. You propositioned every woman in the place at least once. You exposed yourself to Carla. You mooned Brenda, that lesbian bus driver or security guard or whatever she is. You waited on tables and insisted on paying for just about everything that anyone ordered. You were a party animal."

"Did I make a total fool out of myself?"

"No, I didn't think so. You got pretty loud, but what the hell, it was your party, and you were paying for it. Nobody complained, not to me, anyway. You ran up a pretty hefty tab, though. I helped you out as much as I could, but it's still well over a hundred bucks, maybe even two. You were buying beer for people who still had full cups. Nothing but Shiner."

"When did we come over here? I don't remember being back here at all."

"Oh, I guess it was about 3:30 or 4:00. You wanted to tie me up. You were pretty insistent about it. You don't remember that, either, huh?"

Steve looked at Dixie to make sure she was not kidding. "No, I don't. I'm sorry, Dixie. I hope I didn't do anything dumb."

"No, it was okay. I think you felt a little impatient with me for a minute or two. You said that Carla would let you do it. I said, 'Well, I guess you could go over and ask her.' You dropped it pretty quickly after that."

"Damn it. I'm really sorry, Dixie. I can't believe I said something that stupid to you."

"Hey, don't worry about it, Steve. It's okay. I've been told worse. It hurt my feelings a little bit, but I knew you were loaded. And I know you weren't trying to hurt me. Forget it; it's no big deal. Listen, how about some breakfast?"

Steve grimaced. "Thanks, but no thanks. Maybe later. So what happened after that? God, I hope it doesn't get any worse."

Dixie laughed. She put her arm around him and pulled him against her. "No, it was just fine. We had sex—pretty good sex, actually, and then you rolled off of me and closed your eyes and 'Poof,' you were dead to the world." She laughed again. "Listen, all in all, nothing bad happened. No cops and no boyfriends out to get you. Believe it or not, I don't even think you owe any apologies. I can't honestly say that's how I like you best, but you were nice to me, for the most part, anyway. I'm not complaining."

"Well, thank you. I suspect you're being awfully kind. So tell me something, Dixie. Since that's obviously not my best side, what is? How do you like me best?"

"Oh, I don't know. When you're just yourself, I guess. I like it when you sit and talk to me—when you have something on your mind, and you tell me about it or ask my opinion. I like it when you sit at that corner table and read and then bring your book over to the bar and say, 'Hey, listen to this, Dixie.'

"I like it when you make love to me gently, and you rub my body and tell me I'm lovely. I like it when you lay your head on my tummy and tell me you like its softness. I like it when we get up and eat breakfast together, and you compliment my cooking. I don't know, Steve, I guess I like you best when you're just you. Sometimes when you drink a lot you turn into someone else. I'm not saying you turn into a bad guy or anything like that, but you're not you. Am I making any sense?"

"Yeah, you are. You know, you asked me once before to take a look at my drinking. Are you asking me to do that again?"

"No. I made that pitch once. It's not my place to do it again."

Steve closed his eyes and hugged Dixie tight. "I really care about you, Dixie," he said softly. "I trust you, and I respect you. I don't want to lose your friendship. I hope you'll be patient with me."

"Don't worry, Steve. I'm not going anywhere. I like you, too, and I like what we have. I don't expect you to be perfect."

Eventually, Steve and Dixie got up and showered. Over lunch, Steve told Dixie his ideas for The WoodWorks. She applauded the plan and said that her boss at The Roam In, a man Steve had never seen, had a storeroom filled with damaged tables and chairs that he wanted to have fixed but had been unable to find anyone to do the job. She offered to mention The WoodWorks to him.

Dixie left after lunch. Steve straightened up the house. While he worked, he promised himself again that he would control his drinking more closely. The blackout bothered him. It scared him. It was not the first blackout that he had ever had, but it was the worst. He swore to himself that it would be his last.

CHAPTER 18

Steve had a ball bringing The WoodWorks to life. The process challenged him. It rekindled his interest in day to day living and encouraged him to utilize business skills that had lain dormant for some time.

His restructured net worth allowed him to pay off all debts, pay cash for equipment, supplies, and a used pick-up truck, set aside six months' child support, and still have about 90 days' living expenses.

Steve turned to Tucker for help with legal details. Tucker gave him the information he needed but was less than supportive of the plan. "Steve, we need to talk about this. I'm worried about you. First, you turn yourself into a longhaired mendicant and seclude yourself in a pissant little box of a so-called house. Then you give away the farm to Bev because your stupid pride convinces you to stand up and make a point that makes no sense to begin with. And now you want to play with broken wood in your goddamn garage, which I know for certain isn't air conditioned, and I'd bet my ass isn't even heated.

"For Christ's sake, man, we worked our asses off to get our master's degrees so we could get rich and keep our fingernails clean. You need help, Steve. That's all I've got to say. You're a sick pup."

James showed more support. "Yeah, that's far out, man. Putting broken stuff back together. Making ugly stuff look pretty. I like that. Give me a call when you get it set up, man, and I'll come by and check it out. I've got some weed that will be perfect to consecrate the place. And listen, man, when you get ready to buy your pickup, call me; I know a guy who sells used trucks, and I'll talk to him for you. He's a straight dude. The WoodWorks, huh? Not bad for a preppie clothes salesman."

Tommy lit up like a house on fire, crazy wild about the idea. He offered free labor as electrician, carpenter, and machinery expert, and he made Steve promise that he could be involved in setting up shop from start to finish.

Before he embarked on his first major buying spree, Steve called Bev and asked her if he could drive down and pick up his hand and power tools out of the garage.

"I can't believe you would even ask," she said.

"I take it that means 'no,'" he replied.

"You just don't get it, do you, Steve?"

"Well, I guess I do now," he said, and he hung up.

So with Tommy behind the wheel and providing advice and consent, Steve furnished The WoodWorks from the ground up. He bought an air compressor and basic tools at Sears, woodworking tools at an upscale cabinet shop, workbenches and pegboards at the lumberyard, spray gun and refinishing supplies at the paint store, and business cards at the office supply.

Saving the best for last, the boys dropped in on James' friend, who gave Steve a super deal on a 1965 Chevy 1/2-ton stepside pickup. "She reminds me of my great-aunt Cleo—colorful and solid as a rock," Steve told Tommy as they admired the purchase.

"Well, then, from this day forward, you shall be known as Cleo Truck," Tommy said, slapping her on the hood.

Tommy became so excited about the business and involved in the process of setting it up that he hinted to Steve that a partnership might be fun.

"Tommy, I wouldn't partner up with Jesus Christ himself at this point in my life," Steve said.

"Well, hell, man, I don't blame you one bit for that," Tommy said with a straight face. "Who in his right mind would want to be business partners with a psychotically deluded, grandiose madman like him? Talk about asking for trouble."

Instead of a partnership, Steve gave Tommy unlimited use of and access to the shop and its contents.

Ten days following Steve's appearance in divorce court, The WoodWorks opened for business. The day after that, he met Robert Billows—Dixie's boss, and together they delivered two pickup truck loads of broken and bruised furniture to Steve's garage. It was enough work to keep Steve busy part-time for three weeks, and Robert promised more if the first batch looked good.

In the meantime, the more Steve learned about graduate school, the less eager he was to pursue it. The application process appeared daunting. In addition to the usual prerequisites ("complete and return these forms along with official transcripts, etc."), it required steps that intimidated Steve. Those included scoring a minimum of 1100 on the GRE, writing a 400-word autobiographical essay, and sitting before an admissions committee for a full-scale personal interview.

The GRE scared him the most. He doubted his ability to score 1100, even if he studied. The paper sounded tricky—less than a page to introduce himself, outline his professional aspirations, and demonstrate his writing skills. The personal interview occurred only for those who made it to the final cut. The committee was comprised of four tenured professors. "Yeah, it's a bunch of anal-retentive old geezers," Tommy told him.

Tommy took it upon himself to map out Steve's approach. "Don't worry about it, man. I've got a foolproof plan all ready for you. First off, you go today and buy one of those GRE study guides, and you bust your ass for two or three hours a day for about two months. Then you take the test immediately, before you forget everything. That's all there is to it. You'll ace the bastard. I guarantee it.

"Now then, the slippery part—the application. They get about 300 of these damn things a year, and they only interview about 50 applicants. So you either have to be an outstanding applicant who brings his own prestige in with him, which I don't think you are, or you've got to have an angle. Therefore, I've been thinking about an angle for you, and here's what I've come up with.

"We concentrate on the short essay. You're a pretty colorful, interesting guy. You've been around. You survived a violent upbringing, ran loose and crazy on the streets of San Antonio, stole a couple of cars, won some academic awards in an MBA program, and owned your own successful business. Then you ran off and left your starving family, grew your hair long, sold a little pot here and there, became a tradesman, etc., etc. I think you play up that color. You be original, funny, and maybe even a little weird. You wake the old bastards up. You grab their attention.

"Maybe they'll scratch their old bald heads and throw your application into the trash. If so, you'll be off the hook, and you can thank me profusely and buy me a pitcher of Bud at the In. Or maybe they'll scratch their old bald heads and take notice. Maybe they'll read it and say, 'Hell, I think we ought to meet this guy.' Then you can go into the interview and blow them away with your pretty smile and superior bullshit. Either way, it's interesting. What do you think?"

Steve smiled and shook his head. "I think you're a goddamn nut case is what I think. The problem is that you're so damn strange that I can't even tell if you're kidding or not."

"Kidding? Hell no, I'm not kidding. What do you think? I sat around in my shorts and developed this strategy just to humor you? Listen, man, I've seen some pretty damn impressive sons of bitches get turned away from this stupid program, and I think it's because they didn't do anything to set themselves apart from the crowd. They played it straight and got lost in the shuffle. I bet 275 of those 300 autobiographies are interchangeable except for name, sex, and age. 'I was born on June 25, 1950 at the break of day. My father was a lawyer, and my mother taught school. Through Dad's dedication and hard work, I learned values. Mother taught me to love learning. We lived in a middle class neighborhood, where I developed a burning desire to help people deal with their psychological issues.' Give me a barf bag and send me home, man."

Steve laughed. "Actually, I kind of like your idea, but I think I'd like it better if you were doing it instead of me. Really, though, what do I have to lose? If I do get bumped, it's certainly not going to break my heart. I mean, I want to get into the program, but I'm also pretty excited about The WoodWorks, you know? I haven't had this much fun with work since I was a lifeguard at a country club back in college, and all the little girls wanted a piece of my butt.

"So what the hell? I'll give it a try. Maybe not exactly like you have in mind, but I'll work on the 'offbeat' angle and see what I come up with. I'll buy the book this afternoon and write the paper tonight. I suppose you'll edit it for me, right?"

"Yeah, sure. I'll edit the son of a bitch. Ha! This is gonna be fun. We'll knock their fucking socks off. Come on, butt wipe, I'll run you by the bookstore right now, and then I'll buy you a cold one at the In. Old Dixie ought to be getting there pretty soon. We'll test our plan on her and see how healthy her sense of humor is today."

Steve kept his word to Tommy. At 10:00 PM he rolled a joint, smoked half, opened his spiral notebook, and wrote.

STEVE CAMPBELL'S
A SIMPLE CALL TO ARMS

Steve Campbell is no wimp—never was, never will be. His old man slapped the crap out of him one afternoon because he said "uncle" to end a fistfight with an older, bigger boy. Steve was eleven.

"You don't ever, ever quit, goddamn it," he told Steve. "I'll be damned if I'm going to raise a fucking coward for a son. Now you get your ass back out there and kick that kid's butt, or I swear to God, I'll kick yours."

"But Dad," Steve said, "I can't kick his butt. How am I supposed to kick his butt? He's bigger and stronger than me."

"I don't give a damn how you do it. Use a goddamn board on him if you have to, but find a way to do it, or I swear you'll be one sorry little chicken shit."

Steve looked his dad in the eye and shook his head. "No way, man," he said.

His dad backhanded him across the face so hard that it knocked Steve flat onto the floor. He got back up on his feet and faced his dad squarely.

"I'm not going out there, Dad, and you can't make me," he said matter-of-factly.

Old Dad freaked, of course, and Steve paid dearly for his brashness. Mr. Campbell never appreciated the irony of the way the whole thing played out.

As a teenager, Steve roamed the streets of San Antonio with a group of boys who worked hard to earn bad reputations. They went where they wanted and did what they pleased. Other boys gave them trouble; they gave it back twofold. Steve belonged.

About half of those boys never made it through high school. A few of them are in prison today. Two of them are dead.

Steve earned an MBA at a conservative Christian university and set records for academic achievement in the process. He organized that school's first ever anti-Vietnam War protest despite his disdain for hippies and his conservative political convictions. Today, his hair is long, and he eschews politics altogether.

Following graduation from college, Steve opened and managed a successful retail business. He started a family. He walked away from both when it became the honest thing to do. He grieved his losses and then very thoughtfully considered the future. He landed here.

Steve Campbell's life experience has been rich. He is a fascinating man. He has a good mind and a good heart.

The End

When Steve got into bed at midnight, he smoked the rest of the joint that he had started at 10:00 and read the story one last time. He liked it. It was clean and concise.

He considered its truthfulness. "Rich life experience" seemed to fit. "Fascinating man" might fly, depending on one's interpretation of the word "man." "Good mind" was accurate. "Good heart?" He wasn't certain about that one. He hoped it was true.

It occurred to Steve that he had not been drunk in two weeks, since the night of his divorce celebration. He had gotten high every day with some combination of beer and pot, but he had not lost control. At that moment, he felt good about himself.

The next morning he woke up Tommy at 8:30. "You must have done your homework," Tommy said, yawning and scratching. He sat down on his couch and read Steve's paper. As he read, he smiled and nodded. At one point, he laughed out loud and said, "That's pretty good."

When he finished, he handed it back to Steve. "It's cool, man. I'd send it in exactly like that. Boy, I'll tell you what; I'd like be a fly on the wall when those old wheezers pass that one around. I guess if nothing else, we'll find out if they have any courage. Nice job, Steve-o. Real nice job."

CHAPTER 19

Following the burst of energy that opened The WoodWorks and submitted the graduate school application, Steve settled into a routine. He went to class and studied in the morning, worked in the afternoon, and partied and played after dark. He saw Lynn and Eddie every other Saturday and Sunday without fail.

The routine brought order to his life, and despite his commitment to freedom and non-conformity, he felt relieved to be on a predictable schedule.

The remainder of 1973 passed quietly. Steve spent Thanksgiving with Dixie, Tucker, Tommy, Carla, and Carlos, one of Carla's roommates. The six of them chipped in on a traditional turkey & dressing spread at Carla's. Tommy contributed marijuana tea, marijuana brownies, and marijuana sugar cookies. Tucker added two grams of cocaine. Steve brought two cases of beer and two exquisite marijuana tops, compliments of James, who typically declined social gatherings, especially those involving food.

Carla and Dixie cooked. Carlos entertained the group with stories of growing up gay in Abilene, Texas. By dark, everyone was full, drunk, stoned, and flying high. Dixie, who seldom drank or used enough to change her personality, told Steve that she would kill him if he did not take her to his house and fuck her brains out. Tucker spent the night with Carla. Tommy went home alone. Carlos disappeared into the night.

Steve spent Christmas with Lynn and Eddie at Lois and Chester's. When he took them home, he met Bev's new boyfriend.

"I'm an attorney," he told Steve.

"No shit? For crying out loud, Bev, what the hell are you trying to do?" Steve said. "No offense, buddy, but attorneys kind of give me the creeps. Surely you understand."

The man maintained absolute silence and did not crack a smile, but Steve saw the corners of Bev's mouth turn upward ever so slightly. It gave him hope for their post-divorce relationship.

On his way out of town, Steve stopped and called Rachel. He smiled when he heard her voice. "Hey, old girl," he said. "It's Steve Campbell, your summertime lover and partner in drastic life changes."

"Well, I'll be damned. I thought you'd just forgotten all about me. Where the heck are you?"

"I'm in S.A. I figured I'd call to check in with you and say 'Merry Christmas and Happy New Year' and all that good stuff. I thought you might like to get a bite to eat and visit for a little while."

"Well, I've already eaten, but if you want some company, I'll tag along. Or better yet, come over here, and I'll fix you a sandwich or something."

"Ah, excellent idea. I'll pick up a couple of six-packs and head over your way."

"Okay, Steve. But just bring beer for yourself. I'm not drinking these days."

Steve hesitated. "Hmmm. You'll have to fill me in on the details behind that little piece of news."

As he drove to her apartment, Steve tried to imagine an evening with Rachel without alcohol. And the closer he got, the more apprehensive and disappointed he felt. He wondered about the implications. Does no alcohol also mean no pot? Would they be able to communicate without getting high? Would she be less receptive to sex?

"My, my, my, Rachel," Steve said when she opened the door. "You look more beautiful every time I see you. How can that be?"

Rachel smiled and hugged him tightly. "It's so good to see you, Steve," she said. "I miss you."

"I miss you, too, Rachel," he whispered.

"Come into the kitchen and sit while I finish fixing your dinner. Catch me up on you. The last I heard, your divorce was final, but you got worked over pretty good. What else is going on? Did you get into graduate school?"

"No, not yet. My application is in, though, and I feel pretty good about it. I met a guy in Austin who is in that program, and he helped me get everything organized and submitted. I have to take the GRE sometime within the next couple of months, and I'm studying for that. It will probably be April or May before I know anything for sure.

"In the meantime, though, I got my furniture refinishing shop up and running, and that's going really well. How about you? How's your love life?"

Rachel laughed. "It's about a three and a half or four. I'm kind of dating a guy. It's not serious. He's a very divorced doctor with two kids and a Jaguar. I'm mostly window dressing, but he's nice to me. He takes me places, and he's considerate. He's not really a boyfriend, at least not like you were, but he's sweet."

90

"Not like me, huh? Well, what kind of a boyfriend was I?"

Rachel put Steve's plate down in front of him and sat next to him at the table. "Oh, you were pretty intense, old boy. You swept me off of my feet and held me breathless. You were my red hot lover and my best good buddy."

"So what's been going on lately?" Steve asked. "It sounds like you've made some pretty big changes."

Rachel nodded. "Yeah, I have. I've had lots going on. Too much, really. So don't even ask unless you're really interested and have plenty of time."

Steve smiled. "Interest and time are two things I have plenty of, my friend. I'm yours until you run me off. By the way, where's Sammy?"

"He's at my mom's. He's been staying there off and on for several weeks while I've been working through some things. We spent Christmas over there yesterday. I came home by myself last night. I'll pick him up after work tomorrow and keep him here for the weekend."

"Well," Steve said, "you have my curiosity up. Does his being gone have anything to do with your not drinking?"

"In a way, yes, it's all connected. Are you sure you want me to go into it? I'd be happy just to keep the conversation casual."

"No, I do want you to go into it. Come on; let's go sit in the living room. I'll finish my sandwich in there."

When they were settled on the couch, Rachel started. "Well, let's see. On October 30th, about two weeks after the last time you were here, I was at a party with a date, and I got really drunk. I think I was drunker than I ever got when you and I were together. Anyway, this very cute, very hot young guy—couldn't have been more than twenty—started coming on to me. So I ditched my poor, unsuspecting date and brought the kid back here.

"We drank some more. He laid out some coke. And before long, I was ready and willing for just about anything. Then all of a sudden, without any warning whatsoever, he freaked. I mean, he went ape shit. One minute, I was kissing this guy on the mouth, and the next, he was ripping my clothes off and shoving me around the living room. He was throwing things and breaking things—a lamp, a couple of vases, a mirror, stuff like that.

"Needless to say, I was scared to death. I felt like I was stuck in a nightmare. He kept yelling at me, calling me a fucking bitch and a fucking whore and a goddamn cunt. He slapped me across my face really hard, and like an idiot, I tried to slap him back. He hit me right here on my chest with his fist. It knocked me over the couch and onto the floor and knocked the wind out of me.

"Two different times, he threw me down on the floor—once in here, and once in the bedroom—and told me that if I moved, he'd kill me. I thought he would, too. So I'm lying there, not moving a muscle, and he's going through all my stuff—closet, dresser, everything. I have no idea what he was looking for, but the whole time he was mumbling to himself, and cursing me. This went on for over an hour. Then about 4:00 o'clock or so, he started calming down, and I somehow convinced him that if he would just leave, I'd never tell anyone that he had ever been here.

"Anyway, to make a long story short, he walked out—strolled out, actually. I locked the door and all of the windows and called my mom and dad. Mom had Sammy, so she stayed there with him. Dad came over here with a .38 caliber pistol and a 12-gauge shotgun. By then, it was almost daybreak.

"Dad spent that whole day and night with me. We cleaned up the place and then spent the rest of the day watching football on TV. I never saw the guy or heard from him again."

"Man, Rachel, that's the scariest damn story I've ever heard. God, I'm so glad you're okay. You didn't call the cops or anything, huh?"

"No, I didn't. My dad wanted me to, and I thought about it a lot, but I decided not to. I don't know, I thought it might make things worse in the long run. I did call the rape crisis center, though, and they got me hooked up with a counselor who works with women who have been traumatized—raped or battered or whatever. I've seen her once a week since then, and she has been a lifesaver. She helped me work through that experience, plus she's helping me look at some other issues, too."

"Like drinking and using drugs?" Steve asked.

"Yeah, that's one of them. I was very aware during the attack that it never would have happened in the first place if I had not been so drunk. I mean, a lot of things went through my mind. Some of them were pretty ridiculous, I guess, like how ugly I was going to look when they found me, and how nobody would know that I had clothes ready to be picked up at the cleaners. Others weren't, though. Like, I thought about how incredibly stupid and careless I had been, and what a selfish person I was.

"I thought about Sam losing the only parent who has ever cared about him. I swore to God that I would be a better mother if I got the chance.

"You crossed my mind, too, Steve. I flashed on our trip to Colorado. I pictured that little bar in Ouray, where we sat and drank beer all afternoon and listened to country-western songs on the jukebox. I thought about our ride home and wondered if you had gotten into graduate school. Isn't that weird?

"Anyway, in one of my counseling sessions, I happened to mention my being so drunk when the attack occurred, and we spent some time talking about my 'relationship,' as she calls it, with alcohol and drugs—not just at that time, but over the years, you know? The more we talked, the more I realized how much time and energy I've spent getting high and what kind of price I've paid for that. I mean, the whole time you and I were together, we never went a day without getting drunk or stoned, or both. Remember? And it didn't change after you moved away, either. I still got high every day, or just about, anyway.

"You know, one of the reasons I think I was willing to let you go so easily was that I felt guilty about abandoning Sam. But then it didn't really change after you left. I thought it would, but it didn't. To tell you the truth, I thought I would quit drinking and getting high once you were gone. That was my plan. It wasn't a definite, well-thought-out plan, but it was my plan.

"Anyway, about five weeks ago, I quit everything. I haven't been high since November 20th."

"Wow," Steve said. "So I guess things are really different now. I mean, what's it like to be straight for five weeks?"

"Well, it's good, actually. And, yes, it is different. I mean, I haven't turned into some big deal sober wacko, but I do feel better—physically and mentally both. I feel as though I'm keeping my promise to God to be a better mother to Sammy. I feel like I'm really here for him. I'm eating better, and I got back to running every day, which I had gotten away from. And just this week, I joined a gym.

"It hasn't been all fun and games. Sometimes I miss getting high. I'm not sure I could have gotten this far without my counselor's help. I've also been to a few AA meetings, if you can believe that, and I've started spending a little time with a couple of women who I met there."

"No shit, Rachel? This is really a surprise. I just never pictured you as someone with a problem. I know you and I stayed loaded a lot, but that just felt like blowing off steam to me. You know, we'd both been stuck in bad relationships, and hell, you were stuck in that house with your parents. I just thought we were having fun. I remember you saying once that you had some concerns about your drinking and stuff, but I didn't take you seriously. I'm sorry if I caused you a problem."

Rachel laughed. "Oh, no, Steve. Believe me, it did not have anything to do with you. It was me. I was the problem. And I probably still am. It's not like I'm cured or anything. I mean, one of the first things I thought when you called tonight was, 'I bet he has some pot with him.' So don't think you did anything wrong. You didn't."

"That's pretty funny, Rachel, because one of the first things I thought when you said you weren't drinking was, 'I hope she still smokes pot.' I figured you probably wouldn't invite me to spend the night if we didn't get high."

Rachel laughed again. "That's so funny," she said. She paused and then added, "Actually, I do hope you'll stay."

"Well, okay, if you insist. I don't like to see a girl have to beg to get her needs met," Steve said, smiling.

They spent the rest of the evening talking. Steve never drank a beer or smoked any pot. He told Rachel about Tommy and Dixie and Carla. He gave her the details surrounding his divorce, including his embarrassment during the proceedings and his guilt afterwards. He told her about the divorce party and his blackout. He told her about his promise to himself—successful so far—to control his drinking and drugging.

They went to bed around midnight and reminded each other of how good they were together. They went to sleep in each other's arms and stayed that way until Rachel's alarm went off at 6:00 AM.

Steve reacted first. "Turn that damn thing off, and don't even dare think of getting out of this bed," he said.

"Work," Rachel whispered. "Money. Food. Rent. Independence."

"Forget it, girl. You're going nowhere." He kissed the back of her neck and behind her ear.

"Umm," Rachel sighed, as she relaxed against him. She rolled over in his arms and faced him. She kissed his face and neck until she felt him getting hard. Then she reached down and gently stroked him until he was fully erect.

"Lie still," she said. She worked her way down his body, kissing his chest, his stomach, and then the inside of his thighs. She took him into her mouth and sucked him gently until just before he came. Then she stroked him with her hand until he did.

"Whew, Rachel. What a nice way to start the day. Thank you."

"You're welcome, my friend," she said. "Let that be a reminder not to stay away so long."

Steve smiled. "That's a powerful damn reminder."

"I have to get up now, Steve," she whispered. "Stay as long as you like, but I have to go to work." She slipped out of bed and walked across the room.

Steve watched her. She moved so gracefully. "God, you look good, Rachel," he said as she disappeared into the bathroom.

Just before she left the apartment, Steve said, "Hey, Rachel, I might want to talk to you some more about this no drinking and drugging thing one of these days."

"Sure, Steve. Anytime."

As he drove back to Austin, Steve listened to music that reminded him of his summer with Rachel. He tried to imagine her horrifying experience, and he thought about how she connected that experience to drinking and drugging.

"Rachel Anders, sober and straight. Will miracles never cease?" he asked himself.

When Steve pulled up in front of his house, he felt grateful to have a place of his own and a routine to return to. New Year was in the air. Steve had never felt more confident.

CHAPTER 20

Steve and Dixie spent New Year's Eve together at The Roam In, listening and dancing to the music of Doug Sahm's band. They drank moderately, and they rang in the New Year with clear heads. They fell asleep in each other's arms at forty minutes after midnight.

Steve got up before sunrise on New Year's Day and wrote resolutions for 1974. They reflected his optimism. He had made a good start with The WoodWorks, and he resolved to work diligently to make it a respectable and successful business. Feeling hopeful about his prospects for graduate school admission, he resolved to be painstaking in his academic and intellectual pursuits. Having had no bad episodes with alcohol or drugs since his blackout in mid-November, he vowed to maintain control of his alcohol and drug use.

He decided that 1974 would be the year to get serious about his physical health. He recommitted himself to eat good food and exercise regularly.

Steve served Dixie breakfast in bed. As he watched her eat, he felt affection toward her that went deeper than trust, respect, and friendship. When she finished eating, he pulled her to him, held her tight, and caressed her.

"What's going on with you this morning, lover boy? This is awfully nice," she whispered.

He grinned. "I don't know, Dixie. I just feel good today. I'm glad you're here with me to share the good feelings." He kissed her. They made love tenderly.

The morning of January 1, 1974 was the perfect beginning to a new year. It felt promising and friendly. Steve felt good about himself. His new life was actually working. The high bottom drunk had figured it out. He got high every day without it causing problems.

Alcohol and drugs were simply a part of his culture. It was a culture that he understood, felt a part of, and fit into. If anyone had accused him of being a substance abuser on the first day of 1974, he would have said, "No way, man. That might have been true at one time, but those days are history."

95

CHAPTER 21

The optimism and confidence with which Steve began 1974 extended through winter and into spring.

Steve registered for two more courses. He took the GRE in February and scored 1210. The graduate program invited him to interview in March. During the interview, the Admissions Committee members did not mention his essay.

"I don't know if they're anal or not, Tommy," he said afterwards. "But they sure are doddering old farts. I know they must be brilliant men, but they seem a little beyond their prime. One old bird kept losing his train of thought, so the guy sitting next to him got frustrated and started finishing his sentences for him. Then the first one got pissed and told the second one that he had missed the point entirely. I'm telling you, man, with a little work it could have been a Marx Brothers routine.

"And speaking of the Marx Brothers, what's with the eyebrows on those old guys? How do human beings make eyebrows like that? They were like forests."

UT offered Steve enrollment into the graduate program the following month. He accepted despite reservations about the sincerity of his commitment.

The WoodWorks became a gathering spot for high bottom drunks. Tommy loved the place. He showed up most afternoons with a six-pack of off-brand beer in hand. He pitched in and helped whenever the need arose. He worked on personal projects most weekends.

James dropped by a couple of times a week. He never failed to bring good pot and never rested until everyone on site was stoned. Those afternoons often turned into elaborate intellectual bullshit sessions, with Steve working halfheartedly or not at all, and James and Tommy delighting in each other's genius. Steve usually just listened, in awe of and somewhat intimidated by the fascinating interchanges between Tommy the intellectual atheist and James the spiritual wizard.

James arrived one afternoon with a honey-colored chow mix pup. "She needs a home, man, and you need a reliable female presence around here. She's as smart as a whip. She's got a damn sweet disposition, too. And she rides in the back of a pickup like a veteran. It never occurred to me that you wouldn't want her. She belongs here." Steve named her Ginger. She quickly became his friend and companion.

Tucker continued to renounce The WoodWorks as a business endeavor unworthy of Steve's talents. He stopped by occasionally, though, sometimes to visit, sometimes looking for drugs. Usually both. As a favor, Steve became Tucker's middleman for pot, coke, and speed. James supplied the weed; Mario, the convenience store manager, supplied the rest.

Tucker expressed his gratitude by paying Steve top dollar for everything. He started referring to Steve as his "damn fine honest drug dealer." Steve liked the moniker. He also liked the role, which made him feel powerful and important. He quickly added it to his persona and offered his services to a select group of Roam In regulars, who jumped at the chance to buy drugs from someone they trusted. In no time at all, Steve was pocketing about $125 a week cash profit.

The extra money came in handy. It took on greater importance in February, when John informed Steve that he could no longer swing the $300.00 per month under-the-table cash payments and that he would not be able to resume them anytime in the foreseeable future. Steve let the matter drop out of respect for his sister, the only other person who knew anything about the original agreement.

To compensate for the lost income, Steve opened the door to a few more customers. His profits doubled.

"Damn, man," he told Tucker, "this drug business is too easy. I think I could make as much as I wanted doing this."

"Don't get too cocky, Steve," Tucker warned. "It may be easy money, but it sure could turn nasty on you. To be honest, I kind of wish you would let it go. It worries me."

Steve laughed. "That's rich, Tucker. You're the one who got me started in this little business enterprise. What's the matter? You're not jealous, are you?"

"Don't be an idiot. What I am is your friend. Believe me, I love having a good, reliable source. But when I asked you to pick up stuff for me, I didn't intend for you to turn into a mobster. I just don't want to see you get your ass in a crack."

Not long after that conversation, Steve's new life took a downward turn that eventually spiraled out of control.

CHAPTER 22

The more drugs Steve sold, the more he stocked. The more he stocked, the more he handled. The more he handled, the more he used. And the more he used, the more he liked using. He took a particular liking to speed, especially methamphetamine.

"Hey, you better watch that shit, Steve," James told him. "Speed is a bad, bad drug. I've seen guys strung out on that drug, and believe me, it's not a pretty sight. It fucks with your whole being, man. It eats away at your core, and it does it fast, before you even know it's happening. I know this isn't my business, but I gotta tell you, man, you're playing with a damn hot fire."

"Yeah, yeah, I hear you, James. I'll keep an eye on it. But there's really nothing to be concerned about. I'm only using a little, and only every once in a while. It's cool."

"Well, it may be cool right now, but it sure can heat up fast. Speed is a punk drug, man. It's dishonest. Actually, it's more than dishonest; it's a goddamn pathological liar.

"Listen, if you want to experiment with alternative drug experiences, let me take you in a different direction. Let me introduce you to LSD. It's a truly serious drug, but unlike speed and cocaine and most of the other pharmaceuticals, it's an honest drug. It's had some bad press over the years, but that's because most people don't understand it.

"See, man, most people use acid just to get high. They do a hit and then they contaminate it by putting alcohol and other drugs, like speed and coke, on top of it. Then they go out and party. It's a serious waste, man. I mean, they get off and everything, but the true purpose of the drug gets totally lost.

"Acid affects different people in different ways, but its proper use is always as a spiritual catalyst. It's not supposed to be a party drug. Some people will tell you different, but don't believe them. They don't know what they're talking about.

"You gotta respect LSD, man, or it can fuck you up big time. It can take your brain away from you. I've seen that happen to a few people. If you respect it and trust it, though, acid can take you places and show you things that few humans ever experience.

"I'll turn you on to some, man. I'll even hang around and guide you through the trip so you'll understand what it's really all about. Then you'll see for yourself what a bad waste of time and energy speed is. In the meantime, lay off that shit. If we're gonna do this, let's do it right." Steve agreed.

True to his word, James patiently taught Steve how to use and appreciate LSD. He stayed with him for the duration of his first two trips and then discussed subsequent ones with him in detail.

"James, when I was tripping yesterday afternoon, I felt as though all the barriers came down. It was like I had total and absolute freedom. I was at that little park over by my house. I was walking in the grass, and I closed my eyes for a minute, and man, I walked right up into the sky.

"It felt like my physical reality changed. It wasn't like a hallucination, either, because I didn't think my body went anywhere. It was just my mind. And listen, here's the good part. I knew that that was me. I knew that my mind was me, that my mind was my essence.

"It's not that my body was irrelevant. It's just that I wasn't my body, and I wasn't limited by anything physical. I was restricted a little bit by my ego, I think, because every once in a while, I had a thought like, 'Oh, shit, I wonder if anyone's watching,' and that thought would take me out of the trip. I could go right back into it, though, as soon as I relaxed and gave myself that freedom."

"Yeah, that's far out, man," James said. "That was a good experience. It's interesting that you mention ego, because when you use acid to reduce the size and power of your ego, you gain more and more freedom from your constraints—physical as well as mental. LSD teaches you that connection. Smaller ego equals fewer barriers. Fewer barriers equal greater spiritual freedom. Spiritual freedom equals stronger ego. Do you get that? It means small ego equals strong ego. Big ego equals weak ego.

"It's an important spiritual awareness, man. And it only really makes sense when you experience it. Once you've had the experience, you know where you want to go, and you can move in that direction even without the drug.

"The consummate spiritual existence is one in which we live free of our constraints, that is, without our protective barriers— our egos. Then we experience the oneness of all. There is no duality whatsoever—no good and bad, no right and wrong, no you and me. There is no separateness, even from God.

"It's tricky, though, man. See, the drug has the power to rip your defenses away from you without your consent. That's why some people have bad trips. Their walls get knocked down before they're ready. I think maybe their souls have been wounded, and their egos are fiercely protecting the wounded souls. When the wounded soul is exposed, it collapses—sometimes into fear or terror, sometimes into anger or rage, sometimes into sadness and grief.

"I don't know, man, I'm still thinking about this part of the whole thing. I haven't completely figured it out yet. That's one reason I wanted to bring you into this experience carefully. I know you had some pretty rough times when we were kids. I was concerned about your ego strength."

Under James' tutelage, Steve had other stunning LSD experiences and no bad trips. He traveled, unrestrained, into the darkness of the universe. While there he saw a very tiny but extremely intense flame. It burned for an instant and then extinguished. He asked the universe what it meant. The universe answered that it represented his life as a human being within the context of his infinite Self.

On another occasion, while camping at the lake, he saw the moon and stars of the night sky in three dimensions. On another, he and Carla dropped acid together, and while making love, their spirits merged into one.

Steve offered LSD to Tommy and Dixie, but both declined.
Tommy said, "No thanks, Buddy. That shit's too mysterious
for me. I'll just stick to beer and weed."

Dixie said, "I don't think so, Steve. I did it a few times back
when, and I liked it for the most part, but I think I'll pass. You
know, you might be careful, yourself. I think there may be more
to it than James is telling you."

Using LSD changed Steve. In the beginning it extended him.
It opened and expanded his mind. He saw that his finite
understanding of the infinite world was vastly limited. It
encouraged him to experience life instead of judge it. It softened
his critical voice. It deepened his awareness of the limiting self
and gave him a glimpse of the spiritual Self. But that was in the
beginning.

James left Austin for two months at the end of April. As
soon as he left town, Steve hedged on his agreement to lay off
speed and began experimenting with LSD in ways that James
had warned him against. He discovered that he could modify and
intensify his experience through various combinations of LSD,
alcohol, pot, and speed. When that happened, he abandoned the
pure experience in favor of the diluted one. He deserted the
spiritual catalyst and partied on top of acid.

CHAPTER 23

As spring turned to summer, drugs stole more and more of
Steve's time and energy. His escalating commitment to using and
selling drugs dramatically altered the lifestyle that he had
embraced that winter. The comfortable predictability
disappeared.

When the academic semester ended in May, Steve filled his
mornings with sleeping late, drinking coffee, getting high,
listening to music, and working to improve his drug business.

He expanded the product line by buying from different
dealers. He expanded the business by selling to more users. He
took great pains to make his products attractive. He
meticulously cleaned and packaged marijuana tops in one-ounce
and quarter-pound bags. He carefully cut coke and speed just
enough to preserve his profits without seriously compromising
the quality of the drug. When his increasing personal
consumption of speed and coke began reducing profits, he
compensated by cutting them to a lower quality and raising their
prices. To his relief, no one seemed to notice the difference in
quality, and no one complained about the prices.

By June 30th, Steve's New Year's resolutions lay in shreds.
He gave little attention and minimal effort to The WoodWorks. He

lied to his customers to cover missed deadlines. He ignored intellectual pursuits. He neglected his health, especially his diet. Speed destroyed his appetite. When he ate at all, he ate fast foods, fried foods, and red meat. His exercise consisted of occasional trips to the lake, where he lay on the rocks and watched women sunbathe and swim.

Also by June 30th, Steve's alcohol and drug use had hit an all-time high. He snorted speed every day. He went through a gram a week and sometimes more. He used LSD as a party drug once a week and sometimes more. He drank enough beer every night to feel hung over and sluggish every morning. He smoked pot off and on all day, every day.

As Steve's bottom dropped lower, his denial shot through the roof.

"For Christ's sake, Mother," he told Lois. "How can you possibly question how well I'm doing? I own my own business, and I'm making good money. I pay all my bills on time. I'm in perfect compliance with every facet of the divorce settlement. I haven't missed a single child support payment or visitation with the kids. I've built a strong, reliable support system of friends almost from the ground up. I have a dog, and I take good care of her. And on top of everything else, in just two months I'll be a doctoral student in counseling psychology. I mean, what do I have to do to look good to you?"

CHAPTER 24

Symptoms, particularly behavioral symptoms, define addiction. The most reliable symptom of addiction is *loss of control*. The alcoholic/addict intends to use according to a plan, and he fails to follow the plan. Closely related to loss of control is *unpredictability*. Once he starts using, the addict cannot predict with absolute certainty what will happen next.

Another reliable characteristic of addiction is *progressivity*. Over time, the addict experiences progressively more frequent and/or progressively more severe problems associated with his or her use of alcohol and drugs.

Progressivity does not mean that everything goes to hell in a hand basket. It just means that over time, things get worse. This is true despite short-term fluctuations in which things get worse and then better, then worse, then better.

As addicts' bottoms sink, they hide behind walls of denial and other defenses. Those defenses protect the addict's right to continue using. Without them, the alcoholic whose bottom is dropping would have to see and admit the truth—that he or she is heading toward trouble.

Alcoholic denial is similar to aging denial. A man looks at himself in the mirror several times a day every day. He cannot see himself aging because it happens so gradually.

On a lark, Steve and Tucker attended their eight-year high school reunion. About two hours into the first big party, Tucker sidled up to Steve and said, "Damn, Steve, why is it that everyone here looks so much older than you and me?"

"I don't know, man," Steve replied. "I've been wondering the same thing."

They looked at each other, smiled, and shrugged their shoulders. Both were privately thinking "...and I'm just being kind to include you in with me."

Alcoholics' and addicts' bottoms move in only one direction—from higher to lower. Imagine a vertical scale, like a ruler standing on end, marked "10" at the top and "0" at the bottom. The numbers signify the level of the alcoholic's bottom. All alcoholics start at the top—at 10. They stay at 10 as long as they experience no problems of any kind connected to their drinking and using. As problems crop up, their scale numbers go down. As bigger problems emerge, their scale numbers go down further. The question becomes, "On a scale of 10 to 0, how low does your bottom go?"

About one or two percent of all alcoholics hit the bottom of the scale. They reach 0. They lose everything and live under the bridge with cirrhosis of the liver and brain damage and then they die. Ninety-eight or so percent roam around between 9 and 1, and their scale numbers fluctuate up and down depending on the temporary circumstances of their lives. Over the long run, however, the overall trend is in the direction of lower bottoms.

Steve started out at the top of the scale just like every other alcoholic. He started drinking alcohol at age seven, when Lois and Henry gave him a small glass of beer every afternoon at 6:00 o'clock to encourage his appetite for dinner. The plan did not work so they discontinued the practice and forgot about it. Steve remembered, though, because drinking the beer changed the way he felt. It made him feel "bigger."

He started drinking on his own at eleven. He sneaked beers out of the refrigerator when Lois and Henry were not home and finished off mixed drinks left on tables and counter tops after they went to bed.

Steve first bought beer at thirteen. He paid a neighborhood friend 50 cents for a quart of Lone Star. Then he arranged for a regular supply by paying the janitor at the neighborhood elementary school a quart of beer to buy him a quart of his own. At thirteen, Steve got tipsy or drunk about twice a month during the school year and twice a week during summer vacation. He threw up in his bed a couple of times, but nothing really bad happened. At thirteen, then, he measured 9.5 on the scale.

In high school, Steve's drinking increased. During his sophomore year, which was his last year at home and in public school, he drank just about every weekend. During summer vacations following tenth, eleventh, and twelfth grades, he partied and got drunk nearly every night.

Heavier drinking precipitated more problems. His smart mouth got him into some fights. He said and did things that he later regretted and for which he felt compelled to apologize. He drove his car while intoxicated, and one night he ran off the road and put a dent in Roxy's fender. Another night, he "borrowed" a stranger's car when he mistakenly thought his friends had left him at a party; the car's owner caught him and beat him up pretty good. He picked up a venereal disease at a whorehouse in Mexico. He cussed out his mom big time when she accused him of being a drunk like his father.

Steve had good reasons to abuse alcohol during his high school years. Most of his peer group partied the same way that he did. And his home life was a chaotic mess. He lived without parental support or supervision. His place on the scale shifted downward to about an 8.

As a college freshman, Steve settled down and applied himself. He and James got drunk once a week or so, which caused a few minor problems, but for the most part, Steve maintained a scale ranking of about 9 for almost a year.

As a sophomore, though, he pledged a notoriously wild fraternity, and his drinking escalated dramatically. His grades slipped; A's and B's turned into B's, C's, and D's. He struggled financially. He wrote hot checks. He lost two part-time jobs. He dented up his car twice. His reputation with women suffered when two different girlfriends broke up with him because of his behavior when he drank. He described himself as "just a young man sowing my wild oats." Nevertheless, he dropped to about a 7.5 on the scale.

As a junior, Steve restricted himself to weekend binge drinking in an effort to bring up his grades. On one of those weekends, he refused to take "No" for an answer, and pushed Bev into unprotected sex. She became pregnant and insisted on getting married and having the child.

Steve acted out his resentment toward Bev by hanging out and drinking with buddies and frequenting topless bars and massage parlors. Bev complained; Steve ignored her. He ridiculed her pleas for him to settle down.

He had his first major blackout during his senior year. He also had his first affair, about which he bragged to some of their friends. When Bev threatened to leave him, he pushed her up against the wall and told her to start packing. He felt profoundly guilty about that incident the next day, but he failed to change his behavior.

103

When he graduated from college, Steve weighed in at about 7 on the scale of 10 to 0.

In graduate school, Steve forced himself to buckle down. He worked very hard, and as a result, sat at the top of his class. He limited his drinking strictly to weekends. Some of those got pretty wild, especially when Lenny or Tucker came to visit, but as often as not, he refrained from getting too drunk to study.

Alcohol-related problems diminished but did not disappear. He had another blackout and woke up in bed with a sixteen-year-old high school girl. Bev caught him half-naked in a closet with a friend of hers during a party at their house. He laughed that one off because nothing had "happened."

Over the course of two years of graduate school, Steve averaged about 8.5 on the scale.

Armed with an MBA, a near-perfect graduate school record, and a silver tongue, Steve landed a position with a major brokerage firm in San Antonio. He immediately impressed management with his intelligence and enthusiasm. Within three months, co-workers called him the company's fair-haired boy.

Steve's head swelled, his ego exploded, and his drinking increased. He started showing up late for work every Monday and leaving the office early every Friday afternoon. He drank beer with lunch. He had a visible affair with an office secretary. People talked. His local manager confronted him about the affair but took no action because of his status with company higher-ups.

Then Steve angered his regional manager with an ill-timed display of drunken arrogance at an office party. When called onto the carpet the following Monday, he reacted defensively and threatened to quit and go to work for the company's main competitor.

Following that episode, Steve's attitude worsened. His drinking increased further. He heard through the office grapevine that he was on loose footing with the company and that his behavior was being "watched" by management. He reacted by packing his personal belongings and walking out. He had been with the firm for exactly nine months.

When Steve told Bev what had happened, she blew up. She refused to listen to his excuses. She confronted his drinking directly, stating flatly that she would divorce him if he did not change. He agreed to manage his drinking more closely. At that moment, his scale ranking sat at 6.5.

Convinced that working for someone else was a waste of time in the long run, Steve drafted John to partner with him in a small business. Together, they borrowed money, bought the clothing store, and worked tirelessly to build it into a successful, profitable business.

Steve reached out for respectability. He and Bev joined a church. He joined the Jaycee's. In public, he drank socially. In private, he got drunk. Bev did not complain. Steve upped his place on the scale to 8.5.

Business profits ushered in change. Steve and John hired one salesman, then another, and another, and then an office manager. Gradually, they spent less time at work and more at play. They lengthened their lunch hour to two and then three. They added beer and scotch whiskey to their daily routine. Steve edged back into hanging out at bars and strip joints and staying out late.

Lenny showed up one night with an ounce of pot. "You want to try this stuff, man?" he asked Steve.

"Hell yeah, I want to try it," Steve answered. "I've been waiting a long time for the right opportunity to try it. Just show me what to do, and I'm there."

Lenny rolled some joints, and he and Steve smoked one after another until daybreak unexpectedly hit them in the face. Steve bought the remainder of the lid from Lenny and started smoking every day.

Bev hit the roof and threw out another ultimatum. "You have to choose, Steve," she shouted. "It's me and the kids or marijuana." Steve agreed to quit smoking. Instead of quitting, though, he smoked on the sly and lied about it.

Steve's old arrogance and unpredictability returned. He had two costly affairs. He disappeared from home for days at a time. He dropped the ball repeatedly at work. John and Sheri complained.

By the time Steve and Bev separated, Steve's behavior, including his drinking, had spun out of control. For all intents and purposes, he was a bachelor on the party circuit. His alcoholic bottom had shifted downward, back to 6.5.

During the six months between his separation from Bev and his move to Austin, Steve got drunk and stoned every day. His moods fluctuated crazily. Bartenders and barmaids knew him by name. He slept with every woman he could get his hands on and never used a condom. He alienated family members. He somehow talked his way out of a certain DWI. He drank and smoked pot when he was alone.

On several occasions, he promised himself that he would monitor his drinking more effectively, but he did not. His symptoms of alcoholism were undeniable, and his denial unshakable. He reached 6, and then 5.5 on the scale, numbers that questioned his appropriateness for membership in the high bottom drunk club.

Steve's relationship with Rachel, his geographical cure, and his first six months in Austin raised the level of his bottom again. He moved back up the scale to around an 8. He still got high every day. He made judgment errors. He had his worst

105

blackout ever. Nevertheless, on New Year's Day 1974, his life had structure and meaning. He had hope. He cared.

The tide turned during the first quarter of the year. He added more dangerous drugs to his diet. He became a small-time dealer. He worked less and drank more.

It turned again during the second quarter. He combined drugs thoughtlessly and dangerously. His personality changed. He lost sight of his goals and sat blind to the fact that he was in trouble.

By mid-summer 1974, Steve's bottom hovered around 6 on the scale and appeared ready to break through previous lows and set new records.

CHAPTER 25

Dixie loved Steve. Had she been younger, she would have expressed her love in ways that Steve could understand. Instead, she expressed concern about his wellbeing.

Dixie saw what was happening to Steve as early as April and May. She watched his drinking increase from her vantagepoint as his weekday bartender and his weekend drinking partner. She accepted that part of him. She observed his experimentation with LSD through the details that he shared with her. She accepted that part of him, too, though she chose not to accompany him on his acid trips.

She worried about his growing dependence on speed. He did not talk much about the speed, and he seldom used it in front of her. Nevertheless, she could spot it on him a mile away.

Speed altered his personality in ways that Dixie found offensive. He acted arrogant and detached. He made flippant remarks that he thought were witty and funny but came across to others as abrasive, mean, and sometimes hurtful. Instead of smiling, he smirked.

One night when Dixie stayed over with him, he slipped out of bed after they made love and never returned. She heard him roaming the house and playing the stereo during the night. The next morning, he nibbled at his breakfast with little interest and seemed not to care when she left earlier than usual.

Throughout late spring and early summer, Steve's moods fluctuated a lot. Dixie fell into the habit of monitoring his moods, and she caught herself modifying her behavior to accommodate his feelings. By mid-June, she felt herself becoming decidedly more guarded. The change was subtle, but it was definitely there. Steve did not see it, but Tommy did.

"What's the matter, Dixie?" he asked her one evening before Steve came into the bar. "You don't seem to be yourself lately. You pissed off at us guys about something?"

"No, I'm not pissed off at anyone, Tommy. Why do you ask? How have I been acting?"

"Oh, I don't know. You don't stand around and bullshit with us the way you used to, and you hardly ever come over and sit with us when we're hunkered down at a table, even when business is slow. I thought maybe one of us had said something to offend you."

"No, it's nothing like that. I've just been in one of my moods, I guess. Don't worry about it, Tommy; it doesn't have anything to do with you."

"Hmmm. I guess it has to do with Steve, then. I've noticed that you're keeping some distance between the two of you. He hasn't said anything about it, but I've noticed."

Dixie grinned and nodded. "You're very observant," she said.

"Well, it's pretty obvious to an old people watcher like me. Anything I can do to help?"

Dixie considered the question. "I don't know, Tommy. Maybe. Just between you and me, I think Steve's drinking and drug use is becoming a real problem. He feels different to me, and not in a good way, either.

"I probably should say something to him about it, but I've tried that before. I don't think he can hear me. I probably shouldn't even be talking about it with you, but you asked. So you tell *me*. Is there anything you can do?"

Tommy thought for a moment and then said, "To tell you the truth, Dixie, I don't know. I really don't. I'll think about it, though. I'll give it some serious thought. I really will."

James returned to Austin in mid-July. One of his first stops was Steve's house, where he reacted strongly to what he saw. After a very cursory "Hello," he walked into the living room, looked Steve in the face, and said, "Man, you're sick. You have drug abuse written all over you. Your eyes aren't right, man, and your karma is all fucked up. You've lost too much weight. What the hell has been going on here?"

Steve laughed and tried to brush it off, but James held his ground. "Listen, man," he said, "you've got to put down the speed or the coke or whatever it is you're strung out on. I've told you about that shit, man. Where the hell is everybody, anyway? Where's Tommy? Why hasn't anyone ripped you up about this? Are they fucking blind?"

Steve tried again to brush it off and change the subject. "Lighten up, James. I haven't seen you in over two months, and you walk in my house and jump all over my ass. Why don't you relax? Tell me about your mysterious trip."

James held his hands up for Steve to stop talking. "Steve, I've been around drugs and drug addicts since I was sixteen. I've seen good guys go down around it. I won't stand by and watch you fuck up that way. What the hell are you thinking, man—that it doesn't show?"

Steve tried another angle. "It's ironic that you, of all people, would jump my shit about using drugs. It's hard to take you seriously when you stay stoned all day every day. Give me a fucking break, man. I'm just blowing off a little steam before I have to settle down and get serious in September. Okay?"

James sat down on the sofa and motioned for Steve to do the same. He waited for Steve's attention and then he said, "Steve, there are all kinds of ways for you to refuse to hear me. You can change the subject, you can switch the focus over onto me, and you can talk about how it's going to change naturally in the future. You could even get pissed off and tell me to get out of your house.

"But none of those distractions will change what I see. They won't change what I'm telling you right now. You need to quit doing amphetamines, man. Pot, and even alcohol, is one thing, but speed is something else. I bet you're using it every day, and I bet you're mixing it with other drugs, including acid. Tell me the truth, man; am I wrong?"

Steve looked away and then he shook his head. "No, you're not wrong, but it's not nearly as big a deal as you're making it out to be."

James nodded and said, more gently now, "That's the way it works, man. It needles its way into your life and gradually takes over. You'll start graduate school in September. School will be really challenging. You'll decide to use just a little bit to stay up and study. Then you'll start using a little more to give yourself an edge in class. Then you'll find some other reason to use a little more. And before you know it you're using it all day long. You'll do a little bump here, and a little bump there. Then you'll feel wired, and you'll need a little smoke or a little alcohol to take the edge off. Then you'll want the edge back. I'm telling you, man, it's a goddamn insidious thing.

"Listen to me, Steve. I'm asking you as a good old buddy. Put it down right now. I'm asking you, man."

Steve nodded. He felt exposed. He felt embarrassed. "Alright, James," he said. "Don't bust a gut. I hear you. I know you mean well. I'll take care of it."

"You'll take care of it?" James repeated.

"Yes, I'll take care of it. I promise."

"Okay, man. I've got your word on this. I'll drop it now. Jesus, a guy can't even take a little vacation without his friends trying to fucking *off* themselves with stupidity."

Steve smiled. "I can still drink beer, can't I, Master?" he said.

James laughed. "Yeah, man, you can do whatever the hell you want as long as you quit using that poison. Come on; let's go across the street. I'll buy you one, and you can tell me what I've been missing out on the last couple of months. Later on, if you want me to, I'll turn you on to some smoke that I brought back with me that will knock you off your goddamn feet."

Steve and James ordered a pitcher. Tommy walked in just as Dixie set it down on their table. The three of them talked until James excused himself, promising Steve that he would see him the next day.

When they were alone, Steve said, "Tommy, James just got all over my ass about my drug use. He asked me why no one around here had said anything to me about it, especially you. What do you think about that?"

Tommy nodded his head and stared into his beer. "Well, Steve-o, since you asked, here's what I think. I think James is an odd one to bring up anything about anyone else's drug use. I would be, too. To be perfectly honest with you, though, I've been thinking about saying something to you for a little while now. Not that I think it's a great big, huge deal, but you do seem to be investing a lot of energy around it lately. And I believe that I see your shadow side more these days. Maybe those two things have something to do with each other.

"I've always been impressed with how well you handle your buzz. You know that. You've certainly never said or done anything to offend me. But I do know this; you're getting kind of skinny behind that speed, and it does seem to affect your disposition. And, too, you turn up kind of strange, like I don't know you very well, for a day or two after those acid trips of yours."

Tommy looked at Steve and shrugged his shoulders. "That's what I think, my friend. Take it for what it's worth. I ain't your keeper. What you do is pretty much your business. But like I said, you did ask."

Steve leaned back in his chair and took a swig of beer. He swirled the beer around in his cup and took another swig. "You know, Tommy, the weird thing is I don't always like the speed. I mean, sometimes I love it; sometimes it's the greatest thing in the world. Other times, though, it's nasty. I feel wired and strung out. Lately, there have been days when I don't really want to do it, but I go ahead and do it anyway. And, too, the acid trips haven't been the same ever since I started mixing the acid with other stuff. I don't know, I guess it really is time to back up a little bit."

They were quiet for a few moments, and Tommy topped off their cups. "You know, Steve, I've probably been more concerned about your retail business activities than I have been with your using. I'm pretty familiar with the ins and outs of the drug trade, you know, and my experience has been that it's assholes like you that get busted.

"It happens like this: Your little one-ounce and one-gram customers get popped accidentally, and to save their own butts, they rat you out in the blink of an eye. You, on the other hand, won't rat on your source, for whatever reason—loyalty or fear or whatever. So you take the goddamn fall. They don't really give a shit about you because you're so small-time, but when you don't cooperate, they go ahead and punish you to avoid coming up empty. And you're probably not making jack shit anyway because you're selling just enough to pay for your own personal stash. Am I ringing any bells here?"

Steve laughed. "Tell me something, Tommy. Will I get to be as smart as you when I'm a big time graduate student?"

"Yeah, sure you will, Steve. I wouldn't have let you get into it if it weren't so."

Tommy smiled at Steve. "You're a good guy, man. You're cool. Take it easy, why don't you? You've got a lot coming up on you pretty quick. The graduate program takes a lot of effort, at least in the beginning, and I'd like to see you enjoy it.

"And one other thing before I shut my trap. Talk to Dixie. I get the feeling she might need a little reassurance from you. That's all I have to say, if you can believe that. Now, my friend, I'm going to leave you with the last cup of beer in the bottom of the pitcher, and I'm gonna go set my old butt down in front of an Adlerian psychology book. I'm gonna deepen my understanding of how to help wild men like you and James get your shit together and lead respectable, productive lives."

After Tommy left the bar, Steve felt uncomfortably alone. He felt humbled—not humiliated, but definitely humbled. He thought about Dixie. He wondered what she had said to Tommy. He felt his shame rise, and then his ire, as he pictured them talking about him behind his back. He felt butterflies in his stomach as he pictured himself talking to her about it.

He finished off the pitcher and walked back to his house. He sat on the porch with Ginger for a few minutes and then the two of them went into The WoodWorks. There were tools and supplies scattered around on benches. Debris covered the floor. Two chairs sat in glue clamps from when Steve repaired them several days before. A table sat stripped and ready to sand.

He put the tools away, swept the floor, emptied the trashcans, and straightened up his supplies. He removed the clamps from the chairs and touched up the glue lines and other scratches.

While he worked, the conversations with James and Tommy ran over and over through his head. The graduate school/speed

110

use scenario outlined by James described his current use patterns. He was not using that much over the course of a week—only a gram and a half or so, but he snorted a little every morning and bumped it every so often during the day. He moderated the intensity of his buzz with bong hits, joints, and beer.

He spent at least part of every day anxious and vaguely irritated. He slept erratically. He worked in the shop just enough to keep his customers at bay. He spent little quality time with Dixie, and when they were together, he secretly judged her.

He had to force himself to eat. His jeans sagged around his waist and butt. When he looked closely in the mirror, he saw gray circles under lifeless eyes.

Steve sat down and pulled Ginger onto his lap. "Well, old girl," he said, "what are your complaints? Better give them to me now while I'm still flattened out."

Ginger licked his face. He scratched her head and neck. "I better listen to these guys," he said softly. "They're right, you know? I felt a lot better, and happier, when you and I first adopted each other than I do today. What was that, five months ago? That was just before I started doing speed. I hate to say it, old girl, but I'm going to have to do it. I'm going to have to put it down. I don't want to, but I'm going to have to.

"And you know what else? That's not all. The rest of the problem is there's no way in hell I'll ever quit using anything I'm keeping around the house for sale. That means shutting down business. Not that it will matter much money-wise. I'm not really making all that much anymore."

He sat quietly for a moment and then stood up and said, "Come on, Ginger, let's get busy."

Steve walked into the house and pulled his dope box out of the closet. He inventoried. Sale items included ten bags of pot, six grams of coke, three grams of speed, and ten hits of acid. Personal stash included two and a half bags of pot, one and three-quarters grams of speed, and four hits of acid.

After handling everything and considering the different possibilities, he transferred one gram of speed from personal stash over to sales in exchange for one bag of pot. Then he called Tucker.

"Hey, man," he said. "I've got a hell of a deal for you. I'll give you my last six cans of that juice that you like for five bills. You gotta do it now, though, because this is a going out of business sale." Tucker grabbed the deal.

Steve walked next door to the convenience store and asked Mario to take back the four grams of speed at a discount from the original price. He agreed.

By 6:30 that evening, Steve convinced himself that he had done everything necessary to address "the problem." He now owned no cocaine and less than one gram of speed, which he designated "for very special occasions only." He promised himself that his speed and coke buying days were over. Furthermore, he promised himself that he would never again mix other drugs with acid.

From where Steve stood, the problem was handled. His promise to James was kept. He was back to basics—beer and pot, plus the spiritual catalyst—LSD.

Now he needed to smooth things over with Dixie.

CHAPTER 26

That night, Steve slept well. The next morning, he got up early, ate breakfast, took two bong hits of pot, and took Ginger to the park, where they played together for the first time in weeks. Steve ate a good lunch, took a bong hit, napped for an hour, and then called Dixie. She agreed to meet him at his house before going in to work.

When she arrived, Steve was in his shop working on a display case that was ten days late. He dusted himself off and gave her a hug. "Sorry about the mess," he said.

"No problem, Steve. Actually, I'm glad to see you out here working. I missed you at the bar last night. Are you okay?"

Steve laughed. "Yeah, I'm pretty good. It's funny, though, that you thought something might be wrong just because I missed one night at the bar. I guess that should tell me something about my habits, right?"

"I didn't mean it like that. It's not like you've never missed a night at the bar. I guess I was just thinking about you last night, and I kept looking for you to walk in. I'm sorry; I didn't mean to imply anything."

"Hey, forget it. Anyway, that's not what I wanted to talk to you about." Steve looked down at the floor for a moment and then said, "Listen, do you want to go in the house? It's awfully hot out here."

"No. This is fine. Actually, I kind of like it."

"How about something to drink then? You want me to get you a Coke or something?"

"No, I'm okay. Really."

"Well, here, let me get you a chair. Or listen, are you sure you don't want to go inside?"

"Yes, I'm sure, Steve. What's the matter? This is starting to feel kind of awkward."

"I'm sorry," he said. "I'm a little nervous, I guess." He pulled up two chairs and placed them facing each other. "Here, let's sit down. I'm not as good at being straightforward as you are. So anyway, here it is. James and Tommy both said something to me yesterday about how much speed I've been using. James jumped all over me. Tommy was more tactful, but he said that he had been thinking about it for a while.

"He also said that I should to talk to you, so I figured that you must have said something to him about me. So, I don't know, I guess I thought I should at least bring it up. Anyway, that's what I wanted to talk to you about."

"Okay, Steve. I don't mind talking about it. Is there anything in particular that you want to say to me or ask me?"

"Well, yeah, I suppose so. I mean, well, I felt a little weird about a couple of things. One is the obvious. I feel embarrassed that anyone would think they needed to confront me about something like that in the first place. To tell you the truth, I didn't have any idea that anyone had even noticed anything.

"I mean, I knew that I was using quite a bit. I wasn't really trying to hide it, but I didn't know it showed, either. You know what I mean? But the other thing was the thought of the two of you—you and Tommy—talking about me behind my back. I don't know, Dixie, I guess I felt really weird about that. Actually, I felt kind of angry." Steve paused. "There's a question in there somewhere, but I'm not sure what it is."

Dixie nodded. "Do you want to know what I said to Tommy?"

"Yeah, I guess so. You don't have to tell me, but I am curious."

Dixie took a deep breath. She spoke slowly and clearly. "Steve, I told Tommy that I think you're drinking and using too much. I told him that I think it's affecting your behavior and your personality in negative ways. I also told him that I should be talking to you about it instead of to him. I think I was right about that. I'm not sure, though, because the truth is, I probably shouldn't be talking to anyone about it. It's really none of my business. I have no right to judge you or criticize you or try to change you in any way. Besides, you and I have talked about this twice before. I'm sorry that it came up again."

Steve hesitated for a moment and then said, "So, then, as far as you're concerned, it's not just the speed."

"I really don't know, Steve."

"Well, what do you think, Dixie? I mean, I'm asking you. I'd like to know what you think."

Dixie contemplated the risk, and then she answered Steve's question. "Alright. For what it's worth, here's what I think. A year ago, you were sweet and shy. We spent some great afternoons together. We played, and we talked. It was fun. It was easy. You seemed to like my company, and I loved yours dearly. I looked forward every day to seeing you walk into the bar.

113

"When we made love, I felt appreciated and accepted by you. You were gentle. I loved the attention. Sometime in the fall, you started drinking more heavily. You started acting cocky. The incident in the bar, when you announced that you were screwing me all over the place, hurt me. I overstepped my boundaries and suggested that you take a look at how much you were drinking. I think you did.

"Then, the divorce party happened, and it was fun, but it was also unsettling to me. Your drinking that night brought out another side of you that made me pull back and protect myself a little more. I overstepped my boundaries for the second time and told you that I liked you best when you weren't drinking so much.

"After that, it got better for a about a month or so. The time we spent together around New Year's was wonderful. You were present, and I felt really cared for. And even though that level of intimacy scared me a bit, I let myself go with it. I trusted it.

"And then, I don't know what happened. Right after that, you started going away. At first, I think it was the speed. You acted more confident, but it felt pretentious and superficial to me. Then, when you got into your acid trips, you darkened. You withdrew from me, not physically but emotionally. I felt like an outsider. You quit talking to me, or at least talking with me.

"Since then you have become so moody—sullen one day and haughty the next—that I don't know what to expect from you, and, quite honestly, it's been a couple of months since I've really, honestly looked forward to seeing you day to day.

"When we make love these days, I feel more tolerated than appreciated and accepted. I do not feel very cared for.

"Actually, Steve, I've been slowly pulling away from you, but I don't think you've noticed.

"If there's a bottom line to this diatribe, it would be something like the following: I've been around people with alcohol and drug problems all my life. Both of my parents were alcoholics. My brother is a cocaine addict. Both of my husbands had serious problems with alcohol and drugs. I've even questioned my own drinking from time to time.

"I know what these things look like, Steve, and I believe that you are smack dab in the middle of a very big alcohol and drug problem. There, I've said it. Now I've overstepped my boundaries for the third time. I'm sorry."

Steve did not respond immediately. He looked at Dixie and then at the floor and then back. He took a deep breath and released it slowly. "I, uh...." He shook his head back and forth. He stood up and took a few steps and then turned back.

"I don't know what to say, Dixie. I mean, I want to defend myself. I feel like I should defend myself, but..." He stepped back to his chair and leaned against its backrest on his hands. "I just don't know what to say."

Dixie stood up, walked over to him, slid her arms around his waist, and hugged him gently. He returned her hug tentatively. After a minute of silence she said, "Do you want me to go?"

Steve nodded. "Yeah, I guess so. Not because I'm mad at you or anything, but I feel like I need to be alone to think about this. I feel pretty taken back by what you said. It wasn't what I expected."

"May I ask what you did expect?"

Steve gave a little half-laugh and said, "Well, a lot less for one thing. I don't know, maybe that you were concerned about me and wanted to make sure I was okay. At most, ask me to slow down on the drug use and be aware of my behavior."

Dixie nodded her head. "Those things are certainly true, Steve, but they just touch the surface. I believe that you deserve a more honest answer than that from me. I think I owe you that, even if it scares you away."

Steve backed out of Dixie's hug and looked at her. "You haven't scared me away, Dixie. I just want to sit with this awhile. Okay?"

"Sure. Let me know if you want to talk some more, or if I can help."

"Okay. Maybe I'll see you at the bar later."

Dixie left. Steve sat down. "Jesus Christ, this is getting out of hand," he said. "I'm getting beat to a pulp here. Am I really that screwed up? Is that possible?"

Steve locked the shop and walked into the house. He opened a beer and took a long drink. Then he sat down on the sofa and rolled a joint. After taking a couple of hits, he got up, shuffled through his records, and put B.W. Stevenson on the stereo. He smoked some more and finished off the beer. Then he stretched out across the sofa.

He closed his eyes and drifted into a familiar, soft, safe place. Jumbled thoughts floated through and around him. The music wafted behind.

Steve felt the solitude close in around him. He felt rejected and forsaken. He understood that Dixie, James, and Tommy meant well, that they acted in good faith. Still, he felt hurt. He felt wounded. He felt small. He felt ashamed.

"Once again, not good enough. Defective merchandise," he whispered to himself.

He closed his eyes and recalled another time in his life when he felt judged, abandoned, alone, and unworthy.

He was sixteen, a high school sophomore, living at home with his parents. Lois and Henry had been at each other's throats for days. Following a loud late night shouting and

115

shoving match, Henry threw some things in a suitcase and stormed out of the house. Steve followed him out the front door and told him that if he was moving out, he wanted to go, too. Henry clapped him on the shoulder and said, "Okay. I'll talk to you tomorrow."

The next morning, Henry rented a room at The Countryside Motor Hotel, about five miles from the house. Steve moved in that afternoon.

Steve did not choose to live with his dad because of his affection for him. His decision to go with Henry reflected first, his ambivalence about living alone with Lois. He knew that scenario all too well. Secondly, he wanted to know his dad outside of Henry's and Lois' twisted relationship. Finally, he thought he saw an opportunity to finally score Henry's approval.

He anticipated a storybook father and son deal—a couple of bachelors doing their thing. He pictured himself and Henry sharing restaurant meals, poolside chats, and late night man-to-man talks. He never thought to ask Henry what his expectations were. Apparently, though, they were very different from his own.

Steve and Henry lived at The Countryside for two months. During that time, they never ate a meal together, sat together at the pool, or had a late night talk. Indeed, they never talked at all. Not once. For all intents and purposes, Steve lived alone.

At night, he watched TV alone while sipping bourbon from half-pint bottles that he hid under his mattress. He went to sleep during or shortly after The Johnny Carson Show. Henry came in between midnight and 4:00 AM. He tried not to wake Steve.

Steve left for school at 7:30 AM. He ate breakfast alone at The Pancake House, lunch at school, and dinner at a restaurant or with Peggy Sue Martin and her family. He came home to an empty room every day, sometimes right after school and sometimes later. Henry did not know the difference because he was not there, and he did not ask.

Steve and Henry interacted once a day, every day before Steve left for school. The scene never changed. Steve shook Henry's arm until he opened his eyes.

"Hey, Dad, can I have some money for food?"

Henry leaned up on one elbow and said, "Hand me my pants from over there on the chair."

Henry handed Steve some bills and said, "How's it going, son?"

Steve took the money and said, "It's going okay. See you later."

Weekends were much the same. Steve worked as a grocery store package boy every Saturday, so their Saturday morning routine mirrored the others. Henry seldom came home at all on Saturday night so they had no Sunday morning routine of any kind.

116

By the end of week two at The Countryside, Steve admitted to himself that he had made a very bad mistake. He called Lois and asked if he could return home. She unloaded on him.

"You have some nerve," she said bitterly. "A decent boy would never turn his back on his own mother, especially after she's been treated with such cruelty as I have been. What makes you think you can toss me aside when I need you the most and then just drop back in when things don't go your way? What makes you think you can break my heart and then pretend that nothing ever happened?

"Well, I'll tell you what you can do, Mr. Big Shot. Since you like that bastard so much that you prefer him to me, then you can just live with him. You might as well; you're just like the son of a bitch. You don't think you are, but I know both of you, and you're just alike."

Six weeks later, Steve asked again. This time, he apologized and asked her to please forgive him. She relented. He moved out without telling Henry goodbye. Four months later he left San Antonio to enter boarding school.

Steve found out later that Henry had used Steve's decision to leave Lois and live with him as ammunition in his war against her. "Look at you," he screamed at her, "you're a pitiful excuse for a human being. You're worthless. You're not even a fit mother, for God's sake. Your own goddamn son can't even stand the sight of you! You make him sick, and you make me even sicker."

The whole Countryside Motor Hotel experience became a piece of the puzzle that molded Steve's self-worth. From Henry, Steve heard, "You are not valuable. You are not worthy of my time and effort. The truth is, you are worth about one minute every morning and five bucks a day for food. That's all."

From Lois, Steve heard, "Love and worth are conditional. My love and your worth depend on your behavior being acceptable to me. You have value if I say you have value."

Steve took these messages and turned them into two fundamental precepts. #1 was, "You are defective and worth less—much less." #2 was, "Never, under any circumstances, ever let anyone know about #1. If you do, you will be rejected and abandoned."

"That's it," Steve thought to himself. "Dixie and them know my secret. I screwed up and let them see the real me. No wonder they're disappointed. I would be, too."

He opened his eyes, stared at the ceiling, and recalled Lois' indictment. "...just like the son of a bitch!" he whispered to himself. "...just like the goddamn son of a bitch." It was his worst nightmare. If it were true, he would end up bitter, cynical, and alone, loving no one and being loved by no one in return.

"Please God, don't let that happen to me," he said out loud to the empty room. "Please don't let me be Dad."

He slowly sat up. The house was deadly quiet. He looked at his watch. It was only 6:45. He lit and smoked the last of the joint. His buzz returned, but it felt flat and dismal. He put Elton John's *Madman Across the Water* on the stereo and turned the volume high.

He walked into the bedroom, lay down across the top of the bed, and listened to pieces of the first cut.

Pretty eyes,
Pirate smile.
You'll marry a music man...
Now she's in me,
Always with me.
Tiny dancer in my hand...
Hold me close, my tiny dancer.
Count the headlights on the highway.
Lay me down in sheets of linen.
You've had a busy day today.

Steve's mind flooded with pictures of Rachel, dancing alone, her eyes closed, her head, her hair, and her body swaying fluidly to the music.

"I'll call her tomorrow," he thought. "I'll find out how she did it, and whatever she did, I'll do, too. I'll get clean, like her; at least for a while anyway. That's a promise. First thing in the morning."

Steve dropped off to sleep. He dreamed that he was dancing, alone, in a large, empty room. The music was the most beautiful he had ever heard. It filled the room. It filled his head. He knew the music. He felt it. He saw it in his mind. But his body could not catch the beat. His movements felt awkward. He felt embarrassed and afraid that someone would see his awkwardness. But try as he did, he could not stop dancing.

CHAPTER 27

Steve was awakened abruptly by loud knocking on his front door. He turned on the bedside lamp and looked at his watch. It was a little after 11:00 o'clock. Reluctantly, he went to the door.

"What the hell are you doing, man? I've been pounding on your door for five minutes," James said as Steve unlatched the screen door and let him in.

"I was sound asleep. What the hell's going on, James? Is something wrong?"

"No, man, nothing's wrong. You got any cold beer?"

"Yeah, help yourself. Bring me one, too."

James brought two beers back to the living room. "Take a look at this weed, man," he said. He handed Steve an ounce bag of the most beautiful, plump, sticky, red-haired marijuana tops that he had ever seen.

Steve nodded. "That's some damn fine looking smoke, alright. Where the hell did you come up with it?"

"This is local stuff, man, grown just east of here. That's where I've been. I'm selling this shit by the pound, man. I want you to take some of it. I've got enough that I can front it to you and see how you do. This bag is a gift, compliments of the grower. Why don't you roll one up? I think you'll be pretty impressed."

Steve rolled a skinny joint, lit it, took a hit, and passed it to James. "Your timing is bad, James. I'm thinking about quitting everything for a while, starting tomorrow."

"What do you mean? You're not going to sell any more dope, or you're gonna quit getting high?" He passed it back to Steve.

"Quit getting high," Steve said as he took another hit.

"Yeah? Well, that's cool, man. Just use this bag as samples, then. You don't have to smoke it."

Steve laughed. "Yeah, right. Man, you weren't kidding. This is awesome weed. I'm already getting off." He hit again and handed it to James, who smiled broadly and waved it off.

"I told you, man!" he said. "It's some fucking unbelievable, wild shit. I'm telling you, Stevey, you can sell this shit like it was the end of the world. Listen, I'll leave twenty one-pound bundles of it with you. Give a couple of tops to your buddy at the convenience store. He'll be begging you for as much as you can give him. Spread a little around to a few of those guys at the bar. Give some to Tommy, too. You might be surprised what he can do with it. All I need is eight-fifty a pound. You ought to be able to double your money at that price."

"Man, I don't know," Steve said. "That's a lot more pot than I'm used to having around here. I'm a little nervous about it. How about if I took five pounds instead of twenty?"

"I'll tell you what. I'll give you ten. Believe me, you won't be sorry. You'll be selling the finest dope in Austin. I guarantee it. Now, tell me about the other thing."

"What other thing is that?" Steve asked.

"Not getting high, man. You said you were going to quit getting high."

"No, I said I'm thinking about it. I'm just thinking about it. I've already quit the speed, thanks to my impertinent friends, so maybe I'll just give up everything for a little while. Get clean, you know?"

"Yeah, sure, man. That's cool. See what that feels like. I think you ought to do it. Get real healthy and all that shit. I've done it a few times myself. It's far out. I mean it. You could use a change like that right now."

"Well, we'll see. Anyway, in the meantime, this is some truly spectacular weed. I am stoned on my ass."

James laughed heartily. "Far out, man. Okay, listen up. I'm gonna go out to my car and bring in a bag. Just sit tight till I get back." He walked to his car and returned with a large, black suitcase containing ten pounds of fresh, clean marijuana tops. Each pound was individually wrapped in plastic wrap, in the shape of a small leg of lamb. "Beautiful, no?" he asked Steve.

"Beautiful, indeed," Steve agreed. They laid the ten bundles carefully in Steve's bedroom closet, handling each with the care normally reserved for young infants. When the transfer was completed, James left. "I'll touch base with you in a few days," he said. "Call me if you need anything."

Steve sat on the edge of his bed and finished his beer. Then he finished James,' which was half-full. He pulled his dope box out of the closet and picked out the last remaining vial of speed. He held it at an angle up to the light and thumped the bottom of it with his fingernail. It was not quite full. He popped off the top, dumped a small amount onto the mirror, and chopped it out with a razor blade. He snorted half into each nostril.

He stepped into the bathroom and looked at himself in the mirror. He brushed back his hair with his hands. "Tomorrow it will be different, right? Am I right or am I right?" he said. He turned off the lights and walked across the street to The Roam In.

"How's it going?" he asked Dixie without looking at her directly.

"Okay. We've been pretty busy. How are you doing? You want a beer?"

"Yeah, give me a pitcher," he said.

"Expecting company?" Dixie asked.

"Nope. Just thirsty. I didn't think that would be a problem."

"No problem at all, Steve. It's coming right up." Dixie drew the pitcher, set it on the counter, and walked back to the other end of the bar.

Steve sat at a back table by himself, drank his beer, and outlined a new plan of action on the back of a napkin.

Tomorrow—Friday
AM—Call Rachel
Talk to Tommy & Mario @ pot
Finish display case
NO alcohol or drugs

Saturday
AM—Deliver case

120

Deposit $ before noon
PM—Ginger to lake
PM—See Rachel in S.A.???
NO alcohol or drugs

Sunday
AM—Drop acid—KEEP IT PURE—
NO alcohol or other drugs

Monday thru Thursday (Routine)
AM—Read, study min. 2 hrs/day
PM—Work in shop min. 5 hrs/day
        (NO EXCEPTIONS)
NO alcohol or drugs

Friday
IF successful week, THEN
AM—Study
PM—to lake w/ Ginger
One joint ok
4 beers max ok
Dixie spend night? Carla?

Saturday & Sunday
S.A. with kids
Play it by ear on alcohol & drugs

Steve read and reread the plan. It was reasonable,
responsible, and do-able. He stuck the napkin in his pocket and
left the bar without saying anything to anyone. He drove
downtown to a warehouse district punk rock nightclub and
drank until it closed at 2:00 AM. Afterwards, he stopped by a
pool hall and shot pool with drunk strangers until 4:00. Then to
The Omlettry for breakfast. He walked into his house in time to
avoid seeing the sun come up. He put Ginger in the back yard
and then went to the phone.
    "Hello?" Rachel answered. Her voice sounded soft and
sleepy.
    "I'm sorry to wake you up so early, Rachel. It's Steve."
    "Steve? What time is it?"
    "It's obscenely early. Five-thirty, about. I need to talk to you
for a few minutes. Can you handle it?"
    "Yeah, I guess so. What's the matter, babe?"
    "Are you still sober, Rachel?"
    "Yeah."
    "How are you doing with it?"
    "I'm doing good. Why?"
    "Can you tell me how you did it?"

"Uh, yeah, I think so, Steve. But probably not off the top of my head at 5:30 in the morning, and maybe never in a brief phone conversation. Do you want to come down and talk?"

"Yeah, I do. How about tomorrow, late afternoon or early evening?"

"Okay. Yeah, that will work. Listen, are you all right? You sound awfully...down...flat, kind of."

"Yeah, well, I'm pretty tired. Been up all night. I'm okay, though. I'm going to bed as soon as we get off the phone. I hated to call you so early, but I wanted to catch you before I crashed. Anyway, I'll see you tomorrow, okay?"

"Okay, Steve. Take care of yourself."

"Yeah, you too. And thanks."

Steve stepped out of his sandals and his jeans, climbed into bed, and slept until three in the afternoon, when Tommy banged on the back door.

"What the hell's going on, man? I was getting a little worried about you. I've been working out here in the shop for a couple of hours. Damn, you look like hell, Steve-o."

"Yeah, well, I feel like hell, too. Hey, come in here, man. I want to show you something." Steve opened his closet and pulled out one of the bundles. "Take a look at this shit, man. Tell me what you think."

Tommy carefully unwrapped the package and fingered the tops. "Very nice. Where'd you score this little sweetheart?"

"I've got ten of them. I need to sell them and get them out of here."

"How much?"

"A grand apiece. What do you think?"

"For this particular product, I think that's a real fair price. I'll take them."

"You're shitting me!" Steve said. "You'll buy all of them at once?"

"That's right. Are there any more where this came from?"

"Yeah. Plenty of them, I think. How many do you want?"

"I'll take up to fifty of them if you can deliver them to me here."

Steve looked at Tommy in disbelief. "Just like that? You want to buy fifty thousand dollars worth of pot? Hell, I have to twist your goddamn arm to buy me a fucking beer, and you want to buy fifty thousand dollars worth of pot? You kill me, man. I mean it; you fucking kill me. I'll see what I can do."

"Yeah, let me know. I'll be over at my house. Call me there."

Steve called James. His mind raced as he thought about the money—$7500 for five minutes' effort. James answered the phone on the first ring. "Hey, James," he said. "You know those things you showed me last night?"

"Yeah, man. Those tie-dyed t-shirts. What about them?"

"Could you bring me over forty more?"

James hesitated. "Uh, yeah, man. I could do that. Are you sure you need that many?"

"Yes."

"Okay, then. I'll see you in a little while."

Steve sat on his bed and stared at the wall. "Son of a bitch," he said out loud. "I hit the fucking jackpot."

The deal went off without a hitch. James delivered the packages; Steve called Tommy; Tommy showed up with cash and took delivery; Steve called James; James picked up his cash. At 9:00 PM on Friday night, Steve held seventy-five $100 bills in his hand.

He no longer felt tired, depressed, hurt, abandoned, or ashamed. He was stoked. His failure to finish the display case never crossed his mind. Neither did staying sober and straight.

Steve slipped a sample of the new weed into his pocket and walked across the street to The Roam In. When the bar closed at 2:00 AM, he had orders for 16 lids at $75.00 each.

CHAPTER 28

Steve called Rachel as soon as he woke up Saturday morning. He told her that he had an intestinal virus and had been up almost all night, going at both ends. She offered to drive to Austin, but he told her that he did not want her to get sick, too.

When she asked him about his phone call the previous morning, he told her that he was in the process of evaluating his alcohol and drug use and that he wanted to consider all of his options, including not using at all. "I promise I'll give you a call as soon as I'm feeling better," he said.

Steve walked next door and showed Mario the sample bag. Mario's eyes lit up like the headlights on a car. He made a couple of phone calls and then ordered five pounds at $1200 each.

Steve called James and arranged delivery. Then he sat down at the table and figured his profits. "This is un-fucking-believable," he said. "Ninety-six hundred bucks in less than 24 hours." He wondered how much James and Tommy were making. "Lots more than me, I'd bet."

James arrived in two hours, holding the same black suitcase. "Enjoy this while you can, Stevey-boy, because we're already at the tail end of it. I trust you've made enough to pay for your first year of graduate school."

"Yeah, I've done pretty well," he said. "I'm kind of disappointed, though. I didn't know it would disappear so quickly. I was hoping to do even better."

"Yeah, well, I know what you mean. I thought it would last longer, too. But this is good, man. This is the way to do it and survive. Get in and get out quick. Don't get greedy. I've still got a tiny bit left if you want it."

"Well, let me have one more pound, then. I want to keep a half in the freezer for personal stash."

James smiled. "A half pound of this weed goes a long way, Steve. Sounds like you decided against sobriety."

The statement caught Steve by surprise. He looked at James and laughed. "Oops," he said. "I guess I forgot about that. I must still be thinking about it."

"Yeah, I can tell," James said. "You know what, Steve? I was completely clean and sober for six months after I got out of prison. I was never clean while in prison, but I lived in a halfway house after I got paroled. It just so happened that the only halfway house in Austin at the time was a drug rehab house, so that's where I went.

"They did urine screens three times a week. I didn't want to screw up my parole so I stayed as clean as a king's elbow. I also had to go to group counseling and AA meetings. And I'll tell you what, man, it wasn't too bad. I learned a lot, and I met some damn good people, including a really far out counselor that I came to trust. I still check in with him from time to time just for good measure.

"I grew to respect sobriety. I truly did. I didn't necessarily want it for myself, but I did learn to appreciate it. I still clean up for a couple of weeks or so about every six months. In fact, I just spent the last two months totally straight. You know when we went over to The Roam In the other day? That was the first beer I'd had since I left town at the end of April.

"Anyway, I think you ought to check it out. You know, Steve, you told me Wednesday that you would quit using speed. You gave me your word. Then you told me Thursday night that you had, in fact, done that. But you know what? It's just Saturday, and unless I've lost my touch, I'd say you didn't quit using it at all. I can feel it on you right now.

"What I'm saying is, maybe it's more of a problem than you're allowing for. Think about it, Steve. Hang loose, and I'll grab that last pound for you."

Steve spent the rest of the afternoon and evening filling orders and collecting cash. He ended up selling everything he had—the new stuff and the old, except for four ounces of the new pot, his remaining personal stash of speed, now down to a half gram, and ten hits of LSD.

He counted his cash several times. Almost $12,000, and most of it pure profit. He hid it in the back of his bathroom linen closet, on the top shelf, folded into a ragged beach towel, under a

124

set of sheets. "Nest egg," he said as he carefully closed the linen closet door. He felt happy and relieved.

He walked across the street to the bar and ordered a beer. It was a typical Saturday night at The Roam In. A country-western band played loud music. University students in khakis and Izods drank beer, smoked cigarettes, and checked each other out. He did not recognize a single face, but the beer tasted good. He drank two quick ones and walked out.

He looked down the street at Tommy's house; it was completely dark. Same thing at Carla's. He ambled home. He put Simon and Garfunkel on the stereo, took two bong hits, and went to sleep on the sofa with Ginger at his feet and *The Sounds of Silence* in the air. He slept through the night.

CHAPTER 29

On Sunday morning, Steve sat down with a pot of coffee and the crumpled bar napkin on which he had outlined a new schedule for himself the previous Thursday.

"Are you ready now, Steve?" he asked himself. "Are you smart enough and strong enough to take your own advice? I hope so, buddy, because the time has come. Everything is in place. You still have all your friends. At least I think you do. Hell, I hope you do. You have The WoodWorks, which is sitting there waiting for you. You have a little financial security tucked away. And you have a good, simple, reasonable plan right here in front of you. Today is the day, my friend. Today is the day to get back on track."

He ate a bowl of cereal, fed Ginger, straightened the house, and took a shower. Then he unplugged the telephone and took one hit of acid, as called for in the plan. He kept it pure—no alcohol, no pot, no speed. It worked.

That night Steve slept like a baby. On Monday morning, he woke up feeling energized and strong, confident that nothing could derail him from his plan. Monday went exactly according to schedule, with zero alcohol and zero drugs. When Tommy dropped by the shop Monday afternoon, Steve turned down free beer.

Tuesday came and went without a slip. On Wednesday, James stopped by, and before he left, he complimented Steve on how good he looked. Thursday followed right in line. "There's nothing to this," Steve told himself. On Thursday evening he drank a tonic and lime at the bar, and he talked to Dixie for about an hour. He thanked her for her patience and for caring enough about him to tell him the truth.

By Friday morning, Steve's confidence soared. The high bottom drunk had turned it around again. He felt like a winner. He had stood by his plan to the letter. He had worked hard in the shop and delivered out over $400.00 in finished work. He had read and studied every morning. He had grocery shopped, cooked for himself, and eaten well. He had not drunk a drop of alcohol or touched any other drug in four days.

He called Rachel and thanked her for her support and her inspiration and promised to call her back soon to get together and compare notes. He invited Dixie to dinner Friday night. He cooked homemade lasagna and served it with wine by candlelight. They made love. It felt like old times.

"I can't believe I slipped so far off my path," he told Dixie the next morning. "When I think back, it seems almost like a bad dream, like I stumbled and fell into a hole and got trapped there. And apparently, everyone could see what was happening except me."

Dixie stirred her coffee for a moment and then looked up. "Steve, what's to prevent you from falling into that same hole again?"

He smiled. "Dixie, I feel so good right now that I can't imagine screwing it up. I think I just had to go through the last couple of months to get it out of my system. And I think I did. I'm really not worried about it."

Steve quickly modified his napkin plan to allow reasonable daily consumption of beer and pot. Nevertheless, he lived the next five weeks strictly by the book. He studied every morning, worked every afternoon, and partied and played with friends and lovers every evening. He got high but not too high every day, and without negative consequences of any kind. He used LSD as an agent for spiritual insight once a week. He took no speed or cocaine. He dealt no drugs. He experienced no surprises, no problems, and no complaints.

Then on the morning of Friday, August 18th, without warning or reason, the bottom fell out. Steve got up on the wrong side of the bed. He felt irritable and irrepressibly restless. He cursed the back door when it momentarily stuck and yelled at Ginger when she got in his way.

He had coffee for breakfast and struggled through the restlessness to log exactly two hours of study time. For lunch, he had two hamburgers and a milk shake at a greasy spoon joint down the street from his house.

After lunch, he rolled a joint and smoked half of it. Then, with no forethought, no hesitation, and no remorse, he chopped out and snorted two lines of speed. He opened a beer and walked out to his shop, where he failed to accomplish anything for forty-five minutes. Finally, he just stopped. "Fuck this shit," he said to himself. "I deserve a goddamn break. I've earned it."

126

He locked the shop, walked into the house and packed up for the lake. He included a towel, two joints, his half-gram of speed, and six beers. He left Ginger behind.

Driving to the lake, Steve ruminated on what had gone wrong. "This isn't fair, goddamn it," he muttered. "I don't deserve this shit. I did everything right. I kept my promises. I followed the schedule. And what do I get for it? I get this fucking bull shit!" Then he glanced upward toward the sky. "What's going on here, God? Is this a test? Is it a trick? Or maybe you're really just a fucking asshole who gets off on screwing with people's lives. Which is it, huh? Just as I thought. You're not even there."

Before walking down the path to the water, Steve bumped his speed buzz with two small hits. When he got to the water's edge, he sat down, guzzled one beer, opened another, and smoked a joint.

When the drugs kicked in, he mellowed a bit, but even the sun and the water and the buzz did not relieve his agitation completely.

On the way home, he swung by Tucker's office and convinced him to leave work and start Friday night a little early. Tucker had a gram of coke, which they mixed together with Steve's half gram of speed. Within an hour they were off to the races.

They bar hopped until midnight and then landed at Tucker's favorite spot, an upscale nightclub filled with hipsters in hairdos and trendy clothes. Steve looked out of place with his long hair and jeans and sandals, but he attracted the attention of a pretty, slightly plump Hispanic woman, who went home with him and yelled "Sweet Jesus" throughout her very substantial orgasm.

Steve's Saturday morning hangover left him feeling weak and dull. Nevertheless, he was polite to his date, whose name he could not remember and who seemed not to remember his. He fixed her coffee and toast and drove her back to the bar, where her car had spent the night amid many others. He kissed her, thanked her, told her she was pretty, and took her phone number.

On the way home, Steve decided that since his run of good behavior had already been demolished, he would take one more day off from his routine before getting back on track.

He bought a gram of speed from Mario and then called Tucker, who had gone home alone the night before. They spent the rest of the day shooting pool, drinking beer, smoking pot, and snorting coke and speed. Before falling into bed at 3:00 AM, Steve reminded himself that he would get back on schedule the next day. That did not happen. Instead, he dropped acid and polluted it with pot, alcohol, and speed.

127

On Monday morning, Steve lay in bed and thought about the previous three days. He had not eaten a real meal since Friday noon. He had not showered since Thursday morning and had not brushed his teeth or combed his hair since Saturday. He shuffled into the bathroom and looked in the mirror.

"Good God Almighty," he said. "You are one disgusting son of a bitch. I don't even know you, do I?"

He showered, brushed his teeth, cleaned his fingernails, rubbed lotion on his skin, and put on clean clothes. After coffee and a bowl of cereal, he felt a little more alive. He apologized to Ginger for his neglect, and to show her he meant it, he gave her a bath and took her to the park.

Later in the day he washed Cleo Truck and washed and dried his clothes at the Laundromat. By evening, he felt recovered. He stopped in at The Roam In and drank two beers. Dixie seemed glad to see him. She knew nothing about his three-day binge.

CHAPTER 30

Steve awoke Tuesday morning thinking about how close he was getting to the start of graduate school. He counted thirteen days and then felt a shiver of anxiety shoot through his body.

He pictured himself surrounded by people more intelligent, more experienced, more interested, and more committed than he. He recalled how out of place he had felt with Tommy and his peers. He imagined his embarrassment at not being able to do the work. Another wave of anxiety hit him, and for a moment he felt ill. "What the hell am I doing?' he thought. "I must have been out of my ever-loving mind to make that commitment."

Then he had another thought. "Wait a minute. This is ridiculous. I don't have to do anything I don't want to. I can back out any time I choose. It's not a big thing." Those thoughts gave him comfort.

During breakfast, Steve weighed his options in light of his current situation. He listed his various commitments and considered the importance of each. He thought especially about Lynn and Eddie and considered possible conflicts between weekend visits with them and weekend study loads. After breakfast, he walked down to Tommy's house.

"I hope I didn't wake you up," he said when Tommy opened the door wearing only his underwear.

"It's okay, man. I probably needed to get up anyway. I'm not sure why, but there's probably a reason. You want Java? I'm gonna put some on for myself."

"Yeah, that sounds good. Listen, there's something I want to talk to you about."

"Okay. You know me, always ready for some conversation. Come on in the kitchen and take a chair while I rustle me up a little grub, as they say. What's on your mind?"

"Well, Tommy, I've been thinking a lot about school starting. It's just two weeks until first year orientation week, and to tell you the truth, I'm having second thoughts about going through with it. I kind of hate to start something that I'm not all that committed to in my own mind. You know what I mean?"

"Yeah, sure I do. You're getting cold feet," Tommy said, as he yawned and scratched his butt. "But listen, I'm telling you, man, it's not that tough. You've got to study, you know? I mean, you've got to put your time in and all, but you're a smart guy. Believe me; you'll be fine. Quit thinking about it."

Steve took a deep breath and looked at his hands. "Well, Tommy, maybe I'm not as convinced as you are that I'm all that goddamn smart. And even if I am, I'm not so sure I'll be willing to put the time in. I've got a hell of a lot of stuff going on right now."

Tommy stopped what he was doing and looked at Steve. "So what's the rest of this story? Forget the bullshit about how busy you are; I ain't going there with you. What else are you telling yourself about why you can't do graduate school?"

Steve hesitated and then said, "Tommy, it's not as much about 'can't' as it is about 'won't.' The truth is I'm afraid that even if I'm capable of doing the work *and* willing to make the effort, I still won't be able to pull it off. I won't be able to go the distance without screwing it up."

Tommy was quiet for a moment. "Alright, let me see if I understand. Maybe you're smart enough, and maybe you're not. Maybe you're committed enough, and maybe you're not. But either way, it doesn't matter because you plan to sabotage it and fail. Is that it?"

Steve shrugged his shoulders. "It wouldn't be the first time."

Tommy looked at Steve and said, "Well, then, Steve, my guess is you must have a pretty good idea about how this sabotage will occur. And if that's true, this conversation would go a lot quicker if you just cut through the rest of the crap and tell me how you plan on screwing it up."

Steve bristled. "I think I'm not nearly as insightful about that as you imagine, Tommy."

"Well, I think that might be bull shit, but I'll give you the benefit of the doubt. Let's look at your patterns. When was the last time you spoiled something for yourself that you thought you really wanted?"

Steve flashed on Friday and Saturday's alcohol and speed binge and Sunday's busted acid trip. "Four days ago," he said.

129

"Oh yeah?" Tommy said, raising his eyebrows. "That's good. Fresh material to work with. What was it?"

Steve told Tommy about his three-day flight from sanity and then added, "To make a long story short, Thursday night, I was fine. In fact, I was great. My life had order. Fourteen hours later, I was out of control and cursing at God for fucking me around. Three days after that I could hardly stand the sight of myself in the mirror."

Tommy smiled and nodded. "Cursing God, the trickster; that's a good one. Anyway, getting back to business, tell me real briefly, what other successes have you sabotaged?"

"That's easy," Steve said. "I quit the track team in high school the day after being publicly praised and encouraged by the coaches. On the other hand, I quit the football team immediately after being publicly criticized. I quit playing golf as soon as I broke 85. I quit playing the guitar and singing soon after I got good enough that people started asking me to play in public.

"I tried my best to ruin my college career, but it somehow always pulled itself out of the gutter before I ruined it completely. I did it big time to my brokerage job. I was one of the company's top producers in six months, and three months later I told them to stick it because I was afraid that they were going to fire me. I probably would have fucked up my clothing business, too, but I bailed out before that happened.

"Hell, Tommy, I've been doing it this whole goddamn year. I mean, my life was great on January 1st, but in July, my three closest friends told me I was full of shit. Six weeks ago, Dixie would hardly look at me, and if she knew about this latest weekend binge, I think she might just throw up her hands and say, 'I've had enough.'

"Man, when I moved here last summer, I had the greatest plans for myself. I had optimism coming out of my ears. I mean, everything was going to change for the better. If you would have told me then that in one year I'd be sitting here so afraid of failure that I was thinking about quitting before I even got started, I would have said you were crazy."

Tommy laughed. "Good old delusional grandiosity. It always seems to bite you in the butt sooner or later. Listen, Steve, I'm no goddamn therapist, as you well know, but it doesn't sound so terribly complicated when you think about it. You've already identified fear as the main culprit. All we need to do is figure out and fix whatever's underneath the fear. Nothing to it, right?"

Steve smiled. "Yeah, right; nothing to it," he said sarcastically.

"Well, think about it for a minute. What is it about success and failure that scares you so badly that you scuttle success before it's complete and avoid failure before it begins? What are you protecting so goddamn resolutely? If you're not sure, just take a wild guess."

Steve stared at the floor. "I don't know, man. Myself, I guess. I mean, I know that sounds simplistic, but what I mean is, maybe it's that part of myself that feels inadequate. I don't want anyone to see it. I know this is stupid, Tommy, but I think I'm afraid that if I truly succeed at one thing, then I'll be expected to succeed at everything. And I know I can't pull that off. I'm not that good. I'm certain to fail.

"On the other hand, if I don't succeed at anything, then I won't be expected to succeed at anything else. Now that, I can do. It sounds like planned mediocrity, but let me tell you something; mediocrity feels like a pretty safe place right now.

"Here's another thing. I'm not sure it's just about success, per se. I think it might be more about people knowing about the success. Here's an example: I did really great when I was in graduate school before. I finished with a 4.0, and it was the first time in the history of that program that anyone had done that. Now, I never told anyone about that. Truth is, I would have preferred to keep it a secret. But when I was hired at the brokerage firm, the branch manager introduced me to the entire staff by announcing my record-setting performance. They all clapped and said, 'Wow, and blah, blah, blah.'

"Logically, I should have felt proud, but I didn't. I felt panicky. I suddenly felt compelled to duplicate my graduate school heroics at the brokerage firm. And I did, for a while, but then I sabotaged it. I think I had to, you know? The pressure was overwhelming. It's like, if I wasn't the top guy, then I might as well have been the bottom one. Second or third didn't count for anything. It ate my lunch. Am I making any sense at all?"

Tommy nodded. "Yeah, I'm getting it. Keep going. Don't ramble, but keep your train of thought going. '...Second or third didn't count. It ate my lunch.' Then what?"

"Well, it's simple. Everyone in the office knew how everyone else ranked in terms of productivity because our weekly and monthly sales figures were posted. If I failed, that is, if I wasn't the top producer, then everyone knew it. There was no way to hide. See? That's what I'm talking about. I *am* afraid of failure, but I'm probably more afraid of people perceiving me or knowing me as a failure."

Tommy nodded and said, "Because..."

"Well, because then they would know my secret, that I'm really not anywhere near as good or as smart or as cool as I make myself out to be. That in reality I'm...I don't know, not good enough. I mean, I think I try so hard to look good because I know that I'm really not, and I don't want anyone else to know that. To tell you the truth, I don't even want you to know that, but I guess it's too late now to worry about that, right?"

131

Tommy smiled. "Yep, the cat's out of the bag now. Our very own Steve Campbell ain't perfect, and Tommy knows it. So what happens now? You can't play with me anymore because I know your stupid secret?" He laughed softly. "Just kidding, Steve. Okay, bear with me now while I see if I understand what you're saying."

He spoke slowly now. "Regardless of how it has happened, you have come to believe, or to *know*, that you don't measure up—that you're imperfect, and that at least for you, imperfection is unpardonable. You believe, further, that you can hide this so-called deficiency in your true nature by not taking the kinds of risks that may expose it if and when you fail. Am I in the ballpark?"

"I guess so. I know it sounds ridiculous, but the fear is real, and I think there have been times that it's been debilitating."

"Oh, hell, man, I don't doubt that for a second. I'm not in any way questioning or diminishing the reality of the feeling. It's called *shame*. And it's all too real, as you already well know. Here's some miniature versions of what you're describing; see if they don't sound familiar. 'I don't just fuck up; I *am* a fuck up.' 'Even when I *do* good enough, I *am not* good enough.' 'Underneath this mask, I'm a piece of crap; please don't notice.' And last but not least, 'If you knew me like I know me, there's no way you could still love me.'

"Man, I think when we feel defective on the inside it almost forces us—it compels us—to protect ourselves anyway we can, including what you're describing when you talk about avoiding the perception of failure at any cost. It's like, 'Please, don't see my defectiveness. I'll do anything, including standing on the sidelines all of my life, to keep my defectiveness hidden.' Does this sound familiar at all?"

"Yeah, of course it does. You know it does. So if that's the problem, what's the answer?"

"Well, Steve, I think there may be different answers for different people. A psychologist or therapist might tell you that it's a psychological or therapeutic issue and that intensive, long-term therapy is the key. You know, like, understanding the origins of these messages about defectiveness and perfection and self-protection would provide insight that in turn would relieve the symptoms, like debilitating fear.

"James, the wild metaphysical holy man, would probably describe shame as a spiritual issue rather than a psychological one. He would say it's a spiritual issue requiring a soul-healing spiritual solution. You should talk to him about it. He's as crazy as a loon, but he's a brilliant thinker.

"Myself, I'm more the pragmatic type. I'd take a cognitive approach. Whenever I had those thoughts and feelings about defectiveness and self-protection, I would consciously remind myself that it's just my shame talking trash to me, that I'm recycling thoughts that have found a way to trick me into thinking they are true regardless of where those thoughts originated.

"I'd remind myself further that yes, in fact I am imperfect, just like every other living thing in the universe, past and present. And listen to this, Steve; I'd tell myself that that's a good thing rather than a bad one. It's what gives me my unique weirdness.

"I might even flaunt my imperfectness and check out who does and who doesn't simply accept me, warts and all, the way I am. Then I could choose my friends more wisely."

Tommy smiled. "The truth is, Steve, that's pretty much what I do already. And at least for this morning, that's the approach you've taken. You've exposed your imperfect self to me. And I should probably tell you, I like you exactly the same now as I did an hour ago when I still thought that you were perfect. What do you think of that?"

Steve laughed. "Yeah, you're a pal, alright. Just last month, you were beating me up about my drug abuse. I didn't say so at the time, but that hurt my feelings, especially after Dixie confirmed it. She *really* hurt my feelings. And as a result, I went through this stuff we're talking about. I mean, I felt my shame, if that's what it is. I felt like there was something fundamentally wrong with me, that I wasn't good enough, and that everyone who mattered knew it and had rejected me because of it."

"Yeah, well, Steve, keep in mind the difference between what you *do* and who you *are*. I was talking to you about your drug abuse. That's your behavior—what you were doing. I didn't mean for you to take that personally. I had no complaints about your heart, or your spirit, or your true nature, or whatever the hell you want to call what's on the inside—who you are. I'm pretty crazy about your heart, man; I think it's good. I didn't like the way you were covering over that good heart with the dope. That's all. You see what I mean?"

"Yeah, I do. I see what you're saying. You rejected my behavior, but you didn't reject me."

Tommy studied Steve's face. "You got it. Listen, this is rather complex stuff. Why don't you take a little time and think about it, and then let's talk some more. In fact, I'll make a deal with you. If you'll agree to spend some time with it, I'll do the same. I'll study up on it so I can discuss it more intelligently with you. How does that sound?"

Touched by Tommy's offer, Steve agreed. "It's a deal, and very generous on your part, Tommy. I appreciate it a lot. I really do."

"No problem, man," Tommy said. Then he added, "You know what? You ought to go off somewhere for a few days before school starts. Somewhere that you can be alone, where you can just really veg out. Do some writing while you're there, you know, about whatever comes up, but especially around this issue of your not being good enough the way you are.

"Consider how your family, in particular, gave you those messages about defectiveness and perfection. Who told you that you weren't good enough, and who told you that the only remedy for that was to be perfect? You know, I've got a feeling that that won't be too difficult for you to do. It would be for some people, but you already have very keen insight. Believe me; you do. You've got somewhere you could go, don't you? Your family has a ranch or something like that, right?"

Steve nodded. "My dad has a place in South Texas that's been in his family for three generations. I used to go down there all the time to hunt and fish and drink beer. It's a good place. And yeah, that does sound appealing. Not the writing necessarily, but taking a break from here sure sounds good. Hey, maybe you'd like to go, too. I could teach you the magic of LSD and watch your cynical atheism dissolve into the South Texas cosmos."

Tommy smiled broadly. "You'd like that, wouldn't you? Convert me to some silly religious belief system. Thanks, but no, I better hang around here and protect the neighborhood. You take old Ginger. Talk to her. She'll believe any damn thing you tell her.

"I will, however, give you something to take with you. Listen close because you'll never get a more sacred free gift than this one. The gift is two guaranteed shame busters that you can count on to neutralize any and all opportunities to feel ashamed. Are you ready for them?"

"Sure, lay them on me," Steve said.

"Okay, here they are. The first one is 'Oh, well....' The second is 'So what?'

"You use these most profound thoughts in two different ways. One is external, as a statement in response to criticism from another person. The other is internal, as a statement in response to criticism from yourself. In effect, they remind us not to take ourselves and/or others too seriously. Keep them close and use them often."

Steve hung around Tommy's house for the rest of the morning, drinking coffee and trading stories. They spent the afternoon together in The WoodWorks, working at a leisurely pace, listening to the radio, and sipping beer. It was a good day. Steve felt back on track and under control. He felt excited about going to the ranch.

Section Two:

What Happened

CHAPTER 31

Steve loved The Quarters Ranch. When he was a kid, his grandmother, Marge Campbell, and her father, Mr. J. M. "Pappy" Quarters, took Steve to the ranch often to fish and hunt and "run around like a wild Indian," as Pappy Quarters would say. As an adolescent and young adult, Steve took himself there to do those same exact things.

A family myth said that quarter horses had been named after Pappy Quarters because of his pioneering expertise with the breed. In reality, Pappy was a simple, frugal, hard working ranch hand who spent the first sixty years of his life buying a few acres at a time until he had put together a respectable spread of 4,980 acres. He used the land to raise cattle and grow peanuts. He eventually became a wealthy South Texas rancher and banker. He never trained a quarter horse.

No one lived on Quarters land. The old farmhouse still stood, though barely. Pappy Quarters built it in 1930, when he decided to put his rancher's pride behind him and become a peanut farmer. The house served as home to the same Mexican family for twenty-two years. Between 1930 and 1952, various members of that family worked the peanut fields seven days a week for room and board and a share of the peanut crops.

In 1974, the farmhouse provided basic shelter to hunters during deer season. The rest of the year, it sat empty and dying. The living room and front bedroom offered the only protection from rain and wind. The rest of the house had little or no roof. The back porch and what was once a bathroom lay rotting on the ground.

The front porch sloped downward away from the house. The angle of the slope made for tricky footing, especially when one was drunk and carrying a loaded shotgun. But it gave the house character. It reminded Steve of a big fat woman with an appealing but precarious lap.

Most of The Quarters' land was beautiful only in a South Texas sort of way, with lots of rocks, cedar, and cacti. However, two substantial constant flow rivers bordered The Quarters on two sides. The Frio River provided the south border; the Atascosa provided the east. This arrangement made the southeast corner of the ranch, which Steve called "The Meadows," a paradise.

The Meadows consisted of roughly 200 acres of cool, green ground cover and hundreds of huge cypress, native pecan, live oak, and post oak trees. It offered a haven for squirrels, rabbits, armadillos, and reptiles and birds of all kinds. Gentle, cool breezes made it a respite from the South Texas summer heat.

Steve parked Cleo in front of the farmhouse late Friday morning. He sat for a few minutes, finishing his second beer of the day and feeling grateful and relieved that the old place still stood.

He remembered when the house fared better. He was only six when the sharecroppers moved away, but he still remembered how the mother, or perhaps she was the grandmother, swept the hard dirt front yard with a broom while kids played around her.

He had enjoyed many good times here, both as a child and as an adult. The Quarters Ranch was where he and Henry had spent their best times together on father and son hunting trips. It was where Henry had told Steve "the facts of life." He did not do a very thorough job, as Steve learned later when he needed the real scoop, but Steve never forgot or lost his appreciation for Henry's effort.

Steve had brought Rachel to the ranch once. Like many of their undertakings together, the trip was a spur of the moment decision. They had been sitting at Little Hipp's Bar & Grill, sharing their third pitcher of Shiner Bock and a plate of shypoke eggs, plugging quarters into the juke box, and laughing heartily at each other's stories.

Rachel told one about being so drunk and stoned one night that she didn't realize that her redneck husband was in bed with her, and she masturbated while fantasizing about different men that she felt attracted to. Luckily for her, she never mentioned their names, but instead lumped them together under the rubric "baby," as in "Ooh, baby, baby, baby." After a while, she realized that her husband was sitting up in bed next to her, watching her, wide eyed, and masturbating himself, and saying, "Yes, baby; yes, baby."

After they both came, she hugged him and said, "I thought you might get a kick out of that." He greatly appreciated the new experience, and to show his appreciation, he tried his best to get it up again to make love to her. When that didn't work, he gave her head. It was the best sex that she ever had with him.

That story inspired Steve to tell his own masturbation story. He was sitting in a booth at a particularly sleazy bar, across the table from a particularly sleazy woman, who he had picked up earlier at a crummy pool hall in a rough part of town. They were both drunk, but she was drunk and loud and obnoxious, and to make it worse, her breath was bad.

While she rambled on about herself and her previous boyfriends, and without a clue as to what Steve was doing, he masturbated and ejaculated on the leg of her jeans, which were tucked into black leather cowboy boots. They got up to leave about 30 minutes later, and sure enough, there it was—wet spots and dabs of semen on her lower right pants leg and boot.

She was acting cool and sexy. He was pretending to like her. He took her back to the pool hall and dropped her off at the front door, promising to be right back to pick her up after he scored some cocaine for them to enjoy together later that night. Luckily, she had chosen to call him "sweetie" and had never asked his real name.

Three hours of stories, belly laughs, and cold Little Hipp's draft moved Steve to propose the trip.

"Hey, Rachel," he said. "I've got a great idea. My old man's got a place two hours south of here. It's a big, deserted ranch with a ratty old farmhouse that has a bed suspended on wires from the ceiling. Ever since I was old enough to beat my meat I've dreamed of having a beautiful woman naked in that bed. Inasmuch as you're the most beautiful woman I know, I say let's pack up some beer and some weed and drive down there and take that swinging bed for a ride. Then we can sit out on the front porch and watch the stars move across the sky till morning. We can get there by dark if we hurry. We might even have time to grab a bite to eat on the way. What do you say? Are you game?"

True to her nature, Rachel was, indeed, game. "I wouldn't want to stand in the way of a good man fulfilling a lifelong fantasy. You've got to promise, though, that you won't misfire and get anything gooey on my leg. Is that a deal?"

Steve laughed. "Yeah, I can make that promise. I'll tell you what, though; I wouldn't mind doing that little "Ooh, baby, baby, baby" mutual masturbation routine one of these days."

Rachel laughed. "God, men are so weird. But, sure, what the hell? Why not?"

Steve and Rachel iced down a case of beer and packed eight joints, a bag of pretzels, a can of peanuts, two blankets, two pillows, one toothbrush, and a tube of toothpaste. Three hours after their Hipp's conversation, they sat in Steve's Corvette in the identical spot where Steve now sat in Cleo.

"It looks a little spooky, Steve," Rachel said. "Are there ghosts in there? And if so, are they friendly?"

"Yeah, as far as I know, they're friendly. But if they're not, they will be as soon as they get a load of that beautiful body of yours lying across that bed."

If the ghosts were watching, they got quite a show. Steve and Rachel took advantage of the absolute privacy and safety of the farmhouse and let loose completely. Afterwards, they laughed out loud and kidded each other about their near complete lack of decorum.

They laid the blankets and pillows out on the sloping porch, then opened beers, smoked a joint, and watched the sky. The stars were luminous, and as they crept slowly across the sky, Steve and Rachel shared stories of a different sort than the ones they did at Little Hipp's. Those had been wonderful and funny. These came from nearer the heart.

Steve told Rachel about the night that Bev told him she was pregnant with Lynn. They were barely twenty years old. They had not been together, even for a date, for nearly two months. In his mind, Steve wondered if the pregnancy was really even his, but he never said so out loud. When Bev ruled out abortion, he asked her to marry him. She agreed, but only on the condition that he really did love her. He promised her that he did. He told Rachel about Lynn's birth and about the unbridled joy he felt when he held her for the first time.

Rachel shared with Steve details of her experience with an emotionally abusive father, followed almost immediately by a physically abusive husband. She told him how it felt to be raped by someone she lived with and loathed.

They talked about their children. They talked about death. They talked about God. They talked all night. By morning they were sober and hungry.

Steve took a deep breath. He let Rachel's image linger for a moment in his mind. In a way, he wished that Rachel were there with him again. In another, though, he was glad to be alone.

"Come on, old girl," he said to Ginger. They carefully crossed the porch, which leaned downward a little more than it did the year before. He shoved open the front door and walked into the familiar old dirty, musty-smelling living room with the same old dingy furniture.

"Empty houses age poorly, Ginger," he said. "I'm afraid this one is on its last leg. Today, though, she's still standing. That's lucky for us." He walked through the kitchen, which had lost so much of its roof that it showed open sky. He kicked open the back door and looked down at the rotting remains of the back porch.

He checked out the front bedroom and felt relieved and happy to see that the swinging bed was still attached securely to the ceiling. He lay across the bed and smelled its thick accumulation of dust. By shifting his body weight, he made the bed sway back and forth, back and forth. He thought about the next few days.

The plan was simple. The rest of Friday and through Saturday afternoon he would relax and enjoy being alone with Ginger. They would roam the ranch in Cleo and on foot. He would smoke some pot, drink some beer, do a little speed, listen to music, read, and perhaps do some of the writing that Tommy had suggested.

Saturday evening to Sunday morning he would take what he thought might be his last acid trip for a while. He had packed his last two hits of LSD for the occasion. The rest of Sunday would allow recovery—sleep, rest, reading, writing, and more sleep. They would go home Monday morning, fully rested and ready for the next challenge—graduate school. Maybe they would stop in San Antonio to see Lois and Chester. They might even drop in on Henry for a very quick visit.

Steve walked outside and sat on the edge of the truck bed. He drank his third cold beer and took in the familiar beauty of South Texas—the crystal clear blue sky, the blindingly bright sun, the bone dry, hot air.

He finished the beer and unloaded the truck. As he made trips into and out of the house, he wondered why he had packed so much junk. He carried in a large ice chest full of beer and food, two grocery sacks filled with snacks, a duffel bag containing clothes and toiletries, his sleeping gear, a lantern, a Walkman, a boom box, a box of tapes, four books, and a Playboy magazine.

Lastly, Steve carried in his "toot bag," a small black leather zipper bag containing his drugs and drug paraphernalia. He dumped its contents onto the swinging bed and took inventory. There were eight rolled joints plus an additional half ounce of James' superb pot, a half gram of coke, a two-thirds gram of speed, two hits of purple dragon blotter acid, a mirror, a single-edged razor blade, a short glass straw, a pack of rolling papers, and a miniature bong.

Steve put Seals & Crofts' *Summer Breeze* on the tape player and sank down into the sofa with a beer and a joint. He closed his eyes and drank and smoked and listened.

He recalled seeing Seals & Crofts in concert at Trinity University in San Antonio with Bev. It was one of only three concerts that they could agree on during their six years together. He remembered that after the concert, the two men and their wives remained on stage and invited anyone who was interested to hang around and talk about the Baha'i faith. Steve wanted to stay, but Bev insisted that he take her home. He sulked for the next three days.

As the tape played, Steve drifted into and out of a dreamy, mellow high. When the tape ended, he opened another beer and decided to do a little coke to perk himself up. He chopped out and snorted two lines. It worked immediately. He felt his head and chest open and expand and his mind sharpen. Suddenly feeling exuberant, he stepped out onto the porch and yelled, "Whoever said that drugs are bad for you has never done good cocaine."

He quickly chugged the beer that he had just opened and said, "Come on, Ginger, old girl, old pal; I'll show you around The Quarters Ranch."

He grabbed six beers, two joints, and the coke vial and walked briskly to the truck. He put Ginger in the cab with him, and together they meandered around dirt roads and cattle trails for the next two hours.

Steve sipped warm beer, took hits of pot from ashtray joints, and bumped his high from the coke vial. He turned up the volume on Janis Joplin and The Moody Blues and sang or whistled along with every song. Frequent piss stops let Ginger explore her fascination with an endless number of new smells. Steve felt totally free.

They made it down to The Meadows about 4:00 o'clock. Steve parked Cleo, and he and Ginger walked down to the banks of the Frio. While she sniffed around the water's edge, he threw rocks to the other side. Then they walked back up to Steve's favorite Meadows spot beneath a sprawling oak tree.

Steve lay flat on his back on the cool ground and stared up at the canopy of branches and leaves above him. His body relaxed. His mind spun like a top.

"I'll own this place some day," he thought to himself. "It's promised. Promises do get broken, especially in the Campbell family, but this promise is a sacred one. When it's mine, it will be my security against the world.

"Maybe I'll raise cattle like Pappy. I like that image. Maybe I'll grow peanuts. I like that image better. Maybe I'll be smart and grow marijuana, the most dependable cash crop in the world. If James can do it, why can't I? It's nothing but a damn weed. Yeah, I like that image best of all. Steve Campbell—pot farmer; weed grower.

"Maybe I'll just sell the whole damn place, all except this spot right here. Then I could retire and live on the interest from my investments. That wouldn't be too bad, either.

"Maybe I'll do nothing. Maybe I'll just lie right here and die and watch my body rot into the earth. Maybe I'm dead already and don't even know it."

Steve slowly closed his eyes and slipped into a half-sleep. While there, he dreamed he was flying, not peacefully and gracefully like an eagle, but darting and dodging, fast and frantic, low to the ground, in and out of tight places, around trees and bushes and rocks, mouth set in a grimace and eyes blazing. He glided to a landing on a spot very near where he lay now on his back. He walked closer to himself, resembling a bird as well as a man. With unfriendly, piercing eyes, he glared at himself, asleep on the ground.

Steve's body jerked involuntarily, and his eyes popped open. He sat upright and looked around him, half-expecting to see the birdman staring back. When he saw nothing except for the lovely space, he laughed softly. He wondered what the dream meant but not enough to give it any more thought.

He checked himself out. He felt slightly headachy and a bit woozy, but okay. He slowly stood, a little wobbly, but again, okay.

Steve opened the last beer, which was very warm, and strolled back down to the river's edge. Muddy in spots but clear where shallow and rocky, the Frio was running well for August. Cool air rose from the water. He leaned against a cypress tree and tossed rocks into the river and watched them sink.

They got back to the farmhouse around 6:00. Steve fed Ginger, who gulped down her food. He opened a cold beer and forced himself to eat a sandwich and some chips. He took a couple of bong hits and contemplated the coke and speed. "What the hell," he said to himself. "It's still early. What could it hurt? If I do it now, I'll still be able to sleep later." He chopped out two lines of speed and then added a dab of coke to each one. After snorting the lines, he again felt alert and energetic. He opened another beer and dragged a chair out onto the porch, where he sat until sunset.

When daylight faded into twilight, Steve took a bong hit to boost his buzz, opened another beer, picked up his flashlight and headed east across the field toward the Atascosa River, a half-mile from the house.

About halfway there, he stopped and looked at the sky. It was deathly quiet and perfectly clear. A few early stars made themselves visible. He imagined a spectacular night sky, with shooting stars and wishes coming true. Images of Rachel and Dixie came to him. He wished that one of them were there to share it with him.

Then he thought about the LSD. It occurred to him that even though he had done a lot of beer, pot, and powder over the course of the day, he was in remarkably good shape. He felt clear-headed, alert, and fully present. He had even eaten dinner.

"Why not do it tonight?" he thought. "Why wait? If I do it tonight, I'm assured of a perfect night sky and perfect weather. Then I can relax and recover all day tomorrow and head home Sunday instead of Monday. That way, I could stop in S.A. and see Rachel. Man, why the hell didn't I think of this sooner? It's perfect."

Steve walked quickly back to the house. Once inside, he filled and lit the kerosene lantern. He gave Ginger fresh water. He arranged the living room and bedroom the way he wanted them, with everything he might need in a familiar place and handy. When he felt comfortable with his surroundings, he opened his toot bag and removed a small baggie containing two tiny squares, each about one-fourth the size of a postage stamp, and each picturing a snarling purple dragon.

He stared at the squares. He never did two hits at once, but this time was different. The setting was ideal. He was perfectly safe and completely isolated in a place that he had known and loved all of his life. "I have history here," he said softly. "I will add a page to that history tonight."

He held the baggie up to the light of the lantern and studied it. "This is magic stuff, Ginger," he said without looking her way. "Have no doubt about that. It's magic goddamn stuff."

He laid the baggie down on the table and backed away from it, rubbing his hands together. He looked at his watch. "Just a little after 9:30," he said. "Still early; still plenty early." He picked up the baggie and then laid it down again.

He took a bong hit, opened a beer, and walked outside. He sat down on the porch and leaned against the front of the house. Feeling tentative about starting an acid trip was unusual but not unknown to Steve. James had taught him well to be certain that he felt ready and that the time felt right.

"It's a commitment, man," James would say. "Like all commitments, you don't make it lightly because once begun, there's no turning back. You're in it till it's over."

Steve looked at the sky. No moon yet, but lots of stars. "God, it's beautiful," he said. "If there's such a thing as a miracle, this night sky is surely one. God, if you made this, I thank you."

He chugged the rest of the beer, walked resolutely into the house, and picked up the baggie. "Let's do it," he said. "Let's get this show on the road." He opened the baggie, tapped the tiny squares into his mouth, chewed them thoroughly, and swallowed the speck of paper that remained.

CHAPTER 32

Steve breathed deeply and stretched. "Get ready, Steve-o; here it comes," he said. Slowly at first, then faster and harder as apprehension gave way to resignation, which gave way to surrender. Filling and tightening the jaw and the back of the head and neck. Creeping, then gushing into the muscles of the shoulders, the upper back, and the chest, filling the lungs with heavy, expectant energy. Breathing deeply, deeply; exhaling with the sound of submission and anticipation. Hearing channels open up, followed by the hollow sound of breath flowing through the nostrils, past the ears, and into the lungs. Expansion. Surging energy into the arms and hands. Steve spread his fingers into open fans and stretched his arms upward and outward. Exhaling deeply, audibly. Expansion.

Coming on more. Tongue thickening, saliva heavy, throat closing. Steve stretched up, arching his back, shoulders, neck, and arms. "Man, oh man, oh man," he whispered. He stretched down, touching his toes and then the bottoms of his feet with his fingers. Mind reaching outward and further outward. Expansion.

Waist, hips, buttocks, and groin tightening and filling with expansive energy. Steve rubbed his groin area with his hands and glimpsed upon the promise of a powerful, exploding orgasm before the night turned into morning. "Be patient, Steve," he whispered. Legs, feet, and toes feeling the expansive energy surge. Teeth clenched. "Relax, Steve; relax; go on into it." Breathing deepening. Surrendering to the trip.

Steve wandered through the rooms of the house, observing his perceptions, studying objects and surfaces, watching them move and change. Feeling restless. "It's too early for restlessness," he said. "Relax, man; let it be. Just watch and listen. Everything's cool."

He sat carefully and deeply into the corner of the sofa and closed his eyes. Relaxing. Breathing. Listening. Letting go. Barriers dwindling. Defenses dissolving. Ego vanishing. Awareness expanding.

Steve felt himself slipping away and away and away. Falling into childhood; regressing to infancy. One year old. Lying in Papa Roger's bed; now in Papa's arms. Large man, large hands. Strong hands, working man's hands. Gentle hands, loving hands, cradling Steve against Papa's chest and neck and face. Bearded face, kind face, smiling face, laughing face. Soft eyes, clear eyes, dancing eyes. Baby talk to the baby. "Who's my boy? Hmm? Who's Papa's big boy? Stevey-pooh, that's who." Big, sweet smiles on the face of a big, sweet man.

Tummy tickle, gentle and friendly, on baby's fat tummy. Delighted giggles from baby. Deep, hearty laughter from Papa. Papa's bearded face blowing loud, wet bubbles against baby's tummy. Squeals of baby laughter, arms and legs waving wildly. Gales of laughter from Papa. Smell of Old Spice; smell of the big man's sweat; smell of the earth; smell of Papa. Reassuring smell; reassuring laughter; reassuring presence.

"Hold me, Papa," Steve said softly. "Hold me tight and close so I can smell you and feel your skin against mine. Stay with me. Hold me. Kiss my cheek and my tummy with your rough, bearded face. Nuzzle me into your neck. Hold me against your chest while I rest. Don't let me go. Stay with me. I miss you. I miss you so." Experiencing Papa's essence so intensely, feeling it completely—now, then, here, there. Holding the experience against his heart, until it starts to waver, slipping away, then returning, then slipping away again.

Very reluctantly, Steve let it go. And the tears began. They flowed hard, from deep inside, for his loss, in his grief. "I was cheated," he whispered. Cheated by Papa Roger's early death. Holding his memory. Suffering his absence. Gradually, the sadness faded. Gratitude replaced it. "Thank you, Papa," he whispered. "Thank you for coming."

Steve breathed deeply and opened his eyes. He ran his fingers through his hair; it was damp with sweat. His head tingled to the touch of his hands. He massaged his neck and shoulders and then wrapped his arms around his chest and held himself tightly. Tripping big time now. Off like crazy.

He sat up on the sofa and stared at the opposite wall. Like him, it was breathing, in and out, expanding and contracting. The floor tilted downward toward him, forcing him to look up slightly to see the wall fully. For an instant, he thought the wall would topple over onto him. "Shit, man," he said loudly, fear mixed with awe. The sound of his voice startled him. He quickly sat upright and shook his head from side to side.

Sobered for a moment, he looked at his watch. It was 11:22. "All right," he said. "Still early; still young." He looked at Ginger. She lay still, her head on her paws, her eyes open, alert, and watching him. "Stay close, old girl," he whispered to her.

He relaxed against the back of the sofa. He closed his eyes and listened to his breathing. Floating now. Drifting. Slipping out of himself and hovering. "Go on, man; don't be afraid. You're safe." Gliding slowly and gracefully through the sky, through the darkness. Seeing without eyes. Hearing without ears. Feeling without touch, without body. Awareness without mind. Presence through essence. Knowing. Being.

He heard the question, "Who is God?" and the answer, "Yes." He felt the presence of every man and no man. He saw the presence of everything and nothing in the unity of darkness and light. Was it night or was it day? Yes, no, both, neither. Where? Everywhere and nowhere. How? Every way and no way. When? Always and never. He heard the words clearly, "Being; there is only being." Gliding, floating, hovering. Slipping back into himself.

Steve opened his eyes to the present. The lantern light flickered unsteadily. The shadows felt menacing, frightening, and wholly unfamiliar. "It's okay, Steve; it's just the trip," he reminded himself.

He tried to stand but lost his balance and fell back onto the sofa. He checked himself out. Nothing unfamiliar within the context of the trip. Skin soft and clammy, tongue heavy, mouth dry, eyes difficult to focus, hair damp, muscles weak and slightly achy, fingers stiff, breathing shallow and irregular, pulse quick, balance off. He stood slowly, bracing himself against the front of the sofa.

"Easy does it, man," he said. "We're not in a hurry." He moved haltingly to the table and sat down. He looked back at the floor, which was undulating precariously. "Ha ha. It appears that I can walk on water," he said.

Steve tried to swallow but the heaviness of his spit and dryness of his throat made swallowing impossible. He opened the ice chest and took out a beer. "One beer won't hurt anything," he said. He twisted off the cap and drank it down like water. "One more won't hurt anything, either." He opened another and drank half of it straight down.

"You ready to move around a little bit, old girl?" he asked Ginger. "Come on, baby, let's take a look outside."

He plucked one more beer from the chest. Then he reached into his toot bag, grabbed the vial of speed, and put it in his jeans pocket. He picked up a blanket and walked out onto the front porch. The sky exploded into sight. "Jesus fucking Christ," he murmured.

Transfixed, Steve stared into the incredible depth and blackness of the night. A quarter-moon had risen in the east. The Milky Way made a thick band of light gray across the middle of the vast sky.

Orion, huge and sprawling, triggered the memory that as a child Steve counted on the orderliness and predictability of the three stars of Orion's belt. They were always there and always the same. He smiled and thanked the giant hunter.

Walking away from the house, carrying the beers and blanket, Steve felt more control. Drinking the beer had helped. Fifty yards out, he spread the blanket onto the ground and sat down. He opened and drank the third beer, then reached into his pocket and extracted the vial of speed.

"Just a taste to bring me up," he said. He snorted a small amount into each nostril, then bumped each side with a little more. He lay down facing the heavens. Ginger curled up against his leg.

Eyes open. Mind open. Thoughts racing. Intensely awake. Vigilant. The ground felt cool through the blanket. Breathing. Listening. Night noises, hundreds of them in symphony. Beautiful. Eerie.

Steve closed his eyes and immediately felt his consciousness rise from his body and the surface of the earth and float gently, rocking side to side, a weightless feather in a gentle breeze. He smiled. "I'm weightless," he mumbled.

He settled back down into his body. Lying motionless, he felt his heart beating. Then he felt the Earth's heart beating in sync with his own. He felt the earth at work beneath him. Every particle, every molecule alive and in transition, breathing its own breath, pumping its own life force, moving, changing, generating new life, and dying.

Steve slipped out of his body through the middle of his back and folded himself into the earth. Burrowing slowly toward the center. Burrowing deeper, seemingly with curiosity and purpose. Then gradually gaining speed and momentum. Deeper, deeper, toward the core. Deeper now, and faster. Then faster still. Losing purpose. No destination. No longer burrowing, but slicing through the earth at great speed, then extraordinary speed, until fear grabbed him and told him that he would be unable to stop, unable to retrieve himself. Deeper still. Faster yet. Blinding speed through fields of color. Colors changing—green to brown to red to purple—darker, deeper shades—folding into creases of gray and black—thicker now, and heavier. The colors had sound. He heard them humming. No, wait; not humming, but rather moaning, whining, crying. "They hurt, for Christ's sake," he thought. Crying. Sobbing. Wailing. Screaming. In pain. "Oh, my God," Steve said. "I've gone too deep. I've gone too far." He tried to stop, but he had no brakes, nothing to dig in with, nothing to create resistance. "Oh, God, I've done it this time," he yelled. Fear. Panic. "I wasn't ready. I wasn't ready." He heard the screaming. It pierced his ears and split his brain. His skull started cracking open. He screamed at the top of his lungs.

And then...nothing. No light. No color. No sound. No movement. "Am I dead?" he wondered. He could move at will, but to where? Which way was up? Which way was out? He had no clue. He realized that he had hands, however, and he used them to dig. There was no direction, but no matter; he dug, moving forward toward his hands. "God?" he said. "God? Am I worth keeping?" There was no answer. "God? Do you hear me? Are you there?" Silence still. "Does that mean 'no,' God?" Silence. Digging more, moving forward. No panic. "God, answer me," he said. And then he heard an answer. It was a whisper, or perhaps softer, quieter than a whisper, somewhere within his being. "It's simple." That was all. Then pure silence.

Steve opened his eyes. "It's simple," he whispered to himself. "What's simple?" he thought. He lay perfectly still and quiet, attempting to orient himself to place without disturbing the silence. He moved his eyes but not his head. He felt his body against the ground. He saw the night sky above. Perfect silence. He felt Ginger, breathing, against his leg. He moved his hand slowly to her and touched her; she grunted and shifted her body slightly. His head hurt. His chest felt tight. His throat was sore, and his muscles ached.

He inhaled deeply, exhaled, and tried to sit up. His body felt weak and his balance poor. He lay back down. Confused, disoriented. Nothing looked or felt right. It was too quiet. Too still. Too clear. Too damp. The ground was too cold. The night colors looked wrong. The stars were too dim. The moon shadows were too long. He tried to think. "Acid trip," he said. "But then what?"

Time passed—a minute, two, five. His breathing normalized. More and more of his conscious mind came back, but it felt dull and disordered.

"It's simple," he thought again. "What's simple? What's simple?"

Steve looked at his watch. It read 4:15. "What the hell?" he said. He looked at it again from a better angle. It read the same. He had lost at least three, maybe even four hours. He closed his eyes and searched his mind, trying to remember. "What the hell is going on? Where did I go? How was I gone that long?" he thought.

"Wait a minute. Surely I haven't been asleep. I couldn't possibly have been asleep." He closed his eyes and recalled the trip into the earth. "That was no goddamn dream," he said to himself. "No fucking way."

He tried again to sit up. He made it this time, but he felt very weak and light-headed. Ginger raised her head and sneezed. The sound scared Steve intensely, and his body jerked aggressively to one side. His sudden movement frightened Ginger, who jumped to her feet and leaped backwards.

"Damn it," he said. "I am really fucked up here." In a sitting position now, he drew his knees up to his chest and pulled the blanket around his shoulders. He laid an open hand out for Ginger and scratched her head when she came to him. Then he pulled his arm back under the blanket and hugged his knees against his chest.

"It's simple; it's simple; it's simple," he said. "I don't know, man; this doesn't feel simple. I'm scared."

After a few minutes, Steve slowly and carefully got to his feet. His body trembled. He felt uncoordinated. He balanced himself by holding his arms out and leaning from side to side. Once stable enough to move, he took one step, then another, then another, one foot in front of the other, until he covered the fifty yards back to the front of the house.

As he approached Cleo, he was struck by the thought that perhaps he had gone into a blackout and had, in fact, left the blanket between midnight and four and gone to who knows where. The thought sent a wave of anxiety through him. He slowly walked around and inspected the truck. To his relief, he found no evidence that Cleo had moved. The hood felt cool to the touch, and the ground around the tires appeared undisturbed.

Reluctantly, he retraced his steps back to where he had been lying. Again to his relief, he found the same evidence that he had not left the site.

Stronger now, Steve ambled back to the farmhouse. He went inside and sat at the table with the blanket still around his shoulders. "Something happened, goddamn it," he said. "I don't know what, but it was something. I know I didn't space out that much time." He tried again to concentrate and remember, but other than the frightening trip through the earth, he came up blank.

He held out his hands and watched them tremble. He opened a beer and lit a joint. The beer had no taste, but its frigid wetness soothed his throat. He drank it quickly, opened another, and drank it while he smoked the joint. He longed to feel high, but his brain rejected intoxication. Instead, he felt dull and down and done.

"Man, I can't let it end like this," he said. "If this is going to be my last hurrah for a while, I need more out of it than this." He located his toot bag, took out the coke vial, and dumped its contents onto the mirror. Then he matched that pile with speed. Mixed together, the combination yielded two long, fluffy lines. He snorted them and waited. Still nothing. Nothing but agitation, frustration, and anxiety.

"I'm not going to get there," he said to himself. "It's just not going to work." He stood up and dragged the chair onto the porch and sat and drank beer and waited for the sun to rise.

CHAPTER 33

While he waited for daylight, Steve listed words that fit his feelings. They came easily. Dull. Flat. Shot. Worn. Beat. Spent. Blown. Empty. Hollow. Lost. He wished he were home in his own bed. He pictured himself sleeping, with covers pulled up to his chin to protect him from the attic fan's cool breeze rushing across his body.

He visualized himself getting out of bed and brewing fresh coffee. He pictured warm oatmeal, a banana, and the morning newspaper. He imagined taking Ginger to the park, where they would play and he would study. He pictured himself working in the shop and expecting a visit from Tommy or James or Tucker or Dixie.

Sitting in one of his favorite spots in the world, Steve felt sad and alone.

When daylight broke, he walked into the house. Knowing that sleep was not an option but wanting desperately to relax, he took two large bong hits and opened a beer. He picked up the *Playboy Magazine* and sat on the sofa. Flipping past the articles to the pictures, he paused at the Playmate of the Month. "Way too perfect," he muttered.

Skipping to the next pictorial, he found *Girls of the Southwest Conference*. "Ah, here we go; this is more like it," he said, smiling. He studied several pages filled with pictures of young women from universities with which he was familiar. The one that caught his eye was the hometown girl, Nicole Campbell, from The University of Texas at Austin. He laughed to himself.

"Nicole Campbell, huh? I wonder how we're related. Kissing cousins, perhaps, or a very naughty niece."

Steve stared at Nicole's picture. Very pretty face. Incredibly sexy body. Five feet five with lots of leg. Medium brown hair, long and curly. She wore tight leather pants with matching leather suspenders. The suspenders crisscrossed at her sternum to accentuate perfect, round breasts that sat high on her chest.

"My, my, my, Miss Campbell," he said. "What would you say to our slipping those leather pants down around your ankles and spanking your bottom with the suspenders? Would you like Cousin Steve to do that for you? How about if we lay you down on your back and let Stevey give you head till you come in his mouth? Would you like that? Yeah, I think you would. Then while you're still wet and juicy, we'll flip you over onto your hands and knees and play bitch in heat. How does that sound, little cousin?"

As he spoke, Steve rubbed himself partially erect. "Maybe not all is lost," he thought. "It won't be as good now as it would have been earlier, but at least it's something." He stood and stripped to bare-naked. He held his penis in his hand and smiled. "All right; I'll get it yet."

He stepped over to the table and dumped out the rest of the speed. It made four very heavy lines. He snorted two of them and lit another joint.

While he smoked, he sat on the couch and flipped the page. "Well, look at what we have here. It's a sweet little Baylor Baptist girl." Carol Manners. Blond, of course. Pretty and clean and innocent. "Kissed once, but never been touched," Steve said, laughing softly. "Look at you, Miss Manners; you've still got a little baby fat in just the right places. Maybe I should fuck you gently, the old fashioned way, with me on top and you with your eyes shut tight. Maybe I could get you pregnant and send you home to daddy with sad stories about liars and madmen robbing you of your innocence."

He turned back to Nicole in her leather pants. "Hello, there, little cousin," he whispered. He closed his eyes and pictured Nicole showing up unexpectedly at the next Campbell family reunion. She's dressed in cut off blue jeans with a silver dollar-sized hole in the rear, white tank top, no bra, and Birkenstock sandals. Devilish grin. Eager, playful eyes.

After a minimum of poking and sniffing around each other, they slip away from the party to smoke a joint in the back seat of her car, a restored '55 Buick. Getting high on pot and expectations. Conversations about the *Playboy* shoot and sexual morals, which she rejects entirely. "Morals imply right and wrong, which requires judgment; those are concepts without relevance to sexual behavior between consenting adults," she says.

150

Further conversation about attraction and incest between second cousins, followed by confessions regarding sexual preferences, sexual fantasies, and favorite sexual experiences.

Steve's penis stood fully erect now, responding nicely to fantasy and gentle masturbation. He laid *Playboy* down, closed his eyes, and held Nicole's image tightly in his mind. Stroking himself harder now, his mind returned to the back seat of the Buick. His hands underneath her shirt. His mouth on her hard, erect nipples. Pulling her shorts and her panties down and off. Burying his face in her cunt until she squirms and moans into one orgasm and then another. Entering her briefly and then withdrawing to put himself into her mouth, allowing her to taste herself while she gives him head.

Stroking harder, Steve reached for his climax. Almost there, but losing it; close again, very close, but losing it once more.

"Damn it," he said. He opened his eyes, caught his breath, and glanced around the room. Daylight shone through the windows and door. He relaxed for a moment, then brought his mind back to Nicole, naked, sweaty, and sizzling in the backseat of the car. Kneeling over her, in her mouth, guided by her hands grasping his butt, thrusting deeply into her mouth and throat, again and again and again and again.

Fully erect, close to coming, almost there, but just not quite. Beating himself hard and fast. Out of her mouth now, spreading her legs wide with his hands and entering her, banging against her, over and over. Nicole taking every bit of him, moaning loudly through multiple orgasms. Very close now, very close; "Come on, damn it; come on; come on." But still unable to get there.

Steve opened his eyes again. Frustrated and tired, he looked at his penis. The tip was red and swollen. He slowed his stroke and relaxed, his head and shoulders propped against one arm of the sofa, one leg draped over the back of it, the other lying off the front edge to the floor. He breathed deeply and continued the slower stroke. "Come on, goddamn it," he said. "At least give me this."

Despite his plea, his erection began to soften in his hand. He got up off of the couch and stood still until his balance was good enough to walk over to the table. He snorted the last two lines of speed, opened a beer, and walked out to the front porch. He spread the blanket out and lay on top of it. The early morning sun felt warm and reassuring on his body.

He closed his eyes and sipped the beer. He felt nothing from the speed.

He directed his mind to Miss Manners, the lily white Baylor beauty. Stroking himself gently now, he pictured her lying on her back, on a pallet on the floor, beckoning him to come to her and to please be gentle. Soft and plump, tasting sweet and pure, groaning softly as he enters her, then louder as he picks up speed, and louder yet as he pounds against her, then calling out "Oh, God; oh, God; oh, my God, my God," as she comes for the first time ever.

Stroking his penis with one hand, Steve soaked the middle finger of the other with spit from his mouth, then worked the finger into his anus. Moving the finger gently in and out while holding his feet and legs in the air and spread apart to give himself a larger opening.

He pictured Miss Manners with her face between his legs and her tongue in his anus, moving it in and out and in and out, pushing harder, breathing harder, pushing harder. Licking and sucking his balls now, then the head of his penis. Working her way up the front of his body, her blond hair tickling his stomach and chest, her breasts touching his legs and groin. Sucking his nipples, bringing them erect. Moving up further, her full, soft mouth on his; her tongue reaching for his throat.

She's breathing hard now, wanting him desperately. Mounting him, guiding his penis into her, moving herself up and down, gently at first, then faster. Moaning loudly, coming hard once and then again and then once more.

Touching the edge of orgasm, Steve stroked hard, pounding his fist against his body with each stroke downward and stretching his foreskin up completely with each stroke upward. Holding his finger still, buried deep into his anus. "Come on, goddamn it; come on; come on," he whispered. Pounding himself, reaching desperately now for a climax. "Come on; come on; come on," he repeated.

Finally, frustrated and out of breath, he slowed his stroke. "It's not gonna happen," he said. "I'm beat."

Steve opened his eyes. He moved his hands away from his body and sprawled out on his back on the blanket. "I can't believe it. I can't even get my goddamn rocks off. What a dirty goddamn trick."

His penis remained engorged but lost its stiffness and lay heavily against his abdomen. It felt tender and sore. He fingered it delicately and stroked it again, very gently, with his fingertips, knowing, then accepting that it wasn't going to work. He let go and sat upright.

The sun's heat hit him full in his face and chest. He looked at his watch; it was 8:40. He scooted back and leaned against the front of the house. He finished off the open beer and inventoried his condition.

Physically, he felt used up, very weak and very shaky. His facial, neck, and shoulder muscles twitched; his limbs jerked involuntarily every few minutes. Mentally, he felt actively brain-dead. Constant buzzing in his head competed with random, meaningless, unconnected thoughts. Emotionally, he felt flatly depressed. Given the option of dying where he sat, he very well may have taken it.

He closed his eyes and tried to relax, but images of his failed sexual debacle inundated his consciousness. And as the images came and went, he experienced feelings of intense disgust, self-loathing, and shame. Tears welled up in his eyes as he pictured himself defiling his body. "Only a sick son of a bitch would degrade himself that way. Only a very sick bastard would humiliate himself in front of the goddamn world."

He hung his head between his knees and stared at the porch floor. "I've got to do something with myself, Ginger," he said without looking up. "If I don't do something pretty soon, I'm going to kill myself, either by accident or on purpose. I can't live like this. I just can't do it. I take one step forward and two steps back, then two forward and three back. I win battles, but I'm losing the goddamn war. I never thought I'd say this, and it breaks my heart to say it, but I'm worse than the old man. I really am; I'm worse than Dad."

He looked around and realized that Ginger was not with him. He called her name, then heard her scratch at the front door from inside the house. He leaned over and pushed the door open for her to come out, and when he sat upright again, he felt dizzy and thought for a moment that he might faint. He tilted his head down, and the feeling passed.

"Well, old girl, what now?" he said. "One thing's for damn sure; this trip is definitely over. What do you think are the chances we could make it home alive today? Fifty-fifty? Probably not that good, huh? Hell, you might not even want to ride in the same vehicle with a goddamn pervert who can barely walk from one spot to the next. I wouldn't blame you if you didn't."

Steve considered the options—stay or go? The only reasonable option was to stay put. Driving a vehicle in his present condition would be really, really stupid. Suicidal, perhaps. But if he could beat the odds and pull it off, he could lie down and go to sleep in his own bed in his own home. He yearned for home.

"Let's see what we can do," he said. "If we don't make it, at least we can say we died trying."

Steve moved slowly and deliberately. Despite physical weakness, poor coordination, and bad balance, he collected his gear and packed it into the bed of the truck. Then he closed up the house. As he walked away from it, he said, "Sorry, old friend. Better luck to us both next trip. Try to stay on your feet till then."

He took a cold beer from the ice chest and climbed in behind the wheel. He patted the dash with his hand and said, "Take us home, Cleo. Can you do that one more time? I'll make a deal with you. If you'll get us there in one piece, I'll give you a wash and wax, and I'll change your oil and filter. I promise, and Ginger here is your witness. If you don't get us there, please make sure we don't survive the effort."

He started the motor. As he shifted into reverse, he looked once again at the farmhouse. It looked old and sad. "I know how you feel," he said. He studied his watch. It was exactly 10:10. He backed up the truck and then crept forward onto the narrow dirt road leading to the main gate out of the ranch. They were 170 miles from home.

Steve felt empty and afraid. "I can do this," he said softly. "I've driven fucked up a million times before, and I've always made it home. Surely I can do it one more time."

Moving forward, slipping off the road to the left, over-correcting and slipping off to the right. Stopping for a moment to gather his wits and then starting up again. It took ten minutes to travel the first mile from the farmhouse to the gate, which was locked. Steve put Cleo in Park, opened the door, and got out. Halfway to the gate, he returned to make sure that the gearshift was in Park. "Don't fuck up, Campbell," he said. "Keep your mind right here; keep it here. You can do this." He unlocked and opened the gate, drove through it, then closed and locked it back. Climbing into the cab, he said, "You see? This isn't so goddamn difficult. If you'll just stay present. Just stay focused and keep your mind right here, right now."

The dirt road from the gate to Highway 281 was wider, flatter, and straighter than the one from the house to the gate. Steve stayed on the road easily and quickly gained confidence. He shoved a Jesse Colin Young tape into the player, and for a few minutes, he believed that the trip home might not be as big a deal as he had thought.

As he approached the highway, he saw the Stop sign clearly. His mind reacted appropriately; it picked up his right foot and placed it squarely onto the brake. But in a flash of panic, he realized that the foot had not mirrored the mind's action. In that moment of realization and fear, he slammed on the brake and slid at an angle through the stop sign, coming to rest in a cloud of dust at the edge of the highway. He looked around instinctively. He saw no other cars. No one had seen his mistake.

He felt an instant of relief and then a wave of terror. "Mother fucking son of a bitch!" he yelled. Ginger jumped up from the floor onto the seat. Her eyes were wide open, and she panted heavily. Steve glanced at her and said, "It's okay, Ginger. I'm just a little nervous, that's all." He reached over to pet her and noticed that his hand was trembling. He took a deep breath and said, "We might be in for one hell of a ride after all. One hell of a fucking ride."

Steve straightened Cleo's wheels and backed up so that the front end aligned perfectly with the Stop sign. "Just like it says in the book, officer," he said to himself. He looked to his left and to his right several times and then pulled out onto the highway, pointing north. Eyes wide open. Heart pounding. "Concentrate, Steve; concentrate every second."

Thankful for a deserted road, he moved forward cautiously, gaining speed very gradually, until the speedometer read 50 miles per hour. "I'm a goddamn rocket in slow motion," he whispered.

He stared at the double yellow stripe, just to the left of his left front wheel. "Hold that line," he said. He noticed that his wrists and forearms hurt. He looked at his hands; his fingers and knuckles were white from gripping the wheel so tightly. He loosened his grip. The fingers were stiff and aching. He opened and closed each hand several times. "Relax, old boy. You're doing good. Just relax and concentrate on the road. You can do this."

Jesse Colin Young's voice filled the cab. Steve's mind wandered to the memory of Jesse Colin Young on a twin concert bill with Jimmy Buffett at the Austin Municipal Coliseum just a few months before. He caught the image of Jesse and his band on stage playing and singing, and his little boy, who looked to be two or three years old, toddling out onto the stage toward him. A pretty young woman, presumably Jesse's wife, walked out in pursuit.

When Jesse noticed them on stage, he smiled and strolled over to the child, took his outstretched hand, and gently gave it to the woman. She in turn quietly turned him around and nudged him back from where he came. The child turned and waved goodbye to his dad, who smiled and waved back. The band did not miss a beat. The audience applauded its appreciation.

Steve felt touched by the experience of the adults' patience and tenderness. The memory settled nicely inside of his heart.

Over the top of that memory, however, Steve heard the words, "Rough ride. Rough ride. Rough ride" in his mind. "What?" he said. Then he heard them again. This time they were louder and more urgent. "Rough ride. Rough ride. Damn rough ride." And then, very loud, "ROUGH RIDE! ROUGH RIDE! ROUGH RIDE! FUCK! I'M OFF THE GODDAMN ROAD." His eyes snapped open, and he saw to his horror that he had drifted to the right, out of his lane, off the road, off the shoulder, and into the gravel and weeds that lined the outer edges of the roadway.

He instinctively jerked the wheel hard to the left, and when he did, the truck went into a power slide, with all four wheels perpendicular to the road. He heard himself yelling something but could not hear what it was. He yanked the wheel back to the right, trying to correct the slide, but he over-corrected again, and

155

they flew into an accelerated clockwise spin. They spun around and around for what felt like forever, then drifted to a standstill in the grass and weeds, about ninety feet to the right of the road.

Steve sat motionless, frozen, still gripping the wheel tightly with both hands, staring straight ahead, eyes wide open, jaw clenched, ears ringing, body rigid. Then he heard Ginger yelping and whining and felt her struggling violently to free herself from being trapped on the floor between the seat and his legs. He raised his legs to let her free. Unharmed but highly agitated, she jumped up onto the seat and climbed into Steve's lap.

"Son of a bitch and holy fucking shit," Steve whispered. "We dodged a bullet that time, old girl." He let go of the steering wheel and put his trembling hands around Ginger's trembling body. He took a deep breath and looked up and down the highway. There were no cars either way. "Small favors," he said.

He moved Ginger out of his lap, reached down to the ignition switch, and turned it to the right. Cleo started right up. He smiled and shook his head. "More small favors," he said. He slowly pulled forward and closer to the road until they sat just to the right of the shoulder. Then he killed the motor, opened the door, and stepped out onto the ground. Ginger scampered out after him.

Steve looked in the bed of the truck. His gear was scattered but appeared to be all there. He leaned against the wheel well. "Jesus fucking Christ," he muttered. "What the hell am I trying to do? Do I really want to die today? Is that the program?" He looked to the heavens and said, "Well, God? Is it still 'simple?' Is that still the answer? Damn it, can you help me here?"

He reached into the cooler and got a beer. He sat on Cleo's stepside and took a long swig. The taste of it almost made him gag, but the cold liquid felt wonderfully soothing. He took a deep breath and another long swig.

He closed his eyes and tried to relax. "The irony of this is just too much," he thought. "Here's your intellectually complete graduate student, the soon-to-be psychologist, the new man pursuing his dream within the context of his new life, sitting on the side of the goddamn highway unable to drive 170 miles in a straight line home. Is that ironic, or what?"

He visualized what a ball some conservative South Texas county coroner could have with his body, describing his violent death to the reporter from the *Three Rivers Gazette*. "His name was Stephen Campbell. He was a twenty-eight year old Caucasian male. He died instantly, as close as I can tell. Cause of death was massive head and internal injuries. Took his dog out with him. It's a damn miracle that he didn't take out some innocent family along with him, too.

"Mr. Campbell's blood alcohol level was 3.2, more than triple the legal limit. His body also contained very substantial levels of methamphetamine (that's speed), cocaine, THC (that's marijuana), and LSD. This young man was a walking drug lab. Apparently, he was one of those Austin, Texas hippie types, long hair and all. It's pitiful, really. A damn sorry waste of human life, if you ask me. Like all the rest of his kind that gets caught up in that lifestyle, he was probably some poor innocent mother's son. Anyway, the sheriff has the full report. If you want more details, talk to him. I'm done with my part." Maybe the reporter would make a few phone calls. Probably not.

Steve finished the beer and threw the empty on the ground. He imagined Lois standing over his grave saying, "I told you so, but you just wouldn't listen." He thought about his obituary and his tombstone, and he constructed wording for both.

Speed and coke make me hyper.
Beer and pot slow me down.
LSD's a windshield wiper
That takes my soul downtown.
Cocaine puts me in a frenzy.
Beer puts me to sleep.
LSD rips my defenses
And makes me dream of sheep.
Crystal meth lets me fly,
Just like speeding cars.
Marijuana leaves me mellow
And craving candy bars.
Mix 'um up, suck 'um down,
And stick um up my ass.
LSD, speed and coke, alcohol, & grass.

He opened another beer. Then he dug a roach out of the ashtray and smoked it. With some effort, he coaxed Ginger back into the cab, started up the truck, and slowly pulled forward. Approaching the highway again, Steve took a deep breath and looked south. An 18-wheeler blew past, blasting them with a blanket of wind that bumped and shook Cleo and sent a shudder through Steve's body.

He looked south again. Seeing that the road was clear, he pressed the gas pedal. He pressed it harder than he intended, though, and instead of pulling out onto the highway gracefully, Cleo's rear tires spun in the loose gravel and then burned rubber when they hit the road.

Steve glanced at Ginger. "Here we go, my innocent friend," he said.

CHAPTER 34

Steve resolutely pointed Cleo north. "Okay, Steve, no more fantasies; no more distractions. Just focus on the road."

After a few minutes, he realized that the cab was quiet. "Old Jesse Colin Young must have run out of things to sing about," he said. "Man, I can relate." He stuck Fleetwood Mac's *Bare Trees* into the player and turned up the volume.

Steve's concentration and driving continued to be erratic, but both stabilized somewhat. He kept his eyes open and focused. When he drifted one way or the other, he saw what was happening and carefully corrected the line. He turned right onto Highway 72, a short stretch of two-lane highway leading to Kenedy, his boyhood home.

They reached the Kenedy city limits at 12:25 PM. When he saw the city limits sign, Steve breathed a sigh of relief. "Phase One accomplished, sir," he said. It had taken him two hours and fifteen minutes to travel the thirty-two miles from The Quarters Ranch to Kenedy.

Once inside the Kenedy city limits, Steve drove slowly and carefully across town to the house where he had lived until age six with his grandparents—Mama Rogers, the one he trusted, and Papa Rogers, the one he missed the most. The house had a For Sale sign in the tiny front yard. Steve turned into the gravel driveway and parked alongside the house. He and Ginger got out of the truck and walked around to the back yard. He peered through the windows and saw that the house was empty. He tried the back door, and sure enough, it opened.

Steve's mind immediately flooded with strong memories of his youth. A lump rose in his throat. Tears flooded his eyes. He brushed them away with his hands.

He walked slowly and methodically with Ginger through every room of the house, pointing out to her how each room had functioned—what went here, what went there, who slept here, who slept there, who sat here, who sat there.

When they entered his old bedroom, Steve lay down on the floor in the spot where his youth bed had been. He closed his eyes and let his thoughts drift backwards to better times. He recalled one night when he was four years old, and he threw up on himself in his bed. When he tried to call Mama Rogers for help, his little voice was weak, and it came out barely a whisper. Even so, Mama walked into the room.

When she saw what had happened, she said, "Oh, my goodness, Stevey; you poor, sweet boy," and she bathed him and changed his bed and sat patiently with him until he fell asleep again.

Steve pictured Papa Rogers, his hero. Papa stood tall, beefy, hairy, and strong. He was Steve's best friend. Steve recalled how the two of them went to the Golf Hotel Coffee Shop, five blocks from home in downtown Kenedy, at exactly 7:30 AM, seven days a week. Papa drove his black Ford pickup truck; Steve stood beside him, wedged against the seat back by Papa's big right arm. Papa drank two cups of coffee. Steve ate a roll of LifeSavers. People called them both by name.

Steve remembered the last time he saw his grandfather. It was the day before he and Sheri and Lois and Henry left Kenedy for Henry's two-year tour of duty in Japan. Papa lay in a hospital bed, in a coma, under an oxygen tent, dying. He looked asleep, and Steve talked to him as though he were. He died two weeks later, while Steve and his family were on an ocean liner in the middle of the Pacific. Steve remembered Lois crying uncontrollably. He experienced his own grief many years later.

At some point, Steve dozed off into light sleep. He dreamed that he opened his eyes and saw Mama Rogers enter the room and sit beside him. "Oh, Honey," she said, touching his forehead with her fingertips. "You're so tired, and you seem so unhappy. It breaks my heart to see you this way."

"I'm sorry, Mama," Steve replied. "I don't like for you to see me looking like this. If I had known you were going to be here, I would have cleaned up and put on nicer clothes. I might have even cut my hair. I would never want to disappoint you."

She smiled and stroked his head. "Gosh, Steve, I didn't even notice your hair or your clothes. I noticed your heart. You're distressed. You're hurting."

"Yeah, Mama, it's true. I am. I'm not feeling good about myself at all. I'm going home, though, and when I get there, I'm going to be okay. I'm going to take better care of myself. I'm going to get healthy again. It'll be okay, I think."

"Yes, I'm sure it will be," she said, nodding her head and smiling. "Remember, though, Steve, that it doesn't have to be a big, complicated issue. It's much simpler than you might imagine."

"Yes, Mama. That's what God said. 'It's simple.' That's what God said. What do you think he meant?"

"I think it's a prescription for a happy life. I think it means to always just do the next right thing—to pay attention to what's in front of you and leave the rest alone.

"You know, Steve, when you and Sheri and your mother left here to go off to Japan with your dad, it was the saddest day of my life. And then your Papa died shortly after that. I thought surely my world had ended. But it hadn't. I had an ace in the hole. It was my faith in God. I had a wonderful life, even after those losses. I have no regrets."

"Mama, do you ever see Papa?"

"Yes, of course I do. I see him all the time."

Steve looked into his grandmother's eyes. "I miss y'all so much. I thought I saw Papa last night, but now I'm not sure."

"Yes, I know," Mama said. "You're not sure of anything right now." She took Steve's hand into hers and closed her eyes. Then she was gone.

Steve opened his eyes slowly. He knew that he had been dreaming, and he wanted to remember the dream. As perfectly as he could, he repeated it to himself word for word several times. Then he recalled in minute detail the previous night's regression and Papa Roger's presence.

"Was that really just last night?" he asked himself. "That's hard to believe. Thanks again for the visit, Papa, and thank you, too, Mama."

He nudged Ginger, who lay asleep beside him. "Are you about ready to hit the road, old girl? Let's eat a little something and then get back to it. I know you probably want to get home just as badly as I do."

They left the house and returned to the truck. Steve opened a beer and a bag of chips. He ate a few and gave Ginger a few. They shared a can of Vienna sausages and a sleeve of saltine crackers. He had a granola bar for dessert. To his surprise, the food tasted pretty good, and it stayed down with no problem. He finished the beer and then drank some water.

Steve traveled back roads from Kenedy to Austin. Driving at or under 50 miles per hour the whole way, they passed through Karnes City, Helena, Nixon, Luling, Lockhart, and a few other tiny towns that he did not really see. He drove with the air conditioning on high and with the windows rolled down. He played rock and roll cassette tapes very loud. He talked to Ginger. He stopped and got out of the truck every fifteen or twenty minutes to stretch his body and clear his head.

He bought gas in Leesville, where the attendant glared at him and asked him to pay "in cash, up front, if you don't mind." He drank a beer every hour on the hour as his reward system for staying alive, and he took a hit or two of pot whenever the thought crossed his mind.

Steve parked Cleo on the street in front of his house at 8:12 PM, ten hours and two minutes after leaving The Quarters Ranch, 170 miles away. He turned off the motor, closed his eyes, and sat perfectly still. He was completely spent. His body ached from head to toe. He might have cried but for fear of being seen by the people milling around outside of The Roam In.

After a few minutes, he got out and walked up to the house. He propped open the front door, and while Ginger ran into and out of and around the house and yard, he slowly transported his gear from the truck to the living room floor. Then he locked the front door, opened a can of beer, turned off the light, and sat on the couch.

"Unbelievable," he whispered. "Just totally fucking unbelievable."

He finished the beer, opened another, and ambled into the bedroom. He pulled off his boots and his jeans and sat on the edge of the bed. He stared at the wall and took a long swig of beer. "So...what now?" he asked himself. "Go on like nothing happened? Nothing did, really. When you get right down to it, I went to the ranch, and now I'm safe and sound in my own bedroom. At this point, it's just another Saturday night, right? Or should I get honest, and look at the problem?"

He laughed softly. "The problem? What problem is that? If something isn't working, you just change it, right? God, how many times have I promised changes this year? I'm up and down, up and down, up and down. Today, Stevey-boy, is down; today you found the gutter. Man, if you have any intelligence and courage whatsoever, then you damn well better call on it now, 'cause face it, motherfucker, your life is shit.

"You might be able to get away with it a little while longer if you try really hard, but the truth is...your life is shit."

Steve set the beer on the nightstand and rested his head on his hands. "I've been here for one whole year, and I'm nowhere. In fact, I've probably gone backwards. I don't remember ever feeling this fucking low. So...I ask again, what now? Call Mom? She'll just tell me to quit drinking and using. How about Rachel? She helped me once. Or did she, really?"

Steve finished the beer and looked at the can. "I think you've turned on me," he said. "You don't work very well any more." He walked to the living room and took another one out of the cooler and opened it. Then he walked into the bathroom and looked at himself in the mirror. "Look at you, man. You're disgusting. Talk about death warmed over, I think maybe you *are* dead. And if you aren't, you should be."

He sat on the bed again, picked up the telephone, and dialed Rachel's number. There was no answer. "Thank God," he said, as he laid the receiver down.

He fell back onto the bed and closed his eyes. After a minute, he whispered, "God, thank you for letting me get home. I know I'm a mess, and I'm sorry about that. Can you please help me turn things around? Will you? I'm afraid I'm hopelessly lost. I know I only come to you when I need something. I don't mean to do that. I also know that sometimes I say that I don't believe in you, but that's not true. I do believe in you, regardless of what I say when I'm pissed off at the world. I don't know what else to say except that I'm sorry for being this piece of crap that I am. I'll try to do better, but I need your help. How about it? And, God, I need more than 'It's simple.' That may, in fact, be the answer, but I need more than that right now. Please, I'm asking you."

When Steve opened his eyes, tears blurred his vision. They trickled down the sides of his head to his ears. He wiped them away. He rolled over and laid his head on his pillow. Just as he was dozing off, the phone rang. He picked it up on the sixth ring. "Yeah?" he said.

"Hey, old buddy, where the hell you been? I've been trying to call you all day. And what's the matter? You sound like a real sour puss."

"Hey, Tucker. I'm just tired, man. Very long day, and I'm in bed. What's up?"

"A lot, but to accommodate your fatigue, I'll talk fast. I need a favor, man. I need some smoke. I've got a very, very hot date in about half an hour, and my stash bag is nothing but seeds and stems. You've got to help me out."

"Tucker, you couldn't have called at a worse time. All I have is some personal stash, and not much of that, either. I don't want to sell it, and even if I did, I wouldn't want to fuck with it tonight."

"That's bull shit, man. This is Tucker, not some fucking goofball from the bar. All I need is enough to get her stoned. This chick loves to get high, and I know beyond a shadow of a doubt that if I can toke her up, I can take her down. And I'm telling you, Stevey, this bitch is one hot little number. If you could just see her, you'd be begging me to come over and pick up some of your precious dope. Come on, what do you say?"

"I say get the bitch drunk, and let me get to sleep."

"Ain't the same, man. Come on, I'm begging you. I'm on my goddamn knees. You're the one person, hell, the only person I can count on. Believe me, I'll make it worth your fucking while."

"Tucker, any night but tonight I'd bend over backwards to help you get laid, but I'm telling you, your timing sucks. Call James. He'll fix you up."

"Man, I'm not calling James tonight. I don't know him well enough, and besides that, I don't trust him the way you do. He's got those wild eyes, man. He looks just a little too much like Charles Manson. And don't say I'm exaggerating, either. That one time you dragged me out to his place, I couldn't stop looking over my shoulder. I kept expecting DEA agents to bust through the door with guns blazing. And you saw that arsenal he keeps out there; he's dangerous."

Steve laughed. "He's a good guy, Tucker. He's just a little strange, that's all. Listen, I'll tell you what I'll do, and this is my one and only offer. I'll put a couple of joints in a baggie and put them in my mailbox. You come by and quietly take them out. Don't knock on the door; don't even try to thank me. Go get yourself fucked and come by and tell me about it tomorrow. Is that a deal?"

162

"Yeah, sure; you're a goddamn prince. But make it three or four joints, you cheap son of a bitch. I'll give you details that will make you cream your jeans."

"Yeah, whatever. Anything to get you to leave me the hell alone. You don't deserve this, you know. If you can't get your dick in her without getting her stoned, then you don't deserve to get your dick in her at all."

"You're cute, Campbell. You're a real comedy act. Just get your ass up and put the goods in the box. I won't bother you anymore tonight. Adios, amigo." He hung up.

Steve went into the living room and found his toot bag. He emptied the contents onto the floor. Paraphernalia, empty vials, and a baggie with three rolled joints and about a half ounce of tops. He put the joints, along with one nice bud, into a baggie and stuffed it into his mailbox, just outside the front door. He smiled, thinking about Tucker's frantic search for the pot that would get him laid. He pictured him careening down the road at 90 miles an hour at that very moment, hell bent on picking up the pot and the babe before the whole deal somehow fell through the cracks. "What a stupid fucker," Steve said to himself, still smiling.

He went to the closet and retrieved the rest of his stash. He had one ounce of pot, and nothing else. He took out one small bud and then combined the two bags into one and set it carefully in the back of the freezer. "I'm going to retire you for a little while," he said. "Don't worry, though; I won't forget about you. I'm just going to let you sit a while." Then he rolled the bud into a joint, lit it, opened a beer, turned off all of the lights, sat on the sofa, and relaxed. About halfway through the smoke, he heard Tucker run up the front steps, grab the bag out of the mailbox, and run back to his car.

After he finished the smoke and the beer, Steve went to bed. He closed his eyes, dropped off to sleep, and immediately fell into a dream.

In the dream, he was driving Cleo along an unfamiliar country road. He was sober. He felt fresh, relaxed, confident, and happy.

His hair was cut short. His face was tan. His T-shirt revealed strong, muscular arms. A Brewer & Shipley tape played on the stereo: "One toke over the line, sweet Jesus, one toke over the line."

He glanced to his right and noticed a stranger—apparently a hitchhiker—sitting across from him on the passenger's side of the cab. The hitchhiker's face and hands and clothes were filthy, and he looked dead tired. He stared straight ahead but appeared to see nothing. The muscles in his jaw moved rhythmically as he clenched and unclenched his teeth. He looked beat, and he looked angry.

Steve stared at the man for a moment. He felt apprehensive and confused. He did not remember picking him up.

"What's happening, buddy?" he said to the hitchhiker.

"Fuck off, asshole," the man replied in a monotone. He did not look at Steve or change his sullen expression.

"Where you headed?" Steve asked.

"Straight ahead," he answered.

"What's straight ahead?" Steve asked.

"Hell if I know," the hitchhiker replied.

CHAPTER 35

Steve slept through the night and awoke at 5:45 on Sunday morning. He opened his eyes, glanced around the bedroom, sighed with relief, and whispered, "Thank you, God." When he closed his eyes again, images of the previous two days filled his head.

He saw the decaying farmhouse and the swinging bed, on which he never slept. He saw Ginger's curious, gleeful exploration of unfamiliar territory. He revisited his flying dream while dozing in the meadow of the southeast section of the ranch. Then he shifted into the aborted plan—the very badly aborted plan.

He pieced together his memory of the polluted acid trip. There was the good part—Papa Roger's visit. There was the weird and scary part—the journey into the earth's interior, his intense fear, God's message ("It's simple"), and the mysterious lost hours. Then there was the corrupt part—everything that happened after that.

He pictured the degrading, unsuccessful compulsive masturbation and anal penetration scene on the front porch of the house. He recalled the irrational decision to drive home under the influence of LSD, alcohol, pot, speed, and cocaine and the subsequent terrifying near-accidents. He recalled the stop at his boyhood home and the dream about, or perhaps it was a visit from, Mama Rogers. He retraced the tedious, seemingly endless drive back to Austin. He remembered Tucker's crazy phone call.

Finally, he recalled the brief "retirement ceremony" during which he packaged and stored his personal stash in the freezer and smoked his last joint.

He closed his eyes and dozed off again. He awoke to soft daylight at 6:40. He sat up on the edge of the bed and leaned down to scratch Ginger's head.

"Sunday morning," he said. "Wouldn't you know it had to be Sunday? Who ever heard of quitting alcohol and drugs on a weekend? Why couldn't it have been Monday? Or better yet, Tuesday?"

He stood up and shuffled into the bathroom. He caught a glimpse of himself in the mirror as he walked past. "Pitiful," he muttered. He tried to run his fingers through his hair, but tangles and mats prevented it. "Pitiful, pitiful, pitiful," he repeated.

He let Ginger out into the back yard and gave her fresh food and water. Then he walked into the living room and faced the mess that he had left there. He opened the cooler and found everything either floating or submerged in cool water. There were four beers left.

"Christ almighty," he thought. "Thirty-two beers in thirty-six hours. Oh well, I guess when you figure it by the hour, that isn't so bad." He shut the cooler and walked back into the bedroom. He looked at the telephone. He considered calling Rachel, but he knew that was not the call he needed to make.

"I might as well get this over with," he said. He picked up the receiver and held it in his hand until a fast busy signal reminded him to make the call. He got another dial tone and dialed his mother's number.

She answered on the first ring.

"Mother? Hi. It's me, Steve. How ya doing?"

"Oh, hi, Honey. Gosh, you'll never believe this, but I swear I was just thinking about you not more than two minutes ago. I was going to wait a little while and then give you a call. What's going on? It's awfully early to be calling your old mother, especially on a Sunday morning."

"Yeah, well, I know it, but it felt like the thing to do." He paused and took a breath. "Mother, I have a question for you. I'm a little reluctant to ask it, so let's call it a hypothetical question, at least for the time being. Okay?"

"All right, I can do hypothetical questions. Go ahead."

"If I wanted to go to an AA meeting, how would I go about it? I mean, like, how would I know where to go and when and stuff like that?"

Lois hesitated for an instant and then said, "Steve, it's really quite simple. There's a 24-hour phone number that you can call to get meeting times and locations. If you want, that call can be totally anonymous. No one will ask you for your name, or anything else for that matter. That's one way.

"A better way, though, is to talk one-on-one with a member of AA who goes to meetings regularly and could take you to a meeting as his guest. Either way, it's as simple and painless as it could be."

"Well, how would I go about finding the phone number? I mean, I don't know any AA members except for you and Chester."

"I'll tell you what, Steve. If you'll just sit tight for a couple of minutes, I'll make a quick phone call and get right back to you. How does that sound?"

"Well, I guess it sounds okay, but why? Who are you going to call?"

"I'm going to call a friend of mine who has connections in Austin. It will just take a minute or two. Don't go anywhere; just wait for me to call you back, okay?"

"Okay, but listen, Mother, don't blow this all out of proportion. I'm just curious at this point. Do you understand?"

Lois promised that she did.

Steve hung up the receiver and stared at the phone. "Well, the cat's out of the bag now," he said to himself. "Big mistake. I'd lay odds on it."

Steve walked into the kitchen and started making coffee when the phone rang. It had been less than two minutes since his conversation with Lois. In fact, the call came so abruptly that Steve expected it to be from someone other than his mom. He was right.

"Hello? Is this Steve Campbell?" The voice was relaxed and friendly.

"Yes, it is," Steve answered.

"Steve, my name is Al Bommer. I spoke just a moment ago with your mother, Lois. She said that you were interested in information about AA in Austin and that you would like to attend a meeting."

Steve fell silent. He felt his heart rate quicken and face flush warm. Grasping at his composure, he responded. "Well, I don't know, Mr. Bommer. I did speak with my mom in general terms about possibly being interested in learning more about AA, but I'm afraid she must have jumped to conclusions because I never said I was ready to go to a meeting. Where are you calling from? San Antonio?"

"No, no, I'm here in Austin. And actually, I'm probably the one who misunderstood. I'm sorry about that. It's awfully early, you know, and our conversation was quite brief. Anyway, I'm a member of AA, and your mother and I have a good mutual friend in San Antonio who is also an AA member. She got my phone number from him. I go to meetings very regularly, and to tell you the truth, I'd love to take you to one if you have any interest at all in going. And if not, I'd also be glad to just get together with you and talk."

Steve thought for a second. The process was moving too fast. "Yes, well, that's really nice of you, Mr. Bommer. And I might just take you up on it. In fact, why don't you give me your number, and if I decide I want to go to a meeting or get together with you, I'll give you a call."

166

"Sure, Steve. I'll be glad to do that, that is, if you'll promise to call me Al instead of Mr. Bommer. Just for the record, though, I'm going to a meeting tonight. It's a small group, and it's on your side of town. Please don't think I'm being pushy, but I'd be more than happy to swing by and pick you up about 7:30. We could go to the meeting, and I would have you home by 9:30 or 10:00. Any chance of that?"

"I don't know, Al. I've got a lot going on today. I'd hate to say 'yes' and then have to back out on you. But I'll tell you what. Tell me where the meeting is, and I'll try to meet you there."

"Okay, that would be just fine. It's at the First United Methodist Church, on Berkman Drive, about half way between 51st Street and Anderson Lane. Do you know where that is?"

"Yes, I know exactly where it is," Steve lied.

"Good, good. The meeting starts at 8:00 o'clock sharp. I always try to get there a little early so I can visit with people and drink a free cup of coffee. By the way, I'm easy to spot; I'm old and short and bald. Now, Steve, are you sure you don't want me to pick you up? Sometimes it's very hard to get to your first AA meeting. I remember how it was for me. I was a real knucklehead. I probably slowed down and then drove on past a dozen meetings or more before I finally stopped and walked into one. When I finally did, though, it was the smartest move I ever made. That was seventeen years ago, and I'm still sober."

Steve he held his ground. "No, that's okay," he said. "I'll really try to make it, though. And don't worry; it's not like I've never been in an AA meeting before. Actually, I have. I used to go with my mom years ago in San Antonio. Every Friday night was bingo night where she went, and I'd go with her every now and then." He had, in fact, gone with Lois to bingo night once when he was nineteen years old. He won a five-dollar pot and bought two six-packs of beer with it later that same night.

"All right, then. Do you have a pencil handy? I'd like to give you my phone number, just in case. I'm here most of the time, but if I'm not in, my wife, Ellie, can usually track me down. And Steve, you can call me any time, night or day, if you want to talk. I'd like very much to help."

Steve took Al's number. "Thanks, Al," he said. "I appreciate it. And I'll see you tonight unless something unexpected happens."

He hung up the phone and smiled and shook his head. "Well, you've got to give the old gal credit," he said to himself. "She orchestrated that one like a pro."

Steve was impressed not only with Lois' efficiency, but also with Al Bommer's manner. He seemed like the genuine article—concerned, unselfish, and available. He did not push too hard, but he got his point across. He was not obnoxious in any way.

He even backed off at just the right moment. Steve wondered if AA trained people like Al on how to make that kind of phone call.

It occurred to Steve that Lois may have had the connection with Al prearranged for some time and had just been waiting for "the call" to put the plan into action. He looked at the clock. It was 7:10. The entire episode had taken less than fifteen minutes, start to finish. "Pretty damn impressive," he said, laughing softly to himself.

He walked into the kitchen and resumed fixing coffee. "The question is, what now?" he thought. "What would it really be like not to drink? Not get high? What the hell would I do? Who would I hang out with?" Besides Rachel, Lois and Chester were the only people he knew who did not drink.

He recalled the one AA bingo night meeting that he had attended with Lois. He remembered a bunch of middle-aged and older people smoking cigarettes and slugging down hundreds of cups of coffee. He remembered thinking that there was not one cool person in the whole place except for himself.

Steve cleaned up the living room and put away his gear. He changed the sheets on his bed and then cleaned the kitchen. He "retired" his toot bag to the back of the bathroom linen closet right next to his nest egg. When he finished cleaning the house, he went to work on himself. After a hot shower, shampoo, and clean clothes, he looked at himself in the mirror. "Back among the living," he said.

He poured a cup of coffee, walked outside, and sat on the front porch. It was a nice morning. The sky was clear. The neighborhood was quiet. He felt revived. After a few minutes, he saw Carla next door, guiding her bicycle out of the house. He wandered over.

"Hey, Carla. Thanks for keeping an eye on the house. I appreciate it."

"No problem, Stevey. You're back early. Did you have a good time?"

"No, not really. To tell you the truth, Carla, it was pretty much a nightmare. Where you headed?"

"Going to church like a good girl. Want to come?"

"No, no, no, no, no. Thanks, though. Listen, you wouldn't have time for a cup of coffee would you? I'm buying."

Carla caught the faint pleading in his eyes and said, "Well, a quick one probably wouldn't hurt anything. I suppose God won't mind if I'm a minute or two late."

Settled at the table, Steve said, "Carla, I've been thinking about drinking and drugging. *My* drinking and drugging, to be more exact. I got so fucked up Friday and yesterday...well, you wouldn't believe it even if I told you. I'll just say it's a miracle that I made it home in one piece last night.

"When I got out there to my dad's place Friday morning, I had a real specific plan for the weekend, including what drugs I was going to use and when I was going to use them. It was supposed to be a time for me to just chill out, relax, and get mentally prepared for graduate school to start. Well, let me tell you; that ain't what happened. I'll spare you the gory details and just say it was really bad.

"Here's the thing that bothers me, though, and it leads up to the point I want to make. It seems like I've done that several times this past year. You know, something happens, like I say or do something stupid when I'm loaded, and because of that, I set limits on how much I'm going to use. And then all of sudden, sometimes for no apparent reason, I'm off and running again.

"I don't want to make this a long, boring story, but I do want to ask you something. Do you think I drink and use too much? I mean, have you ever thought I was out of control? Dixie thinks I have a problem with it. Do you? Tell me the truth."

Carla looked at Steve for a moment and answered carefully. "You know, Steve, I really don't know. I mean, I know you like to party. Hell, we all do. I guess we've all seen each other a little over the top a few times. I can't honestly say that I've ever seen you totally out of control, though. Not any more than anyone else anyway."

"Yeah, well, you're probably right. Maybe I'm making a mountain out of a molehill. It was bad yesterday, though. I'd be embarrassed to tell you the whole story. I almost wrecked my truck several times, though, and it took me all day long—ten goddamn hours—to drive 170 miles. I was pretty scared, to tell you the truth. I don't know; maybe I should just cut back, or maybe quit everything for a little while and let my system get good and clean and then see how I feel about it. What do you think?"

"Steve, I wish I knew. I'd love to have the answer for you, but I just don't. For one thing, I'd hate to talk you out of something that might be right for you. I mean, the truth be known, we'd probably all be better off if we didn't drink or use drugs, especially those really toxic ones like speed and cocaine. I mean, I've thought about it before—not for you, but for myself. There have been days when I felt bad about what I said or did the night before, and days when I thought I should cut back. I've never seriously thought I ought to quit altogether, but I have thought about maybe needing to use better judgment."

"Really, Carla? Now that surprises me. I don't think I've ever seen you so loaded that you weren't in control or anything like that. I mean, when did you feel that way?"

"Well, okay, I can give you a couple of examples. One was that night when there were six or seven of us doing shots and bongs, and I took my shirt off and stuck my breasts in Carlos' face. Remember that?

"Yeah, but hell, I just thought that was funny. You know, we were all laughing and playing around. I never thought about that as being out of control or being a problem."

"Well, I did. I thought about it a lot. For one thing, it embarrassed Carlos, and I felt terrible about that. For another, it embarrassed me. It wasn't about being naked. You know me; I'm not modest, to say the least. The point is that I wouldn't have done it if I had not been drunk. I mean, it's no great big deal or anything. It's just an example of feeling bad about something I did when I was drinking, you know?

"The other example that comes to mind right away is the same kind of thing. Remember last Thanksgiving, when I let Tucker spend the night with me? I regretted that the moment I woke up the next morning. And again, it's not about having sex. Hell, you know how much I love sex. It's about the decision to sleep with Tucker. You know as well as I do that he's not my type. He just happened to have the right equipment in his pants when I was too drunk to use better judgment. That was a wrong decision for me. It was a compromise of my values. If it had been you, or even Dixie, I would have felt great about it, but it wasn't. It was Tucker. See what I mean?"

"Yeah, I do. I see exactly what you mean." Steve laughed. "Hell, Carla, if I really tried, I could probably come up with a hundred examples of times like that, when I've done stuff drunk that I'd never in a million years do when I was sober. I mean, it's like Friday night. I planned to relax and get a lot of sleep. Guess how much I got. Zilch. And I know it was because I was too fucked up to stick to my original plan, which, by the way, was a very good one.

"Then yesterday morning, I got in my truck and headed home when I couldn't even walk a straight line, much less drive one. And I know you remember last year when I announced to the world that Dixie and I had slept together. You know, I could have lost a very good friend over that little screw up. I never would have done that when I was in control of myself.

"Anyway, not to change the subject, but you'll never believe what I did earlier this morning. I called my mother, who's been in AA for about ten years, and asked her about AA meetings. She turned around and had an AA guy from here in Austin call me and invite me to go to an AA meeting with him tonight. This was all at 7:00 AM."

"Yeah? Well, are you going to go?"

"I don't know. Maybe. I told him I might meet him there. I don't suppose you'd want to go with me, would you?"

"Umm, I don't think so, Steve. Nothing against AA, but I don't think it would be my bag. What the hell, though, maybe you should do it. I mean, what could it hurt?"

"Yeah, well, we'll see. I'm going to think about it. So...anyway...I hope I haven't made you miss church. It's funny, Carla; I've known you for over a year, and I never even knew that you go to church."

Carla smiled. "Well, I don't broadcast it. It's just something I do. In fact, I guess I better get going. Are you okay?"

"Yeah, I'm fine. I'll let you know what I decide. And listen, Carla, thanks for taking the time. I really appreciate it. I mean it. I owe you one."

Carla laughed. "You're beholden. That is a word, isn't it? Beholden? Anyway, I'll see you later. Be cool." She kissed Steve lightly on the lips and left. Steve stood on the front porch and watched her ride off. "Going to church, for crying out loud," he muttered to himself.

He walked into the house and into the bedroom, where he culled five small roaches from the ashtray. He peeled away the old paper, dumped the contents onto a sheet of new paper, cleaned away the burned edges, and rolled the residuals into a skinny joint. "AA," he thought. "I wonder if you can smoke pot and still go to AA."

CHAPTER 36

Before Steve had a chance to light the joint, the phone rang. It was Lois.

"Did Al Bommer get you?"

"Yes, of course he got me. How could he not? I mean, the phone rang before I could even get the coffee started. Pretty swift move, Mother. In the advertising business, I think they call that tactic 'bait and switch,' and it's illegal. Anyway, I talked to him. I told him I might meet him tonight at a meeting. But I guess you already know that. Am I right?"

"No, Steve, I didn't know that. I'm glad to hear it, though. What are the chances you'll really go?"

"To be perfectly honest, Mother, I don't know. I'm thinking about it. I told him I'd be there unless something unexpected came up."

"Well...something unexpected is almost certain to come up, then. You'll find some good reason not to make it. I've been around long enough to know how these things work. I do wish you'd go, though, Steve. I really wish you'd go."

Steve heard the disappointment in her voice. "Mother, listen; please don't bug me about this. I know how you feel, and you might be right, but I'm already starting to regret having called you about it. I don't even know if I need to go, you know? Nobody else seems to think I do, and these are people who see me almost every day and who know me really well. Just because you think I have a drinking problem doesn't necessarily mean that I do. I mean, I probably do, but I'm not convinced of that."

"So what would it take to convince you, Steve? Why did you call this morning? Something pretty significant must have happened to make you call me at 7:00 o'clock on Sunday morning."

Steve fiddled with the joint in his hand, and the thought of lighting it while he was on the phone with Lois crossed his mind. "It wasn't that big a deal. I mean, I called you this morning mainly because I had a bad day yesterday. What happened was, I went down to the ranch, and I drank more than I should have. That's it. When I woke up this morning, it was on my mind, so I called. I didn't expect to have strangers calling my house and trying to drag me off to AA meetings, for Christ's sake. I was just curious about the process, you know, in case I decided to check it out. Mother, I'm not trying to be defensive, although I'm sure I sound that way. I just don't want it to turn into some big damn issue that we get cross-wise over."

Lois backed off. "Okay, Steve; I wish you trusted me enough to really talk to me about it, but I can see that's not going to happen, not now anyway. So I'll just say my piece and then I'll do my best to drop it. Can you listen to me for a minute longer?"

"Sure, go ahead."

"I've been worried about you and your drinking for a long time, ever since one night twelve years ago, when you were sixteen, and you came home drunk and angry and talkative. I don't even know if you remember that, but I'll never forget it. I believe that it may have been one reason why I eventually got sober, because as you know, I blame myself for a lot of your problems. And it occurred to me that night that you were headed down the same damn road that your dad and I were on. It broke my heart, and for the last two years of my drinking, I never forgot that night, and I never again enjoyed being drunk.

"Steve, I know a lot about alcoholism. I don't know anything about drug addiction, but I do know a lot about alcoholism, and I know a lot of alcoholics. I've watched them come and go in AA for ten years. I've listened to their stories. I've seen them get sober, and I've seen them twist off and lose their sobriety. I've even watched a few die.

"I think by now I know the program. I know first hand what it looks like and what it feels like. I know that no one but you can say that you are an alcoholic. At the same time, I also know that every alcoholic needs help being able to see whether or not there is a problem. Without help, he's almost certain to live in

172

denial about his drinking—about what it's doing to him and what it's costing him, and I don't just mean what it's costing him in dollars, either. Steve, that help can't come from friends, especially drinking buddies. It has to come from someone who knows what the hell he's talking about. Preferably from someone who's been there.

"All I'm asking is that you step back and take an honest look. Right now might be your best chance yet to do that. Obviously, your protective covering—your denial, or whatever it is—around your drinking has cracked a little, at least enough for you to pick up the phone and call me. I don't believe that you would have done that strictly out of curiosity.

"The last thing I want to say is that I love you. I love you dearly, and I want you to have a happy life. I don't mean to meddle in your private affairs. I swear I don't. But I am your mother, and that gives me a certain amount of meddling rights. Don't you agree?"

Steve smiled for the first time since the conversation began. "I guess so. I really don't mind all that much. I know you mean well. I'm not questioning that. And who knows? I might just surprise you. It sure as hell wouldn't be the first time I surprised you, would it?"

"Honey, that's the understatement of the year. Sometimes I think you get a certain amount of sadistic pleasure from surprising me." Lois paused for a moment and then said, "Steve, please go to the meeting with Al. If you won't do it for yourself, then do it for me. Just see what happens. Gosh, what could it hurt? It's one hour out of your life."

"I don't know, Mother. We'll see, and I'll let you know. Please stop worrying, though. I think I must be doing much better than you imagine. Try to remember that. I'll call you later."

"Please take care of yourself, Steve. I love you."

"You, too, Mom. Give Chester a hug for me."

Steve hung up the phone. He laid the joint in the ashtray. For the second time in a little over a year, Lois had candidly and effectively confronted him about his alcohol and drug use. "And the pisser is, she's probably right," he said to himself.

He spent the next few hours working on Cleo, just as he had promised her. He thought about the AA meeting a lot. He tried to picture what it would be like, sitting in a smoke-filled room with a bunch of old sad sacks complaining about their pitiful lives. He recalled the AA meeting scene toward the end of *The Days of Wine and Roses,* when Jack Lemmen stood before the group, embarrassed that his suit coat was missing a button. "Man, I'm just not like those guys," Steve thought. "They're losers, and I'm not like that. I may be a fuck up, but I'm not a loser; I'm not like those old drunks."

A little time in the workshop, a little time cleaning up the yard, a quick walk to the park with Ginger, and the afternoon was gone. Steve was still sober, still straight, and still ambivalent.

At 6:15, he called Rachel. He smiled broadly and sighed with relief when she answered. "Hey, old girl. How the hell are you?"

"Steve, I can hardly believe it's you. You've been on my mind so much lately. How are things?"

"Pretty good, Rachel. Well, fair, anyway. I've been thinking about you, too. I just left you hanging the last time we talked. I called and asked for a favor and then disappeared. I apologize for that. Anyway, I thought you might have time to talk about something."

"I suppose I do. What's on your mind?"

"Well, oddly enough, it's the same thing I called about last time. Rachel, I keep getting unexpected unpleasant surprises around alcohol and drugs, and to tell you the truth, it's starting to hurt. I'm wondering; are you still not drinking or using?"

"Yeah, I'm hanging in there, nine months now. Can you believe that? Rachel the wastrel is nine months sober."

"It sounds like you still feel positive about it."

"Yeah, I do. I feel better about it all the time. It's not as much of a chore as it was in the beginning. But how about you? What's with the surprises?"

"Well, it's crazy. I'll go for long periods of time, I mean like weeks or even months, with no problem whatsoever, and then, all of a sudden, I find myself off the deep end. I did it again this weekend. I went down to my dad's ranch to relax, and before I knew what was happening, I was so fucked up I was doing weird things to myself and making very stupid decisions. I don't want to go into all the details. Just suffice it to say that I'm glad no one filmed it. I mean, here's how bad it was. This morning at 7:00 o'clock, I called my mom and asked her about AA. Does that tell you anything?"

"Yes, it tells me you must have been feeling pretty desperate."

"Hmm. I hate that word, but I guess it fits. Anyway, I thought I might ask you the same question that I asked you before. How did you do it?"

Rachel closed her eyes and took a breath. "Steve, the answer to that question comes on several different levels, and to be fair to you, we would have to sit down and have a fairly long talk. I mean, there's a simple answer, but it's awfully superficial. I just stopped putting alcohol and drugs into my body, period. But that's only part of the answer, and the longer I stay clean, the more I think that perhaps that's not really even the most important part. God, it sounds confusing when I try to put it into a couple of sentences. I mean, I'm not trying to sound like I know a lot about sobriety, or that I'm smart enough to tell you what you need to hear, but I would be willing to get together with you and talk about it if you want to."

"Well, okay, that would be good. Any chance you could do that tonight?"

"Yeah, I don't know why not. Do you want to come down here? Or how about if I meet you somewhere in between?"

They agreed to meet in San Marcos. During his drive down, Steve reviewed the day, which upon review seemed like a long one. There were the two conversations with Lois, the one with Al Bommer, the talk with Carla, and his abstinence—no alcohol or drugs since the previous night. He took the joint that he had rolled that morning out of his shirt pocket and put it in the glove box.

He smiled when he remembered Lois' prediction about the AA meeting. He had, indeed, found something unexpected that would prevent his going. "Imagine that," he said.

Steve got to San Marcos before Rachel, and when she pulled into the parking lot of Rivendale's Café, he was waiting for her.

"God, you look great, Rachel. I mean, really. You must have discovered a secret."

"Thanks, Stevey. You don't look so terribly bad yourself given the nature of your wild weekend. Give me a hug."

Steve put his arms out, and Rachel stepped into them. He closed his eyes and felt her against him. "You feel good, Rachel, just like always. I'm really glad to see you. Thank you for meeting me."

After a minimum of small talk, Rachel did her best to tell Steve about her sobriety. She talked nonstop, except for brief comments and questions from him, for two hours.

She told Steve about her sobriety within the context of three stages. The first was quitting alcohol and drug use, initially through her own determination and will-power, and then aided by the support of other people, including her counselor and two sober women whom she met in AA. She talked about gradually moving through her denial and coming to understand that her drinking and drug abuse had hurt her in more ways and in different ways than she had imagined. She admitted to occasional slips in her resolve to remain sober and talked about the process of regaining that resolve.

The second stage was settling into a sober lifestyle, facilitated during the best of times by open-mindedness and patience, and at others simply by the passage of time. She talked at length about time, not just in terms of having more of it to do more things and be more productive, but also in terms of boredom—having time on her hands that seemed difficult to fill. She told Steve about going to AA meetings, something that she still struggled with at times. She lamented the loss of her old support system—friends who systematically abandoned her as she lengthened her sober time. She also discussed her new one—other sober people she had met and liked and respected and learned from.

The third stage was a process that she was coming to understand gradually—growing and changing on deeper levels as a sober person, or perhaps as a bewildered person within the context of sobriety. She disclosed her discomfort at learning that sobriety itself was just as much about growth and change as it was about not drinking and drugging. She mentioned the twelve steps of AA as a "spiritual path," acknowledging that she had gotten a late start on the steps and was still a beginner.

Rachel told Steve about her efforts to develop a relationship with God. She discussed trying to become a more honest and genuine person, about letting down her defenses in order to understand herself better and to share herself more openly with others. With some hesitation, she shared with Steve her decision to remain celibate until she felt stronger in her sobriety and clearer in her values.

"I really didn't mean to talk so much, Steve, but to be quite honest, this is the first time I've ever tried to talk about being sober and straight in any kind of comprehensive or meaningful way. I'm afraid I've just rambled on and on, but maybe I can summarize it so that it makes more sense. Can you stand about five more minutes of my rambling?"

"Sure, Rachel. I'm listening. Believe me; I am. Parts of it are a little confusing, and a little scary, but I am listening."

"Okay. Here's the deal. I quit drinking and using because I got to the point that I could no longer ignore the bad things that were happening to me when I got high. In other words, I broke through that part of my denial that told me that drinking and drugging wasn't related to my screwed up life—my mistakes, my bad judgment. Then as I stayed sober and worked with my counselor, I started breaking through that part of my denial that told me that drinking and drugging wasn't related to the rest of my screwed up life—my confusion and fear and unhappiness and guilt and loneliness.

"Somewhere along the line, as I continued to stay sober and work on my issues, I started feeling better, in a lot of ways. At first it was feeling better physically, but then it went further than that. I began feeling better inside, too. I felt more positive about myself and more optimistic about my life and my future. I felt brighter and sharper, too, not every minute, of course, but overall. So it's like, there were payoffs, you know?

"Then, other stuff, maybe the really important stuff, started happening. I began thinking differently, and feeling differently.

Partly because I was challenged by others to let that happen, but also, I think, because I wasn't poisoning my brain and my heart.

"Here's an example, and I hope I can make it make sense. One of my major goals when I got sober was to be a better mother to Sam. That meant doing more for him, doing more with him, cooking better meals for him, being nicer to him, not yelling at him, and so on. Different behavior, you know? What's happened over the last few months is that I have come to *feel* differently. With him, it's been to appreciate him more, and love him more, and like his company more. With me, it's been about what goes on inside of me—feeling more patient, more understanding, and more capable of loving and giving.

"As a result of that difference—the one inside of me—I don't *have* to try to spend more time with Sam. I spend more time with him because it's what I want to do. I don't have to try to be nicer to him. I'm nicer to him because I'm a nicer person. And that's the point I'm trying to make. I'm a better mother now because of how I feel, instead of what I do.

"God, I feel like I'm going off on another tangent. I'll just say this. I like being sober, Steve. I like who I am now better than who I was a year ago. Again, though, I need to be honest and say that being a sober person is not always great. I still get lonely. I still get down. And when that happens, I sometimes regret not having the option of getting high. I remember how that felt. I liked it. It softened the hard times, and quite frankly, sometimes I miss it. On the balance, though, I definitely like being sober better.

"So, believe it or not, I'll stop there. Did I make any sense, or did I put you in a coma?"

Steve was quiet for a moment. "Well, I never got bored; that's for sure. I expected a much simpler answer, as usual. I seem to think that things are black and white, but they never are. I'm finding that out more and more as I live this strange life of mine. To tell you the honest truth, though, Rachel, I feel a little overwhelmed, and a bit intimidated. It sounds like so much, you know? I mean, I know enough about myself to know that I'm afraid of change. Not all change. Hell, I could change houses or jobs or physical appearance in a heartbeat. No problem. But the thought of becoming a different person on the inside, even if it's wonderful and good and what I want for myself, is pretty terrifying to me. My friend Tommy says that it has to do with my shame, which lives and thrives in me as fear—fear of succeeding and fear of failing. That means I need to stay the same, as in refusing to change, in order to keep myself protected."

"Yeah, well, Steve, luckily for chicken shits like you and me, the changes I've been describing occur like molasses flowing in the dead of winter. Actually, I'm beginning to understand that they occur over the course of an entire lifetime, and maybe longer. I feel as though I've just begun to scratch the surface of what's possible. The difference for me is that right now I'm willing to scratch. I haven't always been willing."

Steve laughed. "Well, Rachel, I gotta tell you something. I've always thought you were very damn wonderful. You've always been two steps ahead of me. I can see that you still are. Okay, one more question before I let you get away. I kind of agreed to go to an AA meeting with a guy tonight. Obviously, I didn't make it. But the question is, what about AA? If I take the plunge and commit myself to a lifestyle change like you've made, do you think it's necessary to go to AA meetings? I mean, I'm feeling pretty resistant."

"Man, I can relate. AA is still a part of the picture I'm not altogether sure of. I mean, I believe in the program—the twelve steps—and I see and feel the need for a support system made up of people who understand what's going on. In particular, I get a lot from other people who are also sober. I have an AA sponsor—a person in AA who's like my guide—and she really helps me keep my perspective.

"But there are a few things I don't like about AA. I feel as though I've gotten hit on quite a bit, sometimes blatantly and sometimes subtly, and I don't appreciate that. Also, I hate the cigarette smoke; it drives me crazy. There is a non-smoking meeting in town, but it's not convenient for me. And there's a lot of bullshit there. I mean, why wouldn't there be, you know? Again, though, all in all, I think it's helped me.

"So to answer your question, Steve, I don't know if it's necessary or not. In the meantime, though, I'm going twice a week. My sponsor says I should go more often. Does that help cloud the issue?"

It did. By the time Steve hugged and kissed Rachel goodbye and left San Marcos, he felt as though he had hit overload, and he felt more confused than ever.

CHAPTER 37

Driving back to Austin from San Marcos, Steve lit and smoked enough of the joint from the glove box to cop a mild buzz. He parked in front of his house at just after 10:00 o'clock. He found a note on his front door from James telling him to come over to The Roam In for a free beer.

He was surprised to see Dixie behind the bar on a Sunday night. She was surprised to see him home from his trip a day early. They talked for a minute and then Steve sat down at James' table, where James was engrossed in a paperback book.

"What you got there?" Steve asked him.

178

James handed him the book, a beautifully faded paperback copy of *The Autobiography of Benjamin Franklin.*

"It's a masterpiece of American letters," James said. "I read it once a year to remind myself about dignity, honesty, and humility. I recommend it. I didn't expect to see you. Dixie said you were in South Texas till tomorrow."

"Yeah, well, it didn't go so good down there, so I came home last night. Are you sharing this beer?"

"Sure, help yourself. So what happened? Too many mosquitoes and rattlesnakes?"

"No, I just got stupid. I fucked up another acid trip with alcohol and drugs and ended up going stark-raving mad. I don't know, man; I think I've really just about had it with getting high. I'm thinking again about just giving up everything for a while."

"...he says as he pours himself a beer," James said, smiling broadly.

Steve laughed. "Yeah, no shit. That's exactly what I mean, though, man. I think that's why I'm feeling the way I am. I've been saying one thing and doing another too much lately, and I think it's getting to me.

"Anyway, do you remember Rachel? Well, I just spent a couple of hours with her. She's been totally sober and straight for nine months, and man, you wouldn't believe how good she looks and how much better her life is. She's really working on herself, and it's paying off. I mean, she seems almost like a different person, James. It's like there's a different...quality about her, you know, like in her personality or in her spirit or something. I can't put my finger on it, but I wouldn't mind experiencing in my own life what I think I see happening in hers. Do you follow me?"

"Um hmm, I sure do. I've seen that happen to quite a few people who have for whatever reason chosen to explore and embrace deeper spiritual qualities. It's pretty phenomenal, and quite beautiful. I'm glad you were able to recognize it in her. That's a good sign, Steve."

"Yeah, whatever. So what are you doing hanging out in a public place. I didn't think you took too kindly to joints like this."

"Well, I just came by to bug you, and when you weren't around, I thought I might run across the mad atheist over here at y'all's hangout. I tried to talk to Dixie a little bit, but I think she's afraid of me. So I decided to do a little reading and drink a little beer. Now that you're here, though, I can just browbeat you. So, what exactly is it about being sober that scares you so much, Steve?"

"Oh, God, James. Do we have to talk about this any more? I feel like I've been talking about it all day. Twice with my mother, once with a guy from AA that I've never even met, once with Carla, and then for over two hours with Rachel. I'm not sure I

any more fucking insight into my alcohol and drug
, *if* that's what it is. Why don't you just tell me about
.n Franklin."

ld Ben Franklin was a pot smoker. What's the deal about
tin ₒ y from AA? Did you go to an AA meeting or something?"

"No, no. Okay, I'll run through the story real fast, and then
let's shoot some pool or something. It actually started right after
you got back from your dope growing deal, when you and Tommy
and Dixie all jumped my shit about my drug use. Remember?
Well, after that, I was fine. I maintained perfect control for over a
month. No problem whatsoever. Then last weekend, boom; I blew
it out like a son of a bitch. I mean big time, a real bender, and I
felt pretty bad about that.

"So Monday I got back on track and was fine all week. Then
I went down to my dad's ranch Friday morning for R & R. It was
Tommy's idea, and a good one, except that almost as soon as I
got there, all hell broke loose. I totally, utterly, and completely
embarrassed myself, and I was the only one there.

"I barely got home, and I do mean barely. I woke up this
morning full of guilt and remorse about the weekend. I called my
mom and asked her about AA. Well, that was a mistake. She
called a guy here in Austin named Al, who immediately called me
and wanted to sweep me off to an AA meeting with him. I lied to
him and told him I'd meet him there.

"Then I saw Carla, and she and I talked about it for a while.
Then my mother called me back and confronted the shit out of
me. Then I called Rachel, the voice of reason, and we met down
in San Marcos and talked, talked, talked. Now I'm sitting here
with you, just about talked out. That's it in a nutshell."

James nodded. "That's a far-out story, man. People
apparently give a shit about you. That's nice. So are you gonna
go to AA?"

"I don't know what I'm gonna do, James. My mom seems
convinced that I'm an alcoholic. What do you think? You claim to
know all about this bullshit."

"Well, Steve, it's like this. There are many definitions of
alcoholism and drug addiction. According to the one that I
learned when I was in treatment at Steadman House, you are
most definitely an alcoholic and drug addict. In fact, my friend,
you are a classic alcoholic/addict."

"Oh, great. Thanks. And what might that definition be?"

"Well, to start with, according to my old counselor, Cally
Callahan, alcoholism and drug addiction are the same thing.
Alcoholism is simply addiction to the drug alcohol, just like
cocaine addiction is addiction to the drug cocaine. Addiction,
then, regardless of the specific type, is present when you have
certain symptoms. The main ones, as close as I can recall, are
these. First is when you have problems that are caused by using,

180

and you continue to use despite the problems. Second is when you lose control of your use, like when you set limits on your using, and you fail to stay within those limits. Third is when you feel guilty or remorseful about your using or about the things you do when you're using. And fourth is when your defenses, you know, your denial, block your own insight into what's really happening, including the ability to hear what other people see and tell you about yourself. There are quite a few others, but those are the ones that stand out in my mind. How does that definition fit with your behavior around alcohol and drugs?"

Steve smiled. "Here, let me pour myself some more beer before I answer that." They both laughed as Steve topped off his cup. "James, that definition fits not only me, but also damn near everybody I know or have ever known in my life."

"Well, there you go, then. Your mom is right; you *are* an alcoholic, just like she says. Come on, I'll beat you in a game of pool."

James left the bar early. Steve hung around and talked to Dixie until it closed. By the time he went home and to bed, he felt tipsy but not drunk or stoned. He masturbated, fantasizing about Rachel breaking her vow of celibacy for him. He had no trouble bringing himself to orgasm.

The next morning, Steve was awakened by the phone ringing at 7:00 AM. He caught it on the second ring. "Hello, Mother," he said.

"Well, Steve, I just knew you wouldn't go through with it," she said.

"Yeah, well, then, why are you calling? And good morning to you, too."

"I tried to call you last night until 10:30; then I gave up and went to bed. I guess I was hoping against hope that you were serious. May I ask what happened to change your mind?"

Steve laughed softly. "Mother, I didn't change my mind. I never decided to go in the first place. Nor did I commit myself to go, if I remember correctly. Do you remember it differently? I'm just thinking about it. That's all I said. And I still *am* thinking about it. Plus, I wasn't out drinking last night, either. As a matter of fact, I was talking to a friend of mine who is nine months sober and goes to AA. So mind your manners and cut me some slack."

"I'm sorry, Steve. I'm just feeling frustrated and impatient. I know that's not your problem, and I don't expect you to understand how I feel. Who's your sober friend?"

"Rachel," Steve said.

"*The* Rachel? Your old girlfriend, Rachel, is nine months sober?"

"Yep. The one and only."

"So what's her story? I didn't even know she had a problem."

"Well, oddly enough, Mother, neither did I. She figures she did, though. All I know is that she's doing well and seems happy."

"Well, I'll be damned. Do miracles ever cease?"

"Apparently not. I hope they don't, anyway, because I'd like for us to drop this subject, and I think it would take a miracle for that to happen. If we could drop it, you wouldn't be sitting around worrying, and I wouldn't be resenting the sound of your voice on the telephone."

"Steve, you're the one who called me. Remember?"

"Yeah, I know. But Mother, I'm okay. I had a good day yesterday, despite all the phone calls. I have Al Bommer's number. I'll call him if and when the time is right. It's not right yet. Okay?"

"Okay. I'm dropping it as of this moment. That's a promise that I'll do my best to keep. That doesn't mean that you can't bring it up, though. Please remember that I have been there, and I do love you, and I'm available to help whenever you're ready to accept help."

"That's perfect, Mother. I couldn't ask for more than that."

Steve got up and went through his morning routine. He felt good. He ate a good breakfast, and he played with Ginger in the back yard for a short while before going to work at the dining room table.

He was skimming through a psychology textbook that Tommy had given him when James banged on the front door. He walked in carrying a grocery sack filled with books and pamphlets, which he dumped unceremoniously onto the living room floor. Every piece dealt with some aspect of alcoholism and drug abuse.

As he sorted the pile into categories—basic information, recovery, relapse, AA, etc., he talked to Steve as if he were simply continuing the previous night's conversation at the bar, and as if Steve expected the conversation to continue.

"Okay, man," he said, "it looks to me as though we have everything we need here. These resources should answer every question you could possibly come up with about addiction and recovery and Alcoholics Anonymous.

"There are several that define or describe the disease in comprehensive ways. Look here; this one has one of those twenty question lists that should diagnosis your addiction for you in the affirmative. And look, this whole pamphlet is about denial. Here's one on Sex in Recovery. I don't think it has any pictures, though, so don't get too excited. Ah, here's my favorite: *What Do I Do For Fun, Now That I'm Sober?*

"Now, this pile here is strictly AA literature. Here's the so-called Big Book, which is like the textbook of AA, the Twelve and Twelve—that's the steps and traditions of AA, and this one is like a history of the AA movement in America. This notebook here is full of lecture notes from Cally Callahan's lectures. I found his lectures fascinating, so the notes are pretty extensive.

"Anyway, it's all here, and it's all yours."

Steve looked at James incredulously, dumbfounded. "James, I've always suspected that you were certifiably insane. Now it's confirmed beyond a doubt. I didn't ask for any of this shit. I mean, where in the hell did you even get all of this shit, man? Did you rob a fucking alcoholic bookstore or something?"

"Hell, no, man. This is all my stuff from when I was at Steadman House. I knew I'd need it someday, and I was right; today's the day. It's far out shit, man. I've read damn near every page of every book and pamphlet you see here. It's serious stuff. Oh, yeah, I brought you something else, and it might be the most important thing." He handed Steve a business card. It read, in part:

The Recovery Center
Robert J. "Cally" Callahan
Chemical Dependency Counselor

Steve studied the card. "Do you actually think I'm going to call this guy, James? Why would I call this guy? Who is he, anyway?"

"He's a very decent man, Steve. If you're concerned about your drinking and drugging, which you obviously are, he's a good man to talk to. He's not full of bullshit like most of those people you'll be in graduate school with starting next week. He'll talk to you straight on instead of always trying to slip in through the side door. You have questions? He'll give you straight answers. Tell him a lie, and he'll call you on it.

"Hell, it's just a business card, man. Throw it away if you don't want it. Throw all of it away if you want to, or burn it. It's no skin off my nose. In the meantime, though, there it is. It's a gift from me to you. Don't ever say I never gave you anything."

Steve smiled and shook his head back and forth. "I just can't believe this. This is too fucking much. I guess I ought to say thank you, but I gotta tell you something. At this moment, I'd be lying to you if I did. Man, you're worse than my mother."

James laughed. "Oh, well, don't worry about it. I don't need any thanks, especially insincere ones. You'll feel more like thanking me later.

"By the way, man, unless you've already promised yourself into sobriety, I've got something here I want you to taste." He pulled an ultra thin joint out of his shirt pocket and held it up. "You game?"

Steve threw up his hands. "Hell, why not?" he said. "I'm going to have to be stoned to look through this pile of crap. Want a beer to go with it?"

"No way, man. This is some exotic stuff. It's Thai stick. You don't want to fuck it up with alcohol."

They shared the joint. Steve got blasted. James left shortly thereafter, smiling and waving and enjoining Steve to have fun with the literature.

Steve walked Ginger to the park, where they spent the rest of the morning. After lunch, he napped for an hour. Then his curiosity got the best of him. He tackled the pile.

The first thing that caught his eye was the twenty-question quiz. Depending on how he interpreted each question, he gave anywhere from four to fourteen "yes" answers. The scoring key suggested that any two "yes" answers indicated a possible drinking problem, any three to four, a probable problem, and any five or more, a definite problem. "Well, what do you know about that, Ginger?" he said with a wry smile. "No definite problem."

He recognized the "Big Book," a blue hardback named *Alcoholics Anonymous*. Lois' old dog-eared copy was a permanent fixture on top of her coffee table. Steve assumed that she kept it there for his benefit, but he knew she read it regularly. He picked up James' copy and flipped through its pages. Virtually every page contained James' written comments in the margins.

Steve picked up a pamphlet entitled *I Can't Be An Alcoholic Because....* He took it into the kitchen and read it over a cup of coffee. Every page offered something relevant to his situation. One section asked the question, "When did you last go 'on the wagon' and why?" Then it went on to say, "It was undoubtedly because your drinking was giving you some trouble...Drinkers who are not alcoholic do not need to go on the wagon, for they are always able to control their drinking."

Another section stated, "One definition of alcoholism says that people have alcoholism when they continue to drink in spite of their own best interests, and in spite of painful and harmful consequences." Steve recognized that statement as basically the same as the one James had told him at the bar.

Another section quoted an expert, the late Dr. E. M. Jellinek. "...continued excessive drinking seriously affects one's powers of reason, impairs judgment, and destroys the ability to look at one's self critically or to evaluate accurately one's own actions and attitudes, especially the depth of personal involvement with alcohol. This explains why the alcoholic can honestly believe 'I can quit anytime,' when the truth is exactly opposite." Steve recognized the quote as a more complicated version of what James had called defenses that block insight.

He rummaged through the pile again and picked up *Dealing with Denial*. He read it over another cup of coffee. Steve had studied defense mechanisms and denial in two of his psychology classes, and he and James had talked about them many times in reference to LSD's ability to dissolve them, or in some cases to tear them away from the user without his consent.

The booklet described denial as a "mother defense," a complex collection of several or many other simpler defenses, such as rationalization, working in concert to protect the individual from relevant, fundamental personal insight. At that point, Steve flipped through James' notebook of lecture notes and found several pages on denial.

There, denial was presented as a process that occurs strictly on a level below the conscious level, so that the individual is always unaware of its presence. Indeed, as presented by Cally Callahan, if someone is aware of his or her denial, then it isn't denial—by definition. James had written off to the side "...so if I were to say, 'I'm in denial about that,' then I would not be in denial about it at all because I would be demonstrating an awareness of it." The lecture notes also drew an interesting distinction between denial and lying. They described both as representing "untruth," with denial as untruth perceived by the individual as truth, and lying as untruth perceived by the individual as untruth.

Steve set the booklet down and thought about denial in terms of his own alcohol and drug use. "Surely I'm smarter than that," he said. "Even Tommy said that I have keen insight. I know when I get out of control. I don't deny that. I can see that. I'm not blind to it. I know I've had incidents that were alcohol and drug related, but I've always been aware of those. I haven't made excuses about them. I know myself better than anyone else could ever know me. Other people can't see what's in my head; they don't know my motivations or how I interpret things. And I *can* quit anytime I want to. I'm sure of it. All I have to do is really make up my mind to do something, and I can do it. I've cut down and controlled my drinking and using any number of times. Surely a real, true alcoholic or drug addict couldn't do that."

Back to the materials, Steve picked up a pamphlet from the "recovery" pile entitled *The Adventure of Recovery*. It described recovery from addiction as a process of positive change along four dimensions—physical, mental, emotional, and spiritual. As he read through it, he better understood what Rachel meant when she described her recovery process, beginning with the more superficial and moving systematically through "deeper" parts of the whole person. The body gets healthy, then thinking clears up, and then the heart and spirit follow over time if the person is willing and if he or she works at it.

Steve recalled his move to Austin and his expectations regarding personal change. He considered the possibility that drugs and alcohol had been the culprit that had prevented his experiencing the dramatic overhaul that he had anticipated. "Maybe," he said to himself.

Steve took Cally Callahan's card out of his pocket and straightened the edges. He walked into the bedroom and laid it by the phone.

Steve spent a couple of hours in his shop and then fixed his dinner. Just as he sat down to eat, the phone rang.

"Hello, Steve? Al Bommer here. I don't mean to bother you, but I missed you last night, and I thought I better check in with you just to make sure that you skipped the meeting on purpose. I mean, to make sure that you didn't get lost trying to find the church or anything like that."

"No, it was on purpose, Al. I ended up doing something else, but I am still interested in going to a meeting. I think I need to wait until the timing is better, though. I feel as though I'm not quite ready, you know? I'm almost ready, but not quite. Does that make sense?"

"Well, yes and no, Steve. I think I do know how you feel, but I would be surprised if it's what you need. I'm sorry; I hope you don't mind my being so frank, but over the years, I've come to believe that there's no time like the present to do what you think is right and say what you think."

Steve smiled. "I don't mind your being frank. I'll tell you the truth, though; I feel closer today to exploring recovery than I did yesterday, and it's partly because of what I did last night instead of meeting you at AA."

"Oh, I'm very pleased to hear that. To me, one of the most beautiful things that happens in this world is when an alcoholic finds recovery. It's a very extraordinary thing, really, and I've been privileged to see it happen many times since I got sober myself. But, that's another story altogether. So how about tonight? I would be glad to swing by and pick you up and drive you to a meeting. I'd also be happy to just meet you there and take you out for a cup of coffee afterwards if you'd like."

"Yes, well, I appreciate the offer, Al, but to be honest, I doubt that I'll go to a meeting tonight. Maybe another time."

"Okay, Steve. In case you change your mind, though, the meeting is in the same place and at the same time as last night. In fact, there's a meeting there every Sunday night, Monday night, Tuesday night, and Thursday night at 8:00 o'clock. It's a very good group—fairly small, nice people, good sobriety. By the way, just so you'll have it, I picked up a meeting schedule for

you. It lists all meeting locations and times throughout Austin.
I'll drop it the mail to you today if that's okay with you."

"Sure, that's great, and very thoughtful of you. Thank you.
And I have your phone number, too. I'll probably call you
sometime if that's still alright."

"Oh, absolutely, Steve. Absolutely. It would be my pleasure.
And please understand that I mean anytime. I don't even mind
being awakened at night."

After Steve hung up the phone, he thought about Al's
reference to the AA group as having "good sobriety." He
wondered if that simply meant people staying sober or if it meant
people changing.

Steve sat down and ate his dinner. Then he read more from
James' pile of literature until 10:00 PM, when he walked over to
The Roam In. He drank two beers and visited with Dixie for an
hour. He climbed into bed at midnight. He felt no effects from the
two beers or the midday smoke with James. He felt relaxed. He
felt resolved in a way that he had not felt before. He understood,
in what seemed like a real and practical way, not only that he
needed to make some changes in his life, but also that he wanted
to make those changes. He felt ready. Before dropping off to
sleep, Steve said a prayer asking God to help him find his way.

CHAPTER 38

All addicts reach bottom. Some reach low bottoms; others
are lucky and call it quits while their bottoms are still high.
Some never *feel* their bottoms when they hit them; others are
lucky and feel them deeply.

The luckiest addicts might be those who hit bottom
relatively early in their drinking and drugging careers and feel
immediate, intense pain when it happens. Many of those addicts
make and some even follow through with statements such as, "I
hit my bottom the moment I heard the jail door slam; at that
moment I committed myself to do whatever it took to get my life
back." And, "The moment I realized what I had done, I knew in
my heart that I would never, ever take another drink or drug."

Steve did not reach bottom with such clarity and insight,
despite many opportunities to do so. As a teenager, he could
have bottomed out after stealing a car, wrecking his Plymouth,
cursing his mom, or being detained by police as a minor in
possession of alcohol. As a college student, he could have hit
bottom after screwing up his grades, wrecking his Chevy, forcing
Bev into an unwanted pregnancy, or experiencing his first major
blackout. As a young adult, he could have experienced bottom
after losing the respect of his peers, blowing his first career, very

nearly receiving a DWI, or experiencing several major blackouts, one of which cost him dearly.

As a retro-hippie living in Austin, Texas, Steve could have bottomed out many times. He damaged and almost lost a valuable relationship. He had another major blackout. He failed over and over to keep promises to himself and others to control his use of alcohol and drugs. He experienced direct confrontations from close, trusted friends. He almost killed himself during a rest and relaxation trip to The Quarters Ranch.

Although Steve passed up opportunities for sudden, profound insight, he could not ignore the hole that he had patiently and painfully dug himself into. And on the morning of Tuesday, August 29, 1974, Steve Campbell stood very near his high bottom. Recent events—the weekend binge with Tucker, followed immediately by the Quarters Ranch fiasco, the drive from South Texas to Austin, the conversations with Lois, Al, Carla, Rachel, and James, and his digesting James' alcohol and drug literature—had occurred at the right time and in the right sequence. Steve's denial had cracked. It had cracked irreparably.

When he awoke on Tuesday morning, Steve felt rested and at peace. Before getting up, he reflected on the previous two days' adventures in confusion, scrutiny, discovery, resistance, approach, retreat, understanding, insight, and resolution.

He closed his eyes and spoke softly to himself. "So, I guess it's true. I really am an alcoholic and drug addict. Now what?"

He rolled over and looked at the clock on the nightstand. It was 7:45. He picked up the business card by the phone. "Robert J. 'Cally' Callahan", he read. "Chemical Dependency Counselor. What's so great about you, Mr. Cally Callahan, that would make someone like James Shannon stay in touch?" Steve decided to wait until later in the day to call Mr. Callahan, but he gave himself his word that he would make the call.

After walking with Ginger and eating breakfast, Steve spent the remainder of the morning studying psychology, with occasional detours into the alcohol and drug abuse literature. The more he read of that, the more he saw of himself in it. Nothing fit perfectly, but nothing failed to fit at least in part.

Steve was fixing a sandwich for lunch when James walked into the kitchen through the back door.

"Hey, man, don't you knock anymore?" Steve said. "Don't you know that people get shot for sneaking into other people's houses?"

James laughed. "I wasn't sure you'd let me in after I dumped all that stuff on you yesterday. What you cooking up there?"

"A turkey sandwich. You want one? I've got plenty."

"No thanks, man. Got any beer?"

"Yeah, help yourself. Leave a dollar on the counter."

"Right. It looks like there's four of them in here. Can I buy you one, too?"

"No, I don't think so." Steve hesitated, and then he said, "Oh, what the hell; grab me one." And then, almost immediately, "No, wait; don't. I'll take one of those bottles of spring water."

James turned and looked at Steve. "Hey, I didn't mean to confuse you, buddy. I was just trying to be polite, you know? If you'll tell me what you want out of here, I'll get it for you."

Steve stared at the counter top. "I'll have the water," he said. "Thanks, Mr. Helpful and Considerate."

James handed Steve the bottle of water. Then he hopped up and sat on the kitchen counter. "So....?" he asked.

"So...what?" Steve said. He turned and looked at James, who was poker faced. "What do you want to know?"

"So what's new? What's that overworked brain of yours been telling you about yourself? I suppose you've been unable to ignore the reading materials altogether."

Steve smiled. "No, I haven't ignored them. I wouldn't say that I've necessarily enjoyed them, but I certainly haven't ignored them. They're relevant, of course, and not just to me, I might add," he said glancing toward James.

James laughed softly. "Now, why doesn't that surprise me, on all counts?"

"So here's a question for you, James. If I'm an alcoholic, why aren't you one, too?"

"Who said I wasn't, Steve? I don't think I've ever said that, have I?"

Steve stopped what he was doing and faced James. "Okay. Let me meander through my jumbled thoughts for a minute, and you give me feedback. I suppose I am, in fact, an alcoholic and drug addict. You apparently think I am. You also seem to be invested somehow in my doing something about that. You obviously want me to become educated on the subject, and you obviously want me to talk to your counselor friend, Callahan.

"Now, if I admit to my addiction, and I see Callahan, and I follow what I assume would be his recommendations, as well as the recommendations of most of the literature that you dumped in my lap, then I'll be as sober as a Christian judge and going to AA meetings and steadily growing into some physical, mental, spiritual goomba.

"Along the way, however—and this is where it gets really interesting—I realize that it's not just me who has this little problem. It's also at least one of the people who keeps throwing it up in my face. That's you, James. There might be others as well, but that's beside the point. So here you are, perhaps an alcoholic and addict yourself, drinking and drugging every day, encouraging me toward recovery, while at the same time encouraging me to get stoned and drunk. Now, is it just me, or is there something wrong with this picture?"

James suppressed his laugh but smiled broadly. "I love it, man. You're great. You're going to make a damn fine counseling psychology student." He shook his head back and forth and ran his fingers through his stringy hair. "Okay, you want feedback, huh? Well, it's like this, Steve. You and I are addicts, right? We both fit the definition; that's obvious enough.

"Addiction affects you in your particular way, and it affects me in mine. Your negative consequences bug the crap out of you. Mine don't bother me one iota. You hate yourself and your life, at least some of the time, and you figure, quite correctly, I'm sure, that your addiction, or addictions, are a big part of the reason. I, on the other hand, am happy with who I am. I wouldn't trade my life for anyone's.

"You're yearning for something better. I like things the way they are. You want to change. I don't. I'd be happy and proud to see you change if you want to, but that doesn't mean that I want to change along with you. As I've told you before, I respect sobriety. I think it's far out, man, but it doesn't mean that I want to be sober. I get the feeling that you do.

"My answer to the other part of your question is most likely a combination of things. One is just my gaminess—my trickster side, perhaps. You know me. With the exception of you and Tommy and a small handful of other people, I don't particularly like human beings all that much. They fascinate me, however. I think of myself as a student of human behavior. So I'm watching with interest and curiosity how you deal with your love-hate relationship with alcohol and drugs. I see it as a classic conflict—one between your addictions on the one hand and your desire to change on the other. In your case, one of them is bound to win out. I think you're starting to see that, too.

"Another part of the contradiction, I think, is a reflection of my regard for you as a friend. I want you to be happy, but as far as I'm concerned, it's completely up to you whether or not you drink and use. I'll feel the same about you whether you're drunk or sober, stoned or straight. The only thing I've ever jumped your shit about is your affinity for methamphetamine and/or cocaine. Other than that, I want you to know that I'm not trying to push you anywhere you don't want to go. I'm just throwing out some possibilities and watching what happens."

Steve carried his lunch into the dining room while he processed what James had said. They sat down across from each other at the table. "What makes you think I hate my life so much, James? Do you see me moping around here complaining about my life? Do I seem that unhappy to you?"

"I see you questioning and searching, Steve. And yes, I do think you're pretty unhappy, or at least pretty unfulfilled. I see you yearning for a different quality of life—a deeper, more meaningful quality of life. I think that's why you moved here to Austin. I think that's why Rachel's experience with sobriety is so attractive to you. I even think that's why you like LSD so much. It takes you out of your defended, constrained experience by setting you free from your ego—your fear—and lets you feel that deeper spiritual level for a few hours. Doing it with acid, though, just gives you a taste of the real thing. If you don't take the bait and work toward it on a more enduring, day-to-day basis, then all it does is makes you feel dissatisfied with your life when you're not tripping.

"I think you're yearning for freedom, man, but you're afraid to have it. And the way I see it, your addiction to alcohol and drugs plays perfectly into that scenario. It takes care of your fear of freedom because it inhibits, or prevents, your getting free. At the same time, it lets you temporarily, though briefly, change the way you feel about yourself, and while that's happening, it doesn't matter that you're dissatisfied with your life on a deeper level."

Steve took a small bite of sandwich and a long, slow drink of water. Finally, he said, "What do I need with a chemical dependency counselor when I have you here? I thought I was the psychology student and you were the unemployed drug dealer. Turns out you're the psychologist, and I'm just your common, everyday, defensive, ego and fear-driven drug addict."

James smiled. "Nah, man, I don't think you're in the least bit common. In fact, Steve, I think you're pretty damned remarkable."

Steve smiled and shook his head. "Boy, you're really something, James. Do you have any idea of what a pain in the butt you are? Why are you doing this to me, man? Are you so goddamned bored with your own life that you have to fuck with mine?"

James' smile broadened. "Oh, I don't know, man. I'm just trying to keep things interesting. But listen, Steve. What I'm talking about is not psychology. It's spirituality. Psychology is interesting stuff, in an intellectual sort of way, but spirituality is the real deal. It's the heart and soul of things, not the head. It's like, I don't think you're mentally ill; I think you're spiritually depleted. You're not crazy, man; you're hungry.

"Steve, you have the most potent hunger that a human being can have—to become real, to be genuine, to be authentic, to be open. I've given this a lot of thought, man. You know, you and I aren't strangers. I watched you grow up. I spent a lot of days and nights in your house when we were kids. I know where you came from, and it wasn't the kind of place where people learn to be authentic. If I remember it right, it was the kind of place where a guy might learn to fear vulnerability and freedom and to protect himself 24 hours a day."

Steve took a deep breath and nodded. "So what's wrong with where I came from? It was just your typical all-American, violent, alcoholic home as close as I can recall. Do you know something about it I don't know?"

"No, man, that's not it. The alcoholism and violence weren't the problem. They were symptoms of the problem. They were symptoms of your parents' spiritual disease—their lack of faith, their lack of trust, their inability to recognize and experience the inherent worth that comes from being one of God's creations.

"The alcoholism and violence were like an exaggerated defensiveness that tried to cover over the fear and the shame that thrived in your family and throughout your so-called home. Your dad couldn't tolerate his own feelings of worthlessness—his spiritual emptiness. That was his shame. His primary target, the person he chose to blame it on, was your mom. Unfortunately, she bought it. He convinced her that she was worthless, too. Hell, who wouldn't feel hateful and stay drunk under those circumstances?

"His secondary target was you. He didn't do it to you on purpose like he did to your mom, but he still did it. He couldn't help himself.

"And listen, here's the payoff. Even though spiritually you're miles ahead of your parents, you're still protecting that same kind of fear and shame. Man, I think you have to be valued and feel valued as a child in order to feel valuable as an adult. I may or may not be right about that, but I think it's true. Regardless of that, though, if your addiction to alcohol and drugs is preventing your healing on that spiritual level, then it's a very costly cover-up.

"See, Steve, I like you just the way you are. I think you're valuable already. Hell, man, if you liked yourself as much as I like you, then we'd be sitting here having a more superficial, enjoyable conversation than this ultra-heavy bullshit."

Steve smiled. "Well, you've got at least one thing right. It's some pretty heavy bullshit; that's for damn sure. You know, Tommy brought up the issue of my shame. In fact, he told me that I ought to talk to you about it because of your perception of it from a spiritual perspective."

"Oh yeah? Well, good for Tommy. The old atheist has an open mind. Because shame is, in fact, a spiritual condition. There's no doubt about that. Shame might precipitate psychological issues or problems, but in it's pure form, it's a condition that strikes at one's deepest level—the spiritual. It resides at the core of one's being. If you believe and feel that your *core* is bad, then God must be bad, because to my way of thinking, that's pretty much what God is—our core. If God created us in his own image, then that's the image of God. If you're a piece of crap at that level, what does that say about the Almighty? God is Dung! Let's pray to Dung for guidance and healing.

"Anyway, man, some professionals are saying that alcoholism is a disease, you know, like a medical condition. When you talk to Cally Callahan, he'll more than likely take your family history and tell you that you've inherited the alcoholism gene, as well as the consequent alcoholism disease from your parents.

"But here's what I think. Although that may be true for some people, addiction is better described generally as a pattern of behavior that covers up the flawed spiritual core. It's not the only way to cover it up, of course. Some people do it with excessive work, others with excessive sex, others with excessive isolation, others with violence, others with martyrdom.

"Some even do it with excessive success, as in compulsively accumulating fame and fortune. And that gets pretty damn tricky, man. It's like, who's successful because he's well adjusted and happy, and who's successful because he's spiritually depleted—shameful and afraid? Fascinating stuff, huh?"

"Um hmm. It is," Steve agreed. "But here's a question for you. I read in your notes from Callahan's lectures that denial is a universal quality among addicts. What does your denial look like?"

James laughed. "You're quick, man. But if you've picked up on that aspect of denial, then you've probably also picked up on the fact that a person can only see someone else's denial and never his own. That's the definition of denial, if I remember correctly. Who knows, though? Maybe somewhere down the line, during the course of your spiritual recovery, you'll confront me on my bullshit and trick me into getting sober."

"Okay, James. That's about all my feeble brain can take for one day. It's summary time. What do you honestly think I should do?"

"Call Cally. I talked to him this morning. He's expecting to hear from you." With that, James said goodbye, took his beer, and left.

Steve finished his lunch. He wandered into the living room and put a Leonard Cohen record on the stereo. He lay across the couch and listened.

Like a bird on a wire,
Like a drunk in a midnight choir,
I have tried in my way
To be free.

CHAPTER 39

James Shannon respected very few people. And the majority of those that he did respect were historical figures rather than living persons. Robert J. "Cally" Callahan, Chemical Dependency Counselor, was the exception.

Demographically, no two people matched up more differently than James and Cally. Cally was big; James was small. Cally was very black; James was very white. Cally retired from the military; James protested against the military. Other than driving while under the influence of alcohol, Cally never broke a law in his life; James lived outside of the law. Cally respected convention; James snubbed convention. Cally was a mature adult; James, an old adolescent. Cally spoke pure English; James spoke abstract mumbo jumbo.

On the other hand, Cally and James shared the qualities that allowed them to like and respect each other. Both men were honest, straightforward, tolerant, and non-judgmental.

Cally Callahan got sober over a promise that he made to a military policeman who did not really want to arrest him for driving on base under the influence of a lot of alcohol. Cally knew that he was beyond legally drunk and deserved to be arrested. Nevertheless, he leaned against his car for support and told the MP that he had only a little more than a year until retirement, and that if the guy would let him go, he would never touch another drop of alcohol as long as he lived. The MP nodded, relieved to have a reason to walk away from the situation.

Cally kept his promise. It was a matter of honor, and if Cally was anything, he was an honorable high bottom drunk.

Cally went to AA the next day. He went with a willing and open mind, and he connected at once. He listened, and he worked his program of recovery by the book and straight from his heart. Within a year, people sought him out for help with their own sobriety. Even people with longer time in the program than he had looked to him for his wisdom and clarity.

When Cally talked in AA meetings, people sat and listened instead of daydreaming or milling around the coffee bar. Young people—blacks and whites alike—gravitated to him and tried to make him a guru. He diffused their efforts by remaining humble and focused on his own recovery.

Following retirement, Cally moved to Austin, Texas because his wife's family lived there. To fill his time, he attended lots of AA meetings and volunteered time to Austin's chemical dependency treatment community.

Cally's reputation spread quickly. He spoke in AA meetings almost every day. He used his comprehensive understanding of the Big Book and its principles of recovery to go straight to the heart of any topic that came up in meetings. Again, people listened eagerly to what he had to say.

Cally became a professional substance abuse counselor almost by default. He was volunteering one day a week at Steadman House, a small non-profit halfway house for alcoholics and drug addicts, when the agency obtained a large federal grant to house paroled federal prisoners. Cally reluctantly accepted a full-time position working with the parolees.

He stayed at Steadman for three years, working for peanuts and honing his counseling skills. When the State of Texas began certifying alcoholism counselors, he jumped on the bandwagon and added the credential to his name.

Cally left Steadman House in 1972, shortly after James completed his stay there, and established his own counseling and treatment center. He named it The Recovery Center. He ran the business and worked with alcoholics and addicts the same way that he lived his life—spiritually, with honesty and integrity. He turned away people that he felt he could not help. He accepted people who could not pay as much as others. He discharged people as soon as they were ready to leave his care and be on their own. He told people the truth, even when it hurt their feelings. He made decisions based on principles, even when those decisions were imprudent financially.

Steve sat on the edge of his bed and stared at Cally Callahan's card. "Do I really want to do this?" he asked himself. "Do I even need to do it? What the hell can this guy tell me that I haven't already told myself? Damn that James." He took a deep breath and dialed Cally's number.

A gruff-voiced man answered. "Callahan."

"Is this Cally Callahan, the counselor?" Steve asked.

"Yes, it is. Who's calling?"

Negative thoughts flooded Steve's mind. "Intimidating, angry, impatient, and this is James' spiritually enlightened friend and counselor?" He suppressed his impulse to hang up. "Mr. Callahan, this is Steve Campbell. My friend, James Shannon, suggested that I give you a call. He said that he mentioned me to you when the two of y'all talked this morning."

Cally's voice brightened. "Oh, yes, Steve Campbell, James Shannon's friend. Well, well, what do you know about that? I'm real glad to hear from you, Mr. Campbell. What can I do for you?"

"Well, to tell you the truth, Mr. Callahan, I'm not exactly sure. I've had some ups and downs with using drugs—speed in particular, and to a lesser extent with alcohol and pot. I mentioned that to James, and I guess he thought it wouldn't hurt anything for me to talk with you about it."

"Um hmm, I see. Well, Steve, let's get together, then and do that. Why don't you run on over here, and we'll sit down and discuss this little problem."

Cally's response startled Steve, and he hesitated noticeably before answering. "Uh, well, Mr. Callahan, you know, I'm not absolutely convinced that there *is* a problem, at least one that requires counseling. Like I said, I've had some ups and downs, but the truth is that I have it pretty well under control right now. I mean, I seldom get down on myself about it. I just happened to talk to James at a moment when I did have some concerns. I don't know what he said to you about me. He might have blown it way out of proportion, if you know what I mean."

"Uh huh." Cally was silent for a moment, and then he went on. "Actually, Mr. Campbell, James didn't say a whole lot, except that you were questioning your relationship with alcohol and drugs and that you might be calling. I didn't get the feeling that there was any emergency. At the same time, though, James isn't the type of person to be concerned about someone who's just a social drinker."

Steve laughed. "Yeah, I know what you mean. I'm not sure that James has ever even known a social drinker. Anyway, I think his main deal with me has been that I occasionally use a little speed, and he really hates that drug. Earlier this year I was using quite a bit of it, and he jumped all over me about that. Then here recently I had a couple of bad weekends, where I kind of lost control of everything. Before that, though, I really was just fine. I went a long time with no problems whatsoever. So, you know, I'm not sure what I ought to do. I mean, I don't want to waste your time or anything,"

"Yes, well, Steve, I appreciate that, but I wouldn't worry about wasting my time if I were you. This is what I do for a living. I help people look at their drinking and drug use to see if there's a problem. Then if there is, I help them deal with it. Listen, I'll tell you what. Since you seem to be undecided, I'll make it easy for you. I'm planning to be right here in my office doing paperwork all afternoon. I'll be available to see you until about 5:00 o'clock. It's a little after 2:00 now. That gives you almost three hours to think about it. If you decide that you'd like to sit down and talk, I'd be more than happy to see you. If not, that's okay. I've got plenty to keep me busy. How does that sound?"

"Well, yeah, that sounds fine, Mr. Callahan. Maybe I'll see you in a little while."

"Good. And Steve, please call me Cally. Everybody else does."

"Okay, Cally. Thanks."

Steve placed the receiver down gently and stared at the wall in front of him. "You better tread lightly, Stevey," he thought.

"You're edging closer and closer to a point of no return. Are you sure about this? Is sobriety and recovery what you really want?"

He thought about his pot stash in the freezer and the three beers in the refrigerator. He thought about the half joint in the ashtray of his truck. He closed his eyes and imagined being high. Then he imagined that feeling going away and *never* coming back. "Never getting high again," he whispered. Instantly, apprehension engulfed him. Tears filled his eyes; he blinked them away.

"Why did I ever start this?" he said. "Why did I ever open my big, fat mouth?"

After a few minutes, he got up from the bed and mechanically walked outside to his shop. He removed bar clamps from a walnut and pine dresser that he had been working on the previous week, before leaving for the ranch. The dresser was a beautiful piece—a very old, intricately constructed, hand-made original.

Steve ran his hand along the top of the dresser. He pondered the care and patience and precise attention to detail that a true craftsman had given to building it. "I wonder what my legacy will be," he thought. "What will my kids tell their kids? 'Your Grampa Campbell, he sure could hold his liquor, and he could smoke dope with the best of them.' Boy, won't they be impressed."

He sat on the floor and rubbed Ginger's tummy. "Well, old girl, maybe there's no time like the present. This isn't getting any better. I guess it wouldn't hurt anything to go and talk to Mr. Chemical Dependency Counselor. I don't suppose he'll imprison me or anything. I'll give it this one shot and see what happens." Steve closed the shop and walked back into the house. He showered and put on clean clothes. At 3:30 PM he walked into The Recovery Center and introduced himself to Cally Callahan.

"Well, well, well. It's nice to meet you, Steve. Yes, sir, very nice to meet you. Please, come on in and sit down. Would you like a cup of coffee?"

"No thanks, Cally."

Cally moved his office chair out from behind his desk and placed it squarely in front of Steve's. He settled into his chair and looked into Steve's eyes. "So, Steve, I'm real glad that you decided to come by. Just between you and me, I'm a little surprised to see you. You'll have to forgive me for selling you short."

Steve smiled. "Well, Cally, just between you and me, I'm a little surprised myself. I'm finding myself pretty reluctant to press forward with this issue. Well, maybe that's not quite true. What I'm really finding is that I move forward until I come close and then I move back. Then I move forward and then I move back. As I sit here in this chair, I feel kind of like moving back."

Cally's eyes widened and then narrowed as he studied Steve's face. "That's quite an insight, Steve. I would assume from the quality of that insight that you must pay pretty close attention to what's going on inside of you. Would that be a correct assumption?"

As Cally spoke, Steve drew his first impression. "Mid-forties, maybe, but hard to tell. Conservative, that's for sure. Ex-military all the way—neat and clean, short hair, dark suit, starched shirt, solid tie, polished wingtip shoes. Posture correct, but relaxed. Confident and self-assured, but not self-absorbed. A sense of humor, perhaps, but not playful. He doesn't blink, and his eyes don't wander. And despite their intensity, they're kind of soft and accepting. Intimidating, but gracious; tough, but warm. Trustworthy? Yes, I think so."

"Well, I've been told before that my insight is good. Myself, though, I wonder. Like, right now, I'm not exactly sure what the hell I'm doing here."

"Um hmm. Well, perhaps it's just that this is where you're supposed to be right now. I personally believe that things happen the way they're supposed to and that it doesn't always do much good to try to figure out why, why, why. Do you know what I mean, Steve?"

"Yeah, maybe. At any rate, here I am. So am I supposed to talk, or will you ask me some questions, or what?"

"How about if you just relax and tell me a little about yourself? How do you know our mutual friend, James Shannon?"

"Oh, I've known James most of my life. We were best friends in elementary school, when we both lived in San Antonio. I'll tell you what; he was weird even back then. He moved to Austin when we were in about the eighth grade, but we stayed in touch and visited each other pretty often. Then we were in college together until he flunked out. After that, we kind of went our separate ways for a while. I became a businessman, and he went to prison.

"We reconnected briefly after he got out—after he got out of your halfway house, actually—and then when I moved to Austin last year we reconnected again. Our friendship is different now, but it's very good. He's still the weirdest guy I've ever known, and one of the smartest. He's a big part of why I'm here today, which is somewhat of a paradox in itself, because he ought to be here with me, if you know what I mean."

Cally nodded and smiled. "Yes, I suppose so. James is quite a character. He'll certainly keep you on your toes and make you think. I've been trying to corral that guy for some time now. He's pretty elusive, though. But now, what about you, Steve? Besides James' encouragement, what else brings you to me?"

"Well, that's the part I'm not sure about. I mean, when I look at things on a week-in—week-out or a month-in—month-out basis, my life is okay. I really don't have any major problems to speak of, including alcohol and drugs. You know, I'm very responsible. I pay my bills, including my child support. I do excellent work out of my refinishing shop. I see my kids right on time every other week. I have some close friends who I know care about me. I'm in good health and good shape. I'm scheduled to start graduate school in counseling psychology this coming Monday. I mean, if you look at my life like that, it looks great.

"I guess the thing that bothers me is that I surprise myself sometimes, and I don't mean in funny, positive ways. I mean in disappointing and confusing ways. You know, I'll be plugging along with everything under control, and I'll just kind of lose it. This is especially true with drugs, but also to some extent with alcohol. My mom uses a term that fits perfectly. It's 'twist off.' It's like I'll be sailing along, and I'll twist off in a different direction—a destructive one. The last couple of times that's happened, you know, with drugs and alcohol, it was totally out of the blue, totally unexpected.

"It happened just this past weekend, and it really bothered me. To tell you the truth, it scared me. So I started talking to people about it, including James. Well, he jumped on it like a fly on shit. He gave me this lecture about addiction. Then he handed me all of the literature that you must have given him at the halfway house. I read through a bunch of it, and sure enough, it pretty much confirmed what I already figured—that I fit the definition of an addict. That was no great surprise.

"Another part of it, though, is that right before I talked to James, I spent a couple of hours with an old girlfriend who's been sober for nine months, and I was really impressed with what that has done for her. It's like, I found myself really attracted to her new life and new attitude. Anyway, I also mentioned that to James, and he went off again about how he thought my alcohol and drug stuff was discouraging my spiritual growth. I mean, who knows? James might just be full of so much crap, but some of the things he said struck a cord. I don't know, Cally; I could go on and on, but that's it in a nutshell.

"I think the bottom line is this. I know I'd probably be better off if I would just quit everything, just like Rachel, my old girlfriend, did. What I'd really like, though, is to continue drinking beer and smoking pot, but to do it in a controlled way, in such a way as to avoid the problems and the surprises. You know, like drink a little beer three or four days a week. Smoke a little pot three or four days a week. Avoid speed and coke altogether, and do a hit of LSD once in a while, maybe once a month or so depending on what else is going on around me. I mean, that's what I'd really like. If you could teach me how to do that, I'd jump at the chance to work with you."

Cally nodded slowly. "I sure do understand how you feel, Steve. I really do. I've been right where you are. Unfortunately, alcoholism and drug addictions don't seem to work that way. If they did, they wouldn't be such a damn problem. And of course, I'd be out of work.

"The fact is that the nearly universal experience of the addict is the one that you just described. He experiences a problem with his drinking or using, he makes promises to himself about controlling his use so as to avoid having the problems, and then he inexplicably, but invariably breaks his promises. That's the definition of addiction, as far as I'm concerned.

"So if you think about it in those terms, it comes down to this: Are you an addict or not? You can diagnose yourself. If you try to control your use through will power, and you don't succeed, regardless of the strength of your will power, then you probably are. If you try to control your use through will power, and you *do* succeed, then you probably are not. Which is it in your case?"

"Well, Cally, it's both. Most of the time, I succeed. Occasionally, I fail. Regardless of that, though, I understand what you're saying. On the other hand, I'm not convinced that what you're saying is true. See, I think I do a good job controlling my use. I've gone weeks and months at a time with my use under control. I'm not a complete stranger to alcoholism, either. Both of my parents were alcoholics, and my dad still is one. I don't drink like them, and I don't act like them. They were out of control.

"In my case, it's just those occasional times that I lose it, you know? And that's what I'd like to work on. But I hear you saying that controlled drinking and drugging isn't possible for me because I'm an alcoholic and addict. If that's true, Cally, then why is it that I have had so much success with controlling? I mean, really, I'm talking months here."

"That's a relevant question, Steve. But I think a more relevant question might be, 'Why have you ultimately failed every time you've chosen to control your use?' Let's look at it this way. Do you think of those 'occasional times' that you lose control as a problem associated with your drinking and using? Has it been a recurring problem? Would you characterize it as a broken promise? Would you describe it as loss of control? Have you felt bad about it when it's happened?

"You see what I'm doing here; I'm listing the symptoms of addiction in relationship to your behavior. The question is, does your behavior—your perception of your behavior—fit the description? Do you have the symptoms?"

Steve smiled. "Yes, yes, yes, and yes. Obviously, yes, at least in a broad sense. I'm not convinced, however, that I couldn't just decide to quit using everything and be successful at that. I mean, I do have strong will power. I believe that if I *really* put my mind to it, I could quit today and never touch another drink or drug for as long as I wanted to, even forever, if that's what I decided. It's hard for me to imagine that I wouldn't be able to do that. In fact, I really think that now that you and I have talked, I could even do the limit setting routine and be successful at that."

Cally nodded. "Okay," he said thoughtfully. "Just out of curiosity, Steve, have you ever made the decision to quit everything—to quit altogether?"

"No. I mean, I've thought about it, but I've never said, 'Okay, that's it; I'll never take another drink or drug as long as I live.'"

"Well, then, maybe that gives us our starting point."

"What do you mean?" Steve asked.

"What I mean is this. Let's you and me make a deal—a contract. You quit using alcohol and drugs for six months. Start as of this moment. If you're successful, I'll apologize for implying that you're an addict, and I'll dance at your wedding. If, on the other hand, you fail, then you come on back in here and work with me for a while, and together we'll see if we can improve the quality of your life. How does that sound?"

Steve smiled. "It sounds like I'm about to get hooked into something that I'm not quite ready for. But how about this as an alternative? What if, instead of quitting altogether, I set very specific limits on the amounts I do use. Then if I go over the limit, I'll come back and apologize to you for stretching my denial too thin, and I'll work with you to the extent that I can afford it."

Cally smiled broadly for the first time during their meeting. "All right, Mr. Steve Campbell, you've got yourself a deal. I'll get a pen and paper, and we'll write down the terms of this agreement and sign it."

Steve chose a limit of three beers per day three days per week, and one joint per day three days per week. His drinking and smoking days could overlap according to his choice, but he agreed to a minimum of two days per week during which he would remain completely alcohol and drug free. He agreed, furthermore, to abstain completely from all other drugs, including speed, coke, and LSD, until at least the last day of the fall school semester in mid-December. He signed the agreement gladly and confidently. When he walked out of The Recovery Center, he felt as though he had pulled off a hell of a deal for himself, and it had not cost him a dime.

CHAPTER 40

Driving home, Steve felt almost euphoric about his conversation and agreement with Cally. He felt fully resolved and completely in control. He had faced the issue squarely and responsibly. He had discussed the problem, if indeed it was one, with a professional—an expert—and the expert had sanctioned his plan. The plan was written, and it was dead-on realistic and absolutely workable.

Steve's mind raced with thoughts about his good fortune and wellbeing. The drug and alcohol issue was handled. He had financial security, at least for a while. Business was good and would only get better. School started in six days, and he was ready to take it on.

To celebrate, he opened the ashtray and removed the half joint that he had left there Sunday evening. He smoked it with a clear conscience, taking the last little toke after turning off the engine, parked in front of his house. He sat behind the wheel for a moment, giving the pot time to work its way through his body. He relaxed and came on to it nicely. It felt good. He felt good. All was well in the life of Steve Campbell, the high bottom drunk.

He walked across the street to The Roam In and was glad to see Tommy sitting in a booth along the back wall, alone with a pitcher of beer. He spoke briefly to Dixie, picked up an empty mug, and walked over to Tommy's table, where Tommy was reading the copy of *The Eden Express,* by Mark Vonnegut, that Steve had lent him.

When Steve sat down across from him, Tommy dropped the book on the table, smiled broadly, and filled both of their mugs with beer.

"Where the hell have you been hiding, man?" Tommy asked. "The last time I saw you, you were heading down to South Texas to relax, and the next thing I heard, you were back home two days early, looking like hell and complaining about a bad trip. What's the story, old chum?"

Steve smiled. "Well, it's actually kind of a long story, Tommy. I won't bore you with the details, but here's the Reader's Digest version. The trip was a bust; it was a disaster. I got fucked up on a shit load of drugs and alcohol, and in the middle of it, I got lonely and almost killed myself trying to get home. I ran into James and made the mistake of telling him about it, and he bullied me into seeing his old alcohol and drug counselor from when he was in a halfway house year before last.

"I just got back from there; that's why I'm so neat and clean at 5:00 o'clock in the afternoon. But it wasn't bad. To tell you the truth, I like the way it turned out. I agreed to cut back on how much and how often I drink and smoke pot, and I agreed to quit speed and coke and LSD altogether until December. It's a good deal for me, actually. So who tattled on me to you?"

"Carla. She didn't tattle, really. I saw her in her yard yesterday. I asked her if she had seen you, and she said that y'all had talked Sunday morning. I asked her what you were doing back a day early, and she said that you didn't have a good time and that you looked tired. She didn't load me up with details. So you saw a goddamn counselor, huh? That's wild, man. What was he like?"

"Well, Tommy, he was alright. I even kind of liked him. He didn't push anything on me, and we were able to come to this agreement about my drinking and using. I agreed that if I couldn't maintain my part of it, then I'd go back and let him fix me up. I don't know; I'm kind of glad I went to see him. I think it helped me get focused on what I need to do for school."

"That's good, Steve. I'm glad it turned out well. I take it from your behavior that today's one of your drinking days."

Steve smiled. "Yeah, I get three of them a week, plus three smoking days a week, as long as I stay sober and straight two days out of seven. So actually, today is a drinking *and* a smoking day. I get three beers and one joint. It's like I'm on a diet, you know?"

Tommy nodded and said, "Three beers and a joint, huh? So that's nine beers and three joints spread out over five days. You know what, Steve? I think your counselor friend may have pulled a fast one on you, because I'll be surprised as shit if you can pull that off. I mean, I hope you do, you know, but I'll be surprised."

"Thanks a lot for that vote of confidence," Steve said sarcastically. "Why do you say that, Tommy? I think I can do it with no problem at all."

"Well, maybe so, but the way I figure it, three beers isn't even enough to get a buzz on. All three beers does for me is whet my appetite for beer. So that means you only get to feel high three days a week, and that's only if your pot is decent and you drink your three beers really fast. I don't know, man; it sounds to me like you've agreed to stay basically straight for four days a week. I'm not saying you can't do it; I'm just saying it'll be a hell of a lot different from what we're used to. You know?"

"Well, hell, Tommy, the whole point of this is for me to experience something different from what I'm used to. If I wanted everything to be the same, I wouldn't be doing this. I think you might want me to fail because I'm about the only one around here who can keep up with you when you start drinking, and I'm for sure the only one who can put up with your bullshit."

Tommy laughed and filled their mugs. "Yeah, you're probably right about that. So, listen, Stevey, have you ever been to a whorehouse?"

Steve flinched at the abrupt change of subject. "Uh, yeah. Why do you ask?"

"Well, I'm thinking about making a run up to Waco tonight. There's a whorehouse there that I've been wanting to pay a visit to. Now that you're a goddamn social drinker, you'd make the perfect traveling partner. You could drive. In fact, I'll make you a rare generous offer. If we can take old Cleo, and you drive both ways, I'll treat you to any woman in the place."

Steve paused for a moment. "You're putting me on, right?"

Tommy shook his head. "Hell, no, man. I'm not putting you on. I'm as serious as a heart attack."

Steve paused again and then said, "Tommy, is it just me, or is this a little out of character for you? You don't seem quite yourself today."

Tommy laughed. "Is that so? Well, I sure didn't mean to tarnish my sparkling image, Stevey, but the truth is, I keep my relationships with women as superficial as absolutely possible. I'm familiar with most every decent whorehouse in the State of Texas. How the hell do you think I get my needs met? Have you ever seen me with a woman?"

"I don't know, Tommy. I guess I thought you just beat off, like I usually do, except when I can snare Dixie or Carla, which hasn't been too often lately. But a whorehouse, huh? It's been a while, but I have been to a couple of them. There was one in San Antonio called The Big House, and one here in Austin—M & M Courts, out on South Congress. That's not counting the massage parlors in San Antonio or Boystown in Mexico, where I've been a few times over the years."

"Uh huh. I've been to M & M a few times. Hattie's place. She closed down three years ago. Broke my fucking heart. I've heard of the place in S.A., but I never went there. A black club, on the east side of town, right? I think it shut down in about 1967. So anyway, what do you think? You up for it?"

Steve thought about it for moment. "Well, what the hell? Why not? It's not like I have to be any certain place at any certain time. And your treat, huh? That's too rare to pass up, I guess. When do you want to go?"

Tommy's smile widened. "Ha! Good for you, you old son of a bitch. Let's take off in about an hour. We'll buzz over there, hang out for a little while, and still get back in time for the midnight movie on Channel Seven. Sound okay to you?"

Steve's intuition told him not to go, that if nothing else, the timing was off. In spite of that, he said, "Yeah, that sounds great."

An hour later, Steve picked up Tommy, and they hit the road. Tommy brought four joints and an ice chest containing two six packs of cheap beer. He reminded Steve that he still had two beers and a joint coming to him on his contract with Callahan.

Steve did not tell him that he had already smoked half a joint. He also did not remind him that he had filled Steve's mug twice at the bar.

On the drive to Waco, Tommy drank beer and talked. He gave Steve an animated rundown of the best whorehouses in the state. He also told stories of his adventùres in the smuggling business—big deals, bad deals, good deals, and close calls. He chattered almost non-stop until they pulled into Waco. Steve listened and laughed. He drank one beer and took two hits on a joint.

They found their destination, The Quality Stop Motor Inn, a little after dark. On the outside, it was a gloomy, faceless place. On the inside, however, they found a lobby area occupied by seven very young, very pretty, fairly inexpensive women of the evening. The girls greeted them with big smiles and cold beers. Tommy threw down two quick beers and disappeared down a hallway with a black girl who looked to be about twenty and may have been the oldest of the group.

At first Steve maintained his resolve and turned down the beer. Soon, however, a strikingly pretty red-haired girl with freckles, who looked sixteen but claimed to be twenty-one, slapped a cold beer into his hand and told him that he was the best looking man that she had seen in weeks. She told him that she was a natural redhead and could prove it. Steve drank the beer on the way to her room, and after she closed the door, she lit and passed him a joint, which he gladly split with her.

After sex and a shower, Steve drank another beer while he waited for Tommy to settle up with the girls and the man at the front counter.

On the drive back to Austin, Tommy told Steve about his one run at a serious relationship—an early marriage that stumbled and struggled through five frustrating years and ended in a nasty divorce. He had no desire whatsoever to try again. Steve told Tommy his own failed marriage story and shared the fact that in his entire life, from grade school on, he had never been without a steady girl until the present, and even then he had Dixie.

By the time they parked in front of Tommy's house at 11:00 PM, they had emptied the ice chest and smoked the joints. Both men were drunk and stoned. Tommy stepped out of the truck, slammed the door, and then leaned his head back inside the window. "So, old pal, what are you going to do about your deal with the counselor? If I'm not mistaken, you're a little over your limit."

Steve nodded. "Yeah, I've been thinking about that. The way I figure it, though, it's a not problem. I got such a late start today that it's only fair that I officially start the deal as of tomorrow morning. So today just didn't count. I should have done it that way in the first place, but I just didn't think about it. Tomorrow, it counts, and this way I have a fresh start beginning at midnight tonight. That's fair, isn't it?"

"Yeah, whatever. I still say you're fucked. Who the hell wants to drink three goddamn beers? I'd rather not drink at all. I'll talk to you later, man." He wove his way to his front door and disappeared inside. Steve never saw a light go on.

After parking in front of his house, Steve strolled over to The Roam In. He sat at the bar and drank and talked to Dixie until closing. He drank three shots of tequila and three Shiner longnecks before midnight, but after that, he was careful to drink only three more beers. Dixie hinted around at going home with him, but he made an excuse and went home alone.

Once in the house, he took part of a marijuana top from the freezer and rolled a joint. He let Ginger in, turned off all of the lights, locked the house, took off his clothes, and sat up in bed and smoked the joint. Before slipping under the sheet, Steve looked at his watch. It was 2:35 AM Wednesday morning. He had blown through the roof of his contract on Tuesday and had already used up Wednesday's allotment of both alcohol and pot. He was very drunk and very stoned.

"I'll start fresh tomorrow," he said. "Nobody will ever know the goddamn difference."

CHAPTER 41

Steve awakened early Wednesday morning with a serious headache. "Son of a bitch," he said, holding his head and slowly rolling out of bed. He shuffled into the bathroom, then into the kitchen for aspirin and cold milk. Then he returned to bed and slept for the rest of the morning. When he awoke the second time, about noon, he felt lethargic but less hung over.

He immediately recalled Tuesday's conversation with James. One part of that conversation haunted him. It was James' contention that Steve might be using his defenses, especially and specifically his drinking and drugging, to cover up the same kind of fear, shame, and worthlessness that Henry felt. "Why does it always have to come back to Dad?" he whispered. He closed his eyes and rubbed his face with his hands.

He tried to recreate the dialogue with Cally. Several parts stood out above the others. One was Cally's description of the nearly universal experience of the addict, that he makes promises about controlling his use but inexplicably and invariably breaks the promises. "Diagnose yourself," he had said. "Are you an addict or not?"

Then there was the written agreement. Even though Steve knew that he could rationalize a pretty good case for having rushed into an agreement that he was not quite ready for, the truth was that he had entered into the agreement willingly, confidently, and with the understanding that it went into effect at the moment of signing, not the next day. That was the truth, even though it was also true that unless he ratted on himself, nobody would ever know the difference. "Nobody would ever know the difference," he repeated to himself.

On Wednesday, August 30, 1974, a little after noon, lying in bed with the tail end of a hangover, Steve faced an intersection. He understood that, and he visualized it clearly.

Straight ahead sat the road of denial. Taking that road meant more of the same. It meant stopping and starting, stopping and starting, yearning for something different but finding more of the same, talking endlessly with this person and that, making promises and breaking promises, finding resolution and then failure. Ultimately, it meant going nowhere.

To the right sat the road of submission to his addictions. Taking that road meant forgetting about sobriety, accepting life as an addict, quitting the goddamn whining and crying, blowing off the promises, forgetting about change, fucking change.

The road to the left led to...what? Did it lead to Cally's door? Did it lead to Alcoholics Anonymous? Did it lead to something really different than what he had ever known? If so, would it be something better? Would it perhaps be something worse? What did recovery really mean? The road to the left was an unknown. That was his only certainty about the road to the left; it was an unknown.

Somehow, perhaps through the same grace experienced by many thousands of high bottom drunks before him, Steve turned left. He picked up the telephone and dialed Cally's number.

"I'll probably regret this, Cally, but can I come in and talk to you sometime today?"

"Yes, Steve, you surely may. In fact, why don't you just come on over right now?"

"Well, I need to clean up a little bit and eat some lunch. How about in an hour or so?"

"That will be just fine. How about if we set it for 2:00 o'clock?"

"That's good," Steve said. "I'll see you at two."

When Steve walked into The Recovery Center, Cally shook his hand, gave him a cup of coffee, and motioned for him to sit. He studied Steve's face for a moment. Then he said, "I don't suppose you're here to collect an apology from me quite this soon. What can I do for you?"

"Well, Cally, I blew it. I guess you knew I would, but I bet you didn't expect it to happen quite this soon. Anyway, I don't know what you can do for me. To tell you the truth, I don't even know for sure what it is you do here. Why don't you tell me that?"

"Okay. What I do here is alcohol and drug treatment. I work with people like yourself who want to get sober and straight and change their lives for the better. It involves education, both here and at home; and therapy, both individual and group. It also involves going to AA meetings. It requires a commitment from you to follow the rules. You have to follow them to the letter. It takes quite a bit of time and effort on your part, probably fifteen hours a week or more before it's all said and done, and it will cost you about fifty bucks a week for as long as it takes for you to get real."

Steve sat silently, looking at his hands. He felt his resistance rising. "Why so much time?" he asked. "I'm not sure I'll have that much time once school starts next week. And why does it cost so much?"

"Well, I know it sounds like a lot at first, on both counts, but look at it this way. How much time per week do you spend drinking and using? And how much money per week do you spend on alcohol and drugs?"

"I don't know, Cally, but not that much, at least not that much money. Surely not more than twenty or thirty bucks a week.

"Um hmm. Okay, well, let's check that out." Cally picked up a small calculator from his desktop. "You're basically a beer drinker, right? So about how many beers per day do you average, and where do you buy them?"

"Oh, I drink about six or eight a day, more or less, depending on the day. I buy about half of them at the store and half at the bar across the street from where I live."

"Okay, and how about pot? How many joints per day?"

"I'd say about two on the average."

"All right. How about speed, coke, pills, LSD, and anything else you can think of?"

"Well, nothing right now, but over the past six months I'd say a couple of grams of speed and a half gram of coke per month, and a hit of acid two or three times a month. That's on the average."

"Okay, Steve, let's figure it up, by the month, being conservative. At six beers per day, that's about 180 beers a month—90 in six packs, or fifteen six packs at $2.00 each, and 90 singles, at 75 cents each. That's about $97.50 for beer. Two joints per day, or about 60 per month, and you can probably get 50 or 60 very slender joints out of a good lid, so that's about $50.00 for pot, being very conservative. Okay so far? And let's see, two grams of speed and a half-gram of coke per month. That's at least $175.00, right? And we'll just throw in the acid as a freebee. So, the way it adds up, you're spending somewhere in the neighborhood of $325 per month. That's about $80 a week. And my guess is, Steve, that we've just looked at figures for an exceptionally good month."

Steve mulled over the figures for a moment in his head and then said, "Well, you know, Cally, I don't really pay for all of that. I mean, some of it is free because of the way I work it, if you know what I mean. So it's not like I'm actually spending that much month in and month out."

"Okay, Steve, let's be even more conservative. I'll tell you what I'll do. I'll let you pay for treatment at the rate of $200.00 per month, regardless of how many sessions we have. That way, if you get sober and straight and stay that way as a result of treatment, you should come out way ahead on the deal financially."

Steve thought. Cally waited. Finally, Steve looked at Cally and said, "Alright, I'll buy that. Now, the next question is, exactly what's involved?"

Cally described his program. It required one long individual session per week, one short individual session per week, and one group session per week. Homework included reading and writing assignments. The program required attendance at three or more AA meetings per week. It also required total abstinence from all addictive substances at all times. "And finally," Cally said, "treatment at The Recovery Center demands that you cut the crap, tell the truth, and get real."

"Jesus Christ, Cally, that's a lot. This graduate program I'm starting at UT on Monday is going to take a lot of time. I don't know how much, but I know it's going to be a lot. And I still have to work, you know? Does your program have to include everything? I mean, couldn't I just see you individually once a week and go to AA or something like that?"

Cally sat forward in his chair and held Steve's eye. "What we're talking about here, Steve, is a fraction of the time that you spend getting high. Plus, if you stay straight, you might find that the balance of your time—the time not devoted specifically to recovery-related activities—will contain more energy and motivation than you have today, or perhaps more than at any time in your adult life. It is possible that you will have more time for school rather than less. Do you hear what I'm saying?"

Steve nodded. He felt scared. He felt sad. He felt defeated. He did not feel energetic or motivated. He did not feel hopeful. And he was out of arguments. "Okay," he said. "When do we get started?"

"We've already started, Steve. We started yesterday. Now, your next job is a simple one. Tell me something; what kind of stash do you have in your house?"

Well, not much, really. I have about an ounce and a half of box of stems and seeds, and a couple of beers. That's about it. I'm out of everything else."

"Okay, what's your schedule like for the rest of this week?"

"Pretty open, I guess. I work in my shop behind my house. I refinish furniture and restore antiques. I have quite a bit of stuff that's overdue, and I'd like to get a lot of it out before the end of next week. I have two kids who live in San Antonio, and I'll have them this weekend, from noon Saturday until Sunday evening at 6:00 or so. I was thinking about picking them up and bringing them to Austin so that I can still get some stuff done in my shop over the weekend.

"That's about it. After this week, though, it's not so easy. On Monday, I begin an orientation week for school. I think I have to be there Monday through Thursday from 9:00 AM to Noon. Then after that, I just don't know because I won't get my class schedule until sometime during orientation."

"Good. What I hear you saying is that you are wide open for the time being. So here's what let's do. We'll visit for a little while longer today and then we'll meet here again tomorrow morning from 11:00 o'clock until about 1:00. It will be easy, nothing heavy. Now, this is very important, Steve. By the time I see you tomorrow, you will be in your second day of sobriety. Your house will be completely and thoroughly clean of all mood-altering substances. That means everything, even stems and seeds. Can you agree to that?" Steve nodded.

"When I see you tomorrow, I'll have a preliminary treatment plan written, which will outline specific activities that you will be responsible for completing in a timely fashion. Some will be activities that you will do here; the rest will be your responsibility away from here.

"Now, this phone number, the one you already have for me here at the office, is answered by my answering service 24 hours a day. I want you to call me between 9:00 and 10:00 o'clock tonight. The answering service will take your name and number, and I'll call you back within thirty minutes unless an emergency has taken me away from home. How does this sound to you, Steve?"

"It sounds a little overwhelming, Cally. It sounds like it's moving too fast. I'm not sure that I can do this. I mean, I'll give it a try, but I'm not sure that I can pull it off."

"Trying is dying, Steve. Remember that. Trying is dying. As of this moment, we have graduated out of *trying* and into *doing*. I have your word, and I have your commitment." He paused long enough for Steve to look at him. "Agreed?"

Steve took a deep breath. "Okay, agreed," he said quietly.

They talked for another forty minutes. Cally took a brief history of Steve's alcohol and drug use. He asked Steve to connect his use, as best he could, to some of the problems that he had experienced in his adult life. He asked several questions regarding Steve's family and friends. He kept it simple and light. He was warm, reassuring, and encouraging throughout.

When Steve stood up to leave, Cally walked around his desk and put his arm gently around Steve's shoulder. "Steve?" he said.

"Yeah?"

"Easy does it. Remember to breathe. I'll talk to you in a few hours." Cally's voice was soft and gentle.

CHAPTER 42

Steve spent the rest of the afternoon cleaning up and then cleaning out his house. He discarded a box of marijuana seeds and several empty speed and coke vials, a couple of which contained usable residue. He set the beers on the sidewalk in front of his house, knowing that someone would appreciate the find. Then he unwrapped his freezer stash—an ounce and a half of the very best smoke that he had ever had. He handled it tenderly. He smelled it. He felt tremendous sadness at the thought of being without it. "This is insane," he said. "I feel like I'm fixing to sell my own baby."

He thought for a moment about what he had just said. Then he smiled to himself, re-wrapped the pot, and placed it back in the freezer.

He picked up the telephone and called Tucker. "Hey, jerk off, what no good acts of depravity are you up to?" he asked.

"Oh, just trying to squeak by the best I can," Tucker said. "Trying to reconcile in my own mind the fact that I'm neither adequately appreciated nor appropriately compensated for my superior intelligence and wit. Other than that, everything's fine. How about you?"

"Well, old buddy, I've had a very most interesting day. I'm not sure you're ready for this. In fact, you're probably going to shit in your pants, but here it is anyway. I signed up for alcohol and drug treatment about three hours ago. I am now officially an alcoholic and drug addict, standing on the edge of some phenomenal recovery process. How does that grab you?"

Tucker laughed into the phone, but it was not his true laugh. "I think you're full of it, Campbell. Remember to whom you're speaking. Tucker Taylor doesn't fall for stupid practical jokes very easily."

"Yeah, well, I know who you are, asshole, and I swear to God I'm telling you the truth."

Tucker hesitated uncharacteristically and then said, "Steve, the day you really and truly quit drinking beer and smoking pot is the day I'll moon the governor of Texas on the capitol steps in downtown Austin."

"Well, pull um down and show your best side, then, buddy, because it's true. I'm not bullshitting you. In fact, the main reason I called is to tell you to come by the house, and I'll give you a hell of a deal on my personal stash of weed. Bring about ninety bucks with you; you won't be disappointed. This is my first homework assignment from my counselor—to clean out the house of anything that could possibly get me high. It's either sell it to you at a bargain price or flush it down the toilet."

"Campbell, listen to me. We're going to have to talk about this. I'll be there in half an hour. And don't do anything stupid with that stash, like in relationship to the toilet. You hear me?"

"Yeah, I hear your fat ass. You better hurry, though, and bring cash only. I don't want you to stay a long time, either. You're a fun friend and all that, but I need to do this, Tucker, and I don't need you trying to talk me out of it. Not yet, anyway. Do you hear *me?*"

"Yeah, whatever. Goodbye."

Tucker stood at Steve's door before thirty minutes passed. "I gotta tell you something, Steve. I'm about half pissed off about this hair-brained notion of yours. You can't possibly be serious about it. Please, tell me it's a joke."

"If I told you that, I'd be lying."

"Shit! Why, man? What's the deal?"

"The deal is that I have been trying to control my drinking and drug use ever since I moved here last summer, and I just can't seem to do it. Yesterday afternoon I went to see this guy that James knows. He's an alcohol and drug counselor. I signed a written agreement with him that set specific limits on my drinking and drugging. I agreed to drink and use within those limits.

"The penalty, so to speak, for failure to do so was starting treatment. Four hours later, I was hanging out in a whorehouse in Waco, drinking beer and smoking pot. Two hours after that, I was slamming down shots and beers across the street. At 2:00 o'clock this morning, I was sitting in the middle of my bed, drunk and stoned as shit and smoking another reefer. I woke up this morning with a huge hangover and a goddamn guilty conscience. So, I went back over to this counselor's place—The Recovery Center—and I agreed to start treatment immediately. End of story."

Tucker shook his head back and forth. "I can't believe it, Steve. Man, you and I have been drinking together since we were 16 years old. You're my favorite party buddy. I mean, there may have been a time or two when I've thought maybe, just maybe, I drank too much, but never you. You've always been in complete control. I've learned to rely on it. You always drive. You do the talking when cool heads need to prevail. You keep track of things. You hold your liquor better than anyone I've ever known. I just can't help but think that you're jumping the gun, just because you've had a couple of bad days. You know?"

"It's been more than a couple of bad days, man. I've been setting limits on myself and breaking them all year. I mean, I can't even tell you how many times I've promised myself that I was going to control my drinking and then found myself fucked up. Listen, when I left Cally Callahan's office yesterday, I was absolutely certain that I would never lay eyes on his ugly mug again. I would have laid big money on it. That's how confident I was." Steve paused, and then continued. "Tucker, I'm going to give this treatment thing a shot. If it doesn't feel good, then I'll blow it off and throw a big party. So, do you want the rest of my stash, or should we flush it?"

"What do you think?" Tucker said. "How much is there, and how much is it?"

"There's about an ounce and a half. It's the finest weed I've ever run across, and I'm sad as hell to see it go. I don't think we'll see any more like it again, at least not this year. If you want it, you can have it for the ninety bucks I told you to bring. It's worth more. You want it?"

"Yeah, sure I do. But I gotta tell you, Steve, I have a bad feeling about this whole thing. I mean, I want what's best for you. You know that. But I've got a bad feeling about it, like I may just lose my best friend out of this deal. Maybe I'm being paranoid, but that's the way I feel."

Steve smiled. "There's no way, man. Hell, I'm not going anywhere. I'll give you a call in a few days and let you know how it's going. Who knows, I may be asking for my stash back by then."

Tucker laughed. "That wouldn't surprise me one bit. And to tell you the truth, it wouldn't disappoint me, either. Problem is, I'm going home and smoke it all tonight."

After Tucker left, Steve called James and told him the news. "Well, good luck, man," he said. "I think you're doing the right thing. I really do. I'll be checking in on you."

At 9:00 o'clock, Steve wandered next door to Carla's house. She wasn't home. He considered walking down to Tommy's but decided against it.

Steve walked into his house and sat on the couch. It was 9:10 PM. The house was quiet. Steve was sober. He was alone. He felt alone. He put Jim Croce on the stereo and called Rachel. He got no answer. He thought about calling Lois, but that felt premature. He did not want to get her hopes up too high. He called Cally's answering service. Cally called him back within a few minutes.

"So, how's it going, Steve?"

"It's okay, Cally. I don't know what to do with myself, though. The people I want to talk to aren't around, and I'm sitting here on the edge of my bed wondering what the hell to do next. Other than that I'm all right. I got the house cleaned out."

"Good. Good job. You sound sober, and I assume that you are. Why don't you get out of your house for a little while? Take a walk or something. Then go home, take a warm bath, and get a good night's sleep. Read that Big Book that James Shannon dumped on you. Who knows? It might just put you to sleep in a hurry."

"Okay. I guess I can do that. Anything else?"

"No, nothing else; at least not right now. You're doing great. Hang in there. You know now how easy it is to get in touch with me. Call me if you need help. And, Steve, remember to breathe. Stop every now and then and just listen to yourself breathing."

At 9:45 Steve put Ginger on her leash and walked around the neighborhood for half an hour. Then he followed the rest of Cally's instructions. He took a bath and climbed into bed, where he lay wide awake, staring at the ceiling. At 11:30 he got up and drank a glass of milk. He thought for a moment about getting dressed and walking across the street to talk to Dixie but then decided not to. Instead, he picked up James' Big Book and read the Forwards, The Doctor's Opinion, and the first two chapters—Bill's Story and There is a Solution.

His initial reaction to the book was critical. "This reads like a sixth grade reader, for crying out loud." "This isn't me; I'm not like this; I'm not this bad."

On the other hand, he found a couple of passages fascinating. One referred to "...deep and effective spiritual experiences which have revolutionized our whole attitude toward life...." Another described "...vital spiritual experiences...in the nature of huge emotional displacements and rearrangements."

"Now that sounds kind of like a good acid trip," he said, smiling.

Steve noted to his relief that although the book made frequent references to God and to spiritual concepts, it remained clearly non-denominational and did not mention Jesus. "Small favors," he muttered to himself.

Steve finally fell asleep at about 2:00 AM. He dreamed that he was sitting on a huge rock, which protruded from the edge of a shallow, rapidly running river. After a short while of calmly watching the river run, he climbed down off of the rock, took off his clothes, and waded in. The rocky river bottom hurt his feet. The swift current nearly pushed him down several times. He did

214

not know what was on the other side, but for whatever reason, he wanted to reach it. He awoke before getting there.

Steve opened his eyes at 6:00 o'clock on Thursday morning, the beginning of his second day of sobriety, the beginning of the second day of his supposed lifetime of continuous abstinence from alcohol and drugs. He awoke to elevated feelings of doubt, fear, and regret. He rolled over onto his side and looked at Ginger, who was lying on her blanket beside the bed. He reached down and scratched her head.

"What the hell have I done, old girl?" he said. "I should have waited one more day. One more day, and it might have just blown over. I can't believe I jumped into this so easily."

After a few minutes, he got up and let Ginger out. He started a pot of coffee. His stomach felt queasy. His body felt nervous. He slipped on a pair of shorts and walked next door to buy a newspaper.

Mario greeted him with his usual good cheer. "Well, Mr. Steve, how are you today, my friend?"

"Medium, at best, Mario. How about yourself?"

"I can't complain. But guess what, man. My cousin, the guy I get your speed from, and the same guy who bought all of that good pot from you, he got his ass busted Saturday night. The stupid fucker sold an eight ball to an undercover cop. His ass is grass, man. It ain't his first bust, either."

"No shit? Man, I'm sorry to hear that. Damn! Poor son of a bitch. What's he gonna do?"

"I don't know, man. He called my uncle, but uncle's so pissed off about it, I don't know if he's even going to help him out. I guess he'll get a lawyer and try to get out of it, but it don't look too good from here."

"Well, I don't know, man. Let me know how it turns out, okay?"

"You bet. See you later, man. Sorry about losing the speed and coke connection. It was a damn good one."

"Yeah, well, don't worry about it, Mario. I don't really care about that. You take care."

Steve walked back to his house, ate some toast, browsed quickly through the paper, and drank as much coffee as he could stomach. To relieve his anxiety and restlessness, he took a long, hot shower and got dressed. He sat down to study, but he could not stay focused. After 30 minutes, he gave up and walked out to his shop, where he moved things around for a few minutes but could not create any interest in working.

Finally, he put Ginger on her leash and walked to the park. When he got there, he lay in the grass and tried to relax and listen to his breath, as Cally had suggested. Again, though, he could not stay focused, and he could not keep his eyes closed.

Impatience and irritability joined his feelings of anxiety and restlessness.

Steve looked at his watch. It was 8:15. "My God, this has been the longest two hours of my whole goddamn life," he said loudly.

Walking home, Steve recalled another morning, exactly thirteen days prior to this one, when he felt very much like he did now. It was the Friday that he twisted off and binged on speed, coke, alcohol, and pot for three days with Tucker. The memory served as a timely reminder. "Not again," he said to himself. "Not today. I'm going to make it through today even if it kills me, which it very well may do."

Once home, Steve shifted gears. He cleaned up the kitchen and cleaned out the refrigerator, throwing away about a third of its outdated, moldy, and/or simply distasteful-looking food items. He checked the time; it was 10:00 o'clock. He emptied the trash, collected and sorted his dirty clothes for a trip later to the Laundromat, and rearranged the piles of alcohol and drug pamphlets, books, and lecture notes. He opened a psychology book and read a few pages about social attitudes and prejudice.

Finally, at 10:40, Steve locked the house and drove to The Recovery Center. By the time he arrived, his anxiety soared to the point that he felt lightheaded and off balance.

CHAPTER 43

When Steve walked into The Recovery Center, Cally was waiting for him. "So, how do you feel, Steve?"

"Not good, Cally. I've been restless and nervous all morning, not to mention my crappy mood. I'm not sure I like this very much so far."

"Good, Steve," Cally said. "That sounds pretty honest. It's a good start. I wouldn't expect you to feel very good this morning. It will get better very soon. You can count on that. Come on in my office. We've got a lot to accomplish in a short amount of time."

Cally handed Steve a small pile of books, pamphlets, papers, and a three-ring notebook. Steve recognized some of the items as duplicates of those that James had given him.

"First, Steve, let's look through this stack of reading materials. Then we'll go over your preliminary treatment plan. After that, I need to ask you a few questions. Does that sound okay to you?"

Steve nodded.

The stack of educational materials included copies of the *Big Book,* the *Twelve Steps and Twelve Traditions,* and a tiny black hardcover book entitled *Twenty-Four Hours a Day*. There were half a dozen pamphlets—one thick one on denial, one on AA and the twelve steps, one on stress management, one on relationships in recovery, one on spirituality, and one on the disease concept of alcoholism. The notebook contained pages that referred to client rights and rules of conduct, several articles on AA, and a paper entitled "Abstinence vs. Recovery." The front inside sleeve of the notebook held a set of written homework assignments; the back sleeve held a list of AA and NA meetings in the city.

After briefly discussing the books and pamphlets, they went through the notebook. The first page had Steve's name, the date—August 31, 1974, and a blank line labeled "sobriety date." Cally wrote August 30, 1974 on the line. He looked at Steve and said, "This is your new birthday, Steve. It's the date on which you decided on a new and better way of life. It's just as much a day of new life as the one on which your mother bore you. Hopefully, you will come to appreciate this date and celebrate it annually for many years to come."

Cally pulled out a single page from the inside sleeve of the front cover. Titled "Preliminary Treatment Plan," it identified problems, goals, and activities for Steve to address during the beginning stages of treatment. They discussed each individual line.

Problem 1: Steve Campbell is an addict (alcohol, pot, speed), and he lacks genuine insight regarding the significance of his condition.

Goal 1: Become educated and insightful regarding addiction as a primary, progressive, fatal disease.

Goal 2: Move through denial in such a way that you can apply what you learn in treatment to your life in a meaningful way.

Activity 1: Read the first 164 pages of the Big Book of Alcoholics Anonymous.

Activity 2: Read Step One in the Twelve & Twelve.

Activity 3: Complete the written assignment "Step 1: Powerlessness & Unmanageability" & discuss in detail with counselor.

Activity 4: Read pamphlets on Denial and Disease Concept and discuss with counselor.

Activity 5: Ask three knowledgeable people why they think you may have a problem with alcohol and drugs; take notes, and discuss with group.

Problem 2: Steve has no effective support system that will encourage his sobriety. His current support system will try to sabotage his sobriety.

Goal 1: Develop a network of people who understand, respect, and can support your recovery from alcoholism and drug addiction.

Goal 2: Find new interests and activities that support sobriety, recovery, and physical, mental, emotional, & spiritual health.

Activity 1: Attend and record 40 AA meetings in 90 days.

Activity 2: Introduce self in AA at least twice per week, and each time, ask for support from the group.

Activity 3: Obtain a male AA sponsor by the end of September, and call or see him at least once a week.

Activity 4: Call each and every close personal friend and family member; tell them what you are doing, and ask each for his or her support. Avoid contact with those who hesitate or refuse to cooperate.

Activity 5: Read article on Abstinence vs. Recovery twice, discuss in detail with counselor, and develop a written plan for recovery which covers physical, mental, emotional, & spiritual aspects.

"Goddamn, Cally, I have another life, you know. When do you suppose I'll have time to do all this? I mean, I'm behind in work as it is. This doesn't seem reasonable to me."

"I know it looks like a lot, Steve, but let's look at it realistically. How many days per week have you been drinking and using drugs?"

"Well, just about every day, but not all goddamn day long."

"Okay, don't get too defensive on me here. Remember, I'm your partner in this journey, not your enemy. How about if we say that on the average, you spend just three hours a day drinking and doing drugs, and that includes the weekends. Fair enough?"

"Go on," Steve said. "I can see where this is headed, but go ahead."

Cally smiled. "Ah, there's that keen insight again. Anyway, that's all I want from you, just three hours a day. And Steve, if you will do this work and stick to this time commitment, I think you'll be shocked at how much time you have left to catch up on work and perform well in school when it gets going. Deal?"

Steve took a deep breath and sighed loudly. "Okay. I'll try."

"Trying is dying, Steve. We don't try; we *do*. Remember that. We are men of our word, and we are capable of making commitments and living up to the terms of those commitments. We have choices. Your commitment to sobriety is a conscious choice. It's not for either of us to take lightly."

Steve nodded and said, "All right, Cally. I'm in, at least for now. But honestly, I'm struggling with all of this. I wish we didn't have to move so damn fast, and I wish I could get my way some of the time. You know, there's a part of me that wishes that I had never laid eyes on you."

Cally reached over and put his hand on Steve's shoulder. He looked deeply into his eyes and said, "I want to tell you something, Steve. I care about you. I think that this journey is going to be challenging and frightening for you. I think that there will be times when you will want to pull out of it. Nevertheless, you need to know that I have your best interests at heart. And because of that, I'm going to push you forward. Sometimes I'll push you pretty hard. I'll challenge you and challenge you again to tear down your walls and embrace recovery. But I'll also be here for you. I'll support you. You can choose to fail at this challenge if you want to, but I won't let you do that without a fight. Do you hear what I'm saying?"

Steve nodded. "I hear you. I'm just a little scared about this whole thing. I'll be okay."

"That's good, Steve. I like your honesty about the fear. I like it a lot. This is a good start. Now, group is tomorrow night at 6:00. We meet right here. Please be here on time. It's important. Group will run until about 8:00 o'clock. By group time tomorrow, I want you to go to two AA meetings—one tonight and one tomorrow during the day. Just look at the schedule in your notebook. I've circled a few meeting places and times that I think will work for you. We'll set our next individual appointment time after group tomorrow night. Now, in the time that we have left, I'd like to ask you a few questions. Can you handle that?"

"Yeah, why not? I'm already in shock. What else can you do to me?"

Cally smiled. He then continued the interview process that had begun the previous day. He asked about Steve's childhood and his family. He showed particular interest in the time around Steve's sixth year, when basically healthy grandparents, functioning as primary care givers, had been removed and replaced by basically unhealthy parents.

He applauded the fact of Lois' recovery from alcoholism and said that if her recovery was indeed the real thing, then it would play an important role in Steve's.

At 1:00 o'clock, Cally laid down his legal pad and said, "Believe it or not, Steve, we're out of time. You have done well today. You've done very well. How do you feel?"

"Actually, I feel pretty good. I feel a lot better than when I came in two hours ago."

Leaving the center, Steve again felt reassured. When he got home, he ate lunch, changed clothes, and worked in his shop for three straight hours. At 5:30, he called Al Bommer.

"Well, hello, Steve. Of course I remember who you are. I'm old but not yet senile. Actually, I've thought about you quite a bit. I would have called, but I didn't want to be a nuisance."

"Yeah, I figured as much, Al. The truth is, though, I'm ready to go to that AA meeting now, and I thought that you might meet me at one tonight. I was thinking about the one you mentioned last time, you know, the one over on Berkman Drive."

"Why certainly, Steve. I would be delighted. It starts at 8:00 o'clock, as you know. I'll get there at 7:45, and I'll look for you if you will just tell me what to look for."

"Well, I'm your direct opposite, Al. I'm young, average height and build, and I have real long, kind of dirty blond hair. I'll be wearing jeans and a T-shirt."

"Good deal; I won't have any trouble spotting you. And Steve, I am so pleased that you called."

Steve hung up the phone and smiled. "Who knows?" he said. "Maybe this won't be so bad after all."

CHAPTER 44

Steve's first meeting of Alcoholics Anonymous received decidedly mixed reviews.

On the one hand, he liked Al Bommer even more than he expected. The moment Steve walked in the door Al extended his hand and treated him like a long lost friend. He introduced Steve to every individual in the room. He sat Steve in one of the few chairs with a padded seat and never left his side except to fill Steve's coffee cup every time it reached half-empty. He did not try to contain his enthusiasm for Steve's presence at the meeting.

The meeting itself was another story. A wheezing fat man with a bulbous nose opened the meeting by mumbling through several pages from the Big Book. Steve hardly understood a word. Then he asked if there were any visitors or newcomers. Steve's sat perfectly still with his hands in his lap and prayed that Al would do the same. Al did not move a muscle.

The fat man introduced a topic for discussion. The topic was Step Three—the third of the twelve steps, in which one makes a decision to turn his will and his life over to the care of God, as he understands him. Following the introduction, the members of the group spent the rest of the hour talking about God. Steve silently cringed as he heard, "God this, God that, God is good, the grace of God, the will of God, the care of God," and so on, ad nauseam. By mid-meeting, he felt impatient. By the end of the hour, he felt dispirited.

"Bullshit, bullshit, bullshit," he repeated to himself over and over. Had he not feared embarrassment, or had Al not been present, he would have walked out and never looked back.

Toward the end of the meeting, the fat man offered tokens to anyone who had remained sober for different specific lengths of time up to a year. Then he offered a "desire chip" to anyone, especially any newcomer, who acknowledged "a desire to stop drinking one day at a time." He got no takers. Then, to top off the God talk, at the very end of the meeting everyone stood up, held hands, and said The Lord's Prayer.

As they left the building, Al said, "Well, Steve, what did you think?"

"I don't know, Al," he answered. "Parts of it were interesting, I guess, but to tell you the truth, I'm not real big on religion. I mean, I'm not an atheist or anything like that, but I'm not a Christian, either. I guess I just expected something different."

"Yes, well, it's different every night, Steve. Sometimes it's very different. Listen, if you'll let me, I'd like to buy you a cup of coffee, and we can talk for a little while."

"How about if I take a rain check on that, Al? I really need to get home and get some studying done. I feel like I'm behind on everything in my life right now, if you know what I mean."

"Sure, that's no problem. Here, I have something for you." He held out his closed hand to Steve.

Steve extended his open palm, and Al placed a round token into it. On one side it read "One Day at a Time." The other side held a prayer. "It's a desire chip, Steve. It signifies a desire to stay sober. I hope that you'll accept it and carry it with you at all times to remind yourself of the desire for sobriety that got you here to this meeting tonight."

"Thanks, Al. That was very thoughtful of you. I will carry it."

Al smiled broadly. "Good; and listen, Steve, please call me again. And I mean anytime, night or day. I'd consider it a favor to me for you to call."

Steve smiled. "I'll see you again. I'm pretty sure of that."

When Steve pulled up to the front of his house, he saw James sitting on the front steps.

"Hey, dude," he said. "Where you been?"

"Would you believe an AA Meeting?" Steve answered.

"Yeah, I had a feeling that might be where you were. So how was it?"

"Not worth a shit, if you want the truth," Steve said.

"No kidding?" James asked.

"No kidding, man. I mean, James, they sat around for a whole fucking hour talking about religion. I didn't hear one word about staying sober. It was all about religion. Hell, you know me, man. It's not like I don't believe in God, or that I'm not interested in God, but if I wanted to talk about God for a whole hour with a bunch of strangers, I'd go to church. I don't know; I didn't like it."

"Hmm. Well, if I remember right, those AA people can get off on some pretty wild tangents. So how long have you been clean? Two days now?"

"Yep, exactly. Two unbelievably long days. I don't know, man; I'm still not sure that this is the right thing for me. I just wanted to be a social drinker. I don't want to be some fucking priest or anything, you know? I'm not sure that I even like God these days, and I'm damn sure that I don't want to stand around holding hands and praying with a bunch of assholes that I don't even know."

James laughed. "You kill me, man," he said. "First off, you need to understand something about recovery, at least the way Cally describes it. It's not a religious deal, man. It's a spiritual deal. Those are two very different things.

"Religion is all about rules and sins and shit like that. Spirituality is more about attitudes and feelings, especially feelings of being connected with God and other people. It's about feeling good about yourself, too, and who you are in your heart. It's about growth and change that leads to a healthier and happier way of life.

"Steve, you and I talk about spirituality all the time, man. Every time we talk about letting go of ego and experiencing the world free of fear and other barriers we're talking about spiritual concepts. And that's different from religion."

Steve nodded. "Yeah, I guess so. But it seems to me that at that AA meeting, they were talking about religion, and not *just* religion, either, but Christian religion. I mean, they said the Lord's Prayer, for crying out loud. You know, the one we said in Baptist Sunday School?"

"Well, Steve, take a really close look at that prayer some day. Study it line by line, forgetting your prejudice and anger against the Baptist Church long enough to see what it says. You might find that it speaks to you of something other than Baptist religious doctrine. I mean, The Southern Baptist Convention may have commandeered some things that don't really belong to them, but that doesn't make those things theirs. That prayer is bigger than the church. I love that prayer, at least within the context of my own interpretation of it."

"Yeah, I know, and I'm probably sitting here making a mountain out of a molehill. But be that as it may, James, I know what I heard. Man, I could have been at a revival and heard less praise of God."

"Yes, and....? What's your point? I mean, it sounds as though they were expressing their personal sentiments, like they have an understanding of God and aren't afraid to share it. I imagine they were using words like 'faith' and 'gratitude' and phrases like 'God's will.' Am I right?"

Steve didn't answer, and James continued. "Look, the way I see it, man, you have to come to your own understanding of who or what God is. When you've done that, and you're comfortable with it, then it becomes easy to feel and express gratitude without interference from all the crap that we learned as children in our grandparents' churches. Then your spiritual program can help your recovery process. That's true because as you grow spiritually, you feel better about and more accepting of yourself and the world, including those people who understand God differently than you do. And as that happens, there's less and less to cover up with drugs and alcohol."

"Yeah, James, you sound like a man who speaks from experience. I'll ask you the same kind of question that I asked you the other day. What are *you* covering up with drugs and alcohol?"

"I've got my baggage, Steve. Obviously I do. That's certainly no secret from the world. I'm not holding myself out as an example of a highly spiritually evolved person. I stumble along like everyone else. In fact, I do it with enthusiasm. I search every day, and through my search, I hit a few straight paths and a ton of blind alleys. I think, though, that I understand AA and its twelve step program in terms of it being a spiritual path. It's not my path, but the basic principles are the same, and I believe that I understand it. Besides, I don't remember that we were talking about me. Let's stay on you and try to get you over this hump."

"That sounds awfully damn convenient for you, but okay. Listen, I get the conceptual difference between religion and spirituality. I think I do anyway. What I don't see is how I'll work on my spirituality—my spiritual growth—in AA when what they're throwing out is religion in the guise of spirituality. That's my point. If you'll remember, we started this conversation by my saying how much I disliked the AA meeting because it was like a tent revival. Maybe I should be going to the Buddhist meditation center instead of AA. From what I heard tonight, it would sure connect up with my spiritual beliefs a lot more closely."

"Or, Steve, maybe it's simpler than that. For the time being, anyway, maybe you should go to more AA meetings and see if this one is representative of AA generally. Man, I went to about a hundred and fifty AA meetings during my year at Steadman House, and I'll tell you the truth, I don't remember very many like the one that you're describing to me. I'm sure there were some, but they don't stand out in my memory. Actually, I remember more meetings where people were pissed off at God than where they praised Him.

"Another thing I remember very clearly is that meetings were different from meeting place to meeting place, and even from meeting time to meeting time. Man, they took us to one place in North Austin where there were signs on the wall asking people to refrain from cursing. And there was one in South Austin where I swear there were half a dozen bikers in full leathers, and every other word was 'motherfucker this' and 'motherfucker that.'

"I remember one big fat son of a bitch stood up and roared, 'Fuck God if he can't take a joke.' About half of the people in the room curled their shoulders up around their ears as if the place was about to be struck by lightning or something, and the other half roared with laughter. I'm not exaggerating, either. It was funny as shit. Anyway, Steve, I don't think anyone will try to tell you that AA is perfect. I mean, think about it; it's not like a gathering of Nobel Prize recipients discussing the meaning of man's existence. It's a bunch of assholes like you and me wading through difficult times. If praising God helps them along and gives them hope, who are you and I to complain?"

"Yeah, okay, enough already, James. I get your point. I guess it doesn't matter that much anyway; Cally has me going to a meeting every other damn day for 90 days. Can you believe that shit? Doesn't that sound excessive to you?"

"Every other day? You got off easy, man. Most people who work with Cally have to do 90 meetings in 90 days. That's one of his favorite deals. I think it's supposed to lay a foundation that you can't very easily walk away from."

Steve rolled his eyes. "That's insane," he said, shaking his head. Then he asked, "So, tell me something James; how come you did—walk away from it, that is?"

"It wasn't for me, man. Maybe it was the total abstinence part of it, or perhaps it was the fellowship part. As you know, I don't dig people very much, especially groups of people. It did influence my life, though, and I have a lot of respect for AA, especially the twelve steps, which represent a truly profound spiritual path. And there's no one in the world that I respect and trust more than Cally. I've stayed in touch with him continuously since I left Steadman two years ago. I probably see him or talk to him at least once a month. He knows I use, but he never bugs me about it, at least in a serious way. I feel as though he never judges me. He's a good guy, Steve. I'm glad you're working with him."

"Well, tell me this, James. Are you glad I'm getting sober and clean? I mean, hasn't getting high been an important part of our friendship over the years?"

James frowned and looked down for a moment. "Yeah, I've thought about that," he said softly. "I decided, though, that it's not really an issue. You need to move forward, to find your own path. Wherever that takes you, I'm pretty sure that I'll be there with you. And even if we should go off in such different directions that we can no longer connect, then so be it. We'll survive. Our friendship isn't really that important at the moment, Steve. Your spiritual growth and your healing—that's the important thing. Anyway, we became friends long before we ever started using together. Surely we can remain friends when we're not using together again."

"Thank you, James," Steve said. "I appreciate that more than you know. I mean, your willingness to give up one of the few friends you have is pretty damn generous."

"Yeah, well, don't make a big deal out of it," James replied. "You know, this whole thing is going to force me to deepen my own self-examination. I've been kind of coasting lately, but now I feel as though I better get back on track myself. If I don't, you'll end up outgrowing me and not wanting to listen to my outlandish bullshit. What would I do then? I guess when you look it that way, your journey is a gift to you and me both."

Steve looked at James and smiled. "Man, are you sure you don't want to climb into this same boat with me?"

"No, man, that would just be a distraction for both of us. Like I said, though, I'll be watching you. So anyway, listen, man, I need to get going. You do your homework. Cally hates it when you don't keep promises. Have you told Tommy what you're up to yet?"

"No, but I will. He's going to flip his fucking lid."

James laughed. "That's good. His fucking lid needs flipping every once in a while."

Steve watched James drive away in his beat up old Buick. "Jesus, what a character," he said to himself as he waved goodbye.

For the second night in a row, Steve thought about going over to The Roam In to see Dixie, but again, he decided against it. Instead, he sat down and worked on his first written assignment for Cally. The assignment included fifteen questions concerning one's "powerlessness" over alcohol and drugs and the "unmanageability" of one's life resulting from their use. Steve did not fully understand all of the questions; a few simply did not apply to him. He left several blank and jotted down superficial answers to several others.

Steve slept restlessly. He woke up at 6:15 on Friday morning with powerlessness and unmanageability on his mind and nervous energy running haywire throughout his body. He forced himself to eat breakfast. His hunger for coffee was nearly unquenchable. He walked out to his shop at 7:00 o'clock, and despite feeling restless and irritable, he worked hard for two solid hours before returning inside to study.

Sitting still, much less studying, proved to be a challenge. His thoughts continually drifted away from psychology to sobriety, treatment, his treatment plan, the previous night's AA meeting, his conversation with James, the prospect of attending

225

another AA meeting at noon, and his first group therapy session at 6:00.

At 11:45, Steve drove to the Catholic Student Center, just the other side of the UT campus. When he walked into the AA meeting room, he found two young women, three young men, and one older man arranging chairs into a small circle. They all smiled and greeted him. When the circle was complete, Steve sat down next to a nerdy looking guy with thick glasses and a hole in his shirt.

One of the women, who identified herself as "...Patti, and I'm an alcoholic," started the meeting by reading what sounded like the same information that the fat man had read the night before. When she finished reading, she turned to Steve and said, "Today's our lucky day; we have a newcomer. Would you please give us your first name?"

Steve blushed slightly and said, "Yes, my name is Steve."

Everyone in the group smiled and said, "Hi, Steve."

"Welcome, Steve," Patti said. "Gosh, it feels good to have a new face in the group. Not that I don't love these faces who are always here, but, well, you know what I mean." Everyone laughed. "It's just nice to have someone new. Would you be interested in telling us a little about yourself?"

Steve shrugged his shoulders. "Oh, I guess so," he said. "This is only my second AA meeting and my third day of being clean, so I don't really feel as though I have much to say. I just started treatment, and going to AA meetings is part of the deal. I can't really say for sure that I'm an alcoholic, but I guess I'll find out soon enough. I mean, I probably am. My counselor says I am; and my friend, who has been in treatment, says I am; and to tell you the truth, I've even said it myself a few times. I'm just not so sure how truly I believe it. My parents are both alcoholics. I know I'm not like them, but I have had some problems around my drinking and drugging. So, anyway, we'll see. I don't know what else to say, really. My counselor says that I should be honest, so I probably should admit that I'm not all that excited about AA right now. I guess that's about it."

Patti smiled and nodded. "Okay, thank you so much, Steve. You're very welcome here. We meet every Monday through Friday at noon. It's usually just us plus a couple of others who aren't here today, and then occasionally a visitor or someone who's just curious.

"So, anyway, in your honor, I think today's topic will be 'How I got to AA in the first place,' and I would like to start."

Patti spoke for about ten minutes about her alcoholism and her abuse of diet pills. Her story flowed easily. Steve thought to himself that she was remarkably open about her life, which he found very interesting. She had been sober for nearly two years.

The older man, Ralph, spoke next. He identified himself as an alcoholic and addict and acknowledged to Steve that he was a faculty member from the political science department. He, too, was articulate and open. He described his alcohol and cocaine abuse and his family's intervention on him two and a half years prior. He shared his fear and humiliation around the intervention process, in which his two teenage daughters confronted him directly and asked him to change. He talked about feeling very happy and healthy in sobriety. Steve wondered if he felt out of place, being the only real "adult" in attendance.

Clarence, the "geek" sitting next to Steve, identified himself as a pot addict who smoked up to ten joints a day before getting into recovery almost one year prior. Clarence was intelligent, expressive, and funny. Steve laughed along with the rest of the group at his "war stories," one of which had him totally spaced out in class and "coming to" with everyone silently staring at him, awaiting his answer to the professor's question, and him staring back blankly and saying, "Huh? I think I must have missed something."

As the meeting progressed, Steve warmed up to it. He liked what he saw. One person spoke, and everyone else listened. One person shared some part of his or her life, and the rest of the group connected. They cared for each other. It felt real.

Every member included Steve as part of the group. As each member spoke, he or she caught Steve's eye and smiled in an effort to engage him. Every person talked, and Steve related in some way to every story.

One of the women, Sue, described herself as an alcoholic who, like Steve, was new to the group and to sobriety, with just three weeks sober. Sue reminded Steve of Rachel—shy, soft-spoken, athletic-looking, and pretty.

The meeting ran longer than an hour. At its end, everyone stood, held hands, and said the Lord's Prayer. The experience did not irritate Steve the way it had the night before.

When the meeting broke up, Patti approached Steve. "Thank you for coming, Steve. I hope you'll come back."

"Thanks, Patti. I'm pretty sure I will. I live close by, and I start back in school next week, so it's convenient. I'm supposed to go to 40 meetings in 90 days."

"Yeah, I did something like that myself," she said. "I did 90 in 90. I remember that it sounded like an impossible task at first, but I'm so glad now that I stuck it out. I think it made a big difference in my sobriety; it put me on solid footing. Anyway, I just wanted to say 'keep coming back.' That's an AA slogan, in case you didn't know."

"Okay, well, thanks again. Maybe I'll see you Monday."

Steve started to leave, but Ralph, the professor, stopped him before he got out the door. "Steve, I just wanted to say 'welcome.' I remember how hard those first few days and weeks were. I thought you might like to have my phone number, you know, just in case the going gets rough and you need someone to talk to, especially over the weekend."

"Yeah, I'd appreciate that," Steve said. "I don't have any friends in Austin who don't get high. Not that my friends aren't supportive, you know. They are. But except for one guy, I think my friends don't believe I need to be doing this."

Ralph smiled. "That's pretty ironic, isn't it? Anyway, I would welcome your call, and I really mean that."

"Thanks. You may hear from me."

Steve walked away from the meeting feeling good. It was the best and most hopeful that he had felt since beginning this journey.

CHAPTER 45

On his way home from the meeting, Steve stopped at the grocery co-op for a few items. He ended up buying enough food to feed the neighborhood. He bought fruit, vegetables, bread, chicken, meat, frozen dinners, juices, and lots of sugar, including cookies, chocolate, pastry, and ice cream. He envisioned going home and eating it all.

Once home, he jumped into organizing. He made menus for the next seven days. He went through his drawers and closet and sorted his clothes into keepers and losers. He straightened up the kids' bedroom and got it ready for their visit. He sorted and alphabetized his record collection.

He went out to his shop and organized his jobs, rank ordering them into those that were very late down through those that were not yet due. He developed a work schedule that would allow him to complete them all within a month. Then he telephoned every customer and negotiated revised delivery dates. During those conversations, he gave preliminary estimates on additional work. By the end of the afternoon, he figured that he had lined up another month's worth of refinishing jobs.

At 5:15, he reviewed his afternoon. When he realized just how much he had accomplished, he felt remarkably positive, strong, and energized.

Steve arrived at The Recovery Center at 5:58. When he walked in, he found seven other clients, plus Cally, already sitting in a circle in the group room. They seemed happy, relaxed, and friendly among themselves. He quietly took the empty chair and tried his best to look comfortable.

Cally started talking at precisely 6:00 o'clock. He led the group in a relaxation exercise and then a silent meditation. Steve tried, but he could not relax his body. Nor could he quiet the chatter in his head. He felt like he was on speed.

Following the meditation, Cally introduced Steve to the group. "Well, folks, as you can see, we have a new group member. This is Mr. Steve Campbell, who has been sober since about 2:30 Wednesday morning. Steve comes to us on his own volition, referred by a former client. Steve, I don't want to put you on the spot right off the bat, so I'll ask the other members of the group to start by introducing themselves to you. Briefly, please. Who wants to start?"

One-by-one, seven group members introduced themselves by giving their names, sobriety dates, and very brief sketches of their recovery experience. Steve secretly judged and nicknamed each as he or she spoke.

Albert, a middle-aged heroin addict wearing dirty clothes, reported ten months clean. Steve named him "Junkman" and pegged him as the only member of the group who looked as though he belonged in treatment.

Billy, a young gay man, reported six months clean off of "everything known to mankind." Steve immediately disliked and distrusted him. He named him "Fag."

Peg, about Carla's age and size but not as attractive, reported "almost six months without a joint." Steve liked her and called her "Legs."

Jim, a smiling, soft-spoken young black man, had two months free from alcohol and cocaine. Steve named him "Mr. Nice Guy."

Sally, a tough-talking woman in her 40s, reported 48 days without a drink "and not happy about it." Sally had been convicted of involuntary manslaughter for shooting her husband to death with a .38 caliber pistol. She was free on bail pending an appeal of that conviction. Steve called her "Killer" and decided not to cross her.

Robert, a businessman in coat and tie, reported five months sober. Steve gave him the name "Yuppie Man."

Finally, there was Kathy, who introduced herself as a recovering alcoholic, addict, and ex-prostitute with about six months in the program. Kathy looked to be about Steve's age or perhaps a little younger. She was beautiful. Steve tried not to stare. He started to give her the nickname "Hooker" but then decided not to give her one at all.

"Well, I guess it's my turn," Steve said. "My name is Steve Campbell. Like Cally said, this is my third day sober and clean. I'm here because...well, I'm not exactly sure why I'm here. But I made a commitment to Cally to join this program, so here I am. I've started going to AA. I've been to two meetings. I hated the first one, but the one today was better.

"Anyway, I've been drinking since I was 14 and doing drugs for about seven or eight years, mainly pot and speed, but also coke and acid. During the last couple of years, I seem to have gotten a little out of control with it, at least every once in a while. When that has happened, I've said and done some things that I've felt bad about.

"I don't know; I can't honestly say I'm glad to be here, but I'm here nevertheless, so I guess we'll see how it goes."

"Good, Steve; thank you," Cally said. "Alright, group, tonight we're going to talk about denial again. This is out of respect for the topic itself and for group members who are still embracing and protecting theirs. As I look around the group, I see that the topic is relevant to exactly eight of you."

Cally talked for 25 minutes about denial. Steve recognized parts of the lecture from James' notes, and he easily understood why James was so impressed with Cally's lectures. The information was concise and organized. He delivered it powerfully and convincingly.

He described denial as a psychological process that happens below the conscious level, so that the person who is in denial is genuinely unaware of it. He talked about denial being invisible to the person who has it but visible to others around him. He assured the group that everyone has denial, including himself, relevant to any number of areas of their lives. He stated that denial is a natural part of one's defense system, and that defense systems are a natural part of one's psychological makeup.

Cally described methods to facilitate movement through denial toward truer insight and awareness. He stated that movement through denial regarding the nature and extent of one's alcohol and drug abuse represented the number one challenge of each group member during the course of his or her treatment. He emphasized that gradually moving through denial, like walking through fog into clearing skies, opened the door to a more real and genuine Step 1, and that without Step 1, the alcoholic and addict "is simply up shit creek without a paddle."

"The final point I want to make is this," he said. "Group therapy is the most powerful denial buster that you will ever find because you and your peers have the opportunity, *and* the responsibility, to confront each other on your bullshit. It's one thing for me to confront you, but it's another for you to confront each other. The latter is invariably more powerful than the former."

When Cally finished his lecture, he turned to Kathy, the hooker. "Kathy, you've been working hard on yourself. You've learned a lot about yourself and gained good insight. If you will, please, share with the group your experience with becoming aware of your own denial. What areas of your life have been affected by your denial?"

"Well," she said, "my alcohol and drug abuse, of course. I went to great lengths to rationalize and justify using. I told myself that it was just part of the territory I lived in. I convinced myself that I wasn't any worse off than anyone else, but hell, look at who I was hanging out with and comparing myself to. At most, I believed that my relationship with drugs and alcohol was an occasional small problem that I could handle if and when I wanted to. I know now that it was a major problem, maybe even *the* major problem, in my life.

"When I look back on it, I realize that using drugs was one of the main reasons why I stayed in my line of work as long as I did. Easy money from easy men translated into easy drugs. It was a vicious cycle. I worked to buy drugs, and I used drugs to deal with my feelings about work.

"And speaking of work, I had a lot of denial around my work and that whole lifestyle. I think I originally used my lack of education and training as an excuse to justify my work. But I also had a lot of false pride around it. The money was almost frighteningly good, and I was tough enough and smart enough to operate independently, which meant that I kept everything I made. But God, it got old. And that's when the denial really came in, when all that remained was the money and the drugs, and I still used the same excuses as before.

"I don't know, I'm starting to ramble, I guess, but the gist of it is that I honestly believed that I had my life under control. The truth is that my life was a hell of a mess—a *fucking* mess, if you'll pardon the pun. I had no true self-worth or self-respect left, but I was blind to that. My blindness was my denial."

After she finished talking, the group was silent for the better part of a minute, until Yuppie Man spoke up. "Thanks, Kathy," he said. "I know our stories are very different, but I can still relate. In some ways, I feel like I've been prostituting myself all my life, especially when it comes to money. I've been working for the same company for fifteen years, and I can't count the number of stupid jerks whose butts I've kissed because I was afraid of losing my job or not being promoted. And I've done it with a smile on my face."

"I can see how that might be seen as prostitution, Robert, but how is it denial?" Cally asked. "It sounds more like plain old dishonesty, as in manipulation and lying. I say that because you've been aware of what you're doing. Denial implies an absence of awareness."

"Well, I don't know, Cally. Maybe it's not denial, but it sure has affected the way I feel about myself."

231

At that point, Billy, the Fag entered the discussion. "It's denial if you honestly thought that lying was the best thing for you to do. In reality, it never is. Right, Cally?"

"I don't know, Billy, has that been true for you?"

Billy furrowed his brow and thought for a moment. "No, not really. I think that sometimes it's stupid to tell people the truth. Not everyone can handle the truth gracefully."

"Are you thinking of something specific?" Cally asked.

"Yes," Billy answered. "I've known for most of my life that I'm gay, but I haven't always been honest about that. When I told my parents, they wouldn't even talk about it. They wanted me to go talk to their minister. When I refused to do that, they started checking on psychiatrists. Just this Christmas, my mother said 'Oh, you're not still having that problem, are you?' But I guess that's her denial, not mine. Mine is hoping beyond hope that some day they'll understand and accept me as I am. In reality, that will probably never happen. If I keep believing it, though, it's less painful for me."

Group continued without Steve's participation until about 7:45, when Cally said, "Well, Steve, I know you've been listening. How about your denial? What form does it take?"

"I don't know, Cally. I *have* been listening, and I think I understand what everyone's been saying. The denial stuff confuses me, though, at least when I try to apply it to myself. I mean, I know that my drinking and drugging has affected me in negative ways. If it hadn't, I wouldn't be sitting around here on a Friday night. I'm sure that it has affected me more than what I'm aware of right now. I mean, I know I have denial, too.

"But what I'm more conscious of right now is how much I'm giving up. You know, I really like getting high. It feels good to me. It relaxes me, and in a lot of ways, it seems like it makes my life better instead of worse. I mean, it's fun, usually, and it's not always out of control or anything like that. In fact, it's very seldom out of control.

"There's the bad stuff, too; I know that. Like I said, I've said and done things that I've felt embarrassed about. But I've survived those things. I've apologized to people and made it up to them and then gone on. And then there's the money. I mean, who knows how much I've really spent just in the last year on alcohol and drugs? Again, though, I pay my bills on time, even my child support, just like clockwork. I've never been arrested or anything. I make excellent grades in school. I mean, all in all, everything considered, my life works pretty well. Really and truly, no one except my ex-wife has really complained hard about my drinking and drugging. So I don't know...." He shrugged his shoulders. "I guess that's it. Like I said, we'll see what happens."

Billy smiled and spoke up. "Boy, I can tell already; you're going to be a fun one, Steve."

232

Steve's anger shot up instantly. He felt himself blush, and in his best carefully controlled, subtly threatening voice, he said, "Yeah? You think so, Billy?"

Cally stepped in immediately. "Whoa, Steve. Forgive my stepping in, but I think what Billy means is that it will be interesting to watch you gain insight. And not to change the subject, but you look rather angry."

"No, Cally, I'm not angry," Steve said.

"It's nothing personal, Steve," Billy said, grinning. "I certainly didn't mean it in a malicious way."

Group ended at 8:00 o'clock with everyone holding hands and reciting the Serenity Prayer. Afterwards, when the others had filtered out, Cally asked Steve, "So, where do you suppose all of that control comes from, Steve?"

"What are you talking about?"

"The control. What kept you from acknowledging your anger at Billy?"

"I don't know. It's no big deal. My anger is none of his business unless I decided to take it out of his hide."

"Steve, listen," Cally said calmly. "This isn't the place to be a tough guy. Be a tough guy at the bar. This is the place to practice being honest. It's the place to practice being real. Do you hear what I'm saying?"

Steve nodded. "Hell, I'm sorry, Cally. I don't know where the control comes from. I don't think it's always wise to show people your feelings, though. I mean, sometimes it means revealing your trump card. Like with Billy, my first impression is that the guy's an asshole. He's cynical and sarcastic. But he doesn't need to know how I feel about him. If he knows how I feel, then that puts us on even ground."

"Hmm. That's an interesting approach to control. And one that we will look at later, I might add. About Billy, though, give him a chance, Steve. Try not to judge until you have more to go on, okay?"

"Well, I don't know. Anyway, I ought to get going. When do you want to see me again?"

"Monday afternoon at 1:30. Bring your homework, at least your Step One Exercise, and we'll look at it together. Also, call me Sunday morning before 10:00 o'clock. Now, are you okay?"

"Yeah, I'll be fine, Cally. I'll talk to you Sunday."

Walking out to his truck, Steve still felt aggravated. Then he saw Kathy leaning against her car, a 1966 Mustang Convertible, and his aggravation disappeared. He walked over to her. "Nice wheels. The '66 model has always been my favorite."

"Thanks. Listen, I just wanted to welcome you to the group. I know how hard it is to get started. I hope it works out for you."

"Thanks, Kathy. I appreciate that. I felt out of place tonight, but I know it will get better. I hope so, anyway. I just didn't like the way it ended."

Kathy nodded. "Yeah, Billy can get under your skin if you let him, but he's really not bad. Actually, he helps keep the group interesting. Anyway, I was wondering where you're going to meetings."

"Well, I went to one over on Berkman Drive last night, and I didn't like it at all. Today, though, I went to one right across the street from the UT campus, and it was much better. I didn't feel so different from everyone. To tell you the truth, I wish I didn't have to go at all."

"Yeah, I know what you mean. I felt that way for a while. I like going now, though. I feel accepted there, you know, same as here. I feel as though people don't judge me at AA, and that's been a big deal for me. Maybe you would like to go to a meeting with me sometime. I could take you to a really good group and introduce you to some of the people who helped me feel good about AA. It might help."

"Yeah, sure. When?"

"Well, how about tomorrow night? I could pick you up if you want."

"Well, I'm going to have my kids this weekend, but I bet I can find someone to stay with them, so sure, why not? It might be nice to meet some AA people I could really relate to. I'll tell you what. Give me your phone number, and if I can't get a sitter, I'll call you. Otherwise, I'm all yours."

They exchanged numbers, and Steve gave Kathy his address. As he drove home, he wondered what she had up her sleeve. "She must be interested," he thought. "I sure could think of worse things than that, even if Cally didn't approve."

When Steve walked into his house, the phone was ringing. It was Bev. "I can't believe I actually caught you at home on a Friday night," she said.

"Yeah, well, lots of things are different around here these days. What's up? Is something wrong with the kids?"

"No, Steve, they're fine, but there's something I need to talk with you about." She hesitated and then said, "I've been offered a really good job in Denver, Colorado."

Steve fell silent. "Steve?" Bev said. "Are you still there?"

"Yeah, I'm here. I heard you. So what does that mean? What are you going to do?"

"Well, I'm going to take it. I feel like I have to. It's a job with a real future. I can make a better living for me and the kids than I could ever make here. Its just too good of an opportunity to pass up."

"So when are you planning on moving?"

"Well, the actual move will be in about three weeks, but I just found out this evening that the company wants to fly me and the kids up there tomorrow morning for four days. They want to meet Lynn and Eddie and show us around. The company owns an apartment complex, and the job offer includes six months rent free in one of their two bedroom apartments. Plus, they're going to pay for a moving company to pack us up and move us.

"This is a good organization, Steve, and it's a great opportunity for me. I feel really bad about it, though, for you. Especially since you have been so conscientious about seeing the kids and everything. I really hope that we can work through it somehow."

"Yeah, right, Bev. What the hell does that mean? You're going to take the kids to another state, and I have no say and no recourse. I don't suppose you called me to ask my permission. How are we supposed to work through that? I mean, what is there to work through? You get what you want. End of story."

Bev was silent for a moment. "I don't know, Steve. But maybe we could try to talk about it in a reasonable, mature way."

Steve laughed sarcastically. "What's there to talk about? What I hear you saying is that you have made certain decisions that affect my life profoundly. I mean, what if I say, 'No, I'm sorry, but tomorrow and Sunday are my visitation days, and I'll be there to pick up the kids at noon, as agreed upon by you and directed by the court.' What then? Would they be there, waiting for me?"

"No, but..."

"See?" Steve said, interrupting her. "It's a fucking stacked deck. So what do you and I have to talk about in a reasonable, mature way? Answer me that."

Bev did not respond, and after a few seconds of silence, Steve hung up the phone without saying another word. His first thought was to get even. His second was to get high. Fortunately, he had no stash, not even stems and seeds.

CHAPTER 46

Steve cursed the day that he ever met Bev. The anger, hurt, and fear that he had felt during and after the divorce slapped him in the face once again. "Fucked again, goddamn it!" he shouted. "Fucked again by the same goddamn bitch. I hate you, bitch! I hate your goddamn fucking guts!"

235

Several minutes of yelling and stomping around the house brought Steve some solace. He ended his tirade by lying across his bed and crying into his pillow.

At 10:30, he picked up the phone and called Rachel.

"Hey, old friend," he said, "you're home alone on a Friday night?"

"Wow, two phone calls in one week from my old lover, Steve. And who says I'm alone?"

"Oops. I'm sorry, Rachel. Did I call at a bad time?"

"No, I'm just kidding. I'm here with Sammy. What's going on with you?"

"A lot. I was hoping you could talk for a few minutes."

"Sure, hang on a minute, and I'll turn off the TV."

"You know, Rachel, when I left you in San Marcos Sunday night, I really thought a lot about what you said. And as a result of that, I honestly resolved to change the way I used alcohol and drugs. I really felt it, too, you know? I even talked to a counselor Tuesday afternoon. Then, guess what happened. I proceeded to blow it out again Tuesday night. I went right over the fucking top. So I gave up. I signed up for alcohol & drug treatment the next day. I had my first session that afternoon and went again yesterday and then again tonight. And I've been clean for three days, or at least it will be three days in about four hours. Can you believe that?"

"Yes, I can, Steve. And you know what? I'm not shocked. I'm delighted, but I'm not really surprised. I could tell that you've been struggling with it. When you called me so early that morning last month, you sounded horrible. It actually kind of scared me. Then last week, you listened so intently when I told you about my sobriety that I knew you were searching for answers. Anyway, I'm proud of you, and if you were here, I'd kiss you right on the mouth and squeeze the stuffing out of you."

Steve laughed softly. "Thanks, Rachel. That means a lot to me; it really does. I'm pretty confused right now, and your understanding and support gives me a much needed boost. I wish you were here. I would kiss you back and then get on my knees to beg you out of your celibacy.

"Listen, though, I've got something else on my mind, too, and I need to talk to someone about it because I'm about two steps away from getting loaded right now. Do you have a little time?"

They talked quietly for over an hour. Rachel listened well, and while she did not try to diminish Steve's sadness around Lynn and Eddie's moving, she did convince him to consider the timeliness of it. "You have so much on your plate right now," she said. "You've got your business, then there's graduate school, and now you've made this commitment to attend a treatment program and drastically alter your entire lifestyle with sobriety.

Steve, that's an incredible load. I think fewer responsibilities and time demands might be a real blessing in disguise."

Steve and Rachel said "goodbye" with the promise to get together very soon.

Steve slept peacefully. When he woke up a little after 7:00, he felt rested and at peace. He ate breakfast, poured his third cup of coffee, and at 8:00 o'clock, he called Lois.

"Hi, Honey. What's up with you?"

"Well, I thought you might like to know that I started in treatment Wednesday, and today is my fourth day sober."

"Oh, Steve, I'm so glad to get that news!" she said. She covered the phone lightly with her hand and yelled, "Chester, Steve is sober! He's in a treatment program!" Then back to Steve, she said, "Okay, tell me about it. Give me the details."

Steve smiled to himself. "Now, listen, Mother; don't jump to any big conclusions here. I'm sober right now, and I'm in treatment, and I'm going to AA meetings. And I even feel pretty good about it at this moment. But I'm not committed to this process the way you are, or the way you probably want me to be. I mean, I don't want to sound discouraging or anything, but I really don't want you to get your hopes up too high, either. You understand?"

"Yes, okay, I hear you. What I hear is that you are sober today. You know, Steve, we can only be sober one day at a time. I've been sober for almost ten years, but today, I'm sober just exactly the same as you—today. So I'm afraid that you can't dampen my joy, and, I must say, my relief at this moment. So come on, tell me about it."

"Well, believe it or not, James, of all people, gave me the name of a counselor that he had when he was in a halfway house two years ago. He really encouraged me to go talk to this guy. So I did, and I liked him, and to make a long story short, I agreed to give treatment a try. I had my first individual session Wednesday and another one Thursday. I had my first group session last night. I'll see him again Monday afternoon. In the meantime, he has me going to AA about every other day. I've been twice, and I'm going again tonight with a girl I met in group."

"Oh, that's great, Steve. How did you like AA? And did you get in touch with Al Bommer?"

"Yes, in fact, I did call Al. He met me at my first meeting. I liked him a lot, but I hated the meeting. It was like a Baptist revival, and you know how I am about that. The one I went to yesterday was better, though. It was a small group over by campus—mostly students, about my age or a little younger, except for one guy who teaches at UT. They were very nice. They seemed honest, and a couple of them spoke to me after the

237

meeting and gave me their phone numbers. Anyway, it was okay. It wasn't like a Beach Boys concert, but it was okay, and I'll go back there."

"Good. So what is treatment like? You know, when I got sober, there was no such thing as treatment. You could dry out in a hospital, but that was about it. For me and Chester, it was pretty much AA or nothing."

"Well, at this point, if it was AA or nothing for me, I think I might choose nothing. I'm not all that terribly impressed with AA so far, but I'm trying to keep an open mind. I think treatment will be okay, though. I like the counselor quite a bit. He's a retired Army NCO, and he looks and acts the part.

"The good news is I feel like I can trust him. James promised me that he's a straight shooter, and you know James; he doesn't trust anyone. Anyway, I'll see him two or three times a week. One of those meetings is a group with seven other people who are in various stages of recovery. It's a pretty strange group of people, but I think it will be just fine once I get used to it."

"Gosh, Steve, I thought 'treatment' meant that you went several hours a day, every day, or even moved into some place for some period of time. Are you sure this counselor knows what he's doing? Did you check him out?"

"Mother, if I had to go several hours a day, every day, I'd say 'Forget it, Jack.' I think maybe there is a program like that over there, but this is the one he set up for me. Maybe he was smart enough to figure out who I am and not push me too far too soon. He did mention that if this doesn't work for me, there were other options to consider.

"And no, I didn't 'check him out.' I trust James' opinion. I know you don't think much of him, but there's a lot more to him than you know. Anyway, that's the deal. I knew you'd want to know, but I didn't want to tell you about it too soon. I wanted to wait until I felt as though there was a good chance of my sticking with it."

"Well, thanks, Honey. There is no possible way that I could tell you how happy I am that you are doing something like this. And I know you don't respect my religious beliefs, but I am going to be praying for you every single day, whether you want me to or not."

"Mother, I don't have anything against prayer. Hell, pray for me all you want to. I can't imagine that it could hurt anything. The only thing I don't like is when I feel as though someone is forcing their religious beliefs down my throat. That's what I hated about the AA meeting I went to Thursday. I mean, everyone was talking about God as though there's no question about who God is, you know? It really was like the old days in the Baptist Church or in what they euphemistically called 'assembly' at

Baylor. You know, like there's no room for individual interpretation of religion or spirituality. You know what I mean?"

"Yes, I do know what you mean. But I want to tell you, Steve, I've seldom had that experience in AA. I've found great tolerance for individual belief systems, and I think that if you will just keep going to meetings and listening with an open mind, you'll find the same thing. That is, unless AA in Austin is tremendously different from AA in San Antonio and other cities that I've visited over the years. If there's one rule in AA, it's that there are no rules, especially about one's understanding of God. Really, Honey, recovery in AA is about spiritually, not religion. You do know what that means, don't you, Steve?"

"Yeah, I think so. At least I'm starting to. James said pretty much that same thing. Sometimes, though, when he starts explaining things, he goes so far out into left field that I don't know what he's talking about. When that happens, I just start nodding and let my mind drift off somewhere else completely. But, yeah, I'm getting the idea. It's like religion has more to do with doctrine—some particular set of beliefs or rules about God, but spirituality is about your own personal understanding, with or without the rules. Is that in the ballpark?"

"Yes, I guess so. I think of spirituality as something even more than that, though. I think of it as one's overall approach to life. You know, like how you experience yourself and your world and also your God, or your Higher Power, whatever or whomever that may be. I've come to see spirituality as more about attitude and less about doctrine. I think that you can be 'spiritual' even with no belief in God. Gosh, Honey, it's rather difficult to explain. I hope that doesn't make it even more confusing."

"No, it doesn't. I think I understand what you mean, and actually, it makes sense to me. But man, I hate it when everyone stands up and holds hands and says The Lord's Prayer at the end of the meeting. That seems like plain old Christian religion to me."

"Well, Steve, it's just a prayer. And it doesn't mention Jesus, you know. I hope you won't use that as an excuse to stay away from AA. I mean, if it's that distasteful, I guess you could go to the bathroom or something towards the end of the meeting."

Steve laughed. "Yeah, I guess so. Anyway, it helps to talk about it. There's something else, though, that isn't good news. Bev called me last night and told me that she and the kids are moving to Denver, Colorado in three weeks. In fact, they're going up there today to check it out."

"Yes, I know," Lois said. "She called here last night, too. She said that you got angry and hung up on her. I guess that's beside the point, though. I'm really sorry, Honey. How are you feeling about it today?"

239

"Well, not nearly as bad as I did last night. I called Rachel and talked to her about it. That helped quite a bit. Who knows? Maybe it's for the best. Anyway, that's all my news—good and bad. So I think I'll let you go. I need to get busy around here. I've gotten a lot done the last couple of days. Hell, I haven't been this organized since I got to Austin."

"Hmm, isn't that interesting. I wonder how that happened. Listen, Honey, please give this your best effort. I promise you that you won't be disappointed. And please stay in touch. I will do anything to help. Do you hear me?"

"Yes, Mother, I hear you. And thanks."

Steve had a very productive morning. He worked in his shop without taking a break and by lunchtime was well ahead of his schedule. During lunch, he read the pamphlet on denial. Just as he was finishing up, James dropped by.

"I just have a few minutes, but I wanted to take a look at you and see what four days of sobriety looks like on Steve Campbell."

"Oh, yeah? Well, do I pass inspection?"

"Yes, you look pretty good. In fact, you're a fucking inspiration. I'm real proud of you. How's it going on the inside?"

"It's going okay, I guess. It's definitely different, though—very up and down. I'm getting a hell of a lot done, and that feels good. I slept well last night, and I feel good physically today. I like Cally, you know? He's a trip. I've never known anyone like him; that's for sure. How about you? What's going on in your perverted world?"

"Oh, same old shit—a little of this and a little of that. I've been thinking about you getting under old Cally's wing. You know, he can come across like a real hard ass, but I really believe that he has your best interest at heart. Has he jumped your shit yet?"

"No, not at all. He's been very straightforward, but I haven't heard him jump anyone's shit yet. You think he will, huh?"

"Yeah, he will. You can count on it. He probably doesn't want to scare you away this soon, though. When he does, just remember he's doing his job and trying to get you to see beyond your limits. He's unbelievably intuitive. Anyway, listen, man; do you have any weed hidden away anywhere? I'm looking for some personal stash; the shit I have for sale right now isn't worth putting in your fucking pipe."

"No, man, I got rid of what little I had. Sold it to Tucker. Sorry about that. It never occurred to me that you might ever be short of good smoke."

"Yeah, well, that's cool. So do you still hate AA as much as you did night before last?"

"Oh, I don't know, James. I guess I don't hate it utterly and completely. Not yet, anyway. I went to a meeting yesterday that was tolerable. I'm going to a new place tonight. In fact, I'm going with this chick who's been working as a hooker for the last few years. That ought to be pretty interesting. She invited me. I don't know what that's all about, but I'm keeping an open mind, so to speak."

"Hmm, sounds pretty promising. You know, they say you ought to keep your dick in your pants for awhile after you get sober."

"Yeah? And who are 'they?'"

"Hell, I don't know, man. Those who know, I suppose. Listen, man, I gotta run. Things to do and people to see, you know? I'm glad to see things working out so far. Tell that big, black bastard I said 'Hello,' will ya?"

"Yeah, I'll quote you. By the way, James, just out of curiosity, what would you have done if I had had some stash? Did you really think I might?"

"Yeah, I thought you might have held some back. I don't know, really. I probably would have just tried to buy it from you. I doubt that I would have taken it forcefully, but I may have asked to see it and then come back and stolen it from you later. I might have called Cally. Hell, who knows? But it doesn't matter now. I'm glad it wasn't an issue. Take care."

"You, too, weirdo."

Steve spent the afternoon as productively as he did the morning. He completed and delivered a refinishing job for which he collected nearly $500.00. Then he picked up enough new work to keep him busy for another week beyond what he already had lined up in the shop.

As soon as he quit for the day, he walked over to Tommy's house and knocked on his door.

"Well, look who's here. Come on in, Stevey, you old harlot monger, and sit your ass down. How about a cold one."

"Thanks, but no thanks, Tommy. I'm riding the old water wagon. I just want to talk to you for a minute or two before I go home and get cleaned up. Got a minute?"

"Yeah, sure. The old water wagon, huh? Yikes! Sounds very damn ominous if you ask me. Things must have been happening in your life since Tuesday night at The Star Quality Inn, or whatever the hell it's called. But, now, let me guess; I bet you couldn't handle breaking your promise to that counselor. Am I right?"

Steve laughed. "You hit the nail on the head, pal. I went back in and talked to him again Wednesday, and before I knew what was happening, I had committed myself not only to abstinence, but also to counseling three times a week, plus AA meetings every other day. Pretty wild, huh?"

241

"Yeah, pretty wild is right. It's cool, though, I suppose. If you think that's right for you, then what the hell? I sure don't have a problem with it. Personally, I don't think you need it, but you already knew that."

"Yeah, I do, and that's one reason I need to talk to you, Tommy. My counselor gave me a treatment plan, and one of the things I'm supposed to do is talk to friends about this deal and ask them for their support. I don't know exactly what kind of support he's talking about, but you know, one of the things that you and I have been best at in our friendship is getting loaded together. So I'm wondering if you can support me in my sobriety?"

Tommy looked surprised. "Well, sure I can, Steve. Why wouldn't I?"

"I don't know, and I'm not saying that you wouldn't. But I can't do any more of those Tuesday night trips to Waco and stay sober. Denial or no denial, even I know that. Cally, my counselor, says that friends, even well-meaning friends, especially those I drink and use with, may try to sabotage my sobriety. I know you wouldn't do that maliciously, Tommy, but I'm afraid that you might do it unwittingly if I didn't say something about it. What do you think about that, man?"

Tommy's expression turned serious. He looked at the floor for a moment and then back to Steve. He nodded and answered slowly and thoughtfully. "Well, Steve, I think I need to start listening to you with a different ear, one that takes this issue more seriously. I think I need to appreciate and respect your decision to quit drinking and using instead of treating it lightly.

"I don't know, man; your counselor may be right. I'm glad you're willing to talk to me about it honestly. I'll work with this in my own mind, and I'll make every effort to support you. I hope you'll forgive what seems to me now like my cavalier attitude toward what you want for yourself." He stopped and looked at the floor again and then continued. "That's what I think."

Steve raised his eyebrows, nodded, and said, "Gosh, thank you, Tommy. I appreciate that. I didn't expect you to take it that seriously, but I really appreciate the fact that you do. You know, I want your respect and your support. It means a lot to me. So thanks again."

"You're welcome," Tommy said. "So, tell me what I can do to help."

Steve smiled. "Well, the truth is, I'm not exactly sure. But one thing might be for you not to offer me alcohol or pot when we're together. It might even help if you didn't smoke pot in front of me. I don't know, Tommy. I'm just guessing, really."

"Well, Stevey, let's play it by ear. If you think of anything else, let me know, and if you see me trying to sabotage you, then tell me. If I get defensive about that, call me on it. How does that sound for starters?"

"It sounds good. It sounds really good. Thanks again, man."

"No problem. So what's up tonight that you have to get cleaned up for? Hot date?"

"Well, not really, but kind of. A woman from my treatment group at The Recovery Center is going to pick me up and take me to an AA meeting. I'm not sure what to expect, really, because she's very hot, and I think she might have her eye on me. On the other hand, one of our rules at the Center is that we don't sleep with one another. So, hell, I don't know. We'll see. Anyway, I better go get ready. I'll talk to you later."

"Okay, man. Good luck. I'll see you around the old campus. Hey, by the way, have you told Dixie about all of this?"

"No, not yet. Why?"

"Well, she was asking about you the other night—Thursday, I think it was. She said she thought you might be mad at her about something. You must be neglecting her, huh?"

"Yeah, I have been. I'll call her. Thanks."

CHAPTER 47

Kathy Morris, Steve's hot date to a Saturday night AA meeting, could easily have been mistaken for a low bottom rather than high bottom drunk. By the time she stumbled into recovery in early 1974, her life was a horrible-looking sordid mess. The simple facts of her life gave her up as a degenerate—a whore, an addict, and a convicted criminal.

Kathy got a hard and quick start on life. Her parents abused her physically and emotionally from early childhood on. She left home on the eve of her sixteenth birthday, angry as hell and determined to survive completely on her own. She lied about her age and rented a tiny one-room garage apartment the next day. To support herself, she dropped out of high school and took a full-time job selling children's clothes in a department store.

Despite the odds against her, Kathy inched her way forward. She taught herself through trial and error how to live independently. She counted her pennies and scraped by month to month. She borrowed textbooks from the library, studied on her own, and at nineteen passed the Texas High School Equivalency Exam. With her GED in hand, she registered for community college courses, which she attended at night after working all day. She collected college credits for four years, and at age twenty-three transferred to The University of Texas at Austin as a second semester sophomore.

Kathy started dancing in a topless bar during her first year at the university. A female classmate convinced her to sign on part-time at The Wicked Wench, "just until you sock away enough cash to finish out the school year." She was a natural for the job. She had a beautiful face, a terrific body, an adventuresome nature, an angry, rebellious attitude, and a legitimate, almost desperate need for money.

Had she followed her plan and saved her earnings, she could have ditched The Wench in a couple of months. Instead of doing that, though, she became attached to the daily influx of tax-free cash, men's ceaseless adoration, and free cocaine, pot, and alcohol.

She accepted after-work dates with her favorite customers, who paid her generously even though she didn't ask for anything. She did not feel like a prostitute, but she did accept the money.

Within a year, Kathy was soliciting customers during her shift and entertaining them in motel rooms afterwards. She charged a hundred dollars an hour and worked three or four nights a week. She snorted cocaine and drank alcohol every day. She held onto her academic career by a thread. Through it all, she managed to keep her chin up. It was her secret life.

By the end of her second year at the club, Kathy had dropped out of school completely. She danced six nights a week, worked after hours six nights a week, and used large amounts of cocaine and alcohol every day. That lifestyle took its toll physically and emotionally.

Kathy lost weight. She lost muscle tone. Her hair became brittle, and her eyes turned gray. She looked ten years older than her age. She constantly felt tired and depressed, even when she was high. Her rebellious attitude turned into conspicuous chronic anger. She called herself "an angry bitch, and don't forget it." Her spirit withered. Her *secret* life became her *only* life, and she hated herself. She flirted with thoughts of suicide almost every day.

A vice cop who utilized her services on a regular basis busted her in an effort to save her life. She would have paid a small fine and gone free except that she was carrying a gram and a half of coke and blew a blood alcohol level of 1.6. She detoxed in the county jail because she did not have the cash to make bail, and she had no one to call to ask for help.

The county judge offered her probation in exchange for her promise to attend alcohol/drug treatment and find a new line of work. She gratefully accepted his offer. A county social worker got her a job at Motorola, and although her pay was a fraction of what she had been pulling down as a hooker, she quickly began socking away money to go back to school.

Kathy's relationship with alcohol and drugs paralleled the circumstances of her life. Prior to becoming a dancer and a prostitute, she drank alcohol and smoked pot socially. As soon as she changed her lifestyle, she changed her habits. She used cocaine and alcohol at work because getting high was part of the culture. It helped her "fit in." On top of that, getting high felt good. It relieved her mind of problems and let her live with herself. But then she crossed the line into addiction, and she used because she wanted to, needed to, and had to.

When the circumstances of her life changed again following her arrest and conviction, she stopped using altogether. Initially, she remained abstinent because her freedom depended on it. Eventually, though, with the help of Cally and other people who understood and cared, she entered recovery and remained abstinent simply because she wanted to.

When Kathy began treatment at The Recovery Center, she trusted no one and refused to disclose anything of substance about herself. But as she stayed sober and straight, worked on herself, and learned to trust, she let down her guard and revealed her past to her therapy group. Their acceptance and support helped diminish the power of her shame.

Following the experience with her group, Kathy took the next step and told her story to her "home" AA group. Most people, especially those who had been around for a while, just nodded. They had heard it all before. A few people judged her, and several men immediately hit on her. She consciously and decidedly ignored them. She gave herself a six-month reprieve from the company of men.

Luckily for Steve, his timing was perfect. Had he shown up at The Recovery Center any earlier than he did, Kathy probably would not have given him a second look. As it happened, though, she felt ready to meet someone, and he grabbed her attention. She liked the fact that he looked embarrassed when she caught him checking her out during his first group session. When he spoke, she understood where he was coming from. She recognized his yearning, tempered by denial and fear. She imagined a good heart and a gentle spirit lurking behind his protective cover. And for the first time in a very long time, she felt attracted and attractive sexually.

Kathy understood that sexual relationships between group members were forbidden, so she decided to try the next best thing and offered Steve her friendship. She did not know whether or not to think of their going to AA together as a date, but as she drove to his house, she felt apprehensive and excited. She liked the feeling.

Steve sat on his front porch and waited for Kathy to pick him up. While he waited, he pictured her in his mind. He wondered about her ethnicity. Her dark skin, hair, and eyes suggested Hispanic, but she did not "look" Hispanic. Her facial features were sharp and distinctive. She was tall, with slender hips, slender waist, and high, round breasts. "Whatever she is, she's damn beautiful," he said to himself.

Kathy pulled up in front of Steve's house at 7:35. He jogged out to the street and hopped in the car. "Hola, Kathy. Thanks for picking me up."

"Hola, yourself, Steve. "Habla espanol?"

Steve laughed. "No, except for a handful of curse words. Do you?"

"No, not really. I used to, but that was years ago."

"You look very nice, Kathy, very pretty. And you smell good," Steve said. "I hope it's okay to say that."

Kathy smiled and glanced over at him. "Thank you, Steve. Why wouldn't it be okay to say that?"

Steve shrugged his shoulders and held his palms up in an "I don't know" gesture. "I know this is going to sound really stupid, not to mention presumptuous, but I feel like I'm on a date, and I haven't been on a real date in a long time. I don't really want to think of it as a date, though, because I don't want to break any of Cally's rules, at least not during my first week. The man scares the crap out of me as it is." Steve looked at Kathy and added, "God, that really did sound stupid, didn't it? Please, forget I even said anything. Where's this meeting we're going to?"

Kathy laughed. "I'm glad you did say it because now I don't have to. Driving over to your house, I wondered to myself if this was a date or not. I decided that it wasn't, probably because I'm afraid of Cally, too, and I've been working with him for six months. So just to be safe, why don't we agree that this isn't a date and that I'm just giving you a ride to an AA meeting out of the goodness of my heart? How does that sound?"

Steve smiled and nodded. "It sounds good and safe to me. And thanks for laughing with me instead of at me. I want to be cool, you know. My friend, James, who I blame for getting me into this recovery mess in the first place, says the reason I need to always appear cool and in control is because my ego is weak— not only weak, but big and weak. I told him that I thought it was because I'm insecure and afraid. He waved me off and said, 'It's the same fucking thing.' Anyway, maybe I should just start over. So, Hola, Kathy; thanks for picking me up. Where's this meeting we're going to?"

Steve and Kathy talked nonstop until she turned into the parking lot of the South Austin Group of Alcoholics Anonymous.

"Well, are you ready?" she asked.

Steve took a deep breath. "As ready as I'll ever be, I suppose. Of course, if you would rather blow this meeting off and go somewhere else, I wouldn't be disappointed."

Kathy reached across the seat and touched Steve's arm. "These are good people, Steve. They really are. Just hang with me. I won't desert you; I promise."

Steve nodded. "Okay, boss; lead the way."

True to her word, Kathy never left Steve's side. She introduced him to at least twenty people, who welcomed him warmly and seemed genuinely pleased to meet him. The meeting itself went by quickly. When the chairperson asked for visitors, Steve introduced himself as a newcomer, and he blushed when the room erupted into applause, hoots and hollers, and boisterous greetings and welcomes.

When the meeting ended, Steve and Kathy joined four other people for coffee at a small shop down the street from the South Austin meeting house. There, they talked and laughed and got high on caffeine until almost midnight.

"Man, I'm pretty wired," Steve said as they sat in Kathy's car in front of his house. "You want to come in and shoot the shit for a little while? I could fix us something to eat."

"Yeah, why not?" she answered. "I'm pretty much of a night owl anyway. Old habits, I guess. For the last couple of years before I got sober, my workday seldom started before 9:00 o'clock at night and sometimes ran into the next morning. I'm adjusting, though. I'm learning how to sleep at night and work during the day. Actually, I like it very much, and I've never felt better in my life."

Once inside, Steve gave Kathy a quick home tour and then rummaged through the refrigerator. "Thanks for taking me tonight, Kathy," he said. "I really did enjoy it. And I like your friends. They seem happy in their sobriety, and that's a good thing for me to see. You all talked about being sober as though it was a good thing and a fun thing instead of just a necessary thing.

"I can't honestly say that I feel that way, myself, not yet anyway. To tell you the truth, I'd feel a lot more relaxed and normal right now if I was rolling us a joint instead of fixing us a late night snack. You know what I mean? Anyway, how about toast and apples and peanut butter and apricot preserves and cold milk?"

"That sounds terrific," Kathy said. She hopped up onto the kitchen counter and crossed her legs. "Yeah, I'm not always totally happy with sobriety. Maybe no one is all the time. And, yeah, I even kind of miss the old lifestyle sometimes. Not the hooking, I promise you that; but the partying and getting high. There's a curious sort of comfort in living that way. It doesn't ask much of you. It doesn't challenge you to grow. In fact, I think it prohibits the kind of growth that means anything—the kind that Cally demands."

She stopped and thought for a moment. "Don't get me wrong; I love sobriety, at least most of the time. I like myself sober a lot better than I liked myself using. I certainly respect myself more. I just had to get used to the routine, though, you know, the predictability. Like, it's very comforting now to wake up in my own bed every morning, knowing exactly where I am." She laughed. "That probably sounds weird, but it's very significant to me. Anyway, I'm glad I'm sober and straight, at least today. So, Steve, what did you think of the meeting?"

"It was okay. It was good, in fact. Actually, it helped a lot to be there with someone. I felt less self-conscious and more like a part of the trip. That's always been a problem for me; I never feel as though I belong anywhere, except for the bar across the street. But I heard some good things. As a matter of fact, I really appreciated something you said."

"No kidding? What?"

"Well, it was when everyone was talking about 'acceptance,' and you mentioned a part of the Big Book that must go into some detail on that. I think you even quoted the page numbers. I think what I heard you say is that you have to be careful to avoid using 'acceptance of things being the way they are supposed to be' as a way of stuffing your feelings. It was something like that, anyway. I related to it because I do that. Like I always try to stay real calm, and I say, 'Oh, well...' and 'Well, whatever...' whenever something bugs me. Then I end up not dealing with whatever the thing is, and it comes back to haunt me when I least expect it. You know what I mean, Kathy? Am I making any sense at all?"

"Yep. You're making perfect sense, and I know exactly what you mean. Do you have a Big Book?"

"Yeah. It's right in there on the table. You want me to get it?"

"No, keep doing what you're doing. I'll find it." She hopped down and walked into the dining room, picked up the book, flipped to page 449, and read out loud, "'And acceptance is the answer to all my problems today. When I am disturbed, it is because I find some person, place, thing, or situation—some fact of my life—unacceptable to me, and I can find no serenity until I accept that person, place, thing, or situation as being exactly the way it is supposed to be at this moment. Nothing, absolutely nothing happens in God's world by mistake. Until I could accept my alcoholism, I could not stay sober; unless I accept life completely on life's terms, I cannot be happy. I need to concentrate not so much on what needs to be changed in the world as on what needs to be changed in me and in my attitudes.'

"That's the part I was referring to. I love that paragraph of this book. I really do; I love it. But what I meant in the meeting was that I could use that principle to discount my feelings, or worse, to stuff my feelings. I could tell myself that I should not feel upset or angry or afraid or ashamed or whatever in response to the events in my life past or present, because everything that happens is supposed to happen. And therefore there's nothing to be upset or angry about. That sounds a little confusing, but understanding it has meant a lot to me."

"I know what you're saying, Kathy, because I've put a lot of stock into not feeling very much of anything for most of my life. Now Cally tells me that I have to get honest, especially about my feelings, and that having a wide range of feelings is healthy. I said 'okay,' but I didn't really mean it. I mean, I'm fine with the good feelings, but the bad ones? I'd just as soon let them stay hidden, or stuffed, or repressed, or wherever the hell they are.

"Anyway, I'm supposed to be praying and meditating every day as a way of becoming more in touch with my true self. I'm doing it, but I'm not sure I want to be in touch with my true self. The truth might be too painful. And I'm only being a little facetious."

Kathy agreed. "Avoiding the truth has been one of my major life goals, too. I think, though, that I no longer have that luxury. My sobriety—my program—has taken it away. Sometimes I miss it." She stared silently at the floor for a moment. "So how's that great feast coming along? Can I help?"

"Yeah, you can get the drinks. I'll take milk with a couple of ice cubes. There's juice in there, too."

Steve put James Taylor on the stereo, and they sat on the living room floor and munched and talked, first about music and movies, then some more about recovery, and finally about relationships. Steve told Kathy about Lynn and Eddie's eminent move out of state and shared with her his feelings of anger and sadness around that. Kathy sympathized and said that parenthood scared her more than anything she could think of.

At 4:00 AM, Kathy yawned and stretched and said, "I'm sorry, Steve, but I'm afraid I better head home. If I don't, I'm liable to fall asleep right here on your living room floor."

"Well, don't do that," Steve said. "But you're more than welcome to stay. You can take the bed, and I'll sleep in the kids' room."

Kathy smiled and touched Steve's hand. "That's very thoughtful, but I don't want to put you out of your bed."

"Well, we could share it. We could draw a line down the center and take a blood oath not to cross it."

"Ooh, I don't know, Steve. Cally might hang us up by our toenails."

Steve chuckled at the thought. Then he looked at Kathy and said, "I really wish you'd stay. I would dearly, dearly love to see you first thing in the morning when I wake up."

Kathy took a deep breath and placed her hand against her chest. "Yikes," she said softly. "I think my heart just skipped a beat." She paused for a moment and then said, "Steve, I do want to stay, but if we sleep together, we really will have to do it without having sex. I can't risk my standing at the Center, and I don't think I could lie to Cally and the group."

Steve smiled. "Well, this *has* been my week for new experiences. I guess one more wouldn't hurt anything. I just hope sobriety doesn't turn out to be one bizarre new experience after another." He shook his head and laughed. "So do you want something to sleep in? A T-shirt or something?"

"Yeah, a T-shirt will do. You don't have an extra toothbrush, do you?"

"No. You can use mine if you want to, though. It's by the sink."

When Kathy slipped into bed, Steve was lying on his back under the sheet.

"Do you have anything on?" she asked.

"Boxers," he answered.

"Oh, good," she said. "If Cally says anything, we can look at him ever so innocently and promise that we had clothes on." She smiled and kissed him gently on the lips. "Good night, Steve, and thank you. You're a gentleman, and I appreciate that." Then she rolled over onto her side with her back to him.

He leaned up on one elbow, put his hand on her shoulder, and kissed the side of her neck beneath her ear. "Good night, Kathy," he whispered. "Thank you, too. Being with you tonight gives me hope. At this moment, I actually want to be sober."

She slowly reached up, took his hand in hers, and wrapped his arm lightly around her chest. He inched forward until the front of his body touched the back of hers. When he felt her body against his, a shiver ran through him, and he hugged her tightly against him. He willed himself not to have an erection, but willpower failed him. Kathy felt it come up hard against her. "Are you going to be all right, Steve?" she asked.

He was silent for a moment. "I really want to say, 'Yes, everything's cool,' but the truth is I don't think I'm going to be able to do this, not according to our plan, anyway. I thought I could, but I was kidding myself. I better just let you have the bed, and I'll go into the kids' room. Believe me, I don't want to, but if I stay here I'm going to end up either attacking you like a wild beast or having a massive heart attack."

Kathy hesitated and then she nodded her head. "Would you rather I just go on home?" she asked.

"No, I want you to stay. I really do. I promise."

"Okay, Steve," she said. She rolled over and kissed him again on the lips. "I guess I'll see you in the morning. And listen, if it's any consolation, it's not just you. I'm also feeling aroused, and quite honestly, I don't think we stood a very good chance of making it through the night without breaking promises."

Steve laughed. "Yeah, well, thanks for sharing that. It makes leaving so much easier," he said sarcastically. "Man, I can't believe I'm doing this." He rolled out of bed and walked down the short hall to the other bedroom. He climbed into Lynn's bed and closed his eyes.

Fantasies of being with Kathy—of holding her, kissing her, and making love to her—flooded his mind. Twice, he decided to return to her, but both times he lost his courage and lay back down. Finally, he let his fantasies flow freely, and he slowly and quietly masturbated to them.

Steve fell asleep shortly before daybreak. He dreamed that he and Kathy were hand in hand on a well-worn path, deep in the forest. As they made their way along the path, they encountered all sorts of strong sensory stimuli. They met with brilliant colors, strange noises, sharp odors, and air so full of electricity that they could feel it throughout their bodies.

"This is wild," he said to Kathy. "This is really, really wild. Should we turn back?"

Kathy shook her head. "No," she said.

He stared into her eyes. "Are you sure?" he asked.

She returned his gaze but did not answer.

"Well?" he asked.

She smiled and said, "Don't worry." Then she took his hand and pressed his palm against her breast. "Don't worry about a thing," she whispered.

CHAPTER 48

Steve awoke Sunday morning after sleeping only two hours. He lay in bed for several minutes, thinking about his evening with Kathy. He pictured himself in bed with her, his arm around her chest, and the front of his body snuggled against the back of hers. He humored himself with the notion that perhaps he was falling in love, then reminded himself that love probably does not really work that way in real life, especially in sober life. Nevertheless, he allowed himself the fantasy.

By the time Kathy got up at 11:00 o'clock, Steve had eaten breakfast, drunk two cups of coffee, read part of the Sunday paper, and put in two hours of study time. When she wandered into the living room, still wearing his T-shirt, he was lying across the sofa, reading a psychology text and listening to Kenny Rankin on the stereo.

"Good morning, sleepyhead," he said, laying the book down and sitting up to make room for her on the couch. She sat down next to him and laid her head lightly against his shoulder. He put his arm around her, and they leaned back against the back of the couch together. "How do you feel this morning?" he asked her.

She yawned. "I'm still pretty tired, but I feel good. How about you?"

"I'm good, too. You want some breakfast?"

"No, not right now. I wake up kind of slow. Maybe in a little while, if that's okay."

"Yeah, sure. Whatever you want. Hey, you know what? You were in my dream last night."

"Really? Was it a good dream?"

"Yeah, it was. You and I were walking in a dense forest, and all kinds of really wild stuff was going on all around us. There were colors and lights and weird noises and smells and I don't know what all. It was cool, but it was also kind of scary. I don't think you were afraid, though. In fact, I asked you if we should turn around and go back, and you said 'No' and told me not to worry."

Kathy looked up at Steve's face. "What do you think it means?" she asked.

"I think it's about how I'm experiencing my life right now. Lots of new stuff. Lots of unknowns. Kind of scary. And now all of a sudden, there's you."

Kathy snuggled into his side. "I'm glad I was there with you. If I couldn't be with you for real, I'm glad I was with you in your dream." She turned her head and kissed him gently on his neck.

"Thank you for last night," she whispered. "I was disappointed when you left, but I appreciate your doing it. Even without you there next to me, though, I felt your presence. It's been a long time since I've shared a house overnight with someone I care about and feel something for. I've been alone for a long time. During the night, I woke up several times and remembered that you were just a few steps down the hall, and I felt warm and safe. It felt good." She took a deep breath and released it. "Of course, this morning I'm thinking about Cally. I'm afraid he wouldn't like my spending the night here, regardless of what we did or didn't do."

Steve nodded his head and pulled her a little closer against him. "Yeah, you're probably right. I'll tell you, though, Kathy, if we get in trouble for that, my regret level will shoot through the roof. I still can't believe I got out of that bed. You felt so warm and so good. Kind of like you do right now, actually. And believe me, I'm not getting up and leaving the couch no matter what."

Kathy slipped her arm around Steve's waist. "I know you're not. I won't let you."

"You know what, though?" he said. "I'm glad that last night happened the way it did. It's not like I didn't want to do more, because I certainly did, and I still do. And I don't know if we have to tell Cally about it or not, but I feel as though we were pretty damn honest. We kept our promise, at least technically."

Kathy laughed softly. "Yeah, at least that," she said.

"Sorry to change the subject, but what do you have up your sleeve for today," Steve asked.

"Hmm, let's see. It's Sunday, right? Hmm, nothing that I can think of. Maybe go to a meeting. How about you?"

"Well, I had planned to work in my shop, but if you want to hang out together, I'll blow that off. A meeting would be okay. The lake doesn't sound bad, either. Ginger always looks forward to a little swim on Sunday afternoon when I'm not in San Antonio."

"Maybe we can do all of those things," Kathy said. "I need to go home for a few minutes to clean up, change clothes, feed my cat, and do a couple of other little things. Maybe you could do your work while I do that stuff, and then we could meet up at the 1:00 o'clock meeting and then go out to the lake from there."

Steve agreed.

They met at 1:00 at the South Austin group. Many of the people whom Steve met the night before were there. Most of them remembered his name and welcomed him back.

The chairperson opened the meeting and asked the group to accept the topic "gratitude" for discussion. The first speaker stated that he felt grateful not only for his sobriety but also for his alcoholism and the problems that it had created in his life. Steve looked at Kathy and made a face that said, "Yeah, right, and what mental institution did you break out of?"

A later speaker, however, said basically the same thing, but she said it in such a way that Steve understood. "When I came into AA originally, all I wanted to do was quit drinking and using drugs. After the first few meetings, I felt angry and discouraged because no one seemed to be talking about how to just quit getting high. Instead, they were talking about a bunch of stupid, irrelevant bullshit like honesty, open-mindedness, willingness, and all sorts of other spiritual crapparama.

"I remember that I almost laughed out loud once when some idiot boasted of his 'attitude of gratitude.' God, I thought that sounded like something out of a bad TV sermonette.

"Needless to say, I didn't get any better. After a while, and out of desperation, I followed some patient, caring person's advice and got with the program. I 'put the plug in the jug,' went to a meeting every day, read the Big Book, got a sponsor, and worked the twelve steps.

"Well, you know what happened. Before I knew it, I had been sober for some time, and my life was better in all respects. My health had improved, my mind was sharper, and I had some inner peace for the first time in my entire adult life, and I'm not exaggerating, either.

"Naturally I felt grateful. I mean, who wouldn't? But part of the gratitude was, indeed, for where I had come from, because etiologically, it was my alcoholism and resulting need to quit drinking that brought me to AA in the first place. It was the AA program, however—the twelve steps, in particular, and *not* the quitting drinking and using—that had changed who I was and how I felt.

"The point is, had anything been different before AA, including 'had I never become an alcoholic in the first place,' I probably would have missed out on finding such a profoundly satisfying way of life. So I do feel grateful for my recovery, but I also feel grateful for the circumstances that brought me to AA so that I could find recovery."

When she finished talking, Steve looked at Kathy and made a face that said, "Hmm, not bad; I think I get it."

After the meeting, Steve and Kathy drove to Lake Travis for a long afternoon together in the sun. They played, and they talked. They checked each other out and touched each other often. They felt and acknowledged the sexual tension between them. They felt but did not acknowledge their mutual infatuation.

They shared stories about their early years and found intriguing parallels. They also discovered interesting differences, particularly in their handling of the parallels. Both sets of parents were shame driven, angry, abusive alcoholics. Steve felt in awe of Kathy's adolescent impertinence and courage, which demanded that she walk away from her parents. Kathy dismissed it as taking the easy way out. Kathy admired and respected Steve's stoic patience and strength, which allowed him to hang in there without running away. Steve dismissed that as taking the easy way out.

On the drive back into town, Steve asked out loud the questions that they both had been asking themselves. The first was, "What's happening between us?" The second was, "Should we, or perhaps *how* should we, bring this whole thing up with Cally?" They decided that they had no idea what was happening between them but that it sure did feel exciting, as well as rather scary. Then, considering their inability to answer the first question, they decided to put off dealing with the second for a little while. Neither of them felt comfortable with that decision. Nevertheless, they agreed to live with it for the time being.

Just after dark, Steve hugged Kathy tightly against him, kissed her on the lips, and left her at her car at the South Austin AA Group house. For the rest of the evening and into the night, his thoughts and dreams were of her. Picturing her in her bikini, he saw a synthesis of Rachel's and Dixie's most appealing physical qualities. She had Rachel's sculptured figure but without the hard muscles and Dixie's soft curves without the extra flesh.

Talking to himself, he asked, "Is it love, or is it infatuation? If it's infatuation, it's the most intense damn infatuation I've ever felt. This makes Rachel seem like a case of puppy love."

He had experienced infatuation before—at least three times that he could think of offhand. The first was with Pamela Hart. Steve met Pam in the same sixth grade classroom where he met James Shannon. Pam was the proverbial "prettiest girl in school." Steve almost fainted when she passed him a note saying that she liked him as a boyfriend. From that moment on, she seldom left Steve's mind. They passed love notes during the day and talked on the phone at night. They held hands in public and kissed on the lips in private. Steve fantasized about having sex with Pam and masturbated to those fantasies almost every day.

After three months of loving bliss, Pam dumped Steve for a cooler guy in the class next door to theirs. It almost broke Steve's heart, but no one ever knew that.

The second time was with Peggy Sue Martin, Steve's first true love. That time, it was eighth grade "love at first sight" infatuation that over the course of three and a half years grew into true "young love." As an adult, Steve never gave Pam Hart a second thought, but he often thought of Peggy with great affection.

Steve's third episode of profound infatuation happened with Marilyn Cugler. Steve and Marilyn were neighbors through junior high and high school. They were friends, but other than occasional teasing and flirting and a few games of Spin the Bottle and Seven Minutes in Heaven, they never had any serious romantic interest in each other. When Steve came home for Christmas vacation during his high school senior year, however, they suddenly saw each other in a different light, as if meeting for the first time, and for eighteen days, they became absolutely inseparable.

During that time, Steve thought about Marilyn twenty-four hours a day. He thought of nothing and no one else. They ignored their families, which was very easy for Steve, as well as their other friends. They sneaked out of their houses at night just to be together, and they spent many hours in the back seat of Steve's car. Steve and Marilyn never went all the way, but they could have written a book on how to do everything but.

After Steve returned to school, they wrote letters for a while, but their interest waned over the course of several months, and they let their infatuation die a respectable death. They saw each other a few times after that, but the intensity never returned. They settled for fondness, friendship, and excellent memories.

255

Steve never felt infatuated with Bev, and in retrospect, he felt as though he had never loved her, either. She was his wife for six years and the mother of his children. After their separation, he never missed her for a moment. And had it not been for the kids, he never would have given her another thought.

Steve thought of Rachel as his second true love, but never an object of his infatuation. She started out as his transition lover following his separation from Bev and became his friend for life. He never stopped loving her.

In the midst of Steve's recollections of old girlfriends, lovers, and partners, Carla knocked on his door. "Hi, ya, Stevey," she said. "Carlos said you dropped by the other day and wanted to talk to me. I'm sorry it's taken so long to get back to you. How are you doing?"

"Well, I'm doing really good, Carla. When I came over Wednesday, I wanted to tell you what had happened after we talked last Sunday, but now a lot has happened even since Wednesday. Can you sit and talk for a few minutes?"

Steve gave Carla a condensed version of the preceding eight days. He summed it up by saying, "...so now I find myself five days stark-raving sober and totally preoccupied with visions of a beautiful dark-skinned prostitute who I'm honor-bound not to have sex with. And on top of it all, I start a counseling psychology graduate program at 9:00 AM tomorrow morning."

"Man, that's a damn fine story, Steve," Carla said, smiling broadly. "It's not one that you necessarily want to submit to the Christian Science Monitor, but it's a great story. Do you want my impressions?"

Steve laughed. "Well, only if they're sympathetic and supportive."

"Hey, it's me—Carla. Where would I get the nerve to judge a fellow traveler? No, man, here's what I think. To start with, I'm impressed as shit with your five days of sober time, whether it feels crazy or not. And I'm quite touched by your falling in love, or whatever it is, with a hooker. That's definitely cool from this freethinking woman's point of view.

"The main thing is this, though. I say, 'screw your counselor and his structured treatment protocol.' If I were you, I would have to go for the girl. The way I see it, when your heart speaks to you that strongly, you're honor-bound to listen to it, not to follow someone else's rules. I mean, don't you have to follow your heart? Even if it kills you, you die with some sense of meaning and purpose."

Steve laughed. "You live from your heart, don't you, Carla?"

"No, Steve, I'm afraid I don't always. I'm trying, though, and I think I'm learning, slowly but surely."

"That's good, I suppose," Steve said. "I'm afraid of my heart. I'm afraid of being judged for the risks that my heart wants to take. My ego is afraid. It's a pansy; it wants safety."

"Yeah. I hear you. I definitely know that feeling. Well, anyway, I'm all for you, Steve. But listen, if you go with the girl, do you figure it to be a monogamous relationship? I mean, are you planning on cutting Dixie and me off forever?"

Steve laughed. "Carla, I haven't even had sex with her yet. Hell, I haven't even laid a hand on her except in my dreams. So don't go jumping any guns on me; let's leave our options open for awhile."

After Carla left, Steve organized himself for Monday morning. He put together his backpack, laid out his clothes, and read through the introductory packet that had come in the mail the previous week.

When he got into bed and closed his eyes, images of Kathy dominated his thoughts. Her lovely face, her beautiful body, her soft smile, her fresh smell. He envisioned rubbing suntan lotion on her naked body, starting at her shoulders, working slowly down her back to her waist, then gently over her buttocks and between her upper thighs.

He pictured them lying together in his bed, naked, with the front of his body pressed snuggly against the back of hers. In his fantasy, Kathy parts her legs to allow his erect penis to slip between them. Then she touches him lightly with her fingertips. For the second night in a row, Steve masturbated slowly and came easily. Soon after, he drifted off to sleep and slept through the night.

CHAPTER 49

Steve's first day of graduate school offered him no excuses to feel afraid.

Thirty-four students comprised the entering class of 1974. A small handful of those 34 passed Steve's cursory "cool" test. The remaining majority demonstrated fatal flaws of one type or another. Several presented themselves as above the rest; they quickly found each other, stuck their noses in the air, and dropped important names that Steve had never heard before. Several were apparent dweebs and nerds of the first order; they also found each other and huddled together in a group by themselves.

One man was grossly obese and perspired profusely. Four chain-smoked cigarettes. Two were very old. Two were very young. One woman's darting eyes and nervous tic made her look like a dangerous person. Three acted so comfortable, composed, and serene that they appeared bored. A few looked down their noses at Steve's long hair, faded jeans, and sandals. Two—one woman and one man—made subtle passes at him.

As Steve listened to the morning's presentations and studied the orientation week itinerary, he realized that the week's activities were ordered around making students feel welcome, comfortable, and confident. Faculty members took great pains to convince the group of 34 that they were the cream of the crop—the chosen few from among 284 applicants—and that they were therefore virtually assured of success in their graduate school endeavors and their future professional careers.

Steve looked around the room and wondered what universe he was from if this was the cream of the crop. He caught the attention of a fellow longhaired oddball, and they grinned and rolled their eyes in code to each other. The gesture said, "Yeah, right."

Additional orientation week affairs included a sit-down breakfast on Tuesday morning hosted by upper-level students, an informal luncheon on Wednesday hosted by the graduate school dean, a dress-up cocktail party on Thursday evening, and a grand finale "western barbecue" Friday afternoon.

Steve slipped out of the session at 11:45 and walked across campus to the Catholic Student Center for the noon AA meeting. When he walked into the meeting room, everyone greeted him by his name, as if they knew him well.

Ralph, the professor, led the meeting. Everyone spoke, including Steve.

"Hi, everyone. My name is Steve, and I'm an alcoholic/addict." He paused for a moment and then said, "Today is my sixth day sober, and I just realized that today I feel okay about being an alcoholic and being in an AA meeting." He paused again, then shook his head slowly. When he continued, his voice cracked ever so slightly. "I'm surprised to hear myself say that. It's not what I had planned to say.

"I've met some really cool people the last few days—people like y'all and others from the South Austin Group, who seem to really understand and accept yourselves as alcoholics. I feel as though you accept me, too, and that you want me to be here. That means a lot to me. I'm sure you don't realize how important that meeting on Friday was for me. You know, that was only my second meeting. The first one I went to was the night before, and if this one would had been like that one, it might very well have been my last.

"Here's another weird thing; I had a good weekend—a good sober weekend. Man, whoever would have thought that there was such a thing? Not me; that's for sure.

"You know, I can't honestly say that I ever really wanted to be sober. I have to admit, though, it feels pretty good. At least, today it does.

"On a different note, I've got a lot of stuff coming up. Just today, I started orientation week for the program I'm in over here at UT, and the primary activities on two of the next four days involve drinking. One's a cocktail party, and the other is a barbecue with a keg of beer. I suppose I'll be okay, but I've always mixed with strangers better when I was drinking. So if any of you have any suggestions for me about that, I'd be glad to hear them.

"Anyway, thanks for letting me talk. I know I don't sound as good as y'all do, but...." Steve shrugged his shoulders and looked down at his hands. "That's all I have to say."

"Thanks Steve," Ralph said. "I think we all remember how it feels to get started in sobriety, and how scary it is to start talking in meetings. I know I do. But newcomers are the lifeblood of AA. In some ways, you're the reason why we're here. You're the most important person in the room. Without newcomers, we would bore each other to death.

"I went to an AA meeting in Ocho Rios, Jamaica once. There were four natives, myself, and an American woman who lived on the island and had brought AA to the town. These five people were convinced that they were the only five sober people in Ocho Rios. I believe they may have been right about that. Anyway, when I showed up, they were so excited about my being there that they were actually giddy. They kept saying how tired they were of each others' stories and how much they were looking forward to hearing mine.

"So I opened the meeting and started talking about myself, but within a minute, one of the natives broke in and took over, talking very excitedly about himself—his alcoholism and sobriety—for a good ten minutes. Then he said, 'But enough about me; we hear about me all the time. I want to hear about you,' and he gave me back the floor.

"So I started over, but then another guy broke in and talked with great animation about his alcoholism and recovery, including his gratitude for Margaret, the American who had shoved AA down his throat. After about fifteen minutes, he said the same thing as the last guy—that what he really wanted was to hear about me. So I started over again and was promptly interrupted a third time.

"Anyway, before long, I realized what was happening. It wasn't that they were so excited to hear a new story. It was that they were so excited to tell their own stories to new ears. That meeting lasted almost two hours, and I never did tell my story. I'll tell you what, though, I've never seen a happier bunch of alcoholics in my life. To top it off, after the meeting, they all thanked me profusely for bringing them new information. You know, I got a lot out of that meeting. I got a new appreciation of what twelve step work, or service work, means. Without saying hardly a word, I was a very essential part of those people's recovery that day. It's a cherished AA memory for me.

"I'd like to say something else, too. Steve, some folks in AA will tell you that we're not supposed to cross-talk in meetings and that we're suppose to refrain from giving advice. But here at this meeting, we're a small group of people who know each other pretty well, so I'm going to break with that tradition. Being connected with the university, I've been faced throughout my sobriety with obligatory social functions that always involve drinking.

"At first, when I was more vulnerable, I found that what helped me more than anything else was taking another recovering person, especially another AA member, with me as my guest. When I did that, I never felt tempted to have a drink. The other thing that I had to deal with was my self-consciousness about being the only one not drinking alcohol, but that resolved itself when I discovered over time that not only did no one care, but also that almost no one even noticed.

"One other thing that occurs to me is that you're starting in this graduate program at a good time. No one knows you or anything about you. So if you decline alcohol, then as far as they're concerned, you're just a non-drinker. Who knows? They might think you're a health nut or something. You can choose to self-disclose your alcoholism if you want, but that would be your choice. Too, I'd be surprised if the pressure to drink and use drugs goes away when this week's parties end. Graduate programs, especially those in the softer sciences like yours and mine, are notorious for attracting drinkers and pot smokers. Anyway, I just thought I might throw my two cents' worth into your thoughts about how to handle this week. I hope the group will forgive me."

Steve felt enormously grateful for Ralph's input, and he took it with him when he left the meeting and headed toward The Recovery Center and his session with Cally. On the drive over, Steve thought about Kathy and their agreement to withhold all information about their...whatever it was. He hoped beyond hope that Cally would not ask him for any details about the weekend.

"Hello, there, Steve. How are you today?"

"I'm pretty good, Cally. Why? What did you expect?"

"I didn't expect anything, Steve. But I'm tickled pink to see you here, on time and looking well."

Steve laughed. "It's funny hearing a phrase like 'tickled pink' coming out of a big old bad ass like you."

"Bad ass? Hell, I'm a pussycat, Steve. Don't you know that? I thought you were a student of human psychology."

"Yeah, well, I've been talking to James, who said to say 'Hello,' by the way, and he warned me to be careful of you. He told me that before too long, you'll be right in the middle of my shit."

"Well, Steve, our mutual friend, James Shannon, is exactly right. It's my job to be right in the middle of your shit. If you ever catch me backing away from the middle of your shit, you should fire me and find someone else to work with. So, tell me about your weekend."

Steve smiled a little nervously. "Oddly enough, Cally, it was very good. About the only time I thought about getting high was Friday night after group when my ex-wife called and told me that she was taking my kids and moving to Colorado. Even then, though, it was more like a passing thought than a compulsive one."

Cally nodded. "I see. Okay, that sounds good. So you made it through a crisis without using. What did you do instead?"

"Well, I got out of the house for a little while, and I relaxed the way you told me—you know, with the breathing and all. I read Step One in the Twelve & Twelve book. Then I called a friend who lives in San Antonio and who's been sober for about nine months. Then I went to bed and slept all night. When I woke up Saturday morning, I called my mom and told her about being sober. She damn near wet herself."

Cally smiled and looked at Steve over the top of his reading glasses. "Do you always talk about your dear mother like that, Steve? Never mind, I don't need to know that. Okay, so what did you do the rest of the weekend? Briefly, please."

Steve took a breath. "Well, after I talked to my mom, I worked in my shop the rest of the day. James dropped by for a few minutes around lunchtime. That's when he said to tell you 'Hello.' Later in the afternoon I talked to a buddy about my being in treatment, and he agreed to support me fully. That was a good conversation.

"Uh, let's see, then I went to a meeting Saturday night at the South Austin Group. Afterwards, I went for coffee with a few of the people from the meeting. Then I went home. Sunday morning I worked. I went to a noon meeting at South Austin and then to the lake for the rest of the day. Sunday evening, I talked to another friend, and she was also supportive. This morning, I went to my first day of orientation for graduate school. At noon, I went to an AA meeting across the street from campus. And now, I'm here."

Cally closed his eyes and nodded for what seemed to Steve like a long time. "What else, Steve?"

"Huh?"

Cally's eyes remained closed. "What else is there? I get the feeling that there's more."

"Uh, no, that's all, Cally. I mean, what do you think? I'm lying to you?"

Cally opened his eyes and looked at Steve. "No, Steve. Let me ask it this way. Is there anything else that you think you should tell me, but for some reason you're not?"

Steve felt his face blush slightly. He sat silently for a moment and then said, "No, Cally, that's all I have to say about the weekend right now. I might have more later, but that's all I have right now. Is that all right?"

Cally held his gaze for a few seconds and then said, "Yes, I suppose it's all right for now. So let's move on. Let's take a look at your homework."

Steve sighed with relief and pulled the Step 1 worksheet out of his backpack. He and Cally sat down together at the table to analyze it. Cally was not disturbed by Steve's failure to complete all of the questions, but they talked at some length about those that Steve had left blank.

"See, Cally, I don't think I ever drank or used specifically to change my feelings. I mean, I think I got high mainly because I liked it. I liked the way it made me feel, you know? I just liked getting high, and that was anytime, regardless of how I was feeling emotionally."

Cally chuckled. "Now listen to this, Steve. 'I didn't drink or use to change feelings. I drank and used because I liked the way it made me feel. After I drank or used, I felt different from the way I did when I started, and it was a better feeling.' Now what do you hear in that?"

Steve smiled. "Well, it sounds convoluted when you say it, but basically, that's what I think. Maybe I just didn't explain it very well. It's not like I ever said, 'God, I feel like shit; I'm going to get high, and then I'll feel like a king.' I mean, I suppose there have been times when I felt bad, you know, like down or depressed, and I smoked pot or drank some beer and then felt better, but hell, who doesn't do that? I mean, I think everyone I've ever known does that sometimes. Usually, though, I felt good before I ever started drinking or using, and getting high just made me feel even better."

Cally picked up the homework and read out loud the question: "What feelings did you try to change through the use of alcohol or drugs?" Then he wrote next to 1.: "Feeling down or depressed; I used so as to feel better." He showed it to Steve and said, "Okay? See, Steve, nothing will apply all the time, but at least there were times when you felt down or depressed, and you drank alcohol or smoked pot to feel better, and it worked.

"Understand me now; this worksheet is not an indictment. It's sole purpose is to help you understand the true nature of your relationship with alcohol and drugs. See what I mean? Now, look at this." He wrote next to 2.: "Feeling good. I used so as to feel even better," and he handed the paper back to Steve. "See, Steve, what you've just told me is that there were times when you felt bad, and you used to feel better, and there were times when you felt good, and you used to feel better."

Steve nodded. "Yeah, okay, I see that."

"What else, Steve? What other feelings did you sometimes have that were unpleasant to you, and you used something in response to those feelings or as a way to change them?"

Steve thought hard for a good answer but came up empty. "I don't know, Cally," he said.

"Think, Steve. This isn't my homework. This isn't my sobriety. It's yours. Come on, let's get serious."

"I am serious, Cally. I just don't know. I mean, my mind's a blank."

"Okay, no problem. You think about it. I'll wait." Cally sat back in his chair and closed his eyes.

Steve felt anxious and embarrassed. He searched his mind again for a good answer. Nothing came up except jumbled, meaningless thoughts seemingly unrelated to the issue at hand. Finally, out of desperation, and without regard for the truth, he said, "How about low self-esteem?"

Cally opened his eyes, and zeroed in. "I want you to go home tonight and think about this question very deeply. Think about the times that you have gained a sense of relief from using. Think about the times when you have said or thought, 'Man, I need a drink,' or 'Man, a joint sure would feel good right now.' Okay? Before starting this task, though, I want you to do something else that you might not like or be used to yet, but I want you to do it anyway. Sit quietly for a few minutes and listen to your breathing, and then pray for willingness and open-mindedness. That's all—just willingness and open-mindedness. It doesn't matter who you pray to. Just send out the thought. I think that it will come. In fact, I'm pretty sure that it will come."

Steve felt relieved. "Okay, Cally. I'll give it a try."

"Trying is dying, Steve. Remember that. We don't try on this stuff. We do it. Remember—willingness and open-mindedness."

"Right," Steve said. "Willingness and open-mindedness and trying is dying."

Cally praised Steve for his continuing sobriety and his AA meeting attendance. They set Steve's next session for Wednesday afternoon, following the school luncheon.

Steve felt relieved and happy to leave The Recovery Center. Forty-five minutes had felt like hours. He felt guilty about his and Kathy's secret. He felt uneasy about his homework assignment. "Pray for willingness and open-mindedness, and trying is dying. Jeez, is it just me, or is this kind of silly?" he muttered. He stopped for a moment in front of his house, but instead of parking, he ventured a little further down the street and stopped in front of Tommy's.

"Hey, there, Stevey. How was your first day in a big time graduate program?"

Steve smiled. "Boy, did I feel important, or what? You'd have thought it was a meeting of the president's advisory council. What a room full of egos, not to mention the weirdoes and geeks. Other than that, it wasn't bad. That's not really what I came by to talk to you about, though. You got a few minutes?"

"Sure, I guess so. What's on your mind?" Tommy asked.

"Spirituality," Steve said.

"Ah, yes, one of my favorite topics. And I'm proud to report that I do, in fact, have all of the answers. What do you want to know, Steve-o?"

"Well, what I want to know is, Tommy, do you pray?"

Tommy looked at Steve and said, "Oh, I see; you're serious." Steve nodded. "Well, then, yes, I guess so, but not in the traditional sense of the word, and certainly not to some omniscient being. But I do gather my thoughts from time to time and send them out to the universe."

"Well, Tommy, if you're not sending them out to something in particular, why send them out at all?"

Tommy smiled. "Steve, I don't think it matters one bit where or to whom they go. To me, it just matters that I get still and quiet long enough to know what's going on inside of me, you know, deep inside, and that I'm not afraid of or selfish with those thoughts, insights, feelings, inspirations, or whatever, but that I send them out to wherever they might happen to go. Who knows? Within the collective consciousness, they might mingle with yours or with my deceased grandmother's, or with Abraham Lincoln's and form a solution to some nagging little universal problem. Or, more likely, they don't go anywhere. That doesn't matter, though, because I've benefited from the experience. It somehow improves my understanding of myself and my world and makes me a better person—both inside myself and in my relationships with others."

"So you think it doesn't matter whether or not there's a God. It just matters that we learn to behave as though there is. Right?"

"Oh, I don't know about that. I'm pretty convinced that there isn't a God, but I'm quite certain that our purpose in life is to feel good about ourselves and others and treat ourselves and others with kindness and respect. The rest doesn't matter much. I know that I do a better job of that if I'm introspective and if I don't selfishly keep my insights hidden inside of myself. Call it prayer if you want to. I don't much care for the connotation, but I don't get too hung up on words."

"Yeah, okay. You know, it sounds to me like you have a substantial spiritual practice—one that I can understand and respect."

"Well, thanks, Steve. I appreciate your saying that. I'm not afraid of the word spirituality. You know, I have come to know a number of Atheists during my tenure as one, and I haven't met many real asshole Atheists yet. Maybe it's because most of us have not taken the issue lightly. It took me years to acknowledge my beliefs to myself, and even more to acknowledge them publicly."

"Tommy, my drug counselor told me this afternoon to go home and pray for willingness and open-mindedness. He believes that such prayer will help me gain insight into what I guess is my denial around my alcohol and drug abuse. About the only times I've ever really prayed have been times when I was desperate for something to be different than it was at the moment. That's true at least in my adult life.

"You know, I grew up in the Baptist church, and when I was a kid, I was a very committed Christian Soldier. I felt close to God, and I felt it through faith in Jesus. I think I really felt Jesus' presence in my life. I felt something, anyway. I guess it could have been my imagination, but I remember feeling it very strongly. Now, though, I don't feel shit. I gotta tell you, man, I liked it better the other way."

"Yes, well, Steve, I'm afraid that it will never be the other way again, at least not for you. I think you've gone too far toward a more objective truth and too far away from childhood naivete to go home again. And I think that's a good thing. I think we can feel that comfort and inner peace without buying into the hoax that we were a part of when we were kids."

Steve thought about that for a moment. Then he said, "To tell you the truth, Tommy, I'm afraid that I won't be able to find inner peace without the help of drugs. Pot, especially, is the one thing I could always count on. Roll one up and smoke it. Instant inner peace."

Tommy grinned at Steve. "Well, Stevey, if it weren't for the fact that I've agreed to support you in your sobriety, I could certainly fix your little inner peace problem. We could have you feeling spiritual in no time at all." When Tommy saw that Steve wasn't smiling, his own grin faded. "Sorry about that, Steve. I'm afraid that wasn't very supportive at all. You'll have to be patient with me while I adjust to this change in what we do together."

Steve nodded and smiled. "Thank you, Tommy. I'm trying to adjust to it, too. I think it may just take a little time and some practice. In the meantime, we have graduate school. We can talk about that with impunity, right?"

265

"Yeah, but it's hardly worth the goddamn effort. Graduate school is a breeze. Hardest part was getting in. There's nothing to the rest of it. You'll be pleasantly surprised. I'm sure of it."

CHAPTER 50

Steve spent the rest of his sixth day sober with his hands in The Woodworks and his thoughts on women. Kathy occupied most of those thoughts, but his mind also drifted to Rachel and Dixie. He felt guilty about not having seen or talked to Dixie since the previous Tuesday night—the night of the whorehouse run with Tommy and his last taste of alcohol and drugs.

Steve reminded himself that of all people, Dixie did not deserve his neglect. She was a good person and a good friend. Throughout his gradual slide toward bottom, no one had been more genuine—more honest and straightforward—than she had. Nevertheless, she was the only friend that Steve had not talked to about being sober.

Steve watched the clock out of the corner of his eye until Kathy finally called at seven. "Well, Steve, I don't know whether to thank you or curse you. You've pretty effectively dominated my thoughts since about 8:00 o'clock last night. Is it voodoo, or am I just going crazy on my own?"

Steve laughed. "Well, let me tell you something. Whatever it is, you're not doing it alone. I decided last night that I must have a severe case of infatuation. I don't particularly like that word; it implies superficiality, and what I'm experiencing doesn't feel in the least bit shallow. I'm only using it because I'm unwilling to use any of the alternatives that come to mind. Nevertheless, you've sure been on my mind."

"Well, at least we're in the same boat," Kathy said. "That's comforting; I would hate to be doing this alone. Listen, I'm going to eat a bite and go to a meeting. Want to join me?"

"I do, but I have something else that I really need to take care of—a friend that I need to talk to. Maybe we could hook up after your meeting for a little while."

"Okay, but...well, this probably sounds odd coming from an old night owl like me, but on Sunday through Wednesday nights, I like to get to bed early because I have to be to work at 7:00 o'clock those next mornings. So maybe just for a cup of decaf or something.

"By the way, not to change the subject, but I've been wondering all day about your meeting with Cally. You can tell me about it later, but for the time being, did you spill the beans?"

"No, I didn't, but I don't feel good about it, Kathy. He knows something's up. He gave me the evil eye and asked me what I

266

wasn't telling him. I felt embarrassed, and when I left there, I felt guilty. I think we need to talk about it—you and I, I mean."

"Okay, I understand. Well, listen, I better go. Can we meet at the S. A. Coffeehouse?"

"Yeah, I'll see you there a little after nine."

After showering and eating a sandwich, Steve walked across the street to The Roam In. Still early on a Monday night, the place was nearly empty. Dixie was leaning against the back of the bar reading a novel. She smiled cautiously when she saw him come in.

"Well, look who's here. I thought we had lost you, Steve. I don't suppose you'd let me buy you a beer, would you?" she said.

Steve grinned and shook his head. "No thanks, Dixie. I'd love a tonic and lime, though. Listen, I'm sorry that I haven't been by or called. I've really had a lot going on. How are you?"

"I'm okay. Same old, same old, you know? I was beginning to wonder if I might have said or done something to run you off for good. I almost dropped by your shop this afternoon, but I didn't feel comfortable doing that. I wasn't sure it would be okay. Do you mind my asking what's been going on? I mean, the grapevine has been active, as usual, but I'd like to hear it from you."

Steve smiled. "Ah, yes, the good old neighborhood bar grapevine. Well, I don't really know where to start. I guess the biggest thing is that I've been sober and clean for almost a week. In fact, the last time I drank alcohol was in here last Tuesday night. I've been working with a counselor and going to AA meetings every day since Wednesday. That's one reason I haven't been in. I almost came by Wednesday night and again Thursday, but I think I was nervous about being in the bar. I know that doesn't excuse my not calling, but this sobriety thing has pretty well dominated my time. I just told Tommy about it day before yesterday. I was kind of afraid that he wouldn't take it too well, but he agreed to be supportive.

"Anyway, that's the main thing that's been up with me. I started graduate school this morning, but that seems minor compared to the other. I really am sorry for not getting in touch with you sooner, Dixie. I was just thinking earlier today that you deserve better than that from me."

She nodded and stared at him for a moment. "That's all right, Steve. I think I understand." She paused and then continued. "Gosh, my mind is whirling. My first thought is how wonderful it is that you're able to do that—to be sober, that is. I'm proud of you. I think it's what I've been wanting for you. But right on top of that, there's another, very selfish thought that I'm ashamed to even have. I'm wondering what your being sober means in terms of our friendship, or our relationship, or

267

whatever you call what we have. I apologize for having such a selfish thought, but it certainly is in there."

Steve didn't know what to say. He didn't want to say too much, and he certainly didn't want to hurt Dixie's feelings, but since she asked, and considering what was going on between him and Kathy, he felt as though he needed to put up some kind of a wall—even a low one.

"I don't know the answer to that, Dixie," he said. "I know I care about you a lot. That hasn't changed. And I certainly don't want to lose your friendship. But I'm pretty confused about a lot of things right now. I feel like I have a lot of stuff to work through, you know?

"Actually, I'm thinking that maybe we could agree to be just friends for a while. What I mean is, friends instead of friends and lovers. I mean, sex or no sex, I really do think of you as one of my best friends, and I could sure use your support. I don't know, though; what would you think about that?"

"I think I would miss sleeping with you very much, and I feel like I'm getting gently set aside."

"I'm sorry, Dixie. I didn't mean for it to sound that way. I don't feel that way. I feel as though I just need to back off a bit, maybe for just a little while, until I straighten things out in my own mind."

"I understand, Steve. I was just answering your question honestly. I mean, I feel pretty good about myself, but I have my insecurities, too. Actually, I've had the feeling for quite some time that we've been slipping away from each other. I've mentioned it before, remember? But I'm okay, and I am happy about you being sober if that's what you want, even if it does affect our relationship. I guess you won't be hanging around the old Roam In very much, will you?"

Steve smiled and shook his head. "No, it's probably not the safest place for me to be right now. That doesn't mean that we can't see each other, though. In fact, maybe we could go swimming or to a movie or something tomorrow afternoon before you come to work."

Dixie's smile softened, and she took a deep breath. "Yeah, Steve, I'd like that. I'd like that a lot. There's an art house film out at The Village that I've been wanting to see. I was hoping that you and I could see it together."

"Great," Steve said. "Hey, I'll tell you what. If you'll come by over here and pick me up, I'll fix us lunch before we go."

Steve felt greatly relieved when he left the bar. He felt as though it could not have gone any better. Dixie seemed happy, and he was off the hook with her, at least sexually, and at least for the time being while he and Kathy sorted through their feelings toward each other.

As he replayed the conversation with Dixie in his mind, he became aware of another interesting thing that had happened while he was in the bar. He had felt uncomfortable and out of place there. Not only that, he had felt repelled by the smell of stale beer and cigarettes.

Kathy was a little late meeting Steve at the coffeehouse, and he was disappointed when she walked in with another woman in tow. "Steve, I want you to meet Susan," she said. Steve smiled cordially and shook the woman's hand, and they all sat down around a small table.

"Steve, Susan is my AA sponsor. She insisted on coming over here with me. I think she's mad at me because I used the words 'Steve' and 'relationship' in the same sentence. Is that right, Susan?"

Susan cocked her head, raised an eyebrow, and gave Kathy a slightly sarcastic smile. She was a fairly plain looking older woman—mid-forties or so, Steve figured. Had he been describing her to a friend, he might have said that she looked like someone's mother.

"Boy, you sure know how to put a girl on the spot, Kathy. But yeah, quite honestly, I'm concerned. You know, conventional AA wisdom suggests that you wait a full year before you get yourself tangled up in a romantic relationship. I know you have about half that, Kathy, and Steve, I understand that you're still really fresh—new, in fact."

Steve nodded. He reminded himself to avoid defensiveness even though he felt irritated at Susan's statement and her attitude, which felt to him like condescending arrogance. "Yeah," he said. "Brand new—six days. I'm afraid that I don't know much about conventional AA wisdom, however. I just know how I'm feeling right now."

"And how is that?" Susan asked.

Steve shifted in his chair and glanced at Kathy, who shrugged her shoulders very slightly. He looked back at Susan and said, "Uh, could I get either of you a cup of coffee or something?"

Susan smiled at him. "I'm sorry, Steve. I didn't mean to interrogate you. I guess I'm over-protective. Sure, I'd love some. Thank you. Decaf, if you will."

"Me, too," Kathy added. "In fact, I'll help you get it."

They excused themselves and walked into the adjoining room and up to the counter. Kathy slipped her hand into Steve's and gave it a squeeze. He relaxed and breathed. "I'm sorry, Steve," she said. "I probably shouldn't have brought her, but she's one of those Nazi type sponsors. Unfortunately, I tell her everything, and right now I think she's on the war path. She likes to run interference for me because a number of men in AA tried to thirteenth step me when I first came into the program.

She really is over-protective, and she really did invite herself. She brought her own car, though, so maybe if we humor her for a few minutes, she'll go home and leave us alone."

"Well, I won't be rude or anything, but I don't feel compelled to tell her anything. I don't know what all a sponsor is supposed to do, Kathy, but surely she's not privileged to cross-examine your friends, is she? What's a thirteenth step, anyway? Guys hitting on you when you're new to AA?"

"Yeah, that's exactly what it is. Susan says that I need to ask myself if that's what I'm doing to you."

Steve gave Kathy a bewildered look. "You've got to be kidding. I don't feel like I'm being hit on. Shit, I've been hit on before, and it doesn't feel anything like this. I mean, I don't think we know for sure what our motivations are, but I'm quite certain they're not selfish and manipulative. Are they? I don't think they are."

Kathy shook her head. "No, I don't think they are, either. If they were, we would have stayed in bed together Saturday night. Right?"

"Yeah, right. Does she know about that?"

Kathy nodded.

"Does she know about Cally's group rules and our decision not to say anything to him about us?"

"Uh huh," Kathy said. "I don't think that's what has her so uptight, though. What's bugging her is that I told her how attracted I feel toward you. I made the mistake of telling her that it didn't feel just sexual. She's afraid we'll jump into something that will sabotage our sobriety."

Steve smiled broadly and squeezed her hand. "You're so incredibly attracted to me that your sponsor's got her panties in a wad, huh?"

Kathy slapped his arm playfully. "Stop it," she said. She paused for a moment and then added, "Steve, I'm not asking you to act any certain way with Susan. She's the one who wanted to butt in. You do what you want."

They sat down with the coffee. Everyone smiled politely, and the conversation took a decidedly more cautious route. They talked about Steve's graduate program and about his refinishing shop. They discussed his and Kathy's treatment program and their mutual respect for Cally Callahan. It only got specific about "the relationship" at the very end, when Susan was about to leave.

"I take recovery very seriously," she said. "I take it more seriously than anything else in the world. To me, it is the world. When I accept the responsibility of being someone's sponsor, I accept it fully. I'm not a part-timer. Right, Kathy?" Kathy nodded. "So I feel obliged to tell you both that in my experience in AA, when two people jump into an intense romantic relationship too early in recovery, it almost always ends with people getting hurt. It very often ends with people getting drunk. "In early recovery, people need the time and energy to concentrate on their sobriety. A new relationship diverts time and energy away from sobriety. For example, Steve, in your free time during the last couple of days, how much mental energy have you devoted to recovery relative to that devoted to Kathy? Never mind; you don't have to answer that. I think I already know the answer.

"Not only is a relationship at this stage of the game time consuming. It's also confusing. Your feelings are typically raw. Your defenses are coming down. You're vulnerable in ways that you're not familiar with. Do you remember your first adolescent love? Remember how absorbing that experience was? An early sobriety 'love' can be the same kind of experience. That might seem pretty exciting, but what if you two are typical, and it ends badly? Since you've been concentrating on the relationship instead of on recovery, you don't have the solid foundation or the skills to deal with setbacks. Would either of you survive the experience? It's something to think about and to seek advice on.

"You know something, guys? A lot of AA's would disagree with me, but I personally think you'd be better off with a hot and heavy one-night stand than with something you perceive as love. That's my opinion, for what it's worth.

"There's one other thing, and then I'll run off and leave you to curse me behind my back. It's the issue of dishonesty with your counselor and your treatment group. If you are going to break the agreement to which you signed your name, then recovery demands that you face up to it honestly. If you don't, it will eat your lunch in more ways than you can imagine. If recovery has a synonym, it's honesty. You may not have broken the letter of the law, but I believe that you have broken the spirit of it.

"Well, that's my spiel, at least for the time being. Do with it what you will. Steve, I look forward to getting to know you better. You do seem like a very nice man. I can easily see why Kathy is drawn to you. I'm ready and willing to leave now, unless you want me to stay."

Kathy and Steve looked at each other and then back to Susan. "I have a question, Susan," Steve said. "First, though, I want to say that I think it's pretty presumptuous of you to say that Kathy and I are in a relationship, especially an intense romantic one. We've been out together once, and that was to an AA meeting.

"Disregarding that, though, I assume that you've been around AA for some time. Have you never seen an early sobriety relationship work out? I ask because I have. My mother's did. Her husband was one of two people who helped her get sober and into AA in the first place. They got married when she was sober one year and he was a year and a half. That was in 1965, and they've been very happy together, as far as I know."

"I'm not implying universality, Steve," Susan answered. "Not every single one ends badly. It's damn close to that, though."

When Susan was out of the building, Steve laid his hands palms up on the table, and Kathy put hers into them. He lifted them both to his lips and kissed one and then the other. Kathy blinked back tears. "Are you okay?" Steve asked her softly.

"No, I'm not. I feel sad and afraid. Before tonight, our thing—our attraction for each other—was exciting. Now it's confusing and frightening. Ever since I've been in AA, I've believed that my sponsor knew what was best for me. I've never rejected, or even seriously questioned, her advice. Now I don't know what to do. I'm very angry at her for saying those things."

Steve held her hands in his. "Kathy, all I know is that right now I want to be with you. I want to spend time with you. Whether it's attraction or infatuation or something else entirely, I want to explore it with you. If it's a passing thing, then I can live with that. I don't think I'd go out and get drunk and stoned over that. And I don't think you would, either.

"I'm not saying that your sponsor is wrong, and I'm not asking you to do anything that you don't feel good about. I'm just telling you how I feel."

Kathy closed her eyes and nodded. "What about Cally? I don't want to lose the group."

"I agree with Susan about that. Like I told you earlier, I didn't feel right about lying to him, and in reality, that's what I did. At least I felt dishonest. And you know what? When I left there today, I felt angry at him. I think that anger was just exactly what Susan was talking about—my dishonesty eating my lunch in a sneaky way. So I think that if we're going to play this attraction out, then we need to talk to Cally about it. If not, then I don't know."

"I guess I need some time, Steve. I need to pray about it and write about it in my journal. Would that be all right with you?"

"Yeah, sure it would. I may even pray about it myself. Praying is one of my homework assignments anyway."

Steve and Kathy gradually changed the subject and talked for a little while longer. By the time they left the coffeehouse at 11:00 o'clock, their moods were lighter. Steve walked Kathy to her car. He leaned against the side of it and gently tugged at her to come closer. She moved up and pressed the front of her body lightly against his. They kissed romantically for the first time and then for the second and then the third, and they both felt it throughout their bodies. During their third long kiss, Steve slid his hand down Kathy's back to the top of the curve in her hips and gently pressed his fingers against her. She tilted her pelvis up slightly to fit more snugly against his. They both breathed heavily and held each other tight.

"Susan is definitely right about one thing, Steve," Kathy said in a whisper. "These are unfamiliar feelings to me. I haven't felt sexually aroused like this in several years. I can't remember the last time that I wanted to hold someone's body close and tight against mine simply because it felt good."

They kissed one more time, said goodnight, and then reluctantly went their separate ways.

When Steve got home, he got undressed and sat naked in the middle of his bed and prayed. He asked for willingness and open mindedness. "...that's all, God, just willingness and open-mindedness." Then he closed his eyes and fantasized about him and Kathy naked in the back seat of her car in the parking lot of The South Austin Coffeehouse, and he masturbated for the third night in a row.

Steve woke up five times during the night with Kathy in his consciousness. Every time that happened, he prayed for willingness and open-mindedness. "Dear God, or whoever or whatever is out there to hear my prayer, please give me willingness and open-mindedness. I don't fully understand why I'm praying for these qualities, but I'm asking for them as seriously and genuinely as I know how. Thank you. Amen."

CHAPTER 51

Poorly catered breakfast with 40 or so academia types was not Steve's idea of a morning to frame, especially when he had so many other things on his mind. He approached it with forced tolerance.

The room was set up to accommodate seven tables of six people each. With some effort, Steve managed to collect five of the students who had caught his interest the previous morning and bring them together at one table. He did not consciously plan it so, but it ended up being the only table without a faculty member at the head.

Following bad food and weak coffee, each faculty member stood up and briefly described the informal groups that he or she would lead during the remainder of the morning. Despite the fact that they all looked prehistoric, four of the six were quite friendly and witty, and all six seemed exceptionally intelligent. Two of them were even provocative. One of those, the youngest, engaged Steve in conversation and seemed interested in him as a person.

Within the informal groups, the other students appeared to Steve to be very knowledgeable, confident, and articulate. They questioned and confronted each other and the professors, who

273

seemed to enjoy the banter. Steve imagined himself the least academically prepared student in the class of 34 superstars. He hid his feelings of inferiority with a lot of brow furrowing and head nodding.

During one highly intellectual exchange between a student and a professor, one of Steve's new cohorts—another longhaired, blue jeaned man named Ron—caught Steve's eye, shrugged his shoulders, and cocked his head toward the door. Steve followed him into the hallway. "Come here; I want to show you something I discovered yesterday," he said.

They went through a door marked "Employees Only," up several flights of stairs, and through another door marked "Maintenance Employees Only." That door opened onto the roof of the five-story building. Ron reached into his shirt pocket and produced a nicely rolled joint, which he held it up by one end for Steve to inspect. "What do you think, Steve? Should we set fire to this rascal?"

Steve's insides froze. His mind threw out about twenty responses to the offer, and eighteen of them were different ways of saying, "Yes," and "Hell, yes." Two of them were ways to decline, however. One of the two was a simple, "No, I don't smoke." He chose the other one. "Well...no, man, I think I better not," he said. "I have a shit load of stuff to do as soon as I leave here. You go ahead, though. I'll just hang out with you while you do it."

Ron lit and smoked half of the joint with the relaxed gestures of a very practiced pot smoker. He offhandedly offered it to Steve a couple of times, and although Steve waved it off, his mind raced with indecision. His anxiety soared. He felt himself become agitated and then angry—first at Ron, and then at himself. At one point, he decided to go ahead and take just one hit. He hesitated, though, and at that moment Ron squeezed off the flame and slipped the roach back into his pocket. "Whew, boy; good stuff," he said.

"Yeah, it smelled good," Steve answered. "This is a great place. How did you find it?"

"I scout out everything, man. I get the lay of the land, you know? I always have, even when I was a kid. I knew shit about our house that the goddamn general contractor didn't even know about. I had hiding places that my parents couldn't have found with a radar gun. To me, a 'Keep Out' sign is like an engraved invitation." Ron laughed loudly at his own wit. His eyes were already glassy and unfocused. Steve forced himself to laugh also, and in that instant, Steve resented Ron tremendously.

"Well, what do you think, Ron? Are you about ready to go back in and face our academic futures?"

274

"Fuck, no, man; I've had about all of the arrogant, patronizing crap that I can take for one day. I'm gonna haul ass. I'll see you tomorrow."

Steve rejoined the larger group, but he could not regain his concentration. Every time he caught up with the flow of the conversation, his mind shifted to Ron and to the smoke, and his anxiety and agitation rose up again. He faked it the best he could until 11:30 and then unobtrusively excused himself. The moment he walked through the door of his house, he picked up the phone and called Cally.

"Callahan."

"Cally, this is Steve Campbell. Do you have a minute to talk to me?"

"You bet, Steve. What's going on?"

Steve told Cally the joint on the roof story, including his emotional response to the opportunity and the aftermath.

"So you declined your favorite drug despite what I would imagine was pretty intense social pressure to conform. I think you passed an important test, Steve."

"If I passed, it was with a C minus, Cally. I wanted to get stoned. I wanted it bad. And I felt angry at everyone connected with recovery, including me and you, because I didn't have that option. I didn't even know what to say to the guy. I felt so stupid. I didn't even know how to say 'No.'"

"Hey, take it easy on yourself, Steve. You did say 'No.' You said it the best way you could at that moment. Beyond that, though, what do think would have happened if you had simply told him the truth?"

"Cally, at that moment, I didn't know what the truth was. I only knew one thing. I wanted to smoke, and I couldn't."

"What do you mean, you 'couldn't,' Steve? It was your choice. Nobody was stopping you. Nobody even would have known. So why couldn't you?"

"Because I'm doing this goddamn, stupid recovery thing!"

"Well, then, *that* was the truth. 'I really want to smoke with you, but I can't because I'm in recovery from alcohol and drug addiction.'"

Steve became silent and let that sink in. Then he said in a restrained voice, "I'm not sure about this recovery business, Cally. Right now, I don't like it worth a shit."

Cally laughed softly. "Yeah, I hear you, Steve. Believe me, I do. Let me tell you something, though. I have a good feeling about you. I think you have a damn good shot at making it in recovery. Your experience this morning, combined with this phone call, says a lot to me. You aren't shutting yourself off to your experience, and you're not denying the implications of it. You have a lot to learn, naturally, but what I hear is that you're willing to walk though this thing with your eyes and your heart open. I don't know where you get that. I know you didn't learn it in your immediate family of origin. Maybe it was from your grandparents. At any rate, I hear it. So you may not feel like it at this moment, but I think you're doing very well indeed."

Steve took a deep breath and relaxed. "Okay," he said. He breathed again. "Man, I'm very confused about some things, Cally. I can save them till tomorrow afternoon, but I'm damn glad that you were here for me today. I'm not saying that I would have used. In fact, I don't really think I would have, but I can't say for absolute certain. You know what I mean?"

"That I do, Mr. Campbell. That I do. You take it easy, now. Don't forget to breathe. It wouldn't hurt anything for you to talk about your experience with other recovering people. See what they have done with similar experiences. You might even want to think about mentioning it in an AA meeting. You and I also need to talk about sponsorship. I think you may need a pretty strong AA sponsor, and pretty soon, too. At any rate, I'll see you tomorrow afternoon. Call if you need to."

After he hung up the phone, Steve lay back on his bed and closed his eyes. "Willingness and open-mindedness, God. Please. Willingness and open-mindedness. Thank you."

Dixie arrived on time at 12:30. She had made an effort to look attractive, and she had succeeded. Her hair, makeup, and clothes were perfect. She looked very pretty.

"I can still have hugs, can't I?" she smiled and asked. They hugged tenderly, and she held him in the embrace longer than usual. Before letting go, she pressed her body hard against his.

Steve fixed them a simple lunch, and after eating, they sat at the table and talked. Dixie asked questions about his sobriety. She easily grasped the conceptual difference between abstinence and recovery, even though Steve apologized for his own sketchy understanding and explanation of it. She expressed interest in AA and asked him if he would take her to a meeting with him some time.

The movie was French with English subtitles. It was a beautiful, very erotic film, and Steve became sexually aroused several times. During one of those, Dixie reached over and picked up his hand from his lap and held the back of it against her breast. After a few minutes, she laid it palm down on the top of her thigh and laid her hand on top of his. Steve slowly slid his hand around to the inside of her thigh. He squeezed and rubbed very, very gently. He felt her legs part ever so slightly, and although he felt tempted, he resisted the invitation to slide his hand under her skirt. Instead, he patted the inside of her thigh, took her hand in his, kissed it, and held it in his lap for most of the rest of the movie.

On the drive home, Dixie said, "I hope that I didn't offend you during the movie. I was feeling quite passionate."

Steve laughed softly. "Yeah, so was I. I feel as though I'm the one who should apologize, though. I gave you mixed messages in there."

"Yes, I was a little confused, and my feelings did get slightly hurt when you rejected my offer. You handled it well, though, I suppose. I appreciated your tenderness. I have to admit that I wanted more," she said, glancing away from the road for a moment to catch Steve's eye. Steve nodded but did not reply.

Dixie parked in front of Steve's house. "I've got about an hour before I have to be to work. Can I hang out with you till then?"

"Yeah, sure you can, Dixie. Come on in; I'll fix us something to drink."

Steve made a pot of coffee and put a Judy Collins album on the stereo. They sat together on the floor and leaned their backs against the front of the couch. They talked about the movie and then recalled other romantic and erotic movies that they had seen together.

After about twenty minutes, the conversation slowed, and Dixie shifted her body so that she faced Steve. She placed her hand on the back of his neck and gently pulled his face to hers. She kissed him on the mouth, then whispered in his ear, "Steve, please take me into the bedroom and make love to me. I want you so much right now. I want to feel your body on mine, and I want to feel you inside of me. I'll try not to ask you again if that's the way you want it, but please make love to me now."

Steve pulled his face back slightly and looked into Dixie's eyes. He kissed her softly on the lips. Then he stood and helped her up. He led her by the hand into the bedroom. They slowly slipped out of their clothes and into bed. Their love-making was very sweet—gentle, friendly, and unselfish. Afterwards, they lay in each other's arms, legs entwined, and stroked each other's back.

"Thank you, Steve. That was very wonderful. I love lying naked with you in this bed. It makes me sad to think that I might lose that." She kissed him and slipped out of his embrace. She picked up her clothes and walked into the bathroom.

Steve watched Dixie walk across the street and into The Roam In. He reflected on his feelings for her. The words, "fondness" and "affection" came to mind. There had never been a tremendous amount of intensity between them, but always genuine affection. She was a good person and a dear friend; she would make someone a terrific partner. She was smart and interesting. She was reliable and honest. She was kindhearted and considerate. She was a darn good lover.

Steve went back into the house and lay on his bed. He felt twinges of guilt, but he easily convinced himself that he had done nothing wrong. Dixie had needed him, and he had given

277

himself to her. Making love to Dixie was an act of generosity—a kind and loving thing. He reminded himself that he was committed to no one. He had no promises or agreements outstanding. Not only that, no one had been hurt, and no one would ever know the difference.

Satisfied that the issue was settled, Steve went to work on his Step 1 assignment. He prefaced it with a prayer for willingness and open-mindedness, as per Cally's instructions, and he surprised himself by finding answers to questions that he had left blank on Thursday. Answers and insights came easily.

One question that had stumped him completely—"How has the way you feel about yourself been affected by your use of alcohol & drugs?"—offered several interesting possibilities. He wrote, "The most obvious effect has been confusion about myself and loss of confidence in myself, especially when I've made firm decisions to control how much and how often I was going to use and then found myself unable to stick with those decisions. At those times, I've wondered what the hell was wrong with me. There have been times, too, when I felt thoroughly disgusted with myself because of what I've done when I was loaded. There have even been a couple of times when I've looked in the mirror and hated what I saw (actually, when I think about it, it's who I saw—not what I saw). The less obvious thing is that I think I've used alcohol and drugs—getting high—as a way to help me or make me feel good about myself and even to give myself an identity. It's like, I'm not just Steve Campbell, boyish man and good fellow. I'm Steve Campbell, beer drinking, high-flying stoner and honest drug dealer. Anyway, what I'm seeing is that in an effort to feel better about myself—to boost my self-esteem and self-image—through an intimate relationship with alcohol and drugs, I ultimately felt worse. I know it's not normal to look at yourself in the mirror and feel disgusted."

Steve was working in his shop when Kathy called a little before seven and asked him to meet her at the South Austin Group at eight. They sat together during the meeting, and Steve was very aware that he was more attentive to Kathy's presence—her smell, her occasional touch, her reactions to what was being said, and her glances toward him—than he was to the meeting itself. After it was over, they walked outside and sat on the grass in front of the house and said goodbye to people as they filed out and drove off. When everyone was finally gone and they were alone on the front lawn, Kathy asked Steve if he had thought much about their conversation with Susan the night before.

"Yeah, sure I have. I've thought about it a lot."

"And?" she asked.

"...and, well, I'm not sure. I mean, I've had some ideas, but I don't know. How about you? What are you thinking?"

Kathy stared at the grass in silence.

"Kathy?" Steve finally said.

"I've thought of virtually nothing else," she said. "And I hate to admit it, but I think she's right, Steve. I think she's right about most everything she said. I don't want to think that, but I do. For six months now, I've focused on my recovery, and my life has turned completely around. Now, you're in my thoughts so much that my recovery is suddenly on the back burner, and when I get right down to it, that scares me."

Steve's heart sank. He immediately felt angry and afraid. He kept his voice even and reasonable, however, and he said, "So what does that translate into for us?"

Kathy's voice was soft and sad. "I don't know for sure, Steve." She leaned against his shoulder. "What do you think are the chances that we could ease away from the romance for a while and be friends?"

"The truth, Kathy? I don't think the chances are that great. Don't get me wrong. I'd agree to do that before I'd agree to not see you at all, but it sure wouldn't be what I want. It doesn't feel right to me. I don't feel just friendly toward you. Hell, I want you to move in with me—tonight—and never leave my sight again."

He smiled weakly. "Actually, I'm just kidding about that, but you get my drift." He paused for a moment. "I don't want to distract you from your recovery, and I do know what you're talking about. You're on my mind a lot, too. I mean, I didn't even hear what people said tonight, but I could tell you how many times your leg brushed against mine. But even though I know that you're a distraction to me at this moment, I don't think that level of preoccupation will last very long. It will settle out. I'm pretty sure about that. I don't know, Kathy, maybe we could find some kind of middle ground between 'just friends' and 'intense romantic relationship' that would give us the best of both worlds."

Kathy looked at Steve's face for the first time since they sat down. "What do you mean?" she asked.

"Well, like maybe we could spend time together, you know, the same as we would if we had everyone's blessing. We could take our time and explore our feelings toward each other, but set some boundaries around it. For example, I don't really want to do this, but in the spirit of compromise and conventional AA wisdom, maybe we could agree to be together but not have sexual intercourse for some length of time. I mean, we did get into bed half naked with each other without having sex, and we spent the night less than thirty feet away from each other without having sex, and even though that wasn't exactly what I wanted at that moment, I was fine with it. In fact, I respected what we did very much. I got to be close to you all night, but we did what we said we were going to do. We honored our agreement with Cally."

Kathy nodded. "Yeah, that's true; we did," she said.

Feeling encouraged, Steve continued. "You know, in retrospect, I think we could have slept together like we had originally planned. I think I just erred on the side of caution. Regardless of that, though, there's many things we could do, like agree to spend a certain amount of time apart, just working on our own stuff. You can still spend time with Susan, and I can get a sponsor and spend time with him. We might even meet and talk with Susan every week or so and let her give us feedback on how we're doing.

"We could talk to Cally, too. In fact, I have an individual session with him tomorrow afternoon. We could use that session to meet with him and talk to him about this stuff, and you know, see what he suggests. What do you think? Am I making any sense?"

"I don't know, Steve. You might be on to something. Susan did say that it's 'intense romantic relationships' that are the culprit. So yeah, maybe we could just try to relax a little bit and limit or define our relationship in such a way that it isn't a really intense romantic one. Who knows? It may just work. I have my doubts, but it may. Like you said, I can't help but think that my obsessive thinking about you will subside before too long. Surely it will. And Cally's rule is against sexual intimacy specifically. I know that because I went back and read it. It doesn't say anything about not spending time together or not exploring feelings toward each other. So I don't know. We might be kidding ourselves, but at least for right now, I like the idea better than agreeing to stuff our feelings for each other and say we're going to be just friends. Now that I think about it, that doesn't seem like a very honest thing to do anyway."

Steve sighed with relief. He put his arm around Kathy's shoulder and pulled her close to him. When he did, she lifted her face up to his and kissed him softly on the lips. They kissed again, and this time, Kathy parted her lips and teeth. Steve did not hesitate to slip his tongue into her mouth.

Still embracing, they rotated their bodies to face each other. Then they slowly lay down and stretched out on the grass, Kathy on her back and Steve on his side with his body pressed against her. He slid his top leg over her and rested it on her thighs. He leaned his upper body over her and kissed her deeply and passionately.

As they kissed, Steve slipped his hand under Kathy's T-shirt. He slowly moved it up her side and then onto her breast. She breathed in deeply and arched her back slightly to raise her chest against his touch. She made a soft moaning sound in her throat. He rubbed her breast gently for just a moment and then moved his hand under her back and pulled her tightly against his chest. She put both of her arms around him and did the same. They lay together on their sides, in their embrace, rocking gently back and forth for several minutes, each feeling the other's body from head to toe, each reluctant to let the moment end.

It was Kathy who finally interrupted the silence. "This solution of ours might turn out to be rather frustrating."

Steve broke into laughter, and his body relaxed. He released his embrace, and they rolled out of each other's arms and onto their backs. Kathy laughed, too, and the sexual tension between them softened. They were quiet for a minute as they lay next to each other and looked up at the night sky.

"You know what I'm grateful for right now?" he asked.

"What?" she said.

"My prowess at masturbation. I think it's going to come in handy...so to speak."

Kathy laughed hard, and then she said, "Well, I might need a little more practice, but I know what you mean. I masturbated a little when I was a teenager, and I faked masturbation a few times in my life as a woman of the evening, but night before last was the first time that I've brought myself to orgasm as an adult. In fact, it's the first orgasm I've had in a very long time."

"No kidding, Kathy? How long?" Steve asked.

"Close to three years, I'd guess. I know that's not what you would expect, but it's the truth. I've been more genuinely sexually aroused tonight than I was at any time during my professional life."

They lay together in the grass and talked for a while longer. Kathy agreed to attend the cocktail party on Thursday night and "maybe" the barbecue Friday afternoon. Because of work, she declined joining Steve for his Wednesday session with Cally but suggested that he go ahead and tell Cally at least a little bit about what was going on between them and ask him for a Friday morning session that they would attend together. They parted in good spirits, hopeful that they had resolved their "problem" and that they could secure the blessings of the people who were guiding them in their recovery.

When he got home, Steve went to bed and read his Big Book until exactly 2:35 AM, when he congratulated himself on having been completely sober and straight for exactly one week. He dropped off to sleep feeling pretty good about himself.

CHAPTER 52

Steve was awakened from a peaceful sleep at 7:00 AM by a phone call from Lois. Yawning frequently, he gave her an abbreviated blow-by-blow update of his progress in recovery, leaving out any and all reference to Kathy. Lois was overjoyed. She gave him enthusiastic, positive feedback and encouragement. She told him that if he came "home" to see the kids on Saturday and Sunday, she would like to take him to her's and Chester's AA group. He told her that he would let her know.

As soon as he hung up and rolled over to go back to sleep, the phone rang again. This time it was Rachel. Steve sat up in bed, fully awake. "I'm just checking up on you, old friend," she said. "If I woke you up, that's too bad. I owed you."

"Yeah, alright. We're even now. Man, it's good to hear from you, Rachel. Can you believe it? I was one week sober as of 2:35 this morning. I sat up and read the damn Big Book until exactly 2:35, and then I patted myself on the back and went dead asleep. What do you think about that?"

"I think it's fantastic," she said with a giggle in her voice. "Are you going to AA or are you sweating it out the 'white knuckle' way?"

"No, I'm going, every day so far. It's okay, too. I've found a good group—two, actually—where I feel like I fit in. I've met quite a few people. I've gone for coffee after meetings a couple of times. I'm doing all the stuff you're supposed to do, I guess. I'm about ready to get a sponsor, too. In fact, I have someone in mind. Didn't you tell me that you have a sponsor, Rachel?"

"Yeah, I have a good one. I like her most of the time, and I usually trust what she tells me." She paused for a moment and then continued. "I gotta tell you, Steve, I'm really proud of you. Isn't it the most ironic thing you can imagine? One year ago we were getting high together, and today we're sharing recovery with each other. I think that's really cool."

Steve laughed. "Yeah, me, too. Even considering how much I enjoyed getting high with you, it really is cool. Hey, listen, why don't we get together? I'd love to compare notes with you now that I have a better idea of what the hell you're talking about. I'll probably be down there this weekend to see my kids. It's not my regular time, but as you know, I didn't get to see them last weekend. What do you think? Could you squeeze me into your schedule?"

"Well, I'll have to double check my social calendar. Hmm, let's see. Oh, my gosh, it's empty. So yeah, I guess it's a date. In the meantime, tell me how your week has gone since I talked to you Friday night."

Steve gave Rachel a longer version of his blow-by-blow, again omitting any reference to Kathy. They talked animatedly for a half-hour, until Rachel said that she needed to get dressed and leave for work. Steve promised to call her by Friday with his weekend plans, and when he hung up, he felt excited at the prospect of seeing her. He immediately called Beverly, who agreed for Steve to have Lynn and Eddie for a few hours on Saturday afternoon and told him that she would bring him up to date on her plans to move when he brought them home.

"Perfect," he said to himself as he hung up the phone. His thoughts moved immediately to spending Saturday night with Rachel.

Steve went to school at 10:00 o'clock. He absorbed little of the dean's two-hour seminar. His mind drifted, instead, between Kathy and Rachel, with occasional thoughts of Dixie, especially their date the previous afternoon. He fantasized about making love with Kathy on the front lawn at the South Austin AA Group. He imagined sleeping with Rachel in three days.

The informal luncheon was better than the sit-down breakfast. Younger, newer faculty members attended. They were looser, less serious, and more fun than Tuesday's tenured professors. Steve overheard one conversation between a student and a longish-haired, frumpy-dressed assistant professor in which the student asked the professor a very serious philosophical question, and the prof replied, "Oh, hell, please don't ask me to work that hard today. Hang onto the idea, though, and bring it up in class sometime." Steve was happy to learn that it was this group who taught first year students.

He found himself avoiding Ron, who failed to notice, and spent most of his time talking with the "normal" woman who had caught his eye on Monday. Her name was Sheri, like his sister, and she was, in fact, very friendly, very open, and very genuine. Steve confided in her that he was in recovery from alcohol and drug addiction. He appreciated the way that she listened. Even with all of the interesting people and game-playing going on around them, she never diverted her eyes or failed to hear what he said. She seemed interested in the process of recovery, and she very much appreciated Steve's disclosure. They agreed to get together the following week for coffee. Steve figured that he had found a true friend and ally, in stark contrast to his previous day's experience with Ron.

Steve went straight from school to The Recovery Center. Cally seemed glad to see him. "So, Mr. Campbell, one week sober, and you already look like a new man. You have color in your face, and your eyes have life. Tell me, how much do you love recovery today?"

"Funny you should ask, Cally. Because today, I'm pretty damned jazzed about recovery. I'm not all that excited about being here at the moment, but I am glad to be sober today."

Cally smiled. "What, not glad to see me? Well, I never heard of such a thing. But if you're not glad to be here, then you must have one of two things on your mind—either serious stuff that is difficult to discuss, or nothing at all. Which is it, Steve?"

"It's the first, Cally."

"Good. I'm happy to hear that. First order of business, though, is for us to review your progress. Will you please give me your completed Step 1 assignment?"

Steve handed it to him. Cally perused it, smiled and nodded his approval, and laid it on top of his desk. "Now, tell me about your AA meeting attendance."

Steve related his attendance and participation and then gave him updates on his reading assignments and other treatment plan activities.

"Excellent," Cally finally said. "Considering the impressive way that you're progressing, I expect that I will need to add activities to your treatment plan in two weeks. Before you leave today, we'll discuss sponsorship. Now, however, you've brought an issue in with you that you want to discuss. Perhaps it's one that you chose to avoid on Monday."

Steve raised his eyebrows. "Yeah, well, James did tell me that you are quite perceptive, Cally. Hopefully, this isn't as big a deal as I'm making it out to be in my own head, but here it is. Kathy Morris and I have found ourselves pretty attracted to each other, and we want to explore that. However, we also want to abide by your rules for the group. So we thought that maybe you would see both of us, together, sometime on Friday and talk with us about it."

Cally sat silently and studied Steve's face. "How far have you and Kathy taken this attraction, Steve?"

"Well, we've seen each other every day. We've gone to three AA meetings together. We've kissed a few times. And one night we slept in the same house. We started to sleep in the same bed, but then decided against it. At any rate, we didn't do anything. We slept in separate bedrooms. That's about it."

Cally nodded thoughtfully. "I hear you saying that you have not had sexual intercourse. Would you say that you and Kathy have been sexually intimate?"

Steve sighed. "Well, Cally, when I think 'sexually intimate,' I think 'sexual intercourse.' I mean, I feel sexually attracted to Kathy, and when I've kissed her, I've felt sexually aroused. Is that sexual intimacy? I don't know. You tell me if we've been sexually intimate."

Again, Cally became quiet and thoughtful. "Is there something that you aren't telling me, Steve? I ask only because I hear defensiveness in your voice."

Steve took a deep breath, released it, and then nodded. "Last night I touched her breast for a moment. It was literally for only a moment, and then we stopped and talked about keeping our relationship within certain boundaries. We decided that setting appropriate boundaries is one of the things we need help with. Hence, my request that you meet with the both of us."

Cally slowly nodded his head. "Steve, how long have you been divorced?"

"I've been divorced almost a year. Separated one and a half."

"And how many different women have you been with since you and your wife separated? Romantically and/or sexually, that is."

"Well, let's see. About eight, I guess, at least that I know personally and have taken out on dates. I still see three of them, but I think of them more as friends than lovers. There were a few others that were one night stands—women that I picked up at bars or parties and never saw again."

"Uh huh," Cally said. "I'd like for you to give me a brief rundown of your relationship history, starting at the beginning and going through today. Please be brief, but don't omit anyone. Start with your first girlfriend."

Cally listened quietly as Steve listed every female that he could remember being romantically connected with. He started with Diane Gothbert in kindergarten and Jill Dadro in first grade. He progressed through various girlfriends in grade school, including Pam Hart, junior high and high school, including Peggy Sue Martin and Marilyn Cutler, and college, including Bev. He listed various affairs during marriage, and then discussed the present, including Rachel, Dixie, Carla, and Kathy.

He mentioned a total of thirty-four girls and women by name. He specifically omitted the names of two boys with whom he had brief homosexual encounters during the fifth and sixth grades. Had Cally asked about males, Steve would have denied that there were any. He was relieved that it did not come up.

"That's quite a list, Steve. How many of them have you had sexual intercourse with?"

"Oh, all but the first half dozen or so from grade school, I suppose, and now Kathy."

"And your last sexual encounter?"

Steve hesitated and then answered, "Well, it was yesterday afternoon. It was like a favor to one of the women that I think of as a friend. I expect that it will be the last time that she and I have sex."

Cally nodded. "Okay, thank you, Steve. That helps, and I appreciate your willingness to share that part of your life with me. We can explore the issue of you and Kathy more fully on Friday afternoon. I can see you at 2:00 o'clock, and I would like to see you together. Let's move on to something else now. Have you given any thought to obtaining an AA sponsor?"

Steve hesitated. "Cally, are we going to change the subject just like that?"

"Yes we are."

"Well, okay, I guess. Anyway, yes, I have given some thought to a sponsor. There's a guy who goes to the noon

ing at the Catholic Student Center. He's a professor or an ructor or something at UT. He gave me some very helpful vice about going to school functions where they serve alcohol, like tomorrow night when I'll be attending a cocktail party with my whole department. He also gave me his phone number the first day I met him."

"Good. He sounds like a prospect. Do you know how much sobriety he has or whether or not he works the steps?"

"No, not really. I don't know much about him because I've only been around him twice. I like him, though. He had good things to say in the meetings."

Cally nodded slowly. "Steve, I'm going to tell you what to look for in an AA sponsor. You've made a good start by looking for someone with whom you have something in common— someone that you can relate to. With this man, for example, you know what he does for a living, and you've heard him speak in meetings and liked what he's had to say. That's good.

"Now, I'm going to give you some very specific guidelines. First, select a man. Do not under any circumstances ask a woman to sponsor you. Second, ascertain that he has at least one year of continuous sobriety in AA, and don't ignore the 'in AA' part of that. Third, make sure that he not only goes to AA meetings, but also that he reads the Big Book and works the steps. In his step work, he must have completed at least Steps One through Seven, and not in some abstract, intellectual way, but rather in a definable, specific way. This is especially important regarding Step Four, the inventory step, which is a written exercise, not a mental one. Fourth, make sure that he has a sponsor of his own and that he uses his sponsor for input and advice.

"Now, finally, if he qualifies on all of those points, ask him how he prefers to work with sponsees. Ask him how often he likes to talk and get together, and how straightforward and confrontive he is willing to be. You might tell him that you need someone who has time to spend with you and who won't be intimidated by your intelligence or snowed by your bullshit.

"If he resists being interviewed to this extent, you can tell him that you're in treatment and that your counselor has given you these guidelines for obtaining a sponsor. Do you think you can remember all of that?"

"Yeah, I think so."

"All right, then, what else, Steve?"

Steve looked at his hands for a moment and then at Cally. He spoke slowly. "Cally, you aren't going to kick us out of the group, are you?"

"If it's okay with you, Steve, I'd really like to wait and talk about that when we meet on Friday. I feel as though I need to think about it, pray about it, talk with a colleague, and see what happens when the three of us get together. I don't want to leave you in the dark, but I also don't want to jump the gun. Is that all right with you?"

Steve remained silent for a moment; then he said, "Well, I guess I can wait if I have to."

Steve went home and spent the rest of the day working in his shop. James and Tommy both dropped by. They entertained each other while Steve worked. Neither of them offered Steve anything to smoke or drink, but between the two of them, they smoked two joints and split a six pack of Pearl Beer.

Steve didn't say anything, but he felt excluded and discounted, which hurt his feelings and pissed him off. He imagined several times that they were talking about him when he was out of earshot. At one point, he excused himself to go into the house to use the bathroom, and he stayed inside and read a magazine for half an hour. After they left, he closed up the shop, took a shower, ate dinner, and waited for Kathy to call.

Steve and Kathy met and sat together at the South Austin Group. This time, Steve listened, and the meeting chairman unexpectedly asked him if he would like to speak. With his heart pounding, he accepted. "Hi. My name's Steve, and I'm an alcoholic/addict. I feel like I don't have any right to talk because I'm so new to AA, and I don't know my ass from a hole in the ground. I think I'm learning, though, and the last two days have really challenged me to stay sober. Yesterday morning I was in a situation where I really wanted to smoke pot. The truth is I came within a hair's breath of doing it. Something happened at the last possible moment to stop me, but it was just grace because I was ready and willing.

"Then today, my two best drinking buddies hung around my shop all afternoon, drinking beer and smoking pot. I felt very left out. I got pissed off at them because they both know what I'm trying to do. Hell, one of them had a big hand in getting me here to AA in the first place. There he was, though, getting high and acting like I wasn't even there. The weird thing about that whole deal is that by the time they left, I was really glad that I was sober.

"So, I don't know. It's still a mystery to me at this point. At least tonight, I'm glad that I'm here and that you all are here so I have people to learn from. That's all I have to say, except that I'm also in treatment, and one of the things that I'm supposed to do is to ask the group for support. So, I'm asking. Please give me support. That's all. Thanks for calling on me, and thanks for listening."

Some people in the room said, "Thanks, Steve." Kathy reached over and laid her hand on his thigh and gently patted it. She turned toward him and smiled and whispered, "Thank you; that was great."

After the meeting, about ten people thanked Steve for speaking and gave him hugs and words of encouragement. Two men and one woman gave him slips of paper with their phone numbers written on them and told him to call if he needed anything or wanted to talk. He felt grateful for the attention and support.

Steve walked Kathy to her car and told her word for word what Cally had said. He thought he felt her withdraw from him slightly, and he asked her about it.

"I'm sorry, Steve. I do this when I get scared. It's not about you. I promise." She put her arms around him, and they held each other close for several minutes.

Before they parted, Steve reminded her about the cocktail party. She agreed to take her clothes to work with her and come straight to his house from work to change and get ready to go. They kissed and said good night. Steve went home and to bed and was sound asleep at 10:15.

CHAPTER 53

On Thursday morning, Steve took Ginger to the park. As she ran around, he lay on the grass and studied his Big Book. Despite what he characterized as its insipid style, he had begun to appreciate several sections of it, including the one that held his attention that morning—*Chapter Six: Into Action.* He repeatedly returned to one particular line which haunted him. It read, "The spiritual life is not a theory. We have to live it."

He laid the book down and closed his eyes. "It's not a theory; we have to live it," he repeated to himself several times, and then added, "So studying it, learning about it, understanding it, and believing it won't suffice. We have to live the spiritual life. The question is, what does that mean? What does it mean in concrete terms? What is the spiritual life? How am I supposed to *do* spirituality? Do I become a monk? Must I be perfect?"

He closed his eyes and thought, "Whatever it is, one thing's for sure. It's not who I am today, and it's sure as hell not what I'm used to. It's not what I'm most comfortable with. It's not how I've been living for the past ten or fifteen years. It's not lying, stealing, cheating, judging other people, and staying high three-fourths of the time.

"If I'm going to live a spiritual life, we're talking serious change. We're talking genuine change. We're talking character change as well as behavior change—change on the inside *and* the outside. Am I up to that?" he asked himself.

288

The thought, "Staying high three-fourths of the time" made Steve think about James, who Tommy liked to call "the spiritual wizard." James had been Steve's spiritual teacher. But what, he wondered, about the seeming disparity between James' incredible grasp of spiritual concepts on the one hand and some of his behaviors on the other? He stayed stoned most of the time. He dealt drugs for a living, despite being a two-time loser in the federal courts. He discounted and judged other people a lot. In fact, he didn't even like people. "Surely, that's not living a spiritual life, is it?" Steve wondered.

He thought about the curious inconsistency between James' generous encouragement to him to explore recovery and his subtle efforts to sabotage it. He recalled the confrontations, the reading materials, the connection with Cally, the long talks. But then there was James' interaction with Tommy the previous afternoon, when only a blind man could have missed Steve's confusion, hurt, and anger. That behavior had felt mean-spirited to Steve. "I know that's not indicative of the spiritual life," he muttered to himself.

There was also the morning that James dumped the grocery sack full of alcohol and drug-related books and pamphlets on Steve's living room floor and handed him Cally's business card, and then proceeded to turn him on to the most powerful smoke that he had ever had. "The gift was a fine gesture; the other was at the very least unsympathetic," he said to himself.

"So what about James' spiritual life?" Steve thought. "What about the life of the spiritual wizard?"

He contemplated these different images of James and came up with two theories, both of which felt discomforting. One possibility was that James was a fraud—that his spirituality was purely intellectual rather than real, that his spiritual life *was a theory,* and that he understood spirituality and talked spirituality but failed to live it, the way the book prescribed.

"Could that be true?" Steve asked himself. He had always so admired James' fascination with and grasp of spiritual concepts and issues. He felt as though he had learned much of what he knew about spirituality from James.

Steve's second theory brought James' other fascination—the one with drugs—into play. Perhaps James' addiction to pot and alcohol, which he did admit in an off-handed way, fatally compromised his *living the spiritual life.* Maybe it was the addiction itself that was his saboteur in this regard, and perhaps his denial surrounding his addiction prevented him from seeing that. "If that's true," Steve thought, "it might follow that living the spiritual life is just not compatible with alcohol and drug addiction, period. Maybe James can master the spiritual life in theory, and talk about it effortlessly and endlessly, but because of his addiction, he can't live it fully."

Steve sat up and rubbed his eyes for a moment. "When I look at addiction and 'the spiritual life' in that light, what does it mean for me?" Steve asked himself.

The question reminded him of his move to Austin. He remembered how significantly he had expected his life to change promptly upon arrival. He saw that many of the changes that he had in mind—the ones that had to do with him as a person—were, indeed, spiritual in nature. They dealt with values and attitudes and feelings and ways of being in the world.

He recalled expecting to arrive in Austin with an open mind and an open heart, feeling good about himself as a person. A total transformation—that was what he had expected. That, along with his belief that he would leave behind his problems, including those with alcohol and drugs.

"And you know what?" he said to Ginger, who was now lying at his side, "not one goddamn thing happened. Not one thing changed. And it's no wonder; the plans and the expectations didn't have a prayer. Mother was right all along. She called it a geographical cure. She assured me that it wouldn't work, and she was right. Moving from one spot to another didn't change anything but my physical surroundings and my physical appearance."

Steve recalled that during Cally's lecture on denial, he had mentioned geographical cures as a powerful and seductive defense against dealing with real issues, especially the internal ones. He had talked, too, about people, especially alcoholics and addicts, drinking and using as a way to avoid experiencing deeper parts of themselves—parts that they were afraid to look at too closely.

"My shame," Steve said out loud. Both Tommy and James had said in one way or another that shame was a core issue—a spiritual disease. "That probably means that drinking and drugging and geographical cures can prevent my living the spiritual life, if for no other reason than their ability to protect me from having to deal with my shame, or whatever it is that keeps me feeling afraid."

Steve closed his eyes and listened to his breath. He let his body relax. After a few minutes, he picked up the book, flipped back to Chapter 2, and reread a passage that had caught his imagination the first time that he had seen it. The passage read, "...once in a while, alcoholics have had what are called vital spiritual experiences...huge emotional displacements and rearrangements.... Ideas, emotions and attitudes which were once the guiding forces of the lives of these men are suddenly cast to one side, and a completely new set of conceptions and motives begin to dominate them."

"So maybe that's all I need in order to live the spiritual life, Ginger," he said. "A vital spiritual experience; a huge emotional displacement and rearrangement. Well, old girl, what do you want to bet they don't offer any of those in the Sears tool catalog?"

Finally, Steve turned back to Chapter 6, and from the same page that held the line about the spiritual life not being a theory, he read again what Cally had referred to as, "the promises."

The passage read, "If we are painstaking about this phase of our development [referring to Step 9], we will be amazed before we are half way through. We are going to know a new freedom and a new happiness. We will not regret the past nor wish to shut the door on it. We will comprehend the word serenity and we will know peace. No matter how far down the scale we have gone, we will see how our experience can benefit others. That feeling of uselessness and self-pity will disappear. We will lose interest in selfish things and gain interest in our fellows. Self-seeking will slip away. Our whole attitude and outlook upon life will change. Fear of people and of economic insecurity will leave us. We will intuitively know how to handle situations which used to baffle us. We will suddenly realize that God is doing for us what we could not do for ourselves."

Steve closed the book and lay on his back. The sun was already high, and he felt its warmth on his face and chest. He thought about something that Cally had said about AA and the twelve steps. "Many people misunderstand AA altogether. They think that AA is the fellowship. They say, 'I'm in AA' because they attend AA meetings. But AA is more than meetings. It's a program. It's a program of spiritual growth and change—a spiritual path, so to speak.

"The principles of the program lie in the steps. Attending meetings is helpful. Indeed, the fellowship is wonderful. We learn a lot there. It gives us a place to be with and learn from and give back to other alcoholics. But spiritual growth and change—the spiritual awakening that changes our lives and keeps us clean and sober—occurs from working the steps and living according to the principles."

During that conversation, Steve had asked Cally if AA was the only option. "Why can't I just do it at the yoga center or the Buddhist meditation center—places that I already believe in and that I'm already attracted to?" Cally had shrugged his shoulders and said, "You can, Steve. There are many spiritual paths that encourage growth and change. I deeply respect most of them, and I'm delighted that you're attracted to some. I'd like to see you give AA an honest shot also, though, at least while we're working together. If you find it distasteful, then we'll focus on other alternatives. The unique aspect of AA is that it's a path that understands alcoholics in a way that perhaps others do not."

Steve reached over and rubbed Ginger's side. "Maybe I've had it backwards, old girl. Maybe instead of waiting for a spiritual experience to hit me so that I can live the spiritual life, I should concentrate on living the spiritual life, as in following a spiritual path, so that a spiritual experience can better find me." He laughed softly to himself. "I better be careful. This stuff is starting to fit together in pretty scary ways. Come on, Ginger, let's go home."

When they passed the Stop and Save, Steve stuck his head in the door and said, "What's up, Mario?"

"Not much, man. What's up with you? And where you been, anyway? You buying your beer down the street or something?"

Steve laughed. "No, man, I haven't bought any beer in over a week. In fact, I haven't even drunk any beer in over a week. Can you believe that?"

"I guess so, man. What's the matter? You on the wagon or something?"

"Yeah, as a matter of fact, I am. The truth is, I'm not drinking because it got to be a problem. I'm even going to some AA meetings."

Mario's eyes widened. "No shit, man? I have an uncle who goes to those meetings. He got three DWIs, and the judge, he said my uncle better go there every week, and now my uncle has to prove to his probation officer that he goes. He hates it, man. He says all they ever do is sit around and bitch and moan about how bad they used to fuck up when they were drinking, you know? Man, I can't believe you have to go there like my uncle."

"Well, no one's making me go, really, and it isn't so bad. Actually, I kind of like it. Maybe it's because I'm going on my own instead of someone making me, you know? I've met some pretty cool people there. So does your uncle stay sober?"

Mario laughed out loud. "Shit no, man. He drinks beer all the time. He just goes to that AA because his probation officer says he better or he'll put him back in jail. Shit, man, my uncle won't never quit drinking beer. He loves it."

"Yeah, well, I understand that. I guess I love it, too. Maybe I love it too much. Maybe that was the problem. Hell, you know, man, I bought beer in here almost every day. Speed, too, and coke, all the time. It was getting to me, causing problems. And speaking of problems, what's going on with your cousin—the one that got busted?"

"He's still in jail, man. My uncle got him a lawyer, but he won't put up no bail money. I don't blame him, either. Uncle's really pissed off at him, and my aunt's all torn up about it. I feel sorry for her. The lawyer says he's probably gonna do some time.

"I don't get it about you, though, Steve. I've never seen you have problems with drinking. I've never even seen you drunk, man. People come in here all the time fucked up on alcohol and drugs. You've never done that. You always pay with cash, and you're always a gentleman. People around here like you, man. Nobody's ever said a bad word about you, not that I've ever heard anyway. Even old man Burke next door to the bar says you're a nice boy, and you know him; he don't like nobody."

Steve smiled. "Well, thanks, Mario. We'll see what happens. Listen, I need to get to work, man. I'll still come in and buy milk and bread and candy, okay?"

"Yeah, sure, man. And I'll tell you what; you let me know when you start up drinking beer again, and I'll give you your first six-pack free. I'll make it Shiner, too, just like when you first moved in over there. How does that sound, man?"

Steve smiled. "You've got a deal, Mario."

Steve spent the rest of the morning working in his shop. At noon he rode his bike to the Catholic Student Center. All of the regulars were at the meeting except for Ralph and Sue. Steve asked about Sue and discovered that Patti had been in touch with her and that she was drinking again and did not want to return to the group right away. That prompted the chairman, another student named Charles, to suggest that they talk about relapse. Everyone had a story—either a relapse experience of their own or of someone they knew in the program who had "gone back out" to drink or use again. Steve had little to contribute, but he listened hard.

After the meeting, he went back to work, and by 6:00 o'clock, he had completed several small projects, delivered out some finished work, and picked up a good job from a new customer. No one called or came by. He was just getting out of the shower and still had the towel wrapped around him when Kathy arrived with her hang up clothes and an overnight bag in hand.

"I see you got all dressed up for me," she said as she walked in the door. She put her arms around him and hugged him tight. "You better go put some clothes on before I rip that towel off of you and sneak a peek at your naked body."

"Hmm, let's see now," he said. "I can go get dressed alone or stay here and get naked with you. That's a hell of a tough choice, Kathy, but I guess I'll go get dressed like a good boy." He smiled and kissed her lightly on the lips. When he turned to walk away, she patted him on the butt. He kept walking, but he loosened the towel and let it slip down enough to show her the upper half of his butt.

"Very nice," she said casually.

While Steve got dressed and fixed them something to eat, Kathy showered, put on light makeup, and got dressed. When she walked into the kitchen, Steve opened his eyes wide and whistled. She wore a simple, conservative cocktail dress that

293

revealed her figure nicely, but unobtrusively. She wore no jewelry except for silver earrings.

"Yow, Kathy, you look fantastic," he said. "You look very beautiful."

She smiled. "Thank you, Steve. That's nice to hear. You look pretty great yourself. Down right handsome, I'd say. How long has it been since you've worn a tie?"

"Not long enough, and maybe never again. Listen, I figured we better eat a little bit. I don't know what they're serving at this party, except for alcohol. I've heard that it runs pretty freely at these deals. I hope there's not a lot of pressure to drink."

"Don't worry, Steve. We'll be fine as long as we stick together. I'm sure of it." She hesitated for a moment and then added, "Listen, I think there's something that I should mention. My past is no secret to you. I'm not proud of it, but it's there. And Austin is where I worked for over two years as a dancer and a prostitute. Obviously, I did have customers from UT—students as well as a few faculty members. It's not outside of the realm of possibility that someone at this party will recognize me. I would have mentioned it sooner, but I didn't think about it until I was in the shower. I thought you needed to consider that, just in case. If you think it might be a problem, I'd understand if you decided to go without me."

Steve smiled. "That's cool, Kathy. Thanks for bringing it up, but as far as I'm concerned, it's not a problem. I feel excited and proud to have you with me. If it comes up, we'll deal with it. Okay?"

"Okay, Steve."

Kathy was right about their being just fine. Not only did they survive, but they had fun. To Kathy's relief, no one recognized her, and even though she felt out of her element, Steve thought that she mixed beautifully with people, including the geezers, the geeks, and the women. She hit it off immediately with Sheri, with whom she also shared the fact of her recovery. One man, a too-handsome fourth year student, came on to her. She rebuffed him gracefully.

As the party stretched into its third hour, a few people got drunk, a few got loud, and a few acted silly, but they were the exceptions. Indeed, to Steve's surprise, not everyone drank alcohol. Ron, however, got loaded early and stayed that way. He invited Steve and Kathy to join him and a handful of other people on the roof for a smoke. Steve said, "No, we better not, Ron." Kathy said simply, "No, thank you."

The party started thinning out about 11:00 o'clock. Older faculty members left first, then those who were obviously uncomfortable with groups of people, and then the group that included Steve and Kathy and Sheri—those who had fun but drank lightly or not at all. When they left, they left the real partiers.

Walking to the parking lot, Steve said, "Man, this is the first time I can remember ever leaving a party just when it was finally getting good. Free booze, serious drinkers, clandestine groups getting stoned on the roof, and all of the boring old geezers, sticks in the mud, and geeks are out of there." Kathy laughed and patted him on the back.

When they arrived back at Steve's house, he turned off the motor and said, "I noticed that you brought a bag, Kathy. Does that mean that you're going to stay the night?"

Kathy searched his face for a moment and then nodded her head without saying anything. They went inside. "Would you like something to eat or drink?" Steve asked.

"Oh, I don't really care one way or the other, but I would like to talk for a little while if you're up to it."

"Yeah, I'd like that," Steve said. "First, though, let's ditch these stupid clothes and get into something more comfortable. Then I'll make us some hot tea, and we can sit on the floor or on the bed and talk to your heart's content."

They wound up on the bed, both wearing T-shirts and shorts. They talked briefly about their meeting with Cally the next afternoon. Kathy mentioned again her fear of being asked to leave the group. "It's been so important to me," she said. "It's the first place, and the first people, I guess, that I trusted enough to talk about my past—all of my past. And when I felt overwhelmed with shame, Cally and the group accepted me and nurtured me and loved me through it."

"Listen, Kathy," Steve said, "if one of us has to leave the group, it will be me. I mean, I feel like I'm getting into this recovery stuff for real, but the group doesn't mean that much to me. And I'm not trying to be a hero or anything. It's just common sense. You love the group. I don't. Agreed?"

Kathy nodded. "Thank you," she said.

Steve told Kathy about his morning at the park and about the process he went through to understand what he had read in the Big Book about living the spiritual life. He recounted for her his insights regarding James and how those related to himself, his geographical cure, and his shame. He shared with her his yearning for a spiritual way of life in which he could honestly feel good about himself.

By the time he finished talking, he had tears in his eyes. Kathy set her cup on the table and then took his from him and set it beside hers. She lay back on top of the bed and reached her arms out to him. He went into them, and she held him and rocked him gently.

After a few minutes, Steve said, "Stay here. I'll lock the doors and turn off the lights." He got up, and as he walked through the kitchen and living room turning off lights and locking the house, Kathy took off her shorts and T-shirt, pulled back the bed covers, and slipped in under them.

Steve stripped down to his underwear, climbed into bed, and snuggled against her back. When he felt her bare skin against his, he ran his hand down her side to her hips, then moved his hand slowly around to the front of her body and gently rubbed her lower abdominal area just above the top of her panties. He then slid his hand and arm slowly up the front of her body, across her upper abdomen and her breasts, and finally encircling her chest with his arm. He felt her breasts against the inside of his arm and the rise and fall of her chest as she breathed.

His erection was quick and strong, and he did not try to hide it from her. Kathy took his hand in hers. She kissed his palm and placed it on her breast. He gently massaged one and then the other while he kissed the back of her neck and across her shoulders.

"Kiss me, Kathy," he whispered into her ear. She rolled over and faced him. She looked into his eyes, and they kissed tenderly several times and held each other very close. Steve nudged his knee gently at the place where her legs came together. She parted them enough for him to slip his leg between hers. He slowly slid it up between her thighs until the top of his leg pressed against her. He felt the crotch of her panties against his skin. She was warm and damp. He pressed harder, and she responded by rocking back and forth against his thigh.

Steve took a deep breath, released it, and whispered, "Kathy, if we're going to stop, then we better stop now, this very moment, because I'm getting lost in this."

Kathy breathed deeply several times and whispered, "I don't want to stop, Steve. I don't want to stop."

He pulled his face away from hers just enough to see her eyes. "Are you sure?"

She kissed him softly and said, "Yes, I'm sure. I'm absolutely sure."

Steve gently released her, and she rolled onto her back. She laid her hands beside her head. Her body moved fluidly with her breathing, which was slow and deep. He pushed the covers away and sat up beside her. He perused her body. "God, you're beautiful, Kathy," he whispered. She smiled softly and soundlessly mouthed the words, "Thank you."

Steve unhurriedly and deliberately removed her panties and then took off his boxers. He kissed her deeply and rubbed her breasts and stomach and pelvic area with his hand. She spread her legs slightly, and he slipped his finger up into her. She was very full and wet, and she sighed deeply. Steve's excitement and anticipation accelerated, but he kept his movements gentle and slow.

Kathy's breathing grew heavier and more audible as she moved her pelvis to the rhythm of Steve's hands. Then she shuttered and moaned as he removed his finger from inside of her and tenderly rubbed her clitoris. After a few moments, she reached down, took his hand in hers, and guided his finger back inside of her. She held his hand tight and hard against her. "Now, Steve," she whispered. "I'm ready now."

He gently rolled over on top of her and carefully guided himself into her. She moaned and moved with him, slowly at first and then with more energy and purpose. She placed her hands in the middle of his back, pulled him into her chest, and tilted her pelvis up to meet his strokes.

Steve came first, sooner than he wanted, but he kept his erection long enough to stay with Kathy through her orgasm. When she felt him come, she let herself go. She drew her knees up around his waist and pressed her heels into his buttocks, at first pulling him into her repeatedly, then holding him firmly against and deep inside of her as she came. She moaned deeply and began to relax. She lowered her legs and moved more slowly. Then she relaxed completely and released her breath.

They lay in each other's arms for several minutes. Still inside of her, and in no hurry to move, Steve tenderly kissed Kathy's face and neck. She rubbed his buttocks and his back and shoulders. Finally, he slowly pulled out of her and rolled onto his side. He leaned up on an elbow, and brushing a few strands of damp hair away from her forehead, he said, "Hey, there, are you okay?"

Kathy smiled. "Yeah, I'm good. I'm very good. I'm damn good. God, I was really ready for that, Steve."

Steve smiled broadly and then he laughed softly. "It was great, wasn't it? I mean, wasn't it really great?"

Kathy laughed, too. "Yeah, it was really great. I doubt if our friend, Cally, will be very pleased, but right now I feel nothing but total satisfaction from my head to my toes. So for the moment, anyway, I say, 'Too bad, Cally.' All I want to do now is spend the rest of the night in your arms."

Steve kissed her on the nose and said, "There's nothing in the world that I'd rather do right now than sleep with you tonight."

CHAPTER 54

"Kathy? Hey, wake up, sleepyhead."
"Umm. What time is it, Steve?"

"It's about 8:00 o'clock. I didn't know if you had anything you needed to get up and do this morning or not."

Kathy kept her eyes closed and remained quiet for a moment. "It's Friday, right?"

"Yep. Friday morning, 8:00 AM."

"Thank God," she said, as she opened one eye and looked at Steve. "I don't do anything on Friday mornings. It's against my principles. Would you mind if I slept for a while longer?"

"No, not at all. Sleep as long as you like. I'll be around, probably out back in my shop. Okay?"

"Yeah, that's perfect." She slid her arm out from under the cover and took his hand, rubbed it gently against her cheek, and kissed it. "We're still okay, right?" she asked.

He smiled and kissed her on the forehead. "Yeah, we're fantastic. Go back to sleep."

At 10:45, Steve woke Kathy up again. "Hey, you old lazy bum."

"Okay, I'm getting up. What are you doing?"

"I need to go give a couple of estimates for work and then I thought I'd go to my noon meeting at the Catholic Student Center. Would you like to meet me there?"

"I guess so. You don't mind?"

"No, I don't mind at all. In fact, I want you to. Afterwards, we could get a bite to eat and then go over to Cally's together at 2:00. You haven't forgotten about that, I'm pretty sure. Then, I have that barbecue deal at school. It's from 2:00 to 7:00. I feel like I need to at least make an appearance there. You don't have to go if you don't want, but I'd like for you to. Then we have group at 8:00."

"Okay. I'll meet you at the AA group at noon." She lifted her hands toward him. "Come here. Lie down with me and hold me for just a minute."

Steve removed his shirt, kicked off his boots, and slipped into bed. While holding her close, he rubbed her back and her buttocks and kissed her neck and throat. "You have the most incredible body, Kathy," he said softly. "I melt a little every time my skin touches yours. I think I'm under your spell."

When Steve arrived at the noon meeting, Kathy was already there, looking fresh, happy, and spirited. She was sitting and talking animatedly with Patti. "Oh, hi, Steve," she said. "Here, I saved you a seat. I was just catching up with Patti. Believe it or not, she was one of the first people I met when I came into the program. I tried not to like her, but I couldn't help myself. I told her I was a hooker so that she would go away and not bother me, but she just smiled and said, 'Oh, cool. I'm glad you're here. Can I get you a cup of coffee?'" Kathy and Patti laughed heartily over the story.

Steve said hello to Patti, and then spoke to Ralph about sponsorship.

"Yes, I do sponsor one person," he said. "In fact, he's also a graduate student. He's in the engineering department. I'd be glad to talk with you some more about it if you'd like."

"Well, here's the thing," Steve said. "I'm in treatment, and my counselor has given me a whole list of qualifications for a sponsor. I mean, I'm almost embarrassed to go through it with you because it feels like I'd be interviewing you for Secretary of State or something. If you're willing, though, I'd sure like to pursue it. I like what you say in meetings, and I've appreciated your help so far. The advice about the cocktail party was very good. It really helped last night." They agreed to get together and talk on Sunday after Steve got back from San Antonio.

Patti asked Kathy to chair the meeting, and she agreed, even though she felt apprehensive. "Well, my name is Kathy, and I'm an alcoholic and addict. I've been sober and clean for a little over six months. I hate to tell you, but this is the first time I've ever chaired a meeting, so please forgive me if I don't do it right. I was so delighted to walk in here today and find Patti, who I don't know all that well and haven't seen in a long time, but who feels like a good friend nevertheless. She was nice to me and gave me encouragement when I was in my first few weeks of sobriety. It came at a very crucial time for me, and I've never forgotten it. So in honor of that experience, I think that I would like to suggest as a topic for this meeting, the fellowship of AA.

"I attend a lot of meetings, usually at the South Austin Group. I do that because I want to. Meetings are important to me. I feel safe here, and I feel good when I'm with my friends in AA. They know me pretty well. In fact, they know me better than my own family knows me. Unlike my family, though, they accept me for who I am. I have a past that's worthy of judgment, but when I've felt guilty or regretful or bound up in shame, my AA friends have supported me and, I think, loved me.

"If people in AA have ever judged me harshly, it's been without my knowledge. Maybe it's because you all have pasts, too, or maybe it's because in recovery we learn to be accepting of others. Either way, I know this: The AA fellowship welcomed me into it and accepted me long before I was able to accept myself. I'm finally a part of something positive. The only other place I've ever felt like I really belonged was with other people who were as spiritually sick as I was, and all we encouraged in each other was our disease.

"I know that the AA fellowship won't keep me sober. However, it definitely enhances my sobriety. It makes it more worthwhile. I have a lot of gratitude and love in my heart for the fellowship of AA—for you guys, even those of you whom I don't know yet.

299

"Anyway, I hope that's an okay topic, and I hope that every one of you will share so that I can know you by the end of this meeting."

Everyone did share, and Steve left the meeting with a deeper understanding of and respect for the AA fellowship because of it. He, too, wanted to feel like he belonged, like a part of something positive and worthwhile. He also left the meeting with a deeper respect for Kathy—for her willingness and her courage.

Patti joined Steve and Kathy for lunch. They told her about their situation, and she offered them a different perspective than Susan's.

"I know who Susan is," she said. "I've heard her talk in meetings, and I have a lot of respect for her sobriety. I'm sure she's a good sponsor. I also know Cally, and there's no one in the program whom I respect more than him. When he talks, I listen. But they both seem to accept this so-called 'conventional AA wisdom' without question, you know, like it's the absolute gospel that applies to everyone, every time.

"I mean, I'm in no position to question either of those people, but I've seen several 'ill-advised' relationships between AA infants and toddlers work out very well. I've seen a few crash and burn, too, and I have seen a couple of people get drunk because of that. But I think the reason for the failures was the lack of recovery within the individuals. What I mean is, they grabbed onto each other believing that the relationship itself would solve their problems, and so they focused on the relationship instead of focusing on recovery. I guess that's kind of like what you were saying that Susan told you. But that's not the only way that it can work.

"I know one AA couple, in particular. They both came into AA at about the same time, just a little after I did, and they were really raw. They latched onto each other like opposite sides of Velcro. I remember people telling them that they were committing sober suicide. But they focused their attention and energy on getting well together. They went to meetings together, prayed and meditated together, studied the Big Book together, went to an AA conference together, and supported each other's recovery in what seemed to me like a very beautiful way. In other words, they focused on recovery instead of focusing on the relationship, and they did it as a team.

"They also took care of themselves individually. That may have been one of the keys for them. They each had their own sponsor, and they both went into therapy groups, but they were different groups and different therapists. They also went to some AA meetings separately. She went to a women's group one night a week. That's where I got to know her, and that's how I know that the deal between them was real, that it wasn't just show. Another thing they did that was really smart is that they eventually both went to Al-Anon, and that helped them maintain their individuality.

"They actually ended up getting married. I still see them at meetings in North Austin. They seem happy to me. Now, I know this couple might be totally unique, but I don't think they are. I've seen others that look like they're working it out with varying degrees of success.

"You know, in a way, I envy you guys. I mean, knowing what I do about Cally, I don't envy your having to talk to him about your situation. But on the other hand, I'd love to have someone special to share my recovery with. I know there's certain challenges associated with that, but it's been a long time since I've felt what you guys are feeling right now.

"Please believe me, I'm not trying to talk you into anything. I'm not even giving you advice. Please understand that. It's just that I think there's more to recovery and more ways of doing recovery than conventional AA wisdom might allow for. Do you know what I mean?"

Steve and Kathy did, indeed, know what Patti meant, and her opinion felt to them like a breath of fresh air. They drove to The Recovery Center with less fear and greater hope. They had a case to present.

Just before they walked in the door, Steve took Kathy's hand in his and said, "Kathy, I want to tell you something. Just speaking for myself, I'm willing to let go of Cally and the group before I'll let go of you. That's how I feel." He put his arms around her and hugged her, and at that moment, Cally opened the door for them from the inside. He looked serious but not angry.

"Well, come on in, you two," he said. "Let's sit down and have us a talk."

They followed him into his office and sat in a small circle. The three of them remained silent for a few moments while Cally scrutinized both of their faces. Finally, he said, "Kathy, I've been thinking for several weeks now about moving you up to a more advanced group, one that functions on a level much closer to where you are in your recovery.

"It's a group that focuses less on education and basic recovery issues like denial and sober living skills, and more on feelings and unresolved personal issues, including those related specifically to families of origin. Instead of topics such as Steps One through Three, the group works more within the conceptual realm of Steps Four through Nine.

"With six months sober time, you would be the youngest person in the group, but your current level of personal insight, combined with your openness and honesty, would put you right in the thick of things. I believe it's where you belong. You have been outgrowing your current treatment group. It has become too safe, too predictable, and too comfortable. What do you think about that idea?"

Kathy glanced at Steve and then she narrowed her eyes and studied Cally's face. Her breathing became quicker and shallower. She crossed her arms across her chest and drummed her fingertips against her arm. She remained silent for a full minute. When she spoke, her tone was sharp, and she spoke directly to Cally's eyes.

"I'm not sure that I believe you, Cally. And to tell you the truth, I feel very angry."

Her response startled Steve, and he shifted uncomfortably in his chair. Cally did not immediately react. After a few seconds, though, he slowly nodded his head, closed his eyes, and took a couple of breaths. Finally, he responded.

"I'm quite certain that I'm right about this recommendation, Kathy. You're ready to move on. The two of you have made a decision about yourselves. That decision may or may not be a wise one. We'll discover the answer to that in due time. In the meantime, though, your recovery deserves our challenging it to progress beyond the basics.

"Steve's recovery, on the other hand, deserves to get the basics without your watchful eye encouraging him to be further along than he really is. That is a different issue entirely, however. This is not a compromise, Kathy. This is not a simple solution to the problem at hand, if indeed there is one. This is a right decision, one that is clearly in your best interests. I feel it in my heart."

Kathy sat still for a moment and then nodded slowly. "Okay, Cally," she said.

"Steve? How do you feel about it?" Cally asked.

Steve looked at Kathy and said, "Well, Cally, I feel as though I'm the least relevant voice here, really. But if Kathy's okay with it, then I'm sure okay with it. I mean, I know you said that it's not a compromise or a solution to this problem, but it feels like one to me, and there's a part of me that feels very relieved. Of course, there's another part of me that feels very guilty. I figure I'm the one who waltzed in here and stirred up the pot. I know how much the group means to you, Kathy, and it hurts me to see you lose it. So, I don't know. Maybe you could say more."

Kathy looked at Steve. She had tears in her eyes, and the corners of her mouth turned down slightly. "He's right, Steve. I reacted the way I did because I'm afraid to move forward. I've been comfortable and safe in the group for a long time. I need to push on. I knew I'd have to sooner or later. It might as well be sooner. I'm okay. Don't worry about it."

Steve nodded. "Well, what can I say then? I'm so goddamned relieved that I can hardly stand it. I'm excited for you, Kathy. I know how courageous and willing you are. I've seen

302

that part of you, like today when you chaired the meeting despite your fear. I mean, I know you'll be okay, and I trust Cally's judgment about what you should be working on, even if it is scary.

"Actually, it's kind of scary for me, too. You're moving on without me. I feel kind of like the little kid being left behind. You know what I mean? Despite that, though, I'm relieved for myself because the thought had occurred to me that I might want to hold back in the group because of not wanting to look bad to you. I didn't say anything about it to you, but the thought did occur to me.

"Anyway, overall, I feel great. I know that's selfish, but it is the way I feel. At least Cally, here, didn't kill us or anything—not yet, anyway."

Kathy and Cally both smiled. "Okay, then," Cally said. "The two of you need to decide how to talk about your situation in group tonight. I can't predict how the group will react. Kathy, you'll need to be prepared to inform the group that next week will be your last. We'll move you into the new one the following week. It meets on Wednesday night at 7:00 o'clock. I assume that will work for you."

Kathy nodded.

"Okay, then, I feel as though we're done here," Cally said.

Steve and Kathy looked at each other. Kathy started to stand up, but Steve put his hand out as if to say, "Wait a minute." She sat back down, and Steve said, "You know, Cally, I almost hate to bring this up, but I kind of expected you to talk with us about what's going on between us. I mean, I expected you at least to question our judgment and give us some feedback and advice."

Cally smiled. "Steve, I feel good about what we've accomplished here today. You both have been forthcoming and genuine. You have shown empathy for each other. I respect that.

"The other thing is that I'm a realist. Despite some people's opinion, I'm neither a bully nor a magician. I don't feel the need to beat my head against brick walls. We'll look at y'all's relationship. In the weeks to come, we'll look at it closely. I promise you that."

"Well?" Steve said to Kathy as they pulled out of the parking lot of The Recovery Center. "What do you think?"

"Same as you, I suppose. I'm relieved on the one hand. There's no denying we got off easy. But I'm also disappointed. I wanted more from Cally. I wanted that feedback and advice that you asked him about. I don't know, maybe I feel ripped-off, and you know, the more I think about it and talk about it, the more I'm aware that I have not shaken the feeling that this solution may have been a cop-out on his part. He keeps us both in treatment this way, and he does it without even having to deal with the issue. Damn it, I would be bitterly disappointed if that were the case."

"You sound still pissed off, Kathy."

She nodded. "Yeah, I guess I am. I mean, I know I cover up fear that way. It's also how I cover up hurt feelings. Be that as it may, I do feel angry. Very angry." She stared straight ahead. "Steve, I'm going to pass on the barbecue. I need some time to myself. Will you please just take me to my car?"

Steve looked over at Kathy curiously. He saw the anger on her face, and without thinking, he took it personally. Suddenly, his feelings mirrored hers. He looked at her again, and when he spoke, his voice gave away his impatience and irritation. "So what's the deal? Why the hell are you mad at me?" he asked.

She turned her head toward him and shot him a very angry look. "My need for time alone isn't about you! Damn it, I hate it when people do that!" she replied curtly.

Steve didn't answer. His face froze. His mind flipped into defensive overdrive. He immediately understood exactly what was going on. Kathy blamed him for what had happened—for her having to leave the group, and now she was turning on him and punishing him and rejecting him because of it. He felt wounded as well as angry. His ego judged Kathy and told him that the relationship had been irreparably damaged. His critical mind said, "Now we see what she's really like. Goddamn it, I should have know this was too good to be true; I should have known it."

Thoughts of blowing off treatment and getting high burst into Steve's head. Images of dropping Kathy off at her car and going straight to The Roam In dominated his thoughts. Without diverting his eyes from the road and without saying another word, he drove to the Catholic Student Center parking lot and stopped behind Kathy's car. "Okay," he said without looking at her. "Here you are."

Kathy did not budge. Steve looked over at her and saw tears on her face. "Please don't do this, Steve," she said in a broken whisper. "Please don't push me away."

He softened at once. Every negative thought vanished, and he said, "Oh, no, I'm sorry, Kathy. I'm really sorry." He slid across the seat of the truck and put both arms around her and drew her into his chest. When he did, she surrendered against him and broke into sobs. He held her and rocked her. He stroked her hair and kissed her head and the side of her face. "It's okay, Kathy. I'm sorry. It's okay."

When she finally calmed down, she said, "What I really want is some quiet time. I don't really want to be alone. I just want some time to be with myself. It doesn't have to be by myself. Maybe you'd hang out with me for a little while before you go to school."

"Yeah, I'd like that very much. And Kathy, I'm really sorry for being so damn defensive and immature. I don't know what that was all about. It just swept over me; it took me over. Whatever it was, I apologize."

"Let's talk about it later, okay?" she said. She kissed him on the lips and rubbed the front of his shirt with her hand. "I got your shirt all wet," she said, almost laughing.

Kathy got into her car and followed Steve back to his house. When they got inside, Steve made coffee, and they settled in on opposite ends of the couch. Kathy wrote in her journal, and Steve read about half of the book *Gift from the Sea,* by Anne Morrow Lindbergh.

After an hour, Kathy said, "If you still want me to, Steve, I'll go with you to the barbecue."

"Thanks, but I've decided to blow it off. I don't think they'll miss me. They have a keg, and I bet they're all about three sheets to the wind by now. How about a short nap instead? We've got group in a couple of hours, and I feel a little wrung out."

They didn't sleep. Instead, they lay together, held each other, and talked. Steve shared with Kathy his fear of rejection and abandonment, exacerbated by his deep feelings of insignificance. He told her about losing the unconditional love of his grandparents and the unwavering security of their home when he was six years old, and then almost immediately losing the promised love of his mother and father and the promised security of their new life together as a family, all to Lois' and Henry's alcoholism. As he spoke, he felt the loss, and he wept into Kathy's shoulder. She held him and patted his back gently.

While his defenses were down, Steve revealed to Kathy his earlier reaction to her snapping at him in the car—the sudden perceived damage to their relationship and his thoughts of getting high. He acknowledged those thoughts and his consequent withdrawal from her as his ego and its defenses protecting him against the possibility of greater fear and deeper hurt. He asked her to be conscious of his fears and unresolved issues when she expressed her feelings, especially her anger.

"I understand where you're coming from, Steve," she said, "and I'll give you whatever support I can to help you work through your stuff. I can't agree not to be myself, though. I'd wind up a liar if I did. I anger easily, and sometimes I react sharply. You've seen me do it twice today, and if we spend much time together in the future, the way I hope, you'll see it again, and probably with greater intensity than you saw today.

"It's in my nature, I'm afraid. I'm volatile. I'm a hell of a lot better than I used to be, and I'm working my butt off in therapy to deal with it. But, you know, I grew up angry, and I react angrily when I feel threatened or hurt. That's my stuff, Steve, and I'm not done with it."

"Well, at least we both have plenty to work on. At least it's not just me," Steve replied. "Your fury and my shame. Boy, this ought to be pretty damn interesting. If we had any sense at all we'd start filming a documentary."

He smiled at her and kissed her. "You know what would help me, though, Kathy? If you would just remind me from time to time that you're dealing with your stuff and that it's not necessarily me. You know? Because I have a tendency to take things personally, to internalize things, and I could easily interpret your anger as my failure. Okay?"

"That I can do," she said. "I think if we just keep talking—if we just avoid the temptation to keep our issues hidden from each other—that we'll be able to work through anything that comes up." She closed her eyes and breathed. "I have a good feeling about that," she said.

They talked for a few minutes about what they wanted to say to the group. Then they got up, ate some fruit and cheese, and left the house for The Recovery Center. On the way from the house to the car, Steve watched Kathy walking in front of him. He had the feeling that he was falling in love with her. He smiled to himself. "At 2:30, it was over. At 5:30, I'm in love. Heaven help us both," he thought.

CHAPTER 55

Steve was not prepared for the group's reaction to his and Kathy's disclosure. Despite Kathy's warning against his taking the group members too lightly, he expected that like Patti, they would be understanding and supportive—thoughtfully concerned, of course, but beyond that, supportive. In this regard, he misjudged their empathy.

Steve was blind to two factors. First, he had little understanding of group members' deep regard for Kathy, and because of that he failed to predict their grief over her leaving the group. Second, he knew nothing about the power of the group when it functioned within its true purpose, which was for each member to be fully present in the moment and to share on a feelings level in an honest and open manner, even if it ruffled feathers.

Steve and Kathy agreed that Kathy would make the initial disclosure and that they would try to keep it simple and straightforward. So when the time came, she said that she had two things that she needed to tell the group, and she said it briefly.

"Last week after group, I asked Steve to go with me to an AA meeting. I did that because I was interested in him. I also felt attracted to him. Anyway, he agreed, and we went to the South Austin Group Saturday night. We ended up spending the night together, and we've been together as a couple ever since. We have been sexually intimate, which of course is in violation of our agreement with Cally and the group. Steve talked with Cally about this Wednesday, and the two of us met with him earlier today. That's one thing.

"The other is that after next week, I'll be leaving y'all and moving into another group, one that focuses more on underlying issues such as family of origin stuff. Cally says that my move is because of my progress in recovery, not because of my and Steve's 'situation.' I'm leaning toward believing him about that, but I have lingering doubts. At any rate, next week will be my last with y'all. Steve will continue here.

"That's about all I have to say at the moment. I want your feedback, but first, Steve needs to share."

Steve took a breath to calm his nervousness. "Well, I don't really know what to add. I'm...uh...well, I don't know. I feel as though I should apologize, but the truth is that I don't feel sorry. I feel bad for Kathy because I'm aware of how much she loves this group. But I know that she'll do well in whichever group she's in. This thing between Kathy and me has happened. I'm a part of it, and I hope that you all won't hold it against me, or against us. I guess that's about it for me."

Not everyone expressed anger, but several people did. Billy the Fag was boiling mad, and he expressed that anger openly. "I have a couple of things to say," he started. "To begin with, I feel very damn angry. I feel betrayed by you, Kathy. It's not like the issue of relationships between group members has never come up before, and I know damn good and well that I've heard you say how your recovery has to come before anything else, especially men. And now, along comes Mr. Hip, Slick, and Cool, and you're off sleeping with him twenty-fours later. That's betrayal in my book. And what do we get? You go away, and he stays. The way I see it, that's a bad trade. I don't like it. I don't like it one damn bit.

"Of all the people in group, including those who have come and gone, you're the one I trusted the most. You're the one I thought would never betray my trust and the trust of the group. I'm really mad, and hurt, and now I have to grieve your loss. I'm sorry, Kathy, but that's how I feel. I better not say any more just now."

Steve's reaction to Billy's outburst was wildly mixed. On the one hand, he felt fighting mad; his instincts told him to jump out of his chair and beat Billy to a goddamn pulp. On the other, he grudgingly admired Billy's willingness to thrust himself out there with such spontaneity and clarity.

Kathy's reaction was more focused. She knew Billy. She understood and respected his capacity for intense feelings and their honest, open expression. As he blasted away, she maintained eye contact with him. She listened and nodded.

Al, the Junkman, who seldom spoke without being spoken to first, raised his hand. Cally nodded to him. He looked at the floor and talked slowly. "I'd like to say that for the first time since Mr. Billy, there, joined the group, I have to agree with him, at least in principle. It's nothing against you, Steve. I think you'll be all right in due time. You seem kind of full of yourself, but we're all like that to some extent.

"No, it's about you, Kathy. A lot of it's about losing you out of the group. I know that you don't know this, but your being in the group is one of the reasons I've hung in here so long without complaining. I'll miss you more than you will ever know.

"I'm also having a hard time believing that you would break your word to us and to Cally. It just doesn't seem like you. Maybe that's not such a bad thing, though. Maybe I needed to see that even you are just a human being, like me, and like old Billy, there. I've seen any number of people come and go since I joined this group a year ago, and the group has always survived. It will this time, too, but the truth is, I feel a real loss. That's about all I have to say."

Yuppie Man picked it up from there. "I don't feel quite as strongly as Billy either, but I do feel betrayed—by both of you, but mostly by you, Kathy. You've been something of a role model for me, believe it or not. I've looked to you from time to time to help me find my next layer of recovery. It's hard for me to imagine the group without you. I don't know who else to look to. I think you've been a step ahead of the rest of us for a while.

"I guess I don't feel angry as much as I feel sad. I don't want to deny you any hàppiness that you may find, but I sure do question the wisdom of looking for it with a guy who's newly sober. Speaking of which, the thing that bothers me about you, Steve, is that you totally disregarded our feelings. I'm referring to the rest of us here—the other members of this group.

"Apparently, it never occurred to you that we would be deeply affected by your behavior. Really, though, it's not your behavior that I'm complaining about. It's your failure to consider our feelings about your behavior that bothers me. We feel hurt. I feel hurt. Welcome to the world of conscious people and their very real feelings. I hope you'll think about that. That's all."

After Robert spoke, Steve felt embarrassed, and he avoided eye contact with Kathy even though he could see out of the corner of his eye that she was looking at him. He had, indeed, disregarded the feelings of the group members. He had been concerned about Kathy and about himself, but no one else.

Kathy saw Steve's discomfort. She wanted to rescue him, to assure him that this would work itself out over time, that people were just expressing their feelings and that their feelings would change. When he did not return her glance, she reminded herself to just trust the group process and be with her own feelings.

Peg offered a different perspective. Like the others, she expressed sadness over Kathy's leaving the group, and she admonished Steve for failing to appreciate its sacred nature. She also raised the issue of Kathy leaving the group within its larger context.

"I think I heard Kathy say that her move to another group is not a consequence of her and Steve's transgression," she said. "But it doesn't take a mind reader to see that she's not completely convinced of that. And I hate to admit it, Cally, but I'm not convinced of it either. If the two aren't directly connected, then the timing of Kathy's move to another group is phenomenal. The main reason I bring this up at all is that I feel as though if someone has to go to a different group, it should be Steve, not Kathy. He's the new guy; he should hike.

"That's all I want to say right now, except that if I'm angry at anyone, it's not at you, Kathy. It's at Cally. I might be all wet, but that's how I feel."

Sally, the husband-killer, and the next newest member of the group behind Steve, added little. What she did offer was a projection of her own issues. She expressed anger but directed it specifically toward Steve.

"I can't believe all of you are jumping on Kathy's case. Hell, Kathy was doing just great until *he* came along," she said, pointing her finger at Steve. "He's the one who came in here and caused trouble. What the hell did Kathy do? Give her a break. And Cally's not the one who broke the rules. All he's doing is enforcing them. That's his job, for Christ's sake."

Jim, Mr. Nice Guy, the youngest group member and the one who smiled too much, went last. "There's a part of me that's sad, just like everybody else. Kathy, you've been my favorite group member ever since I started, and of course I'll miss you. But there's a part of me that's happy for you, too. I don't feel betrayed. I don't feel as though either one of you did anything to me personally.

"I mean, I don't imagine that the two of you were together late Saturday night saying, 'Let's hurt those people in our treatment group, especially that Jim. Let's be sexually intimate. That will get them good.'

"I know you have needs just like me and everybody else. I don't know, maybe I should feel angry and hurt, but I don't. I know you all think I'm out of touch with my feelings, and I suppose I am compared to some of you, but that's where I'm at right now. Hell, I feel like saying 'Good luck to you both.' Sorry, everybody."

Kathy picked it up there. "Thank you, guys. I appreciate your honest feedback, and I think I understand how you feel. I cringed every time I heard the word 'betrayal.' It's such a harsh word. I suppose that's what I did, though. I made a promise that I failed to keep. It's as simple as that.

"I had every opportunity to keep that promise, too. At one point in our lovemaking, Steve was ready and willing to stop. He even suggested it. I insisted that we go ahead. I made that decision selfishly, based on my needs at the moment, or at least on my desires, and although I do apologize for betraying you—for breaking my word—I should also say that if I had it to do over again, I'd do it the same way.

"I don't know what that says about me as a person, especially as a recovering person, but I know that it's the truth. I'm following my heart with Steve. I'm putting a lot on the line. We'll see how that plays out.

"Beyond that, I'm touched and humbled by your feedback about my role in the group. I never intended to be anyone's role model. I promise you that. My efforts toward recovery—toward genuineness—have been purely selfish. Cally told me when I came in here that if I didn't get real, I was going to die, and I believed him. I thought he was talking about physical death. I know now that he was referring to spiritual death.

"I also know now that I would rather die physically than endure spiritual death. I'm deeply saddened by the prospect of leaving you all. I'm also scared shitless about starting over with new faces and new hearts in the circle. I'll be the new kid on the block. They'll all be steps ahead of me, and that means I'll have to go places within myself that I'm afraid to go.

"I'd also like to say that my heart is telling me to plead for your mercy with Steve. I won't do that, though. I've learned to trust this process, as scary as it can be sometimes, and even though I have a few things to work out with Cally right now, I trust him, too.

"So, Steve, I'll just say to you that these are some of the people who have helped save my spirit, and that includes Billy, who will always tell you the truth. It also includes Al, who looks big and tough but has a sweet heart, and Robert, who's a straight arrow that you can trust, and Peg, who is as real as the day is long, and Jim, who's a beautiful, charming guy who's going to find his feelings soon. It even includes Sally, who will have one of the best AA stories of all times once she finds her heart. I love you guys."

When Kathy finished, the group looked to Steve. He looked at the floor and then at Kathy. "Well, I don't think they will ever

310

care for me as much as they do you, Kathy, and I can certainly understand that.

"I don't know; I'm pretty blown away by the whole process right now. I've never in my life, and I mean even once, sat among a group of people who were so honest and open with each other and took such risks. The experience is totally foreign to me, and to tell you the truth, I'm not so sure that I like it. I respect it, but I'm not sure that I like it. It scares me. I mean, I know a couple of people who I think tell me the truth, but not with such abandon, such spontaneity, and never in front of other people.

"So, anyway.... I've been all over the emotional map tonight; I'll tell you that. I've experienced anger—pretty intense anger, actually—plus fear, guilt, embarrassment, shame, and more anger. My feelings have been hurt, and I've felt discounted and rejected. I've also felt protective of Kathy. I see now that that wasn't necessary.

"I decided a couple of times to leave tonight and never return. Then another time, I decided to force my way in and make you all like me. Right now, I feel as though I could learn a lot from at least some of you, and I hope that happens. That doesn't mean I'm crazy about you, but I do want to stay and work through whatever comes up.

"Finally, I'd like to say that I apologize for my self-centeredness. My ego gets in the way of my considering the feelings or needs of anyone who's outside of my immediate experience. Hopefully, I'll get better. I guess that's all I have."

The group sat quietly for a few moments, and then Cally spoke. "Well, we've made a good start toward working through a lot of issues and a lot of feelings. As usual, you're an amazing group. I applaud your genuineness, and I am in awe of it. We're approaching 8:00 o'clock, but before we end, I would like to briefly address the issue of Kathy's leaving this group for another one.

"Obviously, there is a connection between her moving on and her relationship with Steve. I never intended to imply that there was no connection. The connection, however, is one of timing, not consequence or punishment. Kathy is ready to move on. She needs to move on. She has other work to do, and she will be challenged to do it in the Wednesday night group. I was aware of that well before Steve joined this group. Their decision to enter into a relationship determined the timing of her move. That's all."

Following the group, Steve and Kathy decided that what they both wanted was a break from the intensity—a simple, light, romantic date with no heavy conversation. So they went to a movie, ate popcorn, and drank Pepsi-Colas. Afterwards, they went to an ice cream parlor and devoured hot fudge sundaes.

On the drive back to Steve's house, Kathy said, "Well, I guess we're legitimate now. We're no longer a secret. Do you suppose that will diminish the attraction?"

Steve laughed. "If so, it hasn't happened yet. In fact, I was just this second visualizing you naked in my bed and trying to decide exactly how to ask you to stay with me another night. I have to go to San Antonio in the morning, you know, so I won't see you again until Sunday. What do you think?"

She slid over next to him, placed her hand on the inside of his thigh, kissed his neck, and whispered into his ear, "I think I might just have you for a late night snack."

Following passionate, guilt free lovemaking, Steve and Kathy lay in each other's arms and talked well into the night. Before drifting off to sleep, Steve said, "I hate to tell you this, Kathy, but I think I'm falling in love with you."

"Yeah, I know the feeling, Steve. I know the feeling."

CHAPTER 56

Steve opened his eyes on Saturday morning to the lovely sight of Kathy's face. He carefully pulled back the sheet and looked at her shapely, supple, naked body. Her dark skin contrasted sharply against the white sheets.

"How very lovely," he whispered to himself.

He gently laid the sheet back over her and slipped out of bed. Then he picked up the telephone, tip-toed into the living room, closed the bedroom door, and dialed Rachel's number.

"Good morning," she answered.

"Good morning to you, too, my friend. Sounds like you're up and at 'em early this morning."

"Hi, Stevey. Yeah, I just got back from jogging, and I feel like a million bucks. Are you still coming today?"

"Yes, definitely, but can we leave the time kind of soft? I'm not sure when I have to have the kids home, and Bev wanted to talk to me for a few minutes about their moving."

"I guess so. Listen, how would you like to go to an AA meeting tonight?"

"Well, yeah, sure, why not? I'll tell you what. I'll come by your place as soon as I get free, okay? It shouldn't be later than 6:30 or 7:00. If it is, I'll give you a call. I'm looking forward to seeing you."

Steve woke Kathy up at 10:00 o'clock to tell her that he needed to leave for San Antonio. She coaxed him back into bed, and when he lay down beside her, she rolled over on top of him and playfully penned his arms against the mattress. "What if I won't let you go?" she asked. "What if I shackle you to this bed and keep you here all day?"

He laughed. "Well, in the first place, what makes you think I'd try to fight you off? I'd be hard pressed to complain too much about the discomfort or inconvenience of being shackled to a bed with a beautiful naked woman lying on top of me."

"Yeah, well, I think I'll wait until you have more time to devote to meeting my needs," she said.

Steve gave Kathy an extra key to the house. She agreed to lock it up when she left and to return that evening to feed and visit with Ginger. She put on shorts and a T-shirt and walked him to his truck parked on the street. Carla was sitting on her front porch. She smiled and waved. Steve kissed Kathy on the lips and promised to call her as soon as he got home on Sunday. As he drove off, he looked in the rear view mirror and saw Kathy strolling over to Carla's house. "Hmm," he thought to himself, "I'd like to be a fly on the wall for that conversation."

Thoughts of Kathy and Rachel, mixed with thoughts about love, friendship, sex, loyalty, and right and wrong filled Steve's mind during the drive from Austin to San Antonio. Within the context of his relationship with Kathy, would it be wrong to be intimate with Rachel—an old friend for whom he had genuine and deep affection? Of course not. Would it be wrong to be sexually intimate with her? That, he wasn't sure of.

His conscience said, "You know it would be wrong." His rational mind countered with, "Wait a minute; that's nothing more than someone's old guilt trip. The expression of love through sexual intimacy is sacred as long as it's pure."

He reminded himself that he and Kathy had no agreement whatsoever regarding their behavior away from each other, and that to suggest that there should be an unstated one was rather presumptuous.

"Who could it possibly hurt if Rachel and I spent the night together?" he asked himself.

"Probably no one," he answered, "but then again, perhaps everyone."

He did not resolve the debate. Instead, he told himself that it probably didn't matter anyway because Rachel was celibate. Even so, images of her muscular body floated through Steve's consciousness. He decided that he would play it by ear with Rachel, and if there were a decision for him to make regarding sexual intimacy, he would make it based on what felt right at the moment.

Steve's visit with Lynn and Eddie was short but fun. They had milk shakes at their favorite hamburger joint and played on the playground equipment at the park close to the house. Lynn filled Steve in on the move, about which she knew every detail.

313

"Denver is not so far that you can't come visit, Dad. Mom made the drive in about twenty hours, and you drive faster than her. Our new apartment is big. There's an indoor swimming pool. Eddie and I will have our own rooms, and I can have a dog. I want one just like Ginger, but Mom said maybe we could find a smaller one, like a little poodle. I said, 'No way, Mom. Poodles are wimpy little rat dogs.'"

Later, Bev told Steve about her new job, their new apartment, the new city, and her opportunity for a better life away from the old negative influences. Steve felt certain that he heard her mocking him, saying, "I've won, you son of a bitch," and the thought pushed just about every one of his buttons. His anger flared, and he turned sarcastic and contemptuous. Try as he may, though, he could not penetrate Bev's air of victory and superiority.

"I suppose I'm one of the old negative influences you're talking about," he said.

"What makes you think that, Steve?" she replied.

"Just a hunch. In fact, Bev, I've got a feeling that getting away from me, and getting the kids away from me is one of your motivations for this move."

She smiled and shook her head. "Why do you always think that everything is about you? Maybe this has nothing to do with you. Maybe you never even entered my mind when I was contemplating this move."

"Yeah, right. I believe that. What about my visitation rights? How are you planning to accommodate my legal rights to see the kids every other weekend?"

"That's your problem, Steve. They'll be ready and waiting for you if you decide to come."

"Oh, that's just fucking great! What a tremendous goddamn relief! In light of your willingness to be so conciliatory, let me ask you this. Just how do you plan to collect child support when I'm not getting my time with the children?"

"My attorney and I have already talked about that. He has papers drawn up and ready to file the minute you're late with a child support payment. I've already signed them. I doubt they'll be necessary, but they're ready just in case."

"Your attorney, huh? Is that the fat, ugly little fart who you've been fucking in the same apartment where my children are? Is that the guy?"

"No, Steve, it's a different attorney. Listen, I have a lot to do. Since next weekend is your regular visitation, I'll have the kids ready to go Saturday morning. I'd just as soon you leave now."

Steve glared at Bev. "I hate you for doing this, Bev. I may not be the greatest father in the world, but I love Lynn and Eddie, and you know that. I'll never forgive you for this."

Bev returned his glare. "You're the one who left, Steve. I'm glad now that you did. I'll see you next week. Goodbye."

Driving to Rachel's, in the privacy of the cab of his truck, Steve vented his anger by yelling obscenities. He nurtured his anger by recalling everything he could think of that he hated about Bev, from her squatty body and her mousy hair to her narrow mind, detached feelings, and ice cold heart.

When he got to Rachel's house, he parked Cleo in the driveway and sat behind the wheel with his eyes closed. "Listen to your breath," he told himself. "Relax. Let go of this bullshit. Pray for willingness and open-mindedness. Willingness and open-mindedness."

After a minute, his prayer was interrupted by Rachel's soft voice. "That bad, huh?"

Steve opened his eyes. He nodded. "Yeah, I've really got myself riled up. I let Bev get to me big-time, and I acted like a stupid idiot. Anyway, hi, Rachel. You're a sight for sore eyes—still the most beautiful unattached woman in South Central Texas."

He smiled slightly and shook his head. "Hey, listen," he said, "do you have any cold beer in there? No, wait, now I remember; we don't drink anymore. How about a nice big joint? Oops. No chance of that either, right? Well, how about a hug for a pissed off old friend?" He stepped out of the truck, and they embraced warmly.

"Come on in, Steve. I fixed us a little something to eat before we go to the meeting. I'm in a listening mood, and Sammy's at my mom's, so you can rant and rave if you need to." She put her arm around his waist and led him into the house and into the kitchen.

Steve did not rant and rave, but he did vent his frustration. Rachel listened, nodded occasionally, touched his arm or shoulder at appropriate times, and seemed to understand. When he wound down, she said, "You know what? It sounds to me like you're gearing up to do your Fourth Step."

Steve looked at her and rolled his eyes. "God, does everything have to be couched in terms of recovery? Can't I just be angry at my fucking ex-wife without it being a recovery issue?"

Rachel smiled and said, "Sorry, pal, but I'm kind of in that mind set where there's no such thing as an issue that's not related to recovery. Since we met in San Marcos, I've been going to a lot more meetings and working more with my sponsor on the steps. I'm writing my Fourth Step inventory right now, so it's really on my mind. You'll just have to forgive me."

"I'm sorry, Rachel. Recovery feels kind of slippery to me at the moment. That seems to happen when I get pissed off or feel really threatened. At those times, my commitment to recovery

315

becomes tenuous at best. Just in the last couple of days, I've thought twice about blowing off recovery and treatment and everyone connected with both, and getting good and drunk. It occurred to me on the way over here, as a matter of fact.

"I've been kind of dating this woman who's in recovery. Yesterday she said something that pushed my buttons, and the first thing that popped into my mind was to go straight to The Roam In and get fucked up. Am I just an AA retard? I mean, does that happen to you?"

"Well, I still think about getting high sometimes. Different things seem to trigger it. Anger is one; fear is another; boredom is another. I think it happens to everyone, Steve. It's not just you. I think it's part of the deal."

"Well, at least I feel better than I did. You know, I think I'm so upset because I know she beat me. She's the winner, and I'm the loser, and I can't do a goddamn thing about it. It's the ego monster again. Or maybe it's just another example of powerlessness and unmanageability putting the ego monster in its place. God, I hate that feeling. I used to think that I was in control of everything. What a joke, huh? The ironic thing about it is that in my heart, I believe their moving out of state is probably a blessing in disguise. How weird is that?"

Rachel smiled. She stepped over Steve's chair and gracefully straddled his lap. She put her arms around his shoulders and brought his head against her chest. "You know what, Steve? I love you a lot. I think you're doing great, and I'm very proud of you."

Steve put his arms around Rachel's waist and pulled her closer. Her crotch settled snugly against his, and he briefly imagined them naked in that position. After a minute, she shifted her weight and started to get up, but he gently pulled her back onto him and lifted his face to hers. She kissed him tenderly on the lips and slipped her tongue into his mouth.

After the kiss, she whispered in his ear, "Steve, I've been celibate for six months, and I'm ready to end it. I'd love for you to stay and spend the night with me tonight. I've thought about it all week."

The moral debate that had occurred in Steve's mind earlier in the day returned. It lasted for such a brief moment, however, that Rachel did not hear the hesitation in his voice. "I'd love to, Rachel," he said. "I've been thinking about it, too. Can we just get naked and spend the night in this position on this chair?"

She smiled. "Whatever you want," she said, and she slowly rotated her hips against his lap.

"You better go slow, old girl, or there won't be enough left of me to satisfy even your simplest desire," he said, laughing softly.

"Uh oh. I sure don't want that to happen. How about this for a plan: Let's hit the AA meeting and then come back here and see who can breathe the hardest?"

They straightened up the kitchen and went to Rachel's AA group—the Club 12 & 12. It was a large meeting, with over a hundred people in attendance, most of them older than Steve and Rachel.

Rachel introduced Steve to several people, but she did not know many by name, and very few took the initiative to meet Steve on their own. Compared to his two groups in Austin, the Club 12 & 12 seemed not unfriendly, but reserved and aloof.

The meeting was good, however. The topic was "what recovery means to me." Many speakers equated recovery with abstinence. But several described their recovery more like Rachel had described hers to Steve two days before he got sober, as a process of meaningful internal growth and change over time.

An elegant older woman, who looked to be in her seventies, spoke of her recovery as a miraculous gift that had taken her from desperation to serenity. "My name is Ethel Smith. Today, I am a grateful alcoholic. Once, however, I was a very bitter person—very bitter, indeed. My only reasons for living were to get drunk and to get even with a man—my husband—who had abused me repeatedly and then thrown me aside for a younger, prettier woman. I drank alcohol and developed elaborate plans to emasculate this man—physically as well as emotionally. The more I drank, the more elaborate and vicious my plans became. I was a very insane, very alcoholic woman.

"As many of you already know, I was arrested for and convicted of soliciting a hit man to murder my husband. I have only sketchy recollections of my crime, inasmuch as I was in and out of blackouts during the time. I withdrew from alcohol in a county jail. That part, I remember well.

"I learned about sobriety in a women's prison in Los Angeles, California. Two volunteers from the AA community, both of whom were older than myself, brought Alcoholics Anonymous into the prison once a week, every week that I was a guest there. They brought exactly two hundred and ten meetings over two hundred and ten weeks.

"When I was paroled from that prison in 1954, one of those AA women—her name was Birdie Porter—took me into her home until I obtained employment and was able to support myself. She taught me through the example of her daily life, which ended in 1964, that recovery has less to do with not drinking and more to do with living my life on a daily basis as God would have me live it. Whenever I forget that principle and return to selfish, self-centered thinking, I recall Birdie's generous nature, and I find my way back to the real spirit of recovery, at least as I understand it.

317

"Today, my life has joy and peace. If there are any newcomers here tonight, I would like to suggest something to you. Please don't leave AA until the miracle happens for you. That's not my saying, but I love it and wanted to pass it on. Thank you for listening."

After the meeting, Rachel went to the restroom, and Steve sought out Ethel Smith. He found her standing alone by one of the coffee makers. He introduced himself, and he thanked her for her beautiful story.

"I find myself impatient with sobriety," he told her. "I think I want to be farther along than I am, and I get down on myself when I fall into selfishness and self-centeredness, which I do quite naturally. I did it today, in fact.

"While you were talking, it occurred to me that my impatience probably discourages miracles from happening in my life. Anyway, I wanted to tell you that what you said meant something to me. It helped me, and I appreciate it. Thank you."

"You're very welcome, Mr. Campbell," she said, smiling broadly. "I couldn't be more pleased. Thank you."

On the way back to Rachel's, Steve asked her if she knew Ethel Smith. "Um hmm, everyone knows Ethel. I think she's quite beautiful. Some people feel impatient with her because she repeats herself. I've heard her tell her prison story quite a few times. I never tire of it, though. She puts different twists on it, like tonight when she added the piece about her slipping into selfishness but then reminding herself about her unselfish friend. I've never heard her say that before. I liked it very much. The Big Book thumpers can barely tolerate her. They get up and get coffee when she speaks. What did you think of her?"

"I thought she was fantastic. I talked to her for a minute after the meeting while you were in the restroom. I want her to be my grandmother."

Rachel smiled and kissed Steve on his cheek. "Do that some more," he said to her. She laughed softly, and she obliged, over and over, on his cheek, in his ear, on his neck, and up and down his arm. She kissed and caressed him all the way back to her house, and they started making love the moment they arrived there. Steve pulled into the driveway, turned off the motor, and climbed on top of her across the front seat of the truck. They kissed deeply, and Steve pulled off his shirt.

"Let's at least go into the house," Rachel whispered, laughing. They walked through the door in each other's arms and were naked within two minutes. They started on the living room floor, moved onto the couch, and finally into Rachel's bed. They progressed rapidly through their old familiar routine with each other and were completely spent within a half-hour.

"Whew, God. I don't mean to be gross, but I needed that," Rachel said, lying on her back and staring at the ceiling. Steve propped himself up on one elbow and with his free hand rubbed the front of her sweaty body.

"You're so beautiful, Rachel. Inside and out. I don't understand why you don't have men beating down your door and crawling all over you. What's the deal with that?"

She rolled over to face him. "I don't think other men find me as attractive as you do, Steve."

"What the hell are you talking about? You're one of the most beautiful women I've ever known," he said.

"Well, I think that men do find me pretty, and I suppose that a few would call me beautiful. Men do stare at me sometimes, but I don't think they're attracted to me romantically. Sexually, perhaps, but not romantically.

"I asked a male friend of mine about it one time. He said that it might be because I'm androgynous. I have qualities of femininity and masculinity in roughly equal proportions. I'm strong, both physically and emotionally. I'm efficient and effective in my life. I don't need a man around to fix things or to take care of me. I'm muscular, as you know. You seem to like that, but I don't think that most men do. Men at the gym ogle my body, but they're almost all narcissistic dolts. The men in AA that I find attractive are in the process of finding their feminine sides, and I think I intimidate them.

"I don't know, Steve, I think I might not be feminine enough to be attractive to most men, and I've never been much of a flirt. Perhaps I'm the kind of woman who men look at and say, 'Boy, would I love to stick it to her,' but not the kind who men look at and say, 'Isn't she lovely.' I'm not complaining, though. I like who I am. If there's a man out there for me, besides you, of course, I suppose he'll show up when the time is right."

Steve considered Rachel's self-analysis. He found the qualities that she labeled masculine very attractive. Her athleticism was a definite turn on for him. One of his favorite images of Rachel was of her running, breathing hard, sweating, hair stuck to the side of her face and neck, muscles standing out. He loved her body. When he thought about it, though, he had to admit to himself that he found Kathy's softer body more feminine, and perhaps more appealing.

Rachel had another kind of "hardness" about her, too. She was, indeed, tough, strong, and independent, just like she said. She was also assertive. She knew exactly what she liked in bed. She knew exactly what would bring her to a climax, and she did not mind asking for it. Steve liked that, too. Again, though, he flashed on Kathy, who was more yielding, and he realized that Kathy's softer approach in bed was also more appealing to him. Despite these thoughts, Steve replied, "Rachel, I think that any man who fails to be enormously attracted to you as a woman is stupid, crazy, and probably latently homosexual."

Rachel laughed. "Thank you, Stevey. You can compliment me anytime." She leaned over and kissed him. "Speaking of people crawling all over other people, tell me about your girlfriend."

Steve hesitated. "Well, I wouldn't call her a girlfriend. I've only known her for a little over a week. We've mostly gone to AA meetings together. She used to be a hooker, but now she's six months sober and working a regular job. She's pretty, and I like her, but I don't know if it's going anywhere or not."

"How do you think she'd feel if she knew you were here with me?"

Steve squirmed a little at the thought. "I don't know, Rachel. We're not in the kind of relationship where we have any say over the other's comings and goings." He smiled. "Did you catch the pun?"

Rachel smiled and nodded. "Yeah, pretty cute. You know, Steve, you and I didn't have that kind of relationship, either, but I think I would have felt hurt if you had spent the night with someone other than me while we were together."

"Yeah, well, that's different. Kathy and I aren't really 'together.' We're just getting to know each other. I don't think I'm doing anything wrong being with you. You're my heart pal, Rachel. I love you, and I hope we'll always be intimate friends, whether that includes sexual intimacy or not. Lying here with you feels natural to me; it feels good. Don't you think so?"

"Yes, I do. I'm just giving you the business. Listen, how about a little snack? Food, I mean."

"Sure, as long as we can stay naked so I can look at your muscular, masculine body while you putter domestically around the kitchen in all of your feminine prowess."

Steve and Rachel nibbled at their food and talked for an hour. They made love again at midnight. This time, however, they relaxed and pampered each other. They went to sleep in each other's arms.

CHAPTER 57

Steve awoke very early on Sunday morning in a mild panic. He had been sober for exactly eleven days and two hours, and all in all, it had been an easy ride, with only a couple of legitimate threats to his sobriety and no real compulsive desire to use. But on Sunday morning, lying in Rachel's bed, with her snuggled against his side, he felt as though recovery was closing in on him, strangling him. He felt terrified.

Recovery is a far cry from abstinence. Most alcoholics and addicts enter recovery from addiction just looking for abstinence, just wanting to quit using. And that's exactly what most get. They remain abstinent. If they have the will power to hang in there, that is. Over the long haul, few do.

Abstinence is not a bad thing, of course. Abstinent alcoholics never get arrested for driving while intoxicated because they don't drink. Abstinent drug addicts never get busted for possession of controlled substances because they don't possess drugs. That's an improvement over their previous lives.

A certain percentage of alcoholics and addicts, however, experience the miracle that Ethel Smith talked about—recovery beyond abstinence. Unfortunately, it's a rather small percentage.

Abstinence is an *event*. It takes place at a particular point in time and does not change. The event occurs in the form of the decision, "I quit." The decision occasionally comes from the heart, but more typically it comes straight from the head, at a purely intellectual level. Abstinence represents behavior change and is accomplished through the exercise of willpower.

Steve Campbell, the high bottom drunk, became abstinent at 2:35 AM on Wednesday, August 30, 1974. He was alone, sitting naked and cross-legged on his bed, drunk and stoned. His high bottom had peaked with the ranch trip fiasco and then again with the Waco whorehouse trip and his broken contract with Cally Callahan.

As opposed to an event, recovery is a *process*. It is a process of positive growth and change that touches all aspects of one's being—physical, mental, emotional, and spiritual. It happens not because of, but within the context of abstinence from alcohol and drugs.

Inasmuch as recovery means positive change, it happens best when following some kind of a plan—a path, so to speak. The prescribed path in AA is the 12 Steps, and most recovering alcoholics who sincerely and systematically "work" the steps from one through twelve realize profound change in their lives.

Not all alcoholics who "try" AA experience profound change. This is because they do not work the steps. Indeed, most "put the plug in the jug" and remain abstinent with the help of the fellowship for some period of time. Then they get bored and complacent, and they go back out and drink again. They have no recovery—no positive growth and change. They have only abstinence without recovery, and it does not work.

At its subtlest, AA works thusly: An actively alcoholic man goes to AA because he needs to quit drinking; that is, to become abstinent. He has tried to do it on his own, but his efforts have failed. Recovering alcoholics in AA tell him that he needs to do several things in order to stay sober; that is, to remain abstinent. He must join the fellowship, which means attend meetings. He must read the Big Book, or study the text. And he must work the steps and live according to the principles outlined in the book; that is, stay on the path.

Because he really wants to quit drinking, he follows the advice of these recovering alcoholics. He *walks the walk*. As a result of that, he experiences profound positive change in all aspects of his life. He experiences recovery. Then, as a natural by-product of recovery, he remains abstinent.

Recovery does not happen only in AA. An alternative scenario—one among many—might be the following: An actively alcoholic woman goes to her pastor for guidance regarding her drinking. He counsels her to abstain and to fill the resulting void with activities that will heal her spiritual dis-ease. He suggests that she join the fellowship, which means attend church services and other church-related functions. He encourages her to read the Bible, or study the text. And he tells her to live according to the spiritual principles outlined in the book; that is, stay on the path.

Like the alcoholic man at AA, she does what she is told. She walks the walk, and also like the alcoholic, she experiences profound positive change in all aspects of her life. She experiences recovery. As a natural by-product of recovery, she remains abstinent.

The same story could be outlined for any individual with any spiritual dis-ease who stumbles across any true spiritual path, and for any reason whatsoever actually walks that path. The tricky part is the path walking.

Steve came to understand that on the morning of his ninth day sober. He read it in the book, and it hit him pretty hard. *The spiritual life is not a theory. We have to live it.*

Living the spiritual life is akin to walking the path, or walking the walk. Faking the spiritual life is akin to talking a good line, or talking the talk. Alcoholics without recovery are naturally good talkers; indeed, they are typically selfish, self-centered, slick manipulators. They have to *learn* how to walk the walk, and the learning process can be unbelievably tedious and painful.

Steve's anxiety on the morning of his twelfth day sober was triggered by shame. Two things had stuck with him hard from the night before. One was Rachel's question, "How do you think she (Kathy) would feel if she knew you were here with me?....I think I would have felt hurt if you had spent the night with someone other than me while we were together."

The other was Ethel Smith's statement: "...recovery has less to do with not drinking and more to do with living my life on a daily basis as God would have me live it."

Steve tossed the two ideas together in his mind and came up with the undeniable realization that his spending the night with Rachel had significantly compromised his recovery. It showed his true colors—his glaring selfish self-absorption, which his mind told him sounded like, "Fuck honesty and integrity as long as I get mine." He saw his behavior as the perfect example of gross failure from a defective being, and it manifested spiritually as shame.

Steve quietly slipped out of bed and tiptoed downstairs to the living room. He picked his jeans up off of the living room floor and slipped them on. Then he sat on the couch in the dark and made himself small. He wrapped his arms tightly around his legs, pressed his thighs against his chest, pressed his heels against his butt, and rested his face on his knees. He felt guilty, sad, and afraid.

Images of Kathy filled his mind. Words, phrases, and ideas from Cally and the Big Book and AA meetings flooded his mind. *Spiritual disease. Spiritual experience. Spiritual awakening. God's will. Self-will. Self-will run riot. Willingness. Rigorous honesty. Surrender. The spiritual life—not a theory—we have to live it.*

He heard a noise behind him and looked up to see Rachel. "Are you okay, Steve?" she said in almost a whisper.

"Yeah, Rachel, I'm okay. I'm sorry if I woke you."

"That's alright. I didn't know whether to come down or not. I was afraid that you might have left without saying goodbye."

Steve reached his hand out to her. She took it and sat down next to him on the couch. "I wouldn't do that," he said. "I just woke up with stuff on my mind and couldn't get back to sleep."

"Do you want to talk?" she asked.

He took a deep breath. "I don't know, Rachel; there's so much floating around in my head that I wouldn't know where to start."

Rachel remained silent.

"Rachel, I'm afraid that I can't do this recovery thing, that I don't have it in me," he whispered. "It's too hard. It's too much. It's more than I can do. I think I'm not good enough or smart enough or strong enough for it. I want to go back to the way things used to be. Not the bad things, but the fun and easy things.

"Earlier this year, I'd study in the morning and work in my shop in the afternoon. My buddies would drop by. We'd shoot the shit and laugh and drink beer and get stoned and have a good time. I'd hang out at The Roam In and shoot pool and get high and bullshit with the regulars. There wasn't any pressure to grow or change anything. 'The spiritual life' *was* a theory, one that James and Tommy debated in fascinating, intellectual terms. There was no need to surrender. Willpower was a positive thing. Rigorous honesty was something for nuns and nerds."

Rachel snuggled closer and laid her head on his shoulder.

"Rachel, I think I lied to you last night. I lied to myself, too, but I lied to you more than I lied to me. The truth is that I *am* in a relationship with the woman in Austin. Her name is Kathy Morris. I met her in my treatment group. We went to an AA meeting together the next night, and we've been hanging out together ever since. We've slept together a couple of times. I told her Friday night that I thought I was falling in love with her.

"We've never talked about seeing other people or not seeing other people, but I think that's just a technicality. I know that if she had slept with another man last night, I would feel very, very hurt."

He turned his head so that he could see Rachel's face. "I'm sorry, babe. I really am."

Rachel leaned forward and kissed him on the lips. "I probably did the same thing, Steve. I don't know exactly how I knew it, but in my heart I knew there was more to your relationship than you admitted. I mean, I knew it before I even asked, which means I knew it before we ever took our clothes off.

"The truth is, though, that it probably wouldn't have made much difference to me anyway. I wanted last night to happen. I longed for it, selfish or not, self-centered or not, rigorously honest or not. And regardless of what that says about my recovery, I don't regret last night. I'm sorry that you do, but I don't."

Steve slipped his arm around Rachel's shoulders and said, "It's not that I have regrets about being with you, Rachel. The things I said last night about my feelings for you were absolutely true. I loved being with you. It was wonderful.

"The thing that has my stomach in knots is this incredible mass of recovery stuff. Living the spiritual life, rigorous honesty, positive growth and change. I mean, here I am with perhaps my dearest friend, who I love very much, doing what we've always done with each other—giving of ourselves, making love, sharing from our hearts, and I feel almost overwhelmed with guilt to the extent that I want to run away and hide. I mean, what *is* the spiritual life? What *is* rigorous honesty?

"If you had said last night, 'Steve, I know in my heart that you're in a relationship with that woman in Austin. Therefore, I don't want you to sleep with me unless you can, with rigorous honesty, tell me that being with me tonight is more important than being faithful to her,' I would have assured you that that was the case. And it would have been the truth. Now, this morning, I'm sitting here feeling guilty and feeling like I can't handle the rigors and rules of recovery.

"Honest to God, I love you, Rachel, and I wanted more than anything in the world last night for us to make love and spend the night together. Honest to God, I care a lot for Kathy, and I feel as though I betrayed her by being with you last night. Honest to God, I wish that you and I still drank alcohol and smoked pot and could put on a nice little Sunday morning buzz right now.

"Damn, Rachel, I feel like I'm going nuts. Right now, I just want to blow the whole recovery thing off. I'm not cut out for this. This isn't who I am."

Rachel wrapped her arms around Steve and buried her face in his neck. "Come back to bed with me, Steve," she whispered. "I'll help you go back to sleep. Then later I'll fix us some breakfast, and we can talk some more if you want to. Come on, okay?"

They went upstairs, slipped out of their clothes, and back into Rachel's bed. Steve lay on his stomach, and Rachel gently rubbed his back.

"Relax," she whispered. "Just relax. Let go of all the tension in your body. Let go of all the thoughts in your mind. Relax and let go. Be aware of your breathing. There are no problems, only opportunities to learn. Be here with me now, and relax. Breathe."

Eventually, Steve drifted into sleep. He dreamed that he was floating on his back on the surface of a large body of water. Floating felt simple and easy and natural, as long as he relaxed and kept his arms and legs spread out and away from his body, like spokes of a wheel. When he tensed up or drew his limbs in against him, he started sinking, and every time that happened, he started to panic. Instead of panicking, however, he heard the words, "Relax and be open," and he immediately floated again—freely, easily, and peacefully.

When Steve awoke, Rachel was sitting up in bed reading a booklet. "What time is it?" he asked her. "And what the heck are you doing?"

"It's a little after 10:00 o'clock, you old early riser, and I'm reading *The Grapevine*. It's a little booklet that's published by AA headquarters in New York. This is an old copy that a friend gave me. I've just run across something that I want to read to you as soon as you're really awake."

"What's it about?" he asked.

"It's about you."

Steve rolled over and propped himself up on one elbow. "Well, hell, if it's about me, you better go ahead and read it to me."

"Okay, here goes," she said. "This is from 1962, and it was written by Bill Wilson himself. 'Our very first problem is to accept our present circumstances as they are, ourselves as we are, and the people about us as they are. This is to adopt a realistic humility without which no genuine advance can even begin. Again and again, we shall need to return to that unflattering point of departure. This is an exercise in acceptance that we can profitably practice every day of our lives. Provided we strenuously avoid turning these realistic surveys of the facts of life into unrealistic alibis for apathy or defeatism, they can be the sure foundation upon which increased emotional health and therefore spiritual progress can be built.' There, what do you think of that little piece of wisdom, crazy man?"

"Can I see that?" Steve took the booklet and read the paragraph twice. Handing it back to Rachel, he said, "I think it's pretty scary that you found that this morning. Were you looking for it? I mean, had you read it before and remembered it?"

"Nope, I read it for the first time five minutes ago, just before you woke up. Quite a coincidence, huh? Does this answer a few of your questions, or what?"

"Yeah, it does that. You know, I told Ethel Smith last night that my impatience with sobriety, or recovery, probably discourages my progress, you know, like I think I should be perfect before I even know what perfect looks like. What that paragraph says to me about me is that I need to accept who I am right now before I can expect to become different. I need to accept myself, not judge myself. Humility first, and then growth and change. Then humility again, followed by more growth and change. What do you think? Does that sound right to you?"

"Uh huh. Listen to these words: 'Realistic humility; acceptance; foundation; progress.' There it is, except for this additional little piece, which was the part that caught my eye in the first place: 'Don't use the truth as an excuse to get high; use it instead as a catalyst for awareness and then growth.' Forgive my paraphrasing, but that's what it says to me.

"What I saw you doing this morning, Steve, was convincing yourself that you aren't good enough for recovery, so why try. What this says to me is that we can look at the present situation, and if it doesn't honestly feel right to us, we can say, 'Ah, here's why I need to work on my recovery. This is why I'm in recovery. If I were already perfect, I wouldn't need to work on recovery.' See what I mean?"

Steve smiled and nodded. "Rachel, if I didn't know better, I'd swear you're really my guardian angel disguised as this beautiful, smart, recovering alcoholic woman."

"Yeah, well, what you don't know won't hurt you. So, are you ready for breakfast?"

"Just about, but first, I'd like to lie here with you for a few more minutes."

Rachel laid down her booklet and snuggled into Steve's arms. "I'm yours," she whispered. They made love—warmly and tenderly, with sexual intimacy but without sexual intercourse.

CHAPTER 58

Before Steve left Rachel's, he wondered out loud why they had ever broken up in the first place.

"We had to, Steve," Rachel said. "You remember that, don't you? We didn't have any other choice. We were heading off in different directions, and it wouldn't have worked to do it any other way. Plus, had it happened differently, what do you think are the chances that we'd be sober today? My guess is, slim to none. Anyway, I love having you as my good, good friend."

Steve stopped by Lois and Chester's on his way out of town. Lois made quite a fuss over him. She would not let him rest until he had given her the details about his treatment program and his progress in recovery. Following the report, she wanted to know about Bev and the kids, and finally, where he had spent the night. He told her the truth.

"Oh, Honey, do you think that's smart? You know, you're supposed to avoid romantic relationships for your first full year of sobriety."

Steve smiled and raised one eyebrow. "Yeah, like you and Chester did?"

"Well, that was different, Honey. We were older, and we were very careful not to compromise our recovery programs. We never slept together until our honeymoon. Did you know that?"

"No, I didn't know that, but it doesn't matter to me one way or the other. Rachel and I are good friends, Mother. We're not in a romantic relationship, nor do we plan to start one. Anyway, there's a woman in Austin that I kind of have my eye on. She's also in the program. Don't worry, though; I'm not in any hurry to get bogged down in some heavy romantic doo-daa."

"Steve, you're the most hard headed person I've ever known. Do you have an AA sponsor yet?"

"Not quite, but I'm going to meet with someone later today to discuss it. Why?"

"Well, I hope to hell that you get someone who will set you straight on these things and not let you ruin your chance at sobriety. You need to concentrate on yourself right now, not on some damn stable of women."

Steve laughed. "Stable of women? Mother, you're a riot. Listen, I *am* focusing on myself. I'm learning more and more about recovery and how I need to approach it. As a matter of fact, I learned a lot this weekend. Rachel and I went to a meeting last night, and I heard some things that I don't think I'll ever forget. And this morning, we read some stuff out of *The Grapevine* that helped me understand some stuff that had been driving me nuts.

"I mean, I'm having ups and downs, but all in all, I think I'm doing pretty well. I'm even working on the Steps. I think I've done

Step 1, maybe not perfectly, but I do believe that I'm an alcoholic, and I can see that my alcoholism has caused me problems. Isn't that Step 1?"

"Yes, Steve, it's Step 1 *if* you understand what being an alcoholic means. It means that you can never drink again without having those same problems return. It's easy to say, 'I'm an alcoholic' if you ignore the implications of that statement. That's why Step 1 goes on to also say, 'powerless over alcohol.' If you know you're powerless over alcohol, then there's no misunderstanding about the nature of the relationship between you and the drug. Alcohol has all of the power, and you have none. Do you see what I'm saying?"

"Yes, I see what you're saying, and I'm not far from there. I mean, I'm not so thoroughly convinced of it that I'd bet my life on it, but I'm not stupid. I've done some written work that has shown me how deeply involved with alcohol and drugs I was and how costly it was to me. I know I wasn't a social drinker and that when I tried to be one it didn't work, at least in the long run.

"Cally, my counselor, keeps reminding me that this is a process, that my coming to accept my alcohol and drug addictions will take some time if that acceptance is to be real. He discourages people from just jumping on the bandwagon and saying, 'Oh, yes, of course I'm an alcoholic; otherwise I wouldn't be here.' He wants people to go through the process of understanding and admitting and accepting their alcoholism on a deeper level. And I think that's what I'm in the process of doing.

"Also, Mother, I'm seeing more and more that I can't do recovery by myself, that I do need help with it. I feel like I'm being open-minded. I'm listening to people. I'm reading the Big Book and learning from that. I'm going to meetings every day. I'm seeing my counselor and going to my treatment group. I'm trying new ways of looking at things. I'm trying to change. I feel like I'm moving closer toward sanity, whatever that is. Now, isn't that what Step 2 is really about? Accepting help and learning?"

Lois studied Steve's face for a moment. "I guess you'll need to be patient with me, too, Steve. Your approach to sobriety is so different from what I experienced. I don't know, maybe it's more psychological and sophisticated. I was just so defeated that I walked into AA and surrendered. That's all there was to it. I wanted my life back, and I didn't need "a process" to understand how sick I was. There was no doubt in my mind regarding my powerlessness over alcohol.

"When I saw Step 1, I said, 'Of course I'm powerless. I'm completely powerless. I've proven that to myself over and over. I've tried to control my drinking many, many times, and I can't. And unmanageable? Are you kidding? I've alienated everyone that I've ever loved, and I'm about two-thirds dead!'

"As you know, I didn't go to treatment. I didn't have a counselor. I didn't have group therapy. I had the Big Book, the Steps, the fellowship, and a sponsor who told me what to do. I never questioned any of those sources. I did what I was told because I didn't know what else to do.

"So, I don't know, Steve. I know I tend to over react. Of course, you already know that. I'll tell you something, though; I would give anything, even my life, to see you overcome this disease. I feel responsible for your unhappiness, as you also already know. Now, though, I see you with a chance for something better, while you're still a young man with your whole life ahead of you. Please, just don't throw away this chance. Please take it seriously. That's all I'm asking."

Steve made it home around 4:30. He called Kathy as soon as he walked in the door. He had grappled on the drive home with the question of whether or not to tell her about Rachel, and although he had not decided for sure, he was leaning towards doing it. When she did not answer the phone, he called Ralph. They agreed to get together to talk about sponsorship after Ralph's regular Sunday night AA meeting. Steve agreed to meet him there.

In the meantime, he had a few hours so he worked on organizing his time to accommodate his busy life. By separating his responsibilities into functions—school, work, recovery, and social, he developed a schedule that committed roughly 30 hours per week to school, 20 hours per week to each of the other three activities, eight per day to sleep, and four or five per day for busy work and "nothing." Reduced to a weekly schedule, his life looked manageable.

While he worked, Steve tried several times to call Kathy, and each time, when he failed to get an answer, his anxiety rose a little higher. Just before leaving for his meeting at 7:45, he tried for the last time. When she did not answer, he hung the phone up hard and said, "Where the fuck is she? She knew I was going to call."

On his way to the meeting, Steve obsessed on Kathy's absence. It occurred to him that perhaps she had somehow discovered his whereabouts the night before and was avoiding him because of that. He could not imagine how that could have happened. The one thing he knew for sure, however, was that she was avoiding him, for whatever reason.

During the meeting, Steve's thoughts repeatedly drifted back to Kathy. He pictured her at her apartment, not answering the phone because she knew it was him calling. He pictured her out with friends, perhaps at the lake, having too much fun to remember her agreement to see him when he got home from San Antonio. Finally, he pictured her with another man, acting out her newly reawakened sexuality. By the end of the meeting, Steve was totally obsessed.

"Do you want to go somewhere and get a cup of coffee, Steve?" Ralph asked.

"Yes, but listen, I need to make a quick phone call first."

"Okay. I hope nothing's wrong. I noticed during the meeting that you were pretty distracted."

Ralph showed Steve the phone and walked away. Steve dialed Kathy's number and got no answer. "Son of a goddamn bitch," he whispered to himself.

Settled into a booth at a nearby cafe, Ralph said, "Maybe you would like to talk about something other than sponsorship, Steve. You seem more than distracted. You seem downright agitated."

"Yeah, I feel pretty agitated, even though it's probably nothing more than something I've manufactured in my own sick mind. It's relationship stuff. Why don't we talk about sponsorship first, and then if there's time we can talk about the other."

Steve laid out Cally's job description for sponsorship. Ralph met all of the requirements except that he no longer spent significant amounts of individual time with his sponsor. He told Steve that his approach to sponsoring was to be very available to the sponsee but to leave it pretty much up to him to ask for time together.

"If you're looking for someone to run roughshod over you and your recovery, then I'm probably not your man. On the other hand, if you want someone to be available to you and honest and open with you, then it will probably work out just fine. I'll treat you like an adult and like a friend, not like a child.

"I hear other AA sponsors talk about their 'babies' and their 'pigeons.' I don't care for those terms. I think of us simply as men who are working together toward a better way of life. I'm no genius, and I'm far from perfect. If you can live with that, then I would be glad to work with you. If not, then no hard feelings. We can just be friends."

Steve felt comfortable with Ralph's approach. They shook hands on the new partnership.

That settled, Steve brought up Kathy. "This other thing is eating my lunch, even though I'm sure it's just in my mind. I'll need to back up and give you a little history, but I'll keep it as brief as I can."

"Take whatever time you need, Steve. I'm not in any hurry. If this is going to be my first challenge as your sponsor, I'd like to do a good job with it."

Steve smiled and relaxed. Then he talked non-stop for forty-five minutes. He gave Ralph a condensed history of his life since leaving Bev. He touched on his relationship with Rachel, the geographical cure move to Austin, his relationship with Dixie, the ranch trip, the Waco trip, his commitment to treatment, and his relationship with Kathy.

He told him about his and Kathy's conversations with Susan and Patti and explained the implications of their relationship on the treatment process with Cally. Finally, he talked about the weekend with Rachel and his return home to find Kathy missing.

"The dilemma that I came home with was whether or not to confess to Kathy about sleeping with Rachel. Now my mind has Kathy out there fucking other men, and the original dilemma is no longer an issue. Anyway, that's where my mind has been since about 5:00 o'clock this afternoon, wondering where she is and what she's doing, when she's supposed to be with me. I know how insane this all must sound. I feel like some damn insecure teenager. I actually feel kind of embarrassed about it, but it's exactly the kind of situation that I could see myself drinking over. So, what do you think, sponsor?"

Ralph sat back in his seat. "Well, first of all, I think we're going to have a lot of fun working together. You remind me an awful lot of myself—an impatient, compulsive control freak with an over active imagination. In that regard, I offer my understanding, as well as my sympathy. Beyond that, I think you have tremendous insight for a young man with less than two weeks of sobriety. I honor you for that.

"Now, about advice. I would be inclined to keep it simple. First, the easy part. Do not 'confess' anything to Kathy. As I see it, your only real transgression is in your own mind. My guess is that at this point, confessing could only hurt her, not to mention yourself. And there's no need to create pain for anyone. I'm certain that there is a lesson to be learned from this situation, but I doubt that it has anything to do with throwing your guilt off onto someone else.

"Now, that brings us to your crazy thinking, which you have described as powerful enough to get you drunk. Let me ask you this, Steve. Do you pray, and if so, what do you pray for, and to whom?"

"Yeah, I suppose I do pray. My counselor, Cally, told me to pray for willingness and open-mindedness, and that's all. I'm not sure about the recipient of those prayers. I just throw them out there."

"Well, okay, that's good. Have you remembered to do that this evening?"

Steve smiled and shook his head. "Not even once."

"Okay, then, I'd like to suggest that you do several things, starting immediately. First, remind yourself to pray, and add 'patience' to your request. So you'll be praying for willingness, open-mindedness, and patience, and you will be doing that a lot. Okay?

"Second, remind yourself of what you already know—that your mind is playing games with you—fucking with you, so to speak. I believe that with your insight, you can easily intervene on that process by reminding yourself of what's going on. You know, 'My mind's doing it to me again.' Then take the power away from your crazy mind and give it back to your rational mind.

"You may want to reinterpret your experience by simply honoring your feelings and consciously changing what you say to yourself. Here's an example: When your mind says, 'She's out fucking some other guy, and I hate her for it,' honor the feelings—the fear and anger, and replace the original statement with ones that are based more in truth.

"Here's what I mean: 'I feel insecure because she's not home to take my call.' 'I feel afraid when I can't get in touch with her.' 'I feel panicky when my mind goes into overdrive and tells me things that probably are not true.' You get the idea, don't you?

"The next step of that process is to simply ask yourself—your deep, inner self—for feedback and answers. Then get quiet and still and see what happens. Maybe you'll get something, and maybe you won't, but I think you will more often than not.

"I don't know for certain if this process will work for you, but it has done wonders for me. It helps me to keep my feet on the ground.

"Finally, I want you to read the story in the Big Book entitled *Doctor, Alcoholic, Addict,* by Dr. Paul O. It starts on page 439. Pay particular attention to the last four or five pages."

Steve nodded. "Okay, Ralph, I think those are good suggestions. I'm familiar with the story, but I'll read it from start to finish. Anything else?"

"Oh, I don't know, Steve. Trite stuff maybe. Easy does it; one day at a time; keep it simple. The party line, you know?"

Steve laughed. "You haven't warned me of the dangers of being in a relationship in early sobriety yet, Ralph."

"Well, Steve, I do believe they're there. In fact, I think you're experiencing the direct evidence of that right now. If you can live with it and continue your recovery, fine. If not, then we'll try to figure out together how to pick up the pieces."

They said good night and went their separate ways. Instead of going home, Steve drove by Kathy's apartment. Her car was in its regular place, and he could see from the parking lot that her apartment was dark. Though tempted to just go home, he decided to stop.

"If there's a problem, I might as well find out now," he said to himself.

He knocked on her door. When she did not respond, he knocked again, harder. After a minute he heard Kathy say, "Who is it?"

"Kathy, it's me—Steve."

Kathy unlocked the door and opened it. She was dressed in short pajamas and appeared to have been asleep. "Steve, come in. Come in and sit down. I'm so glad to see you. I had given up on talking to you tonight. Did you try to call me?"

"Yeah, lots of times. You weren't home. I was worried."

"No, I was home. The stupid phone wasn't working. I guess it's been dead all day, but I didn't know it until just before 8:00 o'clock. At first, I wasn't worried about you because I knew that you were going to try to see your mom and all. Then, when it got late and I hadn't heard from you, I thought maybe something was wrong.

"Anyway, I decided to go to an 8:00 o'clock meeting at South Austin, and just before I left, I decided to call you to see if perhaps you were home but for some reason just hadn't called. I knew you wouldn't forget, but I thought that maybe something had happened. It even occurred to me that you might be mad at me for some reason. Anyway, I picked up the phone, and it was as dead as a doornail.

"So I went next door and called you from their phone, but there wasn't any answer. I went on over to the meeting, thinking you might by chance be there. Then on my way home, I stopped and tried to call you again. That was about 9:30. I tried one more time from next door about a half-hour ago. Then I gave up and went to bed. Anyway, I'm really sorry. Are you okay?"

Steve put his arms around her. "Yeah, I'm okay," he said softly. "Now that I'm with you, I'm just fine. God, Kathy, you won't believe what I've put myself through. I am such an idiot. Listen, I know it's late, and you have to get up early, but could we talk for just a little while? It would mean a lot to me."

Kathy made some tea, and they talked. Steve told her about his afternoon and evening. He told her about the frustration and the fear and his mental gyrations around those feelings, including imagining her with another man. He apologized for thinking the worst, and he owned it as his own issue.

"It makes me sad to think that you could see me that way, Steve, even when you're upset. I appreciate your trusting me enough to tell me about it, though. I know that's a risk for you. I want to tell you something about me, though. I'm not like that. Don't confuse my previous line of work with who I am today. I want to be with you. I don't want to be with anybody else. If that should ever change, I will tell you. I promise you that. For now, though, I'll be true to you. You can count on that." She kissed him on the lips and put her head on his shoulder. "Do you understand what I'm saying?"

"Yes. Thank you, Kathy."

They talked until midnight. Steve went home alone. He prayed for willingness, open-mindedness, and patience. He went to sleep feeling grateful for his sobriety.

Section Three:

What It's Like Now

CHAPTER 59

Sunday night ended in gratitude. Monday morning promised routine. Steve awoke early, and before his feet hit the floor, he reminded himself to pray, and his prayer for willingness, open-mindedness, and patience felt genuine. Before he closed it, he said, "I know I'm not supposed to ask for anything more, but God, it would help me if I had a better idea of just to whom or what it is I'm praying. Maybe you would help me with that. I'm not looking for some big deal burning bush or anything, just a better understanding. Things are going pretty good for me. Thanks."

He took Ginger for a brisk walk, did yoga postures for a half hour, ate breakfast, and straightened up the house before riding his bike to his first graduate school class at 9:00 AM.

The class, Social/Developmental/Personality Psychology vestibule, was about what Steve had expected—information-heavy lectures elaborating on four textbooks totaling over 1600 pages. The instructor, an assistant professor, and low person on the academic totem pole, was a woman about Steve's age in her second year with the department. She seemed bright but insecure. She promised the class of ten that every student who came to every class, read every assignment, and participated in every class discussion in a thoughtful manner would almost certainly receive an "A" in the course. "No problem," Steve thought to himself.

After class, he rode to the Catholic Student Center, where a small group of four assembled. Ralph suggested that Steve chair the meeting.

"Is that legal?" Steve asked. "I don't even have two weeks yet."

They all laughed. "Everything is legal in AA," Clarence said. "I could come stoned if I wanted to, as long as I have a desire to quit drinking."

After reading the introductory materials, Steve said, "Well, I'm Steve, and I'm an alcoholic/addict. I feel awkward chairing a meeting, even with you guys. I feel as though I haven't earned the right to do this yet, like I haven't experienced enough to qualify. Nevertheless, I do have a topic that I'd like to know more about, so I guess I'll throw it out there for discussion, and maybe I'll learn something.

"This morning when I woke up, I said a prayer. That's not so unusual in itself. I mean, I've been praying ever since I started recovery, mainly because my treatment counselor told me to. This morning was different, though, because not only did I say words that I've been instructed to say—asking for willingness, open-mindedness, and patience, but I also felt as though I meant them.

"It was like I really did want to become more willing, open-minded, and patient. It was a small difference—a qualitative difference—but I was pretty struck by it. It felt as though I was communicating with something besides my own sick brain. So I took the prayer a little further and asked whoever or whatever might be hearing my prayer to help me understand him or her or it or them or whatever the hell is out there. I mean, prayer is pretty confusing to me because I have no understanding of or connection with whomever or whatever it is I'm praying to.

"I've talked about prayer and about God to friends many times. One of my friends is an atheist who appears to have a regular spiritual practice that sounds strangely like prayer to me. Another friend is a spiritual genius of sorts who talks about spirituality constantly but doesn't seem to live it on a daily basis.

"I grew up pretty religious, as a Christian. And I believe that as a kid I felt the presence of God in my life. There was even a time when I thought I might devote my life to religious work. That was when I was young, before junior high school even, but I remember it as feeling very real. I lost my faith somewhere along the way, though. I even became bitter toward my early religious beliefs, although I don't know why.

"Anyway, I don't mind praying to something that I don't understand or feel connected with. It feels pretty weird sometimes, though. It feels pretty empty, actually, and a little stupid. Like I said, though, it felt better this morning, and I liked the feeling a lot. It was subtle, for sure, but I know that it was there. I wish that I could express what the feeling was, but it doesn't lend itself to description very well. It was like...like a sleepy puppy...you know, like friendly and kind of soft and warm.

"So anyway, that's my topic, if in fact there is one in there somewhere. Maybe it's prayer, or maybe it's God, or maybe it's something around the connection between the two." Steve smiled and shook his head back and forth slowly. "See what happens when you turn a confused, newly sober alcoholic loose as chairman of an AA meeting? Perhaps one of you guys will rescue me. What do you think? Who wants to talk?"

Ralph reached across Patti and patted Steve on the knee. "You're doing a very good job, Steve," he said, smiling.

Clarence's approach to prayer and God was very pragmatic. He memorized specific prayers out of the Big Book and other AA literature. He said each one at a certain time each day. He described his God as one reminiscent of the God of Steve's youth—The Father, Creator of Heaven and Earth, Overseer of His

336

creation, Rewarder and Punisher, angry a lot of the time, and holding very high expectations of His flock.

Steve pictured Clarence's God as the old white-haired, white-bearded cloud sitter, with calculator in hand, recording transgressions, making judgments, and meting out punishments. "This one deserves to be addicted to pot," He says, pointing a long, thin finger at Clarence.

Patti's prayer life was heart centered and feelings generated. She described communicating with God freely, whenever the feeling hit. She talked about having lost all connection with God as her alcoholism progressed but finding it again during recovery. She felt close to God much of the time, particularly during morning prayers. Patti's God was more feminine in nature—nurturing, forgiving, caring, and holding few expectations of Her flock. "God really is love," she said.

Steve pictured a big, fat, smiling black woman, rocking back and forth in her porch rocker. "I love you, honey child," She says, with her arms encircling Patti and holding her close against her enormous bosom.

Ralph described his approach to prayer as an ongoing, unrehearsed, deeply internal dialogue. He spoke of "the God within"—the "perfect moment" at the spiritual core of all beings. He also referred to this spiritual core as "the perfect Self," "the true Self," and simply, "the Self." He spoke of the unity of all living things, held together as one by that perfect core. He talked about using his breath and conscious awareness of his breath as prayer, as one way of bringing himself to be present in and with each moment.

"When I'm fully present in the moment, fully conscious of my being, then I feel my oneness with God—the God within me and the God within you," he said. "When I'm not present, I don't seem to feel that. I know it's there, of course, but I don't really feel it.

"When I drank alcohol and used cocaine, I did not feel it at all. I yearned for it, but I didn't feel it. Indeed, I think that alcohol and coke put up a wall between me and God, which to me means that they put a wall between me and my Self.

"Like you, Steve, and perhaps you, too, Patti, I felt a connection with God at an earlier time in my life, in my youth. But along the way, something happened to that. Maybe like so many other kids in our culture, I started learning to feel bad about myself, and because of that, I felt the need to put up walls for protection. I lost my humility. I acquired defenses. The self that I developed a connection with then was my ego—my defended self.

"By the time I reached college, I lived in those defenses. I was arrogant. I was judgmental. I was a perfectionist. I was secretive. I was sneaky. On a deeper level, I was afraid. And I was ashamed of myself. Alcohol, and later cocaine, gave me moments of relief. At those times, I felt at peace, but they were false moments. They did not take away the wall between me and God, like I wanted them to. They just put a temporary cover over some of the most painful defenses. They ameliorated the fear and the shame.

"I think that for me, the whole process of recovery has been one of taking down those walls, of lowering the defenses, so that reconnection with God was possible. I'm certain that reconnection never would have happened as long as I was using alcohol and drugs to cover over the pain. When I was high, my prayers were cries for help, and they were sent outside of myself. Today, they are more likely to be expressions of gratitude and simple requests for guidance.

"I do have a couple of standard prayers that I mumble off and on during the day. One is like yours, Clarence. It's from Step 11; "God, please grant me conscious knowledge of your will for me and the power to carry that out." The other asks for the spiritual qualities that I most respect; "God, please give me faith, courage, and humility." I direct those prayers to the place inside of me where I can feel God's presence—to my true Self, which is more assessable to me now than it was when I was drinking and using.

"If I've been rambling, I know you'll forgive me. I need to do that from time to time to remind myself about my own spiritual program. I think you gave us a good topic, Steve, and I appreciate your chairing the meeting and bringing up an issue that is central to my recovery."

After the meeting, Steve thanked Ralph for what he had shared. "Your God and your prayer life is one that I think I could live with," he said. "I believe it's one that might work for me. It's like what I would imagine a Buddhist God would be if there were such a thing. How would you feel if I just borrowed it and used it as my own until something better comes along?"

"I think that's a great idea, Steve. Be my guest. My God is your God."

Steve left the Catholic Student Center and headed straight to The Recovery Center. After the mandatory treatment plan review, Steve detailed his weekend for Cally. He started with the good news—having obtained a sponsor and at least a temporary understanding of God. Then he moved on to the more controversial but predictable topic—the two episodes of sexual intimacy with Kathy. Then he hit on the more substantive issues—the angry, immature conversation with Bev, spending the night with Rachel, his Sunday morning panic and subsequent insight, and his Sunday afternoon insanity around Kathy and its resolution Sunday night.

"As you can see, Cally, I had a busy weekend, with plenty of opportunities for growth. I feel good today, though, especially following the noon meeting. But I was a mess on Saturday and a crazed madman yesterday. The thought of getting high occurred to me more than once. I believe that if Rachel had pulled out a joint and lit it at 5:00 o'clock Sunday morning, I might very well have smoked it with her.

"You know what, though? I'm beginning to understand the inherent danger in focusing a lot of energy on relationships instead of recovery. I mean, I think that if I avoided intimate relationships altogether right now, the recovery work would be a breeze. Know what I mean?"

Cally nodded. "Yes, I do. And it's an interesting thought, but probably an unrealistic fantasy, at least for someone like you, Steve."

"What do you mean, Cally? Is there something wrong with me that I don't know about?"

"No, no, there's nothing wrong with you. All in all, I think you're doing remarkably well. The quality of your insights around recovery still amazes me. I've seen people work their programs for months—years, even—and still not grasp some of the connections between abstract concepts and their personal lives that you seem to grasp with relative ease.

"For example, through the passage from *The Grapevine,* you caught the real meaning of the term humility. It simply means *truth.* You saw that, and you saw the implications of it for your recovery. Truth, and *then* growth. No truth, no growth. Personally, I find that remarkable. Like they say, though, the proof is in the pudding. We'll see now how that insight changes your life."

"So what's my problem, then?" Steve asked. "What did you mean when you referred to me as 'someone like you?'"

"Well, all I meant was that I don't believe you will let recovery be a simple process. Some people do. Some walk into my office and surrender. Their poor old egos have been shattered. In effect, they say, 'I'm beat. I have no resistance left. Tell me what to do, and I'll do it.' They never question anything. They're open. They walk the walk one foot in front of the other, and they never look back. Those people are a counselor's dream. They make me look good, you know, like I know what the hell I'm doing.

"You, on the other hand, are the type who insists on learning through the school of hard knocks, from your own mistakes. You have great promise, but you're more of a challenge. That is, if you stick around long enough. Do you want to hear more?"

"Yeah, sure, what the hell? I might as well know what I'm up against."

339

Cally waited until Steve looked him in the eye. "Are you sure, Steve? You might not like it."

Steve hesitated. In his mind, flashing red signs, like the ones on Sesame Street, said, "DANGER." Nevertheless, he shifted his weight in his chair and said, "Go ahead, Cally. I mean, how terrible could it be?"

"All right," Cally said. "I've got a hunch about you, Mr. Campbell. I've got a hunch that deep down inside, you're scared to death of recovery. You understand that recovery means a whole lot more than staying abstinent from alcohol and drugs. You know it means that you really do have to change, and not just your behavior, but also inside, in your mind and in your heart.

"For that to happen, it means that you have to deal with your issues, including the deep, dark ones. Ultimately, it means that you have to get real. You have to let go of that protective cover of yours and get real. You used the phrase *humility— realistic humility*—earlier. That phrase captures the spirit of what I'm talking about quite well.

"Now, I realize that you've known all of this stuff all along. At least you've known it intellectually. I think that now, however, it's starting to sink in and really grab your attention. Like it did on Sunday morning, when your scared-shitless defense system— your frightened ego—tried to convince you that you just were not cut out for recovery and that you could go back to the good old days when drinking and using was nothing but fun. Of course, the irony of that fantasy is that for you, it's probably never actually been nothing but fun.

"So what do you do with all of those contradictions? You want sobriety. You want something better than what your parents had and better than what you, yourself, have had up to this point. You're drawn—strongly drawn—to a more spiritual way of life. You're fascinated with the idea of a spiritual awakening. You yearn for genuineness. I can feel it in you. Your intuition is telling you that the path you've found, the one you're tip-toeing around on right now, is probably the best shot you've ever had at the kind of life you long for.

"But something inside of you is firing off like wild. It's telling you to beware, because you've got a lot at risk—a hell of a lot at risk. You already know what it feels like to be hurt. You've been deeply hurt before, and you learned very well how to protect yourself from letting it ever happen again.

"Do you want me to continue?"

Steve smiled defensively and shrugged his shoulders. "Why not? You've gone this far; you might as well put it all out there."

"Okay, then. There are two parts left. One is this: Your defense system is a sneaky one, Steve. Yours is the kind of defense system that is smart enough to know what a defense system looks like, and it does not want to be that obvious. It's the kind of defense system that I call *slick*.

"Being slick means being dishonest, but in such a way that it looks and feels honest. Some people are good at it. Some are really good at it. Seasoned politicians seem to be some of the best; they can tell you what you want to hear without lying and without telling the real truth, and your natural tendency is to believe them because they seem so genuine.

"My belief about you, Steve, is that in your dedicated effort to avoid being hurt, you learned how to *appear* genuine without assuming the risks inherent in actually *being* genuine. You learned how to *appear* honest, open-minded, and willing without taking the risks involved in *being* honest, open-minded, and willing. That, my friend, is slick.

"You came about that defense system honestly, of course, out of a legitimate need to protect yourself from being crushed by your parents' rage and fear. But as defenses tend to do, yours carried over into your adult life, far beyond its original legitimate need. Why? Probably because it works so well to keep you safe.

"You see, Steve, your defense system lets you look good, and for those of us who have shame and fear at the core level, appearances are damn near everything. Now, though, it's starting to crumble a little bit, and you are caught in the horns of a dilemma. You have to let it crumble if you're to have what you're drawn to, which is sobriety, recovery, and genuineness—in short, a spiritual life.

"But the flip side is that if you do let it crumble, it will also leave you vulnerable. And if you're vulnerable, that is, if you are humble, honest, open, genuine, et cetera, you open yourself up to being hurt. On some level—an unconscious level, perhaps—you are painfully aware of that, and that part of you is saying, 'No fucking way, man; not in this lifetime. I've worked too goddamn hard to build up this protective cover just to let go now.'

"So what do you suppose happens to the *real* Steve Campbell—the one underneath the defenses, the one that the defenses are duty bound to protect? Well, that ushers in the second part of this story. The defense system goes to work to find distractions. Alcohol and drugs were perfect. Alcohol and drug addictions keep you stuck in your defensive posture for the rest of your life. But now, all of sudden, your real self—your Self, as your sponsor calls it—has intervened, and the alcohol and drugs are suddenly gone.

"Hmm, well then, how about food? No, your daily operating defense system—your ego—is too appearance conscious to become a compulsive over-eater. Gambling? No, you're too tight with a buck for gambling. Well, then, there's always work. Nah, your ego has adopted this 60s persona, and compulsive work would not fit in with that at all.

"But say, how about relationships—women and sex? Now there's a good possibility. They're a great distraction. They will certainly dominate your time and energy, especially if we turn it into an addiction and make it two or three or four women and become romantically and/or sexually involved with all of them. Surely, at least one or two won't act right, which leads you to feel threatened and to obsess over them. Indeed, it might even get so crazy that you will be compelled to start using again. Then your defense system has it made. No more threat of recovery, genuineness, vulnerability, and the spiritual life."

Cally made strong eye contact with Steve, who had been looking at the floor more than at Cally. He continued. "I think perhaps women are the perfect distraction for you, Steve. They're certainly a socially acceptable one, especially if all of them are beautiful and desirable. While they dominate your thoughts and feelings, you avoid recovery. Your issues get triggered, of course. They don't get resolved, though, because you remain defended. You remain slick. Consequently, you avoid true growth and change. You don't achieve genuineness. You don't risk getting hurt."

Cally took a deep breath, exhaled, and looked at Steve. "Hopefully, I did not go too far with that story. I would hate to scare you off before you really got started here."

Steve narrowed his eyes. "I don't know if you went too far or not. It doesn't feel good, though, and it doesn't give me credit for the work I've done or the progress I've made. What do you want from me, Cally? Do you want me to blow off my relationships with women? Do you want me to abandon Kathy? Do you want me to submerge myself in recovery and disregard the rest of my interests and responsibilities? Is that what you want? Because if it is, you're shit out of luck."

"Those are all relevant questions, Steve, but the one I will answer is the one about what I want from you.

"To start with, I want your word that you will hang in there with me, and with the group. I want your word that you will listen to what I tell you and consider it with as much open-mindedness as you can muster. I want your solemn word that you will not run away when the going gets rough. I want you to promise that you will work with me, that you will consciously and courageously lower your defenses when they scream to be raised.

"You see, Steve, you are the one who is insisting that your recovery be challenging, and that makes my job more challenging as well. I will have to take risks with you that I don't take with everyone. But I do not want to lose you in the process."

Steve thought for a second and then nodded. "Okay, Cally, you have my word. I'll hang in there with you. Understand this, though: I will not allow myself to be abused, not by you or anyone else. And I won't promise to accept everything you say just because you say it. I don't believe in you that strongly, not yet anyway. But I will listen. I'll listen with as open a mind as I possibly can.

"I believe that I want recovery more than you think I do, but I don't have a damn thing to prove to you. The way I see it, Cally, you work for me. I hired you to help me. I'm paying you for that help. I trust that you'll do the best job for me that you can. If that means confronting me with a truth that I can't see, then I can live with that. At least I think I can. Now, what else?"

"Three things," Cally said. "First, add the word *humility* to your basic prayer for help, and pray many times every day. When the prayer doesn't feel genuine, start over, and keep saying it until it does. Second, address your Treatment Plan—Problem 2, Goal 2, Method 5. Address all parts of it, and have it written by next Monday.

"And third, back off on your romantic involvements. I'm concerned about your relationship with Kathy, but I'm not alarmed. When you add your friend from San Antonio and your friend from the bar and your next door neighbor into the mix, however, it's too much.

"Ideally, you would not even be dating right now, but I'm realistic enough not to ask that of you. So I want you to explore your feelings, your values, and your conscience and make some choices and set some limits. What does each relationship mean? What will you do with whom? How will you get honest with each? I want you to write down thoughtful answers to these questions and bring them in when you come on Wednesday for our short session."

"All right, Cally. I think I can handle those things. Anything else?"

"Yes, Steve, I want to compliment you on the work you've done and the progress you've made. Believe me, it has not gone unnoticed or unappreciated. Indeed, it is because of your work and your progress that I am able to be as open and honest and confrontive with you as I am. I can't take off the gloves with everyone, but I feel as though I can push you. It's okay with me when you push back."

Steve left The Recovery Center feeling pensive. "Slick," he thought to himself as he drove toward his house. "God, I hate the sound of that word." He pictured a used car salesman in white patent leather shoes and matching belt.

CHAPTER 60

Steve's new schedule had him in his shop from 3:00 to 7:00 on Monday afternoon, so as soon as he arrived home from The Recovery Center, he changed clothes and went to work.

James dropped by at 3:30. His eyes were bloodshot, and he smelled like marijuana. Steve reminded himself to relax and pay attention to business. He closed his eyes for a moment and said, "Okay, God, now is when I could use a little willingness, open-mindedness, patience, and humility."

"Well, you don't look any different," James said. "How are you feeling?"

"You don't look any different either, old buddy, and I'm feeling great," Steve replied, as he continued working.

"How's it going with old Cally Callahan?"

Steve smiled. "You sure did have him pegged. He's a dangerous S.O.B. He rips your defenses away from you, slips his message in while they're down, and then puts you back together before you know what hit you. He did it to me today.

"He told me that I'm slick, James. He said that I'm dishonest while appearing honest. He also said I'm using women and sex to keep me distracted from the issue at hand, which is the recovery process. I've been thinking about that ever since I left there today."

"Well, is he right?" James asked.

Steve laughed and nodded. "Of course he is. I guess I'm more concerned with how I come across to people than with being who I really am with people. If it's a question of image or truth, I go for image. Keeps me safe, you know? Pretty sorry state of affairs, huh?"

James laughed softly. "Yeah, there's no doubt about it, Stevey. You're just a goddamn human being. Listen, man; who do you know that's always open, honest, and real? Go ahead, name one person."

Steve laid down his tools and looked at James. "I guess I had you pegged as someone who thought of himself in those terms."

James smiled and shook his head. "Not me, man. You've got me mixed up with someone else."

"I guess I'm a little surprised," Steve said. "You always seem so damn sure of yourself."

"Yeah, well, that's not the same thing as open, honest, and real," James said, laughing. "I mean, I do pretty well. I tell the truth, you know, and for the most part I don't give a rat's ass about what people think of me. You know that. Like I've told you before, though, man, I've got my issues. It's not like Cally never jumped my shit. He used to say that I hide behind my brain.

344

"Cally says you're slick. He says I'm intellectual. You use women and sex. I use information. Hell, man, everyone has an ego. Everyone has defenses that work for him, or against him, depending on how you look at it. Our families, our institutions, our culture—none of them encourage, or even permit, total openness, honesty, and genuineness.

"Besides that, evil really does exist, man; at least I think it does. I think we live in a pretty damn dark world, myself. I think we *have* to protect ourselves sometimes, or we'll get eaten up. The best I can hope for is to be able to choose when to put up my defenses and when to take them down.

"The trick is learning first, how to recognize the sons of bitches. Second is how to take them down. And third is being willing to do that when it's appropriate. I think what happens to most people is that they learn how to put them up and keep them up all the time. They just go into denial. They never learn how to recognize them or how to take them down. When they're challenged to do that, they freak out because their egos tell them that any crack in the defensive wall is dangerous.

"You know, Steve, Cally has his stuff, too. Ask him about it sometime. I don't think he'll deny it. In fact, if you pay attention, you'll see it. At different times, he'll be more open or less open. He has his games, too. One of his favorites is the one that it sounds like he pulled on you today. He goes for the jugular, and while he has your throat lying open on the table, he sneaks in a piece of something or another. Then he smoothes the whole thing over as if nothing has happened. He gets what he wants from you, and you end up grateful that you survived the experience. How open, honest, and real is that, huh?

"Anyway, I think our journey is *toward* genuineness, not *to* genuineness. We take down part of the wall, see how it feels, take another part down, see how that feels, put a little piece back up, see how that feels, take a chunk down, see how that feels, et cetera, et cetera. We do that for the rest of our lives. Hopefully, we get to a place where we're consciously aware of how we protect ourselves, and we choose to leave that protection down most of the time. That's what I think, anyway. In the real world, at least."

Steve nodded. "Yeah, that makes sense. I just keep bumping up against my impatience. My sponsor told me to add patience to the list of things I pray for every day. Cally told me to add humility. So now I'm praying for willingness, open-mindedness, patience, and humility."

"That sounds like a damn good prayer, Steve. Hell, man, maybe you're going to make it in sobriety. It wouldn't surprise me if you did."

Steve smiled. "Well, it might not surprise you, but it would surprise some people. You know what, though? Talking about it helps. When I stay in my own head, you know, thinking, without sharing my thoughts with anyone, I work myself into massive confusion and crappy feelings. When I talk to someone, though, I generally come to some kind of resolution or understanding. Even as abstruse as you can be sometimes, you're usually able to say things in ways that I can understand. And even though I wonder about your experience of spirituality on a daily basis, I respect your opinions and insights."

James scratched his head and looked at Steve curiously. "You wonder about my spirituality? How's that, Steve?"

"Well, yeah, I mean, you're so knowledgeable and articulate, but there's also things about the way you live your life that don't seem to fit. You know what I mean; we've talked about it before. You stay stoned all the time. You deal drugs. You isolate yourself. You're an admitted game player—a trickster, I think you called it. I mean, that's not honest, is it?

"Here, this may not be a good example, but it's recent. It just happened last week, when you and Tommy hung around here all afternoon drinking and smoking dope right in front of me. That was mean, James, or at least thoughtless. I felt put down. I felt as though you were mocking me, or mocking my sobriety. I don't know, I should have said something about it, I guess, but I didn't want to piss anybody off. Anyway, where was your spirituality then?"

James nodded. "Yeah, I guess that wasn't too cool. I thought about it later myself. I decided that it might be an example of what Cally told you to beware of—subtle forms of sabotage from people who profess to support your recovery.

"You know, Steve, my conscious mind says that I support you fully and unconditionally. Then I go and play a game like that, which was passive-aggressive at best, and it makes me aware of deeper, unconscious motivations at work. I've lost a smoking and drinking partner, and instead of my grief coming out as sadness, it came out as judgment, intolerance, and anger.

"When something like that happens, though, my responsibility to myself as a spiritual being is to look at it honestly—to recognize what I did, accept it as who I am at this point in time, and then use that understanding and insight to make myself better. You know? I mean, what more can I do? That's how I learn about myself. That's how I grow spiritually. Anyway, regardless of all that, I am sorry about that little deal, Steve.

"That other stuff is just me, man. I sell drugs, and I do it honestly. I tell people exactly what they can expect, and that's what I deliver. I sell the shit at a fair price, I'm never jealous of anyone else's profit, and I only sell stuff that I believe isn't dangerous. I've never sold a gram of speed or coke or smack in my life. I never will.

"And it's true, I do isolate. The reason, at least as I understand it, is simple. I just don't care that much for that many people. I don't know why I don't; I just don't. For me to hang around with a bunch of people would be phony as hell.

"Furthermore, man, I'm not trying to be perfect. As far as I know, there was only one perfect person, and that was Jesus. And I ain't him. If you expect yourself or me or Tommy or Cally or anyone else to be perfect, then I'm afraid you're setting yourself up for a major disappointment. I seem to remember a line in the Big Book about that. It's in that part, I think it's Chapter 5, that they read at the beginning of every meeting. It says something about our claiming spiritual progress rather that spiritual perfection. Does that ring a bell?"

"Yeah, it does," Steve said. He was quiet for a moment and then he added, "Thanks for the explanation and the apology, James. I appreciate both. Sometimes I get to thinking that things are supposed to be a certain way. I forget that there's more gray than there is black and white. Sometimes I hold people up to standards that aren't realistic. I do it to myself, too."

James left at 5:00 o'clock. Steve felt so good about his talk with James regarding his and Tommy's behavior the previous week that he decided to also bring it up with Tommy. He walked down the street to Tommy's house and knocked on the door. Tommy's truck was there, but there was no answer.

"I bet he's at the bar," Steve thought to himself. "If I go in there, I'll have to deal with Dixie, too."

Talking to Dixie was inevitable, but Steve wanted to do his homework assignment from Cally—exploring his feelings, values, and conscience regarding Kathy, Rachel, Dixie, and Carla— before he talked to any of them. He left a note on Tommy's front door and went home to work on the assignment. He wrote a full page on each and then a summary.

He started with Rachel. He loved Rachel as truly as he had ever loved anyone. Maybe more than anyone except his kids. He shared himself more openly with Rachel than with anyone else he had ever known. She was his true heart pal. His conscience with Rachel was clear. She knew what he knew. He did not feel the need to keep many secrets from her.

He didn't completely understand his love for Rachel, though. He knew that it was real and that it ran deep. He knew that he never wanted to lose her friendship. He also knew that his love for her lacked, and had always lacked, the intensity of his love, or infatuation, for Kathy. He wanted to continue a sexual relationship with her, too. He felt willing to abandon that, however, if it became inappropriate for either of them. The sex was great, but it wasn't the basis for his feelings or for the friendship. It was not what he valued most about their relationship.

Next, he looked at Kathy. He knew intellectually that the relationship was too young to honestly call his feelings for her "true love." But "infatuation" did not do justice to the intensity of his attraction to and feelings for her. With Kathy, Steve felt a sense of promise. He secretly fantasized that they would marry and spend the rest of their lives together, "happily ever after."

His conscience with Kathy was not clear. There were issues. One was Rachel. If he and Kathy were to have a meaningful relationship, she needed to know about Rachel. Another was his kids. Kathy had shown only minimal interest in them, and Steve feared that she might feel toward Lynn and Eddie the way he had felt toward Sammy when he and Rachel started their affair.

A third issue was Kathy's past. As much as he hated to admit it, her life as a prostitute mattered. It was not irrelevant to him, not if the relationship was going to be a long term, committed one. He needed to get honest about that, but he dreaded bringing it up. That feeling made him realize that he lacked trust in both himself and her.

Finally, Steve questioned how attracted to Kathy he would be if she were not so drop dead beautiful, and he still did not know her ethnicity.

Dixie and Carla were easier. Steve had never loved either, though his affection and respect for both was quite strong. He knew that he and Carla would remain friends regardless of what transpired between him and Kathy or him and Rachel. His "other relationships" seemed of little interest to Carla.

As he wrote about her, Steve was struck by his feeling of trust for her. She seemed to have no expectations of him. Perhaps because of that, he felt free to be just himself with her. He knew also that Carla was a transient in his life. She was young and free. She would move on and forget that he ever existed. With Carla, then, Steve's conscience was perfectly clear. He loved her as a friend and occasional sex partner, but he felt no romantic love for her.

Dixie held a special place in Steve's heart. Maybe his feelings for her came closer to love than his feelings for Carla, but they were a far cry from the love he felt for Kathy or Rachel. Dixie was a good friend and a good sex partner. That is what she had been from the start. The only time he had felt as though it might be more than that was on the morning of January 1st, after they had spent New Year's Eve together. Even then, though, he had not mistaken his feelings for romantic love.

Steve hated to admit it, but Dixie's age mattered. She would turn 40 while he was 29.

Steve's conscience was clear with Dixie, except for his recent abandonment of her in favor of Kathy. Steve had never misled Dixie, nor had she him. Neither had made any promises, even implied ones. He hoped that they could remain friends, but friends or not, he figured that their sexual relationship was over unless things failed to work out between him and Kathy.

Steve summarized his work: "Carla: She's my younger, uninhibited, fun friend and lover; she's my role model for openness and free spiritedness. In terms of enduring significance, she is neither the past, the present, nor the future. No work required here.

"Dixie: She's a good friend, a comfortable, non-threatening, reliable friend. She's the older woman and experienced lover; she's my role model for mature, straightforward honesty. In terms of enduring significance, she is the past, and a very sweet part of the past. A little work needed here—perhaps just an honest talk.

"Rachel: She's a true friend, my best and most trusted friend; she's a soul mate and friend for life. She's comfortable and familiar, but at the same time, exciting. She's my teacher. We accept each other for ourselves. She's my lover, and I love her, but I am not in love with her. In terms of enduring significance, she is the past and the present; I'm not sure about the future. No work required here, at least not anytime soon.

"Kathy: She's my new friend, my beautiful friend, and potentially my best friend. She's exhilarating, but not yet comfortable. She's my new lover, and I am in love with her. We have lots of ground left to cover, and there are a lot of unknowns. In terms of enduring significance, she is the present, and quite possibly the future. Lots of work needed here—at least several honest, potentially serious talks. Yikes!"

Kathy called when she got home from work at 7:00 o'clock. Somewhat to Steve's relief, she sounded friendly and upbeat. "What'cha doing?" she asked.

"I'm sitting at the table, eating a baked potato, and thinking about you. How about you?"

"About the same. You've been on my mind just about all day. I'm really sorry about yesterday. How are you feeling about it now?"

"I'm fine. It wasn't you, anyway. It was just my own insecurity and stupid, compulsive thinking. As usual, I might add. I'm sorry I judged you. You didn't deserve that."

"Well, thank you. It's forgotten. Can you meet me at South Austin tonight?"

"Oh, I don't know. Hey, guess what? Ralph asked me to chair the noon meeting today, and I did it. My topic was prayer and God. I was nervous, but it went okay; in fact, it went good. After the meeting, Ralph said that I could use his understanding of God until I come up with one of my own. Generous guy, huh?"

"Man, that's great, Steve. Two weeks sober, and already chairing a meeting. I would have been scared to death."

349

"Yeah, well, there were only four of us there, and all familiar faces. Anyway, how about if I pick you up after the meeting and we get some coffee or something? I've got a couple of things I need to take care of tonight, including homework for Cally."

"That sounds fine. I'll see you at nine."

After he hung up, Steve cleaned up and walked across the street to The Roam In. On the way, he prayed for willingness, open-mindedness, patience, and humility.

CHAPTER 61

Steve walked into a nearly empty Roam In and found Dixie sitting with Tommy at a table near the bar. Tommy had a pitcher in front of him, as usual, and Dixie was drinking a cup of beer, which was not usual, at least during working hours. They both smiled and greeted him, but something about their smiles and friendly greetings did not feel right. Steve felt his radar go up.

"Well, I'll be darned. There's my old used-to-be best customer, Steve," Dixie said. "Could I interest you in something cold to drink?"

"Yeah, thanks, Dixie; I'd love a glass of tonic water," he said. She got up to get it from the bar, and Steve sat down. "Can I join you?" he asked Tommy.

"Hell, yes, man. What do you think? Of course you can join us. Park your butt right there."

They looked at each other for a moment, and then Tommy said, "You know what, buddy? It's funny that you should walk through the door right now. Dixie and I were just talking about you. We were wondering how you were doing in your new life as a respectable, law-abiding citizen, and as a sober man. I'm assuming you're still a sober man."

"Yeah, that I am, Tommy, almost two weeks now. That's no big deal, I guess, but there sure is a lot happening in my life. How have you been, man?"

"I've been great. Never better. It's good to be back in school, too. Have you started your classes yet?"

"Uh huh. Had my first one this morning—the social psych vestibule class. I have learning psych tomorrow afternoon and statistics on Thursday. I think you were right all along, Tommy. I don't think I'll have any trouble with these classes, and I don't think I'm any dumber than anyone else is. It was just my insecurity getting the best of me. I feel pretty good about it now."

"That's good, Steve. Yeah, man, that's great. I'm glad to hear it." Tommy looked at Steve and nodded and smiled. "Yeah, I was afraid that you were going to bail out on me for a while there. I'm glad you didn't."

"Yeah, me too," Steve said.

Watching Tommy's body language, Steve realized that Tommy felt as uncomfortable as he, himself, did. Steve thought to himself, "How could two old friends sitting together in their old, familiar hangout feel uncomfortable with each other when the only difference is that I'm not drinking alcohol?"

Dixie returned to the table with Steve's tonic water. She sat down and smiled at Steve and then at Tommy. "We miss you around here," she said. "Just about everyone has asked about you. Even old Brenda, the dyke cop. The other night, she was sitting at her regular spot, and all of a sudden she looked around the room and blurted out, 'Hey, Dixie, where the hell is Steve?' I bet you didn't know you had such a following."

Steve half-smiled. "It's different, not coming over here every night. Honestly, I haven't really missed the bar as much as I thought I would, but now that I'm sitting here with you guys, it sure feels familiar. This place has been like a second home to me, you know? Lots of good memories here. Anyway, I need to talk to both of you guys—separately, if possible. When do you think would be a good time to do that?" He looked at one and then the other of them.

"Anytime for me," Dixie said. "I'm pretty easy to find. The truth is, though, Steve, we need to talk to you, too. Tommy and I have something we want to run by you. We need to do ours together, though."

"Oh, yeah?" Steve said, curiously. He looked at Tommy, who glanced up from his beer and raised his eyebrows, and then back at Dixie, who held his gaze.

"Well...okay. Why don't you go ahead and do it now? I can do my thing with each of you later," he said.

Dixie started. "I'm sure this will come as somewhat of a surprise, Steve, but Tommy and I are talking about seeing what it would be like to spend some time together. Before we do that, though, we want to make sure that you don't have a problem with it."

More than somewhat surprised, Steve felt startled. "You mean, you two are going to start dating each other?"

Tommy smiled, and Dixie answered. "Well, I guess you could call it dating, although that sounds like something younger people would do. I'd call it something like checking out the limits of our friendship."

Steve shook his head as if to clear it of confusion. "Well, I've got to tell you that 'somewhat of a surprise' does not do justice to this little piece of news. I'm *thoroughly* surprised. Shocked might be a better word. I mean, you could knock me over with a feather if you had a mind to. When did this come about? I mean, it's not that I have a problem with it, but, well, to tell you the truth, I can hardly believe it."

Tommy spoke up. "I thought that might catch you a little off guard. It makes sense in a way, though, Steve. I mean, think about it. Dixie and I are peers, you know. We're close to the same age. We have similar backgrounds and similar interests—a few, anyway. We've known each other for a long time—several years, in fact, and we've always liked each other. Plus, Steve...." He hesitated, looked down into his beer cup, and then continued. "Plus, I think we're both kind of grieving the loss of you in our lives, and that's created a bond between us that didn't use to be there."

"What do you mean, Tommy? Did I miss something here? Did I move away or die or something while I wasn't watching?"

Tommy glanced at Dixie and then back to Steve. He took a deep breath and exhaled. "I don't know, Steve, in a way I think perhaps you did. I mean, the Steve that Dixie and I have known for the past year or so is no longer here. But don't misunderstand me, Steve. I'm not saying that in a critical way, and I'm not implying that it's a bad thing. In fact, I know in my heart that it's a very good thing.

"Either way, though, it's a reality. I could feel it happening as soon as you started this new journey into the land of the sober people. Actually, I could feel it even before you started it. And that's the way it ought to be, man. If it was any different, then it wouldn't be real, you know? You get sober, your sobriety means something to you, and you change to accommodate it.

"Anyway, since you started this trip, I've been reading up on it, and I've talked to a couple of people about it. I know it wouldn't work for you to hang out in a bar every day or spend a lot of time with a stoner like me. Hell, I still want you to get high with me, man. I'm sorry, but I do. I'm not blind to the discrepancy between what I say about supporting you and my behavior around you.

"The truth is, man, I've felt a little resentful, and a lot abandoned. That's not about you, of course. It's my issue. I know that. I also know we'll continue to be friends, Steve. I love you like a brother, man. That won't change. But I also know that the nature of our friendship will change. It has to. You know that, and I know that."

Steve nodded slowly. "Yeah, I suppose you're right," he said softly. "I feel sad about it, though." He looked at Dixie. His eyes teared up slightly. "Is this how you feel, too, Dixie?"

She was quiet for a moment and then said, "I'm not sure how I feel about that part of it, Steve. I guess I have faith that our friendship—yours and mine—will continue to evolve into something that's comfortable and right for both of us. I think we've been in that process for some time now, and I think it started before you got sober.

"I've known for quite a while that I need to let go of you, at least in the sense that there's no romantic future for you and me. Really and truly, I guess I've known that almost from the beginning. But surely that doesn't mean that we can't be friends, even good friends. Like Tommy said, I love you. I really do. I love you dearly. You're one of the sweetest men I've ever known. I mean that. There have been times that I've felt as though I loved you more than you loved yourself. I may be wrong about that. It's just a feeling I've had from time to time.

"Anyway, this thing between Tommy and me is uncertain at best. I mean, who knows where it will go? At least for the time being, though, it seems to be falling into place in an interesting and comfortable way. Like he said, we have some things in common that give us a natural dialogue. We're a couple of old hippie underachievers moving though a culture that we don't quite fit into. Our paths aren't the same, but they're both different enough from the mainstream to throw us into the same boiling pot.

"It's rather ironic, though, Steve. You're the one who brought us closer together. We've known each other a long time, but it was our mutual relationship with you—our love for you and our concern about you—that sparked a more meaningful connection between us. Tommy thinks of you as his best friend. You've been my best friend, too, and my only lover for the entire past year. And here we are asking you for your blessing."

"Well, what can I say?" Steve said quietly. "I care a lot about you both. I love you both. Hell, you two have been my closest friends since I've been here in Austin, even more so than James. You and James and Carla, and to a lesser extent, Tucker, are like my Austin family. Last Thanksgiving, when we were all together at Carla's, is one of the best holiday memories that I have from my whole life.

"And talk about irony; it was your damn confrontations that started this alcohol and drug recovery ball rolling in the first place. Especially yours, Dixie. The stuff you said to me in my shop that day really hit me hard. I mean, you were so right on target. That's why it hurt so much. I think the weekend at my dad's ranch, when everything blew up in my face, was just the icing on the cake. It was the nudge over the edge of the cliff. But you guys had already planted the seeds; you're the ones who dragged me to the cliff's edge. Now I'm sober, and you're drinking beer together and talking about your future.

"I don't know, guys, I guess I'll just say 'Good luck,' you know? I don't know what else to say. I mean, I feel happy for you. But I feel sad, too. Everything is changing so damn fast. I feel like I'm on some runaway train, and I don't have the option of jumping off. And even though I'm sure that it's the right thing for me, I'm afraid that it's not all positive like I thought at first. What I mean is, it's costly, too.

"It's not that I want to turn around and go back. I don't. But I'm damn apprehensive about too much change too fast. This right here is a good example of what I'm talking about. I don't want to lose either of you guys. I know it has to be different between us. I can accept that, and it's really okay. But I don't want you guys to disappear. That would be too much too soon."

Dixie touched Steve's arm. "Hey, Steve, we're not going anywhere. You've got my word on that."

Steve nodded and smiled. "Yeah, I know. I know you're not. But thanks for the reminder just the same."

Tommy pushed his chair back. "I think I'll mosey on down to the house for a little while and let you two talk. I'll be around, Steve, if you want to talk to me some more. Just give me a holler."

"Okay, Tommy. Thanks. Listen, you'll find a note on your door from me. Just throw it away. I'll come by in a little while."

When Tommy was gone, Steve looked at Dixie and said, "You and Tommy, huh? I never would have guessed that in a million years."

Dixie looked away for a moment and smiled weakly. "Well, stranger things have happened. How about you and me? Whoever would have put us under the same set of sheets?"

Steve laughed. "I guess you're right. Anyway, Dixie, I need to talk to you about something else. It doesn't seem like quite as big a deal as it did an hour ago, but I still need to do it."

"Is it about your new girlfriend?" She asked.

Steve nodded. "So you already know about her," he said.

"It's a small neighborhood, Steve. Everyone knows about her. I think Tommy and I are the only ones who haven't seen her. I hear she's very beautiful."

"Yeah, well, I'm sorry that you had to hear about her through the grapevine. That was inconsiderate and unfair of me. I should have been the one to tell you."

"Well, Steve, don't worry about it too much. I felt hurt at first, but when I thought about it, it made sense. Maybe I could meet her sometime."

"Yeah, sure, I'd like for you to. I think you'll like her. She's honest and up front, like you. She has very little bullshit about her. I met her at my treatment center. She's been sober for about six or seven months. She's had a pretty interesting life."

Dixie hesitated for a moment and then said, "It doesn't really matter, I guess, but I suppose that this was already in the mill when you and I were together last week."

"It kind of was. The beginning of it, anyway. How about you and Tommy? Was that in the mill last week when we were together?"

354

"No. When I left your house Tuesday, I knew that a major shift had occurred in our relationship. You had put me on notice the night before, but after Tuesday I knew it was real. I talked to Tommy a little bit about it the next night. I think we got to commiserating about missing you. That might be when we started looking at each other in a different light. How weird is that?"

Steve smiled. He reached over and placed his hand on top of hers. "Dixie, I want you to know how much you've meant to me over the past year, and how much you still mean to me. I meant it when I said that I love you. You're not like any friend I've ever had. I don't know, maybe it's your...maturity, and I mean that in a positive way. I probably trust you more than any woman I've ever been with, maybe even more than my friend Rachel in San Antonio.

"Also, I'm going to miss our sleeping together. You're a good lover. Actually, you're a fantastic lover. And I'm talking about more than just the sex. I always felt comfortable with you. That hasn't always been the case for me, if you know what I mean."

"Thank you, Steve. I feel very much the same way about you. You're a good guy. I have no regrets, none whatsoever."

Steve left The Roam In and walked down to Tommy's. They talked for a little while, and before long, the conversation became relaxed and friendly. Tommy was pretty high, but he refrained from drinking and smoking while Steve was there. He promised to work on his prejudice against Steve's sobriety, and Steve promised to let Tommy know when his prejudice showed.

They talked about Dixie and about Kathy. Tommy acknowledged his fear of being in a relationship, even with someone as non-threatening as Dixie.

"I'm probably crazy to go back on my word to myself," he said, "but do you know what? I think I've always wanted to get closer to old Dixie. I respect her. She ain't no silly bitch who wants something from you. She looks you right in the eye when she talks to you, and I know she's not trying to manipulate me. With Dixie, I think that old saying is true: 'What you see is what you get.' I like that."

Tommy was quiet for a moment and then said, "You know, Steve, I think Dixie would still rather be with you than with me, but maybe over time that will change. And you know, if I'm anything, I'm patient."

Like Dixie, Tommy wanted to meet Kathy. He had heard from both Carla and Mario that she was a knockout. "Yeah, she's beautiful," Steve said. "But that's not even the best thing about her. She's honest, like Dixie. She's as real as the day is long. She's had a tough damn life, and she's never had much help.

"I think she's the genuine article, man. And I think I love her. In fact, I think I love her more than I've ever loved anyone. I know I might be extremely premature making a statement like that, but that's the way I feel today."

The conversation played out just about the time that Steve needed to leave to meet Kathy. When he left Tommy's house, he felt relieved, and he felt a sad. He had turned another corner in his recovery, with friendships retained but redefined.

CHAPTER 62

Steve stepped inside of the South Austin AA group just in time to stand in the circle and say The Lord's Prayer with about 40 other high bottom drunks. He caught Kathy's eye midway through the prayer. Her quick, friendly smile warmed him from head to toe. They made it to the coffee shop about 9:30.

"How's your sponsor been treating you?" Steve asked.

"She's okay. I think once she said her piece and saw that we listened, she let up. She's not stupid. What does your sponsor say about us?"

"Well, he's rather philosophical about it. He says that we'll just see how it goes. If it goes nicely, as planned, then he'll share in my joy and good fortune. If it falls apart, we'll work together to repair the damage.

"You know, I think I got lucky when I got Ralph for a sponsor. He's very different from Cally. He's easy going, and his spiritual program is one that I understand and relate to. I think he'll be there for me, but he won't bug me to death or try to run my life. Cally wanted me to find someone who would watch me like a hawk and question my every move. I think I'll just let Cally continue in that role and let Ralph be my friend and advisor. One Nazi is enough for me."

Steve hesitated for a moment and then continued. "Kathy, there's something else I need to talk to you about. Do you feel up to a serious conversation?"

"I guess so, as long as it isn't something terrible that will break my heart or something so complicated that it takes all night."

"No, I don't think it's either of those. In my writing today, a couple of things came up that I feel as though I need to get out into the open. One is about my kids—Lynn and Eddie."

Steve told Kathy about his fear that his having children would eventually encourage Kathy to back away from the relationship, particularly in light of her seeming lack of interest in them. He told her about his reaction to Rachel's son, how he thought that Sammy's presence in Rachel's life had been a roadblock for him. He made it clear that the kids were an important, permanent part of his life, and that even though they were moving out of state, he would be no less connected to them.

"I've never been around kids, Steve," Kathy said thoughtfully. "I don't know how I feel about them. I didn't have any younger siblings, and I've never really had any friends with children. I've never even babysat. I don't know, maybe they just scare me. I'm not sure how to be around them. I don't know what they do or what they like or how they feel.

"You know, part of the problem is that I was never much of a child myself. I don't remember childhood things. I lost my childhood because of the family I was born into. I spent my so-called childhood just trying to survive without pissing anybody off."

Steve nodded. "I understand what you're saying. It's kind of sad, though. Kids are great. They're pure, you know? They're honest. They haven't picked up all the bullshit that they'll eventually find and use to protect themselves. I lost a lot of my childhood, too, but I did get to be a kid for a few years before my parents remarried and moved us away from my grandparents' house.

"God, what a shock that was. One day I was a kid, and the next I was slammed into adulthood. When I lived with my grandparents, they took care of me. All I had to do all day was play. From morning till night, I just played. All of my needs were taken care of, almost like magic.

"We lived in a very small South Texas town, and by the time I was four or five years old, I could pretty much come and go as I pleased. I had relatives all around me. I had another grandmother, two sets of great grandparents, aunts and uncles, cousins. Hell, I'd cruise all over the neighborhood on my tricycle, dropping in on people, getting snacks, playing with my cousins. Man, it was so great. Anyway, I didn't mean to get off onto memory lane."

Kathy smiled. "That sounds like a wonderful way to be a kid. I'm sorry you lost it." She reflected silently for a moment and then said, "Steve, please don't misunderstand me. I'm very willing to check it out. Actually, I've thought about your kids quite a bit. I've wondered when I would meet them. I'm just a little nervous about it; that's all. I've heard that kids don't take too kindly to 'the other woman.' Even so, maybe I could meet them before they move, and we can see how it feels."

Steve nodded. "Yeah, I'd like that. Listen, why don't you come with me next weekend when I go to San Antonio to see them? It might be your last chance for a long time. We could do something special, like maybe we could go camping. They really enjoy that. It would be fun for all of us."

Kathy thought about it for a moment. "Okay; I better warn you, though. You might be asking to see me at my worst. Not only have I never been around kids, but I've never been camping, either. A double virgin—that's what you'll have on your hands with me."

Steve laughed. "A double virgin, huh? Well, that makes us even, because I've never been with one of those. It sounds like something to handle with great care and patience. We'll have fun. I'm sure of it."

"So what else do you have on your agenda for us to talk about?" she asked.

Steve took a breath. He almost stopped there but then decided to continue. "Well, a little while ago, I mentioned my last girlfriend, Rachel. Since it appears as though you and I are setting our sights on a real relationship instead of a brief fling, I feel as though I need to tell you about her.

"She and I pretty much lived together for several months before I moved to Austin last year, and we've stayed friends since then. We see each other every once in a while, and we talk on the phone occasionally. She still lives in San Antonio. She's also sober—almost a year now. She helped me a lot when I was thinking about getting sober myself. Anyway, the reason I need to tell you about her is that I want to be able to continue being friends with her, and I want to do that out in the open, you know?"

Kathy was quiet. She started to say something, but then she stopped. Finally, she said, "Just out of curiosity, Steve, did you see her this weekend?"

Butterflies filled Steve's gut, and he blushed slightly. "Yeah, I did," he said. "She took me to an AA meeting Saturday night."

Kathy looked down into her coffee cup. "Did you sleep with her?" she asked.

A jumble of thoughts exploded in Steve's mind. He remembered his sponsor telling him not to confess anything, not to create hurt for anyone. He also recalled the importance of rigorous honestly. He thought about trustworthiness, faithfulness, and self-centeredness. He caught an image of himself and Rachel sitting on the couch together at 5:00 AM Sunday morning. Then he took his best guess about what to do, and he answered honestly. "Yes," he said.

Anger flashed in Kathy's eyes. The ferocity and intensity of it shocked Steve. "I see," she said sharply. "On Friday night, you told me that you love me. Twenty-four hours later, you slept with another woman—an old girlfriend that you want to continue seeing while you and I develop a 'real relationship.' That's goddamn tough to swallow, Steve.

"No wonder you judged me and suspected me of sleeping with other men. It makes sense now. You were projecting your own bullshit values onto me. And of all the stupid things, I actually felt guilty. I did nothing, and I felt guilty. I bet I felt

worse than you did. God, I feel stupid. Stupid, stupid, stupid!"
She shook her head and stared out the window of the coffee shop
into the darkness.

Steve's initial shock at Kathy's angry reaction sank in and
turned into fear and shame. He felt like a very bad child. He
wanted desperately to run and hide and cry. His heart rate
soared, and he blushed brightly.

When he spoke, his voice cracked. "Kathy, I'm sorry. I'm
very sorry. I didn't think I was doing anything wrong until the
next morning, and then I felt terrible. I mean, we hadn't talked
about not seeing other people or anything, and it just kind of
happened. It's not like I planned it or anything. She and I hadn't
slept together since last Christmas. I didn't mean to hurt you. I
promise, I didn't. I swear I didn't."

Kathy turned her head and looked at him. Her jaw was set;
her eyes were narrow. She spoke through her teeth. "Well,
believe me, Steve; you did. I feel like such a fool. I feel
humiliated. I think the best thing that we can do right now is not
talk about it. When I get this angry, I'm prone to say things that I
later regret. Just take me back to my car. Maybe we can talk
about it later."

"All right," Steve said meekly. As they walked to Steve's
truck, his mind raced. "God, I can't believe I'm such a goddamn
fuck up," he told himself. "When will I ever learn to keep my
goddamn, stupid, fucking mouth shut?"

They rode in silence to Kathy's car. Steve glanced toward
her several times, but she never looked in his direction.
Gradually, his thoughts calmed and became more rational. "This
is her stuff," he told himself. "This isn't really about me. I didn't
do anything to her."

He drove slowly and waited, hoping that she would calm
down before they got to her car. When they pulled into the South
Austin AA Group parking lot, he turned off the motor and looked
at Kathy. Her face had softened.

"This isn't right, Kathy," he said gently. "We shouldn't be
leaving this thing hanging like this. I mean, as much as I hate
anger and arguing, as much as it scares me, I would rather you
go ahead and let me have it so that maybe we could talk this
thing out. I really don't want you to leave yet."

"I know," she said softly. "This isn't about anger anyway,
Steve. It's about trust. I've been reminding myself that the
intensity of my anger is a reflection of the intensity of my fear.
More than anything in the world, I fear being used and being
made a fool of. Maybe I was the one who was projecting. Since I
felt committed to you, I assumed that you felt the same way.
Apparently, you didn't."

"I do now, though, Kathy. Any doubts that I had about that
disappeared after we talked Sunday night at your apartment,

when you told me that you only wanted to be with me and that you would be true to me. If we had had that conversation Friday night instead of Sunday night, then I would not have done what I did. I'm sure of that. And if it makes any difference, I promise you that it won't happen again."

Kathy nodded, but she looked down at her hands instead of at Steve. "How many times did you cheat on your wife, Steve?"

"That's different, Kathy," he said strongly. "It's completely different. In the first place, I didn't love my wife. I resented her. I never intended, nor did I promise, to be faithful to her. In the second place, I stayed drunk and stoned the whole time we were together. I'm not the same man today that I was when I was with her, and besides that, you're not her."

Kathy closed her eyes and said, "I don't know, Steve. I'm sure I'll be okay, but for right now, I really want to go home and go to bed and not think about it. I'll call you tomorrow." She glanced quickly at Steve and then got out of his truck and into her car.

Steve did not move. Kathy started her car and pulled forward to the exit. When she got there, she stopped. After sitting at the exit for a few moments, she put her car in reverse and backed up to Steve's truck. She got out of her car and walked up to his window. She leaned in and kissed him lightly on the lips.

"Thank you for telling me the truth, Steve," she said. "I know you didn't have to do that. I appreciate your honesty."

"Wait a minute," Steve said. He got out of Cleo and put his arms around her. He gently pulled her close to him. "I really am sorry, Kathy. I adore you. I want us to have an honest and trusting relationship. I give you my word that I will do everything within my power to make that happen, including being faithful to you. You can count on that."

Kathy nodded slowly. "Thank you," she said. "I'm sorry that I over reacted. I love you so much, Steve. I want this relationship to work, but I don't know how to do relationships any better than I know how to do kids. I don't know the rules. All I know is that I have these incredible feelings for you, and I'm afraid that you'll get tired of me and leave."

Steve stepped back and leaned against the door of the truck. Kathy relaxed into his arms. He breathed deeply into her hair. "I'm not going to leave, Kathy," he whispered. "I promise you that from the bottom of my heart."

Kathy slipped her arms around his waist and hugged him tight. "Okay," she said.

"You forgive me, then?" he asked.

Kathy nodded. "Yes, I do. But please, Steve, please don't make a fool out of me."

CHAPTER 63

"God, what an emotional roller coaster," Steve said to himself as he lay in bed. He revisited the conversation at the coffee shop and recalled Kathy's vicious look. "That, my boy, was the look that could kill," he said out loud. "And then, right on the heels of the look that could kill, she says 'I love you' for the first time. I hope to God you haven't bitten off more than you can chew because that, my friend, is one hot-blooded goddamn woman."

Steve got up very early on Tuesday. According to plan, he split the morning evenly between work and study. As soon as he arrived at his noon AA meeting, he cornered Ralph.

"I think I need to talk," he said. "I probably should have called you last night, but it was so late that I decided to give you a break."

When their afternoon schedules did not mesh well, Ralph invited Steve to come to his home for dinner.

Steve's afternoon learning psychology class promised to be more challenging than social psych, but manageable. No tests, but quite a bit of reading plus two papers—a literature review and an original, creative effort on some aspect of learning theory.

The instructor was another young woman—very bright, articulate, enthusiastic, and confident, but ugly as a troll and dressed for a Halloween party. When Steve walked into class he found Sheri sitting in the front row. He joined her, and they talked during the breaks and for a little while after class.

Sheri asked about Kathy. Her inquiry was cordial, but she said it in such a way that Steve thought she was feeling him out regarding the exact nature of the relationship.

"Yeah, she's great," he said. "We haven't been together very long, but we feel very drawn to each other. I guess if we were in high school, I'd say we were going steady. Since we're in grad school, though, I'll call it a committed relationship. I *can* have friends, however, and I hope you and I will explore that option."

Ralph lived in South Austin, not far from Kathy's. On his way there, Steve swung by Kathy's apartment and left a note on her door that read, "Hi, ya, Kath. I'm at my sponsor's house loading up on free dinner plus all the advice I can handle (and man, can I use it). I'll see you later at S.A. Group, or after. Your ever lovin—Stevey."

Ralph and his family were delightful hosts. Ralph's wife, Marilyn, was very gracious, and his two teenage daughters were friendly. The older one, a seventeen-year-old high school senior, was quiet, a little chubby, and plain. The fourteen-year-old, a freshman, was just the opposite—outgoing, spontaneous, funny, and cute.

During dinner, the funny one asked Steve if he was a hippie.

"Well, I try to be, but sometimes it doesn't work," he said.

She tilted her head to one side and said, "What the heck does that mean?"

After dinner, Ralph and Steve went outside on the back patio. "So let me guess," Ralph said. "Relationship problems, right?"

Steve laughed. "Of course. What else would have me needing to call you at midnight? I did exactly what you told me not to. I told Kathy that I slept with Rachel. That gets me ahead of myself, though. I wanted to tell you the whole story."

Steve told Ralph about seeing Kathy late Sunday night and about the dead phone. Ralph laughed about that and asked, "Tell me something, Steve. Did you pick up and check out the receiver and the wall plug while she wasn't watching, just to verify her story?"

Steve smiled and answered, "No, but I thought about it. In fact, I probably would have if I could have been absolutely certain that I could have gotten away with it. Damn, man, how do you already know me so well?"

He related the meeting with Cally and Cally's charge that Steve was using women and sex as a distraction from recovery. He detailed Cally's description of him as "slick' and his challenge to Steve to move beyond looking and sounding real to actually being real.

"Do I come across that way to you, Ralph?" Steve asked.

"No, not to that extent," he said. "On the other hand, I think that just about everyone who has had a less than perfect life and less than perfect role models can be rather slippery from time to time. You know, we learn how to protect ourselves. We learn what works for us, and we practice that until we get good at it.

"Personally, I would rather be slick than violent or stupid or silly. I also think that if you take a room full of people chosen at random off of the street, you might find that the alcoholics in the group are generally the best defended—that is, the slickest.

"No, to tell you the truth, Steve, I perceive you as quite genuine in your early sobriety. I don't feel as though you've tried to bullshit me at all. Like everyone else, you have a lot to learn—about recovery, about yourself, about genuineness, about everything. So do I. So does your wise friend, Cally.

"That's what recovery is. At least that's the way I see it. The definition of recovery that I got in treatment is that recovery is a lifelong process of positive growth and change in all areas of one's life. That includes the physical, mental, emotional, and spiritual parts. Hell, what if you got it all the first two weeks? What then?"

362

Ralph smiled. "Actually, I would be surprised if your Mr. Cally Callahan didn't use that same speech with a lot of his clients, and maybe all of them. I wouldn't take it too personally if I were you. I'd certainly listen to it, but I wouldn't let it get me down.

"Now the part about using women and sex as distractions from the business at hand, he might have hit on something there. After all, you didn't go to bed last night or come over here this evening in a crisis over your relationship with God. And what was the focus of our conversation Sunday night? It wasn't powerlessness, unmanageability, or the God of your understanding. It was women and sex."

Steve nodded. "Yeah, that's right. But do you see that as a major problem?"

"Well, I wouldn't say that, but I think it's a flag. It's a flag that we should pay attention to. We want to see you broaden and deepen your recovery. How far can we go with that while your mental, emotional, and spiritual energies are fully invested in your relationships with women and their bodies?"

"Yeah, I know," Steve said. "But listen, let me tell you the rest of the story and then see what you think."

He described his written work around Kathy, Rachel, Dixie, and Carla and his subsequent conversation with Dixie and Tommy. Then he related in detail the encounter with Kathy, including her specific question to Steve about whether or not he had slept with Rachel, as well as her instant, angry, quick-tempered reaction to his answer and her soft forgiveness and confession of love, less than thirty minutes later.

When Steve finished, Ralph raised his eyebrows and smiled. "Well, if nothing else, it makes for a damn good story. But let's make sure I get the gist of it. What you're telling me is that except for your discomfort with Kathy's explosiveness and unpredictability, you feel as though you're close to solving the puzzle of your involvement with these four women.

"Your neighbor is not a problem because she'll be cool with whatever you want, including a non-sexual friendship. The bartender is going off in a different direction entirely, and therefore, you're off the hook with her. Your friend in San Antonio is a little more uncertain. In fact, you're a little ambivalent about your relationship with her, but at least for the time being, you're willing to put her on hold while you explore your feelings for Kathy. And you're hot as a firecracker for Kathy, but she scares you to death. How did I do?"

"You hit the nail on the head, as usual. The deal with Rachel is okay. I mean, we went eight months without having sex with each other. I'm sure that she would be fine with a non-sexual friendship. And although it's not at all what I want, I think she'd even be okay with not seeing me for a while if that was necessary. After what happened last night, my guess is that the only way I could see Rachel would be on the sly. I doubt seriously if Kathy is all that open to me seeing her now that she knows we spent the night together. God, the way she reacted last night, I'd almost be afraid to even bring it up."

Ralph smiled. "Which of Kathy's reactions scares you the most? Is it the first one, or is it the last one? The anger or the intimacy?"

Steve cocked his head curiously. "The first, obviously. Why do you ask?"

"Well, Steve, think about it for a moment."

Feeling caught off guard, Steve thought hard before answering. "I know that intimacy—true intimacy, anyway—is difficult for me. That's no secret. What scared me last night, though, was the anger, especially the sharpness and intensity of the anger. I hate it. I really do; I hate it. Maybe it reminds me too much of my family and the way I grew up. I never knew what to expect then, and I'm not anxious to have to deal with that again, at least not if I don't have to."

Ralph was silent for a moment, and then he said, "Steve, I want to try something with you. Call it a pop quiz, except that there are no right or wrong answers. I want you to close your eyes and relax for a moment."

He waited until Steve looked relaxed. "Okay, now, in your mind, picture this scenario: You're Steve Campbell, a recovering alcoholic/addict who has worked his program diligently and gained full benefit from the effort. Hold that image in your mind for a moment. Now, because of your honest effort and your progress, you are open, honest, and genuine. You play no games and carry no bullshit. You're just open, honest, and genuine. Okay?

"Now, with those qualities present in your life, how do you handle the following situations? First, what do you do about Rachel?"

Steve pictured Rachel in his mind, sitting cross-legged on her couch, wearing khaki shorts and a white T-shirt, smiling her beautiful, shy smile. "Well, I tell her the truth about my feelings for Kathy. I tell her that I've promised to be faithful to Kathy and that I intend to keep that promise. I ask her to be my friend within that context. I tell her that I love her. Then I really do keep my promise."

"Okay, now what do you say to Kathy about Rachel?"

Steve imagined himself sitting at his dining room table with Kathy. She's wearing the same faded purple T-shirt that she wore the night of their first date, and she looks lovely. "I say, 'Kathy, Rachel is my friend. As my friend, I love her. It's not the romantic love that I feel for you. I intend to continue my friendship with Rachel. It will remain an intimate friendship, one that includes affection, trust, and respect. It will not, however, include sexual intimacy of any kind.'"

"Okay, now what do you say to Kathy about her anger?"

Steve flashed once again on Kathy's angry eyes and volatile nature. "This is tougher, but I say, 'Kathy, your anger frightens me. I know your anger is part of who you are right now. Therefore, I need to accept it without judging you for it. Furthermore, I know that my fear is my issue, not yours. Please be patient with me while I work through my stuff; I'll do the same with you.'"

Ralph told Steve to open his eyes, and he waited for him to focus. "Steve, that all sounded good to me. It sounded honest, simple, and clear. But listen, I didn't ask you to do this as a rehearsal for your next conversations with Rachel and Kathy, but rather as a way for you to become clearer in your own mind about what you think and feel on a little deeper level.

"I should also tell you that I agree with everything you said. I think it would be an unfair compromise for you to abandon your friendship with Rachel because of Kathy's insecurity, or whatever it is that triggers her anger. However, I do think that keeping your promise—the one about fidelity—is important. In fact, I think it's pertinent to your recovery process. We make promises and we keep them. We're honest. We stand accountable. And that's not a burden. It's a gift—a gift to us, the ones who make the promises.

"Beyond that, you need to understand that Kathy is human. She's not perfect. Like the rest of us, she has her issues. She has character defects—shortcomings—just like you and me. You'll never have an honest, open, genuine relationship with her if you try to keep her up on a pedestal. She's beautiful, smart, interesting, fun, and good in bed, but she's also got baggage. In fact, she might have a lot more baggage than you imagine.

"Kathy's recovery is a lifelong process just like everyone else's. I don't think you ought to ask her to hide who she is. If you know you can't handle her personality, including her anger and her unpredictability, then give her, and yourself, a break, and move on. If you ask her to be perfect, then she will just improve her ability to hide who she really is from you. Then what do you have? Just another dishonest relationship.

"By the way, under the circumstances, I believe you did the right thing by telling Kathy the truth about sleeping with Rachel. She asked you a direct question. You either had to lie, tell the truth, or refuse to say. Considering who she is, that last option might have cost you your life, and I think it's always wrong to tell outright lies, even if our conscious motivation is to spare someone pain.

"Anyway, I've given you more advice than I like to give, especially since I'm not even certain that it's good advice. It's just

365

what I think. Take it or leave it. There will be no hard feelings on my part either way."

Steve nodded. "Okay, Ralph, I think I'll take it. At this point, your take on things has got to be better than mine."

Steve left Ralph's in time to see Kathy after her meeting. They sat on the steps outside of the South Austin Group house and talked. "So how did it go with your sponsor?" she asked him.

"It went really good, Kathy. He's a smart man. He's a political science professor, you know, but he really knows a lot about people. He's very intuitive. It's almost like he's known me for a long time. He says that's because we're so much alike, but I think it's because he's so present.

"When I talk to him, it seems as though he tunes right in to me. He hears exactly what I'm saying. Like tonight, I was rambling on about some writing I did this afternoon, and when I finished, he summarized what I had said in about five sentences. I feel his presence when I'm with him. It's quite powerful. He's gentle though, and humble.

"I'm sure that's all connected to his spiritual path. He calls himself a Zen Buddhist. He says that the primary focus of his spiritual practice is to be fully present in and with every moment. I really like that. I would like to be more like that."

Kathy looked at Steve and said, "I think you *are* like that, Steve. When we're together, I feel like you're very present. You're a terrific listener. I think you're very intuitive, too; you're very insightful. Even Cally says so. I mean, look at how far you've come in sobriety in just two weeks. I've seen people still in a fog after two weeks, and look at you. You're growing by leaps and bounds."

"Do you really think so, Kathy? I mean, I'm really trying, but I get so confused. Like today, Cally confronted me about my defenses. He said I'm slick. Man, I hated the way that sounded. When he said it, I thought of used car salesmen in their white shoes. It really made me stop and think, 'Am I just a damn phony who has everyone fooled?'

"Ralph said not to worry too much about it, but the problem is that I can see where Cally's coming from. I don't want people to know me or feel about me the way I know and feel about myself. I like it when people think I've got my shit together. I like it when people think I'm smart and confident and cool and tough and emotionally strong. Rightly or wrongly, that *does* keep me safe, and damn it, I like it that way.

"Kathy, I don't want people to see all of my character defects. I don't want them privy to my insecurities. My insecurities are none of their damn business." He glanced at Kathy, who had leaned her head on his shoulder as he talked. "I'm sorry; I didn't mean to get off on a tangent."

She put her arms around him and hugged him. "I like it when you tell me how you feel. I want that from you. I don't want to be with someone who shows me only what he wants me to see. That's not real. To me, it's a lie.

"I understand your insecurities; I relate to them. And I believe I can love all of you, even those parts that you don't like about yourself. That doesn't mean that I won't sometimes feel angry or disappointed or hurt, but in my program of recovery, it's alright to feel all of those feelings."

She sat up and look into Steve's eyes. "Which reminds me, I feel as though I owe you an amends for last night. Not for getting angry; I've warned you about me in that regard. But for nurturing the anger in my mind and keeping it alive and for cutting at you the way I did. I'm especially sorry for asking you about your cheating on your ex-wife. That was a low blow, and I knew it. I felt hurt, and I wanted to hurt you back. I'm sorry."

Steve nodded and said, "Thank you, Kathy. I appreciate your saying that. You know, I doubt if I'll ever learn to love your quick temper. It scares the shit out of me, if you want to know the truth. But it is part of who you are, and I know that it would be wrong and ultimately damaging to our relationship for me to ask you to hide it from me. I'm not as far along as you are in my emotional recovery, so I can't say with complete honesty that I'm capable of loving all of you. That's my intention, though, to learn how to accept you and love you as you are with no expectations that you'll change. I know you're working on yourself, and I believe in you wholeheartedly.

"I would probably be a lot better off if I were more spontaneous with my feelings the way you are with yours. I keep a lot bottled up inside. I'll try not to do that with you, but it might take me a while."

Steve went home alone and fell asleep before midnight. He slept through the night, missing the 2:35 AM anniversary of his second week of sobriety.

CHAPTER 64

Steve's third week sober, like the two before it and several that followed, reminded him of the roller coaster ride at Playland Park—slowly up, quickly down, and full of unpredictable curves.

Except for an hour at the park with Ginger, an AA meeting at noon, and forty minutes with Cally, Steve devoted Wednesday to work and study.

Cally praised Steve's written work and his progress on treatment plan goals. He laughed out loud when Steve told him about Dixie and Tommy.

367

"I love the irony involved in the solutions to many of life's little problems," he said. "It never seems to fail; you become ready and willing for answers, and BAM, they lay themselves right there at your feet, despite your own best efforts to screw them up."

Cally listened intently to Steve's condensed version of the angry eyes story.

"I'm glad you were able to work through that one," he said. "You might as well get used to it, though, Steve. Kathy will most likely continue to shove your fear right in your face. She's not one to edit her thoughts and feelings to accommodate your unresolved shame and fear. If you're up to the challenge, it will accelerate your growth. If you're not, it's liable to eat your lunch."

"I don't think I like the sound of that, Cally," Steve said.

Cally laughed softly. "I'm sure you don't, Mr. Campbell. Yes, sir, I'm sure you don't."

Later, Steve met Kathy after her meeting. They sat at a small table in the back corner of the South Austin Coffeehouse and talked about the weekend camping trip. Steve reassured her that he wanted her to go, even though the weekend would be his last with the kids until Thanksgiving or Christmas.

He perceived her misgivings and asked her why she seemed hesitant. She reiterated her concern that she would not know how to act around Lynn and Eddie. She still worried that they might not like her.

"They'll like you, Kathy," Steve said. "Why wouldn't they like you?"

"I don't know, Steve. I've thought about it a lot since we discussed it Monday night. The thing is that I have this hunch about kids, that they can see through people. To be perfectly honest, I'm afraid that Lynn and Eddie will see through me. With adults, I can get by on my charm and my looks, but I'm afraid your kids might not buy it. They may be smarter than that."

"What the hell are you talking about, Kathy? According to Cally, I'm the one who slips through life and relationships by mastering effective defenses. I'm the one with shame and fear at my core, the one with something to hide, the slick one. What do you have to hide? You're the honest one."

Kathy snickered. "Yeah, right. You think you have a corner on the shame core market just because Cally's been on your ass about your defenses. Well, I'll let you in on a little secret, Stevey. You don't. I have my own shame. Cally's been on my ass about my defenses for six months now."

Steve studied her face for a moment. "Kathy, I've never heard you talk about yourself in those terms," he said. "At least I don't remember it. I thought you felt good about yourself. I mean, you're the independent one. You're the one who had the confidence to walk out on your abusive parents, the one who put herself through night school. You're the one who opens her mouth and tells the truth, the one who's spontaneous with her feelings. Hell, you're the one who everyone in group loves and uses as a role model."

Kathy shook her head slowly. She frowned and stared into her coffee cup. "You're giving me a lot more credit than I deserve," she said softly. "Think about it, Steve. I was a topless dancer in a sleazy bar. Men put dollar bills in my g-string and copped a feel in the process. I was a prostitute. I went to bed with men I didn't know and faked orgasms for money. Then I spent the money frivolously and used a lot of it to buy cocaine and alcohol.

"How many women who truly love themselves would do drugs every day and sell their bodies and their pride four or five nights a week for two years? How many confident, healthy women would demean themselves that way? Answer me that."

Steve hesitated. There it was—the other issue with Kathy about which he had questions and problems. He saw his chance to kill two birds with one stone—to discuss the issue with her and be supportive of her at the same time. A part of him wanted to go ahead and tell her the truth, as in, "Yeah, that's the other thing I want to talk with you about." But a wiser, more patient, and better-defended part tried coming in through the back door.

He said, "I can't answer that, Kathy, but maybe you would like to talk about it."

She became silent and stared out of the window for a moment. Then she turned her head and looked him in the eye. He saw a spark of anger. "Is it something you want to talk about, Steve?"

"Wait a minute. I didn't say that," he answered.

Kathy looked away and nodded. "You do though, don't you? I wondered how long it would be before it came up, before it became an issue."

"Whoa, Kathy. I didn't bring this up at all. I just meant, 'would you like to talk about it within the context of how you feel about yourself.' I didn't say it was an issue for me."

She became quiet again and then said, "Tell me the truth, Steve; is it an issue for you?"

Steve saw the bright red "DANGER" signs flashing in his head. "I wouldn't call it that, Kathy," he said. "It's not like a big deal or anything. I mean, it's not irrelevant. Nothing about you is irrelevant to me. I want to know and understand you better just like I suppose you want to know and understand me better. I guess I figured we'd talk about it one of these days, but I didn't bring it up as an issue to talk about. You're the one who did that."

Kathy's voice turned strong and direct. "Steve, you're doing it. You're doing it right now. You're doing what Cally calls being slick. You're dancing around an issue that you know is important to you, but you're trying to make it sound like it's no big deal so you won't look bad or so I won't get mad at you. Am I wrong or right about that? Tell me the truth."

Steve fell silent. He didn't know what to say. The truth was that she was precisely right, and he felt embarrassed to have been caught and confronted.

That wasn't all, though. He also felt as though he had been backed into a corner unfairly, and he felt angry and defensive about that. He took a breath to relax.

"No, you're not wrong, Kathy," he said. "But I didn't bring it up. Maybe I would have sooner or later, but I didn't tonight. If you want to know the truth, it seems to me as though you're the one who has the issue here. You're the one who jumped on this and the one who's being defensive. It feels like you're trying to blame me for something that I didn't do. I just asked you if you wanted to talk about it because you brought it up. That's all."

To Steve's relief, Kathy backed off. "Okay," she said. "You're probably right. I'm sorry. I do have an issue here, and I do feel defensive about it. I've been waiting for it to come up, almost from the beginning. The truth is that I want to talk about it. I want it out on the table. I want all of it on the table. I don't want this topic to come back and haunt me because either or both of us were afraid to discuss it. We don't have to talk about it right this minute, but I want to do it soon—very soon."

"That's fine," Steve said. "I think we ought to wait, though, at least until we're more open and receptive to each other. You know, I want to talk about my past, too. There are some things I want out on the table as well. Like, do you really want to know how many times I cheated on my ex-wife? If you do, then I want to talk about that."

Kathy nodded. She closed her eyes for a moment and then said, "This isn't easy, is it?"

"What isn't easy?" Steve asked.

"This relationship. It isn't easy. When we started, I thought it would be easy. I thought we would just coast along in sweet bliss forever and ever. That was my fantasy. I guess it was also my denial. Even when Susan warned us about the difficulties that we were almost certain to encounter trying to do a relationship in early sobriety, I still thought it would be easy. I guess I just wanted it so badly.

"Now I'm starting to wonder if we can pull it off. I mean, little things are erupting into arguments, and it seems like we have so much to work out and so much to work through. I'm starting to feel overwhelmed. Worst of all, I'm afraid that my true colors are starting to show. I know that my quick temper and my anger are hurtful to you, but obviously that's not enough. I've been lying awake at night, regretting things I've said and making empty promises to myself about how I'll act the next time we're together. I'm afraid that I'm going to scare you away, if I haven't already."

Tears came to Kathy's eyes. She tried to blink them back, but they tumbled out onto her cheeks. Despite feeling discouraged, Steve reached across the table and took her hand in his.

"Look at me, Kathy," he said. "I've said it before, and I'll say it again. I'm not going anywhere. I do get scared, but I'm not running away. I'm right here with you. It's where I want to be. We'll work through this stuff. It's hard, like you said, but I believe we can do it." He lifted her hand to his lips and kissed it.

Kathy nodded but said nothing. They remained silent for a few moments. Then Steve said, "I want to tell you a story, Kathy. I had an aunt and uncle who lived in Waco. Their names were Leonard and Anne. They're both dead now.

"Uncle Leonard was the younger brother of my grandfather—the one who raised me when I was little and died when I was six. Papa Rogers and Uncle Leonard were two years apart. Uncle Leonard looked just like Papa, so much so that they could have been twins. That might be one of the reasons why I loved him so much.

"Anyway, when I was in college in Waco, Leonard and Anne were very nice to me. They treated me like favorite family, and I got very close to them. I remember one Sunday, when I was a freshman, they picked me up at my dorm to take me out to lunch. When I opened the front door of the car to get in, Anne slid over into the middle of the seat next to Uncle Leonard. He smiled and patted her knee gently with his hand, and he said, "My, my, you sure have nice knees for an old lady." Anne smiled back and winked at him. I thought it was one of the sweetest things I had ever seen in my life. I'll never forget it.

"Later that afternoon we were at their house, and I had a chance to talk to Uncle Leonard in private. I asked him what the secret was to having a successful, long lasting marriage.

"He thought about it for a minute, and then he said, 'Well, Steve, the first thing is that you have to find someone that you really love, someone who grabs your heart. I don't think you can make yourself love someone who doesn't grab your heart. That's the first thing.

"But the real secret is that once you connect with that person, and you make a commitment to her, you never leave. You decide right up front that you will never walk away. You remove that option from the picture. Then you hang in there and deal with whatever comes up, and you just don't leave. No matter what happens, you just don't leave.'

371

"I remember feeling a little disappointed. I thought his answer was simplistic—very unsophisticated, you know? Now I'm not so sure. He and Anne loved each other very much. That was obvious; it was palpable. You could see it and feel it.

"They had their tiffs, of course. I saw her, especially, get pretty annoyed at him from time to time. Once when we were eating dinner at their house, he started telling me a dirty joke. At first, she just gave him 'the look.' When that didn't work, she said, 'Leonard, please.' When he ignored her that time, she stood up from the table and said, 'Leonard, I will not be treated with disrespect,' and she walked out of the room.

"He frowned and looked down at his plate for a second. Then he looked at me and said, 'Excuse me for a moment, Steve.' He went into the kitchen where she was, and I heard him say, 'I'm sorry, dear. I was being thoughtless. Please forgive me.'

"She said, 'Certainly, Leonard. Thank you.' And they walked back into the dining room as if nothing had happened. It was just so simple. That's the way they were with each other.

"Anne died first, about three years ago. She wasn't supposed to. Uncle Leonard had heart problems, and everyone, including him, expected him to go before her. He had a heart attack and died about six weeks after she did. I think he didn't want to be in this world without her."

Kathy smiled. "That's a beautiful story, Steve," she said softly. "Thank you for sharing it with me."

"You're welcome. Kathy, my sponsor says that in recovery, we make promises, and we keep them. He says it's that simple. Do you believe that?"

Kathy nodded. "Yeah, I think it's that simple. Why? What made you think of that?"

"I don't know. It just came to mind. Maybe because I tend to complicate things. I think too much. I analyze the hell out of everything. I look for hidden meanings, and I project a lot. I take things too seriously and too personally. I'm really going to try to lighten up. I'm going to try to remember just to observe the events in my life instead of placing myself at their center. If I can do that, maybe I won't feel so threatened when you get angry."

Kathy nodded. "That would help me a lot," she said.

Before leaving the coffeehouse parking lot, Steve and Kathy embraced warmly.

"We made it through another one, didn't we? We're okay, aren't we?" Steve whispered.

Kathy squeezed him tight. "Yes," she said softly, and then added, "Can I spend the night with you tomorrow?"

"Sure you can, Kathy. You can spend the night with me anytime you want."

On his drive home, Steve thought about the AA slogan, "Keep It Simple."

"I need to remember that one," he said to himself.

CHAPTER 65

Following his schedule, Steve worked Thursday morning until 10:30 and then studied through lunch and until time for his afternoon class. The course, Research Methods & Statistical Analysis, held the reputation as the killer for first year students.

The course instructor was an associate professor on his way up in the department. He was fairly young—mid-thirties, perhaps, but he acted formal, impersonal, and autocratic. Following his lecture required Steve's total concentration. Every time he drifted away from it, even for a moment, he found himself lost for at least five or ten minutes.

Steve took some solace in the fact that he was not the only one who felt challenged and confused. Several times when the instructor turned his back to the class to write on the board, Steve noticed a couple of other students rolling their eyes or shrugging their shoulders at each other, as if to say, "Beats the hell out of me."

After class, he overheard a student express concern to the instructor about the difficulty of the lecture and his inability to follow it. The instructor responded, "This is a graduate course, Mr. Carlton. It's a difficult subject and a difficult class. I suggest that you prepare for it with that in mind. If you have specific questions, you may bring them to me during my office hours, which are listed on your syllabus."

"But sir," the student replied, "this is supposed to be a vestibule class."

Looking and sounding annoyed, the instructor said, "'Vestibule' means passageway. A vestibule class prepares the student who lacks adequate skills in a subject to erase his deficiencies and move into more advanced studies. Vestibule does not mean easy. If you put forth the effort to learn this subject, you will do fine in this class. If not, you will fail."

When the student left the classroom, Steve smiled at him and said, "What a warm hearted guy, huh?"

The student shook his head. "If you ask me, he's a goddamn arrogant, egotistical asshole," he said.

After class, Steve bought groceries, straightened up his house, cleaned the bathroom, and changed the bed linens, all in anticipation of Kathy spending the night. She tapped on the front door at exactly 7:00 o'clock. She carried a smile on her face and an overnight bag in her hand.

"Got room for me in there?" she asked.

373

Steve laughed. "I've got just enough room for you and nobody else." He took her bag and set it on the floor. He stepped up to her and put both arms around her waist. "It's tight quarters, though. You'll have to stay exactly this close to me except in the event of an emergency."

"Does the fact that I'm about to pee in my pants qualify as an emergency?"

Steve put a thoughtful look on his face and said, "No, that means that you get...TICKLED." He grabbed her on both of her sides, dug his fingertips into her ribs, and tickled her wildly while she screamed in laughter and writhed against him.

"NO, STEVE," she yelled. "STOP IT! I'M NOT KIDDING! I'M GOING TO PEE IN MY DAMN PANTS! I'M NOT KIDDING! STOP!"

Laughing hard, Steve let her go. She ran into the bathroom and slammed the door. From inside, she giggled loudly and yelled, "You did it, damn it. You made me pee in my pants. What the hell am I going to do now?"

He walked up to the closed door and said in a normal, serious voice, "Take them off and come in here and help me fix dinner. I won't look. Scout's honor."

She cracked the door and peeked out at him. He could see her bright, smiling eyes and flirtatious smile. "You wish," she said. "You're going to have to do me a favor now, you bad, bad boy. Go in there and open my overnight bag and bring me a clean pair of panties. The yellow ones."

Steve grinned at her. "Yes, ma'am. Whatever you say, ma'am." He opened her bag and picked a pair of yellow cotton bikini panties from among four pair. He rubbed them in his fingers and then against his cheek. They gave a hint of fragrance.

"Here you go, piddle-pants," he said, handing them to her through the crack in the door. "Do you need any help getting them on?"

"No, I can manage that by myself. Thanks to you, though, I'm going to have to get into the shower before I get dressed again. And since that's your fault, you should have to get in here and bathe me."

"I see," Steve said. "You're a devious one, you are, Kathy Morris. Sweetly devious, but devious just the same." He slipped out of his sandals, pulled off his T-shirt, and unbuttoned and stepped out of his Levi's. "Well?" he said.

"What are you going to do—shower in your underwear?" she asked, still peering out from behind the door.

He shrugged his shoulders and pulled off his underwear. "Okay, here I am, naked to you and the world, ready to atone for my sins."

She opened the door a little bit more, as if to let him in, but then she stopped. "Oh, never mind," she said, and she slammed and locked the door.

Steve laughed. "You dirty dog," he yelled.

Kathy opened the door all the way. "Just kidding," she said, smiling.

She stood naked and beautiful before him. He put his arms around her and pressed his body against hers. "Um, that feels nice," he whispered.

They held each other for a few moments, until Kathy said, "So, what do you say? Do you want to get in the shower with me?"

Steve laughed softly. "What do you think?" he said. He started the water, and they climbed into the tub. They took turns soaping and rinsing each other, working slowly, and stopping frequently to embrace, touch, kiss, and tease each other until they both felt intensely sexually aroused.

During Kathy's final rinse, Steve stood behind her and slipped his arms around her waist. He moved his hands slowly up and down the front of her body, from her shoulders to her breasts, across her abdomen to her pelvic area and between her legs, then back up slowly to her shoulders.

He gently kissed the back of her head and neck. She reached both hands behind her and placed them on his buttocks and pulled him tight against her.

She turned her head slightly toward Steve's face. "Make love to me, Steve," she whispered. "Do it here, now."

"How do you want to do it?" he asked softly.

"From behind," she said, "with your mouth first, and then the rest of you." She slipped out of his arms and down onto her hands and knees. Steve kneeled behind her. She lowered the front of her body by resting on her elbows and forearms. Then she arched her back, presenting herself to him like a cat. He went down on her eagerly from the rear.

Over the sound of the water from the shower, he heard her breathing heavily and moaning through her breath. After several minutes, he leaned over her and whispered, "Tell me when you're ready, Kathy."

She answered immediately. "I'm ready," she said. "I'm ready right now. Do it now."

He slipped into her easily and stroked deeply. He worked slowly at first, holding her hips on either side with his hands and guiding her into his rhythm. She moaned with every stroke. They gradually quickened their pace, and Steve felt Kathy tensing and relaxing, approaching an orgasm. He thrust himself into her harder, and she opened to him even more. He came a moment before she did and was nearing the end of his orgasm when her body quivered, and she moaned loudly. She backed herself up hard against him, pressing her body into his to achieve maximum penetration. She raised the front of her body for a moment and then lowered it again and relaxed.

Steve stayed in her, but moved more gently, until he felt her relax completely. Then he stopped stroking and massaged her shoulders and her back with his hands. Finally, he leaned over her carefully and kissed her back and the back of her neck. "You okay?" he whispered. "You're not drowning or anything, are you?"

"Oh, God," she said, and she laughed weakly. "I hope that was anywhere near as good for you as it was for me." She moved forward slightly so that he came out of her. She turned the water off and then turned around slowly and sat in the tub facing him. She reached out for him. He leaned over, laid his arms on top of her shoulders, and kissed her on the forehead and then the mouth.

"It was incredible for me," he whispered. "It was the best. I've enjoyed sex many times, but I've never enjoyed it more than that."

"Me neither," Kathy said. "That was the strongest orgasm I've ever had. I thought I was going to pass out for a minute there, and I didn't even care. How are your knees?"

Steve laughed. "They hurt like hell. How are yours?"

"The same," she said. "Are you about ready to get out of here?"

"Yeah." He unfolded his body and stood up and then helped Kathy to her feet. He pulled back the shower curtain and grabbed two towels. Ginger was sitting just inside the bathroom door with her head cocked, looking at them with a puzzled expression.

"Don't worry, old girl. Everything's okay. She wasn't trying to kill me. Hurt me, maybe, but not kill me. I don't think so, anyway." He turned to Kathy. "Were you?"

Kathy laughed. "Shut up, you big baby," she said.

Steve finished drying off. "So did you work up an appetite? I grocery shopped this afternoon. The refrigerator is full of goodies."

"Yeah, I'm pretty hungry. What time do you think it is?"

Steve walked into the bedroom and looked at the clock. "It's a quarter to eight," he said.

"Hmm, I bet if we really wanted to, we could make it to an AA meeting," she said. "Are you interested in that?"

Steve thought about it for a moment. "I'll go if you really want to, but to tell you the truth, I'd rather just hang out here with you."

Kathy nodded. "Okay, that's cool; we can go tomorrow. Hey, I have an idea. What if you and I had our own meeting? You know, just the two of us. We could make some coffee, pick a topic, and share with each other. We could do it after dinner."

Steve laughed. "Yeah, I could go for that. You have to pick the topic, though. I'll make dinner, and you chair the meeting."

They slipped into shorts and T-shirts. Kathy put a Jim Croce album on the stereo. Steve fixed huge servings of rice and steamed vegetables, and they ate and listened to music and talked quietly. After dinner, they cleaned up the kitchen, and Steve brewed a pot of decaf."

"So what's our meeting topic going to be?" he asked.

"Well, I've been thinking about that," she said. "You know how the Big Book says that our stories disclose in a general way what we used to be like, what happened, and what we're like now? I think this might be a good time for us to talk about 'what it used to be like and what happened.' How does that sound to you?"

Steve hesitated. He thought he understood what Kathy meant, and the last thing he wanted was for them to get into something heavy that could ruin a very nice evening together. "Can you be a little more specific?" he asked.

"Steve, I want to pick up where we left off last night. I want to tell you my story and answer your questions."

Steve was silent for a few seconds. "This is important to you, isn't it?"

She nodded. "Yes, it is."

"Well, okay. Let's go for it."

Kathy poured two mugs of coffee, and they settled onto the floor in front of the couch.

"I know you've heard some of this already," she said, "but I'd like to just go through it from start to finish. Then I want to talk about any part of it that you're interested in or curious about. Okay?"

"Okay. I'm all ears."

For the next two hours, Kathy talked, and Steve listened. She omitted nothing of any substance from her story. She cried through parts and laughed through others.

As Steve listened, he realized that much or most of her story sounded and felt painfully like his own. There were the alcoholic parents, the abuse, the rejection, the shame and fear, the confusion and self-doubt, the feelings of separateness and isolation, the anger and alienation. There was the inexplicable, almost desperate need to feel accepted by others, especially by the father who abused her, the ever-widening and deepening web of defensiveness, the eventual emotional toughness, the loss of spiritual connectedness, the futile search for meaning and purpose, the alcohol and drug abuse, and the denial.

A few parts of her story were very different from his. She talked about standing up for herself and confronting her abusive parents. She discussed her incredible drive to survive and her unyielding commitment to complete independence, especially financial. She told of her failure to attract or experience a meaningful romantic relationship prior to meeting Steve.

Only one part of Kathy's story was tough for Steve to hear. That was her life as a prostitute. And knowing that Steve needed to understand and accept that part of who she was, Kathy provided details. She included a lengthy account of her gradual slide into prostitution and her concurrent slide into alcohol and drug dependence. She told him about the strongly seductive nature of the money and the attention lavished upon her by men, many of whom were her father's age and older.

She mentioned the mechanical nature of the work and her almost frightening capacity for dishonesty with the men who doted on her.

She shared with Steve her process of emotional and spiritual decline, from tough, proud, resourceful woman trying to improve the quality of her life to angry bitch, distrustful of and resentful toward everyone with whom she came into contact. Through tears, she related her inability to look at herself in the mirror without feeling literally sick to her stomach.

"The night I got busted, I had been on about a three day alcohol and coke binge. I had not eaten in two days. I was a wreck. I was a very sick woman. The cop who busted me was a regular customer. He was a vice cop, but he liked me because I was an independent. I think he had a thing about pimps and the women who worked for them.

"He told me that he was busting me because he couldn't just stand by and let me kill myself. He said he didn't want to have me on his conscience. I told him to fuck himself and that I didn't give a shit what he did. When I realized that he was totally serious, I screamed at him that he had a puny little dick and that he was the worst fuck that I had ever had.

"He just shook his head and said, 'Yeah, right.'

"I was so strung out that I didn't even bother to empty my purse before he cuffed me. He would have let me flush the coke, but I didn't even care enough to mess with it. When they booked me, he asked them to do a breath test on me. I blew a 1.6. He said later that he did that because he thought it would encourage the judge to send me to rehab if there was some tangible evidence that I had a drinking problem. He didn't know about the coke in my purse.

"I detoxed in the county jail. A few weeks later I had my first meeting with Cally. I don't know why, but Cally believed in me from the moment we met. Maybe it was because by the time I saw him, I was beat to a pulp. I was ready for anything. He could have told me to mop the floor with my hair, and I would have done it.

"When I look back on it now, I think that prostitution is something that happened to me. I mean, I know I'm responsible and accountable for my decisions and my behavior, but when I think about that part of my life, it seems hardly real anymore. I know now that is not who I am. It's something I did, but it's not who I am. I may never be completely free of the shame that I feel, but I know in my heart that I have value as a woman and as a human being. I'm no longer a whore.

"So there it is, Steve. I'm willing to elaborate on any part of the story and answer any questions you might have. No holds barred. Nothing's sacred."

Steve shifted his position on the floor and looked into his empty coffee cup. "Can I get you another cup of coffee?" he asked softly.

Kathy laughed. "Yeah, thanks," she said.

"What's so funny?" Steve asked her.

"Oh, I guess I expected a little tougher question than that."

Steve smiled. "Yeah, I bet you did. I'll be right back." When he returned with the coffee, he sat down beside her, close enough for their legs to touch.

"Well, girl, it's a hell of a story. Thank you for sharing it with me. While you were telling it, I was thinking about how similar our stories are. Change a few details here and there, and they're damn near the same, especially the emotional stuff. Anyway, I don't think I have any questions for you, at least not right now. I mean, I do have a little perverse curiosity about a few things, but it's not relevant to this discussion.

"I do want to share something with you, though. I'm not absolutely positive about this, but believe it or not, I think that the biggest problem I have with your having been in that line of work has to do with my own insecurities. I mean, you've been with so many other men—men who are handsomer, smarter, bigger, stronger, richer, funnier, more sophisticated, more interesting, and everything else than me. Surely you've been with men who were better, stronger lovers than I am. You've had all of this experience with sex that I haven't had, and I'm afraid of coming across like an amateur. I'm even self-conscious about my size, if you know what I mean.

"Anyway, that's one thing. I'm afraid I won't stack up well against other men, especially since there have been so many to compare against.

"The other thing is harder to talk about, but you said you wanted it all on the table so here it is. It's about you and the way you are with me when we're together romantically and sexually. Kathy, please don't get mad at me for saying this, but I need to know that you're being spontaneous and real with me and that you aren't using some technique on me that worked for you with the men who paid you. I need for you to be a woman who loves me and responds to me from her heart. I want us to be fresh and new with each other. In a way, I wish we could be beginners with each other. And I'm sorry for having ever thought this, but on a couple of occasions, I've caught myself wondering, 'Is this real, or is it a professional technique?' I didn't want to have that thought, and I felt ashamed of myself for it, but the truth is, it was there. Do you know what I mean?"

Kathy grew silent for a moment. Finally, she nodded and said, "Yes, I do know what you mean, and I'm not angry. My feelings are hurt, but I'm not angry." She wiped a tear from the corner of her eye and then continued. "It never occurred to me that you would think I was doing a number on you, that I was just screwing you instead of making love with you.

"Other things occurred to me, but never that. I thought you might judge me from a moral standpoint, or worry that I had been diseased, or even be concerned that I did what I did because I was a man-hating, money-hungry bitch. But I never thought that you might think I was being dishonest with you. I also never thought about my past from the perspective of your insecurity." She paused for a moment and looked at the floor.

"Steve, you are fresh and new for me. I think of you in a totally, totally different way than I thought about the men who paid me. It's not even within the same realm of conscious thought. This whole experience is fresh and new for me.

"Believe me, I have never compared you with anyone. I have no reason to compare you with anyone. It would be like comparing a vitamin C pill to a fresh orange. There is some kind of basic connection between the two, but they're just not comparable.

"Steve, I have never been in love before. I've never honestly said the words 'I love you' to another man. I've repeated words to men who asked me to say certain things to them, but they were just words connected in a sentence. I've never opened my heart and said those words from that place inside, not until I said them to you. I've had sexual relations with many men, as well as a few women, but you're the first person that I have ever truly made love with.

"When I was a teenager, acting out my anger against my parents and all men everywhere, I screwed a few guys just to be bad. I didn't like it. After I left home at sixteen, I dated a few guys because I was lonely and because I thought that's what I was supposed to do. I let them sleep with me so that they would like me and not just dump me.

"Then after I got my GED and started night school, I didn't have time for men, and that was a relief, because to tell you the truth, by then I wasn't particularly impressed with them. Besides that, I was driven to achieve something, and relationships of any kind would have been a distraction.

"It wasn't much different when I was at UT. I had a few dates. Sex was infrequent. It was better, but it didn't mean much to me. Then when I got into dancing, and then prostitution, sex became totally meaningless. I used the word mechanical earlier, and I promise you, that's a perfect description of what I did with men. I developed techniques, and I used them.

"But Steve, I don't use techniques with you. The thought hasn't even crossed my mind. Everything that I've done with you has been spontaneous and from my heart. I mean, obviously I learned about sex through my experience with sex, just like everyone else. Just like I imagine you did. Maybe I'm good at it; I don't know. But I don't have a bag of tricks. I did at one time, but not anymore.

"You and I have made love through sexual intercourse three times, and those have been three very wonderful experiences for me. I've had orgasms each time. And you might think that wouldn't be such a big deal for someone who's been in as many different beds as I have. But do you know that for the last two and a half years, the only other orgasms I've had have come from my own hands? *Never* did I experience orgasm with a client, and I mean not once. They never knew that, of course, but that's the way it was.

"Steve, I went two years without an orgasm of any kind. When I entered recovery and got reacquainted with my body and my mind, I started masturbating every once in a while. I did it initially out of curiosity, and then for pleasure. When you came along, and we got into bed together that first Saturday night, and I felt your arm around my chest and your erection coming up against the back of my leg, I thought to myself, 'Maybe it's time for me to experience some of the pleasure that other women my age have been experiencing for years.'

"You know, Steve, if you look at my sex life outside of my stint as a professional, you're more experienced than I am."

Steve put his arm around Kathy's shoulder and kissed the side of her head. "Thank you, Kathy," he said softly. "I appreciate everything you've said. I'm a little in awe of your story. You have amazing strength, more than I've ever even dreamed of having. No, I take that back. You have exactly the strength that I've dreamed of having.

"I'm glad now that you pushed ahead with this. I think you were right to want to clear the air. You're a miracle in the truest sense of the word, and I'm deeply grateful that you're in my life."

"Thank you, Steve," she said.

They sat quietly for a few moments and then Kathy reiterated her readiness to answer Steve's questions. "I would rather do this now than to have it pop up a month from now," she said.

Steve looked into Kathy's eyes and asked, "Are you sure?"

Kathy nodded. "Absolutely."

"Okay," he said. "Were you ever abused by customers? Like, did anyone ever beat you up or anything?"

"Yes, I got knocked around a couple of times. I was never hurt badly, but I picked up a few bruises. I was actually very lucky. What else?"

Steve hesitated and then said, "Kathy, did you ever get pregnant?"

She shook her head. "No; I never got pregnant, and I never contracted a sexually transmitted disease. Again, I was exceedingly fortunate. Go ahead; what else?"

"Did your dad or mom ever sexually abuse you?"

"No, not exactly. But my dad never passed up a chance to look up my skirt, down my blouse, or through the shower curtain. And one time when he was drunk and angry at the world, he ripped a bath towel off of me and prevented me from covering myself while he ridiculed my body. I was thirteen. Next question?"

"If you could turn the clock back to, say, the day before your sixteenth birthday, when you ran away from home, would you do anything differently with your life up to this point?"

Kathy thought for a minute, then shook her head slowly. "I don't think so, Steve. I probably should, but I don't believe I would. As horribly as I have lived much of my life, I just don't think I would change it. Isn't it strange, though; I'm surprised at my own answer to the question. Anyway, keep going; next question."

Steve shook his head. "We don't need to do this anymore, Kathy. If you think of anything else that you want me to know, you can just tell me. Okay?"

Kathy started to respond, but Steve stopped her. "Wait a second," he said. "I just thought of something I've been meaning to ask you, but I keep forgetting. It's on a different subject altogether."

"All right; fire away."

"What is your ethnicity?"

Kathy smiled. "Do you want to hear something funny? That is the other issue that I've been waiting for you to bring up."

Steve held up his hands as if to block Kathy from attacking him. "Hold it," he said. "I swear to God, it isn't an *issue*. I'm curious, and that is all. It is *not* an issue."

Kathy laughed and pushed him away. "Mock me, buster, and you will pay dearly for it. I'll get you in your sleep, if I have to."

Steve fell backwards, laughing. "Please, God," he yelled, "don't let Kathy's ethnic heritage be an *issue*."

When they stopped laughing, Kathy said, "If you must know, I'm a cur. At least that's what some of the kids from my old neighborhood called me. My mother is one-half Hispanic— Mexican-American to be exact—and one-half Cherokee Indian. My father is pure Anglo—German-Irish, I think."

Steve nodded and smiled. "You have the most beautiful skin I've ever seen," he said.

Kathy narrowed her eyes slightly and looked intensely into Steve's eyes. Then she smiled and said, "Thank you, Steve."

She sat up straight and breathed deeply. "Okay, Steve, this is your last chance. Do you have no more questions? One from your perverted curiosity, perhaps?"

Steve laughed. "Oh, I don't know; one, maybe. You've been with women?"

Kathy smiled and nodded. "I should have guessed. Yes, I've been with other women a few times. I did it for men who wanted to watch. And no, I am not a lesbian. Nor am I bisexual. It wasn't an unpleasant experience, but I did it for the money."

"Why should you have guessed that I'd ask that?" Steve said.

"Because men are fascinated with the thought of two women making love. The number one sexual fantasy of the vast majority of men is to have sex with two women at once."

Steve smiled. "I see," he said. "Isn't that interesting?"

They were silent for some time. Kathy laid her head on Steve's shoulder. He kissed the top of it and said, "I really do love you, Kathy. I love everything about you. I adore you. I'll tell you my story sometime soon. I don't want to do it tonight, though. All I want to do tonight is lie in bed with you snuggled up against me."

Kathy turned her face up to his and kissed him gently on the lips. "I love you, too, Steve. You're my sweetheart. You're my first true love. You're also a sweet and gentle sober man, and I'm proud to have you as my lover. Now, as chairperson of this private little meeting of Alcoholics Anonymous, I declare it closed. Will you pray with me?"

Kathy offered her hands. Steve took them in his, and together they said The Serenity Prayer: "God, grant me the serenity to accept the things I cannot change; courage to change the things I can; and the wisdom to know the difference."

After the prayer, Steve and Kathy rinsed out their coffee mugs, brushed their teeth, slipped out of their clothes, and settled into bed in each other's arms.

"Sweet dreams," Kathy whispered.

"You too, babe," Steve replied.

CHAPTER 66

On Friday, Steve and Kathy attended a noon meeting at the Catholic Student Center and then ate lunch with Steve's sponsor. When questioned by Kathy about his opinion of early sobriety relationships, Ralph said, "Well, Kathy, I guess I'm not real big on general rules that supposedly apply to everyone all the time. I figure you're pretty much where you're supposed to be while you're there. I believe that if we stay present, we'll learn what we need to know.

"I remember one morning about a year or so ago, I was listening to a cassette tape over my earphones. It was a Bonnie Raitt tune—a beautiful, sad one. I was in kind of a slump at the time, feeling kind of down and kind of lonely.

"Anyway, I closed my eyes for a moment and said a simple prayer. I said, 'God, why am I here?' Well, believe it or not, the answer came instantly. In my mind, I heard the words, 'So you can listen to this song.' I don't know, I always seem to come back to that same basic principle. Pay attention to what's in front of you. The rest is an illusion.

"That's probably more of an answer than you were looking for, and I apologize for that. My wife says I tend to pontificate, even when I'm not in the classroom. At any rate, y'all certainly do make a lovely couple. No one could deny that."

When Kathy told him that she was a former UT student, he asked her why she dropped out and if she planned to return.

"I dropped out because I lost interest. I lost interest because of my addictions and the rest of the drama going on in my life, which siphoned off my energy and left little for school. I didn't want to show disrespect for the process by hanging on with a second- or third-rate effort. I do plan to return, though. I love school, and obtaining a college degree is one of my goals."

"You know what, Kathy?" Steve said. "I don't even know what you were studying in school."

Kathy smiled. "Well, I was in the School of Business. I figured that since I was an entrepreneur, so to speak, I should learn how to run my business more efficiently." She paused for a second. "That was a joke; don't you get it? Anyway, the truth is, I was interested in the fashion business. My goal was to become a buyer for a major department store. I envisioned myself home based in Dallas or Houston and traveling to the major world markets. A jet setter—that's what I wanted to be. Pretty funny, huh?

"Now, though, I really don't know what I want to do. I might stay with business, but in an area other than marketing; something like human resources, perhaps. Or I might do something very different, like social work. I'm not worried about it right now. It will be a while before I put together the resources, and I'm in no hurry."

"How about you, Steve?" Ralph said. "Do you really want to be a psychologist?"

"I don't know, Ralph. I think my ego does. When I started back to school last year, my conscious thoughts about studying psychology were basically unselfish. I thought I had something to offer, you know? I wanted to work with people and be of some help.

"I'm seeing other sides of it now, however. I think my *unconscious* motivations were not quite so pure. On that deeper level, I may have just wanted another layer of protection. I mean, what better protection is there than to 'see all and know all' about other people? To listen to their secrets and give them learned advice? To see through their defenses and lead them to the truth? Man, talk about power! What better protection is there than that? Hell, you even get a badge in the form of the doctorate degree, which goes up on your wall."

Steve laughed and shook his head. "Boy, isn't it ironic that I've spent my entire life building great walls of protection, and now my goal is to admit powerlessness and practice lowering defenses to achieve genuineness. Go figure.

"You know, I remember when my friend, James, and I were kids. He was way ahead of his time. By the sixth grade, he already had self-awareness. He was a true individual who didn't give a shit about what people thought of him. I, on the other hand, cared more than anything in the world about what people thought of me.

"James told me one time that I seemed like two different people to him. The first was the one that hung out with him and raised hell and had fun. The other was the one who needed to be popular.

"He said that the first me was his friend—his buddy—but the second wasn't. He liked, understood, and related to me the one way. But he couldn't reconcile the phoniness of the other. I didn't understand or appreciate his insight at the time. I do today, though.

"Another part of my motivation for starting graduate school had to do with self-knowledge. I think I had the notion that if I would study psychology at that level I might find out what was wrong with me. In that regard, graduate school would be a painless substitute for therapy.

"Anyway, I'll forge ahead with the graduate program and see what happens. I realize that I have a lot of work to do on myself before I could ever work with others. I have time, though, and the intellectual exercise can't hurt anything. The truth be known, Kathy would probably make a much better psychologist than I would."

After lunch Steve and Kathy went swimming at Barton Springs. They talked very little, choosing instead just to relax with each other in the sun. They left in time to clean up and make it to group at 6:00.

Cally lectured briefly on emotional recovery in sobriety. He distinguished between thinking and feeling, but within the context of the connection between the two. He emphasized that one's thinking process—one's attitudes, beliefs, and opinions—dramatically affects one's emotional process, which in turn affects one's thinking process, which in turn affects one's emotional process, etc, etc.

"The place to intervene on upset feelings is at the thinking level," he said. "If I'm willing to challenge the veracity of my beliefs and attitudes on an ongoing basis, especially when I'm feeling upset, then I have a good chance of resolving those feelings. You see, I'm capable of holding on to some pretty irrational beliefs. After all, they're nothing more than a reflection of all the ridiculous crap that I've learned during my life, mostly from well-meaning people and institutions that did not know what they were talking about in the first place.

"For example, where did I learn about how two people in an intimate relationship are supposed to be with each other? I learned it primarily from my mother and father—two people who may never have had a truly intimate moment in their lives, at least not one that I ever witnessed. What I learned from them was that I'm supposed to bring home the bacon and rule the roost. In turn, my wife is supposed to take care of the house, the children, and me, and on top of that, do whatever else I tell her. Now, if I believe that, if I truly believe it, and my wife doesn't follow the script, how do you think I'm going to feel? Yeah, I'm going to go around mad as hell, and I'm going to blame my anger on her.

"Here's another example. Suppose I meet an attractive woman at a party one night, and I see her on the street three days later. I say, 'Hello, Betty; how are you?' and she looks at me and wonders who I am and where she knows me from. If my expectations are that people, especially attractive women, are supposed to always pay attention to me and remember me and remember my name, then I'm going to have some upset feelings around this situation. I'll probably judge her, and I'll tell myself that she's not treating me the way I deserve to be treated. I'll probably feel hurt and angry.

"But it's not her behavior that precipitates my feelings. It's my attitudes and beliefs about her behavior. Now, there's the culprit. The way I know that's true is this: If I don't have those expectations of people, and if I don't have those beliefs, then I can simply acknowledge that some people are attentive and some aren't and that it doesn't have anything to do with me personally. Then I won't have any reason to feel upset. There's no judgment to be made. Now then, if I see her on the street, and she doesn't remember me, then I figure she's one of those who isn't very attentive, or at least wasn't the night we met. That's about her, not me. My ego won't get involved, and my feelings won't be hurt."

Robert raised his hand and asked, "Cally, how are we supposed to intervene at the thinking level while we're in the middle of those feelings? Hell, when someone hurts my feelings, it pretty much consumes me until I somehow get over it."

Cally nodded. "That's a good question, Robert. Here's what I do: I have a couple of stock questions ready at all times. These are questions that I ask myself as honestly as I can. One is, 'What am I telling myself about this situation that's causing me to feel upset?' Another way of putting it is, 'What are my unreasonable expectations about this person or situation?' Or, 'What are my irrational beliefs about this situation?' The other question is, 'How am I taking this situation too personally or too seriously?'

"Let me go through it for you. The sequence is this: Experience the event; feel the feeling; ask the questions; gain insight. This process allows you to have your feelings, accept responsibility for them, and gain insight into yourself that will help you on your next go-round with similar situations.

"Of course, it's not always that simple. Sometimes we'll need help answering the questions with honesty and insight. That's where other people figure into the equation."

Steve raised his hand. "Cally, how would you define emotional recovery? Or better yet, how would you define emotional health?"

Cally thought for a moment and then said, "Steve, I've heard many definitions of emotional health, including those that describe it in terms of the absence of symptoms of emotional disturbance or disease, and I'm not so sure that any of them are any good. But if I had to define it, I'd say that emotional health— emotional recovery—has an awful lot to do with the way we experience and deal with feelings.

"I would say that we're approaching emotional health when we're able and willing to feel, share, and resolve a wide range of feelings, both positive and negative. A lot of it has to do with lowering defenses and risking pain. Words that I associate with emotional recovery are the ones that we talk about in here all of the time: Openness, honesty, and genuineness."

Sally spoke up. "Hell, Cally, why would I want to feel painful feelings when I don't have to? I've spent a good part of my life learning to avoid that kind of thing. I figure I don't have to feel anything I don't want to. I can just shut it off and think about something else. I don't think whining and crying all over the place is so emotionally healthy. I think it's stupid."

Cally smiled. "Yeah, Sally, a lot of people would agree with you. Remember, though, just because you stuff a feeling away doesn't mean it's gone. It's still in there, and stuffed feelings are tricky little bastards. They always seem to find a way of sneaking out. Oftentimes, it's sideways. You stuff your anger at work and then go home and yell at your kids and kick poor old Fido. Stuffed anger can give you ulcers, too, even when your diet is decent.

"Stuffed feelings encourage you to judge critically yourself and other people who are just being themselves. Angry people develop righteous indignation and complain about things that have nothing to do with them. What I'm saying is that stuffed feelings are pretty darned toxic.

"Regarding your second point, Sally, I'm not a proponent of whining and crying all over the place, either. What I'm suggesting is that we treat our feelings with dignity and respect. When we have them, we recognize them, honor them, interact with them, see what we have to learn from them, and when appropriate, share them with others. You know, when you share your feelings openly and honestly with other people, they lose their power over you. When they hit daylight, they tend to dissolve, kind of like vampires do. When they stay hidden, they fester."

Following Cally's lecture, the group took a break and then returned for group therapy. Kathy's leaving the group took center stage, but most group members said that they had done the bulk of their work around her leaving the previous week and were prepared to let her go. This allowed their good-byes to be genuine and tender. They wished her well and looked forward to reconnecting with her as they advanced to the next level of work themselves.

Billy apologized to both Kathy and Steve for his angry outburst, which he knew now failed to consider anything but his own fear of rejection and abandonment. He went on from there to talk about his parents' inability, or unwillingness, to love him and accept him unconditionally.

"The bottom line is that they want me to be someone I'll never be," he said. "Mainly, they want me to be straight. They want me to have a wife and kids. They want me to be masculine, to be a real man. They look upon me as defective. I feel their disapproval and disappointment; I see it in their eyes.

"It's not the same look I get from South Austin rednecks. It's not that angry or intolerant. It's more like, 'I feel sorry for all of us in our failure.' The worst part about it is that there's a part of me who buys into it. There's a part of me who yearns to give them what they want, and that part of me feels ashamed of who I am. I think that's one reason I hate to lose Kathy out of the group. I know she accepts me just as I am. She doesn't judge me, she doesn't feel sorry for me, and she doesn't coddle me or condescend to me. She just accepts me. Kathy, I love you for that."

Just before group ended, Al asked if he could recite a poem for Kathy. "I didn't write it," he said, "but I've known it for so many years that I think of it as my own. At any rate, I'd like for you to have it, Kathy.

"There once was a dachshund, oh so long,
That he hadn't any notion
How long it took to notify
His tail of his emotion.

"And so it happened that while his eyes
Were filled with woe and sadness,
His little tail went wagging on
Because of previous gladness.

"You've given me a lot of gladness, Kathy, and for that, I'll always be grateful."

After group, Steve and Kathy drove to her apartment, where she packed for their weekend camping trip with Lynn and Eddie.

"I don't even know what to take, Steve," she said.

"Just throw in whatever you'd take to the lake for a couple of days plus a pair of jeans and a pair of boots. I've got everything else. You might also want to bring one extra change of clothes for when we run by my mom's on our way home."

"Your mom's?" Kathy said. "Who said anything about going to your mom's? I rather reluctantly agreed to go camping with you and your kids, but I did not agree to go to your mother's house."

Steve laughed. "Hey, man, it's no big deal. I just want her to meet you. We don't have to hang around or anything. Just a buzz in and buzz out kind of thing."

Kathy shook her head. "Boy, I hate to say it, Steve, but you don't know shit about women. I want to be at my best when I meet your mother. I want to look my best. I don't want to meet her after two days of camping. I won't even have a chance to shower and wash my hair.

"And I'll tell you something else, old boy. Your mom wants me to be at my best when she meets me, too. She doesn't want to think her son is hanging out with some old scag with dirty, stringy hair, and wrinkled clothes. That is, unless she wants to dislike me regardless, and from what you've told me about her, I doubt that's the case."

"Hey, wait a second," Steve said. "Don't you think she could just look past the stringy hair and wrinkled clothes to what a terrific person you are on the inside?"

Kathy laughed. "God, are you dumb. She's your mother, Steve. You're her only son; you're her baby. She wants you to be

389

with someone who's good enough for you, and I mean good enough by *her* standards. And my guess is that anything less than a goddess wouldn't be good enough.

"Listen, maybe I don't know what I'm talking about here. Maybe I'm working off of television stereotypes. But one thing I do know is that when I meet your parents, I want to make a good first impression on them. First impressions are very powerful. They're hard to change, in either direction."

"Okay, okay," Steve said. "Let's just play it by ear. Let's see how the weekend goes, and we can decide about seeing my mom after we drop the kids off Sunday afternoon. I think you have the wrong idea about camping, though. We won't be out in the wilderness somewhere. We'll be at a state park. There will be bathrooms and showers there. But don't worry about it. We'll just see how it goes, okay?"

"Okay, but don't count on it, Steve. And I mean it; do you hear me?"

"Yes, I hear you," Steve laughed. "Come on, throw some stuff in a bag, and let's get going. I need to pack the truck so we can get an early start in the morning. Besides, I'm hoping we'll have time for a little wrestling match before we go to sleep tonight. What do you think? Any chance of that?"

Kathy smiled and put a thoughtful look on her face and said, "Why don't we just play it by ear? Let's just see how the rest of the evening goes and then decide."

When they finally got into Steve's bed, they took their time and made love gently and playfully.

Before drifting off to sleep with Kathy in his arms, Steve whispered, "I can't believe we found each other. I really just can't believe it."

CHAPTER 67

During the drive to San Antonio, Kathy was quiet, distracted, and a little irritable.

"Hey, Kathy, I promise you it's going to be alright. Nothing could please me more than for the kids to see through whatever protective cover you throw up for them, because then they'll see what a wonderful person you really are. Believe me; there is nothing for you to worry about."

She nodded. "I know. I'll be okay. I suppose she'll be there?"

"Who, Bev?"

"Yeah."

"Yes, I'm pretty sure she will. You're not worried about her, too, are you?"

Kathy glanced at Steve and said, "Sorry, but I guess I am—a little, anyway. Maybe it's a woman thing." She looked down at her hands and closed her eyes. "Steve, maybe I shouldn't have come. It's your last couple of days with them for a long time. Not just the kids, but Bev also. Don't y'all have things you need to talk about?"

Steve reached across the seat and touched Kathy's hand. "Come on, Kathy," he said. "I want you with me. I want the kids to meet you before they leave. I want them to know who I'm spending my time with. I want you all to know who I'm talking about when I say Kathy and Lynn and Eddie—the names of the people I love.

"Hey, if you were a casual friend or a temporary fling, then it wouldn't matter. But you're neither, and it does matter. Listen, let's just do this: Let's stay present, stay conscious, be honest, go with the flow, and watch what happens. Let's try to let go of any and all expectations we have of how this is supposed to turn out. Okay? Let's be Buddhists for the day. Let's just be present and observe."

Kathy smiled and squeezed Steve's hand. She took a deep breath and released it. "Okay, I'm alright. It's all about acceptance, right? Nothing happens in God's world by mistake, right? I'm not in control. I'm just along for the ride. I'm an observer. No expectations and watch it unfold, right? Nothing to it, right?"

She took her hand out of his and gently punched him in the shoulder. "You have a creative imagination and a ton of denial. I'll do my best, though."

They arrived at Bev's mid-morning. As soon as they walked in the door, Lynn and Eddie gave Kathy the once over and then ran downstairs and out to the truck to see Ginger. Bev went out of her way to be cordial and pleasant, and Kathy reciprocated. When Kathy went to the bathroom, however, Bev said, "Well, Lynn told me you had a girlfriend and that she was coming with you. I would have thought that you would want to spend your last weekend with the kids alone."

"I wanted them to meet her. It felt important to me," he said, calmly.

"Why? You're not serious about her, are you?" she asked.

"What's that supposed to mean, Bev? Why wouldn't I be?"

She shrugged her shoulders and frowned. "She doesn't seem much like your type. She's too clean, and definitely too nice."

Steve shook his head. "I don't even know how to respond to that one, Beverly, so I think I just won't. Listen, I'll have the kids home tomorrow afternoon by five. We'll be at Blanco State Park. Do you know exactly when y'all are pulling out next week?"

"Yes. The moving van will be here Tuesday. We'll stay at my mom and dad's Tuesday night and leave Wednesday morning."

Kathy reappeared. "Thanks, Bev," she said. "I hope I'm not interrupting anything."

"Nope, you aren't interrupting a thing," Bev said. "I was just telling Steve that you seem very nice. Anyway, y'all have a good time, and I'll see you tomorrow. Be sure you're back by five, Steve. The kids and I have plans tomorrow night."

Steve, Kathy, Lynn, and Eddie piled into Cleo's front seat. Ginger took her regular place in the back. Lynn sat next to Steve. They made small talk for awhile. Steve asked questions about school and grandparents and the move to Denver. Kathy listened, and before long, she loosened up and relaxed.

During a lull in the conversation, Lynn looked at Kathy and said, "Are you in love with my dad?"

Kathy glanced at Steve. He smiled and raised his eyebrows but kept his eyes on the road. Kathy smiled and said, "Yes, I think I am. In fact, I'm pretty sure of it. Is that okay with you, Lynn?"

Lynn considered the question for a moment and then said, "Yes, I guess it's okay with me. Are you going to marry him?"

Kathy shifted her position slightly so she could see Lynn's face more fully. "Now that, I don't know. Your dad and I haven't talked about it. We haven't known each other long enough to make that decision. If we did decide to get married some day, though, would you come to the wedding and stand up in front with us?"

Lynn smiled broadly and said, "Yes, if my dad would come up to Denver and pick me up." She looked up at Steve. "Would you, Dad?"

"Yeah, sure I would. No problem."

"Me, too?" asked Eddie.

"Yes, you, too, big guy. We would drive up there to Denver and pick you both up and bring you back here to Texas. We'd get married, and then we'd take you back to Denver."

"But what if we wanted to stay in Texas with you and not go back to Denver?" Lynn asked.

"Well, gosh, I don't know, Honey. I guess we'd have to talk about that with your mom."

Once inside the park, they selected a campsite. Steve set up camp while Kathy, Lynn, and Eddie walked around and investigated the campgrounds. When they returned, Lynn was hand-in-hand with Kathy on one side, and Eddie was hand-in-hand with her on the other. All three were smiling and laughing, especially Kathy, who seemed very relaxed and cheerful. She caught Steve's eye and winked.

They spent the afternoon in near-constant motion. They played tag, hide and seek, Frisbee, and horseshoes. They played on the jungle gym and swam in the Blanco River. By early evening, they were all tired. Lynn read a comic book to Eddie while Steve and Kathy cooked hot dogs and beans for dinner.

"Looks like you've found a couple of new friends," Steve said to Kathy quietly.

Kathy smiled. "Yeah, I think so. They're great, and they're so funny. When Lynn and I were changing out of our swimsuits, she was really checking me out. I thought I might have made a mistake getting naked in front of her. So I asked her if anything was wrong. She just shook her head and said, 'No, I was just looking at your boobies. They're big. Mine are little tiny, but when I get older, they're gonna be big like yours.'"

"What did you say?" Steve asked, smiling.

"Well, I just said, 'Yeah, I bet they will.' I mean, what else could I say?"

Steve laughed. "That's funny. You've got big boobies. Listen, I can't tell you how glad I am that y'all like each other and are getting along so well."

"Yeah, me, too. There's nothing to it. I feel a little foolish about having been so uptight about it. They're a lot easier to be around than most adults I've known."

After dinner, they all went for a walk and then talked and told stories until the sky became dark. The kids bedded down in the tent and went to sleep quickly. Steve and Kathy spread a blanket outside and snuggled together under the stars.

"I can't believe how much and how quickly my life is changing," Steve said. "The last time I laid out under a Texas night sky, I was tripping on acid and on the front end of my own version of the weekend from hell. Cally said that weekend was when I hit my bottom. I didn't quit using then, but it set the wheels in motion for me to get into treatment.

"Now I'm lying here under another Texas night sky, just a few weeks later, and look at me. I'm clean and sober, I'm with you, and I'm madly in love. It's almost unbelievable."

Kathy snuggled under Steve's arm. "I've never laid on a blanket under a Texas night sky with someone I love before. I like it. It's beautiful. I feel safe and happy. Do you think we could get away with making love out here?"

"What, right out here in the open? In front of God and the whole universe?"

"Yes, in front of God and the whole universe."

"Well, I think we could do it if you promise to keep your moaning and groaning down to a minimum. I'd hate for Lynn and Eddie to go home with an X-rated story to tell."

Kathy laughed softly. "Now that, I can't promise, but I'm willing to try."

They slipped out of their clothes and made love quietly and tenderly on top of the blanket under the stars.

During lunch the next day, Lynn asked Kathy if she was a model. Kathy smiled and said, "No, sweetie, I'm not a model. Why did you think I was a model?"

"Because you're pretty, and you're tall like the women I see on TV. My mom is short. She couldn't ever be a model, but you could be."

"Well, I don't think I'll ever be a model. But you know what? I'd like to be a mommy someday, and I'd like to have a little girl just like you. You're very pretty, too, and you're very nice. I'm glad to have you as my friend."

Lynn smiled from ear to ear. "I think you should marry my dad, and then when you have a little girl, she could be my little sister. And I could help take care of her. I help take care of Eddie all the time."

Kathy nodded. "Well, you never know. It may happen someday. I don't think it will be anytime real soon, but maybe someday." She glanced at Steve, who was listening to the conversation. She expected a reaction, but he gave none.

Shortly after lunch, while Steve and Kathy broke camp and packed the truck, and Lynn and Eddie played on the swings, Steve said, "Speaking of babies, there's something I've been wanting to ask you, but I've been a little embarrassed. It's about birth control. Are you taking care of that?"

"Yes," she said. "I started taking the pill the Monday morning after our first date. I guess that tells you something, doesn't it? Anyway, I don't need any surprises. I doubt if you do, either. Since we're talking about babies, though, how would you feel about having another one someday?"

Steve stopped what he was doing and looked at Kathy. "I'm not sure, Kathy. I've thought about it a little bit since we starting saying 'I love you,' but I'm just not sure. Do you really want children?"

Kathy looked down for a moment and then at Steve. "I think so. It's kind of a scary thought, but a comforting one, too. As you know, I've never been around babies. I've only held one a couple of times. When I did, I felt a mixture of warm love and impatience.

"I don't know, I think maybe all kinds of dormant feelings are being awakened in me. That's your fault, you know. Before you came along, I was happy to be a fiercely single, completely self-centered, sober celibate. Now look at me, making love unashamedly under the stars and talking about having babies."

Steve laughed. "Hey, all of this baby talk reminds me of something. How are you feeling about stopping at my mom's?"

Kathy smiled. "Oh, what the hell. I'm on a roll, right? If your kids like me, maybe your mom will, too. I want to clean up first, though, and that is not open to compromise."

They dropped off Lynn and Eddie at exactly 5:00 o'clock. Bev agreed to stop in Austin on their way through town on Wednesday morning for final good-byes.

Driving to Lois and Chester's, Kathy asked Steve, "Does your mother know about me?"

Steve looked surprised. "Sure she does. I mean, that's why we're going over there, so that y'all can meet each other."

"No, I mean, does she know about my past?"

"Oh, that. No, I didn't tell her about that. I don't think of it as a secret, but I didn't tell her. Do you think I should have? I mean, I will if you think I should. I'm pretty sure she can handle it."

Kathy did not reply immediately. When she did, she spoke cautiously. "I think I would rather she didn't know, at least right away. I mean, if she were to ask, I would tell her the truth. I'll tell you, though, Steve, she won't like it. I can almost guarantee you that. I don't care how cool she is, she won't like the idea of her son being in a relationship with a hooker, even a nice, retired one. You can bet the farm on that."

"Well, we'll see. Remember, we're observers. We're Buddha's, right? Stay present? Stay conscious? Be honest? Go with the flow? It's worked so far," Steve suggested.

"All right, Steve," Kathy said. "But don't say I didn't warn you."

When they arrived at Lois', she had dinner made and waiting for them. "I know I wasn't supposed to do this, but gosh, how often does a mother get to cook for her only son and his friends once they get grown and out of the nest?"

During dinner, the conversation stayed light. They talked about the camping trip and the kids. Steve told Lois and Chester about graduate school, including the stories about Ron and the rooftop smoke and the cocktail party. They asked about treatment, and Steve talked a little about that. Finally, during dessert, Lois asked Kathy to tell them about herself.

"What would you like to know, Lois?" she asked.

"Oh, I don't know. What kind of work do you do?"

"Nothing glamorous," she said. "I work on an assembly line at Motorola. I don't plan to do that forever, but it's okay for now. I have some college credits, and I plan to return to UT when I can afford it."

"Kathy put herself through junior college plus a year at UT," Steve added. "She didn't have any help from anyone, even her family."

"Really?" Lois said. "Well, I admire you for that, Kathy. It's tough for a woman trying to make it on her own these days. I tried it when Steve's dad and I divorced. I don't think I could have made it if it wasn't for this sweet man right here." She touched Chester's arm. "He saved my life. I was living in a little

395

old garage apartment and working at a job that didn't pay diddly, and I was trying to stay sober to boot. Chester came by every day and took me to an AA meeting and out to dinner. Then he sat with me and encouraged me to hang in there and trust the process. He was my angel."

Steve and Kathy looked at Chester. He smiled and nodded his head. "It was my pleasure," he said quietly.

"May I ask how long you've been sober, Lois?" Kathy asked.

"I celebrated ten years on September 5th, exactly three days after Steve told me that he was in a treatment program. How about you?"

"I've been sober and clean for almost seven months. I've been in treatment the whole time. That's been a great help to me. It's where I met Steve."

"Yes, he told me that. You're so lucky to be in a treatment program. I think it would have helped me a great deal if I would have had that opportunity. How did you happen to get into treatment?"

Kathy hesitated. "Well, it's kind of a long story, really. The greatly condensed version of it is that I got into some legal trouble, and the judge offered me treatment instead of jail. I was happy to comply, and of course it turned out to be a real gift, for which I'm very grateful."

"Would it be too rude of me to ask what kind of trouble you were in?" Lois asked.

Before Kathy could answer, Steve stepped in. "Mother, for crying out loud; give it a rest, will you? Kathy's here to meet you, not tell her life story."

"I'm sorry, Kathy," Lois said. "Please forgive me. I didn't mean to interrogate. I was just interested. I was arrested once myself, but I wasn't fortunate enough to be sent to treatment. The judge merely admonished me for my behavior. He looked down his nose at me and told me to get my act together and be a lady.

"He sent me home in my husband's custody and ordered him to keep me out of trouble. To tell you the truth, I would have been better off in jail. I was drunk again before the sun went down. After that, my husband reminded me of my shameful behavior on a regular basis. He did that until I finally moved out. He didn't know it, but he did not have to remind me. To this day, I've never fully forgiven myself."

Kathy nodded. "Yes, I understand. I imagine that it was even more difficult for you because you were not only a woman, but also a mother. I suppose that turns up the heat even more. I was very much alone. I had virtually no contact with my family. And I had no friends except for the shallow relationships that develop among people who drink and use together.

"I lived alone with my cat. I had no one to answer to and no one to impress. Anyway, Lois, the truth is that I was arrested for prostitution. I didn't really want you to know, but I guess it's just as well."

After a brief silence, Lois said, "You know, Kathy, you would think that one of these days I would learn to keep my big mouth shut and my nose out of other people's business. But I guess I never will. You should probably know that about me. Would you like another piece of pie or more coffee?"

Kathy blushed slightly. "Maybe another cup of coffee, if it isn't too much trouble."

"Me, too," Steve said. "How about you, Chester? More coffee?"

"Yes, I suppose so," Chester answered. "There's nothing like a good cup of fresh, hot coffee to settle the nerves." He smiled kindly at Kathy. "Wouldn't you agree, Kathy?"

Lois stood up from the table. "I'll put on a fresh pot. It will only take a few minutes. Kathy, maybe you would like to help me. I think we can trust these men to be alone for a few minutes," she said.

Once in the kitchen, Lois closed the door to the dining room and went to the cupboard for the coffee. When she did not immediately say anything, Kathy went ahead and spoke first. "I'm sorry Lois. I'm sure you're disappointed."

Lois turned to face her. "No, dear," she said. "I'm not disappointed. I asked you to come in here with me so that I could apologize for prying into your private business. That's what I was doing, obviously. I could tell by the way you and Steve look at each other that something pretty big is brewing between you. I'm afraid that my maternal curiosity got the best of me. I'm very sorry. I hope you will forgive me."

Kathy smiled. "Of course. Thank you, Lois. You're very kind. I'm not so sure that I would be so understanding. Perhaps when I'm further along in my program."

"Yes, well, I'm not so sure that I would have been as honest as you. You're quite courageous. I admire that in a person."

On the drive home, Steve and Kathy discussed their time with Lois. When they pulled into the parking lot of Kathy's apartment house, Steve said, "Well, I've got to say that all in all, I'm pretty damned impressed with both of you. Especially you, Kathy. You never cease to amaze me. You stand up to your fears, and you walk right through them. It's incredible. You're incredible. Do you know that?"

She shook her head. "No, I don't feel like I'm incredible at all. I feel as though I plod along, and sometimes I hit it lucky. That's what this weekend felt like—like I hit it lucky with your family. I like them all very much. I even liked Bev. She was very gracious."

"Yes, she was. Don't turn your back on her, though, Kathy. Don't make the mistake of trusting her too far. You're a threat to her, and she knows it. The minute Lynn tells her how great you are, she'll go on the offensive. If she ever finds out about your past, she'll use it against you to the absolute max. Believe me on this one. She's cunning and smart, and she's terribly insecure. That's a dangerous combination."

Kathy nodded. "I'll remember that." She scooted over next to Steve and put her arms around him. "You know what? I'm going to miss sleeping with you tonight. The last three days have been wonderful. You want to come up for a little bit? I'll fix some tea."

"I'd like to, Kathy, but I have Cally Callahan homework to do, and it's going to take some time. I'll miss you, too, though. How about if I meet you tomorrow night at your meeting?"

"Okay. I love you, Steve."

"I love you, too."

Steve walked Kathy up to her apartment and said good night. Driving to his house, he thought about how great his life was. He felt happy. He felt secure. He felt confident. He felt good about himself. Some of the promises that he had made to himself when he took his geographical cure to Austin in August, 1973 were actually coming true in September, 1974.

CHAPTER 68

Steve completed his Callahan Treatment Plan assignment a little before midnight, and even though he missed Kathy's body next to his, he had a peaceful night.

He awakened to a familiar 7:00 AM telephone call. He picked up the phone and said, "Hello, Mother. Did anyone ever tell you how predictable you are?"

"Good morning, Steve. I operate best on predictability. It contributes to my sanity, which does get threatened from time to time."

"Meaning what, Mother?"

"Meaning you should have told me about Kathy before I stuck my foot in my mouth. You sat there and let me embarrass myself and her."

"Damn it, Mother, it wasn't my place to tell you about Kathy. Her past is her business. Anyway, if you'll remember, I asked you once to back off, and you didn't listen. In fact, you did more than not listen. You forged ahead with your own story that said loud and clear, 'I've shown you mine; now show me yours.'"

"Steve, that's not fair."

"Well, maybe it's not fair, but is it wrong?"

Lois hesitated. "Well...I don't know," she said. "I just wish you would have told me so that I wouldn't have embarrassed her like that."

"Don't worry about her embarrassment, Mother. It was fleeting. She accepted your apology, and she left there liking you very much. She had a good time. I probably shouldn't ask, but besides the obvious, what did you think of her?"

Again, she took a moment to answer. Finally, she said, "Steve, I have to say, I have mixed feelings. On the one hand, I couldn't help but like her. She's a very lovely young woman. But when she said the word 'prostitution,' I almost choked on my food. I mean, she's such a beautiful, intelligent person; why in the world would she ever become a prostitute? I can't even imagine that."

"I don't know, Mother. Why would anyone slip off into self-destructive behavior? Why are you an alcoholic? Why am I? Why did you let Dad beat you up for twenty years? Who knows?

"To me, the issue is not 'What have you done?' Especially not, 'What did you do while you were active in your addiction?' The relevant question is 'Who are you?' And I'll tell you this: Kathy is a wonderful person. She's not just beautiful and intelligent. She's warm-hearted and genuine. She's very honest and very real. I don't think she has a phony bone in her body.

"And you know what else, Mother? I love her."

"Honey, how do you know that? You hardly even know her."

"I feel it, Mother. I feel it in my heart. I love her in a way that I've never loved anyone."

Lois sighed. "Well, like I said, I did like her. And I respect anyone who can turn his or her life around. I just wish she hadn't been a prostitute."

"Well, you can wish all you want to, and it won't change a thing. Anyway, it will give you a chance to work your program. You'll get to practice open-mindedness, tolerance, non-judgement, acceptance, and all of that good stuff. What did Chester say about her?"

Lois laughed. "Oh, you know Chester. He fell in love with her. He called her a breath of fresh air. He said she has a good spirit and that she's a keeper."

Steve laughed. "Man, don't you just love that guy? And he's right, Mother. Just give her a fair chance. You won't be sorry. I guarantee it."

Following his Monday morning class and an AA meeting at the Catholic Student Center, Steve drove straight to The Recovery Center for his individual session with Cally. He told Cally about his weekend and then they tackled his homework.

"As I remember it Steve, your treatment plan assignment ᵹed you to read and discuss the article *Abstinence vs.* ₁ᵥₑcovery and then develop an action plan to address your physical, mental, emotional, and spiritual recovery needs. So tell me first, what did you get out of the article."

"I got a lot out of it, Cally. It's a good article. What it said to me is that abstinence is an event. It's something that I do at a particular point in time; that is, I quit drinking and using. Recovery, on the other hand, is a process of growth and change that happens over time while I'm abstinent, if in fact I work to make it happen.

"The recovery process affects those four aspects of myself that you just mentioned—physical, mental, emotional, and spiritual. Physical recovery is the simplest; mental is more complex; emotional is more complex yet; and spiritual is the most complex.

"The article states clearly that abstinence alone won't cut it, and that for this thing I'm doing right now to be real and meaningful and lasting, recovery must occur. In other words, I have to change and grow, and I have to look at it as a lifelong process."

"All right, Steve; that's very good. Now let me add a couple of things. You probably already know all of this, but humor me. Simply put, physical recovery has to do with taking care of your body to restore physical health. Mental recovery has mainly to do with attitudes, beliefs, and movement through denial toward truth; it requires open-mindedness and willingness to challenge your old ideas.

"Emotional recovery has to do with feelings; it covers learning to deal with them in honest, open, responsible ways, which includes their appropriate expression and resolution. Spiritual recovery incorporates and extends the first three dimensions to include the deeper personal qualities that add up to one's overall attitude toward life—to the way one experiences the world and himself *in* the world.

"Spiritual recovery implies movement in a positive direction toward those qualities which represent spiritual healing and wellness. That includes qualities like honesty, integrity, genuineness, humility, acceptance, tolerance, serenity, courage, faith, etc.

"By the way, it's important to remember that spirituality does not refer only to positive qualities. To my way of thinking, every positive spiritual quality has a negative counterpart. If we're talking about deep personal qualities, then dishonesty is a spiritual quality the same as honesty. Pride is one just like humility is. See what I mean?

"If one's spirituality reflects his attitude toward life and the way he experiences the world and himself in the world, then it

400

becomes obvious that one's spirituality could have a pretty negative twist to it. I saw a bumper sticker one time that said, 'Life's a bitch and then you die.' Now, that's a pretty negative experience of the world, wouldn't you say?"

Steve smiled. "Yeah, I guess it is. That reminds me of some bathroom wall graffiti I saw not too long ago. It was over at The Beer Garden. I was pretty loaded—drunker than hell and stoned on pot and speed. I was standing at the urinal taking a piss, and I looked up on the wall, and there it was—my entire philosophy of life right there in front of my face. It said, 'The whole world sucks. That's why outer space is a vacuum.' I thought to myself, 'Some fucking genius stood in this very spot where I'm standing right now and captured the essence of my belief system right here on this dirty goddamn wall.' Of course, I didn't think about it in terms of it being a reflection of my spiritual nature. Now that I do, though, I realize how negative my attitude toward life was at that moment. I thought I was having fun, but in reality I was empty. I was spiritually bankrupt, as they say.

"Anyway, I don't feel that way today. Today, I feel optimistic about my life. I don't feel as though the whole world sucks at all."

Cally nodded. "I'm glad to hear that, Steve. I'm very glad to hear it. Maybe we'll have time to talk about that some more a little later. First, though, I want to hear how you're planning to attack recovery on the four dimensions we've been talking about. You don't have to read it to me, but tell me your plan."

"Okay, well, the physical part was pretty easy. I love to practice yoga, so I'll do that for at least 30 minutes a day, and I'll end each session with a meditation. I also love to take my dog for walks, especially to the park, so I'll do that at least three, maybe four times a week. I decided, too, that I can use my bicycle for transportation even more than I do now. That will help because I usually ride pretty fast, which gets my respiration and my heart rate up.

"I also committed to cooking for myself at least once a day and to use basic, healthy foods—not necessarily vegetarian, but mostly so. Finally, I'll do another meditation before I go to bed at night. I figure that takes care of diet, exercise, and at least part of stress management.

"For mental recovery, I set out a couple of books to study. One is on Zen Buddhism, and the other is on Taoism. I chose those because they focus on letting go of old ideas—attitudes and judgments and expectations—and encourage going with the natural flow of your life with a curious and open mind. And the Zen, especially, addresses staying conscious and living in the present moment.

"I wrote down two questions to ask myself when I have negative feelings. I took them from your Friday night lecture. The first is, 'What are my beliefs about this situation that are making me feel this way?' The other is, 'How am I taking this situation too seriously or too personally?' I also plan to continue in group, of course, and I get the feeling that my attitudes and beliefs will get confronted in there.

"There's also AA—both the meetings and the literature. I'm going to a lot of meetings. I figure I'll do close to 90 meetings in 90 days.

"Finally, I plan to start my Fourth Step pretty soon. I expect that to yield insights into the way I judge people and interpret situations in unhealthy ways.

"On the emotional level, besides what I've already mentioned about intervening on upset feelings by questioning or challenging my old beliefs and stuff, I feel very committed to do less stuffing. I'm really going to work on being more spontaneous in the expression of my feelings, and I'm going to work on doing that without contaminating it with a bunch of extraneous bullshit.

"You talked the other night about making 'I statements' as a way of expressing feelings appropriately, without blaming other people or situations for the feelings. I went back and found several pages on that in one of the pamphlets you gave me when I first started here, and I plan to use that technique as a way of expressing my feelings more spontaneously, as well as accepting responsibility for them.

"I'm also going to start keeping a journal, and I plan to focus on feelings when I write. I was planning to do that anyway. Then, of course, there's the group and the other people I've met in recovery who seem to live closer to their feelings than the people I was hanging around with before I got sober. I have Kathy, in particular, who doesn't hide her feelings much at all. She's a role model for me in that regard, even though I don't always like the way she does it.

"The spiritual recovery part is scattered throughout everything else I'm doing, but I have a couple of things to add to what I've already listed. One is prayer. I've done pretty well with the prayer you gave me, the one where I'm asking for willingness and open-mindedness, to which we added humility and patience.

"In addition to that, I've started saying the Third Step prayer as well. I figure I'll say it every morning and every evening in conjunction with meditation. It's not that I've developed some great belief in or understanding of God, but I have come to understand that my own selfish will for myself has brought me a lot of grief. I think maybe saying the Third Step prayer from my heart will at least encourage me to operate from a deeper, more authentic place. Who knows? It may lead unexpectedly to faith in something about which I have little or no understanding today.

"Finally, I want to focus on my behavior as a way to encourage internal change. I heard a guy in a meeting the other night say something that made perfect sense. He said, 'Sometimes I can't think myself into right acting; I have to act myself into right thinking.'

"It reminded me *again* that I've spent more time and effort in my life trying to appear emotionally and spiritually healthy than I have actually behaving that way. Like, I'll secretly judge the hell out of someone but act totally accepting of him or her. I'll cover up my prejudices so that people will think I'm open-minded.

"The big show is an effort to fool people into thinking I'm someone I'm not so that they will give me positive strokes, which make me feel better about myself. It's the old 'If you think I'm okay, then maybe I *am* okay.'

"If I can stop worrying about what people think of me and just conscientiously practice being honest, just for the sake of being honest, then I'll become more honest. If I practice being genuine, just for the sake of being genuine, then I'll become more genuine.

"So I'm going to practice. Like, if I hear myself telling a lie, which happens more often than I like to admit, then I'll just back up and say, 'Wait a minute; that's not true. Let me back up and start over.' And when I catch myself being selfish and self-centered, I'll say, 'Oops, that feels selfish and self-centered; let me start over and say it or do it a different way.' And when I find my consciousness scattered out all over the place, I'll close my eyes for a moment and bring it back to the present.

"What I'm saying is that I think if I practice doing positive spiritual qualities, just for the practice, then those qualities will become more a part of who I am. They will become me, and I'll become them, and I won't have to fake it.

"Now, if I put all of this together, you know, all these loosely related parts, then I think I'll have an integrated plan of recovery in which all of the parts complement other parts. I'll be healthier physically, so my brain should work better to confront my irrational thinking. The yoga and meditation complement spiritual growth. The book study does the same thing. The feelings work feeds back into mental recovery and forward into the spiritual, because in the long run it's directed toward deepening my self-knowledge, self-acceptance, and genuineness. Etc., etc., etc. I don't know if that makes much sense to you, but it does to me.

"That's pretty much it, Cally. I might think of other things along the way, but for now, that's what I've got. That's my plan. What do you think? Do I pass the test?"

Cally smiled. "Oh, I'd say you pass with flying colors, Steve. In fact, you have put together a model program. One thing's for sure; it's not a wimpy program. It's a lot. It's all really good stuff, but it is a lot. I hope that you will continue to pray for patience because my experience has been that writing it all down is difficult enough, but following through can be quite a challenge. This program will take a consistent effort on your part. I hope you know that, and I think you do.

"I also hope you understand that even with a consistent effort, you're going to get bogged down sometimes. Recovery is never a perfectly smooth ride for anyone, not even you. Every once in a while, I hear someone in AA say something like this: 'I got sober six years, three months, and twelve days ago, and every single one of those two thousand and some-odd days has been wonderful.'

"The first time I heard that, I wondered what in the hell was wrong with my program, because I sure wasn't having the experience with recovery that that guy was having. I thought, 'Damn, Cally, you must be doing something very wrong.' Now, though, I just shake my head and wonder if those folks are lying in order to look good, or if their denial is so profound that they aren't in touch with the reality of their lives.

"I'm not telling you this to discourage you, Steve. You know that. I just want you to understand that, 'Yes, you can do this work, and yes, it will pay off for you, and yes, you will still have some tough times.' In fact, you will have some very tough times."

Steve nodded. "I understand that. Be that as it may, though, I feel awfully damn positive right now. You know, while I was writing this assignment last night, I felt really excited because as I wrote it, I kept telling myself, 'Yeah, I can do this. I can do this routine. I can ask myself these questions. I can challenge and give up my old attitudes and beliefs. I can practice being genuine. I can express my feelings.' You know what I mean? It just really felt good, and it came on top of a great weekend with Kathy and my kids. It's like, at this moment, all of the planets are aligned."

"Yes, I can tell," Cally said, smiling. "You're on what some people call a pink cloud, Steve. You know, most people who find themselves feeling as good as you do in early sobriety end up falling off of that cloud and getting a little banged up. Some get more banged up than others do. A lot depends on how diligent you are in maintaining your discipline and working your program.

"You've been on an incredibly fast track so far, and you've handled it beautifully. Now, you've outlined an impressive longer-term recovery plan. I believe that if you implement and stay with this plan, you will continue to progress at a rapid pace.

"I need to give you a word to the wise, however. Sometimes, the most dangerous time in a person's sobriety is when everything is great. It's a paradox, I guess. I've seen a lot of people struggle through incredibly difficult times and stay sober, and then just when it all turns around, and everything is rosy, BOOM! They twist off like crazy and get drunk. It's the damnedest thing. Remember that, Steve.

"There's a sentence on page 85 of the Big Book that says, 'What we really have is a daily reprieve contingent on the maintenance of our spiritual condition.' To me, that's a reminder to avoid complacency. Do you hear what I'm telling you?"

Steve did hear. He heard well.

Steve met Kathy at 8:00 o'clock at the South Austin Group. They sat together, and they listened to the meeting. Afterwards, they sat on the lawn outside and talked. They talked about recovery and how their individual commitments to their individual recoveries was one ticket to a meaningful relationship.

CHAPTER 69

Ralph chaired the noon meeting on Tuesday. His topic was "character defects," and he discussed them within the context of the Fourth Step. He read sections of several pages from the Big Book, and then he talked about his experience of writing his own Fourth Step inventory.

"The Fourth Step says that we're to make a searching and fearless moral inventory of ourselves. I was afraid to do this step, because I knew that I had a whole lot of unflattering (to say the least) character defects that I did not particularly want to put the spotlight on. I was especially reluctant to commit the inventory to paper. I imagined the wrong people getting their hands on it, and me finding myself on the front of *The National Enquirer*. What an ego, huh? Like the whole world was sitting around waiting to read about my character defects.

"Nevertheless, I did want to stay sober, and my sponsor convinced me that writing the inventory was a critical part of the program. He said that my character defects would keep me separated from my self—from my true Self, my Buddha Self, which is how I understand God, and that the inventory process would show me what these character defects were. Then when it came time to ask God to remove them, down the line a little ways in Step 7, I would at least have some idea of what I was asking for. Plus, I would have a map of my recovery, right there in black and white. I could watch the progression of my recovery as my character defects were lessened or removed.

"So I studied the part of the Big Book that tells us how to proceed, and with my sponsor's help, I plowed through it. It took me about four and a half weeks. The finished product was exactly forty pages long.

"What I discovered, and subsequently acknowledged about myself, is probably exactly what everyone else already knew about me—that I was full of anger, resentment, and fear. I was selfish and self-centered. I tried to act like I cared about other people, including my family, but the truth is that I was so self-centered that my needs almost always came first. Because of that, I was a master manipulator; I was a dishonest, arrogant bastard who believed that the ends justified the means so long as it always ended in my favor.

"On top of everything else, I was confronted with how terrified I was that people would somehow see through my armor and see the frightened, dishonest, arrogant man that I had become. Even after I finished writing it all down and did my Fifth Step 'confessional' with my sponsor, I was afraid that someone would find my inventory and thereby know the truth about me.

"I no longer feared seeing it published somewhere. I was just terrified that people would find out the truth about me. So I burned it. I set fire to it and burned it up.

"Not long after that, I began experiencing real, honest-to-goodness change. That's when I became able to laugh at myself—at my ego and it's protectors.

"I believe that the Fourth Step is one of the keys to our recovery. It's one of the keys that opens the door to a meaningfully better life in sobriety. Those who decide to skip it, for whatever reason, lose out on a pretty incredible journey, one that had a profound effect on my life."

Other members shared their experiences with the Fourth Step. Everyone's experience was different, but no one reported a bad one. By the end of the meeting, Steve felt ready and willing to start his own inventory process. He told Ralph, and Ralph suggested that they start working on it immediately.

"Let's start tomorrow night. In fact, let's agree to meet at my house every Wednesday evening until you finish it. We can meet during the time that Kathy attends her group at The Recovery Center. That will give us time to talk and work on a regular basis without the distraction of her sitting around waiting for you."

Steve and Kathy met for coffee after Kathy's meeting. As soon as they settled at a table, Kathy said, "I've been wondering if you've talked to your mom."

"Oh yeah, I forgot to tell you. Seven o'clock yesterday morning. She's the most predictable person I've ever known."

Kathy waited for a moment and then said, "Well? Are you going to make me ask?"

Steve smiled. "Ask what? What are you talking about?"

"Come on, Steve. That's mean. Tell me what she said."

Steve laughed. "Well, what could she say? She loved you to death. I told you she would. So did Chester. He told my mom that you were a breath of fresh air and a keeper."

Kathy smiled. "Okay, wise guy, what did they really say?"

"They both liked you very much. My mom sounded a little hesitant at first, but she said it like she meant it. She said it two different times. She said she felt a little shocked when you revealed the circumstances of your arrest, but she said she respected you for turning your life around. All in all, I think she's fine. And by the way, I told her that I love you."

Kathy was quiet for a moment, and then she said softly, "I'm glad it's out in the open, at least with her. I appreciate your telling her that you love me. That makes me feel good."

Later that night, Steve celebrated the anniversary of his third full week of sobriety by sleeping like a baby all the way through the night.

The next morning, he said a heartfelt, tearful goodbye to Lynn and Eddie as they passed through town heading north. When they drove away, he went immediately into his shop, turned on the radio, and started working. He knew that his busyness was a distraction—a defense against feeling the sadness that lurked just under the surface. He reminded himself that his plan for emotional recovery called for feeling rather than stuffing his feelings. Finally, he gave in and let go. He sat down on the floor and cried.

After lunch, he sat on the front porch, stared at nothing, and fantasized about getting high. He recalled letting go of his last few marijuana tops—the ones that he had once retired to the freezer for safekeeping. He closed his eyes and pictured it still there. He pictured himself rolling one and firing it up. Then he imagined coming on to it. He felt the gentle, relaxing high starting at the top of his head and spreading downward throughout his body. He savored the feeling for a few seconds; then he opened his eyes and let it go.

He took a deep breath and released it. "You better not play this game right now, Steve," he told himself. "Getting stoned wouldn't change a thing, not for the better, anyway."

He stood up and opened the door to go into the house but stopped when he heard Carla calling his name. He looked around and saw her leaning over her porch railing and waving her arms crazily. "Hey," she shouted, "I'm taking oatmeal cookies out of the oven in five minutes. Get your butt over here, and bring some milk."

Steve gave her the "okay" sign, walked inside to grab the milk, and mumbled to himself, "Small favors; damn near unbelievable small favors."

While they filled up on warm cookies and cold milk, Steve brought Carla up to date on his roller coaster life. He talked a lot about Kathy. Carla reminded him that they had met.

"Oh yeah, I wondered about that," he said. "I was driving away, on my way to San Antonio, and I saw her meandering over this way. What did y'all talk about?"

"We talked about you, of course. Neither of us told any bold secrets or anything, but I could tell she had stars in her eyes. We had fun agreeing on what a sweet guy you are. Actually, I liked her a lot. I'd like to get to know her better. Maybe you will trust me to become friends with her. She said she doesn't have many friends outside of you and a couple of women from AA."

After a while, Steve mentioned Lynn and Eddie. As he talked about saying goodbye to them earlier in the day, his sadness returned, and he started to cry.

"I'm sorry, Carla; I thought I was done with this shit," he said, wiping the tears away.

Carla moved over next to him and put her arms around him. She pulled him close and said, "Let it out, Steve. It's okay. Just let it out." He closed his eyes, relaxed into her arms, and cried hard.

Carla held him and rocked him gently back and forth. Whenever he started to move or talk, she said, "Shhh, just let it all go."

When he finally cried himself out, he sat up and said, "Man, I think that was the most I've ever cried at one time in my life. Thank you for being so patient."

"You're welcome, Steve," Carla said. "You have a lot of sadness. I could feel it; it runs very deep inside of you. Listen, how about letting me do some bodywork on you? I think it would really help, especially right now while you're so open."

Steve nodded. "Yeah, okay, I'd like that."

"Great; go on into my room and take your clothes off and get up on the table. We'll start with you lying on your back. I'll be in there in just a minute."

As Steve undressed, he recalled having sex with Carla following the first time she gave him a massage. He remembered lying with her in her bed with the overhead light on. He remembered her openness and spontaneity. And by the time he got onto the table, he had a partial erection. He quickly tried to put the memory out of his mind, but at that moment, Carla walked into the room.

"Oops," he said. "Sorry about this, Carla. I couldn't help it. Old memories and such, you know?"

Carla smiled softly. "Don't worry about it, Steve. It's just your body, and I've seen it before. Anyway, we have a different agenda and different rules today than we did last year.

"Close your eyes and relax," she said. She put one hand on his chest and the other on his abdomen. "I'm going to do some pretty deep work on you, so if I start to hurt you, tell me and I'll back off. Otherwise, just keep breathing, and try to focus your awareness on your breath. If any feelings come up, just let them out."

Carla worked on Steve's body for over an hour. When she was finished, she put her face close to his and whispered, "How do you feel, Steve?"

"I feel good. I feel very relaxed—deeply relaxed, and I feel light, and empty. It's a good empty, like I'm clean inside. I feel really good."

Carla nodded. "Lie here for a few minutes and relax. I'll be right back." When she returned, she helped him up and said, "Come with me." She took his hand and led him into the bathroom, where she had drawn a tub of hot water.

"Be careful, now; it's pretty hot," she said. Steve slipped into the water.

"Umm, this feels great, and it smells good," he said. "What's in it?"

"Some scented oils; nothing that can hurt you. Just lie back and relax. I'll check in on you in a little while."

After getting dressed, Steve sat with Carla on the front porch. "Thank you, Carla," he said. "It's been a very long time since someone took care of me like that. When I was a kid, I used to get sick or fake being sick hoping that my mom would show me that kind of attention. She never did.

"My grandmother did a few times. One of my earliest childhood memories is of her coming to my rescue one night when I threw up in my bed. And in fact, she did what you just did; she put me into a tub of warm water." He looked at Carla and smiled. "I feel humbled by your tenderness and your generosity, my friend. I hope I can repay you one of these days."

Carla smiled. "Thank you for letting me care for you, Steve. Not everyone can do that, you know. It was a wonderfully nurturing experience for me."

Steve spent the rest of the day at the kitchen table. He prepared for his Thursday class and then studied the part of the Big Book that outlined Step Four. By the time he met with Ralph at 7:00 o'clock, he had written the title at the top of the first page of his Fourth Step inventory. It read:

Steven Edward Campbell's Fearless and Searching Moral Inventory—A Journal of Depravity

When he arrived at Ralph's house, they went right to work. They started by saying the Third Step prayer together, turning their will and their lives over to the care of a power greater than themselves. Then they reviewed what Steve had read in the Big Book. Then Ralph talked more about his own experience with the exercise.

"Writing the inventory according to the book is magical," Ralph said. "The process is ingenious because it slips us in through the back door of discovery and insight. Instead of just listing our bad traits, we list our resentments against people and places. Then we analyze those resentments to discover what part we played in their formation. That's how we identify our defects of character. It's a fascinating way to approach self-examination.

"At first I couldn't understand why we did this 'through the back door' deal. I argued that I should be allowed to just list my character defects. You know, I figured I knew what they were. I knew that I was a loser—a weak-willed liar and a cheat who had screwed people around to serve my own needs. Why did I have to do all of that damn writing? Especially, why did I have to analyze my anger and resentments against other people as a way of understanding myself? As I got into it, though, I came to appreciate the subtle brilliance of the method.

"I saw for the first time that it really wasn't other people who caused my upset feelings. It was *me;* I did it to myself. It was *my* character defects—my behaviors, my attitudes, my beliefs, my way of looking at things—which were responsible for the way I felt. It was my defensive, over-protective ego. It was my impatience, intolerance, arrogance, and my judgmental nature. It was my false pride. It was my shame, and my fear that other people would see my shame. It was my need to be liked and my fear that I wasn't. It was my egocentrism—my self-centeredness and my selfishness. It was my fear that I would not get what I wanted or needed for myself and my holding on tight to what I already had. It was my dishonesty, including my manipulative nature that fought hard to always get me what I wanted when I wanted it. It was my expectations of other people—my belief that they should be who I wanted them to be and act the way I thought they should act.

"I felt resentful toward other people because of me. And for every one of my resentments, I came to see how my behavior and my attitudes and my beliefs were the root cause of my feelings. By analyzing the resentments, I obtained a clear picture of who I was and what it was about me that kept me separated from my true Self, or God, or whatever you want to call your higher power.

"You know, none of this was anything that I didn't already know somewhere inside of me, but by doing the written inventory, I had it right there in front of my face. I saw exactly why I needed to do all of that writing instead of just sitting down and making a list of my shortcomings. Had I done it the easy way, the exercise would not have been very meaningful to me, if for no other reason than I would not have seen the context within which my character defects worked. Doing it by the book brought the character defects to life. I saw and understood how costly they were to me, and I became more willing to have them removed.

"And here's something interesting, Steve. I never felt bad about what I had written or what I learned about myself. I didn't shame myself for it. I just looked at it, and I remember saying to myself, 'Damn, look at all this shit. God's got a lot of work to do here.'

"I think I was able to take that attitude because I did a pretty honest Third Step. I really did make a decision to turn my will and my life over to the care of a power greater than myself, which I understood to mean a power greater than my own ego."

Ralph's experience inspired Steve to forge ahead. "I'm ready to get going on it," he said. "I mean, I've piled a lot on myself lately, and because of that, I feel a little pressured for time. I'm in a good place right now, though, and I want to keep moving forward."

"Well, it doesn't have to be done all at once, Steve. In fact, what I think works best is to make a good fast start on it in the beginning so that you have an immediate investment, and then commit yourself to a certain amount of time or output every day after that. The daily commitment can be very minimal. It can be ten minutes or two lines or something like that, so long as you're consistent.

"Another good idea is to end each day's work in the middle of a sentence so that the next day, when you pick it up again, you know exactly where you are. That way, you don't have to waste time reviewing what you've already done. I promise you that if you follow these guidelines, you'll have your Fourth Step done before you know it.

"By the way, a good way to get the fast start I was talking about is to get away from everything for a day or two. Go where there are no phones and no TV's and no work. I went to my parents' cabin on Lake LBJ for two days, and I came home with twenty pages done."

Driving home, Steve knew that Kathy would probably be in bed, but he decided to chance it and drop by her apartment. She answered the door in her nightshirt.

"What a treat," she said as she let him in. "I thought you might call, but I didn't expect a personal visit. Where's your overnight bag?"

Steve smiled. "God, I'd love more than anything to stay, but I still have studying to do for tomorrow. I had this great idea, though. How about another camping trip this weekend?" He told her about Ralph's recommendation to get away from distractions to facilitate a fast start on his Fourth Step.

Kathy laughed and said, "What makes you think I wouldn't be the biggest distraction you could ever imagine?" She offered

411

half-heartedly to stay behind. Steve waved off the idea, and they agreed to leave Friday night after Steve's group.

"So how's you're new group?" Steve asked.

"You know what? It was just fine. I felt nervous but not afraid. I felt a little self-conscious, and a little lonely, but all in all I think I'll be okay. The level of work didn't seem that much deeper than that in the Friday night group. The feedback was better, though; it was more honest, insightful, and on target, but that's about it. I feel good about the change. I think we're both better off. I guess I have to say it: "Cally was right.""

At 11:15, Kathy said, "Either come to bed with me or go home. It's up to you, but I've got to get to sleep or I won't be worth killing tomorrow."

Steve took a rain check. "I have my tough class tomorrow, and I want to be prepared," he said. "Let's do it tomorrow."

Steve climbed into bed at 2:00 AM. He sat cross-legged and meditated for fifteen minutes and then he prayed. He directed the prayer, his own bastardized version of the Third Step prayer from the Big Book, inward to the deepest place within himself that he could imagine, as well as outward to wherever prayers may go.

"God, I'm sitting here naked on my bed, offering myself to you, to do with me as you will. I'm asking you to please relieve me of the bondage of self, that I may better know and do your will. Please take away my shortcomings, so that I may somehow be of help to others. Help me to do your will always. God, assuming that it's your will for me, please give me willingness, open-mindedness, patience, and humility. I could also use more faith. I want to feel closer to you, and I want to live a better life. Thanks for listening, if in fact you are."

CHAPTER 70

Despite the late bedtime, Steve got up early Thursday morning and followed his recovery plan. He practiced yoga, meditated, and prayed before breakfast. Then he walked Ginger to the park, where he studied Zen for 30 minutes before going home to study statistical methods until time for class.

During class, he fielded questions from the instructor, and he generated intelligent, thoughtful ones of his own. After class, the professor nodded to him and said, "Nice work, Mr. Campbell."

When Kathy arrived at Steve's house at 7:00 o'clock, she found a nice vegetarian dinner waiting for her on the table. "My, you sure do know how to take care of a girl," she said. "What's this spread going to cost me?"

Steve smiled. "The Campbell Cafe operates on the barter system. What do you have that I want?"

Kathy winked at him and said, "I bet I can think of something I have that you want."

The 8:00 o'clock AA meeting focused on The Serenity Prayer. Most people who shared talked about the first part: "God, grant me the serenity to accept the things I cannot change...." Some spoke about serenity, and others, about acceptance.

One speaker caught Steve's ear. "I've come to understand serenity as a synonym for 'peace of conscience,'" he said. "Speaking just for me, I've found that serenity visits me and stays with me pretty much as long as I'm right with the world. Not when the world is right with me, but rather when I'm right with the world. And that seems to be a function of my integrity— my honesty with myself and with others.

"If I'm doing the right thing according to my conscience, which is as close to a Higher Power as I've been able to get, then I usually feel at peace. There's a little voice inside my head that lets me know what I really ought to say or do, and I have the option of accepting what it tells me or rejecting it.

"When my frightened ego, which I refer to as *the punk,* takes over and dictates how I interact with the world, I invariably end up compromising my integrity. And compromising my integrity messes with my serenity *every single time I do it.* 'The punk' is no friend of mine. He's a tricky little devil, though. Sometimes he convinces me that he's taking care of me, when in reality he's robbing me of my serenity."

After the meeting, Steve and Kathy turned down invitations to go to coffee and went straight home. When they got there, Steve put the teakettle on the stove. Kathy hopped up and sat on the kitchen counter.

"What did you think of the meeting, Steve?" she asked.

"I liked it, at least the parts I heard. My mind wandered off to our camping trip quite a bit, but I really liked what David said about serenity and peace of conscience. I like that idea because it's empowering. It tells me to accept responsibility for my own sense of wellbeing, you know, like the universe is not responsible for my serenity. Rather, I'm responsible for it myself. It's like, 'Okay, if you want serenity, then follow your conscience, and don't compromise your integrity.'

"Ralph said something similar the other day. He said that he believes we're all born with inner wisdom, or innate inner wisdom, or something like that. He said everyone has it, and it's the same in everyone. And we can access our inner wisdom just by consciously deciding to connect with it and listen to it, like through meditation, I suppose. He said that you can call it whatever you're comfortable with. Like, if you're a humanist, you could call it conscience. If you're a Christian, you could call it God or Jesus. If you're a Buddhist, you could call it your Perfect Self or Buddha Self.

"Regardless, though, the idea is that this wisdom is inside, and if you want to access it and use it, all you have to do is go inside and connect with it."

Kathy hopped down from the counter and picked up Steve's Big Book. "That whole idea is right here," she said. "It's here on pages 86 and 87. Listen to this: 'In thinking about our day we may face indecision. We may not be able to determine which course to take. Here we ask God for inspiration, an intuitive thought or decision. We relax and take it easy. We don't struggle. We are often surprised how the right answers come after we have tried this for a while. What used to be the hunch or the occasional inspiration gradually becomes a working part of the mind.' Isn't that basically what you're saying?"

"Yeah, that sounds pretty close. So what David referred to as 'the little voice inside my head' is the same thing as Ralph's 'inner wisdom' and the Big Book's 'inspiration' or 'intuitive thought.' Good for David; he figured it out, and I learned something important."

Kathy returned to her perch on the kitchen counter. "David's a good guy," she said. "He's funny, too. He asked me out once a few months ago. When I told him I wasn't dating, he said, 'Oh, thank goodness. I felt obliged to ask you because you're so pretty, but I didn't really want you to go because I had the feeling that we could become friends, and nothing screws up friendships quicker than dating.'"

Steve laughed. "That's a good one. Do you think it's true, though? I mean, you're certainly my friend. In fact, you're my favorite friend. If something happened to our romance, I'd still want to continue the friendship. Wouldn't you?"

Kathy nodded. "Yeah, I think I would. Maybe David was just saying that because he didn't want to feel rejected. I hope so, because you're definitely my best friend, Steve. Even though we haven't known each other for very long, I feel as though I know you well. I love being with you. I trust you. I love you to pieces."

Sitting on the edge of the countertop, she opened her arms and spread her legs and invited Steve in for a hug. When he stepped up to her, she wrapped her arms and legs around him and pulled him into her. She held him there until the teapot whistled.

They listened to music and talked for awhile, then showered and went to bed. They made love and fell asleep in each other's arms.

The next morning, Steve went through his recovery routine and then worked in his shop while Kathy slept. He woke her up in time for them to go to a noon meeting. Following the meeting, they ate lunch with Patti, and during the conversation, Patti asked Kathy if she would like to go shopping with her at the mall.

"Really?" Kathy asked. "You mean, like this afternoon? To a shopping mall?"

"Yeah. I need a pair of jeans and a couple of other little things, and I'd love the company. I can drop you off wherever you want after we're done."

"Well, I don't know. Steve, what did you have planned for us today?"

Steve shook his head. "Nothing, really. Get ready for the camping trip. Perhaps a little afternoon roll in the hay. You know, nothing that can't wait. You go ahead; it will be fun. When was the last time you had an afternoon with the girls?"

Kathy said, "You're not going to believe this, but I've never been shopping for clothes at the mall with a friend. I worked at a department store in the mall for a few years, but I didn't have any female friends to just hang out with. I've always shopped by myself, and just about everything I own came from the store where I worked." She hesitated for a moment and then said, "Patti, I would love to go shopping with you. You don't mind, Steve?"

Steve laughed. "No, man, I don't mind at all. I'll go home and work for a little while and then I'll get our gear together for the weekend. Have a good time. I'll see you when you get back."

After lunch, Steve kissed Kathy goodbye and watched her smiling face as she drove off with Patti. On his way home, he ran a quick picture of her love life through his mind. Abused by her parents as a child. On her own and basically alone at sixteen. A teenage girl with no mom. A teenage girl with no female friends. Never been shopping at the mall with a pal. Never been in love.

"A beautiful woman with a good heart and a bad past. What an amazing person," he whispered to himself.

As Steve parked his truck on the street in front of his house, he noticed James' car parked down the street in front of Tommy's. His first impulse was to walk down there and see his old friends. His second was to quickly slip into his house before anyone saw him. His third was to quit being silly and go.

As he approached Tommy's door, he heard loud music and loud talking and laughter inside. He hesitated for a moment and then knocked. Tommy opened the door and said in a loud voice, "Well, hell's bells. Look who's here. It's our old friend, our *sober* old friend—the stranger from down the street. Come on in, Steve."

Steve walked into a vaguely familiar scene—James and Tommy and Dixie sitting around the dining room table. The table top held a slew of empty beer bottles, a bag of pot, rolling papers, an ashtray, Tommy's famous hand carved wooden stash box, and his old glass Toker II bong.

"What do we have here? A Friday afternoon TGIF party?" Steve asked.

Tommy laughed. "Yeah, that's as good a reason as any, I suppose. Come on in and sit down. I don't have much to offer you, I'm afraid. How about a glass of tap water and some carrots?"

The three of them laughed heartily. Steve chuckled politely and sat down at the table with them. They were definitely on a roll. James and Tommy were loaded, and Dixie was as high as Steve had ever seen her. They picked up where they had left off before Steve arrived.

Steve listened and smiled, but he felt uncomfortable and out of place. Their jokes were not funny. Their stories were silly and vulgar; a few felt mean-spirited.

Before long, Steve sensed that his presence dampened the mood in the room. He started looking for a way to leave gracefully.

Tommy and James walked into the kitchen together for more beer. When they didn't return immediately, Dixie caught Steve's eye and said, "You've lost your sense of humor, Stevey. I hate to say it, but you used to be more fun."

Steve felt stung and hurt by the remark. "I'm sorry, Dixie," he said. "Actually, I feel pretty uncomfortable, like I don't belong here. I'm not used to being straight when other people are high. I don't know how to act when we're in such different places. I didn't mean to put anyone off or disrupt the party."

He looked down for a moment and then back at Dixie. "What you just said to me really hurt my feelings. I'm trying hard to do something good and right for myself. If I'm different it's because I needed to change. I seem to remember that you told me that several times."

He paused for a moment and then said, "I think I ought to go." He stood up and walked into the kitchen, where Tommy and James had begun a heated intellectual discussion.

"I gotta run, guys," he said. "Y'all take care and stay out of trouble."

"Hey, man, don't run off," Tommy said loudly.

"Yeah, man," James added. "You haven't even told us what the fuck you've been up to."

"Yeah, well, I'll spare you the boring details for now. Drop by sometime, and we can talk more. I'm still around the house and shop most of the time."

When he walked back through the house to the front door, Dixie was nowhere in sight. He started to look for her to say goodbye but then changed his mind. As he closed the front door behind him and stood alone on the porch, he felt profoundly, almost desperately empty.

Kathy and Patti showed up late in the afternoon, smiling and laughing and joking with each other in a light-hearted and attractive way. Their presence stood in stark contrast to what Steve had felt at Tommy's. It prompted him to tell them about his experience.

Kathy listened but could hardly relate. Since getting sober, she had completely abandoned every person she had known while she was using. Her environment had totally changed.

Patti understood, though. "When I was about four months sober, I went to a party where a group of old drinking buddies were. I felt pretty out of place and self-conscious, just like you did at your friend's, but I was determined to hang in there and be a sport, you know?

"Well, by 10:00 o'clock, everyone was pretty blasted. I was standing by myself at the buffet table, trying to look interested in the food. A guy that I had dated a couple of times and had really kind of liked, came up to me and asked me why I wasn't drinking. I thought he really wanted to know, so I told him that I had come to recognize that I had a problem with alcohol and had gotten sober and so forth and so on. He looked me right squarely in the eye and said, 'Well, I gotta tell you, Patti, I liked you a hell of a lot better the other way.'

"It knocked my feet right out from under me. It was all I could do to keep from bursting out in tears right then and there. I mean, I felt as though everything I was trying to do to better my life had just been invalidated. I was crushed. I think I mumbled something like, 'Oh, I see,' or something profound like that, and I immediately said my good-byes and left.

"The minute I pulled away from the house, the dam broke. I drove straight to my sponsor's house, bawling my eyes out the entire way. I woke her up, and we talked for a long time. After that, I felt much better. I'll tell you, though, it was one of the most hurtful experiences of my early sobriety. It didn't threaten my sobriety, but it sure did shake my feelings up."

"That's a good story, Patti," Steve said. "I'm glad to know it's not just me. But what about the old friends? I mean, these three people have been like family to me. We've been really, really close. Do I lose them now? Does it always have to be that way? I mean, that's a very sad thought."

Patti shook her head. "No, I don't think it has to be that way at all. It changes, but I don't think we have to abandon anyone unless we just can't stand to be around him or her for some reason.

"My experience has been that the people who were really my friends are still my friends, but I spend my time with them individually instead of in a group, and I choose when to do that.

417

, I never do anything with any of my old friends on a Friday Saturday night, and I never go to a party when they're all there. Not that I'm in great demand as a guest at their parties, but you know what I mean. But we go to lunch together, or to breakfast, or we meet in the afternoon for a cup of coffee or something like that.

"When we're together that way, it still feels good. I can open up to them in a genuine way, and I've found that when I do, they often reciprocate. I don't know, Steve; it's very different, but it's still good."

Steve nodded. "That makes sense. I hear people in AA talking about our having to completely change our playmates and playgrounds. But maybe we don't have to take that quite so literally. Maybe I can keep a few of my old playmates if I can arrange for us to play on different playgrounds at well-chosen times. I understand why you couldn't do that, Kathy, but maybe I can. I hope so, anyway."

Patti hung around, and the three of them talked away the rest of the afternoon. The girls took Steve to his group at 6:00 o'clock. Kathy promised to finish packing the truck and to be ready to leave for Enchanted Rock when she picked him up at 8:00.

"Tell them all I said 'Hi,'" she said.

"Okay. I'll miss your being there. I'm looking forward to the weekend, though. I feel happy, Kathy."

CHAPTER 71

Cally stood in front of his treatment group. With Kathy gone, the group held seven people—two women and five men. Two addicted to alcohol and five addicted to alcohol and various other drugs.

Steve Campbell sat in the semicircle waiting for 6:00 PM— Cally's exact starting time. He glanced around the room and appraised his peers. Sally (Killer) sat to his immediate left. "She doesn't have a clue," he thought. To her left sat Al (Junkman). Steve nodded his head slightly. "Remarkably solid; remarkably sober," he thought.

Peg (Legs) sat on Steve's right. "She'll make it," he whispered to himself. Next to Peg, there was Jim (Mr. Nice Guy). "He's too damn nice to tell the truth." Next to Jim sat Billy (the Fag). "That's the original uphill climb." And then there was Robert (Yuppie Man). "I'd bet my butt he's sneaking drinks," Steve thought.

The room felt different without Kathy. It felt curiously empty and lifeless.

Steve counted up his clean time. "Twenty-three days," he said to himself. "Doesn't sound like much, but it feels like a very long time."

Cally started his lecture at exactly 6:00 o'clock. "Tonight, my friends, we're going to talk about bottoms," he said with a perfectly straight face. He noticed the smiles and furtive glances, but his serious expression never changed.

"What's so funny?" he asked. "I didn't say 'butts.' I said 'bottoms.' High bottoms, to be exact, as in high bottom drunks, addicts, and junkies.

"Now, why in the world would I want to waste your precious time with such a silly thing as that? Well, it's because that's what you are. You're a bunch of high bottom drunks, addicts, and junkies. You're addicted users of alcohol and other drugs who never made it to the gutter or under the friggin' bridge.

"Now, I know that some of you might not like the sound of that term. Maybe you have your nose tilted a little upward and to the right and don't want to think of yourself as *any* kind of addict, even a high bottom one. Maybe you prefer a more delicate term like 'substance abuser,' which suggests a temporary lapse in judgment.

"On the other hand, maybe you have your nose tilted upward and to the left and prefer thinking of yourself as more of a low bottom sort—you know, a *real* alcoholic or a *real* junkie. You're the guy in the bar who says, 'Keep 'em coming, goddamn it, and holler at me half an hour before last call!'

"Well, my friends, it doesn't matter much where your ego takes you on this one. I've seen my share of high bottom drunks and low bottom drunks, and I see you as the former rather than the latter. And do you know what? That's the problem, because high bottom drunks and addicts are the very worst kind."

Cally paused for a moment and then continued. "Did you catch that? Let me repeat it for you. High bottom drunks and addicts are the very worst kind. That's right. A high bottom drunk is the worst kind of alcoholic you can be if you have serious notions of staying sober and clean."

Again, he paused and perused the room. Steve leaned forward in his chair and stared at Cally.

"You look perplexed, Mr. Campbell," Cally said. "Go ahead; what's your question?"

"Well, it's not really a question, Cally. I'm just thinking about how you've been telling us till we're blue in the face that addiction is a disease, right? So if I give you the benefit of the doubt and acknowledge that you're right about that, then the logical next step would be to say that the more severe the disease, the more difficult the cure. But what I hear you saying is that the *less* severe the disease, the more difficult the cure."

Cally smiled and nodded. "Damn curious, isn't it, Steve? Very damn curious. Well, hang onto your gimme cap and listen up good because I'm about to hand you some information that may just save your life.

"You see, group, Steve said it right. Addiction is a disease. It's a fatal disease. That means that every damn one of us in this room right now, me included, has a fatal disease. Don't ever forget that. Just because it hasn't killed us yet does not mean that it has quit trying or that it won't eventually succeed. But every one of us also has a choice regarding the prognosis of this disease. That's the good news. Now, here's the bad. Statistics—good, accurate ones—predict that one year from today, four of us will be back out there drinking and using again."

Cally paused and took a breath. When he spoke again, his voice was softer. "Do you hear what I'm telling you? That's four of us, and I gotta tell you something, guys, I feel pretty confident that I won't be one of the four. So that means four of *you*. Now, I ask you, does anyone want to volunteer?

"How about you, Robert? If you drink again, your wife and kids are history. How about you, Sally? If you get caught drinking again, your butt is right back in jail. You, Billy? Do you think you can live through another one of your month-long binges? How about you, Al? Are you ready to try the street again? Do you even have any good veins left? Let's see; how about you, Peg? Are you ready to roll your motivation and your future up into your next joint? You, Jim? You're young enough. You only have one DWI. You could probably get at least one more before they send you to prison. Or perhaps you, Steve. You're just getting started in recovery; maybe you should drop out before it becomes too important to you."

Cally leaned against the front of his desk and waited.

Robert finally rescued the group from Cally's silence. "Okay, Cally, I'll bite since it looks as though nobody else will. I thought Steve's comment made sense. Are you just trying to scare us, or do the grim statistics really have anything to do with our high bottoms?"

Cally smiled broadly. "Well, now, that's a damn good question, Mr. Johnson. Thank you for asking it, because I'm fixing to give you the answer, and it makes me feel good to know that you're interested in what I am about to say.

"As you all know, we diagnose addiction by the presence of symptoms. I believe that someday we'll have a more precise diagnostic tool, but for the time being, this is what we have. Some of the primary symptoms are as follows: One, when someone continues using alcohol or drugs even when his use precipitates negative consequences. Two, when one experiences loss of control over his use; that is, when he intends to use a certain amount or with a certain frequency, but instead he uses a larger amount or with greater frequency. Three, when someone becomes compulsive in his use and preoccupied in his thinking about his use. Four, when denial prevents him from seeing the relationship between his use and his problems. And five, when one has withdrawal discomfort while abstaining from using for a period of time. There are others, but those are the most reliable.

"Now, most people who drink alcohol, and most users of most drugs, have no symptoms of addiction. They are social drinkers and social users. They don't experience negative consequences associated with their use of alcohol or drugs. When they use, nothing bad happens, period.

"Since they experience no problems around using, they have no reason to limit their use, in terms of either frequency or amount. They never even think about setting limits. Amount and frequency simply are not issues. Social drinkers drink a small amount and feel satiated, or fully satisfied. They have no desire to drink more than that amount, and they don't. To drink more would feel stupid to them because it might create an unpleasant experience for them.

"So social users are people who do not experience negative consequences from their use and do not lose control of their use. They do not sit around and think about using, and their bodies never feel discomfort as a result of their going for periods of time without using.

"Sometimes, however, people who are normally social users slip into alcohol and drug abuse. Abuse is *not addiction*. Abuse is *misuse;* it's usually *overuse.* The misuse is typically situational, and it usually occurs within a limited time frame. Sometimes it takes on the appearance of self-medication. The condition being medicated can be physical, like pain, but more often than not it's psychological or emotional.

"People self-medicate depression, fear, anxiety, anger, stress, boredom, etc. I've seen young people medicate substantial parts of their emotionally painful adolescence and old people medicate their emotionally painful old age.

"Abuse oftentimes does precipitate negative consequences, and occasionally, those can be quite severe. However, the abuser is usually capable of seeing the relationship between his behavior—that is, the drinking or using, and the result of his behavior—that is, the negative consequence. In other words, he does not have the kind of alcoholic denial that prevents his seeing cause and effect. More importantly, though, he is also capable of controlling his use in order to avoid experiencing those negative consequences from recurring.

"Here's a typical abuser profile: The abuser feels self-conscious and out of place at a party so he drinks to deal with his anxiety. He gets high and says and does stupid things. The next day he feels remorseful, and he realizes that his drinking

421

precipitated his inappropriate behavior. He promises himself that he will never repeat the experience. And here's the key; he doesn't. He keeps his promise. He has learned his lesson.

"Again, now, what is the key characteristic here? He learned his lesson; he does not recycle his behavior. He makes a promise, and he keeps his promise.

"Alcoholics and addicts cannot do that. Oh, they can make promises. Yeah, they make plenty of promises. They make them to themselves and other people. They just can't keep them. Therefore, not only do they experience negative consequences associated with their use, but they also experience at least some of the same ones over and over. They recycle them. They don't learn their lessons.

"Alcoholics and addicts make promises, and they break promises. Alcoholics and addicts, even those whose denial does not prevent their seeing cause and effect, set limits all the time, but they cannot live within those limits. The intention is there. And actually, intention is an important factor. They set limits within which they intend to live, but addiction—the disease—prevents their following through.

"Now, I know you see the difference. Before the abuser crosses over the line into addiction, he can control his use. He does control his use. After he crosses over the line into addiction, he doesn't. It's not that he doesn't want to. It's that he can't.

"The alcoholic/addict loses control because he or she isn't capable of control, at least not over the long run. He can have very strong will power, but it doesn't work over the long run. And that baffles him. He swears to himself that he will drink only a certain amount at the party. Then he inexplicably wakes up the next morning with a hangover. He can't believe it. But you know what? He keeps trying. And he might very well experience a period of success. Eventually, however, he will fail. Why? Because he has the disease of alcoholism, and loss of control is a symptom of his disease."

Cally stood silent for a moment.

Billy raised his hand. "So what's the deal about the line, Cally? What makes one person cross over it into addiction and another not? Is that where heredity and genetics come in?"

"Well, that's the $64,000 question, Billy, and as yet, I haven't seen any utterly convincing evidence of an incontrovertible answer. Some say it's the activation of a biochemical error in the brain and that within those who are genetically predisposed to the disease, that error has always been just sitting there waiting to be activated by the consumption of alcohol and drugs."

He paused for a moment. "Let me say that again. A biochemical error in the brain triggered by drinking and using among people with a genetic predisposition to addiction. That would mean, of course, that some people are born already set up to become alcoholics and addicts. All they have to do to trigger the disease is drink or use.

"That explanation makes perfect sense for the alcoholic who grew up with alcoholic parents, like you, Steve, and you, Peg. But what about all of the others? Billy, your parents don't even drink, if I remember correctly."

Billy nodded. "Yes, but my grandfather died of alcoholism when he was in his fifties. I think that's one reason why my mom and dad don't drink. My dad did at one time, but after my grandfather died, he quit."

"Okay, well that fits, I guess," Cally said. "I've seen the disease skip a generation many times, perhaps for that very reason. Anyway, to my way of thinking, the issues of biochemical errors and genetic predisposition do not mean much to us in this room at this time. It's a fascinating theoretical question, and I believe that researchers will figure it out someday, maybe even within our lifetimes.

"The relevant issue for us is symptoms. I believe that if you have symptoms of the disease, then you have the disease. I guess that's not absolutely, unquestionably, necessarily so, but it's a pretty damn good bet. Hell, I'd put my money on it.

"Now, what's nice about this situation is that you can diagnose yourself quite simply by asking yourself the questions. "Did you continue to drink and use even after it started causing you problems? Did you do that in such a way that you experienced some of the same problems more than once or twice? Did you ever intend to drink or use a certain amount but end up drinking or using more than that amount? Did you ever make promises to yourself or someone else about your use and then break the promises? Did you ever sit around thinking about drinking or using when you could have been spending your time more productively? Did you ever feel guilty or remorseful about your use or your behavior when you used? Did you have any physical or psychological discomfort when you went two or three or four days without drinking or using? Did you ever have memory loss associated with your drinking? Is there any evidence of alcohol or drug problems in your family?

"If you have any lingering doubts about whether or not you have this disease, take the test. Ask yourself the questions. If the answer to some of them is 'yes,' then my guess is that you have addictive disease."

Steve raised his hand. "Okay, Cally, I'm pretty sure that all of us here recognize the symptoms. I know I do. I have most of them. In fact, I probably have all of them except for the withdrawal symptoms. And at least for right now, I'm willing to entertain the notion that the symptoms diagnose the disease and that I have it. I also accept what you said earlier about us being high bottom rather than low bottom drunks.

"So here's my question. Why the hell does that put us at greater risk? I still think the fact that I did not sink to the lowest bottom raises rather than lowers my chances."

"Good question, Steve, and well put. You know, addiction is just like any other disease; some people have a slight case of it, some have a severe case, and most are somewhere in between. Within the context of that fact, the answer to your question starts looking simple. Those with more severe cases are more likely to get help than those with slight cases. That's true not because of their insight, but rather because they screw up so much.

"Their screw ups attract attention, and the attention brings them into treatment. It comes from judges, pastors, social workers, angry spouses, divorce attorneys, angry employers, doctors, and others who have a chance to refer them to help. It's simple: The squeaky wheel gets the grease. That's one part of the answer.

"The other part has to do with denial and surrender. This is where high bottom drunks have the most trouble. And it's the real reason they are so vulnerable to failure.

"You see, in a sense, they're caught somewhere in the middle between alcohol and drug abusers on the one hand and low bottom drunks on the other. Abusers do have problems, and they do have denial around those problems, but both are typically minimal. Furthermore, since they are not addicted, they can control their use. They don't need to surrender because they can quit or control with will power alone.

"Low bottom drunks also have denial. It can be significant, too, but the closer they get to those low bottoms, and the lower those bottoms become, the tougher it is to maintain. Their negative consequences are right in their faces. They have arrests, lost jobs, lost marriages, lost friends, health problems, mental problems, money problems, etc., etc., all the way down to losing everything and living under the bridge. Surrender is almost a forgone conclusion for low bottom drunks. They have to surrender.

"Unfortunately, the vast majority surrender into their disease instead of into recovery. They know deep down inside it's going to kill them, and they decide to let it. They say things like, 'Well, everybody's gotta go some way; I might as well enjoy it.' In effect, they choose to die instead of choosing to live. A few choose to recover—very few, actually. Those who do, though, have little resistance left. They're beat. Their denial is shot. When they enter treatment, they say things like, 'I don't have any fight left in me; tell me what to do, and I'll do it.'

"And that leaves us with you guys—high bottom drunks. When I get you, you're denial is intact, and part of that denial has you fairly well convinced that you can survive on will power. Is your denial strong? Yes! Are you ready to surrender? Absolutely not! Which makes sense when you think about it. You have not had enough really severe negative consequences to break down your defenses, and you're still able to experience some short-term success with limit setting. With denial intact and defenses hitting on all eight cylinders, what else would you be but vulnerable?

"You know, it wasn't that long ago that high bottom drunks did not demand much respect from the recovery field. Old timers in AA tell stories about men showing up for their first AA meeting and being sent away because they still owned a car and a watch. They believed, so the story goes anyway, that to introduce individuals to recovery before they hit a low bottom would doom them to failure.

"Gradually, though, counselors started playing around with the idea of working with high bottom drunks—those who were on their way down but had not gone very low. Overall, I would say the process has been interesting, but the results have been mixed.

"High bottom drunks like yourselves almost always do well in treatment. That's true for several reasons. One is that you usually have some kind of external pressures on you to at least comply. Another is that you're generally intelligent and at least somewhat curious. Also, you get peer pressure from within the group, and peer pressure is always a powerful motivator. Finally, as you comply with the program and work in group, your insight increases to the point that you break through some denial and make a verbal commitment to stay sober. I think of this process as something like compromised denial and a hint of surrender.

"When you leave treatment, though, and the heat is off, it's often a different story. You start compromising your recovery programs. You slack off on your AA meetings, you quit reading the literature, you forget about your sponsor, you quit praying and meditating. And you know what happens? Your denial returns in full force. Then what do you think happens? You rationalize a return to controlled use.

"You say things like, 'Well, I know I had a problem at one time, but I know so much more now, and I understand everything so much better now, that there's no way that I could ever let myself return to the way it was before I went to treatment. I've learned my lesson. I'll be all right now. I'll control it.'

"So, to make a long story short, high bottom drunks are vulnerable to relapse because of strong denial and weak surrender. That is why I keep banging home the importance of a consistent, patient, long-term approach to recovery. That's also why I go on and on about the difference between abstinence and recovery. If you go back to drinking and using, you not only lose your sobriety. You also lose your recovery. And what's the definition of recovery? Improvement in the quality of life along four dimensions—physical, mental, emotional, and spiritual.

"If there is one critical event that must occur in the life of the alcoholic who recovers from his disease, it's acceptance of his problem. Step One says 'We admitted we were powerless over alcohol—that our lives had become unmanageable.' It does not end there, though.

"Over time, with continued growth and change and personal insight, that admission goes deeper. It becomes acceptance. It moves from the head to the heart. And at *that* point, your chances for true recovery greatly improve. If you abandon growth and change before that happens, your chances for true recovery greatly diminish. If you desert your program, which for most of you right now is the Twelve Step program, then about the best you can hope for is abstinence, which translates into uncomfortable, unfulfilling sobriety.

"Okay, now, I have thrown a lot of information your way. Do you have any questions?"

The room was quiet for a moment, and then Peg said, "Cally, it sounds to me like you're saying that if I'm planning to stay sober, I need to live the rest of my life with my back against the wall. That doesn't sound very appealing to me."

Before Cally could respond, Steve added, "Yeah, I was just thinking the same thing. Is recovery supposed to be fear-based? I mean, I wasn't planning on a lifetime in AA. I came in here seeking freedom, not bondage."

"Okay, those are good questions," Cally responded. "No, recovery is not supposed to be fear-based, although a dose of healthy respect for any fatal disease seems appropriate to me. Let me remind you that this disease does not go away just because you get sober. You will always have it. You won't always have the symptoms, but you will always have the disease.

"You don't need to fear it, though. You can approach it positively rather than negatively. Approach it from your strength, not your weakness. A strong recovery program is preventive. Continuous personal growth rules out relapse. And it does not have to always be centered in AA, Steve. It does need a spiritual basis, but there are many very profound spiritually based programs out there. For example, what are you attracted to besides AA?"

"Well, I *am* attracted to AA, but I'm also attracted to Zen Buddhism, Taoism, and yoga. I feel as though those paths will be more enduring for me than AA, at least in the very long run."

Cally nodded. "So be it. You know, there is no wrong way to grow and change along spiritual lines. Far be it from me to try to dictate anyone's spiritual path. I like AA because it works for me, and I see it working for other alcoholics. To me, it's a complete path. The Steps support my spiritual growth, and the fellowship supports my sobriety. I fit in there. I feel at home with other alcoholics who are growing and changing along the same lines as me. Plus, it's convenient. There are meetings all over town— morning, noon, and night.

"Are there any other questions?"

Billy raised his hand and said, "Cally, I know this has come up before, but I would like for you to address it within the context of this lecture. I know I'm an alcoholic, and I know that I was addicted to coke and speed. But I never had a problem with pot. I was never compulsive around it or anything. In fact, I always had the feeling that pot was good for me. It mellowed me out. Why can't I just smoke pot and leave everything else alone?"

"Well, Billy, what happens when we cross that line from abuse into addiction is that we not only become addicted, we also become *addictive.* We become highly susceptible to all addictive substances. If we try to substitute a different addictive substance, like pot, for the one that caused us problems previously, like alcohol, then one of two things invariably happens. Either we become addicted to the new substance and it becomes our new drug of choice, or we use the new substance and it compromises our judgment to the extent that we go back and use our original drug of choice.

"This phenomenon is called cross-addiction, and I can't tell you how many times I have watched it happen. In fact, I have never seen, even once, an alcoholic or addict be successful in his or her attempt to control the use of any addictive substance once he or she has become addicted to any other addictive substance. Not in the long run, anyway.

"Now, that is the answer to your question, Billy, but it brings up another, equally relevant issue. If we're sincere in our recovery work, if we're moving forward along our spiritual path of growth and change, then we'll feel less and less need to medicate away our feelings. We won't need pot or alcohol or any other substance to deal with our issues. If we *do* resort to self-medication, then our progress will come to a screeching halt. Indeed, we'll start going backwards. An addict cannot recover from addiction while he's using addictive drugs. It just doesn't figure.

"Now, I want to make one last point here, and I want you to listen up good and hear me out.

"As you know, recovery is a process; it's a journey. And part of the journey concerns our attitudes about sobriety itself.

"In the beginning, most of us want to be sober in order to avoid the problems caused by drinking and using. We say, 'When I drink or use, I do stupid things and get into trouble, and I can't afford to live that way any longer. Therefore, in order to avoid problems and stay out of trouble, I need to stay sober.'

"But, if we diligently and patiently press forward on our recovery path, then at some point we cross a magical line into a whole new attitude, in which we want to be sober in order to retain the benefits of recovery. *Then* we say, 'When I stay sober and work my program, I feel great, and I want to live this way for the rest of my life. Therefore, I don't want to drink or use again because if I did, I would surely lose what I have now.'

"Please, guys, hang in there until you get the gift of the latter attitude.

"Okay, we have time for one more question," Cally said.

Sally spoke up. "So you're saying that even after I finish this program and get cleared by the courts, I can't even drink beer?"

Cally slowly walked over to Sally and stood in front of her. He bent over slightly so that she had to look him in the face. "That's right, Sally," he said. "If you are going to have a better life in the future than you had in the past, you cannot even drink beer."

Sally look him right in the eye and said, "Well ain't that a goddamn crock of shit."

CHAPTER 72

On the drive to Enchanted Rock, Steve recapped Cally's lecture for Kathy. When he finished, she said, "You know, I got that information, but I got it piecemeal. I like it better the way he packaged it together for y'all. It makes a stronger point that way. Tell me something, though, Steve; do you buy it?"

Steve thought for a moment. "I'm not sure, Kath. I mean, the package does fit together well, even though it's obviously based mostly in theory. I don't know; I should probably just accept the whole thing as the unblemished truth and never even question it."

"But...?" she said.

"But, I'm just not sure. I kind of wanted to ask him about LSD, but I chickened out. I guess that in the back of my mind somewhere, I have the notion that I could still do a hit of acid every once in a while. I mean, supposedly, LSD is non-addictive, and I think I had some genuine, profound spiritual insights while I was using it.

"For a while it was my spiritual path. When I didn't pollute it with other drugs, it was a true catalyst for spiritual growth.

428

And it probably would be even more so when I'm mentally, emotionally, and spiritually healthier going into it." He glanced over at her. "I hope it doesn't bother you for me to talk about this."

Kathy looked down and said, "To tell you the truth, Steve, it does. It scares me."

"How does it scare you, Kathy?"

She was quiet for a moment, and then she looked up at him and said, "It scares me because I'm afraid that if you think about getting high like that, you might really do it, and if you start getting high, I'll lose you. You'll go away. Then I'll go away."

Steve smiled. "Hey, I'm not going away. I'm not going anywhere without you."

"That's not what I meant, Steve. What I meant was that if I'm staying straight, and you're getting high, we would not be in the same place anymore. I would be here, and you'd be somewhere else, so to speak. If you go away from recovery, and I stay in recovery, we would be worlds apart. It wouldn't work, at least not for me."

"Wait a minute, Kathy. I didn't say anything about abandoning recovery. I'm just talking about an occasional non-addictive acid trip, the whole idea of which would be to deepen and broaden my spiritual growth."

When Kathy did not answer, Steve looked over at her and said, "Well?"

She closed her eyes and shook her head slowly back and forth. "That's just denial, Steve," she said

Steve looked back at the road. "I see," he said. "So what you're saying is that if I use acid occasionally, *you* will go away—literally. Well, then, let me ask you this: What would happen if I relapsed? Would you abandon me then, too?"

"That's not the same, Steve. If you relapsed, and you wanted to return to sobriety, then I would stand by you and help all I could. If you started using again, though, for whatever reason, and wanted to continue using, then yes, I would probably leave. It would be too threatening for me.

"I'm committed to sobriety. I never thought I'd have a life as good as the one I have now as a recovering person. I won't jeopardize my recovery for anything. Not like that. Not even for you."

Steve fell silent for a full minute. Finally he said, "I know intellectually that what you're saying makes sense from the standpoint of your recovery, but it still hurts my feelings. I feel discounted and unimportant, like a goddamn second fiddle."

"I'm sorry, Steve. I didn't mean to hurt your feelings. I just want to be truthful with you. When I was about a month sober, I heard someone in an AA meeting say, 'This is a selfish program.' I did not like the sound of that. In fact, it really bugged me.

"So I asked my sponsor, Susan, about it. What she told me was that when we're in recovery, our recovery has to come first. If we don't put our own sobriety first, then by definition, something else is more important. And nothing can be more important than our sobriety. Without it, we're useless to the world and everyone in it.

"What that means to me is that I have to take care of myself in my sobriety before anything else. If something comes into conflict with that, then it has to go. And I know that being with someone who is using, even occasionally, would threaten my sobriety.

"Steve, you would not like me the way I used to be, and I'm not talking about my line of work, either. I'm talking about who I was as a person. I didn't take care of myself. My attitude stunk. My heart was closed. I wasn't a nice person to be around. I was manipulative and cynical. I didn't trust anyone. And I despised myself.

"I will do anything to avoid ever being like that again. I've gotten a taste of what it feels like to be free, and I feel surrendered into this new way of life. I don't always like every moment of it, but overall, it's an incredibly better world for me. I intend to stay in it.

"I love you very much, Steve. My heart races a little every time I lay eyes on you. When we're together, I feel as though a part of me that has been missing all of my life is no longer missing. I feel complete. But Steve, if you were using, you wouldn't be the person who makes my heart skip. You would be someone else, someone I've never even met.

"Please understand that I'm not putting you on notice about this; I'm just trying to be honest."

Steve took a deep breath and released it slowly. "Okay, I understand. I'm all right now. I mean, it's not like I've been sitting around thinking about using. I haven't. It just occurred to me today when I was over at Tommy's. You know, James was there. He's my oldest friend, and the one who taught me how to use acid. I guess it triggered something. Then it came up for me again during Cally's lecture when Billy asked about smoking pot. Don't worry, okay? You're a lot more important to me than an occasional acid trip."

"Well, thank God for that," Kathy said, smiling for the first time during the conversation. "I'd be devastated to know that you would dump me for a relationship with LSD.

"What you just said, though, is exactly what I'm talking about. Your thoughts about using were triggered when you were with your friends who were using, even though you felt turned off by the way they acted while they were high. It's what Cally refers to as 'euphoric recall.' Something familiar triggers fond

430

memories of getting high without also triggering the bad memories.

"I don't know, Steve; it just scares me. It's like playing with fire. I believe that right now we have something rare and sacred. We're sober, and we have a spiritual path that we can walk together. I don't want to lose that."

Steve patted the seat next to him, and Kathy slid over and snuggled against his arm.

"I love you, too, Kathy," he whispered. "I also appreciate and respect you."

After stopping for a bite to eat along the way, Steve and Kathy arrived at Enchanted Rock at 11:00 o'clock. They finished setting up camp a little after midnight and were under the covers by 1:00.

Before falling asleep in each other's arms, Steve reminded Kathy that he needed some space and privacy during the next two days in order to accomplish his primary goal for the weekend—a solid start on his Fourth Step. Kathy generously agreed to sleep until at least noon to give Steve his time alone.

Steve slept for about three hours. He got up a little before 4:00 AM, slipped into some clothes, packed his Big Book, a notebook and pen, a flashlight, an apple, and a jug of water into his backpack, picked up an extra blanket, and quietly left the tent.

He and Ginger made their way to the main trail and then up the gradual slope of Enchanted Rock to the top. He found a comfortable spot off to one side, where he spread his blanket and lay on his back under the fading night sky.

He closed his eyes, sought his heart, and prayed for willingness, open-mindedness, patience, and humility. He also prayed for honesty and genuineness. He asked to be guided. As best he knew how, he surrendered his will to that of a power greater than himself. Then he let his mind and body relax, and he listened to his breathing.

He quickly became aware of the expansive silence. Gradually, however, he awoke to the universe of life that surrounded him, that engulfed him. He felt it above him and below. He listened, and he heard it. He felt it throughout his body and in his heart. His awareness expanded. He became fully conscious and fully present. He felt connected, an integrated piece of the universe, one with his world, and one with God. It felt like a seamless unity.

He slowly opened his eyes to the first light of the new day. He felt exhilarated and inspired. Thoughts—robust, fluid thoughts—filled his mind. He opened his notebook and started writing. The words flowed from his mind onto the paper without hesitation.

I listen to the trees, and they say:
  "Stand tall, and yield.
  Stand alone, and stand together.
  Be tolerant and flexible.
  Be true to yourself.
  Be brave, and be patient.
  With time, you will grow."

I listen to the wind, and it says:
  "Breathe.
  Take care of yourself—body, mind, and spirit.
  Take time.
  Be quiet.
  Listen from your heart.
  Forgive."

I listen to the sun, and it says:
  "Nurture others.
  Radiate your warmth outward.
  Give of yourself without expectations."

I listen to the creek, and it says:
  "Relax, and flow.
  Tend to what's important, and let the rest go.
  Keep moving; do not be hesitant or afraid.
  Lighten up.
  Giggle."

I listen to the hills, and they say:
  "Be there.
  Be honest.
  Be trustworthy.
  Be true, genuine, and real.
  Do what you say you will do.
  Speak from the heart.
  Don't cheat."

I listen to the birds, and they say:
  "Set yourself free.
  Sing."

I listen to the clouds, and they say:
  "Be creative; be expressive.
  Let your spirit move.
  Let yourself be light and gay.
  Laugh.
  Let yourself be heavy and sad.
  Cry."

I listen to the sky, and it says:
   "Open up.
   Let go of the boundaries & barriers that you have created to
      protect yourself.
   Love yourself as you are; it opens the door to change.
   Experience change.
   Fly."

I listen to the flowers and small plants, and they say:
   "Be humble; be simple.
   Respect the beauty of small things.
   Respect the beauty of humility & truth.
   Let go of perfectionism.
   Practice acceptance."

I listen to the bugs and flying insects, and they say:
   "Work; be productive.
   Use your hands.
   Focus on what is in front of you.
   Ignore the past, and forget the future;
   Only the present is real."

I listen to the moon, and it says:
   "Love.
   Share love; make love.
   Allow yourself to be loved.
   Be gentle, kind, and understanding.
   Be romantic; touch and caress.
   Use candles."

I listen to the stars, and they wink and say:
   "Play.
   Dance.
   Be silly; have fun."

I listen to the Earth, and it says:
   "I am your mother.
   I give you life.
   Respect all that is around you.
   Be especially respectful of the very young and the very
      old, for they are both very near God.
   Find beauty in all things—living and not, including
      yourself; for we are all one—not separate.
   Give up the belief that you are a higher form of life;
      there is no higher form of life.
   We are equal because we are the same.
   Love and nurture your children; cook good food for

them, and hold them very close to you often.
Hold me close to you often as well, and I will hold
    you in return; I will support you.
When you return to me, I will welcome you,
    and I will set your spirit free.
Have faith."

Steve laid down his pen. He stared at the pages that he had scribbled. He felt curiously sad, but also at peace. He lay on his back on the blanket and looked at the sky.

"Thank you," he whispered. A tear trickled down the side of his head. He closed his eyes and dozed off and dreamed.

In the dream, he stood alone with Ginger outside of a very large, very old apartment building that was being readied for demolition. When he looked closely at the front of the building, he saw himself staring back from inside—from five or six different windows scattered around on several different floors.

The looks on his faces were somber. He started to yell at the demolition crew chief to stop because people remained inside, but before he found his voice, the explosion erupted, and the entire building crashed, in slow motion, straight down to the ground.

When the dust had cleared enough to see the rubble, he stepped forward, and as expected, he discovered several bodies— all himself—in the rubble. The bodies were mangled and lifeless. He felt sad, and tears streamed down his face. He knew, however, that he had to walk away from them, and he did.

By the time Steve came down from the top of Enchanted Rock, the sun stood high in the sky. Kathy sat inside the tent, propped up on pillows, reading his Zen book. He climbed under the covers next to her, and when he discovered that she was naked from the waist down, he playfully grabbed the book from her hands, threw it aside, and pulled her down beside him.

After making love, Steve told Kathy about his morning on the rock. When he read her the poem, she wept.

Steve and Kathy devoted the rest of the weekend to joyful play. They swam and hiked and cooked and ate and talked and laughed and made love. They prayed and meditated together. They fantasized about the future. Steve taught Kathy yoga postures. She read him a short story. Steve worked on his Fourth Step.

On the drive back to Austin, Kathy asked Steve how he was doing with his grief over Lynn and Eddie leaving Texas. He told Kathy about his afternoon with Carla—the cookies, the cry, the comfort, the bodywork, and the bath.

"I probably should not even ask," Kathy said, "but I'm sitting here wondering if you ever had a sexual relationship with

434

Carla. I wouldn't bring it up at all except that when I met her, I immediately liked her and thought that she and I could become friends. I think she also wanted to open that door.

"At the same time, I got the feeling that she had a secret. She didn't say anything, but the vibes were there. You don't have to tell me, Steve. I was just wondering."

"It's okay; I'll tell you. Carla and I did have a sexual relationship. We didn't have a romantic relationship, but we did have a sexual one. We had sex infrequently, and it ended the day I told her about you, which was right after you and I met. She's a really good person, Kathy, and I think y'all could be great friends. Does the fact that she and I had sex ruin it for you?"

"No, but knowing the whole story puts us on equal footing. If she knew, and I didn't, the secret would put a wall between us. It wouldn't be fair to either one of us. So will I be running into any more of your former lovers?"

Steve smiled. "'Former lovers' makes me sound like a real Lothario."

Kathy laughed. "You're probably thinking, 'What a strange issue for her to raise; the former prostitute is concerned how many of my former lovers she's apt to run into.'

"I just don't want to make a fool out of myself. I mean, if you introduce me to one of your old girlfriends, I would like to know that she's an old girlfriend. I don't know what the big psychological explanation for that is, but I know that it's important to me."

"Okay, well, you'll probably run into one or two more women I've slept with, but you won't run into any that I love like I love you. The woman who was at Tommy's house on Friday— Dixie, who is dating Tommy now, is someone whom I had a relationship with. Actually, we were pretty close for a time, but we never mentioned love or a future beyond friendship.

"And I hope that someday you will meet Rachel, my friend from San Antonio whom we've discussed a couple of times. I did love Rachel, and I suppose that in a way, I still do. I was never in love with Rachel. I never wanted to live with her or have a romantic future with her.

"Of course, you've already met Bev, and unfortunately you'll probably have to be around her from time to time.

"That's about it. That's my stable of women, as my mom once referred to them. Now, though, I am yours. I'm all yours. You've got me wrapped around your little finger, and I'm as helpless as a newborn baby."

"Yeah, right," she said. "You're smitten, and you're my slave."

"That's exactly right, my dear," he said in a serious tone of voice.

"You know, Kathy, I would like for you to meet the rest of these friends of mine. I don't want us to pal around with them or anything, but they're all good people, even though they do drink and use like a pack of wild animals.

"James is my oldest friend in the world. You probably won't like him very much, but he's pretty special to me. Tommy has been by best friend for the past year. He's a very kind and generous man. He really helped me get settled in Austin and get hooked into graduate school. Dixie is a warm, loving, honest woman. Tucker's kind of superficial, but he's a funny, charming guy who will tell you how beautiful you are three or four times every time you're around him.

"I don't know; maybe we could invite Carla, Tommy, Dixie, James, and Tucker over for dinner some night and not serve alcohol. Do you think you could handle that?"

Kathy nodded. "Yeah, I could probably handle that. Maybe we could include Patti, you know, to balance the scales a little."

"Yeah, good idea; and maybe Sheri, too. Remember her? She's the girl we talked to that night at the cocktail party. You liked her a lot."

The more they talked about the dinner party, the more excited they became. They decided to do it the following Friday night, in celebration of Steve's one-month sober birthday.

When they arrived back at Steve's house on Sunday evening, Steve asked Kathy to stay the night and leave for work from there on Monday morning. "In fact," he said, "why don't you just never leave?"

"What does that mean, Steve?" she asked.

"Well, it means I want you to stay here with me."

"Are you asking me to move in with you?" she said.

Steve nodded. "Yes, I am. What do you think?"

"What do I think? Well, I think, 'yeah, okay.' Actually, I think it's a fantastic idea. Ask me how I feel, though."

"Okay. How do you feel?"

"I feel scared shitless, my friend. I feel happy and excited and hopeful, but scared out of my ever-loving mind."

CHAPTER 73

Between Monday, September 25, 1974 and Wednesday, February 28, 1975—the date of Steve's six-month sober birthday—Steven Campbell and Kathryn Morris, high bottom drunks of the first order, worked through the odds against them to become a team committed to recovery.

During that five-month period of time, Steve and Kathy matured both individually and as a couple. They walked the walk

436

of their recovery program. They became physically, mentally, emotionally, and spiritually healthier. They struggled, and they flourished. They made tough decisions that set the course for the rest of their lives.

Kathy's move to 2905 Columbus was a snap. Kathy packed, and Steve loaded and transported a pickup load each night, until they carried in the last few boxes late Thursday night.

They toasted their hard work, great courage, and questionable judgment with apple pie a la mode and French Roast coffee at an all night bakery and coffee shop in the heart of downtown Austin. When they got home, they got on their knees together, held hands, and prayed for guidance. Then they put Leonard Cohen on the stereo and made love on the living room floor.

They gave their dinner party the next night, the eve of Steve's one-month sober birthday. Everyone came except for James, who dropped by earlier in the day to leave his regrets.

He told Steve, "You know me, man; dinner parties just aren't my bag." He handed Kathy three bottles of non-alcoholic sparkling apple cider and said, "I thought you might like something festive for the party."

Patti arrived several hours early and helped with the cleaning, cooking, and set up. Steve went to his therapy group at 6:00 and made it home just before guests arrived at 8:30.

Dinner was great, and the party great fun. The group mixed surprisingly well. Tommy and Tucker slipped out onto the back porch after dinner and returned with bloodshot eyes and goofy smiles. No one else got high, and no one mentioned alcohol.

Kathy hosted the party beautifully, not because of her experience and expertise, of which she had none, but because of her heart. She easily and solidly connected with Carla, who made everyone at the party dance with her at least twice—one fast dance and one slow one.

Kathy and Patti both fell in love with Sheri, who they nicknamed 'NASCO,' which stood for 'naturally straight and cool.'

Tommy entertained the group with funny stories about how bad he used to be. Patti told him that if he ever happened to venture into AA, he would have a prize-winning drunkalogue. He suggested that she not hold her breath.

Dixie kept her distance at first but warmed up as the night went on. Tucker was his usual charming self. He unsuccessfully hit on Carla, then Sheri, and finally Patti. As predicted, he hailed Kathy's beauty repeatedly. When he left, he announced that if Steve did not marry her within a year, he would have to intervene and marry her himself.

Steve picked up his one month sobriety chip the next night at the South Austin Group. He and Kathy celebrated at the

South Austin Coffeehouse with the same group of people with whom they had gone to coffee on the night of their first date. Kathy's sponsor, Susan the Nazi, joined them, and to Steve's surprise, she smiled once or twice.

As before, they talked about recovery. This time, however, Steve had something to contribute to the conversation. Instead of the insecure, curious new kid, he felt like part of the group. He felt strong in his sobriety and confident in his recovery path.

Following their first weekend as housemates, Steve and Kathy settled into a simple routine. Their daily schedules meshed perfectly, and because of that, they were able to spend good quality time together at night and on weekends.

Wednesday became Steve's day and evening without Kathy. Friday became her day and evening without him. He spent his free days in UT libraries and his evenings with Ralph and Ralph's family. Kathy spent hers sleeping until noon and hanging out with Patti or Sheri or Carla in the afternoon and evening.

Steve and Kathy adjusted well to cohabitation. They wove their way through all of the standard roadblocks. Issues that they had never thought to discuss before moving in together confronted them almost immediately. There were big ones, like money: "Who pays for what and when," and smaller ones, like day-to-day responsibilities: "Who does what and when."

They discovered each other's nasty little habits. Kathy turned out to be a bathroom slob. She left wet towels on the floor and her makeup scattered around on the counter. She seldom put the cap back on the toothpaste, and she squeezed the tube in the middle. During her periods, she left cardboard tampon sleeves on the floor beside the toilet.

Steve's perfectionism drove Kathy up the wall. His shirts had to be folded a certain way. The silverware and dishes and pots and pans had to go in their exact places. And he complained about dirty clothes on the floor, even when they had been there just overnight.

On the other hand, they tried hard to please each other and to be considerate of each other's needs and peculiarities. They ate breakfast together nearly every morning and went to bed together every night. Their sex life remained exciting and fun.

They supported each other's recovery. They continued attending AA meetings, both together and alone. They stayed in treatment, and they saw Cally once a month as a couple. They prayed together often. They confronted each other's blind spots as lovingly as they knew how. They comforted each other's pain. They played together. Most importantly, they talked. They talked openly and honestly. Their love for each other grew stronger. They became a solid team.

Steve religiously kept up with his daily recovery plan. He practiced yoga and meditation. He walked Ginger and rode his bike. The healthier he got, the more he desired whole foods, and before long, he and Kathy turned to a strictly vegetarian diet.

When he finished studying the two books that he had chosen for mental recovery work, he found two more to take their place. With Cally's, Ralph's, and Kathy's help, he continued to question his old ideas and beliefs. As he did, he found that most of them were grounded in ignorance, fear, and false pride. The more he confronted them, the weaker they became. And the weaker they got, the more his defenses weakened as well.

Week by week and month by month, Steve became more open, honest, and real. He felt more, and more deeply, and as he realized that the feelings did no permanent harm, he challenged his old beliefs even more strongly. He learned to laugh at himself. He also learned to forgive himself, and as he forgave himself, he became more forgiving of others. And by February 28th, he had tentatively extended an olive branch to his dad.

Steve continued meeting and working with Ralph. They got together every Wednesday evening during the time of Kathy's therapy group, and they developed a bond of trust that helped carry Steve through the valleys of his first half-year sober. When Steve got bogged down in his Buddhist and Taoist spiritual studies, Ralph gave him clear, simple explanations. Steve found his own Higher Power and returned Ralph's to him.

Ralph patiently guided Steve through the Twelve Steps. Steve completed his Fourth Step inventory on February 1, 1975. He read it to Ralph from start to finish the following day. Having identified his character defects in the inventory and coming to understand them better through sharing and discussing them with Ralph, he became willing to let them go and earnestly prayed that they be removed.

That prayer frightened him tremendously. He worried that God might really hear it and comply with the request, leaving Steve naked and defenseless to the world. Ralph reminded him that in effect, he was praying to his inner Self—his true Self—his Buddha Self—his eternal, enlightened Self—and that that wise part of his being would never trick him in a mean-spirited way.

When he recovered from his fear of losing his defenses, Steve generated his list of the people whom he had harmed, especially through his addictive behaviors, and became willing to make amends to them all. He began making those amends in earnest on March 1st, the day following the evening that he took his six-month sobriety chip.

Steve's old friends gradually came around. They learned to accept his sobriety and support his and Kathy's recovery. Following the dinner party, Tommy and James both started dropping by The Woodworks again. Their visits came less frequently than before, and they had a decidedly different feel to them. Nevertheless, Steve enjoyed and appreciated them, and he got to where he looked forward to seeing "the guys." Only Tucker held out hope that Steve's sobriety was just another one of his phases.

Tommy went out of his way to establish new common ground on which he and Steve could stand. He brought some of his own furniture to the shop and asked Steve to help him do the repairs that were beyond his skills. In turn, Steve asked Tommy for help with his graduate studies, especially Statistics and Research Methods. At semester's end, Steve gave Tommy credit for his A in the class; it was one of only four A's in the class of twenty students.

James painstakingly reestablished himself as one of Steve's teachers. He studied every piece of scholarly work relating to addiction that he could find, and during his visits to the shop, he patiently explained his findings to Steve. On several occasions, he made Steve sit down beside him, and he drew elaborate diagrams and charts, all from memory, to help Steve understand the concepts, as well as the implications of those concepts for his recovery.

When James first started the lecture sessions, Steve listened politely but felt as though he was humoring James by doing so. As they progressed, however, he realized how much effort James put into the exercise, and he treated each visit with greater respect. James never arrived high or got high when he came to "teach."

Dixie stopped by The Woodworks on two different Wednesday afternoons—one in October and the other in early November.

On both occasions, she knocked before entering and said, "Don't worry, I just dropped by to say 'Hello.'"

Steve reciprocated. After he had been sober for three months and had secured Kathy's blessing, he dropped by The Roam In from time to time to visit Dixie. By his six-month birthday, he again thought of Dixie as a close friend whom he trusted and in whom he could confide.

Dixie liked talking about sobriety. She asked probing, thoughtful questions and stayed with them until Steve answered them to her understanding. Steve asked her if she was interested for herself or for Tommy. She replied, "Neither, really; I'm just curious." Steve and Carla helped Dixie move into Tommy's house the week before Thanksgiving.

Carla and Steve remained close friends, but Carla and Kathy became best pals. By the end of 1974, Carla spent almost as much time at Steve and Kathy's house as she did her own. Kathy trusted Carla with Steve because Steve and Carla demonstrated their trustworthiness.

Tucker continued to struggle with Steve's new lifestyle. Consequently, Steve saw him only very occasionally. Just before Steve's three-month sober birthday, though, Tucker dropped by the house and spent the better part of an afternoon.

"You're having a hard time with me being sober, aren't you?" Steve said.

"Well, I'll tell you, Steve-o; I've given this question a lot of thought, and here's the way I see it. You don't drink alcohol, you don't do drugs, and you don't chase skirts. And that's 'never' and 'under no circumstances.' Am I right so far?"

Steve smiled and nodded. "Yeah, so far, so good. What's your point?"

"Well, my point is this; I have three reasons, and *only* three reasons, for being on this planet. The first is drinking alcohol. The second is doing drugs. And the third is chasing down pussy. You take those three things away from me, and I'm on my hands and knees, begging you to put a .38 caliber bullet right between my eyes."

Steve laughed, but a part of him did not think the story funny. "So does that mean that you and I no longer have anything in common?" Steve asked. "I mean, we've been friends since we were 16 years old. We've been through hell and back together. Surely there's more to our friendship that booze, drugs, and women."

Tucker shook his head and waved his hand at Steve. "Hell, man, don't take everything so damn seriously. We have tons of shit to talk about. There's.... Well, there's.... Hmm, now that I think about it, we don't have a fucking thing in common anymore. Don't worry, though, old friend, I'm a very patient guy. And I've known you long enough to know that you'll come to your senses one of these days. You and me, we're not done raising hell together. Trust me on this one."

Later that night, when Steve told Kathy about the conversation, she looked at him and said, "You know, Steve, Tucker is a funny guy, and there was a time, not too long ago, that I would have found that story hilarious. But I'm afraid that coming from him, there might be a little too much truth to it for it to be funny."

Steve thought for a second and then said, "Hopefully, you're referring to the first part of the story and not the last part. I mean, are you afraid that I'll be going back out to drink and use with Tucker?"

She smiled softly and slapped his shoulder. "Shut up!" she said. "Of course I'm referring to the first part."

Steve missed Rachel. He thought of her often and always fondly. They did not see each other in person, but they talked on the phone at least twice a month. She continued on track with her recovery and celebrated her one-year sober birthday on

November 20th. Steve sent her a birthday card and a refrigerator magnet with the recipe for alcohol-free frozen daiquiris printed on it.

During their phone conversations, they talked candidly about their personal lives, and they helped each other think through personal problems. In a moment of weakness, Rachel expressed sorrow over the seriousness of Steve's relationship with Kathy. She admitted that in the back of her mind she had thought that someday they would find their way back into each other's lives.

Throughout the first six months of Steve's sobriety, Lois monitored his progress like a hawk. She gave him a little too much unsolicited advice, but Steve accepted it as Lois' way of making amends for her failure to mother his needs when he was younger. He also benefited from her wisdom, gained through her ten years of sobriety.

Over the months, Lois' respect and affection for Kathy grew. The issue of Kathy's past quickly became a non-issue. On February 28th, when Steve received his six-month chip, Lois asked him if he and Kathy were ever going to "legitimize" their live-in relationship. He interpreted the question as Lois' way of saying that she accepted Kathy's presence in his life.

Steve reconnected with his dad very cautiously. The process stretched Steve's willingness to pray for and practice patience, acceptance, and humility. He kept expecting Henry to change, and when that did not happen, Steve felt discouraged and backed away.

Henry did not care that Steve was sober. It meant nothing to him. Indeed, like Tucker, Henry felt as though Steve's sobriety broke their strongest common link. Steve continued to work on the issue within himself, however, and he came to understand, intellectually at least, that Henry, too, was a product of his upbringing and that he did the best he could with what he had to work with.

Steve's first semester of graduate school ended in December, and even though he did extremely well in his classes, even to the point of making a name for himself among first year students, he felt ambivalent about continuing. He didn't mind the work. Indeed, he enjoyed the intellectual challenge and worked hard without complaining.

His ego loved the attention that his achievements brought. However, he did not connect well with other students. He made a few friends but got close only to Sheri. His peers centered their lives around each other, the department, and the larger academic community, while Steve centered his around Kathy and recovery. Given the choice between coffee with a graduate school peer and coffee with another struggling alcoholic, his loyalties and his heart lay unquestionably with the alcoholic.

Besides that, he already loved his work. The Woodworks filled his needs. It supported his creative side as well as his practical, business side. It offered him autonomy and freedom of movement. Plus, it made him a decent living—enough to live a simple, debt-free life without breaking into his $12,000 nest egg, which on February 28th remained wrapped up in a towel on the top shelf of the bathroom linen closet.

Tommy convinced Steve to stay in school. Tommy reminded him that the hardest part of graduate school was getting admitted. He sagely suggested that to drop out early would probably slam shut all doors to reentry. He also reminded Steve of his old pattern—dropping out of things as soon as he tasted success in order to avoid future failure. Steve heard both points and accepted Tommy's advice.

Steve continued in treatment with Cally Callahan, and he learned to trust Cally explicitly. The individual sessions, especially, never failed to yield insight. Cally pushed Steve to his edge over and over. Steve not only responded, but he also kept coming back and asking for more. Cally helped Steve work through his issues with Henry. He helped him identify and embrace his injured inner child and injured inner adolescent to the point where Steve learned to invite them both out to heal and to play.

Steve also learned to appreciate and trust his treatment group. And as his trust for the group deepened, he opened up more, became more real, and addressed more difficult issues. He discussed his shame. He wept openly, without covering his face with his hands. He tackled his barriers to growth and change. He listened to feedback from his peers and gave straightforward, honest, insightful feedback back to them. He learned to respect and love Billy.

By the end of February, the group had changed a lot. Peg moved up into Kathy's Wednesday night group. Robert and Al left treatment completely but reported staying sober in AA and NA, respectively. Billy hit a rough spot and underwent a major relapse, whereupon he moved into a more structured program that met four nights a week. Jim matured emotionally and started making progress in his recovery. Sally did not mature emotionally and made little progress of any kind. By Steve's six-month birthday, the group had picked up five new members. Steve served as the backbone of the group.

Steve and Kathy drove to Denver to spend Thanksgiving with Lynn and Eddie. They picked them up on Friday morning, enjoyed leftover Thanksgiving dinner at Luby's Cafeteria at noon, and spent the rest of the day at the Cheyenne Mountain Zoo in Colorado Springs. The next morning, they hiked halfway up and then back down the Pikes Peak Barr Trail. That night, they said goodbye and headed home. They met Bev's boyfriend and found out from Lynn that he was also Bev's boss.

The four of them—Bev, Terry, Lynn, and Eddie—returned to Texas for a week at Christmas. Steve and Kathy got the kids for two and a half of those days. They spent them together as calmly as possible in Austin. They opened presents at daybreak on December 26th. They threw a small dinner party on the 27th. Lynn attached herself to Sheri. Eddie fell head over heels in love with Carla. Steve and Kathy took Lynn and Eddie to two AA meetings and introduced them to many of their sober friends. Bev and Terry disapproved.

Whereas 2905 Columbus served as a hub for alcohol and drug abuse through August 1974, it became a hub of activity around recovery through February 1975. Patti became a fixture around the house on most weekends. She spent many Saturday nights on the couch or in the kids' room. When the weather was really, really cold, she shared the bed with Steve and Kathy, with Kathy in the middle.

Small groups of high bottom drunks often converged on the house following meetings of the South Austin Group on Saturday and Sunday nights. On some of those nights, Steve and Kathy went to bed before the group dispersed only to find them still there the next morning, sitting around on the living room floor, still drinking coffee and chattering away.

Steve and Kathy occasionally took in new AA members who needed a safe haven for a week or two until they got stable enough to return home or find a place of their own.

Kathy celebrated her one-year sober birthday on January 22, 1975, and the next day, at Susan's suggestion, she agreed to sponsor a nineteen-year-old alcohol and drug addicted woman who had also been a prostitute. Kathy moved her and her one suitcase of belongings into the house and paid for her to start treatment at The Recovery Center. The girl made progress at first but then disappeared without a word on February 20th. Kathy felt sad and disappointed but not discouraged.

On the evening of Tuesday, February 27, 1975, Steve and Kathy bundled up in their warmest clothes and climbed the stairs to the top of Austin's highest point, Mt. Bonnell. They carried a heavy quilt, a thermos full of hot chocolate, and two insulated mugs. At the top, they sat on the stone wall and watched the Colorado River flow through the west side of Austin.

"So how are you feeling on the eve of six months sober?" Kathy asked. "Are you happy? Do you still love me?"

Steve smiled. "I'm as happy as a fool, and I love you like crazy. You're still the most incredible person I've ever known. I owe you a lot, you know. You're a big part of the reason I've come this far in sobriety. You've been my teacher. You're my inspiration."

"Quit it; you're embarrassing me, Steve," she said softly.

Steve laughed. "You know, I'll never forget walking out of my first therapy group six months ago and seeing you leaning up against your Mustang. I didn't know you were waiting for me, but you looked so lovely standing there. I believe it was the next night, when you spent the night at my house and we didn't sleep together that I fell in love with you. I remember we were in my bed, and you took my arm and wrapped it around your chest. I lay against your back and smelled your hair. I felt your breasts against the inside of my arm. I tried with all my might not to get an erection, but it came up anyway, right against the back of your leg. Do you remember what you said?"

"Yeah, I asked you if you were going to be okay. I tried to sound cool and calm, but the whole time, I was trying to will my heart to beat softer so you wouldn't feel it pounding against your arm. You must have been too concerned about your erection to feel my heartbeat. What I really wanted was to roll over and devour you.

"Then, after you said you weren't going to be able to sleep with me, and you got up and went into the kids' room, I lay awake for a long time. I wanted you to come back, but I knew it was best that you didn't. I respected you for not pressing the issue that night. You could have. I was very vulnerable—very ripe for the picking, so they say.

"I think that's when I fell in love with you, too, Steve. It was that night. For days after that I couldn't get you out of my mind. I dreamed about you, daydreamed about you, and fantasized about you."

Steve laughed. "I think I masturbated every day for weeks." He shook his head thoughtfully. "It's been a pretty wild six months, hasn't it, Kath?"

"Um hmm, pretty wild. We've done well, though. We've worked hard, and we've changed. You know what? I'm twenty-six years old, and for the first time in my life, I have friends. For years, I just had acquaintances; then when I got into AA, I had acquaintances and a sponsor. Now I have friends that I love very much. You taught me how to do that, Steve. You gave me that precious gift. Thank you."

"You're welcome. Maybe that should be my topic for the meeting tomorrow night. 'Friends.' Or maybe it should be 'Change.' Or maybe I shouldn't even think about it and just wait and see what comes up."

"I think that's the best idea," Kathy said. "By the way, I was thinking about giving you a half-year birthday present tonight, and I kind of wanted to give it to you up here, under the stars. What do you think? Are you man enough to brave the cold?"

Steve smiled and shook his head. "You never cease to amaze me, Kathy. But what the hell, I'm game if you are."

445

CHAPTER 74

Steve rang the bell at exactly 8:00 PM and opened the meeting in the traditional way. Then he took a deep breath and said, "Hi, everybody; my name is Steve, and I'm an alcoholic/addict. I'm chairing this meeting tonight because it's the first day that I qualify to chair a meeting under the guidelines of the South Austin Group. I was six months sober at exactly 2:35 AM this morning."

The members of the South Austin Group of Alcoholics Anonymous clapped and hooted for Steve. He blushed and grinned at Kathy, Patti, and Ralph, who sat together in the front row, almost directly in front of him.

"I'm not going to tell my whole story tonight," he said after they got quiet, "but I do want to talk a little bit before I open the meeting up for discussion. As most of y'all already know from knowing me and listening to me talk in and around meetings, this has been an incredible six-month ride for me, with lots of ups and downs. Tonight, I'm happy to say, is definitely an up.

"I'm not the same man today that I was six months ago when I first visited this little South Austin wood frame house. The first time I attended a meeting here at the South Austin Group, I was exactly three days sober, and I was not here to learn about sobriety. I was here as Kathy's guest, or really as her date. It was our first date, and to tell you the truth, I didn't give a damn where we were, as long as I was with her. We just happened to be here.

"At any rate, I didn't walk through the doors of AA with an open mind or an open heart. My defenses were up; my denial was strong. I was afraid and resistant. I was cynical, especially about AA. In fact, the very first AA meeting I attended, two days before I came over here, turned me off so much that I'm surprised now that I ever went back. And do you know why I was so turned off? Because they talked about God, and I wasn't interested in talking about God. I especially wasn't interested in talking about God with a bunch of losers like you guys.

"You know, though, this program is full of paradoxes and ironies. I was talked into exploring recovery by a guy who isn't sober and never plans to be sober. He knows he's an addict, but he doesn't want to change. He knew that I did, though. So he gave me materials to read, referred me to a counselor, and talked to me endlessly to soften my resistance to AA.

"I'm not sure why I even listened to him. I had every right not to; I mean, the guy is an absolute, total pothead. I also can't say why I read the materials he gave or met with the counselor he recommended. I just did. He wasn't the only one who intervened on me, but he was the one who got through to me. And today, I'm grateful to him. His name is James, and I hope that some day he'll join us here.

"Anyway, before I came to AA, I was a mess. My life wasn't working, and I didn't know why. I knew I was struggling with alcohol and drugs, but I could not grasp the connection between that and my messy life. That's true even though I had hit my bottom just days before I showed up here. Of course, I didn't know then that I had hit bottom. Hell, I didn't know there was such a thing. Thankfully, I know it now.

"Since my story isn't one of absolute devastation and utter pain and woe, my counselor says that I'm a high bottom drunk. I'll tell you, though, I hurt a lot of people when I was using. I especially hurt the people that I professed to love. I may not have been a classic alcoholic, but I *was* a classic selfish, self-centered son of a bitch. And on some level, I knew it, too. Even when things were going my way, I had a deep down awareness that something just wasn't right. I hung in there, though. I was a trooper. I kept telling myself that I could control my drinking and drugging and learn to use like a reasonable, sane man. I know now how insane that belief was.

"I also know now that I've been an alcoholic ever since the day I started drinking, and I've been a drug addict ever since the day I started using. I didn't need practice to cross that line, and I didn't go through stages. I always drank alcohol to get drunk and used drugs to get high.

"When things got really bad in San Antonio, where I was living, I left my family, including my two children, and moved to Austin. My mom, who has been in AA for ten years, told me that moving to Austin was just a geographical cure. Well, I couldn't have cared less what kind of cure it was; I was going.

"That was a year and a half ago. And of course my mom was right. That move was supposed to fix everything, but as cheap cures go, it didn't. Indeed, over the course of the next thirteen months, it got worse, until I hit my so-called high bottom during a four day run last August.

"Two of those days happened at my dad's ranch down in South Texas. I had planned a nice, little weekend of rest and relaxation with a few of my favorite drugs, but it didn't work out that way. I stepped off of a deep end that weekend, and by the time I got back home, which was an absolute miracle in itself, I was busted. I felt disgusted with myself. I remember looking at myself in the mirror and feeling sick to my stomach at the sight of my ugly mug. I remember saying out loud to myself that my life was shit, and nothing more. Then I did something that night that I hardly ever did except in deep crisis situations. I prayed.

447

"The next morning, which was a Sunday, I did another rather desperate thing. I called my mom. She instantly put me in touch with a sober man here in Austin, a very nice man named Al B., whom I'm certain some of you know.

"After talking to him for a little while, I called another friend of mine who had been sober about ten months. She and I got together that night, and she talked to me about sobriety nonstop for two solid hours. Believe it or not, I listened. I listened first, because I knew she cared and second, because she made sense.

"A few hours later, I met up my friend James—my perpetually stoned guardian angel—in the bar where I hung out. We drank beer and talked at some length about my situation. The next morning he showed up with a counselor's business card and a grocery sack full of pamphlets and books on addiction and recovery. I sat down and read some of them, and I gotta tell you, some of the information blew me away. I went to bed that night resolved to take care of my problem. I even said another prayer asking for guidance.

"The next afternoon, I met with the counselor, and with his advice and consent, I set some specific limits—written ones, mind you—on my drinking and drug use. I left there feeling very optimistic, very confident. Eight hours later I was drunk and stoned out of my mind. That was the night of Tuesday, August 29th.

"A little while later, I rolled and smoked my last joint. I took my last hit at 2:35 AM. That was the morning of August 30th, six months ago today. I've been sober and straight since then. I went to my first AA meeting the next night. That was the meeting that I mentioned earlier. I met Al B. there; he gave me my desire chip in private after the meeting since I didn't take one during it.

"I went to my second AA meeting the next day at noon. That's where I met my good friend, Patti, and my sponsor, Ralph, who are sitting right in front of me here. Then I went to my first treatment session that same night. That's when I met Kathy.

"The following night, a Saturday, I came here to the South Austin Group with her. After the meeting, we went for coffee with a few of you guys, most of whom are here tonight, I'm happy to say, and I listened while you talked about recovery. I heard you say that recovery was a gift and not a curse. That was hard for me to believe, but somehow it got through. Maybe it was because you simply told the truth from your own personal experience. At any rate, I believed you.

"After that, things just kind of fell into place for me. I don't know why, really. I'm sure it wasn't due to my superior intellect or my exemplary mental and emotional health, and in the beginning, at least, it wasn't due to any real willingness or open-mindedness on my part. Maybe it was just grace, because for some unknown reason, I put my resistance aside and did what I was told. I didn't have to. No one held a gun to my head. I just did. That was very out of character for me. I've always prided myself on my rebellious nature. Nevertheless, I went to work on my recovery, and I've worked pretty hard on my recovery during these past six months.

"I kept coming to AA—three or four times a week here with Kathy and three or four times a week at my noon meeting at the Catholic Student Center, across the street from UT. I went to more than 90 meetings in my first 90 days. I've met nearly every week with my very generous and excellent sponsor, and as a result, I've completed Steps One through Eight, and I'm ready to get going on Step Nine.

"I've also been in treatment the whole time, and if you know Cally C., then you will appreciate what kind of hell I've been through with him. Even that, though, has been a positive rather than negative experience. It's just another part of my recovery process. You know, when your counselor smiles real big and congratulates you every time you feel emotional pain and shed a few tears, it makes the experience a little more palatable.

"I pray and meditate every day, and I honestly try to live my life moment to moment as I believe God would have me live it. I'm not successful in that particular effort, but I do make the effort.

"So I really haven't been sitting on the sidelines the last six months. I've been a participant in this experience, and I believe that the consistent effort has paid off, because I love my life today. I mean, I still have a ton of unresolved issues. And I know that six months sobriety is no big deal. I know I'm still just on the threshold of recovery. But I also know that I'm a different man today than I was six months ago, when I sat alone, confused, afraid, drunk, stoned, naked, and cross-legged on my bed in the middle of the damn night, praying for help from a God that I neither trusted nor understood.

"I have a Higher Power today, one that I actually love and trust and do not fear. I'm in a wonderful relationship, and I feel grateful every day for that. It's the first really healthy relationship that I've ever been in. Kathy and I work on recovery together. I believe that our recovery is the foundation upon which our relationship sits. My life has stability today. I feel secure. For the first time since I was six years old, I'm not continually glancing over my shoulder out of fear of who knows what.

"I mentioned earlier that I moved to Austin in order to fix everything. Well, can you believe it? Things are slowly but surely getting fixed. I'm finding what I moved to Austin to find. I'm finding myself—that is, my real self, and that feels good. I'm a happy man. I feel truly blessed.

"Well, I've talked longer than I intended. I'm going to shut up now and open the meeting for discussion. I would like to suggest that the topic for this meeting be 'growth and change' because I think that's what recovery is all about. Thank you for listening, and thank you for your sobriety."

CHAPTER 75

Following his six-month sober celebration, Steve continued to walk the walk. And because he did, he stayed sober, and his life got better. In what seemed like the blink of an eye, six months in recovery turned into three years in recovery.

Steve celebrated each of his next three birthdays—one year, two years, and three years—at the South Austin Group. He chaired the first two of those annual birthday meetings, but on August 30, 1977, the third anniversary of his sobriety, he felt quiet and reflective. He decided to let someone else have the honor of chairing that night, and he sat in the group with his favorite sober friends. They were all there to help him celebrate.

Once the meeting started, and people began sharing, Steve relaxed and let his mind drift around and through the three years of his sober life. A lot had happened. A lot had changed.

He glanced over at the man sitting on his immediate left. Here was Tucker, the guy who lived to drink, drug, and chase loose skirts, sitting next to him in an AA meeting, drinking coffee, fidgeting, glancing at his watch every few minutes, stroking his beard, listening and analyzing, judging and trivializing.

Steve drove Tucker to his first round of treatment in January 1977. Tucker's sister had called Steve's house on a Sunday afternoon and asked him to come out to Tucker's parents' place on the lake because Tucker was so intoxicated that they were afraid he was going to hurt himself. Steve piled him into Cleo and drove him to an alcohol & drug rehabilitation hospital. Tucker puked on the floor on the way there.

When they arrived at the hospital, Tucker refused to go in. Steve lost his patience and threatened to beat the hell out of Tucker right there in the parking lot. Tucker laughed at him and invited him to try. Steve punched him hard in the chest and knocked him flat onto his back. Steve helped him up, and as he got to his feet, he looked at Steve and said, "What the fuck did you do that for?"

Tucker stayed in rehab for 28 days and left with his denial intact. He was arrested for DWI five months later. That time, he admitted himself to outpatient treatment at The Recovery Center,

450

where Steve now worked as a counselor under Cally's supervision.

Tucker did not bring much of himself to treatment. Indeed, he tried his best to keep it light. One night, Cally asked him to relate to the group something about his experience of being charged with his second DWI.

Tucker said, "Well, when I was in court waiting to be sentenced, the defendant just before me was an old alcoholic named Brown, who had a *real* problem with booze. Mr. Brown was being prosecuted for his *fourth* DWI. He was standing before the judge with his attorney on one side and the prosecutor on the other.

"The judge, a wrinkled old fart who despised DWI cases with a passion, looked down his nose at poor old Mr. Brown and barked, 'Mr. Brown, I've seen you in my courtroom before, haven't I?'

"Brown looked up at him with this contrite expression on his face, and with a backwoods Texas accent, said, 'Yes, your honor, you have. Three times.'

"The judge became very stern, and he said, 'Mr. Brown, explain to me, if you will, how it is that you would stand before me for the fourth damn time.'

"Brown looked down at the floor and then back up to the judge and said, 'Well, your honor, I've had four DWIs.'

"Well, the judge's eyes got as big around as saucers. His face turned red, and he shouted, 'Mr. Brown, what the hell is your problem?'

"Brown didn't flinch or anything. He just thought for a moment, and then he looked the judge right in the eye and said, 'Your honor, my problem is alkehol and women.'

"When he said that, about half the people in the courtroom laughed out loud. My attorney leaned over to me and whispered, 'The funny part about this whole scenario is that old Mr. Brown is probably the only man in this entire courtroom who really and truly knows what his problem is.'"

After the group finished laughing at Tucker's story, Cally pressed him to relate the experience to himself in some personal way. Tucker couldn't do it.

"Hell, it's just a funny story," he told Cally.

On August 30, 1977, Tucker had been 26 days without a drink or drug. And to his credit, he was complying with the written conditions and expectations of his treatment program. He was saying and doing the right things, and because of his wit and charm, he looked pretty good on the surface.

Steve didn't buy it. Neither did Cally.

"Don't worry too much about Mr. Tucker Taylor, Steve," Cally said. "I know you love the guy, but we don't want to push him beyond his limits too soon. If we do, he'll run like a

451

jackrabbit, and then where would we be? No, I'm just biding my time, waiting for the right moment to nail old Tucker Taylor's ass to the floor."

Steve visualized the scene—Tucker in a full sweat, his denial collapsing around him under Cally's intimidating gaze. "Poor son of a bitch," Steve thought to himself, and he chuckled softly. Tucker glanced at him and whispered, "What the hell's so funny?"

"Nothing, man," Steve whispered back. "I was just thinking about something; it wasn't about the meeting."

Tucker shrugged his shoulders and went back to listening and analyzing, judging and trivializing.

Steve glanced to his right, past Kathy to Carla, who was glowing. Her seventeen-month-old son, Able, sat quietly in her lap, playing with the buttons on her shirt. "Our sweet, sweet boy," Steve thought. He nudged Kathy and pointed to Able and then to himself. Kathy reached over and lifted him off of Carla's lap, gave him a quick hug and kiss, and handed him to Steve. Steve smiled and whispered, "Hey, ya big boy; who's your best pal? Huh? Stevey-Pooh, that's who."

Carla dropped out of UT in March 1975. She slipped into a brief period of very heavy partying that lasted through June. It took its toll on her, and for most of that three-month period of time, she avoided Steve and Kathy. She moderated her drinking and using considerably as soon as she suspected that she might be pregnant, and she quit using altogether the day she got the results of the test. She asked Kathy to take her to AA the next day. On August 30, 1977, she was a little more than two years sober and straight. Her recovery was rock solid.

Carla was not sure who Able's father was, and she really didn't care. She birthed him naturally with the help of a midwife on the living room floor of her own home on March 25, 1976. Steve and Kathy were with her from start to finish—from her first labor pain to her first nap with Able snuggled in her arms. Dixie and Tommy arrived about halfway through, and Patti came towards the end.

Tommy hung around in front of Carla's house, drinking longneck Budweisers and walking back and forth between Carla's front porch and The Roam In. Kathy caught Able, and Steve cleaned him up shortly after his birth. The experience was one of the most moving of Steve's life.

Within a month of Able's arrival, both of Carla's roommates moved out. After much soul searching and praying for guidance, Steve and Kathy moved out of 2905 Columbus and into 2907 Columbus with Carla and Able. Steve and Kathy took care of the finances. Carla stayed home and took care of Able and the house. The four of them became a family. Steve adopted Able in his heart and grew to love him every bit as much as he did Lynn and Eddie.

While Steve held Able on his lap, reflecting on Able's birth, he thought about Tommy and Dixie. Tommy had been so funny while Carla was in labor. He refused to enter the room until Able was clean, nourished, and asleep, and by the time that happened, Tommy was loaded to the gills.

Tommy and Dixie had to work through a lot to stay together. They hung in there, though, and on August 30, 1977, they had been together as a couple for nearly three years. Tommy's alcohol and drug use moderated somewhat during that time. Dixie's increased a little. They never discussed marriage.

Tommy completed graduate school and, to the department's utter dismay, obtained his license to practice psychology one year later. He took a part-time position at the Austin State Hospital working with long term, backward nut cases. They loved him. He also continued to turn occasional lucrative drug deals and visit prostitutes once or twice a year.

He and Steve remained friends. When Steve and Kathy moved into Carla's, Tommy worked tirelessly until the move was complete. When Steve moved The Woodworks from the old garage into the new one, Tommy engineered the whole process. He did the wiring, the layout, the move, and the set up. His first project in the new shop was to design and build Able's first "big boy bed." He gave it to him on his first birthday.

Steve and Dixie remained friends, too. They confided in each other and helped each other better understand the ins and outs of their respective relationships. She continued to work her same shift at The Roam In, turning down numerous offers of better money to work at other bars or to manage that one.

"I'm happy where I am, doing what I'm doing," she always said. In February 1976, Dixie accidentally got pregnant, but she miscarried before anyone knew about the pregnancy. She shared the experience with Steve only after the fact and asked him to not tell anyone else. Later that year, she had an affair with a younger man that lasted six months. She gained weight.

Dixie and Kathy never really became friends. Consequently, the two couples did not spend a lot of time together. They had quite a few common links that put them all in the same place at the same time, but for the most part, Tommy and Steve had each other, and Dixie and Steve had each other, and that's about as far as it went.

As Steve thought of Tommy and Dixie on his third sober birthday, he wished that they were in recovery, too. Their drinking and pot smoking didn't bother him nearly as much as it had during his first year of sobriety, but still...Carla was there, and Tucker was there. "Wouldn't it be cool if we were all here together," he thought.

Of course, James was not there, either. James moved to northern Oregon on August 31, 1976, the day after Steve's second sober birthday. James got busted for possession of marijuana with intent to distribute in March of that year. The story made the front page of the City and State section of the Austin newspaper. It was his third felony charge, which in the State of Texas meant a possible life sentence as a habitual criminal if he was convicted. This time, though, James got lucky.

He had stored four hundred pounds of weed in a friend's barn, where he had previously stored several boxes of his personal belongings—mostly books and tapes. Someone tipped the cops, and James was stunned to find two federal agents, a state trooper, and a city cop snooping around the barn, looking for an easy way in, when he drove up to it in the middle of the afternoon. The cops were not waiting for him; it was just bad timing.

James had the key to the locked barn on a string around his neck. He contended that he was there looking for a certain book packed in a box back in the back corner of the barn. He swore that he knew nothing about the marijuana. The district attorney dropped the charges against him four months later, when that key turned out to be the only piece of real evidence that they could come up with.

After that, James decided that he could use a respite from "the land of the idiot redneck monsters." He chose Oregon because of its lax attitudes and laws regarding pot and also because a certain spiritual community with whom he had corresponded for several years lived there. The community studied and lived by the teachings of a deceased Sufi master named Hazrat Inayat Khan. When James informed them of his interest in studying with them, they welcomed him and offered him a place to live. He waited until the day after Steve's second sober birthday and then drove off in his old Buick.

Before James left, Steve asked him who was going to take his place. "Who will be my teacher now?" he asked.

James laughed his hearty laugh and said, "Oh, don't worry, man. He'll show up, and he'll put my puny understanding of things to shame."

When James left, Steve cried. The next day, Cally called Steve and invited him to come and work with him at The Recovery Center.

Steve and James corresponded occasionally. James' letters were masterpieces of classic James Shannon meanderings. They could not compete, however, with James Shannon meanderings in person.

As Steve thought about James on that evening of August 30, 1977, he missed him greatly. "So full of genius, so full of shit, and so full of love," he thought to himself.

454

Steve glanced at his watch. He had managed to daydream and reminisce his way through about half of the meeting. Able lay sleeping in his arms; Steve kissed him tenderly on the forehead.

As he looked at Able, he thought about Rachel and wondered what she might be doing right then. Perhaps she was holding her own sleeping baby. He wondered if she was sober.

Rachel married a dentist on Christmas Day, 1975. He was twelve years older than she. He wanted a family right away, and in response to his wish, Rachel gave birth to Annie on September 27, 1976, nine months and two days after Rachel and Randy's wedding day.

Annie looked just like Rachel. She quickly became the apple of that family's eye. Sammy doted on her constantly. Rachel talked about her incessantly.

Randy respected Rachel's sobriety, but he could not understand her need to continue in AA after they were married. He wanted her home with him, where she belonged, instead of hanging around smoky rooms with people of questionable morals. She resisted his pressure for six months but eventually relented and gave up her sober support network, except for her monthly phone conversations and occasional visits with Steve.

She drank a glass of champagne on New Year's Eve, 1976. Nothing bad happened. After that, she drank socially—wine at dinner parties and a few drinks or beers at social functions. She got drunk at a party in April 1977, and in a room full of people that included Randy's father, she told Randy to fuck off in a very loud voice when he ordered her to shut her mouth, get her coat, and leave with him to go home.

The episode shocked them both, and following it, Rachel remained abstinent for about three weeks. Then she got drunk one night at home alone while Randy attended his weekly poker game at a friend's house. She repeated the experience the following week and the week after that. Randy never suspected a thing.

Two weeks later, he left for a five day backpacking trip in Arizona. Rachel left Sammy and Annie with her mom and stayed drunk for three days and nights. She crashed and fell apart on the third night. She called Steve at 3:00 AM and begged him through tears and slurred speech to help her.

Steve and Kathy made it to her house in San Antonio the next morning at 6:30. The three of them spent the day together. Kathy helped Rachel clean herself up, and then she tackled the house, which smelled of vomit and stale urine. Steve cooked a mountain of fresh vegetables and made Rachel eat until she complained.

Rachel drank coffee and cried. She wallowed in guilt and shame and wished out loud that she were dead. Steve and Kathy browbeat her into going with them to an AA meeting that evening at her old group. Rachel reluctantly took a desire chip and reconnected with her old sponsor, who agreed to stay with her that night and then keep daily tabs on her for a while. Again, Randy never knew that anything had happened.

When Steve called Rachel about a week later, she was drinking again. She swore that she had it under control. He talked to her again a week after that. She gave him the same story, but he could tell from her voice that she was intoxicated.

When he called her in July, she told him that she was sober again and going to meetings. Randy had threatened to leave her and take Annie with him if she did not straighten up and fly right. He flatly refused her pleas that he attend Al-Anon. "You're the one with the goddamn problem, not me," he had said.

When Steve talked to Rachel on August 21st, she was sober but struggling. She had again discontinued her meetings and had not talked to her sponsor in a month. He gave her the name of a counselor in San Antonio that he had gotten from Cally. She said that she would think about calling her.

As Steve thought about Rachel, he realized that he felt not only sad but also guilty. He had not been much of a friend to Rachel since Kathy had come into his life. He remembered the last time that they had spent the night together, when he had awakened in a panic, and she had helped him get his feet back on the ground. The experience had been a meaningful and powerful part of his very early sobriety.

Steve closed his eyes. "God, please be with her," he whispered to himself.

Able roused and started to cry. Steve handed him back to Carla, who opened her shirt and gave him her breast. Steve watched him nurse for a moment. "Always hungry for the old teat," he whispered to Kathy. She winked at him and returned her attention to the meeting.

As the image of Carla nursing Able lingered in his mind, Steve thought of his own mother. Lois continued to dote on Steve's sobriety. She and Chester drove to Austin once or twice a month. They fell in love with Carla and completely in love with Able. For Able's first birthday, Lois hand-stitched a quilt to fit the bed that Tommy had built. She never once criticized the living arrangement.

Not long after Steve and Kathy moved in with Carla and Able, Lois relented and gave her blessing to his chosen lifestyle. It came on a Saturday afternoon, as she and Steve sat on the front porch of Steve's house.

"You know, Steve," she said softly, "I've never understood very many of your decisions. I suppose I don't need to start now. You seem happier than I've ever known you to feel. So, what do I know, right?"

456

Lois never forgot Steve's sober birthdays. His third was no exception. She called him at exactly 7:00 AM on August 30, 1977 to tell him how much she loved him and how proud of him she was.

As he sat in his birthday meeting, not hearing a word being said, Steve reminded himself of how lucky he was to have Lois as his mother and Chester as his stepdad. He felt especially grateful for their sobriety. He wished that Henry could find his way into recovery, but he accepted the fact that the chances of that happening were slim to none.

His drifting thoughts settled on his own two kids. "I have a sober parent, and so do they," he thought to himself. He and Kathy saw Lynn and Eddie twice a year in Denver: Two days at Thanksgiving and three during Lynn's spring break; and twice a year in Austin: Two days at Christmas and a month during the summer.

Bev married her boss eight months after arriving in Denver. They bought a very large, very expensive home in the Cherry Hills section of the city. They belonged to the country club and drove Mercedes sedans. Steve sent her $300.00 child support every month.

Lynn called Able her "littlest brother" and Carla her "favorite aunt." She still talked about moving back to Texas to live with Steve and Kathy. She promised that Eddie would follow her there. Steve brought it up with Bev once, and she just laughed.

"I can't even believe you would suggest such a thing, the way you live," she said. "You and two women and an illegitimate child in a ramshackle old house across the street from a bar. Do you really think that's a healthy environment for small children to grow up in?"

He really did.

He looked at his watch again. In fifteen minutes, Ralph would present him with his three-year sobriety chip. Ralph had given him every chip except his first—the desire chip, which he still carried. Ralph had been there at one month, three months, six months, one year, two years, and now, three years. Steve figured that in their three years together, he and Ralph had spent about 130 Wednesday evenings in Ralph's home, working on sobriety and deepening their friendship. They also had been camping numerous times and had spent a week together backpacking in the Colorado Rockies.

Patti turned around and caught Steve's eye and smiled. She looked very happy. Her husband, John, was a great guy. He was six years sober, and an honorable man. Patti fondly said that he was a long time coming, but well worth the wait. Steve and Kathy and Patti and John called themselves "best couple friends."

Steve looked over at Kathy and thought to himself that she looked even more lovely that evening than she had the night he first saw her in Cally Callahan's treatment group. He leaned over and whispered in her ear, "It's my birthday, and you know what that means."

She turned her head and whispered back, "Right now? Right here? Are you certain about this?"

He smiled broadly. "No, you maniac," he whispered. "On Mt. Bonnell at the stroke of midnight."

She nodded and made an "Okay" sign with her hand.

After three years together, Steve loved Kathy with all of his heart, as she did him. They had been through easy times and hard times, but they never questioned their love for or their commitment to each other. They considered marriage from time to time but never thought it necessary. They figured that they would get around to it when the time came, maybe if and when they decided to have a child.

In the meantime, Steve had his life, and Kathy had hers, but their life together as a couple came first, and their lives together with Carla and Able as a family came second.

On August 30, 1977, Kathy stood just one week away from reentering The University of Texas to complete her college degree. She had waited to return to school until she decided on a career path. That decision came about as a result of her willingness to follow her heart, put one foot in front of the other, and do the next right thing.

Soon after her first sponsee disappeared, never to be seen again, she took on another alcohol and drug addicted prostitute who expressed a desire for recovery. This time, she maintained better boundaries and had better luck. She spent two days on the telephone and found a halfway house that agreed to give Sue room, board, and counseling in exchange for help in the kitchen and around the house. Kathy also found her a minimum wage part time job at a thrift shop where, as part of her compensation, she could buy donated clothes at half of half price.

Sue stayed sober and off the streets, and the day after she picked up her six-month chip, she and Kathy started a support group for other recovering alcoholic, drug addicted prostitutes who wanted to stay sober. For several weeks, the group consisted of Kathy, Sue, a pot of coffee, and a fruit and bread plate. By the end of summer, however, the group had attracted five regulars who seldom missed a meeting, plus several others who came and went.

By the end of 1976, Kathy had become a reliable community resource for recovering alcoholic, drug addicted prostitutes. In addition to the weekly support group, she volunteered time to the Travis County Jail, where she took the message of recovery to prostitutes interested in hearing it.

Kathy also became known as someone who could effectively line up services for women who were unable to pay for them. In

458

December 1976 and again in January 1977, Kathy stood up in court on behalf of women whom she believed were absolutely sincere in their desire for a different way of life. At each appearance, she presented to the court a thoughtfully constructed plan to rehabilitate the woman in lieu of incarcerating her. Kathy's plans included treatment and support services from public and private agencies that had agreed to help the women upon their release.

Following her second court appearance, the Travis County Judge hearing the case invited Kathy to his chambers to talk. After hearing bits and pieces of her story, he strongly encouraged her to get a degree in social work and continue her work with that population of women on a professional level. He offered to make some phone calls on her behalf.

Kathy agreed on the spot. She obtained the application forms from UT the next day and returned them the following week. The UT School of Social Work not only accepted her for the Fall, 1977 term, but also awarded her a tuition and textbooks scholarship.

Steve took Kathy's hand in his and laid it on top of his leg. She leaned over and said, "Where have you been for the last hour?"

He smiled and whispered back, "All over the map, just thinking about the past three years and the people who made them interesting. You're at the top of the list. I love you, you know."

She nodded. "Yes, I know. I love you, too."

Steve felt good. He felt happy. At that moment, he felt complete. "What a difference a little time, a little help, and a little work can make," he thought to himself. He flashed on his infamous ranch trip, followed two days later by the whorehouse jaunt with Tommy and his broken contract with Cally.

"Nothing happens in God's world by mistake," he thought, referring to one of his favorite lines from the Big Book of Alcoholics Anonymous.

He turned around and caught Cally's eye and did a Groucho Marx eyebrows routine at him. Cally nodded back without cracking a smile. "How can that man keep such a straight face?" Steve thought.

Steve went to work for Cally at The Recovery Center in September, 1976. The way Steve remembered it, Cally did not offer him a job. Rather, he called and told him to come work for him.

"I need you over here," he said. "How soon can you start?" Steve started the next day.

As Steve expected, Cally was a good boss and a great mentor. He was knowledgeable, honest, direct, available, and patient. He challenged and encouraged Steve every day that they were together. Steve felt honored to be Cally's apprentice. He worked hard and learned fast, and Cally came to rely on him quite heavily. Indeed, Cally was anxious for Steve to finish school so that he could give him more responsibility.

In terms of school, Steve had about one year left, most of which would be devoted to completing his dissertation research and write up. One major part of the dissertation—the literature review—was complete, and the rest was in outline form.

Following graduation, projected for May 1978, he needed a year of clinical internship before he could test for his license. Cally promised to provide the internship at The Recovery Center by hiring a part time licensed psychologist to provide the proper supervision. In the meantime, Steve expected to become certified as an alcohol and drug abuse counselor before the end of the year.

The Woodworks remained open, but by August 30, 1977, it had become a very part time effort for Steve. He accepted jobs only from previous customers, and only when those customers did not require definite completion dates. Tommy spent more time in the shop than Steve did.

Nevertheless, Steve still felt attached to The Woodworks, as he did to Cleo, who got a brand new 350 cubic inch Chevy engine in July 1977. Buying that motor was the first and only time that Steve had used any of his $12,000 drug deal nest egg.

Kathy nudged Steve out of his daydreams as the meeting drew to a close. The chair asked for all August 30th birthdays to please come forward and be recognized. Steve was the only taker.

CHAPTER 76

Steve and Kathy and Ginger climbed the stairs to the top of Mt. Bonnell a little after midnight. Steve and Kathy sat on the stone wall overlooking the river; Ginger disappeared among the bushes and trees.

Steve put his arm around Kathy's shoulders and snuggled against her side.

"It's beautiful up here tonight," Steve said

"Yes, it is," she said softly. "I love it up here, especially when it's late, and we're by ourselves. It's so peaceful."

After a few moments of silence, Kathy said, "I liked what you said when you got your chip. It was short and sweet, simple and clear, and from your heart. You've gained humility over the three years that I've known you."

Steve chuckled. "Does that mean you thought I was full of it when we met?" he asked.

Kathy punched him lightly in the stomach. "You know what I mean," she said.

Steve kissed her lightly on the cheek. "Thank you, Kathy. Actually, I feel humble tonight. I have everything in the world to be grateful for. Four years ago, I moved to Austin expecting my life to change completely, and magically. You know—move to Austin and watch the phenomenon occur.

"I thought I would wake up my first morning here and be a different man. I thought I would look different, act different, think different, feel different, and generally *be* different. Magic, you know?

"The looking different part was easy enough, except for the hair; that took a while. The acting different part was do-able; I pulled that off pretty well, at least for a while. The rest was a total bust.

"My opinions and beliefs ran much deeper than I ever imagined. I mean, I could act like a liberal a lot easier than I could think like one. And my feelings didn't change at all. I just kept them stuffed the way I always had, except for my resentments, of course.

"And as for the deeper stuff, well, you know how that played out. The miracle in my imagination had me waking up that first day having changed overnight into an honest, open-minded, genuine, patient, generous, tolerant, thoughtful, and kind man, filled with meaning, purpose, and self-esteem. What I woke up with was the same damn jerk I went to sleep with the night before."

He paused for a moment. "Actually, it wasn't all bad. I made some good friends, and we had some good times. Over all, though, it got worse. By the time I had been here a year, I was disillusioned and very confused. God, I was lucky, though. Those good friends, who were damn near as confused as I was, wouldn't let me go down the tubes completely without a fight. It sure could have gone the other way.

"When I talked to my mom this morning, she said something that bothered me a little bit. I've thought about it off and on all day. She said she believes that those of us who find recovery from this disease are 'the chosen few.' She said that when you think of all the millions of people with alcohol and drug problems who never get help and never get sober, it makes you wonder why we did.

"She thinks it's not just random and that grace seems to be selective. She doesn't understand why, of all people, she should have been so fortunate and that she has never felt deserving. She feels grateful, but not deserving. Then she said she was more grateful for my sobriety that she was for her own.

"I told her that I didn't think I would even be sober if she had not gotten sober first."

461

Kathy lifted her face and kissed Steve softly on the lips. "I'm grateful for your sobriety, too, Steve. I don't know about grace, especially selective grace, but I do understand how your mom feels. I've felt that way many times.

"Tonight, though, I just feel like the luckiest girl in the world. If anyone would have told me five years ago that on August 30, 1977 I would be sober, happy, and in love, I would have laughed in his face and said, 'There is no way in hell that will ever happen.'

"Anyway, if you weren't sober today, I sure as heck wouldn't have you up here with me. I might have to sit here and make love to myself instead of having you here to do the honors. Which reminds me, are you about ready for your birthday present?"

Steve smiled. "As usual, I'm ready if you are."

At about 3:00 AM, Steve and Kathy walked up the front steps of the big, old frame house at 2907 Columbus, and quietly opened the front door. They tiptoed through the living room and into Able's bedroom. They stood over his bed and looked at his sweet face. "God, I love that little rug rat," Steve whispered.

They slipped quietly out of Able's room and past Carla's open door. "Hey, guys," Carla said softly, "what the heck have y'all been doing till 3:00 o'clock in the morning?"

Steve and Kathy looked at each other and smiled. "We got naked up on top of Mt. Bonnell," Kathy answered.

"Oh, okay," Carla said. "Sounds good. Goodnight. I love you."

"We love you, too, Carla," Steve whispered.

They walked into their room, slipped out of their clothes, turned on the ceiling fan, and climbed into bed and under the top sheet. Kathy lay on her side with her back snuggled against Steve's front and his arm around her chest, holding her close. He felt her breasts against the inside of his arm. They fell asleep in that position, as they had nearly every night for almost three years.

Steve dreamed lucidly that night. In the dream, he had died. He stood in a long hallway, in front of a door with the name "The Interviewer" painted across the outside. He knocked, and from the other side, he heard a man's voice say, "Come in, Steve."

He opened the door and entered a very simple room with two chairs, facing each other, in the middle. A pleasant-looking man sat in one of the chairs. "Please, Steve, have a seat," he said.

Steve looked at the man and said, "Are you The Interviewer?"

The man smiled and nodded. "Yes, I am," he said.

Steve took a deep breath. "So, I'm dead?" he asked.

The Interviewer smiled. "Only in a manner of speaking, and only in the least important sense."

Steve nodded. "And you're going to interview me."

"Yes, that's the idea. Are you ready?"

Steve thought to ask whether or not he had a choice, but instead he said, "Yes, I suppose I am."

"Good," The Interviewer replied. "My question is this, Steve. Now that you have perfect insight, how would you do life differently if you were to start fresh and do it all over again?"

Steve thought for a moment and then answered, "Jeez, I don't know. I mean, now that I'm here, and everything seems to have turned out okay, I'm not sure I would change that much. I guess I would do it pretty much the same way as I did.

"All in all, I dug my life. I mean, I did a lot of colossally stupid things throughout it, but to tell you the truth, I'd probably do them all again. Like, I would still choose to be born into the same screwed up family. It was definitely where I needed to be. I would still choose to become a troubled, disaffected youth; that was fun, in a mystifying kind of way. I would still become an alcoholic and addict. After all, that was my door opener, you know? I would still enter into that crazy, bad marriage; angels were born from it, and I see now how relevant that is. I would definitely do the whole recovery trip again. There's no question about that; it was great. I guess I would even still choose to die young. I mean, after all, I'm glad to be here now. So...no major regrets, I suppose."

When The Interviewer did not respond immediately, Steve looked at him closely and said, "What's the matter? Is that the wrong answer?"

The Interviewer laughed heartily. "Oh, Lord, no, Steve; it's not that. There are no wrong answers any longer. Wrong answers imply rules, judgment, and ego. You're no longer hindered by such distractions, and your answers are simply honest ones. But you did answer a different question than the one I asked. You answered the 'what' question. I asked the 'how' question."

"I don't think I get what you mean."

"Well, Steve, I did not say, 'What would you have done differently?' I said, 'How would you have done it differently?' See the difference?"

"Oh, okay; I think I get it now. Well, let's see. Within that context, if I had it to do all over again, I would have more fun with it all. You know; I wouldn't take life so damn seriously. I would do it with a better sense of humor all the way around.

"I would also do it more genuinely. I would let the walls down, or perhaps just never put them up in the first place. I would take a lot more chances, especially with people and animals and plants and flowers and trees. I would be more honest and spontaneous. I'd laugh louder and cry harder.

463

"I would live with more curiosity, too, and with fewer distractions. I would do it with more consciousness and with fuller presence. I would pay more attention to whatever was right in front of me. I would think less, figure out less, and simply observe more.

"I would be a better listener. I would stay more heart-centered, and I'd listen to that inner voice that my friend, David, used to talk about. I would live more courageously and with genuine faith.

"Mainly, though, I think I would just keep it simple and have more fun. Is that closer to what you mean?"

The Interviewer nodded. "Yes, that's what I mean, Steve. The 'who, what, where, and when' really don't matter all that much. The 'how,' though, and to some extent, the 'why' are important. If those deeper parts of yourself remain fairly constant and true, the others are pretty incidental. You know, that old saying, 'We teach people how to treat us' is essentially true, regardless of who it is we're with or what we're doing or where and when we're doing it.

"Yeah, I guess so," Steve said. "When I think about it like that, though, there are a few 'what's' that I might, in fact, do differently. For example, I think I would intervene, physically if necessary, at least once or twice when my dad beat up my mom. I would spend more time with my grandparents before they died. I would probably learn more, especially in the areas of history and anthropology, and I would learn to speak Spanish.

"I would go ahead and sleep with Marilyn Cugler. I would rock climb and skydive. I would grow flowers. I would also grow and cook more vegetables. And I'd definitely drink more water.

"I would talk to strangers. I would dance. I would stay up later and sleep fewer hours. I'd read more poetry, and I'd take a turn at writing some, too. I would let my dog, Ginger, sleep in my bed. I would hug Kathy and Carla and Able and Lynn and Eddie and my mom and Chester till their ribs ached and they begged for mercy. I would tell Kathy how much I love her many, many times every single day.

"Man, I better stop. Now that I'm on a roll, this list could go on forever, and I know that's not what you're looking for. I guess a list of 'whats' like this is just a waste of time, right?"

The Interviewer laughed. He reached over and gently patted Steve's knee. "It's okay, Steve. I like your list a lot. And besides, there's no such thing as time."

EPILOGUE

The true statistics around alcohol and drug abuse are anyone's guess. Probably, though, somewhere in the neighborhood of ten to twenty-five percent of people over the age of fourteen in the United States have an alcohol or drug problem of some kind or another. If nicotine and caffeine are added into the mix, as they should be, the numbers go up dramatically.

A small percentage of alcohol and drug addicted people receive treatment for their disease. Most simply die from it. Of those who do receive treatment, about half or more drink or use again within the first year. Seventy to eighty percent drink or use again within five years.

Addiction is a powerful disease. It is insidious. Recovery is powerful, too. The problem is that a lot of people find addiction, while few alcoholics and addicts find recovery.

Steve Campbell, the high bottom drunk, beat the odds. He stayed sober. At least he stayed sober for three years. And although three years sounds like a long time, it really isn't when you're talking about recovery.

In fact, Cally Callahan would smile and say, "Yeah, well, three years is a pretty good start, but the truth is it's just a dress rehearsal for the real thing. We'll see what's going on in the life of our Mr. Steve Campbell when he's six or seven years out of the gate. That, my friend, is when the shit hits the fan. Yes, sir, that's when it really gets to be fun."

About the Author

Charles Roper lives in Buda, Texas, a pinpoint dot on the map about ten miles south of Austin. He resides there with his wife, Joan, two of their four kids, three dogs, four cats, a ferret, a cockatiel, and some-odd fish. His other two children are grown and have families of their own.

By trade, Dr. Roper is an addictions counselor. He began working in that field in 1983, the same year that he got sober and into recovery from alcohol and drug addiction. He opened Solutions Counseling & Treatment Center in Austin in 1985 and operated it successfully until 1994, when he sold it to a large hospital corporation. That's when he officially became a writer.

Charles worked on *High Bottom Drunk* for the better part of five years. "I got the idea for *High Bottom Drunk* in 1990 while on a solo hiking trip in the Colorado Rockies. It was 'a God thing' as we say in recovery meetings. I prayed for direction for my life, and the book, including the title and opening paragraph, popped into my head. I knew in my heart that I would eventually write the story."

People have asked Charles how much of *High Bottom Drunk* is autobiographical. He replies, "Oh, about two-thirds or so, but I'd be pretty hard-pressed to say exactly which two-thirds it is. I'm afraid that if I did that, my mom might disown me. And I'm not kidding about that."

And what's on the horizon? Dr. Roper is working on his second novel, *Elephants in the Living Room, Tigers behind the Doors,* a story about living in (and surviving) a violent, alcoholic family. *Elephants... & Tigers...* is written from the perspective of a 16-year-old boy.

You can contact Charles Roper by e-mail:
chasroper@highbottomdrunk.com

Or through Small Change Publishing Co.:
smchange@austin.rr.com

Life Without Embellishment